# DRAGC

## FATE'S FOI

BOOK 3

Shae Ford

For Grandaddy Ford and Grandma Jo; Papa Amos and Grandma Myrtle

If there's any wisdom, love, or mischief in our family today,

It's because y'all started it

# TABLE OF CONTENTS

# PROLOGUE
## FATE'S WILL

Argon the Seer stood alone at the edge of a battlefield.

The sun fell before him. The red trail of its dying light filled the sky, barely illuminating the ground at his feet. He could still see them, though ... the countless bodies that blanketed the earth like ash.

Swords lay scattered. Torn, faded banners rose and fell weakly in the evening wind, their staves still propped against the bodies of their bearers. The glint was gone from their armor; their bright gold breastplates faded to shadow against the fallen sun. The twisted black dragons hung dully to their chests.

The crest of Midlan now lay dead with its army.

Argon was the sole survivor. He walked among the dead, his eyes fixed upon the jagged line between the crest of bodies and the reddened sky. His feet moved surely through the wastes. Steel and flesh parted around his legs like smoke: wisping away as he passed, coming back together behind him. Argon could not feel the breeze that stirred the banners, nor the faded warmth of the sun.

He knew the battle wasn't over quite yet. He knew something was coming.

No sooner had this thought crossed his mind than the vision began to shake. The earth trembled violently, its quaking grew more fierce with every passing second. A mound of bodies rose into a hill as the shaking continued. It swelled, blistering until a column of fire spewed from its top.

Argon shielded his eyes against the bright yellow of the flames — flames that burned hotter than any he'd ever felt. He covered his face with his robes to keep the heat from singeing his flesh. Only when the fires abated did he dare to look.

A figure had appeared upon the hill of bodies. It stood in the charred bowl the fires had left behind and seemed to carry both the dawn and the night: its robes were the deepest black, its head wreathed in bright yellow flame. The figure stood silently — a wicked grin fixed upon its face.

"Turn back," Argon cried.

He knew this specter's name, heard it whispered among the many legends of Midlan. It was a wraith that traveled freely between the ruins of the past and the chaos of the Veil — a spirit known as the Firecrowned King.

Argon's blood chilled when the specter turned its empty eyes upon him, but he raised his hands in defiance. "You have no business among the living!"

The Firecrowned King didn't move. The pits of its eyes and its horrible grin stayed locked on Argon. Slowly, it reached inside its blackened robes.

Argon tensed, the beginning of a spell formed upon his lips. But it wasn't a sword the Firecrowned King drew — it was a die. The die fell out from between the sharp tips of the specter's fingers, spinning as it rolled towards Argon's feet. He watched it clatter and clink over the dead, striking hard in places where he'd simply passed through.

At last, the die came to a stop before him. Argon studied it closely. His fists clenched at his side when he saw the die's familiar weathered edges. Symbols covered its ivory skin. They moved constantly — swirling, drifting across the die's many faces. But there was one symbol that shone clear.

It was carved into the face that'd landed upwards: an image scrawled in lines that shimmered like blood. There was only one die powerful enough to wake the dead, and Argon knew he had no hope against its will.

Defeat dragged him to his knees. Argon stared at the die's painted message — an image of a tiny sword cleft in two — and *felt* its intentions before his mind had a chance to grasp them:

Change, great change — an act that would send tremors across the six regions ... and render even the sword useless.

Dread filled his chest in an icy rush. When he looked up, he saw that the Firecrowned King watched him silently, grinning. "Please," Argon whispered. "Please, for the sake of all the living, go back to the river. Forget your task — sleep in peace."

The flames around the Firecrowned King's head seemed to swell as it stood taller upon the hill of bodies. "Move aside, *Seer*." It hissed the word mockingly; yellow light flared up behind its teeth. "I have been summoned."

Two great, black wings erupted from the specter's back. They unfurled, covering the sky in shadow and stirring the earth with a mighty wind. Swords, shields and bodies flew into the air as the wings rose skyward. When they snapped back down, the whole battlefield flew forward like a wave.

Argon was crushed beneath it.

*******

Something wet coated his lips. Argon raised his head slowly and tasted the wetness with the tip of his tongue. It was warm, slightly metallic.

Blood.

The red stream began at his nose, where something deep inside had ruptured. The pressure faded a bit as he woke; the blood stopped its trickling. He could feel the warmth begin to cool, crusting onto his skin and among the strands of his long, gray beard.

Argon groaned aloud. He'd known something was about to break. He could feel trouble churning in the future, a changing of the tides. But he'd hoped with all the desperation of mankind that he'd been mistaken — surely Fate wouldn't have intervened twice in one lifetime.

Now there was no doubting it. The darkening of his bowl was the first sign of her coming: the last vision he'd been able to draw up was of the boy in the Endless Plains — the boy from the mountains who had no future. Sending Eveningwing to his aid was the last help he'd been able to offer. After that, the waters had gone dark and his visions had abandoned him.

He'd thought perhaps that Fate was only punishing him for toying with the King, for protecting the mountain boy. But it turned out she had something worse in mind.

Visions were the second sign of her coming — not the visions he scried for himself, but otherworldly bursts rife with her will. Argon could do no more than weather them. He was tossed back and forth, sliding from the Veil and into the future like a cup upon a ship's table. He had no power to rise, no strength to take the helm. He was Fate's bonded servant. And when she summoned him, he had to answer.

Her visions hadn't always troubled him. The last time he'd been summoned, Argon had sat in the quiet and allowed Fate's will to come to him gently. Her words slid behind his eyes as softly as a dream.

But his body was not as strong as it'd once been. This last vision had struck with such force that he knew it would take days to recover. He was ragged on the inside and the out.

Argon's eyes struggled to adjust to the dim light. The room should've been brighter. He'd lit candles and placed them all about his desk. They'd been part of a ward he'd cast to make certain he wouldn't be disturbed. But as he looked around, he realized his spell had been undone: every flickering light was extinguished ... save for one.

A single candle burned upon his desk, its flame barely illuminating the space before it. Faded letters lay softly across the thick, yellowed pages of a book — a book, Argon suddenly remembered, that he'd been trying desperately to read.

*The Myth of Draegoth* was its title. It was a legend of how the first King came to be, how he'd tamed the Wildlands and turned them into the Kingdom. The words were simple enough for a child to read. Argon had waded through far thicker tomes with ease.

But there was something ... strange, about this book. Cold air slid across the back of his neck — an air too cold for a spring evening. Perhaps the young mages had been right about this book, after all.

Perhaps it truly *was* cursed.

The chill had only made it halfway down his spine before Argon saw the dark puddle that stained one of the *Myth*'s pages. He'd collapsed upon the desk, and the blood from his nose had leaked out across the words.

He soaked the blood up with the sleeve of his robes, swearing under his breath. But the damage had already been done: a brownish stain now set behind the words. Its bleary edges faded them even more. Though Argon had to strain to read it, he thought he could still make the message out:

*From the bonds of magic pure and earth's most gleaming vein, the archmage did forge the King's salvation: a protection called the Dragonsbane.*

No sooner had he finished reading than the flame of the last candle hissed and went out, as if a pair of invisible fingers had snuffed it.

Argon sat very still in the darkness left behind. He didn't dare move; he didn't dare breathe. Even his heart seemed to hush its beating. The flames and the shadows of Fate's vision rose starkly before his eyes, alive in their fury. He could doubt no longer:

Something was coming.

# CHAPTER I
## THE FIRECROWNED KING

King Crevan did not know the hour.

He blinked against the mist that filmed his eyes until his chamber walls came into focus. Red vines covered the stone in front of him. They seemed to grow as he watched: crawling across the bumps and chips, racing along the mortar lines. The vines moved strangely, though — growing *downward* instead of up. He wondered where they might be going.

Crevan followed the vines' snaking path to the floor, where they ran into the body of a soldier.

It was a guard of Midlan, fully dressed in gold-tinged armor. His body was crumpled around the butt of a spear, his hands frozen in death — still grasping at the shaft that hung out of his chest. The twisting black dragon on his breastplate seemed to squirm in the firelight. It wriggled against the splintered wood, dancing with the flames.

Crevan watched as the vines crept towards the floor, finally coming to rest within the dark puddle that blossomed beneath the soldier's chest. One by one, each branch of the tangle sank inside the puddle.

Now it was impossible to tell. Anybody who saw them would think these vines had grown *up*wards from the puddle, but they would be wrong. Crevan alone knew their secret. He'd been chosen, privileged to watch them bloom ...

The vines changed suddenly: their twining skin turned green and sprouted heavy leaves. Moonlight burst from between the mortar lines — cold and ghostly pale. The wall's heavy bricks hurtled backwards. They fell soundlessly onto the thick grass beyond where the moon scored them white. Hums rose from the markers, the whole earth trembled with the voices of the dead. They were calling for him, cursing him —

A breath rattled from Crevan's chest as he fought the madness away. Slowly, the mist retreated to the edge of his vision. These weren't vines: they were lines of blood. They hadn't bloomed, but had erupted from the soldier's chest. He'd come into Crevan's chambers unannounced, bursting in with stomps and bellows. It was the soldier's intrusion that'd caused the mist to rise ...

He couldn't remember what had happened after that.

The hearth fire was nearly burned out. Darkness was creeping in. Crevan had ordered the windows in his chambers to be sealed with stone and mortar. She was coming for him, coming to finish what she'd started. He wasn't going to give her an easy way into the fortress. But with the windows sealed, the darkness was thick.

He didn't want to be trapped among the shadows.

Crevan clawed his way to the door and shoved it open. Light from the hallway flooded in. The servants had added more sconces to the wall: now the many torches were spaced hardly a stone apart. Though it was drowned in fiery light, the hallway wasn't safe enough. There were too many doors for her to hide behind, too many ways she might slip in. He had to get somewhere safe.

A large onyx dragon stood guard over his chambers. He pressed a spine of the dragon's tail and stamped his feet impatiently as a wall slid to the side, revealing a narrow passageway.

It was only after the wall had closed behind him that Crevan allowed himself a steadying breath. Nobody else knew about these passages. Here, he could move safely.

Some of the tunnels were chamber-sized, some were hardly big enough to crawl through. They wound around the castle in unpredictable patterns. Crevan had spent years memorizing their twists and turns. He knew which paths to follow merely by glancing at the wear on their steps, or the coloring of their bricks. It wasn't long before he'd made his way to the throne room.

He slammed the creaking door behind him and shoved the tapestry aside. The servants must've just come in: the torches were fresh and the hearth fire roared. There was nowhere for the shadows to hide.

A plate of food sat upon the mantle, but Crevan shoved it away. The silver plate clattered onto the floor; the hot meal the cook had prepared spilled across the stone. Crevan snatched the goblet that had sat behind the plate and downed half its fiery contents in two quick gulps, grimacing as the liquor steadied him.

Drinking took the edge from his madness. The guard in his chambers was only the most recent victim ... Crevan had lost control before.

The great table in the middle of the room lay broken upon its side. Splintered stubs were all that remained of its legs; its top bore the deep gashes of Crevan's sword. Nearly every chair in the room had been shattered — splintered against the walls or hacked to pieces. Only one seat remained, and he kept it planted beside the hearth.

Sometimes, when the red mist faded, he would sit in that chair and watch the flames do their work ...

"Your Majesty. We finally meet."

Crevan drew his sword and spun, leveling it at the hearth chair. When he saw the creature perched upon it, the blade nearly slipped from his grasp.

It was a skeleton — a corpse. Its bones were blackened, as if the man the bones belonged to had been burned alive in a fire. The robes draped across its shoulders were scorched at the hems and so littered with holes that Crevan could see the curve of its spine peeking through the tears.

A skull set atop the spine, its face frozen in an unsettling grin. In place of its eyes were two hollow pits, so wide and deep that they seemed to be trying to swallow him. The crack between the skeleton's ever-bared teeth glowed with the bright yellow warning of a furnace. Dancing tongues of flame sprouted from its forehead, temples, and across the base, ringing its skull in a burning crown.

14

"It's you," Crevan breathed, hardly daring to believe it. "The Firecrowned King."

He knew the legend of the specter of Midlan well. It had begun during the reign of the second King — who claimed the ghost of the first King had appeared to him late in the night, robed in dusk and alive with flame. The specter charged the second King with a great task and in exchange, had offered him an eternal crown.

But he'd failed.

Every King since had sought an audience with the specter of Midlan. It became tradition for a new King to spend his coronation night alone, waiting in the throne room. If he was truly worthy of the eternal crown, the specter might appear and charge him with a task. Those who went on the specter's errands were often killed or gripped in madness. None had ever completed his task.

Crevan feared he was already mad. He downed the rest of his drink and shut his eyes tightly. But when he opened them, the specter was still grinning.

"I assure you I'm quite real, Your Majesty." The Firecrowned King's bare ribs expanded with its breath — cracking slightly to reveal the molten yellow of its marrow. "See?"

Crevan wasn't fooled. "If you're truly the Firecrowned King, why didn't you appear to me on my coronation night?"

The specter twined the sharp tips of its fingers in the bed of its lap. "You hadn't yet proved yourself," it whispered.

Hadn't yet proved himself? No King since the rise of the whisperers had managed what Crevan had done. This specter was a plague, a vision. He threw the goblet aside and raised his sword —

"Ah!"

Burning pain seared his flesh. He wrenched himself from the specter's grasp and stumbled backwards. His arm stung as if he'd laid it among the coals. But when he rolled up his sleeve, he saw no wound.

"I know what you fear, Your Majesty. I know the question you whisper into the darkness. But you aren't losing

15

your mind ... you're mad with *rage*. And you should be," the specter said, reclining in its chair. "Ultimate power should be yours. The entire Kingdom should kneel at your feet. But instead, a final enemy taints your crown. You'll never be anything as long as she lives."

Crevan clutched his wounded arm tightly and stepped back, inching towards the hidden door. "Have you come here to mock me, specter?"

"Not quite," it hissed. "The old Kings once conquered these lands with the help of their mages, and theirs was the only voice of rule. My master has been watching you closely since you took the throne. She knows you plan to return the Kings to their former glory. You've defeated the whisperers. You've bound the mages to your will. Thus far, you've managed to control your Kingdom with the help of your Sovereign Five ..." its ghoulish head tilted, "but now they've begun to fail you."

Crevan knew what the Firecrowned King spoke of. Behind the veil of mist were the worried faces of his stewards. They were faded thoughts — memories made more distant by the anger that consumed him. But he could still hear bits of their panicked messages:

*... merchants have overthrown Reginald ... supplies from Lord Gilderick are running unusually late ... Sahar's shipment never arrived ... no word from Titus ...*

The Firecrowned King cracked its bony neck, startling Crevan from his thoughts. "Yes, your throne is crumbling out from under you — while you fret over a single enemy. Such a weak King will never be worthy of my eternal crown."

"The Dragongirl is no common enemy," Crevan growled. "My army can't stop her, my mages can't find her — she's even blinded my Seer! She is a beast without equal, and she's sworn to kill me." The dull tips of his fingers brushed involuntarily across his scar — the raised, jagged cut that sliced through his beard and stopped just short of his throat.

He'd been a fingertip from death.

"Without equal?" Tiny sparks flew from the jagged crack of its nostrils as the specter snorted. "Oh, now there's

16

where you're quite wrong. For hidden in the maw of your fortress is a hunter even *she* will fear."

Crevan forgot his pain. "What hunter? Where do I find it?"

The specter's frozen grin suddenly became more menacing. "In the place you swore you'd never go again."

Crevan sank back on his heels. His tongue was so dry he could scarcely form the words: "You mean ...? No," he growled when the Firecrowned King nodded. "There's nothing in that chamber but curses and spirits. I won't be lured to my death."

"Death will take you eventually, *mortal*, whether I lure you to it or not. Mankind has but a dot of ink with which to leave its mark. A careful quill-stroke will surely fade, but a line pressed boldly may last an age." The Firecrowned King spread its emaciated arms. "How will you die, Crevan?"

He didn't get to answer.

The molten yellow lines of specter's marrow swelled as the charred bones spread apart, expanding until they cracked. Rays of light shone through the ever-widening rifts in its skull. They flooded the room with heat that singed the hair on Crevan's chin.

He threw an arm over his face as the specter exploded. A blast of flame and light knocked him backwards. The torches sputtered, the hearth fire choked and went out. Darkness swallowed the room.

Crevan lay paralyzed on the floor for hours after, covering his eyes against the many faces that watched him from the shadows.

# CHAPTER 2
## FROME'S REFUGE

"To victory!" Uncle Martin cried. "To the end of a treasonous, treacherous tyrant — may Gilderick's evil rot with him!"

The pirates raised their tankards high and took a hearty drink. They'd spent the last few days dragging their weary bodies down the highway through the Endless Plains. Now they were settled for the night in Frome's Refuge — a tiny fishing village that sat on the border of the High Seas. With their homes lying just before them, the pirates were in high spirits.

Fortunately, there were plenty of spirits to go around.

"Roll out another barrel, my dear. Brave men should never go thirsty!" Uncle Martin said, waving his cane at the nearest tavern girl. She quickly obliged — and returned from the cellar to a chorus of cheers.

They'd packed Frome's tiny inn so tightly that Kael thought the walls had actually started to bend outwards. There were smiles on the pirates' lips; many of their faces were tinged with a cheery glow. They sang and crashed their tankards together, toasting a hard-earned rest.

Not long ago, he might've been overwhelmed by the chaos. He might've retreated upstairs rather than try to brave the drunken revelry and constant roar of noise. But somewhere along the way, it'd all changed. Now instead of a rumble of nameless sounds, Kael heard the voices of his friends.

A familiar squeal drew his eyes to the other end of the table, where Captain Lysander had his face buried amongst Aerilyn's golden-brown curls. He tickled her neck with the scruff above his lips. She tried to fight him off, but to no avail.

"Let me go, you horrible rogue!"

His lips only moved more vigorously. When she tried to squirm away, he pulled her into his lap.

It wasn't long before she was nearly breathless with laughter. "Stop it! You're supposed to be — *gentle* with me."

"I *am* being gentle," he insisted.

He pressed his forehead against hers, grinning as he teased her about one thing or another. She pulled playfully at the waves of his hair. There was a glow in Aerilyn's face that had been growing steadily over the past few days. Lysander rarely took his eyes off of her anymore — let alone his lips.

"It's all sunshine and sparkles now," Uncle Martin warned from across the table. "But in a few months, there'll be a lump the size of a garment crate between you. It'll be a lot harder to steal a kiss, then."

"It's a good thing I'm an excellent thief," Lysander murmured from around Aerilyn's lips. He pulled back, an indignant look on his face. "And that *lump* is my future son — or daughter," he added quickly. "I'd be fine with a girl."

"Blasted right, you would be," Aerilyn said with a glare.

When Uncle Martin came up from his drink, he'd added another full, foamy layer to his mustache. "They're a blessed curse, children. On the one hand, they fill your house with laughter, the patter of tiny feet and so on. But on the other, your wife's figure is never quite the same. It's always bittersweet when a woman becomes a mother."

"You are wrong!" This vehement cry came from Nadine — the desert woman who'd joined them on their travels. She had skin the color of sand and stood at only a child's height. The contents of her tankard had already begun to take affect: she swayed dangerously in her chair as she scolded Uncle Martin. "In my culture, motherhood is sacred. There is no higher honor."

"I wasn't talking about the sacredness of childbearing," Uncle Martin insisted. "I was merely mourning the loss of an exceptional figure."

"Nothing will be lost!" Nadine swept her arm to the side and likely would have tumbled off the bench, had Aerilyn not caught her by the front of her dress. "She will grow more beautiful in the coming months than ever before, until she shines with the light of a thousand stars!"

"Well, I'm rather looking forward to *that*," Lysander said.

Aerilyn giggled.

Uncle Martin ranted on as if Nadine had never spoken: "And it's not just the woman who loses her figure. I used to be a thin man — now look at me!" He slapped the slight belly that protruded from his tunic. "It never goes away, either. Once you've got it, you'll be buried with it."

Lysander rolled his eyes and very firmly declared that would never happen to him. But moments later, Kael glanced over and caught the good captain staring worriedly at his stomach.

An argument erupted at the table ahead of him, drawing his eyes away. Something strange had happened to Battlemage Jake: he hadn't quite been himself the last few days — a fact that hadn't gone unnoticed by his companions.

They'd all tried to cheer him up. Lysander kept him busy, Uncle Martin kept his tankard full, Nadine and Aerilyn had even asked about his research. They were able to coax a smile from him every once in a while, but it never stayed for long.

Now poor Jake was trapped between Morris and Shamus — both of whom staunchly believed that a full belly could cure any ailment.

"Here, have a plateful of these roasted potatoes," Shamus, the master shipbuilder of Copperdock, said. "Aye, shovel those down and they'll keep you full for days."

"I don't feel like potatoes," Jake mumbled. He stabbed half-heartedly at his plate, eyes distant behind his rounded spectacles.

"Well, how about some soup?" Morris pinched a steaming bowl between the nubs of his arms and lifted it carefully towards Jake. "Broth is good for the innards, lad. It'll warm your heart — ouch!"

The soup sloshed to the side and onto the tender flesh of Morris's arm. He yelped and dropped the bowl directly on top of whatever gravy-covered slice of meat had been on Jake's plate.

He sighed. "I don't feel like soup."

"How about some bread?"

"No, thank you."

"A nice mince pie'll cheer your belly," Morris croaked around a mouthful of dough. "Leastways, it cheers mine!"

"And the onions will clear your head," Shamus added.

Morris frowned. "No, *garlic* clears your head. Onions make you smart."

"You've been out of the water too long, you crusty old seadog. Carrots make you smart — garlic keeps the goblins away."

"There's no such thing as goblins."

"Well, there's no such thing as merfolk, either —"

"Merfolk are real! They only come out when it's rainy, though. So it's hard to spot them ..."

While they argued over which food would keep what imaginary creatures at bay, Jake slumped further in his chair. The next time Kael glanced over, he had his arms flat on the table and his head buried deep.

"He'll be all right."

Kyleigh's voice was little more than a murmur, but her words drew him in.

The flames behind her eyes smoldered as she stared at Jake; a slight smile bent her lips. "It seems our mage friend has finally come across a problem he can't solve ... but he'll manage. He'll be back to scribbling in that journal of his before you know it."

Kael certainly hoped so.

He sat close to Kyleigh. Their arms rested on the table between them, pressed together from elbow to wrist. He could feel the incredible warmth beneath her skin: it passed through the scales of her armor and the fibers of his shirt, sealing them together.

No matter where he looked, he kept her in the corner of his eye ... and no matter where he went, he would keep her in his heart.

A hawk's scream cut over the top of them, followed by a clatter of bones striking the table. The inn was so crowded that Eveningwing had decided to stay in his hawk form for dinner. Now he sat in the rafters and screeched for seconds.

"Go find your own meal," Silas growled.

Eveningwing's piercing eyes locked onto him. Silas glared and wrapped his arms protectively around the small flock of baked chickens he'd been busily devouring.

It had come as no great shock to Kael when he discovered that Silas was a shapechanger. The glowing eyes that sat beneath his dark mat of hair fit a lion much better than a man. What *did* surprise him was the fact that he'd chosen to follow them out of the plains when he didn't much care for any of them — a fact he reminded them of nearly every hour.

Eveningwing screeched again.

Silas's arms tightened around his prey. "If you wanted to eat human food, then you should've worn your human skin," he said haughtily.

Kyleigh slapped his arms away and grabbed one of the chickens. "You have plenty to share."

Silas hissed at her.

She leveled the carcass at his nose, brandishing it like a sword. "Do that again, and I'll really give you something to mew about."

Silas glowered a moment before he shrugged and went back to his meal. Kyleigh tossed the chicken into the rafters — where Eveningwing snapped it up.

Kael's eyes trailed across his companions once more. He sat quietly, drinking in the noise of their chatter ... trying to burn every detail of their faces into his memory.

"I think I'm going to turn in," he finally said.

Kyleigh nodded. "Sleep well."

He returned her smile with a fleeting one of his own before he trudged upstairs.

With so many of them holed up together, they'd had to squeeze in wherever they would fit. Kael shared his tiny chamber with a crowd of pirates. Their bedrolls were packed end-to-end all across the floor, creating a lumpy, uneven maze with very little bare space in between.

Kael had his things in the spot closest to the door. He knew this meant he was likely to get trampled when the pirates finally came upstairs, but he was all right with that. He wasn't planning to sleep for long.

"Evening, Thelred," he said as he slipped off his boots.

He got no reply.

Thelred had claimed the room's only bed. He lay atop the sheets, one arm slumped across his eyes and the nub of his leg balanced upon a stack of pillows. The plate of food Aerilyn had brought up for him lay untouched on his bedside table.

As Kael stared at the bandages around Thelred's knee, the room dropped away and thrust him into a memory: he heard the blast of Finks's spell and saw Thelred's blood paint the walls.

*It'd all happened too quickly — nobody could've possibly moved fast enough to save him*, his mind whispered. But the memory lashed him again.

The force of colors and sounds, the raw red of the blood and Thelred's piercing screams — nothing could erase what his eyes had seen, what his ears had heard. He found no solace in the assurances of his mind, nor any comfort from the mouths of his friends.

For the memory spoke the truth.

With the black beast finally thrust from his heart, he felt as if a window had been opened before his eyes. He'd spent days combing through the memories of what he'd done in the plains. He saw the tattered edges of his plans, worn frail by his anguish. His face burned fiercely each time he reached a tangle in the threads — a mistake that could've easily been avoided.

23

There were many worn patches, many bunched-up knots. He watched himself fumble through that season of his life with his lip curled over his teeth. He'd fallen so easily to his sorrows — he realized that, now. He saw his recklessness and his apathy for what they were: the twin wings of his great black weakness.

It reminded him of the stories Roland used to tell — the ones that always ended badly. The heroes he'd spoken about had all had one great flaw. Their weaknesses slowly consumed them as the tale went on and by the end of the story, they'd paid dearly for their mistakes.

That was what burned Kael worst of all. He deserved to pay the price for what he'd done. Instead, he'd walked away unscathed. The pirates and giants filled the grave he'd dug for himself. Others bore his wounds. It should've been *him* lying broken upon that bed, but it wasn't.

Thelred was a monument of his mistakes, the embodiment of all his errors —a living reminder that he'd been selfish. And Kael knew he had no more hope against his weakness than any of Roland's heroes. The path he was on would eventually end. But no matter where it ended, Kael would be standing there alone. He alone would pay the price.

Of this, he was determined.

*******

*A knock on the door woke him.*

*He was back in Gravy Bay, asleep in one of the stuffed chairs in the mansion's library. Someone pounded on the front door — three sharp raps. Kael pulled himself from the chair and trudged out into the hallway.*

*His eyes were still heavy with sleep. Though he tried to blink it back, the darkness kept creeping in. The next time he opened his eyes, he was standing at the front door.*

Knock, knock, knock.

*"Hold on," Kael muttered as he fumbled with the door's latch. It felt much heavier than usual. The door groaned and almost seemed to fight him as he tugged it. When he finally*

*pulled it open, he blinked at the man standing on the other side.*

*He was incredibly thin, with a lank mop of hair and eyes like pits. Angry waves of red and orange billowed up behind him. Screams rode the ash-thickened air, drifting in from the village below.*

*Gilderick smiled — as if he could feel the terror that gripped Kael's chest. Hundreds of shadows gathered behind him. They were taller than men with eyes that burned white-hot. Their arms and chests glistened with the wet blood of the villagers.*

*"I knew I'd find you here."*

*Gilderick's lips didn't move, but Kael could hear his voice in the depths of his ears — as if it'd spoken from within him.*

*"Come with me," Gilderick whispered. "And don't worry about your friends ... they can come, too."*

*His pitiless gaze swept over Kael's shoulder, and he saw his friends had gathered behind him. Their bodies were shadows; their eyes were white and lifeless. He screamed as their arms wrapped about him, but they didn't stop.*

*Lysander and Thelred pulled down. Aerilyn kicked the legs out from under him. It was Kyleigh who grabbed him by the roots of his hair and jerked his head back — forcing him to lock eyes with Gilderick.*

*"This will only hurt a moment." His gaze widened, coiling around Kael's soul. "Yes, little Wright — with your strings in my hand, I'll bring the Kingdom to its knees!"*

*******

A loud gasp startled Kael from his sleep. He choked against the lingering panic of the dream. It took several moments of deep, steady breathing to calm the thudding of his heart.

The room was dark and still. The small fire had burned down to a few feeble coals. As his eyes adjusted, he could see the shadowy forms of the pirates scattered all around him. He watched their burly chests rise and fall with their snores. When he was certain they were all soundly asleep, he stood.

He'd packed his rucksack a few nights ago. The giants had given them so much food for the journey home that he was certain nobody had noticed his pilfering. He had enough food stashed to travel for a few weeks.

After that, he'd be on his own.

A common room littered with the bodies of sleeping pirates blocked his path to the front door. He had to pick his way across them, slipping between bedrolls and rucksacks as he crept towards the door. He was nearly there when he accidentally stepped on a creaky plank.

It squeaked loudly beneath his boot. He waited, breathless, listening to the grunts and snores. When he was certain nobody had heard, he eased his boot off the floor.

The plank creaked again.

Kael's lips moved in silent swears as he skipped over the last of the pirates and went for the door — which moaned like a northern wind when he opened it. He shut it as quietly as he could, hoping to mercy that the pirates slept on.

A plat of mud and filth wrapped around the inn like a moat — a large pigsty that gave all of Frome's Refuge a very distinct stench. Kael crossed the narrow planks of wood that hovered over the reeking mud and jogged for the cover of the trees.

He felt strange as he ran beneath the shadows ... lighter and heavier all at once. He knew he was doing the right thing. In fact, he was certain of it. So why did his legs fall so heavily? Why did his boots scrape against the ground? It was strange how something right could still leave a bitter taste in his mouth.

"What in blazes are you doing?"

Kael was so startled that he leapt sideways into a tree. "Kyleigh!"

Her blackened armor hid her well in the shadows. But he could tell by the tone of her voice that she was glaring. "So

I'm not allowed to leave *you* without telling, but you're allowed to leave me. Is that how it works?"

There was no point in asking her how she'd known. No matter how careful he was, she always seemed to be at least two paces ahead of him. "I have to do this."

She raised a brow. "Really? You *have* to sneak off in the dead of night and leave all your friends wondering what's become of you?"

"Yes. They can't know where I've gone."

"I think they'll be able to guess."

"I killed one of the Countess's agents," Kael said through his teeth. "I think she knows what I am and even if she doesn't, Gilderick *certainly* knows — he knows everything." Anger bubbled up at the memory: Gilderick sitting inside his head, thumbing through the whole story of his life as if he'd had every right to it. Kael took a deep breath. "I don't know what all he learned, but he could very well know what I plan to do next. And if that's the case, he could easily follow —"

"Or he could be dead."

He wasn't. Kael knew in his heart that a snake like Gilderick wouldn't die so easily. But he couldn't explain this to Kyleigh. "Even if he's dead, what about the Countess? How long before she sends her army after me? If she tells the King ..." Kael ran a hand through his hair, fighting against all the many little worries that crawled up his stomach, trying to stuff them back into the depths. "We had a slim chance against Titus, but we can't face Midlan. I won't be the one who brings the rulers down upon us. The pirates will be safe in the Bay. The giants can take care of themselves. As for me," he met her eyes, "I'm going home."

"Kael —"

"I won't change my mind. Scold me all you want, but you know this has to happen."

After a moment, she looked away. She turned to stare up at the gaps of sky between the branches, her face unreadable. "I know," she said heavily. She reached beside her and pulled a rucksack out of the brush. "That's why I went ahead and packed."

That was the absolute last thing he wanted. "You aren't coming with me."

"You can't stop me."

He glared at her. "If you come along, Shamus will follow. You know he will."

"I've already taken care of it."

Kael eyed her warily. "What did you tell him?"

"That you and I are running away together, of course," she said with a smirk.

He hoped the shadows would mask the sudden burn in his face. "You shouldn't have done that."

"Well, it was the truth."

"*Well*, now he thinks we're —"

"It doesn't matter what he thinks. That man would've followed me to the far corner of the Kingdom without a second thought. Now he won't. I told him it was an absolute secret," she added with a grin. "Which should give us a few months to gallivant around the Kingdom in private —"

"*Kyleigh!*"

"What?"

"This isn't a game." He dragged a hand down the side of his face, concentrating on the pressure of his fingertips to keep his voice even. "I left the mountains to find an army. That was my only task, and I've failed — I've failed Tinnark, and I've failed Amos and Roland. Now half the realm knows what I am and I've got no choice but to run, empty-handed, to the one place in the Kingdom where I won't be followed. You came looking for me because you thought I could help you destroy the Five." His hands fell away. "I've got nothing to offer you, Kyleigh. Not anymore."

She stared at him for a long moment. "Are you finished?"

"Finished with what?"

"All this moping and slumping about."

"I'm not —"

"You are. And speaking as someone who's been in trouble on more than one occasion: there's always a way out. Don't give up just yet."

"How can I not? I've lost everything."

"Not quite everything — you'll always have me."

Though he fought it fiercely, a reluctant smile bent his lips. "Yes, whether I want you or not."

She laughed, and his face burned again ... though this time for an entirely different reason.

Apparently, Kael hadn't shut the inn's door as well as he'd thought. He heard the far-off screech of its hinges and a loud *bang* as it slammed against the wall.

Kyleigh pulled him away before he could look back. "Let's go."

So he followed her into the night, leaving Frome's Refuge and his friends behind him.

# CHAPTER 3
## OAKLOFT

The next few days passed by in relative calm. Kael found himself on a boat once more, surrounded by the quiet of the seas.

They traveled with a small fleet of merchants bound for the Grandforest. Crates filled with wares from the seas littered the deck, each one marked for trade. The sailors were pleasant enough, though they were far tamer than the pirates: there were no rowdy ballads, water was served alongside their salty dinners, and the lanterns went out obediently at nightfall. Still, Kael couldn't complain.

Once he'd proven that he knew his way around a ship, the merchants were happy for his help. The helmsman even gave him a few hours at night to steer ... and these were the hours he dreaded most.

It was in the quiet watches of the night that Kael's thoughts turned to Tinnark.

For so long he'd had to keep his village at the back of his mind. There'd always been something else at hand — a task he had to finish, an obstacle he had to overcome. He hadn't allowed himself much time to worry over Amos and Roland. He'd had to push his anger aside.

Now there was nothing in his way. Now when he looked up, the mountains loomed a few paces ahead. He could see their ice-crusted peaks, he could imagine that Titus and his army was hidden somewhere among them. He saw the shadows their ironclad bodies cast against the rocks ...

But he couldn't reach them.

It was such a horribly constant occurrence that he ought to have considered it a gift — for Kael was certain that no man in the history of bad luck had ever had a more endless streak than his. Only *he* could've stood so close to the thing he wanted and somehow have been further away than ever. Only *he* could've spent seasons gathering an army to have it ripped away at the last.

*You're doing the right thing*, he told himself.

But why did the right thing always have to rear its head in such a difficult place? Though it was comforting to know that his friends in the lowlands would be spared a battle for the mountains, it made his stomach churn to think that Titus would go on ruling simply because there wasn't a force in the realm powerful enough to stand against him.

Kael supposed it was only in stories that good overcame evil. Perhaps in the real Kingdom, men had to choose between what they wanted and what was truly best. Had he known what was best, he would've gladly done it. But the future was as shrouded and quiet as the seas. For now, his heart was his only helm — his guide across the dark and to the distant hours ahead.

One of those hours would see the dawn break over his choice to leave his friends behind. Only then would he be able to see if he'd chosen well.

******

One morning, just as the mist began to rise, Kael saw they were close to land. The helmsman emerged and sleepily waved him from the wheel. "This bit is tricky," he muttered as he turned the ship towards the trees.

A vein of sea slipped between the shoreline and became a wide river. At the captain's orders, the merchants drew oars from below deck and put their backs into paddling. The river's waters flowed lazily, but the current still slowed them.

For an hour or so, the banks sat far enough apart that it was like being in the middle of a lake. But the further the boat cut into land, the narrower the river became.

Trees hemmed the water on either side. Their trunks were thick and their branches stretched across the river,

31

meeting and twining together in its middle. The canopy of new leaves that sprouted from their skin blotted out the sky — only shreds of morning light made it through their wall. But as enormous as the trees were, their roots were the most dangerous part.

They stretched out from the walls of dirt at the river's edge — knotted vines that were nearly as big around as Kael's waist. They sank into the murky water and disappeared, only to pop up again a few feet later, their knots covered in moss.

Kael kept a wary eye on the roots as they snaked in and out of the river. He knew they would be every bit as unforgiving as sharp rocks. If the helmsman strayed too close to the shore, those knots would chew through the bottom of the boat and drag them into the murky depths.

"I hate this place," the helmsman muttered. His knuckles were white about the wheel as his eyes shifted up to the trees. "Blasted cursed, it is. There's no sky, it's too quiet. We haven't even made port yet and we've already picked up a ghost!"

Kael tried not to roll his eyes. The merchants had been going on for days about how their boat was haunted. A few lids had been pushed off some of the barrels; something had gotten into a cage of chickens. Every once in a while, they'd find bits of bone lying around. But instead of blaming it on the rats like any normal crew, they'd immediately claimed it was a ghost.

"The forest holds them back," the helmsman went on. "When a man dies, his spirit's supposed to float free. But they can't float out of the forest. They get stuck — tangled up there." He pointed to the thick canopy above them. "Sometimes its years before they pull themselves out. Sometimes its hundreds of years. And in the meantime, they haunt the living realm. Are you sleeping in the woods tonight?"

"I was considering it," Kael said, his mouth suddenly dry.

The helmsman's lips pressed into a firm line. "Well, I don't have to tell you, then. You'll hear it for yourself when night falls."

Not surprisingly, that didn't make Kael feel any better about the journey.

He looked away from the trees and saw that Kyleigh had emerged from below deck. Her rucksack lay in a heap upon the floor and she was slumped miserably over the railing, head buried in her arms.

"We're nearly there, thank Fate," she muttered when Kael stepped in beside her.

Poor Kyleigh. He wished he had one of Amos's tonics with him. It might've tasted foul, but it would've helped to calm her stomach. "How did you know we were close?"

She turned and pressed her back against the rails. Little sunspots drifted across her face and neck, igniting her eyes in a fiery green. He was sorry when she closed them.

"Those blasted waves had stopped knocking us about, so I knew we'd reached the river. And if we've found the river, then Oakloft can't be far ahead," she murmured, her voice a little rough. "Try not to think too much about that old helmsman's tales. He's just trying to get the better of you."

Kael hadn't realized she'd heard. "I wasn't thinking about them."

"Oh?"

"No. In fact, I'd already forgotten."

She smirked, but didn't reply.

They fought their way up the river for another hour or so, until the banks became treacherously narrow. Kael's toes curled tightly and the merchants' voices grew louder as they navigated their way around one final turn. At last, they popped free.

The current slowed considerably as the river widened. The banks stretched further apart, giving them plenty of room to steer. From above, Kael imagined it must've looked like a swollen lump inside a snake's belly.

The trees drifted back and little houses cropped up along the shore. The houses were short and squat, their beams carved from the branches of enormous trees. Many of them looked to be rather old, as well: their walls were covered in leafy vines and thick carpets of moss blanketed their roofs.

There was a small clump of docks in the thickest part of the river. Several boats already bobbed at port, their decks either being emptied or filled. A few of the merchants from the seas were dressed in blue tunics with a gold serpent etched upon their chests.

"Why are they still wearing Duke Reginald's emblem?" Kael wondered aloud.

"I'm not sure. It's probably just some sort of disguise. If news of the Duke's death hasn't reached the Grandforest yet, I imagine Chaucer wants to keep it that way." Kyleigh watched them for a moment more before she casually drew up her hood. "Still … I think we ought to slip out of town quickly."

Kael agreed.

They were taking the longer route to the mountains: through the Grandforest's many winding roads and into a pass marked as King's Cleft on his map. It would lead them closer to Midlan, but Kael would take his chances. He wasn't going to risk going through Bartholomew's Pass again.

"We'll meet in the woods outside of town," Kyleigh said, and he nodded absently.

They'd decided it would be best to separate rather than travel through Oakloft together. Of all the Sovereign Five, Countess D'Mere was the most mysterious. The others had all had some reputation of cruelty or greed. There'd been no doubting what they were. But the Countess was different.

She traveled freely through her region, usually in a carriage and with only a handful of guards. She spoke with her people directly. She stayed at inns and often invited common folk to dine at her table. Three of the merchants he sailed with claimed to have kissed her hand. Everywhere he turned, Kael got the same answer: Countess D'Mere was as just as she was beautiful.

And yet, people had a nasty habit of disappearing in the Grandforest. Anyone who opposed the Countess would undoubtedly vanish — only to turn up a short while later, having died from some unfortunate accident. There was never any proof that she was responsible, of course. Most wrote the accidents off as bad luck, or blamed them on competing merchants. But Kael wasn't so sure.

He remembered D'Mere's icy gaze all too well — the cold indifference with which she'd watched him beaten. Her agent, Holthan, had stalked him for hours unseen. He'd been incredibly strong, as well: it was only by sheer luck that Kael had managed to escape his grasp.

Now Holthan's body lay burned along with Gilderick's army. The Countess had probably figured out what had become of him. There was no way Kael could hope to pass through her region unnoticed.

He expected her spies to be watching him — from the moment he stepped off the boat, until he ducked into the shadow of the mountains. Kael was counting on it. In fact, he wanted D'Mere to see him. If she knew he was in the Grandforest, she wouldn't send her agents to the seas.

And his friends would be safe.

The sailors lowered the ramp and Kyleigh slipped past them without a word. Kael had gone to follow when the helmsman grabbed his arm.

"You're headed north, aren't you? You look like you've got a little mountain blood in you," he muttered, his eyes flicking to the top of Kael's head. "Listen closely now, lad: spirits aren't the only trouble in these woods. Word is that merchants have been disappearing along the northern paths. There's a swamp up that way — a cursed, festering mound of filth and sick. They chased all the barbarians into it a couple of decades back. Wanted to get them clear of decent folk —"

"I'll be careful," Kael said shortly. He knew if he stood there a moment longer, he was in real danger of knocking the helmsman's teeth through his lip.

"Half of the caravans headed to the Valley don't make it," he called as Kael marched down the ramp. "They find the bodies later ... all pale and torn to shreds, not a drop of blood left in them. If you ask me, it sounds like the barbarians are starting to leak out of the swamps. Everybody knows they can't resist the taste of human flesh."

It sounded to Kael as if *everybody* knew nothing. Heated words formed upon his tongue as the helmsman babbled on, but he managed to hold them back. He was relieved when the noise of the village finally drowned his voice.

The mossy houses swept by; the dirt moved quickly under his feet. He kept his head down and stayed on the widest path, the one he was certain would lead him into the woods. Kyleigh would be waiting for him there — in the shelter of the trees and away from the eyes of the village guard.

The walls around Oakloft were twice a man's height and wrought from thick planks of wood. They were every bit as mossy as the houses. From a distance, it looked as if the town had been surrounded by a giant bush.

The wide gate was propped open. A few guards wandered back and forth across the creaking ramparts, spears propped against their shoulders. Kael planned to dart by them quickly. He would keep his head down and walk as if he had important business — exactly how Uncle Martin slipped past the kitchen maids.

His plan was a good one. Unfortunately, he made it to the gates just as a caravan pushed in from the other side.

Wagons and horses and hordes of men tromped through, blocking up the gates. The bulk of their party pushed Kael to the side. He knew he would have no choice but to wait his turn. He went to lean up against one of the bushy walls — and leapt back with a yelp.

A ragged man was tucked behind the leaves, sitting cross-legged with his back against the wall. The man's skin was so dark with filth that Kael would've been less surprised to spot him crawling out of a chimney.

"Sorry. I didn't see you there."

The man didn't reply.

36

His mane of scraggly hair ran directly into his scraggly beard. His head was bent as if he'd fallen asleep. Between the angle of his head and the severity of his hair, Kael couldn't see his face.

"Can you hear me? Are you all right?"

When the man still didn't respond, Kael looked closer. His clothing was made up entirely of rags: bits of trousers, shirtsleeves, and what looked suspiciously like stockings were all knotted together and fashioned around his boney frame like bandages.

He was unnaturally still. Kael had gone to tap him on the shoulder when a knobby hand shot up and clamped around his wrist. "I thought you were dead!" Kael gasped, ripping his arm free. "You could've just said you were all right instead of grabbing me like ... oh."

*Oh* was all Kael could think to say. For when the man raised his head, he saw that another set of rags had been bound tightly across his eyes.

He was blind.

"I'm sorry. I didn't realize —"

"Are you going to the mountains?"

Shock stole Kael's breath. Filthy though he was, the man's voice was commanding and clear. He carried his words as if each one had been made to fit into the next — as if he'd measured every lift and fall into a perfect sound.

After a moment, his bandaged head tilted to the side. "Hmm ... now there's an answer I've not heard before."

"What answer?" Kael said carefully.

"No answer." The blind man cracked a smile. Surprisingly, he still had all of his teeth. "I've asked the same question to every man who's passed through these gates. And for all the time I've sat here, I've heard nothing but *nos* and *not todays* and even a few *nevers*. I've not been met with silence before. So perhaps silence means ... yes?"

"No, I'm not going to the mountains," Kael said firmly.

The blind man slapped his hands to his ears — rattling a shower of dust from the wilds of his hair and onto his shoulders. "*Lies!* Words flung halfway out, a bird caught by the feet as he struggles for the open window. Flee, little bird. Flee!"

"I'm sorry, but I'm not going to the mountains," Kael said again. When he tried to walk away, the blind man wailed all the louder.

"No, oh no. He's trapped! More beats of his wings, desperate fluttering with the blue sky just beyond —"

"I'm not lying."

"— but he can't escape. Something holds him back." Then without warning, the blind man spread his arms out wide and howled: "Fly! Fly, little bird! Wing into the sunlight and leave the gilded prison at your back! Use your beak, use your claws!"

By this point, people were beginning to stare. The merchants at the tail end of the caravan walked with their heads turned back and their mouths agape. Two of the guards peered curiously over the ramparts.

Blast it all. This was the last thing Kael needed.

He tried to walk away quickly, but the blind man latched onto his ankle. "Flee! Flee, little b —"

"*Yes* — all right? Yes, I'm going to the mountains. Now for mercy's sake, will you please shut it?"

"That depends ..." his filthy head cocked to the side, "will you take me with you?"

Kael didn't want to have a blind man fumbling along behind him the whole way to the mountains. In fact, he couldn't think of anything he wanted less — except, perhaps, to be caught by the guards and turned over to the Countess.

Almost on cue, the blind man started to wail.

"Stop it. Stop — *fine*!" Kael hissed. "You can come with me."

His smile returned immediately. "What wonderful news! Just let me gather my things ..." His knobby hands patted the ground around him furiously, finally coming to rest atop a mossy hill. "I've been waiting a long while for someone to take me to the mountains," he said as he dug his hands into the moss. "Ages and ages, it seems like."

Kael didn't believe him — until he tugged hard on the hill of moss and a filthy rucksack burst out. "How long has that been sitting there?"

"It sat down when I did, of course. What a silly question." The blind man raised his hands. "Now help me up."

Kael pulled him to his feet. "Come on," he grumbled.

He'd taken several steps before he realized that the blind man wasn't following. He stood back near the wall, holding his hands out before him as if he read a book.

"Something very heavy rests upon your shoulders, traveler," he said after a moment. "I heard it in your steps when you first approached. *Ah, here's a man who's walked the earth*, I thought to myself. *Here is a man who understands the importance of the prints he leaves behind, because he's already left so many.* I've heard only a few such steps. Usually they belong to men with hands that are crusted hard with age. Your hands are surprisingly young." Kael could hear the dry rasp as the blind man rubbed his fingers together. "And yet ... they're slick with blood."

Without another word, the blind man swooped the filthy rucksack across his shoulders and stumbled forward. He latched onto Kael's pack with his knobby fingers and held on as they passed through the gates.

Kael wasn't sure how deep into the forest they walked before Kyleigh materialized from the trees. When she dropped her hood, he could read the surprise clearly on her face.

"We're probably going to die before we get there, anyways. So what does it matter?" Kael grumbled before she could speak.

Kyleigh shrugged. "Fair enough. But may I at least ask *why* we've added a blind man to our party?"

Kael sighed heavily, and swore he could almost feel the weight sink down upon his shoulders as he said: "I couldn't leave him behind. He knows too much."

# CHAPTER 4
## THE SPIDER AND THE BARD

As soon as Oakloft's gates were out of sight, Kyleigh led them off the road and into the shelter of the woods. It wasn't long before the Grandforest swallowed them up.

Giant trees towered all around them. Many of their branches sat so heavily that they sagged to the ground. The thick shade cast by their hulking tops strangled most of the grass, leaving the ground to be taken over by dirt and moss.

Dry whispers fluttered down occasionally — the far-off sound of a breeze that stirred the trees' tops. But for the most part, the world beneath the branches was eerily quiet.

Kael's ears began to ring after a while, as if the pressure of the silence was every bit as painful as a sharp howl. His lungs burned and he realized that he'd been holding his breath. When he exhaled, the noise of his breathing was frustratingly loud.

While he struggled not to make too much noise, Kyleigh traveled easily. She moved *with* the silence of the woods: her boots rose and fell, carrying her in a rolling walk across the shady ground. Her shoulders turned occasionally towards the trees. She would tilt her head to the side, slowing her pace a bit as she watched the branches.

Kael thought she might be searching for something — or perhaps she was just unsettled by the quiet. In any case, she was beginning to make him nervous.

"Are we in danger?" he finally hissed.

"Hmm ...? Oh, no. Not at all."

"Then why do you keep looking around?"

She spun on her heels and walked backwards a few paces. He was relieved to see her smiling. "I was just listening to everybody. It's been a while since my last walk through the forest."

"Listening to everybody?" Kael wondered if he'd missed something. He stopped to look — and the blind man collided with his back.

"Have we arrived? Have we reached the mountains?"

Kael had gotten so used to the tug of the blind man's hands upon his pack that he'd actually forgotten he was there. "We haven't even been traveling for a day! Of course we're not at the mountains."

He stumbled back a step when the blind man's grip tightened. "We're still in the forest? Oh, then we must move on! I don't like these trees — they're treacherous."

Kyleigh clutched a hand to her lips — but didn't quite cover the corners of her smile. "No, surely not! There's nothing worse than a treacherous tree."

Kael didn't think it was funny. He knew how hysterical the blind man could get, and he certainly didn't want him to start yelling again. "You're just imagining things. Trees can't be treacherous."

"Oh, but they can!" the blind man insisted. "The trees see everything, but they say nothing. I wonder how many vipers hide amongst the leaves? How many cutthroats and thieves? They must've watched countless men be murdered, must've heard countless screams. Yes, they hear and they see, but they do nothing to stop it." His knobby hand trembled as he swept it above them. "Think of the stories they might tell us ... if only they would speak."

At that very moment, a gust of wind rattled through the branches. It stirred the leaves and carried their whispers downwards ... well, Kael *supposed* it was the wind that had moved them. But though the trees swayed, the gust never quite reached the floor. He heard the wind, but couldn't feel it.

Little bumps rose unbidden across his arms as the leaves continued to whisper. Perhaps the helmsman had been right: perhaps there *were* spirits trapped in the trees.

41

"Blazes," Kyleigh murmured as the air went still. "You're quite the storyteller, aren't you?"

"I was a bard, once. Many years ago," the blind man said. He urged Kael forward. "Move, young man! We should put these woods to our heels."

Their pace quickened after that. Kyleigh talked to the blind man for the rest of the day. She tread carefully through their conversation and her questions came in tiny spoonfuls, as if she could somehow sense lunacy behind his bandaged face.

"You said you were a bard?"

"A singer of songs and a teller of tales, yes." He inhaled deeply through his nose — and exhaled across the back of Kael's neck. "Spring's nearly ended, now. It'll soon be summer. Then autumn. Find a mate, raise a brood, head south for the winter. It's remarkable how our lives change with the seasons, isn't it? Every winter we survive wilts us a little more. A man's first spring is considerably greener than his last."

His words made Kael's skin crawl for a moment before he forced himself to be reasonable. It was the blind man's unusual voice that made his words sound important. If Kael stripped it back, he could hear the insanity.

"Why did you stop being a bard?" Kyleigh said.

It was a wasted question. Bards were known to be wanderers, and the blind man couldn't travel if he couldn't see. He'd stopped when the lights went out — that was the obvious answer. But it wasn't the answer he gave:

"In my dreams, I see a land of welcome — a refuge I can't quite reach. I've felt the jagged shadows stretch across my head. Their promise shelters me against the gales that would carry me away. I see them clearly when I sleep: clouds impaled upon its spiny back, unbranded skin, high peaks dressed in frosted cloaks ... but their embrace is warm to some." The blind man's shaggy beard twitched upwards as he smiled. "The mountains are calling me ... and I long to answer."

This time, Kael didn't let himself be tricked by the blind man's voice. He listened carefully, peeling the tone from his words until he could hear the answer clearly: "So you've given up being a bard so you can travel to the mountains."

The blind man's smile fell slack. "If you prefer to simply swallow it whole, then yes. But if you let it soak, let it simmer —"

"Why would you have to give up barding to travel to the mountains?" Kael cut in. "It seems to me that telling stories along the way would get you there faster. You could earn enough coin to get there on your own instead of having to beg for someone else to take y —"

The blind man whistled over the top of him. He warbled at the treetops so loudly that the birds began to sing back. They whistled, chirped, and squawked, each one replying in its own tongue.

Their song was so loud that Kael had to plug his ears against it. "Stop trying to avoid the question! Just answer me plainly —"

"Oh, hush," Kyleigh said. Her arm wrapped about his shoulder and her hand clamped over his mouth. She pulled a finger from his ear and held him by the wrist, forcing him to listen.

To Kael, the birds' cries were an unintelligible mash — a song goaded into racket by the blind man's warbling. But Kyleigh seemed to be enjoying it.

She was standing so closely beside him that he could feel her breathing against his shoulder. Her chest caught mid-rise — as if she was reluctant to make any sound, even to breathe.

He could see her open-mouthed grin from the corner of his eye. There was a brightness in the green of her gaze as she watched the trees, and he didn't want to see it snuffed out. So he stood quietly.

At last, the blind man's song ended. The birds chirped a few moments more. The space between their cries lengthened, as if they were calling out and waiting for an answer. But as the moments passed and they heard no reply, they began to quiet. The birds hushed their song and the forest grew still once more.

"What's your name?" Kyleigh said when the blind man's whistling ended.

"Hmm, now there's a question I've not heard in a long while ..." He was silent for a moment. Then he snapped his fingers — so loudly that Kael jumped. "*The beggar at the gates*. That's what the people of Oakloft used to call me."

Kyleigh frowned. "That can't be your real name."

"My *real* name? Ah, well ... oh, that's back. That's a quite ways back ..." He muttered to himself for such a long moment that Kael thought he might've tumbled off the edge of the pit. "Baird!" he finally exclaimed.

"Baird the Beggar-Bard," Kyleigh said with a smile. "That's got a peculiar ring to it. I'm surprised you forgot it."

"As am I," Baird murmured. Then he tugged on Kael's pack. "And what's your name, young man?"

He said the first name he could think of: "Jonathan."

"Hmm ... is that truly your name?"

"Yes."

"Then why do you thrust it out of your mouth like a friend shoved in an arrow's path?"

"I don't thrust it anywhere. That's my name," Kael said shortly.

The tangled edges of his beard scratched across his ragged tunic as Baird shook his head. "No, that can't possibly be it. A man's name ought to sound at home upon his lips."

"He's got a point, Kael," Kyleigh said.

He shoved her.

"*Kael*," Baird murmured, testing it. "Yes ... that sounds about right. And what about you, young lady? What's your name?"

"Kyleigh."

Baird's hands snapped open and Kael stumbled forward with the sudden change in weight. "No, it couldn't possibly ... " He walked towards Kyleigh, hands outstretched. But he stumbled just before he reached her.

She caught him by the elbows and pulled his thin body up with ease. "Careful. You don't want to —"

"Kyleigh Swordmaiden."

Her shoulders stiffened when Baird grasped her face. The calloused edges of his thumbs ran across her brows, down the bridge of her nose and along the line of her chin. When his fingers brushed her lips, Kael decided that he'd had enough.

"Stop touching her. What do you think you're —?"

"He's looking at me," Kyleigh said from around his fingers.

When his hands had traced over every inch of her face, he leaned back. "Hmm ... no lines, no scars, no touch of age. You're as beautiful as you were the first time I saw you. You were in the company of great warriors, then. I could only watch from afar." His hands fell down her neck and came to rest upon her shoulders. He squeezed them tightly. "Kyleigh Swordmaiden — hero of the realm and dishonored knight. Here's a woman who understands the changing of the seasons better than anybody."

Kael was more than a little surprised. He knew that Kyleigh had been a knight — but she made no mention at all of being a hero. "What does he mean, *a hero of the realm*? What did you do?"

"She slew the Falsewright! She cleft his head from his shoulders with her mighty sword! The King's tried to bury it. His scribes have tried to strike it away, to twist the tale." He held up a finger. "But I remember. *I* know the truth."

Kael had no idea what Baird was talking about. When he looked to Kyleigh, she shrugged.

*Cracked*, she mouthed, tapping the side of her head. Then she put Baird's hands on her pack. "Let's keep moving, shall we?"

"Yes, we need to find a safer place to rest before nightfall!" He stuck his shaggy face into her pony's tail. "Your scent is much more pleasant than Kael's."

She laughed.

They walked away, and Kael followed slowly. For a man who claimed to be blind, Baird could see an awful lot — and there was absolutely no doubt he was hiding something.

*He's crazed*, a voice inside his head said. *He's only rambling.*

Though Kael wanted very much to believe it, he couldn't quite convince himself. Behind that voice was a wall of clouds: they rumbled, their billowing skin brightened by the storm trapped within them — a storm that might pass or break.

Either way, Kael was resolved to be ready. And in the meantime, he wouldn't let Baird out of his sight.

*******

Night came upon them quickly. The heavy cover of the trees strangled the light long before the sun had set. Kael thought they ought to make camp before things got any darker. But Baird thought differently.

"No, we must press on! I don't trust these trees. We need to find an honest place to sleep."

He wailed so loudly that Kael feared they would be heard from the road. So they walked for another hour, going from tree to tree while the beggar-bard rambled on about how he could hear *treacherous whispers* in the leaves.

Darkness had completely overtaken them by the time Baird finally stopped. He wrapped his arms around an enormous oak and pressed an ear against its bark, smiling through his beard. "Hello, dear fellow. Stand sentry over us tonight, will you? Though you're probably an old hand at the watch. Don't need me telling you how it's done. I wonder how many travelers have sought shelter beneath your welcoming arms? Hundreds? Thousands, perhaps?"

He rambled on, but Kael wasn't listening. The oak had a wide canopy of limbs and a trunk that bulged up at the top, making it look a bit like a monster's mouth gulping down a clump of smaller trees. Still, it wouldn't be a bad place to spend the night. At least there was plenty of dried wood lying around its base.

He dropped his pack and started gathering limbs immediately. "I'll get a fire going."

Kyleigh set her pack next to his. "And I'll find us something to eat. The forest is thick with animals this time of year. I should be able to hunt —"

"No!" Baird cried.

Kael dropped his limbs. Kyleigh drew her sword.

"You can't shed blood in these woods! It isn't safe!"

Kael swore. "Oh, for mercy's sake — don't scream unless it's important."

"It *is* important. Do you want to call the Huntsman down upon us? He roams the forest north of here. His hounds bay for fresh blood. He's always hungry, always searching ..."

Kyleigh slipped Harbinger back into her belt, an amused look on her face. "I think the bard's trying to take us with his tales."

Kael agreed, but Baird was insistent.

"It isn't a tale — it's the truth!" He stumbled over to them and grabbed Kael by the front of the shirt. His voice was deathly quiet. "People have been disappearing since the start of spring. *Bandits — it's only bandits*, they said. Then a week ago, a caravan from the seas passed through my gates. Dozens of footsteps, the heavy tread of armored feet and the clang of weapons filled my ears. I heard the barking of soldiers and the coarse banter of hired blades. They were determined to make it to the Valley.

"Yet for all their steel, only one man returned. He burst through my gates in the deadest hour of the night. Madness gripped his limbs. I could feel it in the tremors of his hands when he grasped my shoulders, the crazed strength of his arms as he shook me. He screamed that hounds had devoured his caravan ..." Baird twisted his knobby fingers tighter into Kael's tunic. "But dogs only do the bidding of their master. It's not the hounds that are to blame — it's the Huntsman!"

Kael was seriously considering knocking the beggar-bard unconscious when Kyleigh stepped in. She peeled Baird's hands free and pulled him away. "All right, I won't do any hunting," she said as she led him over to the oak. "Just sit quietly while we get a fire started."

"A small one?"

"Yes, a small one."

It only took Kael a moment to strike flame. Once the fire was built up, Kyleigh gave Baird some of her rations. Then she grabbed Kael by the front of the shirt and pulled him into the trees.

"What do you plan to do with him?" she whispered once they'd made it out of earshot.

"Well, I *was* going to quietly abandon him at the next village. But now I'm thinking it might be kinder to just club him over the head and save the next man the trouble."

Kyleigh didn't smile. She crossed her arms and looked back in the direction of camp. "I pity him," she said after a moment.

He was on to her. "No you don't. He knows something about you, and you're just trying to keep it a secret."

She snorted. "Don't be ridiculous. If that were the case, I would've already killed him."

He believed her.

"Still … I'm curious." She propped her fingers on her chin, but didn't quite manage to hide the curve of her smile. "I think we ought to take him with us."

"You can't be serious." He rolled his eyes when she nodded. "Kyleigh —"

"Oh, come now. All he wants is to go to the mountains."

"Yes, and how many people have you come across that are eager to get to the mountains? I'm telling you — the whole thing reeks."

"I don't smell anything."

"Well you wouldn't, would you? You'd rather believe he had this magical dream about the friendly, forgiving mountains — but I *can't* believe it. So now I've got to be worried for both of us."

"I'm perfectly capable of sniffing out trouble for myself. If he was dangerous, I would be able to sense it." She tilted her chin. "Won't you help a poor old blind man?"

Kael threw up his hands. "I don't think he's even blind! What if this is has all been an act? We know nothing about him. He could be anybody — a thief, a spy, an assassin, an agent of the Countess."

Kyleigh groaned. "Not this again."

"What?"

"You're going on about agents and assassinations — this was exactly what you did with our friends from the Grandforest, remember? And they turned out to be perfectly harmless."

"This is different."

"Is it?"

"Yes," Kael said, though now he wasn't sure. Perhaps Kyleigh was right: perhaps he was being too hard on Baird. But he wasn't going to risk finding out. "We're not taking him with us. We'll give him some coin for food if you like, but we're leaving him at the next village. I don't want him following us around — I don't trust him."

She shrugged. "Very well, then. I suppose if that's your choice —"

"It is."

"— then I'll respect it."

Good. That was precisely what he wanted her to do. But for some reason, the way Kyleigh marched back to camp made him feel as if he'd done something wrong.

They returned to find Baird beard-deep in his dinner. The strips of dried meat the giants had given them for their journey to the seas were coated in a special blend of oil and spices: a few minutes over the fire, and the meat was as hot and juicy as the day it'd been made.

Baird shoveled his rations in at an alarming rate, stuffing the meat down his gullet with both hands. As he chewed, he brought the next strip to his nose and inhaled deeply. "Hmm, pork? Yes, I'm quite certain this was a pig — and a handsome fellow, at that. He was well fed and rather large, judging by the thickness of the fat. I smell a hint of grassy meadows and boundless skies in the crispest bits of skin. Wherever did you find such a creature?"

Kael shot a look at Kyleigh — who pointedly ignored him.

They ate in relative quiet, with Baird's smacking the only noise between them. Kael hardly took his eyes off the beggar-bard. He peered at the hairline folds in his bandages, trying to glimpse beneath them.

"Where did you come from, Baird?"

He looked up from his meal, and Kael saw there was a large gathering of crumbs tangled in his beard. "Hmm ... a bard doesn't care about where he's been — only where he's going. He makes his home wherever he lies, sleeps with his head pointed down the road. To him, there's no beginning and no end. All his steps carry him in a circle."

Baird smiled, but it was only because he couldn't see the look Kael gave him. "You still haven't answered me."

"Shall I ask *you* a question, then?" Baird's head tilted in Kyleigh's direction. "How do you know the Swordmaiden?"

Kael shrugged. "I met her, and now I know her."

"All right." Kyleigh waved a hand between them, cutting off whatever reply Baird had at the ready. "We've all learned some interesting things about each other. Let's call it a draw for the evening, gentlemen."

Baird raised his hands. "Our fairest companion is right. Let's finish our meals with only happy banter, shall we?"

Kael was about to suggest that he keep his mouth shut for the rest of the evening when a rather large spider drifted down from the branches above them. Its black legs curled lazily about its string, gliding down until it finally came to rest — perched directly atop Baird's next bite of meat.

Kyleigh reached to swat it away, but Kael grabbed her arm. They watched breathlessly as Baird brought the meat to his lips, the spider still perched atop it. Kael's toes curled in his boots and he looked away as both meat and spider disappeared into Baird's mouth.

He hoped the bard would notice, hoped he would gag and spit the spider out. But judging by the loud crunch that followed and the look of horror on Kyleigh's face, he didn't.

"Hmm," Baird said as he swallowed. "Well, that bite wasn't nearly as pleasant as the last."

Disappointment sagged at the bottom of Kael's chest. He'd been hoping to catch Baird in a lie: very few men would've willingly downed a spider. But if Baird wasn't truly blind, then he was at least very committed to his tale.

# CHAPTER 5
## AN UNEASY ALLIANCE

Countess D'Mere watched as the King stalked the length of the darkened throne room. His boots struck the ground hard. At each cutting turn, his face became more twisted. Crevan had called the Five to Midlan again.

But this time, D'Mere was the only one who'd answered.

Duke Reginald was dead — overthrown by his managers and murdered in his own dungeon. There'd been no word from Lord Gilderick. When D'Mere's guard hadn't returned from his ... errand, she'd known something was amiss. Her spies were already on their way to investigate. But after what had happened to Sahar, the news likely wouldn't be good: the desert people were already singing of how the Baron lay in pieces among the glittering ruins of his castle.

As for Titus ...

"Why hasn't he answered me?" Crevan spat.

Two stewards lay dead upon the floor, their limbs curled piteously in drying pools of blood. These stewards were the ones who'd drawn the unfortunate lot of having to tell Crevan what had become of his Kingdom.

D'Mere trailed her gaze across the frozen shock on the stewards' faces before she answered carefully: "You said you weren't able to reach his mages. Perhaps that means he didn't survive the winter, Your Majesty."

"No ... no, he's far too good. He wouldn't die that easily."

Crevan's fingers trembled as they scraped down his jaw. There was a flicker of his old self behind his eyes. It was sharpened and bolstered by his madness — stretched into a beast that had all of his cunning, but none of his calm.

D'Mere knew her best option would be to remain still.

"This is all *her* doing." Crevan spat each word, his face burning redder by the second. "I know the Dragongirl is responsible. She senses my blindness. She knows she's got the run of my realm."

D'Mere inclined her head. She kept her face smooth, but her mind was alive with thought: *His* blindness? *What had Crevan meant by that?*

"As always, Your Majesty, my army is at your dispos —"

"No, an army won't do any good. We've tried armies, we've tried mages, we've tried beasts! Nothing can stop her!"

D'Mere had to focus harder than ever to keep her surprise from showing through. Had Crevan just admitted to having monsters? If he had, she knew she probably hadn't been meant to hear it. So she stared at the hearth while he ranted on, trying to keep her gaze as distant as possible.

Suddenly, Crevan quieted. "There *is* one last thing I haven't tried ... but, no — he means to trick me! I swore I'd never return to that chamber. It's an evil place, a cursed place. The vines will strangle me. The earth will drag me down — it'll pull me into my grave, force me to become like ... like ... *them.*"

D'Mere tried not to breathe. The second steward hadn't died because of his news — he'd died because he'd interrupted Crevan. She wondered if there was any truth to what the King had said or if he simply rambled on in madness. But though curiosity strained her lips, D'Mere managed to keep them tightly sealed.

"She's torturing me," Crevan went on. "She swore she'd end me — but first, she's going to make me watch as everything I've worked for crumbles beneath me. She's going to pay me back ... and Titus knows this." Slowly, the red drained from Crevan's face. His next pacing steps were considerably lighter than those before. "I know what Titus is doing — yes, I see it now. He'll hide behind the smoke of the Dragongirl's rampage until I step too close. Then he'll attack. He's trying to catch me in one of his cursed traps ... he's trying to lure my army into the Unforgivable Mountains. He means to steal my throne.

"Titus sits at the threshold of winter. He knows my soldiers would never survive the climb and even if they did, the cold would finish them. But he knows his betrayal will anger me. He hopes to goad me into sending my army to his door." Crevan's voice fell to a deadly hush. "And once it's defeated, he'll march on Midlan to claim his prize."

D'Mere could no longer keep her eyes away. She watched as Crevan slipped deeper into his thoughts. One finger traced the jagged scar through his beard, turning the white to red where he pressed.

"He's forgotten," Crevan murmured after a moment, grinning. "He's forgotten that I chose him — and I choose a servant as much for his weakness as his strength. How else could a man hope to break a larger beast?"

He turned to D'Mere as he said this, and she answered smoothly: "Titus must be stopped, Your Majesty — both for the sake of your crown, and your Kingdom. I'm prepared to do my part."

"Good." Crevan stalked over to the broken table, where a letter lay half-torn upon its top. "The new chancellor of the High Seas — this *Chaucer* — has already written to me. And rather than have the waves churn red with the blood of his people, he's pledged his allegiance. I'm sending an envoy to the seas to forge the details of his surrender."

"Make sure they're spelled out carefully, Your Majesty," D'Mere said with a hard smile. "The men of the seas can't be trusted."

"How right you are, Countess. And as you've already got such a ... talent, for this sort of thing, I was hoping you'd join them. Help convince Chaucer that it's in his best interest to do exactly as I say."

She nodded. "Of course, Your Majesty."

Crevan's grin stretched against his scar, testing it so forcefully that D'Mere thought the skin might split anew. "Titus will defeat an army at the mountain's top, but it won't be Midlan's. And when he comes charging down to take my throne, in the very moment when he thinks he's won ..."

The King crushed the letter between his fingers, and D'Mere understood.

# CHAPTER 6
## THE WILDLANDS

They'd hardly gone a few days into their journey when Kael discovered a problem: in his rush to get to the mountains, he'd forgotten about the Earl's castle.

The castle sat on the other end of the King's Cleft — a natural gap in the bowl of the mountains guarded on either side by wide, sloping hills. Patrols from Midlan often used that path to reach the Valley, but he thought they had a pretty good chance of avoiding them. It wasn't as if there were many places to hide in the Cleft. If they saw a patrol coming in or out, they could simply wait until the path was clear.

But there would be no avoiding the Earl's castle.

It sat deep inside the Cleft, perched in the shadow of the mountains and at the edge of the Valley's gentle hills. He'd read that the castle had originally been built to keep bandits from slipping in and out of the Valley so easily, and it did its job well. Perhaps a little *too* well. Even from the map, he could tell they were going to have a difficult time passing through the Cleft without being spotted.

So while they traveled, Kael spent most of his time with his nose stuck between the pages of his favorite book: the *Atlas of the Adventurer*. He scanned carefully over its many detailed maps, trying to find someway around the Earl's castle.

He hoped he might spot some little path he'd missed before. He thought he'd find a narrow road that ran beside it, or something that cut along the ledges of the Cleft. But there wasn't so much as a trail scrawled anywhere near it.

Though his stomach twisted tighter with every step, Kyleigh assured him that he worried over nothing. "Titus is still in the mountains. Nobody's seen him in the Valley since the day he marched through. The castle's probably abandoned."

Kael wanted to believe her, but he couldn't. A castle that large wouldn't have sat empty for long, and the odds that somebody friendly had claimed it were depressingly slim. "You don't happen to know of any other way through, do you?"

"Sorry. I've always traveled a ... different route," she said with a quick glance at Baird.

She pointed to the sky, and Kael took her meaning. "Well, then why don't we try it your way?"

"I can't."

"Why not? We could be at the mountains in no time at all."

"I do love a good shortcut," Baird called cheerily.

Kael jerked a thumb behind him. "See? We're all in agreement."

Kyleigh shook her head. "It's far too dangerous. The moment we tried going that way, the gates of Midlan would burst open and the King's army would swarm. It would take ages to lose them."

"Hmm, I don't like the sound of that," Baird mumbled.

Kael ignored him. "You could outrun them easily. I know you could," he said when she glared.

"It's not that simple," Kyleigh growled. "I traveled that way so often before because I had to. I could never stay anywhere for long because the King ... knew. It was like he knew where I'd be before I even knew it. The only reason I managed to escape is because I used the shortcut."

It didn't make any sense. "If that's true, then why hasn't he been chasing us this whole time? Why haven't we had Midlan breathing down our necks?"

"I don't know." The fire in her eyes was suddenly more like candlelight than a blaze. "I expected him to chase me. I thought you and I were going to have to use the shortcut eventually. But it all just ... stopped, the day we left the mountains. I'm not sure why." Her brows furrowed as she studied the clouds. "We've been fortunate so far. I'm not going to do anything to catch the King's attention — certainly not while we're so close to Midlan."

"Yes, I agree with the whole skin of my heart!" Baird chirped from behind them. "Let us tread with the soft steps of shadows and leave not a blade bent behind."

"Why does Crevan hate you so much?" Kael said after a moment. "What in Kingdom's name could you have possibly done to him?"

Baird cackled. "He reached for her, but she knocked his hand away! The whole castle saw —"

"Shut it, Baird!"

They'd shouted at the same time.

"I told you — I tried to kill him," Kyleigh said shortly. Then she quickened her pace, pulling Baird along behind her.

Kael couldn't be sure, but he thought the back of her neck might've looked slightly pink.

They traveled in uncomfortable silence until midday — when the sky opened its gullet and a thick spring rain washed down upon the forest. Baird wore his rucksack on the front of his chest and walked, hunched over it like a lean-to for nearly half a mile.

He never once complained, and not even the rain could dampen his chattering. But as Kael watched him stumble along, guilt made him miserable. All he could think about was Roland: with the knobs of Baird's knees and his swollen fingers, the way he more shuffled than walked — it all reminded him of his friend.

If anybody ever came across Roland soaking wet, Kael knew he would want them to stop and help. So with a sigh, he shrugged off his cloak.

It took him several moments to pull Baird's rucksack back into place and drape the cloak across his thin shoulders. "Oh good, I'm so glad you thought to bring a spare," he said as Kael tugged the hood over his shaggy mane.

"Yes, well, I try to think ahead," Kael said shortly.

Once he'd gotten Baird all settled, Kael marched back up to Kyleigh. Her head turned towards him for a moment as they walked. The shadow of her hood covered her face completely, so he had no idea what she was thinking. And she didn't offer any explanation.

She probably thought he was a fool for giving up his cloak.

A few hours later, he'd begun to agree with her. The rain fell warm and thick, spilling from the canopy above them in hundreds of weeping falls. It soaked into his clothes and rubbed raw patches across his skin. By late afternoon, the only bits of him that weren't soaked were the parts of his arms and wrists that were covered by his gauntlets.

They were the gauntlets Kyleigh had given him — the ones she'd made from her scales. The way the rain washed down their blackened tops reminded him of water sliding from the oily back of a duck.

He understood now why Kyleigh hadn't packed a cloak: covered head to toe in dragon scales, she must've been plenty dry.

"Well, there's no use in slogging on," Kyleigh declared suddenly. The shadow of her hood turned to face the trees. "The two of you ought to find us someplace dry to sleep."

"Where are you going?" Kael said.

She didn't reply. Instead, she jogged into the thicket — running until the woods swallowed her up.

He supposed she would be all right. Kyleigh knew the forest better than he did, after all — and he seriously doubted that she would run into anything more terrifying than she was. Besides, he was too wet to worry.

It didn't take them long to find shelter. After a few minutes of searching, they came across an ancient tree that had toppled over onto its side. Decay had been eating at the tree's innards for a while, leaving a hole that looked like a monster's bite mark. The flecks of its bark were as big as the shingles of a roof, and the rotted out space in its middle was the size of a respectable house.

The half-moon cave it left behind could have been home to all sorts of creatures. Kael was surprised to find it empty. The first layer of the wall was too rotted to burn. He dug beneath it until he came across a dryer patch. He cracked the deadwood off in strips and tossed it into a pile. Once he had a fire going, there was nothing left to do but wait.

"Hang my cloak near the flames — I want the wool to be dried by morning."

Kael had been hunched beside the fire, painstakingly wringing the moisture from his shirt when Baird's sopping cloak struck him full in the face. "You have to warn people before you start flinging things everywhere," he snapped as he hung the cloak on a jutting bit of the wall.

Baird spread his arms wide. "Sorry, but I thought *I* was the blind one. You ought to be able to see anything thrown your way."

"Yes, well, where I come from we don't just throw things without fair warning."

"I see. And where did you say you came from again?"

"I didn't."

Baird leaned against the wall behind him and whispered: "Oh, he's clever."

Kael used the small fire to warm their food. Once his hair stopped dripping, he took the *Atlas* out and went back to studying the maps.

The rain slowed to a steady drizzle. Late afternoon drifted into early evening. Baird prattled endlessly about the quiet flutters of the flames and the way the warmth kissed the walls. But other than that, the day was mostly pleasant.

"When should we expect the Swordmaiden's triumphant return?" Baird said loudly, pulling Kael's gaze from the maps.

He wasn't sure when Kyleigh would come back, and he couldn't see why it ought to be triumphant. But he knew one thing for certain: "She'll be back eventually."

"Eventually? Oh dear, what a span and space of time that is ... *eventually*." Baird snorted. "Time keeps a steady gait, young man. It stops for no one. Each step is measured in a moment, a breath. There's no place for vagueries upon its path —"

"Vagueries?"

"You've got to be *specific* about where you plan to turn. You must know how many steps it'll take to get there. Otherwise, the moment might just pass you by." Baird frowned as he added: "Many a man has wasted away waiting for *eventually*."

Kael sighed. "Fine. She'll be back soon."

"Soon?" Baird snorted again. "*Soon* —?"

"Look — if she wanted to leave me, then she would've left a long time ago. Kingdom knows she's had the opportunity."

"Hmm, yes. I must admit I thought it strange that the Swordmaiden would trouble herself with one so frail. She used to keep the company of great warriors. Either she's more disgraced than I thought ... or you are not nearly as frail as you seem."

Kael didn't like Baird's smile — and he liked his words even less. Slowly, he reached for the dagger at his belt. "Who are you?"

"I'm Baird the Beggar-Bard —"

"No. Who are you *really*? Kyleigh thinks you're harmless. I'm not so sure." Kael drew the dagger and leveled the point at Baird's chest. "Tell me the truth."

"I heard the muffled rake of steel parting its leather bonds." He smiled. "Why waste my breath when you mean to cut it short? Plunge your knife into my heart. Go on, be quick about it."

That was it. Kael was tired of playing games.

With one quick movement, he lunged and ripped the bandages off Baird's eyes. The beggar-bard yelped and threw his hands over his head. Kael pulled them away by the wrists, exposing his face. What he saw made his heart shudder to a stop.

The lids of Baird's eyes were red and sunken in, shut tightly against the world. Hairline scars ran in lines from their bottoms and stopped just short of his cheeks. They looked like a trail of tears — frozen in time, forever branded into his flesh. Old age hadn't claimed Baird's vision.

His eyes had been cut out.

"I'm sorry. I had no idea ..."

Kael placed the bandages in Baird's hand, and his knobby fingers curled about them tightly. The other hand traced his scars. "I had no choice," he whispered.

Kael could hardly breathe. "Wait a moment — *you* did this?"

"With a sharp rock and in the dark underbelly of the night. I had no choice," Baird said again. His fingers trembled down the frozen line of tears. "I knew too much. They planned to turn me over to the Falsewright — and he would've got it out of me. Oh yes, he had his ways. I had no choice! The first was easy." He drew a half-moon around his left eye. "Just more pain than any man should ever have to endure and, ah ... darkness.

"The second was more difficult." His finger hovered over his right eye, trembling. "It wasn't the pain I feared — it was the darkness. A window closed never to be opened. A thousand sunsets wasted against my lids, a thousand faces I would never see again. I had not the courage to face the darkness ... but I had no choice. I had no *choice!*"

He clutched his face, dissolving into wails. Kael grabbed the bandages from his hand. He wrapped them around Baird's eyes and bound them tightly. It was only after they'd been covered for a moment that his wails began to quiet.

Kael wanted to sink into the floor and disappear. Kyleigh had been right to pity Baird. She must've been able to sense the pain beneath his madness, the darkness behind his lids. Kael should've listened to her.

Instead, he'd tortured a blind man for no reason. "Baird, I'm so —"

"Do you want to hear a story?" Baird was leaning against the wall, smiling as if nothing had ever happened.

Kael was too relieved to argue. "Yes."

"Very well, then. I'll do a bit of barding." Baird's weathered fingers gripped the knobs of his knees. He was quiet for such a long moment that Kael thought he might've fallen asleep. Then quite suddenly, he began:

"Long ago, in an age when the earth was young and the first grains of time had only just slipped through the glass, two lands were born to Fate. The first rose from the sea in the shadow of the setting sun, and so she called them the Westlands. It was a dark place, a quiet place. Fate cast her die and the symbols for power, greed, and war landed upon its shores. Kings fought against Kings. Mages rent the land with their spells. Men cried out to Fate, and she answered. There was always much to cast for in the Westlands."

Kael had gone back to his reading at the first mention of Fate, but the story slowly drew him in. The words came alive on Baird's tongue. He closed his eyes and images passed before him — blooming out of the dark in bursts of color and sound.

The battered shores of the Westlands rose in his mind. Blood burned his face as he joined the Kings in battle; he could hear the mighty roar of the earth as it crumbled beneath the mages' spells. All around him the gaunt faces of men turned skyward. He listened to the thunder as it split the clouds — no, not thunder. It was the sound of Fate's die rolling across her great table.

His heart slowed its beating and his lungs held their breath. His ears tuned to each bounce and roll. Sweat drenched his brow as he begged for the die to land in his favor ...

*It's only a story.*

Kael's eyes snapped open. He ground his palms against his head and tried to focus on the wall in front of him. It was only a story. He wasn't going to let himself get pulled back in ...

His eyes shut in the middle of this thought and Baird's voice drowned his ears: "The second land born to Fate was as fair as his brother was fierce. Strength, wisdom, and order fell here — a strange cast of the die. They made the land grow thick and gave life to the trees. White rivers burst from the rocks, their waters swift and chilled. Great storms rose from the depths of the northern seas and lashed the earth with their fury. There were no wars, no mages or Kings. The greatest danger was the land, itself. And so Fate called them the Wildlands.

"For all their beauty, the Wildlands stood empty. So Fate fashioned creatures to live within them. She gave them hooves and wings, teeth and claws — they were sure-footed and strong. There were creatures that could reach the highest peak and the lowest depths of the sea. They would never conquer the land, but live *with* it. Of this, Fate was determined.

"But the wars in the Westlands grew more fierce. Powerful mages drove mankind away and kept them pressed against the desolate shores. The Kings began to try to cross the seas, looking for a new land to settle — and Fate knew it would be only a matter of time before the die landed in their favor. So she traveled deep into her brother's realm in search of guardians to defend the Wildlands.

"Death, who loves to bargain, gave her fourteen souls in exchange for this: once each year, Fate must turn her face from the Wildlands and allow Death to rule. It's a bargain they've kept to this very day."

"Who were the fourteen souls?" Kael said. He knew full well which day Fate turned her face from the earth, but he hadn't heard anything about the souls. And he didn't want Baird to skip over it.

Baird's head rose from his chest slowly, as if he woke from a deep sleep. "I'm getting to that. Be patient, young man."

Kael shut his mouth.

"They were the souls of seven men and seven mages — heroes who'd proven themselves worthy during their lives in the Westlands, but had perished before their time. To the seven men, Fate gave great strength and long lives. They would clear the land of monsters so that their offspring might grow in peace. They would protect the people of the Wildlands. And so the seven men became known as *knights*.

"To the seven mages, Fate revealed all the secrets of the earth. The mages forgot their language of spells and instead learned the groaning tongue of the wilds. They were to be intercessors, voices that would speak for the land and protect its secrets from the children of the knights — who might unwittingly destroy them. The seven mages each received a token from Fate, a token of dark and terrible power: they would forsake their human souls and become like animals. So they were called *barbarians* —"

"Shapechangers." Kael didn't remember standing up. He was vaguely aware of how his fists were clenched. His nails dug into his palms, but the fire that filled his head numbed the pain. "They're shapechangers — not barbarians."

Baird's head lifted again, his bandaged face tilted in Kael's direction. "No, they're ... friends of yours?"

When he didn't reply, Baird smiled triumphantly.

"Your words came from somewhere very deep — bursting as if they rode the last wind of a long journey. But still potent, despite their climb. Such a powerful stand against one small word could only mean friendship." He leaned against the wall as if he'd uncovered a great secret.

But Kael had uncovered a secret as well. He smiled back and said simply: "You're a whisperer."

# CHAPTER 7
## The Huntsman

Baird's mouth went slack. "I ... how did you know?"

"I have my ways," Kael replied.

It was the only explanation. Even Roland with his growling voice had never told a story that sounded so alive. If a whisperer could command others by the power of his words, then surely he could entrance them.

"You're a craftsman."

Baird slumped against the walls. "Oh Fate, I've failed you! He's going to turn me over to the King. Now I shall never reach the mountains —!"

"I'm not going to turn you over to anybody," Kael said quickly, before he could work himself into wails. "I just thought ..."

He caught a flash of movement out of the corner of his eye. A shadow stood outside their shelter, hanging near the edge of the trees. Kael was still trying to figure out what it was when the shadow slipped away.

"Wait here."

He grabbed his bow and slung the quiver across his shoulder. The rain had stopped, but the air was still damp. His boots pressed carefully into the soggy earth as he inched towards the tree line. His eyes swept across the brambles; his thumb traced the fletching of a nocked arrow. He was prepared to draw back at the first sign of danger.

A long moment passed and the shadow never reappeared. Kael wondered if he'd only been imagining it. He was about to turn back for the shelter when the snap of a twig drew his gaze to the left.

Two glowing eyes watched him from the brambles, and Kael recognized their haughty light immediately. "Silas?"

The halfcat didn't reply.

"How did you find us? When did you ...?" Then he remembered how the door had slammed open the night they left Frome's Refuge, and how rations kept disappearing from the merchant's vessel. He suddenly figured it out. "You stowed away and followed us to the Grandforest. Why didn't you just —?"

A low, rumbling growl came from Silas's hairy throat and the glow of his eyes dimmed as he slunk half a pace back into the shadows.

"You want me to follow you?" Kael guessed.

Silas blinked.

"Why? Is something wr —?"

"Kael? Oh, Kaaael?"

He turned — and was alarmed to see Baird stumbling from the shelter, nearly bent double under the weight of their packs.

"Kael?"

"Over here, Baird!" He grabbed the bard by his knobby wrist and latched him onto the hem of his tunic.

Silas growled again. His full furry head stuck out from the brambles, now. And Kael knew by the way his whiskers bunched up around his nose that he was getting impatient. "All right, we're coming."

"Coming where?" Baird said from behind him.

"Going, I mean," Kael said quickly. "We're moving on."

"Why?"

Kael wasn't sure. "Just march, will you?"

Silas moved effortlessly through the trees, and Kael had to walk quickly in order to keep the flicking end of his tail in sight — a task made more difficult by the fact that he had Baird dragging down on his tunic.

They'd gone several yards when Silas came to a halt. He turned back, facing the direction they'd come, and crouched.

Kael mirrored him. Orange light from their fire glowed faintly through the hairline cracks in the rotted shelter. Now that evening had darkened it, he thought the monstrous tree looked a bit like a log glowing in a hearth.

Just when he was about to ask Silas what they were waiting for, a large shadow passed above the shelter. It floated across the toppled tree, its blackened skin eclipsing the fiery cracks.

For a long moment it did nothing but circle. Kael lost track of how many times the shadow went around. Then without warning, it disappeared ... and something far more troublesome took its place.

He heard their heavy footsteps before he saw them: three monstrous, hunched creatures — three devils of the night. They lumbered up to the shelter, dragging themselves forward on their front claws while their backs followed at a hop. One by one, they slipped inside. Kael could see their shadows moving around as they searched.

Baird must've been able to sense that something was wrong. He spoke at hardly a whisper. "What is it?"

Kael's tongue stuck to the back of his throat. "Monsters," he choked.

"What sort? Trolls? Goblins?"

"Worse." Kael watched in horror as one of the monsters trotted out with Baird's sopping cloak gripped in its jaws. It swung the garment about violently. He could hear the faint ripping of thread at it broke across the seams.

Somehow, Kael forced himself to turn. "We should ..."

But the space beside him was empty. Silas was gone.

The other two monsters loped from the shelter and joined their companion. They growled to one another as they tore at the cloak. He could hear their sharp breaths as they dragged their noses across the wool. Then all at once, they stopped.

The monsters' heads swiveled behind them and they took off at a gallop, panting loudly as they vanished into the shadows cast by the trees.

It was only after they'd gone that Kael realized just how tightly he'd been clenching his fists. He knew they had to get moving. They needed to find Kyleigh. Where in Kingdom's name had she run off to?

When he turned, he saw Baird's mouth parted slightly beneath his beard, as if he'd been about to say something. "What is it?"

"I ... that is ..." He licked his lips. "Do you ever get the feeling someone is ... watching you?"

Baird spoke as if there was a hand clamped around his throat. His face went pale beneath his beard. His limbs stiffened with a dead man's chill. Kael's heart thudded in his throat as he leaned to peer over Baird's shoulder.

Two glittering eyes peered back.

A monster crept out of the darkness. It looked exactly like the wolf monsters in Bartholomew's Pass — except this creature was a mix between a man and a hound. The monster's fingers were swollen around a set of short, dark claws. A saddle of black fur sprouted in uneven patches down its twisted back. The tattered remains of a tunic and chainmail hung across its chest. The links of the armor had melded into its skin, clinging like scales to its torso and shoulders.

Kael stood, frozen, as the hound raised its head in their direction. Waves of loose skin fell over its eyes. The flesh bulged and swelled as if its face had been badly burned. A man's nose, stretched so widely that it had split down the middle, flared as the hound sucked in the night air.

Thick folds of skin hung off its cheeks and sagged on either side of its mouth. Monstrous teeth smacked together, their sharp white tips dripping as the swollen nostrils breathed in. Then it arched its neck and let out a blood-chilling howl.

Kael knew what was coming next. There wasn't time for anything else: he kicked Baird aside and sent an arrow straight into hound's drooping mouth.

Its gangly limbs convulsed as the arrow's head erupted out the back of its skull and drops of blood sprayed in an arc behind it. A breath later the monster landed — dead — at Kael's boots.

"What in Kingdom's ...?"

His ears cringed against a familiar sound: a howl drifted through woods, rising and falling over the trees. More howls joined the first. They filled the damp air with a song of wails.

Baird moaned and clutched his beard. "It's the Huntsman. His hounds bay for blood!"

Kael didn't have time to argue. He grabbed Baird around the arm and hauled him into the trees.

Howls filled the woods at their backs — a song of wails that rose and fell in a constant stream. Soon they became like the breath of a steady wind, the growl of a storm growing closer. They shrilled until the forest fell silent. The cry of owls, the fluttering of the leaves, even the crickets' song went hushed. It was as if every tree held its breath, as if they knew they were about to witness a slaughtering.

Meanwhile, the hounds pierced the air in a chorus of desperate yelps. *No more!* They seemed to wail. *Please — no more!*

Every bump that rose across Kael's skin trembled against the baying. They bunched together so closely that it made his hide go taut over his bones. He stumbled forward as the joints of his knees struggled to bend, fighting against the strangling grip of his skin.

His heart thudded in his ears; the tips of his fingers went cold as he ripped through the thorns. His breath slid out between a dagger's edge of space. Then quite suddenly, the howling stopped.

"What is it? What's happened?" Baird hissed.

"I'm not sure."

Kael glanced back over his shoulder, but couldn't see a blasted thing. The moon cast a weak light around them — hardly illuminating anything beyond a few feet. With the baying stopped, their steps sounded impossibly loud. He grit his teeth and charged on. If they wanted to live, they had to keep moving.

Kael wasn't sure how long they ran. He dragged Baird by his elbow and fought madly through the tangled mane of the forest. A thick wall of brush rose in front of him, stretching far to either side. He dropped his shoulder and charged through with all of his strength.

Vines grasped at him. Wiry branches whipped him across the face. He grimaced as he felt himself lose one of his curls. When he finally burst from the wall's grasp, he was off balance. He stumbled into a dark clearing and heard Baird crash behind him with a yelp.

"Baird?" Kael hissed.

The leaves were woven so tightly above them that not even the moonlight could filter through. He couldn't see his fingers well enough to count them. He stepped around and swung his hands before him, hoping he'd stumble upon the beggar-bard. He thought he'd found him, once — but it was only his rucksack.

He called again, but Baird didn't answer. So Kael had no choice. He dug through his pack until his hands found a lantern and flint. He struck the flint against his dagger and was relieved when the sparks finally caught onto the oil-soaked wick.

Gnarled roots stretched out in every direction. Their tangled shadows fled from the lantern's pale flame and seemed to wriggle like snakes. He found Baird lying behind him, his body crumpled beneath his filthy rucksack.

The beggar-bard groaned and his scraggly head lolled as Kael shook him. "Are you hurt?"

Baird clutched piteously at his face. "Oh, I'm wounded! Oh, it aches!"

There was an impressive amount of foliage lodged in his mane and a few hairline bramble scratches cut from his beard. There might've been one, perhaps *two* drops of blood weeping from the largest scrape, but that was it. "I think you'll live," Kael muttered. "Come on, we'd better get moving."

But Baird wasn't listening. He grimaced as his knobby fingers edged down to his wound. "What's this? It's sticky, and it smells like ..." He brought a stained hand to his nose and the skin beneath his layer of filth went white. "Blood! *Blood!*"

As if Kael's heart hadn't been pounding hard enough already, the wails that tore from Baird's throat nearly made it stop. "*Shhh!* Shut it!"

Baird clamped both hands over his mouth and moaned between his fingers. "What will we do? What can be done ...? You must leave me, young man!" he said suddenly. "Go, flee into the woods and may Fate protect you. Take this with you." He thrust out his filthy rucksack. "Guard it well!"

"I'm not leaving you," Kael said. He'd dealt with Crevan's monsters before, and he doubted very seriously that they were interested in the blood of a beggar-bard. "We haven't heard anything in a long while. They've probably given u —"

A roar, and Baird was gone — flung several feet away by the monstrous, fleshy mass that slammed into him. A cry tore from Kael's throat as he sent an arrow into the hound's back.

The monster yelped and arched away from Baird. It twisted around and the pits beneath its drooping brow locked onto Kael. Then it charged.

No sooner did he get an arrow nocked than he heard thundering steps behind him. He threw himself to the ground just as a second hound burst from the woods.

Twin yelps pierced his ears as the hounds collided. Bright red blood leaked across the first hound's back. He could see it glistening at the base of the arrow buried in its shoulder. The second hound wrapped its jaws around the wounded hound's throat and tore — showering the root floor with a spray of blood.

There was no time to be horrified, no time to panic. Kael tried to block the sounds from his ears and charged for Baird.

He clung tightly to the filthy rucksack as Kael dragged him to his feet. His bandaged head turned back as they ran; his mouth hung open beneath his shaggy beard. "I hear the crackling of sinew and the shriek of muscle torn from bone.

Are they ... eating each other? What madness could drive a dog to eat his brother?"

"They aren't dogs," Kael gasped. "Keep m —"

The breath left his lungs and his feet left the ground. He managed to catch a tree on the shoulder — the only thing that saved him from splitting his head. The tree whipped him around and drove him belly-first into the knotted floor. The world was still spinning when he forced himself to stand.

A third hound had flown from the woods. Now it stood over Baird, towering on its hind legs. The knots in its throat bobbed up and down as it screamed. The second hound joined its song and rushed to meet it — a fleshy chunk of its brother still gripped in its jaws. The hound that stood over Baird snapped its head down for the feed.

And Kael's arrow struck its throat.

The howl broke into a gasp. The second hound screamed and fell upon its dying brother. It ripped and tore, lapping at the gushing veins while its brother wriggled helplessly beneath it. Their massive bodies were between Kael and Baird. He couldn't reach him with the hounds in the way.

So he fired again.

The last hound arched back as Kael's arrow struck its side. It screamed in pain and spun, nostrils flared above its gaping mouth. Kael grabbed another arrow. He nocked it tightly. The hound leapt, its fleshy jaws bared around its teeth and claws curled for his throat —

A burst of white light erupted in the clearing. The hound flew backwards as if it'd been struck. Kael shut his eyes tightly, grimacing as the ferocity of the light stabbed his lids. He could feel it in his ears, pressing against his skin. Just when he thought he could bear it no longer, the light vanished.

When Kael opened his eyes, he saw an astonishing sight: a forest man stood over the mangled body of the hound. Though he was past his middle age, thin cords of muscle stretched across his limbs. An animal's hide knotted about his waist was his only clothing.

Around his neck he wore a wooden medallion. He held the medallion from his chest and the blinding light faded into its center, leaving nothing but silence in its wake.

"Sleep, Abomination," the forest man rumbled. "I rid your body of its cursed soul."

The hound flailed its limbs; its monstrous mouth froze in a silent howl. White light seeped from its eyes, its drooping ears. The light turned liquid as it slid across the hound's skin and dulled, sinking into the ground. Then at last, its twisted body went still.

A familiar moldy smell struck Kael's nose as the last of the light went out. It wasn't as strong as the stench he was used to, but there was no denying what it was: magic.

Kael kept his bow drawn taught and the arrow aimed at the forest man's back as he got to his feet. "Who are you?"

"Graymange, the wolf shaman," he said without turning.

Shaman? Kael let the bow go slack. "You mean you're one of the shapechangers?"

"Yes."

It made sense. Baird mentioned that the shamans had given up the power of the mages. The spell he used must've been some sort of ... earth magic, he supposed. At least it didn't smell as foul as normal magic.

Graymange knelt before the body of the hound. His hand shot out quickly — prodding and snapping back, as if its skin was hot. "*Abomination*," he hissed.

Perhaps Graymange had never seen one of Crevan's monsters before. Kael took a cautious step forward. "The King does this to them. It's some sort of spell —"

"No, this is different. These creatures aren't shapechangers ... they lust for *human* blood." Graymange scowled at the twisted body of the hound. "Our land is ruled by order: things that were meant to be, traveling the paths they were meant to follow. But these creatures should've never been born. They have no paths to follow. They live only to interrupt our order. Their very existence is Abomination — they must be stopped."

Those sounded an awful lot like the things the Tinnarkians used to say about Kael. He stepped away from Graymange quickly and went to check on Baird.

The beggar-bard must've cracked his head on a root: he was unconscious and snoring heavily through his beard, but otherwise unscathed. Things certainly could've been worse.

He heard a low grunt and turned in time to see Graymange tugging at the collar that was clamped around the hound's throat. "Help me, Marked One."

Kael took two steps before his legs froze. "Wait a moment — how did you know I was a whisperer?"

He grunted something that sounded like *Emberfang*, but that couldn't have been it. "Why don't you just spell it open?" Kael said as he leaned over the collar.

"Our magic isn't like the magic of the mages. I command *order*, not power."

Kael wasn't sure what that meant, but he was focused too intently on the collar to ask. He'd expected it to look like all the others had. But instead of iron, this collar was made of solid gold.

He grasped it and wasn't surprised to feel the familiar itch of magic. What *did* surprise him was that he didn't see the milky white film of a spell wrapped around it. Instead, hairline ripples folded all along the metal — like the marks that wind left in the sand.

The ripples were a dull red and glowing. He supposed it must've been some sort of spell. He scratched at them, but they didn't break. Even when he tore the collar into two, the ripples glowed on. It was as if the magic had somehow *melted* into the gold ...

"Quickly, Marked One — we will gather the other collars. Then we must be gone," Graymange barked. He scooped Baird' knobby body effortlessly onto his shoulders and set off into the woods. Kael stuffed the collar into one of the rucksacks and followed at a trot.

*******

Something was chasing them.

Graymange never said it aloud, but Kael knew by the way he wove them around that he was trying to muddle their trail. He dragged them through thickets and past enormous trees, toting Baird easily across his shoulders. They circled the decaying body of a deer — and the smell was so potent that Kael could taste it in the back of his throat.

At one point, they stopped at a shallow cave. A great tree sat on the hill above it. The roots that stretched from its base hung over the cave's mouth like a curtain. Graymange sat Baird on the ground and went inside the cave. He rubbed his bare shoulders against the roots and his back against the rocky wall. Then he scooped Baird up and set off again without a word.

A wide river flowed just beyond the cave. Kael's toes curled as he watched Graymange slip into the water, but he forced himself to follow. The current was fairly gentle; the murky waters were surprisingly warm. At its middle, the waves came up to Kael's waist. He stepped carefully, keeping both packs raised over his head and out of the river's reach.

Baird's boots dragged a half-moon in the water as Graymange turned.

His face betrayed nothing, but Kael thought he could see the question in his eyes. "I'm all right. Keep going."

The bottom of the river was covered in a thick layer of sand and grit. He concentrated hard on staying balanced while fighting against the current, and he was doing rather well. Then he stepped on a fish.

It must've been sleeping in the sand. The fish's slippery body twisted violently beneath his boot and in his surprise, Kael leapt back. The moment his feet left the ground, the river tried to sweep him away. Luckily, he managed to hook his foot around a root before he got carried too far.

"I'm fine," he said as he righted himself. "I even managed to keep the packs dry — well, mostly dry," he amended, when he saw the dark stain on one of their bottoms.

A chorus of screams sounded off in the distance. Kael's blood chilled the waters around him, but Graymange didn't look at all worried. He closed his eyes as the howls continued.

"Further than before ... their calls aren't as sharp, the wails not as long. We've fooled them." He opened his eyes and sloshed over to Kael. His sharp chin jutted over his shoulder. "Watch closely, mountain child."

Kael could just make out the bank they'd left behind. His heart thudded worriedly as several hounds galloped up to the shallow cave. Their warped bodies disappeared beneath the shadow cast by the tree — but he could hear the snapping of wood as they tore at the root curtain.

From where Kael stood, it didn't look as if they'd fooled the hounds at all. In fact, they were right on their trail. "We've got to move on."

"Patience," Graymange murmured.

"*Patience*? This is hardly the time for —"

"Sleep, Abominations!" a loud voice boomed.

Kael shut his eyes just in time to spare them from a burst of white light. Yelps cut through the air, fading to whines as the light raged on and then at last, to silence.

A tall man stood outside the shallow cave, a medallion hanging from his upraised hand. Kael only got a glimpse of him before the light went out. He couldn't be sure, but it looked as if the man's whole back was blanketed in a mat of hair.

"Come, Marked One."

"Where are we going?"

"Why do humans waste so much breath on questions," Graymange growled, "when their legs could easily carry them to their answers?"

Kael picked up his feet.

# CHAPTER 8
## EMBERFANG

It was near dawn when they finally stopped.

Baird had woken a mile or so beyond the river and began to loudly exclaim that something smelled like a wet dog. And because he'd seen absolutely no point in trying to reason with the beggar-bard, Kael had whispered him unconscious.

They'd trudged on silently for a mile more — or as silently as they could with Baird muttering in his sleep. Kael's ears strained over the endless stream of his prattle and the noises of the woods, listening for the cries of the hounds. But he didn't hear so much as a yelp.

At long last, Graymange led him through a line of trees grown so closely together that they'd nearly formed a wall. Their dark shadows draped over his head and their branches creaked grumpily as he squeezed between them. Kael was relieved when he finally made it to the other side.

But his relief didn't last for long.

A large clearing stretched out in front of him. The moonlight kissed the rain-soaked ground and made it glitter; trees surrounded it in a blackened wall. He might've thought the clearing was a beautiful sight — had it not been for the bodies piled in its middle.

It must've been some sort of camp. There were tents set up near the edge of the clearing, and he could see the faint glow of fires. But now all of its armored residents lay in a bloody mound upon the grass.

Kael squinted and thought he could see a gold wolf's head through the dark smears on one of their tunics. His stomach twisted into a worried knot. "What are the Earl's men doing in the Grandforest?"

"I don't know what an *Earl* is," Graymange said as he passed by. "The world of men means little to me — my business is with the Abominations. These swordbearers stood in my path. Now, they have been dealt with."

A hooded figure emerged from between the tents, hefting a soldier's body across its shoulders. With a grunt and a mighty heave, it tossed the body onto the top of the pile. Then it turned to Graymange, crossed its arms and said:

"Well, it's about blasted time."

"Kyleigh!" Kael didn't know whether to be furious or relieved. So he marched towards her at a half-stomp. "Where in Kingdom's name have you been?"

She waved a hand at the mound of bodies. "Here, mostly. It takes a long while to stack them this neatly."

He pulled her hood away so he could glare at her properly, and saw she was grinning. Something must've been horribly wrong with him — either that, or he'd been more relieved than he'd thought. For though he tried desperately to hold it down, his mouth seemed to have a mind of its own: it bent upwards before he had a chance to stop it.

Kyleigh's grin broke into a laugh.

"I'm still angry with you," he insisted. "It isn't fair for you to go running off on secret errands all the time —"

"Secret errands?"

"Well, you might at least tell me where you're going," he grouched when she laughed again. "One of these days I'm going to get entirely fed up with your nonsense, then you'll be sorry."

He was rather surprised when she grabbed him by the collar. Her fingers burned the skin beneath his throat and made his blood run hot. Her eyes blazed with something that wasn't quite anger — but still every bit as dangerous.

His ears trembled against her voice as she growled: "Is that so?"

"Yes," he managed to choke.

She smirked. "I'll take my chances."

Her hand twisted tighter in his shirt. The fires nearly overwhelmed him. She shoved him away and for a moment, the heat faded. But then the smile she gave him brought the flames roaring back.

It happened in a blink, a breath — one spark that fluttered down his shirt and seared his flesh. She tucked it away quickly, but that smile left a mark. He felt a raw patch in his mind as it burned itself into his memory.

He just wasn't sure why.

"You had nothing to worry about. You know very well that I can take care of myself. And I left you in excellent hands," she said.

Kael snorted. "If you're talking about Silas, then I —"

"Silas?" Her brows arched high. "When did you see Silas?"

Kael was confused. "He turned up at the shelter a while after you left. Granted, he ran off just when things started to get thick. But had he not called us out when he did, those hounds would've found us."

"*Hounds?*" Kyleigh growled.

"I'd been watching them closely, just as you asked," Graymange said when she glared at him. "The Abominations came too near, so I led them away. But then Blackbeak spotted the light of a fire. He called them back. I returned as swiftly as I could, Emberfang."

Now it was Kael's turn to be shocked. "*You're* Emberfang?" When he saw how pink she'd gotten, he suddenly understood. "That's your shapechanger name, isn't it?"

"She belonged to the Fang pack, and so she was named as one," Graymange said in answer. "Long ago, three pups were born to the Mother Wolf: Fang, Mange, and Howl. We are their descendents."

"This is no time for stories," Kyleigh snapped when she saw the question forming on Kael's lips. "Graymange — take that human back to the den."

He scooped Baird up and jogged off in the direction she'd pointed, leaving them on their own.

"Did you manage to find me a collar?"

The sharpness hadn't quite left her voice. Kael dug through the rucksack until he came across a twisted strip of gold. He held it out to her, but she didn't take it.

She stumbled backwards and a curse hissed between her lips. The way she stared at the collar made him wonder if one of the spirits of the dead had just floated down from the trees. "What is it?"

"Dragonsbane," she whispered, her eyes still wide.

"What —?"

"Don't," she said sharply, when he took a step forward. "Don't bring it any closer."

He stood still while she paced. She swiped the loose strands of hair from across her eyes and her face was far paler than usual. He couldn't hear the things she muttered, but he could see how worried she was.

If Kyleigh was worried over something, it meant he ought to have been terrified. But he wasn't. For some reason, her fear forced him to be calm. He supposed one of them had to be. "What's dragonsbane?" he said quietly.

"Gold forged with mage blood — an ancient metal with impossible power."

"What power?"

"An everlasting spell: the essence of magic bound in gold. It's especially useful against dragonscales — which is why it's called *dragonsbane*." She scratched absently at her armor, as if she could feel the metal's bite. "I've only ever seen it forged into weapons and armor ... but Titus seems to have found a new use for it."

Kael felt as if the whole earth had just fallen out from under him. "These collars — those monsters — they belong to *Titus*? How can you be sure?"

"The only place I've ever seen dragonsbane is in the Unforgivable Mountains."

*And Titus rules the mountains*, Kael thought.

He remembered what Graymange had said about the hounds — how they hunted human blood. They'd had armor melded into their skin; they took the shape of dogs. Then all at once, it struck him:

81

"Bloodtraitors," he moaned. His stomach dropped when Kyleigh nodded. "Mercy's sake ... Titus is turning his army into shapechangers."

"It was bad enough before," Kyleigh said quietly. She stared down at the collar. "But this is worse. This changes everything."

Kael didn't understand why things should've been any worse. These collars might've had magic in them, but they'd broken easily enough. He tested a bit of the golden skin with an edge of his dagger and a thick strip peeled off. They weren't even as strong as the iron collars.

When he said as much, Kyleigh sighed. "Dragonsbane wouldn't be any good against stronger metals — the gold weakens it. No, it works best against flesh ... and scales." She scratched uncomfortably at her elbow. "You don't have to be a mage in order to wield dragonsbane, which means Titus won't have to rely on anybody else. His army will be bound directly to him. Blazes ... *blazes* ..." Her eyes darted wildly as she paced, as if she stood before a ravine she had no way to cross.

Kael thought furiously. "What if we destroyed it? I know it would take a while, but if we could break it piece by piece —"

"Dragonsbane is *immortal* magic. It can be melted down, but never destroyed."

Kael wasn't so sure. There wasn't a thing in the Kingdom that was truly unbreakable — even the winds chewed at the mountains. Dragonsbane must have a weakness ... and he had to find it.

He held the collar in his hands for a moment, trying to ignore the itch long enough to get a good feel of it. The red, glowing ripples seemed to slosh around when he tilted the collar. It was as if the ripples were still liquid — as if the gold had soaked them up ...

That was it. That was exactly what had happened: the gold had soaked up the mage blood like water into a rag.

Kael held this thought firmly in his head as he grasped either end of the collar. He squeezed the dragonsbane between his fingers and had to hold his breath as the blood began trickling out. He twisted it, wringed it until every last ripple had been drained from the gold. Then he tossed it away.

"Gah!" He flung an arm over his mouth and concentrated on breathing in the sweat-stiffened cloth of his shirt. "Did that do it?"

Kyleigh picked up the now-misshapen lump of gold and turned it over in her hands, her mouth agape. "What a strange creature you are, Kael the Wright, to solve great problems with such simple answers."

His face burned hot under her look. He wanted to say that it wasn't all *that* — he just hadn't wanted her to have to worry anymore. He didn't want her to be afraid. But his tongue was too swollen to form the words.

Kyleigh hurled the gold into the pile of bodies and said: "Let's finish this."

"Finish what, exactly?"

She waved, and he followed her back to the soldiers' camp. Stacked inside one of the tents was a large number of clay jars. They were small and squat, but surprisingly heavy.

He lifted one of their lids and his nose was immediately flooded by a horrible stench. It was a bitter, far-too-flowery smell — like the milky sap of an enormous weed. He coughed violently as the scent itched his throat. "Ugh! What *is* this?"

"Sap from swamp trees," Kyleigh said.

The liquid inside the jar moved slowly as he tilted it. "It looks like honey."

She smiled in amusement when he coughed again. "Yes, and it'll stick like honey, too — which allows it to melt flesh rather nicely."

He choked on his coughs. "Come again?"

"You said you're tired of me leaving you out of things. So come on, then." She bent and hoisted a jar in either hand. "Let's make some mischief."

They emptied the small tent in a matter of minutes, hauling the jars out and hurling them onto the pile of bodies.

83

Amber liquid oozed from among the shattered clay, slowly drenching every crevice. When they'd thrown the last of the jars Kyleigh grabbed a branch from one of the smoldering fires and led him into the trees.

Kael peered through the shadows. "Where's Baird and Graymange?"

Kyleigh pulled an arrow from his quiver. "We'll meet up with them in a bit. Hold this for me, will you?"

He took the branch warily, careful not to touch its glowing end. "What are you —? Hey!"

She ripped a good amount of material from the bottom of his tunic and began knotting it onto the arrow's head. "Sorry, I needed kindling."

"Well, I happened to like this shirt," he muttered, tugging on its ragged hem. "I'd just finally got it broken in."

"Is that what you call it when you never wash something? *Breaking it in?*"

She grinned when he glared.

Once she'd finished her knot, she grabbed the smoldering branch from his hand and brought it to the arrow's head. She worked gently — coaxing the embers with soft, steady breaths. Kael watched as the ragged material caught with flame and the fire's light spread across her skin ...

"Kael?"

His face burned when he realized she was staring at him. "What?"

"I asked if you would do the honors," she said, holding out the flaming arrow. "Aim right for the middle of the pile."

He did. And the sap caught so furiously with orange-blue light that it made the trees rattle. Kael's hair blew back from his forehead and he watched in shock as the fires roared. "I thought you didn't want to be noticed! What was the point of doing all that?"

"Payback," Kyleigh growled.

Her eyes shone so fiercely in the angry light that he was afraid to ask her what she'd meant.

*******

From what Kael could gather, the shapechangers were in the middle of some sort of war: the shamans hunted the Abominations, and the Abominations hunted the shamans.

Apparently, they'd been warring all spring — though Oakloft had seemed peaceful enough. He found it hard to believe that an entire village could carry on without knowing there was war raging all around it.

"Shapechanger battles are quiet affairs," Kyleigh said when he mentioned it. "They kill precisely who they mean to, and they kill them quickly. There's hardly ever any burning or pillaging. You wouldn't have even known there was a battle going on, had you not wandered into the middle of it."

"I was *chased* into the middle of it," he reminded her. "And since we're already here, we might as well do something about it." He turned to Graymange — who was busily stripping the feathers off the carcass of a large goose. "What can we do to help?"

"This is the shamans' task," Kyleigh said firmly before Graymange could reply. "It's none of our business."

The halfwolf inclined his head.

They were hunched inside Graymange's den: a shallow bowl dug into the earth beneath a bramble patch, forming something like a makeshift cage. It was the very early hours of the morning. Pale, grayish light leaked through the gaps in the thorns. Baird's muttering drifted in an endless stream from where he lay curled up against one of the thorny walls, still soundly asleep.

Kael watched as Graymange stripped the last of the goose's feathers away with a quick, practiced swipe. He cracked off one of the legs and offered it to Kyleigh. He offered the second to Kael.

"You don't have to eat that," Kyleigh said when he took it.

He'd always dreamed of being able to sit among the shapechangers. If Roland were here, he wouldn't hesitate to join them. So Kael didn't hesitate, either. He took a bite of the goose and the raw flesh squished inside his mouth. It was wet and chewy. He'd been half-expecting it to taste like death, but it didn't. If anything, it was slightly bland.

"I like this human," Graymange said approvingly. Then he sunk his teeth into the goose's chest.

When the meat was gone, Graymange went to work on the marrow. Kael tried not to stare as the halfwolf cracked the bones between his teeth and sucked their juices dry. He decided to give it a shot — and very nearly cracked a tooth in half.

Kyleigh didn't even bother. Once she'd picked her bones clean, she tossed them back into the pile.

"Why do you never eat the marrow?" Graymange said.

She shrugged. "I've never much cared for the taste."

Kyleigh sprawled out on the ground, hands tucked beneath her head, and Graymange's eyes roved over her. "Does it feel odd to you?"

She shrugged again. "A little, I suppose."

"Does what feel odd?" Kael wondered.

"Not long ago, the Fangs and the Manges fought over the same hunting grounds," Graymange said.

"You were enemies?" Kael guessed.

"Friends and enemies are human things. Wolves are loyal only to their packs — and what isn't food is merely competition."

Kael was still confused. "But I thought you were the wolf shaman."

"I am. And when the sun sets upon my life, a new shaman will be born among the wolves. He will stay with his own pack, whether it be Fang, Mange, or Howl. And in the spring, when the wolves come together and live peacefully for a time, he will perform the ritual on all of their young — so that they may be reborn into their second shapes.

"The Fangs have been unbeatable for many passings of the sun, as you can imagine," Graymange said, nodding to Kyleigh. "But Bloodfang was fair. After his pack had their fill of prey, the Fangs would leave for a time — giving us all a

86

chance to hunt on the best grounds. Other alphas wouldn't have been so generous."

The mood grew solemn quickly at the mention of Bloodfang. Guilt chewed at Kael's heart as the silence dragged on.

"I've been told what you did for him. I know that you sent Bloodfang to the eternal woods."

Kael raised his chin and immediately found himself snared in the unreadable lines on Graymange's face.

"It was a mercy," he whispered. "Being caged is what we all most fear: to have our claws tied, our voices hushed, to be trapped with nothing but stone beneath our feet — *that* is death. Bloodfang's pack was gone. He was chained and alone. Now his spirit is free to roam the wilds once more, free to hunt with those he loves. It was a mercy."

Kael wasn't sure what to say to that. He was afraid that if he tried to say anything at all, the thing that struggled inside his chest might punch its way out. So he clamped his mouth shut and nodded.

He was thankful when Graymange's eyes went back to Kyleigh. "I knew the moment you set foot among the trees. The forest sang with your coming, as it always does."

"It's good to be back," she murmured. "I thought the shamans had abandoned the Grandforest."

Graymange inclined his head. "When the King drove our people into the swamps, we had no choice but to flee. Our magic must be kept safe," he said, touching the wooden medallion at his chest. "But I sensed a strange black cloud over the forest this spring ... a great and terrible storm riding on shadowed wings. Something had changed — our order had been interrupted. Now I see why." His fingers curled around the goose's ribcage. Its bones snapped into little pieces as he clenched his fist. "Blackbeak has loosed Abomination into our world."

"Who's Blackbeak?" Kael said.

"The crow shaman," Graymange barked. Then his head swung to Kyleigh. "I caught the scent of the bear not long ago. The shadow of the hawk follows me. The fox and lion won't be far behind. It seems the black cloud has called to all of us. With their help, we'll put an end to Blackbeak."

Kyleigh nodded, her eyes on the ceiling.

Kael did a quick sum: that was only six. He could've sworn that Baird had said there were seven shamans. "What about the ... sandpipers?" he finished lamely. He couldn't bring himself to ask about Kyleigh's family — not when he saw how very pointedly she was glaring at the briars.

"Sandpipers?" Graymange rumbled.

"I read about them in a story once," Kael explained. "Quicklegs the sandpiper was the one who saved Iden the Hale from the ... uh ..."

His story trailed off as Graymange stared at him. There was no softness to the edge of his gaze, no curtain over his eyes. "You speak of an ancient time, human. In the elder days, our talismans were strong. There were many families — so many that every child of the forest could belong to a flock or pack if he wished. As the world of men crept into our woods, fewer of our children wished to undergo the change, and families like your sandpipers died out. The shamans were the first in these woods, and now our families are all that remain."

Kael was still trying to wrap his head around it. "Talismans?"

Graymange held the medallion from his chest. There was a wolf carved into its surface: its neck was arched back and its mouth opened in a howl. "The token that holds our magic, that allows us to perform the ritual. We shamans only perform it on our own kind — those are the rules. And we've never strayed from our law ... with one exception.

"Blackbeak gave himself up to the human King many years ago. He traded his freedom for power. He has always lunged for whatever trinket sparkles brightest." Graymange's eyes went dark. "Blackbeak has been using the ritual on our children for years, changing them before their time. They often go mad. Some are consumed by their animal souls. Such a deed is unforgivable. But what he's done now is ... *Abomination*.

88

"Blackbeak has begun to perform the ritual on humans — creatures with no shapechanger in their blood. They are reborn as strange things. Some, like the creatures you saw tonight, are so twisted by evil that they have no place among the worlds of beast or men. They don't answer to order, but do only as they're commanded."

Graymange sank into a crouch and began moving towards the den's entrance. "Soon, this will all be ended. Once the shamans have dealt with Blackbeak, there will be no new births. Then we will hunt and destroy the Abomination that remains." He stopped to look at Kyleigh.

She shook her head.

The halfwolf sighed heavily. "Very well, then. I thank you for your help with the swordbearers, Emberfang. I know you don't agree with the shamans' decision ... but we are grateful for your help. Return to the road quickly if you don't wish to fight. The hour has nearly come. Soon the forest will be filled with our war."

He slipped through the briars and disappeared without another word.

For not the first time that day, Kael was confused. "Why *wouldn't* we fight with the shamans? Why wouldn't we help them hunt Titus's Abominations?"

She gave him a hard look. "You shouldn't use a word if you don't understand its meaning. I'm all for fighting Titus — it's the way the shamans are going about it that troubles me. Perhaps you'll understand one day ... but I hope you never have to. Now get some sleep," she grunted, rolling over so he faced her back. "We've got a long walk ahead of us."

That was the end of it. Kael knew he would get no more out of her, so he didn't waste his breath. Instead, he tried to sleep.

He'd had every intention of using his rucksack for a pillow, but its bottom was still sopping from having been dipped in the river. So he grabbed Baird's instead.

It was a mistake.

Not only did the filthy rucksack reek of mold, but it was also rife with all manner of noisy lumps. No matter how he turned, the pack made some sort of noise: it crinkled or rustled, sometimes it groaned. Sharp corners dug into his scalp.

Finally, Kael lost his patience. He thrust his hand inside and ripped out the thing that'd been crinkling beneath his neck.

It was a letter. He turned it towards the faint beams of light that drifted through the briars, trying to see whom the letter had been addressed to. There was a seal on its folded back. He ran his thumb over the wax and felt something stamped into its surface. He tilted the seal into the light ... and the crest of Midlan leapt out.

Kael's tongue stuck to the back of his throat at the sight of the twisting black dragon stamped into the wax. What was Baird doing with a letter from the King? Had he been right about him being a spy?

The possibilities whirred inside his head as he turned the letter over. He strained to read the words scrawled across its front. Each one was written in dark ink, looped and flourished at their ends. Kael was so mesmerized by how the letters danced that it took him several moments to read the message:

*His Majesty, Crevan — Sovereign King of Midlan — bids you open this message immediately.*

The words rang inside Kael's head and down to his fingertips. Before he could grasp what was happening, his thumb slid beneath the fold of the letter. It moved slowly towards the wax seal —

"No!"

Fury blinded him as someone ripped the letter from his hand. He gasped, trying desperately to snatch it back. "I'm supposed to read that! He says I'm supposed to open the message immediately!"

A pair of strong arms wrapped around his shoulders. He lunged against Kyleigh's hold, moving her an inch. She said something in his ear, but he couldn't hear her. All he could hear were the shrilling words of that letter:

*Open this message immediately! Immediately! Open this message —!*

"You don't have to open the message," a new voice said. The power behind it drowned out the shrilling words. "You don't have to open the message."

As he came out of his fury, Kael recognized the voice as Baird's. He had his knobby hands planted on either side of Kael's head; his bandaged face was mere inches away. He said the words again and again, letting them fade a little each time until they were only a whisper.

At last, the letter's voice disappeared and Kael's body relaxed. When Kyleigh released him, he collapsed. "What in Kingdom's name was that?"

"You shouldn't fiddle with things that don't belong to you," Baird said as he crawled away. He snatched the rucksack up, stuffed the letter inside — and promptly sat on it. "You would've gone to Midlan, had you read it. You would've marched through those gates and straight to your death."

"What are you talking about?" Kael said. He was shaking, now. His limbs trembled with the lingering power of the message. There was no doubt in his mind that he would've done whatever that letter had said, had Kyleigh not held him back.

Baird *tsk*ed and shook his head. "Just like all the others."

"What others?"

Kyleigh sighed in exasperation. "The whisperers, Kael. How do you think Crevan got them all to go to Midlan at the end of the War? Did you think he just asked nicely?"

Kael had never given it much thought. He'd always just assumed that the whisperers had gone because Crevan was King, and to ignore him would've been treason. He supposed he should've realized that such a powerful race wouldn't have been fooled so easily.

Now that he knew the truth, a sudden thought made his toes curl. "But why would Crevan force them to go to Midlan?"

Kyleigh's eyes went dark. "Why do you think?"

*The King summoned the whisperers to Midlan, where they were never heard from again.* That was how Amos had told the story. He'd never said for certain what had become of them. And in his heart, Kael had hoped that they'd only been captured. But the look in Kyleigh's eyes told him the truth:

Crevan had killed them all. He'd killed every last one.

"Whispercraft," Baird said, slapping a hand to the side of his rucksack. "A summons written by the Dog, himself."

"Who's the Dog?" Kael wondered.

Baird grinned. "Not the most talented craftsman, not by far. But he was a loyal pet. Whatever the King asked of him, he would wag his little tail and hop to obey — that's why they called him the Dog. He had another name, but I've forgotten it. Something like … *Horace*, perhaps? No, that doesn't sound quite right. *Magnus*? No. *Bertrand*? Ah, dear me, I think I'm getting further away …"

"Maybe it'll come to you if you sleep on it," Kyleigh muttered after he'd rattled off several other names.

Baird looked as if she'd just suggested he stop breathing. "Sleep? I can't possibly sleep — not with that little thief lurking about!" He jabbed an accusing finger at the wall to Kael's right. "Besides, I've only just woken up."

Kyleigh groaned as she curled into a ball and pulled her hood over her head. "He won't go through your pack again. I'm sure he's learned his lesson … haven't you, Kael?" she growled after a moment.

He certainly had. Now he understood why Morris had warned him to be careful with his words. He'd had no idea that whispercraft could be so powerful. "Why do you even keep that letter?"

"It's no harm to me. *I* can't see it," Baird said with a shrug.

"But other people can."

"Well, then perhaps *other* people should keep their eyes on their own things."

"It's dangerous," Kael insisted. "Why don't you burn it and be done with it?"

Baird gasped indignantly. "This letter is history, young man. *History*. No self-respecting bard would burn a piece of history. Besides that, it's a powerful bit of whispercraft," he added with a sly grin. "One never knows when it might be useful."

# CHAPTER 9
## MERCHANTING

The afternoon sun rose high, spreading its warmth across Gravy Bay. Golden light fell from between the clouds and filtered through the mansion's windows. It climbed slowly along a desk in the library, creeping forward with the minutes until it finally came to rest among the strands of Captain Lysander's wavy hair.

He sat hunched over at his desk, a small mountain of unopened letters lying at the edge of his reach. A fresh sheet of parchment rested between his arms. One hand held the parchment down while the other was poised above it, gripping a quill.

Drops of ink slid from the tip of the quill and splattered onto the blank white of the page, but Lysander didn't seem to notice. His stormy eyes weren't on the parchment: they were locked on the window.

Sunlight shone brightly and the sea sparkled back. Lysander's chest rose and fell with the crashing surf; his gaze grew more distant. His hand lowered slowly until it finally came to rest ... squarely in a puddle of ink.

"Swindlers! Thieves and pickpockets, the lot of them!" Uncle Martin stormed as he marched into the room. "Our fathers would roll in their watery graves if they could see us now — *roll*, I tell you."

"Be that as it may, you're still going to have to pay the chancellor for those goblets," Lysander murmured without taking his eyes from the window.

"Oh, I'll gladly pay him. But it won't be coin he gets," Uncle Martin swung his cane in a dangerous arc, "it'll be blood!"

"Excellent. Why don't you take a crew and explain that to his armada?"

Uncle Martin snorted through his mustache. "Maybe I will. I'd rather be strapped to the bottom of my ship than have to bow to the will of that stony-eyed monster —"

"Fantastic idea. I'll get the rope."

"We're pirates, blast you — not coin-fondling merchants!" Uncle Martin's shoulders went straight as he gripped the cane to his chest. "You'd do well to remember that, *Captain*."

No sooner had Uncle Martin's stomping steps faded than two more sets shuffled in. The first pair belonged to Battlemage Jake. He leaned to watch Uncle Martin storm down the hallway and said, with no small amount of concern:

"You don't think he'll really attack Chaucer, do you?"

"That man is all mast and no sail," Lysander replied.

Eveningwing sprinted past Jake and bounded onto the middle of Lysander's desk, startling his gaze from the window.

"What have I told you about perching wherever you please?"

Eveningwing cocked his head to the side. "You don't mind it when I'm a hawk."

"Yes, well, you're a good deal lighter then," Lysander grumped as he pulled a book out from under his toes. "And your feet aren't nearly as filthy. Now what's this all about? I'm very busy."

Jake shoved his spectacles firmly up the bridge of his nose. "Captain, we've come to ask you, one last time —"

"Are those lady's gloves?"

Jake stretched out his hands. A pair of black leather gloves covered him from the tips of his fingers to past his wrists. The seams were stretched almost to the point of splitting. They squeaked piteously as he flexed his hands.

"It was an accident."

Lysander raised a brow. "How does one *accidentally* wear a pair of lady's gloves?"

95

"I wanted to make a new impetus, one that wasn't so childish," Jake said shortly. "I was just practicing with the gloves, but it wound up working rather well. I had to use a spell to make them a little larger. They aren't perfect, but ..."

He stretched a hand out and a tail of green flame rippled to life on his palm. Then he slapped his other hand on top of it, snuffing it out. "See? Like a sword and a shield."

"How so?"

"Don't bother," Eveningwing said, picking at the feathers that sprouted from his elbow. "He'll say the same thing twenty times and then get ruffled when you don't understand."

Jake made a face at him. "I couldn't have possibly explained it any clearer. But we're not here to talk about my gloves." A knot bobbed up and down his throat as he swallowed. "We've come to ask you, one last time, if you'll reconsider."

Lysander groaned and slapped a hand to his face — smearing a good deal of ink across his stubble. "This again? No, I'm afraid I won't. I've told you a hundred times that Kyleigh knows what she's doing. If she chose to leave, then I'm sure she had a very good reason."

"But they've got no chance at all," Jake insisted. "They need our help."

"No chance at what? You don't know where they've gone." He sighed at Jake's look. "How many times must I tell you? Kyleigh would never try to take back the mountains alone."

"But Kael would. That's *exactly* the sort of thing he would do."

Lysander snorted. "Kyleigh would never let him. No, I'm sure they've gone off on another errand. We'll attack the mountains next spring, just like we planned."

"Dig your head out, Captain," Jake said, with a surprising amount of scorn. "You know full well where they've gone. If you sit around and do nothing, you'll be sentencing them to death —"

"Enough!"

Lysander's fist came down hard upon the desk. The noise startled Eveningwing so badly that he jumped into his hawk form and bolted out the window. Jake's spectacles slid a considerable length down his nose, but he made no move to push them back.

Lysander sighed heavily. He dragged a hand through the waves of his hair, leaving a streak of ink behind. "I know you're concerned about them. I think we all are. But she always comes back — and when she does, I have no doubt that she'll bring Kael and that horrible little cat-man —"

"Silas."

"— with her. We aren't going to go charging into the mountains looking for them, and that's my final word on the matter." He leaned back, jutting out his chin. "Now if you pester me about it again, I'm afraid I'll have no choice. I've already had to lock Nadine in her room because she wouldn't behave. Am I going to have to do the same with you?"

"Assuming you could find a lock that would hold me? No, Captain," Jake grumbled. Then, as he turned to leave: "I just hope you're right."

The moment Jake had marched from the room, Lysander sagged in his chair. His eyes were distant by the time they reached the window. There was a sharpness behind the storm, now — a rumbling in the clouds. He stared, unflinching, until a soft knock drew his eyes away.

"Have you come to scold me as well?"

Aerilyn smiled as she crossed the room, her pale blue gown sweeping the floor behind her. One hand rested absently on the small bump beneath her dress. "That all depends. Have you done something worthy of a scolding?"

"Perhaps," Lysander said as he pulled her into his lap. They sat quietly for a moment: her arms around his neck and his ear against her chest. "I'm doing the right thing. I know I am."

"Of course you are."

"I've managed to keep my people fed, my men out of trouble, and my wife indescribably happy," he said with a smile. "The winds have stopped howling and the weather's

97

finally fair. There's absolutely no point in marching across the Kingdom looking for trouble — not when I've got everything I need right here." He pulled his head from her chest. "Right?"

She kissed him on the chin. "Right. You've earned yourself some peace."

"I couldn't agree more."

"There's no reason why you shouldn't spend the rest of your days comfortably, trading for goods instead of killing for them."

"Absolutely," Lysander said — though the word came out sounding as if he'd strained it through his teeth.

"We'll go to the chancellor's parties together and make all sorts of friends. I'll need to buy you some proper dress wear, of course. You'd look so handsome in a fur-trimmed coat," she added with glowing smile. "They're a little itchy at first, but you'll get used to it." Her eyes flicked down to the smear of ink across his cheek. "Oh dear, what have you gotten yourself into?"

Lysander sat rigidly as she scrubbed at the ink with her thumb. Sparks flashed behind his eyes. "We wouldn't have to go to *all* of the balls, surely."

She laughed. "Don't be ridiculous, my love. If we don't go to the balls, how can you expect your son to marry well?"

"Come again?"

She sighed. "If we ever want any respect at all among the merchants, we'll have to find him a lovely woman of good standing to marry. And if we have a daughter, we'll need to get her betrothed as quickly as possible. Otherwise all the wealthy old men will be taken," she added with a wink.

Lysander's smile didn't quite have the same shine as it'd had before. "I'm worried about Kyleigh and Kael," he blurted out.

Aerilyn raised her brows. "But I thought you said they'd be all right?"

"There's war brewing in the Kingdom. I've heard all sorts of nasty rumors at the chancellor's castle: Midlan has fallen unnaturally silent, Titus's thugs are carving up the mountains, and everybody's convinced there's all manner of evil running wild in the Grandforest. It's all such a sudden, terrible business. I never could've seen it coming."

Aerilyn gripped his arm. "Oh, that's horrible! You ought to go after them — at least as far as the Valley. There's no telling what sort of mess they might've gotten themselves into."

"Ah, but if I leave, who's going to take care of the merchanting? You're in no state to handle all of the writing, all the squabbling back and forth —"

"I have an idea," Aerilyn said lightly. She slid off his lap, took him by the hand, and led him down the hall.

As they wound their way through the mansion's elaborate passageways, a soft trail of music rose to greet them. It was muted at first. But the closer they got, the more the notes began to stand out. The song was sharp, pounded out with force and finality. It rang through the halls like the steps of an army — one with its will bent against the destruction of all in its path.

The louder the music became, the more Lysander slowed. "Ah, I don't think he's quite ready yet, my love."

"Don't be ridiculous. He's more than ready."

"But he said he doesn't want to be disturbed. He's been very clear on that, and I think the least we can do is —"

"If you leave him alone, he'll rot in there," Aerilyn said firmly. "He'll waste away until you come in one day and find his bones hunched over that foolish instrument. If there was ever a man who needed to be disturbed, it's Thelred." With that, she latched onto Lysander's arm and pulled him through the ballroom doors.

The music slammed to a stop.

"I told you not to come in here!"

Thelred sat at the bench of a small piano. The hair on his face had grown long and there were plates of half-eaten food scattered all about him. His eyes were rimmed red, his fists were clenched tightly atop the piano's keys — and his only clothing was a rumpled, filthy nightshirt.

Lysander managed to take two steps in before he staggered backwards. "What in high tide is that smell?"

"He hasn't bathed since we got back from the plains," Aerilyn said.

Thelred returned her look with a glare. "It's nobody's business whether I've bathed or not."

"He hasn't been going for his walks, either," Aerilyn added, crossing her arms. "Morris said you're supposed to walk on it at least twice a day. How do you ever expect to get used to —?"

"I don't want to get used to it," Thelred said sharply. "Do you think I ever want to be seen like this?"

He jerked his leg out from under the piano. A thick leather band was strapped on just below his knee, held tightly by a tangle of lacing. Below that was a wooden stick: it was nearly as thick as a man's arm and with a knob on the end for walking.

Thelred's glare slipped as Lysander met his gaze. He tugged down roughly on his nightshirt — though the hem fell well short of his wooden leg. "I can't sail, and I can't fight. I'm no good for anything anymore. So you might as well just leave me to my music."

Lysander watched him a moment more before he clasped his hands smartly behind his back. "Sorry, Red, but I'm afraid I can't do that. Our friends in the mountains need my help. And while I'm away, I expect you to run the merchanting."

Thelred looked as if a stiff wind had just blown up his nightshirt. "But ..."

Lysander held up a hand. "The latest shipment from the plains should be halfway here by now. Once it arrives, you'll need to take it to the castle. Sell Chaucer his bit — at the most ridiculous rate possible — then sell the rest in the courtyard. Keep the men in line while you're on the chancellor's grounds. And make sure you don't get caught stealing anything."

"There shouldn't be any stealing to begin with," Aerilyn cut in, glaring.

Lysander planted a swift kiss on her cheek. "Isn't that what I said?"

Thelred struggled to his feet. "Wait, I don't —"

"Put on some trousers and get to work," Lysander called as he strode through the door. "That's an order, Red."

"Aye, Captain," he mumbled. Once Lysander had disappeared, Thelred turned his glare on Aerilyn. "I suppose I have you to thank for this."

He plopped down on the bench with a grunt. While he fumbled with the laces on his wooden leg, she leaned casually against the piano. "I should be thanking *you*, actually."

Thelred's fingers froze to the laces, and his head rose slowly. "What do you mean?"

She shrugged. "It's simple, really. We're all worried sick about Kyleigh and Kael, Lysander's completely miserable — and as long as he's here, he'll go on treating me like I'm some frail thing that might crumble to bits at any moment," she added with a frown. "An adventure will give him something to do ... and while he's away, you and I can run the merchanting business."

"You're going to help me?" When she nodded, he rolled his eyes. "You're daft if you think I'm taking you anywhere."

"Oh, you'll take me. I have every confidence you will. Because if you leave me here alone with Uncle Martin and all these nosy maids," she dragged her hand across the piano's keys in an ominous climb, "I'll pull every single string out of your ridiculous instrument. One at a time."

He glared at her.

She smiled sweetly.

"Fine."

"Wonderful! Oh, I'm so happy you've agreed. And it's probably best if Lysander knows nothing about this," she added with a hard smile. "Just in case."

She dragged her hand down the piano's keys as she left, tinkling one obnoxious strand of notes at the end. Thelred glared at the doorway long after she'd gone.

In the end, he threw up his hands and stomped out behind her, muttering curses as he went.

# CHAPTER 10
## FATE'S FORSAKEN

The further north they went, the more spread out the trees became. Slowly, the undergrowth thinned and the oaks grew slimmer. Rocks covered much of the ground and large pines began to take root between them. But though the forest had shrunk back, Baird's prattling never ceased.

"I fell asleep so quickly I don't even remember closing my eyes! There's no peace quite like a long night's rest."

The beggar-bard had reattached himself to Kael's pack — and he talked from sunup till sundown. His words ran in such a constant stream that if he ever stopped to take a breath, the sudden quiet would jolt Kael from his thoughts.

"It's strange, but I always know I'm asleep because things suddenly get brighter. I see colors and shapes, the smiling faces of long-lost friends. Ah, I hope death isn't nearly as dark as life!"

Kael figured if he couldn't be left alone to think, he might as well join in. "What happened to your friends?"

"The Whispering War claimed most of them, though a few died after. They reached the ends of their yarn all too soon. Fate's crafted a story for each of us, you know." He tapped a knobby finger to the side of his head. "She labors with patience at her loom, weaving every moment of our lives into a brilliant tale. Our tapestries go on until she reaches the end of our yarn; some of our lives wind up rather frayed at their hems. It pains me to say that most of my friends' stories ended all too soon. What is it about war that kills the young?"

"It probably has something to do with the swords," Kael said.

"Or the arrows — or all that bothersome fighting in close spaces," Kyleigh added with a smirk.

Baird didn't seem to notice their teasing. "No, no it happens *before* all that. Why do the young answer the battle horns? Why are they so quick to draw their swords? If you ask me, war is in their hearts long before the lines are drawn. It's a lust that need only be awakened."

"Did you fight in the War?" Kael said after a moment.

There was a rustling noise as Baird's shaggy head slung to the side. "No, I was never much of a fighter ... *love* was always my poison of choice."

Kael was immediately sorry he'd asked.

Kyleigh grinned. "Is that why Fate struck you blind, then? Did you spoil one too many noblemen's daughters?"

"*Kyleigh!*"

But Baird just laughed. "No. There might've been one or two noblewomen along the way, but my true love was always in telling of tales. Stories take on a life of their own, don't they? They're creatures carried gently by word and voice, but never quite bound. Long after the last line falls hushed, I can still hear the clang of swords and the cries of my heroes — proof that they travel even beyond the tongue. Yes, stories speak to us like none among the living can."

"I suppose," Kael said. Though he tried to act indifferent, he couldn't quite manage it. Those were the words he'd always felt inside his heart.

*******

Nothing Kael said could convince Kyleigh to join the shapechangers' war. Anytime he asked, she would glower and say that he'd only regret it. She said she was doing what was best. She insisted he ought to trust her. So he had no choice but to follow her to the road.

After another day of battling their way through the thicket, they tumbled out of the undergrowth and onto a wide dirt path. At least following the road meant that there was a little space between the trees: sunlight fell through unfettered, warming them against the forest's gloom.

Kael was buried very deeply in the *Atlas* when he suddenly ran smack into the unrelenting wall of Kyleigh's shoulders. Before he could ask her why on earth she'd stopped, she shoved him back with her elbow.

"Get off the road."

"But we've only just got —"

"Screams!" Baird cried, cupping a knobby hand against his ear. "A song of pain and fright!"

Kael slung his bow from across his chest. "Is it the hounds?"

"Dozens of different voices, some great and some small. They roar and bark and yip and yelp, each one crying: *Help me!*" Baird tugged hard on his pack. "We must turn away! We must be gone!"

"Are you mad? If someone's in trouble, we ought to help," Kael said.

Kyleigh was too busy cursing under her breath to hear him. She grabbed Baird by the wrist and pulled hard, dragging them both towards the brush. "That meddling old wolf ... I'll kill him!"

"What do you ...?" Kael's words trailed away as he caught a faint echo in the distance.

It was the sound of wailing — the anguished screams of men and women, the cries of animals in pain. Though the forest tried to strangle them, Kael could still hear the terror in their pleas.

"No, get into the bushes," Kyleigh said when he took a step forward. "They're coming to us."

He followed her reluctantly into the trees and crouched, waiting. Baird curled upon the ground behind them and cradled the filthy rucksack against his chest. He covered his ears, groaning softly. But at least he stayed quiet.

As they waited, the screams began to grow louder. Soon Kael had to grip his bow tightly to keep from charging out. The wails of the hounds had chilled his blood — he'd heard the evil in their bays. But these screams were different.

105

Instead of chilling, his blood burned against them. He felt the anger rising up long before he saw the cart.

It rolled slowly down the road, flanked on either side by a company of soldiers. The cart's wheels clattered as it bounced along the path. Its bed squeaked piteously. But even the rattling of its axle couldn't quite drown out the cries of its passengers.

Men and women filled the cart's bed to either end. He could tell by their flaming red hair that they must've come from the Unforgivable Mountains. They wore rough spun clothes instead of armor, and he realized with a jolt that they must've been common folk — villagers Titus had captured during his march.

His blood began to bubble dangerously when he saw how they'd been thrown into the cart. The villagers had been stuffed inside metal cages and stacked on top of each other like cargo. Their fingers curled through the wiring. They pounded the bars with their fists. Every few moments, their human wails would become the cries of animals — they would convulse in the middle of their pleas and their skin would erupt in feathers or fur.

Kael realized that must've been how the armor had gotten melded to the hounds' skin: they'd been twisted back and forth so many times until the iron had finally become a part of them.

A horde of Earl Titus's soldiers guarded the cart. They kept a steady march, their helmeted heads turning to search the trees. One soldier jabbed the butt of his spear in amongst the cages. He laughed when he heard a yelp.

Kyleigh hissed in warning, but it was too late. The molten bubbles inside Kael's chest burst with spouts of flame and carried their fury straight to the top of his head. He could do nothing to stop himself. Anger roared in the tips of his fingers as he stepped out from the bushes. His eyes locked onto the soldier ...

And he sent an arrow straight through his laughing mouth.

Kyleigh said something that was far from ladylike as she drew up her hood, but Kael wasn't listening. His eyes were already on the next target.

Soldiers fell helplessly to his arrows. Rage numbed him and his limbs moved in a deadly pattern. His eyes went from patches of flesh to the gaps between plates of armor, leading his hands in a charge.

Kyleigh ran out from behind him and threw herself into the fray. She cut the horses free and they thundered madly from her scent, eyes rolling back in terror. When the cart's driver made the very serious mistake of trying to fend her off, she ripped him from his seat — and directly onto the point of her sword.

Kyleigh leapt to the top of the cart. She dodged the soldiers' spears with ease, spinning and ducking out of their path. A few tried to climb up the cart's side only to find Harbinger waiting for them. The sword's curved white blade bit through their necks, singing sweetly as the soldiers' heads rolled down their backs.

They'd managed to thin out a considerable number before the soldiers changed tactics. They clumped behind the cart, putting the caged people between themselves and Kael's arrows.

It was more of an inconvenience than anything. Kael nocked an arrow and strode in a half-circle, his eyes peeled for the first bit of skin peeking out from behind the cart — and perhaps it was because he was so focused on the soldiers that he didn't see the monstrous shadow cross over his boots …

Or hear the wind whistling off its great, glossy wings.

The back of his head struck the ground hard. Shock chased the numbness away. He managed to catch a glimpse of the canopy above him before something large blocked his vision.

It was black and stank of rotted meat. He felt a sudden pressure on his shoulders — and with the pressure came pain. Horrible pain. It was so sharp and sudden that Kael

107

cried out. He dropped his bow and twisted to look at the things that dug into his flesh.

They were sharp, scaly talons. A face came down to his — a man's face, but horribly twisted. His nose stretched into a point, dragging his upper lip out with it. Human teeth hung from the nose's bottom. They were yellowed and wet with drool. The jaw jutted nearly as far as the nose, forming something that looked like a beak.

No, it *was* a beak. Kael saw the talisman hanging around the monster's chest and knew immediately who this creature was — who it had to be:

Blackbeak.

Two beady eyes stared down at him. They shone every bit as clearly as glass — he could see the shocked white of his own face reflected in their pupils. A long gray tongue smacked between the pointed nose and jutting jaw as Blackbeak screeched: "Kill you! I'm going to kill you!"

Kael tried to move his arms, but the talons cinched down tighter. They dug against his bones and kept his hands pinned to the ground. His eyes were bleary with pain. He could hardly see by the time Blackbeak's head snapped down —

"Away! Be gone with you!" Baird cried.

His first blind swing missed fantastically, but the second struck true. Kael heard a *thunk* and gasped as the talons pulled free. Baird swung his rucksack into the crow shaman's head again, littering the ground with a shower of glossy feathers. Blackbeak screeched and hopped away, holding one of his massive wings up like a shield.

With Baird swinging blindly all around him, Kael saw his chance. He pulled himself to his feet and retrieved his bow. The gashes in his shoulder weren't as deep as he'd feared. They pierced his skin to bleeding, but hadn't gone much deeper. He still had the strength to draw his bow.

"Run, young man!" Baird cried, swinging his rucksack in a wild arc. "Run! I'll hold him back!"

Blackbeak dodged his next swing and jumped, lashing out with both feet. His talons caught Baird in the gut and sent him tumbling backwards.

Kael fired with a cry, but Blackbeak dodged. His feathered head jerked out of the arrow's path and his beady eyes locked onto Kael. He'd spread his wings and arched his neck for the kill when a roar startled him away.

A black bear lumbered out of the woods, shaking the leaves with its throaty bellow. The bear threw itself on the remaining soldiers. It swatted their bodies aside with its claws and crushed their limbs between its teeth.

A reddish hawk fell from the sky and raked across Blackbeak's face. It dug in with its talons and tore clumps of his feathers out with its beak.

A wolf's howl pierced their ears. Blackbeak screeched at the sound and took off. He shot into the sky with a blast of his feathery wings. His talons kicked beneath him as he tried to gain speed. The hawk followed in wide, dipping arcs — ripping out clawfuls of his feathers with every pass.

Kyleigh leapt down from the cart, her eyes on Kael. "Are you all r —?"

"Look out!"

A soldier lunged from behind the cart and swung for her middle — and for half a moment, the world stopped turning. Kael's horror became disbelief as he watched the soldier's sword break across her armor: the blade shattered like glass and the hilt jolted from his hand.

Kyleigh hardly glanced at the soldier as she ran him through. "Dragonscales, remember?" she said, thumping a hand against her chest.

Kael was still trying to force his heart back down his throat. "Well, I didn't know they would do *that*."

She raised a brow. "What did you think they did?" Her fingers hovered above his wounds, but she didn't touch them. "Can you heal this?"

He nodded. "It's not as deep as it looks."

They heard a muffled grunt as the bear crushed the final soldier beneath its claws. A scruffy gray wolf had his nose pressed against the ground where Blackbeak had stood. His pointed ears twitched as the hawk returned to circle overhead, crying softly in greeting.

"I can't believe you, I really can't — I told you we wanted nothing to do with this!" Kyleigh shouted at the wolf.

His lip peeled back over his fangs in what could've only been a sheepish grin, and Kael suddenly understood: Graymange had told them to return to the road knowing full well that the Earl's men were marching through. He'd used them to take care of the soldiers so that the shamans could have a clear shot at Blackbeak.

Kael wasn't sorry for it. He would've killed those soldiers, anyways. "You're just cross because he outsmarted you."

Kyleigh's eyes blazed as they locked onto his. "Am I? You have no idea what you've done."

He thought she might've been overreacting a bit. So what if they'd killed a load of the Earl's men? They already had at least two rulers chasing after them. What was one more?

He spotted Baird lying a few yards away. He was curled upon the ground, his arms wrapped tightly about his middle. Kael jogged over to him. "It's all right," he said as he turned the beggar-bard over. "The monster's gone and all the soldiers are dead. There's no reason to ..."

"Baird!" Kyleigh fell on her knees beside him and pulled his hands away. Her face fell when she saw the dark red mass that stained his middle.

Blackbeak's talons had left a deep gash in Baird's stomach. His flesh was cut as raggedly as his bandages, now — peeled away from his middle in angry strips, their edges soaked scarlet.

"It seems ... it seems my time has come. My yarn is at its end," Baird said with a smile that made his lips shake. "All is as Fate wills it. Ah! Just promise me," his bloodied fingers wrapped tightly around Kael's arm, "promise you'll take good care of my possessions. It's time. Yes — it's time." Then he laid back and shut his eyes.

Kael knew he wouldn't pass immediately. Gut wounds were a slow, painful way to die. Some of Amos's patients had suffered for hours before they finally let go. He'd given them what they needed to sleep, but insisted he could do no more.

"Busted limbs are one thing. But a deep wound is quite another," Amos had always said. "When a man takes a fatal wound, he knows it. He expects to die. And if I bring him back from the dead, he'll know what I am." He'd glared as he added: "We live in a hard time, boy. Letting one man die might mean I'll live to save a hundred others."

Now, as Kael stared down at Baird, he heard those words again. He knew it would be safer to do what Amos had done — to let Baird pass on and keep his secret to himself. It would be the easier thing, the wiser thing.

But he wasn't certain it would be the right thing.

He grabbed onto Baird's knobby wrist and let the smooth calm of sleep flow through his memories. He focused on the feeling of peace, the warm embrace of the darkness and the easy passing of dreams. Slowly, Baird's lips stopped their trembling and the harsh lines around his face went smooth as he fell asleep.

"He was wise, this human," Graymange said from behind them. He crouched, his eyes on Baird. "*All is as Fate wills it.* May he pass on peacefully — his death was meant to be."

*Meant to be.*

Those words ground with such force against Kael's ears that he knew he could never do what Amos had done. He could never sit with his hands twined in his lap and let Fate have her way — not when he had the power to stop her.

Baird might've been a strange man. He might've been a little crazed. He might very well have been a spy or an agent of the Countess, for all Kael knew. But against everything — against all sense and every ounce of his reason — he ... *liked* Baird.

Now that the beggar-bard's voice had gone silent, he realized what a relief his prattling had been. What would Kael do if he didn't have to turn around every five steps and tell Baird to quit whistling at the birds? What would he worry over if he no longer had to worry that Baird would trip over a rock, or run headlong into a tree?

He knew exactly the sort of things his mind would dwell on. He knew the darkness that would fill his days. And as completely mad as it sounded, he *needed* Baird ... in fact, he wasn't sure if he could make it up the mountains without him.

"Your powers are great, Marked One," Graymange growled as Kael placed his hands on Baird's wounds. "But you should never change the will of Fate just because you can. One day you will have to answer for your meddling."

Kael wasn't afraid. He took a deep breath and prepared himself to concentrate. "I don't care what Fate wills. Baird will live today because *I* mean him to."

After that, the world slipped back.

Everything he'd read on anatomy came rushing to the front of his mind. He worked on the slippery surface of organs first. Then his fingers wrestled with sinewy cords of muscle: binding them and pulling them tightly until they hung in place. If he ever got stuck, he would wait — and the image or passage he needed would appear before his eyes.

As he pinched the last bit of skin together, he came out of his trance. The words and images still hovered like reflections across his eyes. He had to blink several times to clear them. But when they finally passed, he saw Baird was mended. The patch of skin that showed through his rags was stained red, but healed.

"Well done," Kyleigh said. She sat cross-legged before him, staring blankly at Baird's gut.

Kael winced as his trance faded and the ache of his wounds crept in. "Is Graymange angry with me?"

"Probably," Kyleigh said with a shrug.

"Where'd he go?"

She nodded behind her. "To deal with the newborns. Now that we've taken care of those soldiers, they'll have no problem getting rid of them."

He didn't like the edge in her voice, and he liked the look on her face even less. He turned where she glared and saw three people had gathered around the cart.

Graymange stood in the middle, flanked by a man on one side and a woman on the other. The man was thick-limbed and had long, black hairs growing out of his back. The talisman around his neck bore the image of a charging bear.

The woman on Graymange's other side wore nothing more than two strips of hide: one around her waist, and the other around her chest. Kael couldn't see what was on her talisman, but judging by the red feathers that hung off the hooks in her ears, he assumed she must've been the hawk shaman.

The three shamans stared at the people inside the cages. Some cowered away from their gazes while others reached out, begging to be set free.

"Now you see what Blackbeak has done to our world, brothers. You see how he's spat upon our order. His evil must be laid to rest." Graymange lifted the talisman from his chest, and the other shamans mirrored him. "Let us purge this Abomination."

Light blossomed from their talismans, and Kael knew what was about to happen. "Wait — stop!" He leapt to his feet and charged blindly for the cart, throwing an arm over his face to shield his eyes from the light. He didn't stop running until he'd smacked into the cart's side.

A few of the caged people grasped his shirt, pleading with him. A young woman sobbed in his ear. They moaned as if they spoke with their last breaths:

"Please ..."

"Don't hurt us —"

"Mercy!"

All he could hear were the cries of the Tinnarkians. He'd tried so desperately to bury that horrible night away that his memories were badly faded. Darkness covered many of the images. But though he could no longer see the flames, he could still hear the screams.

They were burned to the walls of his ears — a single plea from the Earl's captives would've been enough to stir them to life. Now so many cries raked against the walls that the memories had been stoked to a roar. His shoulders stiffened as he turned to face the shamans; his fists clenched tight.

Kael hadn't been able to save his village, but he could save the caged people. "I won't let you kill them."

"You've done enough, Marked One," the bear shaman thundered. Though they stood only a few paces apart, he spoke at a yell. "These creatures are our responsibility. We must purge the land of their Abominable spirits."

Kael pointed to the golden collars around the people's necks. "They didn't mean for this to happen, they didn't ask for it. They're being held captive by a spell."

The hawk shaman's pupils sharpened to points. "These Abominations were never meant to exist. They weren't born of Fate. They were created by men — born to destroy."

"If we let them go, they would belong nowhere," Graymange said. "They would have no pack to guide them, no alpha to rein them in. You've seen for yourself what happens when Abomination takes hold. You've seen how they devour all in their path. They'd terrorize the realms of both beast and men."

Kael tried to keep his voice even. "This is different. The curse hasn't taken these people yet — they still have a chance. I know men who've been trapped under this spell. I've seen how it twists them ... but I've also seen what they become once they're set free. You could be sentencing good men to death."

"They're Abominations!" the bear shaman thundered.

"They deserve a chance!" Kael said back.

The hawk shaman glared. "It's not your place to decide. Fate has set her rules. And we must follow them."

The shamans weren't going to budge. They watched calmly while Kael's fists trembled at his sides. He knew what

114

he had to do. A small voice in the back of his head that he was charging straight to his death, but he didi

When he spoke again, his words were whit was born on the day of the first snow — the day when Fate turns her face from the Kingdom and allows Death to rule. Fate couldn't see me the day I was born, and she can't see me now. I was never meant to exist. According to your rules, *I* am an Abomination. So if you're going to kill them," he pounded a fist into his chest, "then you're going to have to kill me as well."

The shamans didn't move. They stared at Kael for a long, inscrutable moment, and he stared back.

At last, Graymange spoke: "One of Fate's forsaken ... and yet, you bear her mark. What a strange child you are, Kael of the mountains — both chosen and forgotten, deserving of both life and death. How will the shamans answer you?"

Kael didn't know how they would answer. As far as he could tell, none of their faces so much as twitched. He was beginning to get worried when Graymange sighed.

"Very well, the shamans are in agreement. You will be spared — and these creatures will be given a chance."

Kael was so surprised that it took a moment for the words to sink it. "You're going to let me free them?"

Graymange nodded. "And we're going to help you. We've been given a rare gift today — a chance to step off the path. If Fate can't see you," he added with a growl, "it means she can't see us, either."

# CHAPTER II
## A GREATER PRIZE

Titus sat alone in his throne room. Wind howled across the narrow windows above him. They drew the gusts in through their slits and strained them — made them gasp and plea. They rose to a high-pitched wail before quieting, fading like the screams of a man hurled from a cliff.

The throne Titus sat upon was carved from a solid piece of stone. Even with the thick furs draped across it, he could still feel the cold. But that was of little concern to him. His mind was on more important things.

He touched the golden collar wrapped around his throat, watching as visions of lands and beasts flashed behind his eyes. When he'd found those savages hiding at the mountain's top, he'd hardly been able to grasp it. He thought the dragonslayers of old were a myth. But the moment he saw their golden weapons, he knew he'd stumbled upon an ancient treasure:

Dragonsbane.

The golden metal was an eternal spell, capable of being melted down and re-forged to serve any purpose. It was magic the common man could wield. But most importantly, it gave Titus complete control over his army of beasts.

Crevan was forced to rely on his mages. He had to trust someone else to keep watch over his monsters. But with the dragonsbane around his neck, Titus could join them. He could walk among them. He could watch through their eyes. The things they saw moved behind his lids when he closed them. He could hear their voices murmuring in the depths of his head.

At first, it'd startled him. It was strange to be able to see through so many eyes, to hear so many different voices speaking all at once. But the power he'd gained had made it worth the visions, and worth the many sleepless nights he'd spent sifting through them. Never before had he been able to command his army with a thought, an utterance. Now they were truly pieces on a board — unspoiled by cowardice, not limited to their own feeble wit. They were his pawns.

And Titus moved them at will.

Four of his hounds had perished in the night. When Titus woke, it was only to find that their windows had vanished. One of his beasts circled the smoldering remains of the camp he'd sent into the Grandforest — the camp that'd been responsible for supplying his army with firebombs.

His stores had been burned up ... and his soldiers devoured in the flames. It was an act too clever for the bandits, a message wrought too furiously to have been a coincidence. Titus had known from the moment he saw their blackened corpses that he was being offered a warning.

Now as he watched through the eyes of his newest collection of beasts, he saw a gathering of half-naked barbarians standing before him. Their arms were crossed and their eyes locked onto the slim body of a boy.

Titus watched the scene as if he looked through a many-faced jewel: he saw the same picture presented in dozens of different angles. A pair of enormous hands appeared in one of the windows, and he focused on it.

*I hope you know what you're doing*, a thunderous voice bellowed.

The world spun and a young man's face filled his vision. He had reddish brown hair and wore the rough clothes of peasants. His mouth sat in a firm line; his features were sharp and distinct, as if they'd been chiseled from the mountainside. But it was the brows that caught Titus's attention.

The way they bent down over those eyes — eyes with an edge every bit as sharp as his face ...

117

He knew it. He'd known it all along. Crevan had been so intent on claiming the throne that he hadn't been able to see it. He'd been so confident in his little scheme that he'd thought the Wright had truly fallen into his trap.

But Titus had known better.

The young man's eyes stayed on his for a moment before they shifted to someone in front of him. *Try to keep its claws pinned back. I'd really rather not have my face split open.*

His hands reached out, his eyes brightened as he focused. Then like a lid slammed shut over an eye, the image went black.

Cold air ached his teeth as Titus grinned. "Attack," he whispered.

These new beasts weren't used to Titus's voice. He'd taken a risk by sending his slaves to the Braided Tree — a risk he was certain would yield a near-limitless supply of beasts. But the slaves weren't as obedient as his wolves. They needed to be ... broken.

They didn't want to attack the young man: they were afraid of him. But Titus wouldn't be ignored. He'd learned early on that in order to control his beasts, his voice had to be the loudest — his will had to be the strongest. He had to grip their reins tightly, to rule as *alpha* over his army.

"Attack," he said again, this time louder than before.

Madness weakened these newest beasts. They were tossed back and forth between their human and animal selves like wreckage in the seas. After awhile, they began to grasp Titus's command. They clung to the force of his will to keep from being dashed among the waves.

*"Attack!"*

They raked the young man's face with their claws and gouged his fingers with their teeth. He swore like a pirate each time he bled, but he didn't stop. One by one, the windows of Titus's beasts went dark as the young man freed them. The last things Titus saw before the vision dimmed were those eyes.

They held him suspended over a vat, threatening with their calm. Titus had looked into the eyes of many men over his lifetime. Mostly he saw fear; sometimes there was hatred. Their gazes were always either above him or below — either glaring down in rage or pleading upwards. Only a few, a very few, had ever managed to meet them.

When he looked into the eyes of that mountain rat, he saw his own soul reflected back. There was a rare brand of fight in this boy, one he hadn't seen in many years. Titus was going to enjoy this challenge immensely.

He opened his eyes. All of the little windows faded back and the frozen walls of his throne room rushed to fill his vision. A creature sat before him: a man and a falcon twisted into one. Only a small portion of Titus's army had taken the shape of birds — which was rather disappointing, as he'd found his little falcons to be especially useful.

They weren't built for battle. The falcons were only about half the size of humans, but they were fast, quick-witted, and nearly impossible to hit. Their sight was sharp and focused. He'd gazed through their eyes as they'd circled the walls of Midlan, itself — watching from behind a veil of clouds.

"What is it, Earlship?" the falcon screeched. Its small voice struck the walls sharply. Black eyes consumed a large portion of its face — its warped beak-nose took up the rest. "Kill? Spy?"

For a moment, Titus hesitated. His patience had served him well thus far. He'd spent years convincing Crevan to give him the mountains, months slowly changing his army. Now his forces were more beast than man and Midlan had begun to crumble. If he did nothing more, Crevan would fall on his own ... and Titus's patience would earn him the crown.

But now there was a greater prize at stake — something only the death of this mountain rat could earn him. Titus knew he would have to move quickly to claim it.

"Tell D'Mere that I've changed my mind. I'll do as she asks ... but I expect a vial of her poison in payment. She'll know which one I mean." Titus pulled the golden medallion from around his neck — the one with the Earl's symbol engraved onto its surface — and held it lightly. "Wait in the

119

forest for as long as it takes her to prepare it, and don't answer any questions."

He tossed the medallion onto the floor, where the little falcon scooped it up with its clawed feet. "Yes, Earlship!" It shot away, squeezing itself through a narrow window and out into the cold.

Titus knew he'd done a dangerous thing, aligning himself with Countess D'Mere. She watched the shifting of the Kingdom's pawns a few moves ahead, as Titus did. They'd both seen the day when Crevan's pitiful campaign against the Dragongirl would consume him. They'd known his failures would drive him mad — and known that his madness would leave him vulnerable.

Now the hour of change was fast approaching, and each had something the other needed: D'Mere had given him the use of her shaman — and in exchange, Titus would spare her people from the coming storm. She'd promised him even more. She'd been willing to offer practically anything ... all he had to do was hand over his medallion.

Titus frowned. He knew D'Mere planned to use him as bait. She would goad the King into charging up the mountains, where she no doubt hoped that either the bloodshed or the howling winter would eventually claim them both. Then the path to Midlan would be opened to her.

Yes, he was certain her next moves would carry her close to the throne. But she would fail.

Titus's thumb dragged through the tangles of his beard. He broke into a grin as he tried to imagine the look on D'Mere's face when she realized that she'd been fooled.

She'd only let him use the shaman because she believed it would mean his beasts would be tied to his mages, and that their bonds could be easily broken by death. She didn't know about the dragonsbane. She didn't know that his army would answer only to him, that he could witness everything they saw — that not even death could sever their chains.

But he was very much looking forward to the moment when she would discover it.

Titus's grin twisted into a snarl. No, not even *that* thought could please him. A few hours ago, he'd been content with the idea of becoming King ... but this mountain rat had tainted his victory. Now the throne of Midlan felt like a hollow prize.

There were greater spoils to be claimed. Fate had given him the rare chance to right a monstrous wrong — to have his defeat boiled down and recast into a scepter worthy of a King. He would've been a fool to turn such a gift aside.

Titus closed his eyes again, searching until he came to a window that sat high above the green mesh ceiling of the Grandforest. Clouds reddened by the light of the evening whipped past his eyes, smearing the sky with their blood.

"I need you to watch someone for me," Titus said. He drew up an image of the boy's face and passed it on. "Don't attack — only watch. Keep your eyes on him and wait for my command."

The clouds tilted on their side as the falcon changed direction.

Titus opened his eyes. His hands curled around the throne's jagged arms and his mouth broke into a wolfish grin. His voice bounced off the icy walls as he growled:

"You can't protect him any longer. This one is *mine.*"

# CHAPTER 12
## THE PLAGUE OF VINDICUS

They'd been climbing along the cliffs for hours. When Kael tried to see how much further they had to go, drops of sweat rolled into his eyes. "Are we nearly there?"

Kyleigh's head appeared over the ledge above him. "We're getting close."

Kael had to choke his frustration back. They'd been *getting close* for at least the last hour. He didn't know how much longer he could be expected to stay civil. He knelt and tried to hold still as Baird clambered onto his knee.

"A new day, a new dawn. This is a season of fresh beginnings. Try to enjoy the climb, young man," he said as he felt for Kyleigh's hand. When he grasped it, she pulled him up.

Baird had slept through the afternoon and evening, only to wake in the gray hours of the morning. After all he'd been through, Kael expected him to be full of *hmms* and annoying questions, but he'd been surprisingly quiet. He'd run his hands down the bloodstained hole in his shirt, his mouth parted slightly beneath his bandages.

When Kyleigh managed to find him a fresh tunic among the soldiers' gear, he asked Kael to help him put it on. One by one the filthy strips of rags fell away. Kael stared at the red, raised mark that ran down the middle of Baird's chest and found he was still a little surprised.

"I thought your stories were special."

"Whispercraft," Baird had admitted as he tore the last of the rags free. "Most craftsmen prefer to work with their hands — they only ever dabble in words. Yes, their days are wasted on iron and stone while words are cast by the wayside. A tragedy, for there is no greater material." He smiled widely. "Words are powerful and dangerous things —

122

uttered in an instant, yet lasting for an age. They touch the heart, change the mind, and feed the spirit. With nothing else can the truth be bent. The man who understands this may hold the whole realm captive upon his tongue."

Kael was quiet for a long moment. He remembered the few times when his words had come out as whispercraft: he'd used them to set Aerilyn's heart at ease, to convince the giants to go along with his plan ...

"Why didn't you force me to tell you the truth? You could have asked me anything you wanted, and I would've had to answer."

The tangles of Baird's mane had fallen over his bandages as he whispered: "He holds the whole realm captive, yes. Kingdoms rise by his words ... and fall at a slip of his tongue. He understands this," Baird pressed a finger to his lips, "and so he chooses his words carefully."

An uncomfortable feeling had crawled beneath Kael's skin. "You mean you can't always control it? How do you stop your words from becoming whispercraft?" he said when Baird nodded.

"I keep my lips sealed against that which might be troubling, that might be tempting. The only way to truly stop a word is to keep your mouth *shut*," Baird had scoffed. "You remember that, young man."

Kael had thought the beggar-bard ought to take some of his own advice. Still, as ridiculous as Baird could be, he'd felt there was some truth in his words. "That reminds me of something my friend Morris said to me once —"

"Morris?" Baird had erupted in cackles. "Oh yes, he would know better than anybody. Morris the Dog would know better!"

Kael had rolled his eyes. Baird had been trying to remember the Dog's name for days. Guesses had been pouring from his mouth in a near-constant stream: he'd heard of *Haply*, *Riad*, *Carfol*, and *Dewey* the Dog all over breakfast. He wasn't at all surprised that Baird had latched onto *Morris*.

"Morris the Dog!" he'd sing-songed as he pulled the shirt over his head. "Morris the Dog! Morris the Dog!"

Hours had passed since then. Now the sun had climbed high over the treetops, and Baird had discovered a new phrase to chant: "Toil will sharpen our relief, sweat makes the last step so sweet. Yes, enjoy the climb, young man. Enjoy it!"

Kael had officially run out of patience. "If he tells me to *enjoy the climb* one more time, I'm going to shove him off a cliff," he muttered as Baird's knobby ankles disappeared over the ledge.

He'd been talking to himself, but Kyleigh must've heard. She stuck her head back over and grinned down. "Already regretting that, are you?"

He was beginning to regret a lot of things — not the least of which had been accepting help from a halfwolf.

When Kael had told the shamans which way they were headed, Graymange had taken it upon himself to help. "I've heard rumors of a great pack of swordbearers who've claimed the den at the Valley's mouth. You'll never escape their eyes. I can show you a better path."

Kael had glanced at the bear and hawk shamans. "All right … but what about your war with Blackbeak? I don't want to get in your way."

"Each summer, the King travels from his den and makes a journey into the swamps. Blackbeak knows this, and he knows he'll have no choice but to answer when the King calls. That's the price of his treachery." Graymange's lips bent back over his teeth, baring them in two sharp rows. Kael might've thought it was a grin, had his eyes not been so unsettlingly dark. "My brothers are gathering at the place where we'll end him. I will take you to the path … and return with time enough to purge Blackbeak's spirit."

At that moment, Kael had thought it sounded like a pretty decent plan. But now he was beginning to regret it.

Graymange's way had taken them much longer than he'd expected. He led them off the trails and straight into the thickest, most tangled part of the woods. Kael spent most of

124

the day leading Baird carefully around each bramble and rock — a task made more difficult by the fact that every time a bird whistled, the beggar-bard would stop to answer.

Kael was tired, sore, and bramble-whipped. And now they seemed to be climbing straight up.

"Here," Kyleigh said.

Kael stared at her hand, but he didn't take it.

He'd spent most of the day before freeing all of the caged people. They seemed to have no idea what was going on: the villagers were terrified of the shamans and even more afraid of Kael.

They'd begun fighting the second his hands touched their collars and didn't stop until he'd broken the dragonsbane in half. He'd been bitten, scratched, and kicked in the shins more times than he could count. A few thanked him once they'd been set free, but most had simply dropped into their animal forms and bolted for the woods. By the end of it, evening had settled and Kael was completely exhausted.

So while the shamans had gathered in a circle to talk, Kael had gone in search of someplace to sleep. He'd found Kyleigh and Baird camped a ways from the road, nearly hidden among the thick shrubs.

The beggar-bard had been sleeping peacefully beneath a soldier's cloak. Kyleigh had managed to get a small fire going, and Kael had stumbled over to it gratefully.

"I'm sorry I left you on your own. I just ... I couldn't bear to watch," she'd said without looking up.

He'd walked in a wide arc around her and dropped the armful of dragonsbane collars he'd been carrying onto the ground. He'd planned to wring the blood from them — as soon as he'd healed the gouges in his shoulder.

Kyleigh's lip had curled at the sight of the collars. Her brows bent low as she jabbed a stick among the embers. "Perfect. *Now* do you understand why I didn't want to help them?" Slowly, her expression softened. "It isn't your fault. I should've told you, I suppose. But I didn't want you to think ..."

Her words had faded when she finally looked at him. Her eyes had wandered across every bitten, scratched-up inch of his face. When her lips parted, he'd thought she'd been about to scold him.

"Look, I know the shapechangers think those people were Abominations, but I couldn't let the shamans kill them. They deserve to have a chance — every creature deserves a chance. I'm not sorry for it," he went on, when she did nothing but watch him. "You can tease me all you want, and I still won't be sorry."

"Well, then I suppose there's no point in teasing you. I'm going to have a chat with the shamans," she'd said as she got to her feet. "Watch Baird for a moment, will you? It'll give you a chance to lick your wounds."

"I'm not a dog —"

Kyleigh had grabbed him under the chin and planted her lips against the side of his face — so quickly that he wasn't even sure it'd happened. He might've doubted it forever … had it not been for the burn.

Fire spread across his cheek as she walked away. It sank beneath his skin and stayed hot throughout the night. Even now, he could feel where her lips had been. He knew that if he took her hand, those flames would rise up once more.

And he wasn't sure if he could survive the blaze a second time. "I've got it. I don't need your help."

She shrugged. "Suit yourself."

He got one foot planted and found a crack to slip his hand into. He was looking for the next hold when he realized Kyleigh was still watching him. "Haven't you got anything better to do?"

"Well," she glanced over her shoulder, "not particularly. Baird is reciting poetry to a rather scraggly bush, while it looks as if Graymange is … relieving himself on it." She laughed and propped a hand against the side of her face. "That's one thing I don't miss about traveling with wolves. They're always stopping to mark where they've been."

"I feel sorry for that bush," Kael said as he pulled himself up to the ledge.

"A little wolf water isn't going to hurt it."

"No, I meant about the poetry."

Her brows arched high and her smile gave way to laughter. "I can't believe it — Kael's finally told a joke. Come here, you."

Before he could protest, she grabbed him by the back of the shirt and pulled him over the ledge.

At long last, they reached the end of their climb. Kael knew it had to be the end when he saw the slick wall of rock in front of him. There wasn't so much as a crack to hold onto. "What now?"

Graymange rose from his wolf form and pointed towards a narrow ledge. "The path is just through there. Follow it out to the end, and it'll lead you to the mountain's road."

When Kael hesitated, Kyleigh slipped past him. She edged out and she leaned forward into a slight crack — making it look as if her head went through the wall. "I see the path ... though it's going to be an adventure and a half getting through all these thorns." She slipped in one limb at a time until the crack swallowed her up.

Kael knew he should get moving, but something Graymange had said troubled him. "There aren't any roads through the mountains. Are you certain we've come the right way?"

Graymange's sunken-eyed stare took him in for a moment before his hand fell heavily on Kael's arm. "Safe journey, mountain child." Then he slipped into his fur and trotted away.

"What a strange fellow," Baird said cheerily. "Sometimes I think I hear two footsteps, and other times I swear there's four!"

Kael sighed. "Come on."

Once he'd made certain that Baird was latched onto his pack, they slipped between the rocks. At its thickest, the crack might've been as wide as a man was tall. But it was filled so tightly with grasping nettles that they had to turn sideways just to squeeze through.

The nettles grew up the walls like vines. They jutted out on both sides and scraped the tops of their heads. Though Kyleigh cleared a path with her sword, there still wasn't much room to squirm.

Baird pulled back suddenly, choking Kael with the strap of his quiver. "Gah! Oh dear, oh me! Some grasping villain has snagged my pack. Hands off, thief! Back — *back* I say!"

The beggar-bard's skirmish with the nettles very nearly got Kael strangled by his strap. "Just leave it, will you? We've got plenty of supplies to go around."

Baird snorted. "Leave it? Listen to him, will you? I can't just *leave* it, young man. Do you have any idea the sort of treasures I've got stashed in here?"

"No, but it can't be anything too valuable. Otherwise you wouldn't have to be a beggar."

At that exact moment, Baird managed to rip his pack free. He also managed to slam one of his knobby elbows into the small of Kael's back. "Did it ever occur to you that I might've been a beggar because I wanted to be?"

An exasperated sigh came from up ahead. "*Why* didn't we think of that? It makes complete sense," Kyleigh said.

Kael hoped she was joking.

Baird shook a finger in the direction of her voice. "It wasn't the most glorious of tasks, but I was chosen for it! Fate never uses the obvious things."

He went to sling his pack over his shoulders in a dramatic arc ... and wound up getting it snared in the nettles above him.

The straps were so fantastically tangled that Kael had to spend several minutes cutting them free. The thorny leaves seemed to protest his every swipe: no sooner did he manage to cut through one of the wiry branches than it would pop up and scrape his fingers in revolt. He was grateful when the crack finally ended.

They clambered out of the nettles and into the rocky land on the other side. Here, the air was much sharper; the pines grew tall. A steely gray sky leered above them, and Kael realized — with no small amount of shock — that they'd made it into the Unforgivable Mountains.

"We didn't have to go through the Valley at all," he said.

Kyleigh clapped him on the shoulder. "That's generally what a better way does — it takes you where you need to be in less time and with less hassle."

He didn't think anything could've been more of a hassle than battling through that thorny crack, but he was too excited to argue.

Kael took deep breaths as they walked. He hadn't realized how heavy the air in the lowlands had been until the mountain breeze slid easily into his chest. There wasn't any sun to burn him, no dampness to settle into his clothes. The constant noise he'd had to endure for the past several seasons made the muffled voice of the spiny forest ring all the sweeter. The scent of pine filled the gaps between the trees. It settled in his nose and made his head feel lighter than the fumes of any pipe.

He'd been amazed by the power of the seas and the bounty of the plains, captivated by the leafy towers of the forest. He could find words to describe how he'd felt in every corner of the Kingdom. But there was no feeling quite like coming home.

"We're here! Oh Fate, we're finally here," Baird said, shaking Kael's rucksack excitedly. Then all at once, he went quiet. "Ah ... where to now?"

Kyleigh gave him an amused look. "You didn't have a plan?"

"No — goodness, no. A bard never plans. He prefers to take his journey one stride at a time, turning where the road bends. I've longed to come to the mountains for years. And now that I'm here," his smile parted wide beneath his bandages, "I plan to enjoy myself."

129

Kael knew that if they weren't careful, their trip could wind up being rather *un*-enjoyable. "We should keep moving upwards." He peeled Baird off his pack and attached him to Kyleigh's. Then he chose a slope that didn't have too many jagged rocks around it and started to climb. "Hold on a moment — let me get my bearings. It shouldn't take too..."

He stopped. The slope in front of him had suddenly ended. It'd dropped away and flattened out, leaving something that looked like a dry riverbed dug into the mountain.

The bed was shallow, but wide enough for carts and horses. It cleft the slopes and crushed the rock. Everything in its path was either pressed down or shoved away — churning the wild earth aside like a footprint in the sand.

There was no end to it. The path cut back and forth across the mountains, climbing until it finally disappeared among the clouds. From a distance, it looked as if some great serpent had wrapped its coils around the jagged peaks — strangling with such force that it'd left a gaping scar behind.

Kael's chest felt empty as he traced the jagged line that had been carved through the mountains' face. The happy chattering of his companions struck him and washed down, like waves crashing against rock.

"Blazes ..."

"What? What is it?" Baird slung his shaggy head about. "Is it bandits? Trolls?"

"It's a road," Kyleigh said as she stepped in beside Kael. "The rumors were true, then. Titus has conquered the mountains."

Baird snorted. "Impossible. The mountains are the heart of the Wildlands — the one patch of Kingdom that still thrives in unblemished beauty. They've got their own spirit about them, the mountains. There's a danger here that can't be tamed. I shudder to think of how many souls haunt these peaks. There must be legions of glowing ghosts ..."

Baird prattled on, but Kael couldn't hear him. He was lost somewhere between wakefulness and sleep. He hoped that if he shut his eyes tightly, he would wake to realize it'd all been a dream ... but he didn't.

The relief he'd felt just moments before was gone, replaced by a pit so deep he couldn't feel where it ended. He forced his legs to rise and fall even though he couldn't feel them. He forced himself to walk the mountains' scar.

How long would it be before towns sprouted up along this road? How long before the sharp sides were blasted out and its veins were gutted for metals? How long before merchants packed the mountains, gazing unknowingly upon sights meant only for the woodsman's eyes?

The burning and the raiding had only marked the beginning of Titus's war: the road would finish it.

Things bubbled inside Kael's chest, growing and bursting with little blasts of flame. Titus had done this. Those toppled trees, the boulders split into two and the steep slopes completely flattened out — they were the Earl's footprints. His road had plowed through all the danger and the wonder of the mountains, leaving a scar in its place.

When they came around the next bend, the molten steel inside Kael's chest suddenly hissed and went out. They'd come across the ruins of a village ... and Titus's road ran straight through the middle of it.

This village was smaller than Tinnark had been: no more than a handful of tiny houses perched upon the slopes. Their doorways were dark and empty — holes that gaped unseeing. The roofs were gone and the tops of the houses were completely open to the skies, burned black around the edges.

Heavy spring rains had filled the cracks that winter had left along their sagging walls. Now in the middle of summer, the houses were warped and wilted. They sagged against their beams, leaning with the weight of the brambles that had grown up along their skin. Their marrow burst with thick veins of mold.

Charred ruins lined the path; the door was gone from a small storehouse and all its contents pillaged. Kael's tongue stuck to the back of his throat as he walked past one sunken ruin after the next. He was standing in the middle of the village when he came across a sight that stopped his heart.

A mass of skeletons lay in the road. Some were intact, but most had been torn apart by animals. One had an arrow hanging from the socket of its skull. Several were pinned to the ground by spears. A few were small ... far too small.

Roland had always said that to try to carve any sort of life from the mountains was like the man who lived inside a pond: he could only survive for so long before he ran out of breath.

"It's a waste of time to ask *if* a man will die in the mountains," Roland had said. "You'd be better off asking *when*."

Kael knew this. And had these villagers been left to live, the perils would've claimed them eventually. Death was just a part of life in the mountains. But this was different. This was ... it was ...

Sickness gripped him. Kael fell on his knees as his breakfast rushed up. Even after his stomach had nothing left, he choked and gagged.

Baird's shuffling steps stopped beside him. His hand grasped until he found Kael's face. His fingers marked his chin and then with the other hand, he pressed a canteen against his lips. "Careful, young man. The body always tries to purge that which it cannot stand. Ill winds, disease, infection ... hmm, but this is different," he murmured as Kael drank. "Unless I'm much mistaken, this is the plague of Vindicus."

Kael had read the story of Vindicus the Broken more times than he could count, and there'd never once been any mention of a plague. When he said as much, Baird gripped his chin.

"Ah, there's where you're quite wrong. You think of scourge and pestilence. I think of a far more fatal plague — a hate that burned so fiercely it consumed the man from within."

Kael's next drink of water went down slowly.

He hadn't thought about it before, but his story was a lot like that of Vindicus: both of their homes had been destroyed, both set out to avenge them. Vindicus had marched to the gates of his enemies alone. Legend said he'd fought for years without food or drink or sleep, hacking tirelessly through the flesh of his foes — letting the rage of the battle fuel him.

He fought for so many years on end that his hand melded to the hilt of his sword, and the blade became known as his Arm. Only after the last of his enemies fell was Vindicus defeated: without the battle's rage, his body gave out — crumbling like dust until all that remained was his Arm.

That was where the story ended. It'd never said *why* Vindicus had crumbled and died. Kael had always assumed that his body had simply worn out. But now ...

"*Hate* was the plague of Vindicus," Baird said quietly. "He let it bubble, let it brew. And so his hatred grew — it filled his veins, filled his heart. Ah, but Hate is a hungry beast: he must always eat. He shrinks quickly with naught to devour, withers more with every hour. As his battle raged on, Vindicus became Hate. And so when the last of his enemies had fallen, he ceased to be. Now I hear the ominous rumblings of that wicked beast inside *your* chest, young man," Baird said, thrusting a finger at him. "You must rise against it. You must never let Hate reach your heart."

The molten iron inside Kael's chest bubbled up in warning as he stared at the bodies. It would be easier to let the fires consume him — to allow his rage to dry all the horrible little wet things that squirmed behind his eyes. Anger was a familiar face, a monster he understood. Yes, it would be easier to give in as Vindicus had.

But at the last moment, Kael rose against it.

Something strong crept from his middle and snuffed the fires out. It held him up, like hope had held the giants. He focused on it as Lysander had focused on the steely gray sky. This feeling was an armor he wore beneath his skin. And for now, it would keep the fires trapped.

Kael decided to bury the bodies in a circle, in the exact order he'd found them. He figured that if they'd chosen to die beside each other, then that was how they ought to sleep.

He dug the graves with his bare hands, willing his fingers through the unforgiving layers of rocky earth. His mind was so consumed with his task that he hardly noticed when stones crumbled beneath his hands.

Kyleigh lowered the bones into the graves and Baird arranged them the best he could. His knobby fingers traced surely down the cracks and rifts, memorizing their shapes. His lips moved wordlessly as he pieced them back together. Then at each grave, just before he covered them, he'd lay a stone beneath their feet.

"In case they come up one short," he explained. "Our lives are all about balance — no one can be purely evil or good. Men who get sent to the river so suddenly don't always have a chance to right their ways. But if they lived just decently enough, this'll be the step that helps them cross."

For some reason, his words gave Kael a strange feeling. His spirit cringed against a biting cold — a cold his heart seemed to recognize, but his body couldn't remember.

They made their camp among the ruins that night. As Kael was drifting off to sleep, he thought he might've heard a soft whisper on the wind: a voiceless murmur, a wordless thanks ...

The relieved sighs of the dead.

# CHAPTER 13
## A STOMP OF GIANTS

Not long ago, Captain Lysander had been cramped at his desk in Gravy Bay, watching the days creep by through the window. Now his stormy eyes gazed upon a completely different view.

Thick trees and a long stretch of sandy beach dressed the land in front of him. Behind the ring of sand was a large gathering of houses. Merchants scurried all about them, hoisting their wares into the waiting lofts. Their voices rose and fell as the haggling grew heated.

Lysander paced down the length of *Anchorgloam*, hands clasped smartly behind his back. The ships anchored beside them bobbed and creaked beneath the waves, speaking to each other about their journeys. He arched his neck to glare at the sun. Then his chin turned south, to where a dark gray line was beginning to fester on the horizon. With a huff, he spun back to glare at the squabbling crowd.

"We should've done this weeks ago, Captain," Morris called from the helm. "I knew that lad was up to something — I can always tell when he's been scheming."

"Good of you to keep it to yourself," Lysander muttered. His stormy eyes flicked to the skies above the village.

"We should leave without them," Nadine called from the bow. "Every moment we waste is one our friends might be in danger. It would be better to sail to them now than waste time waiting for the giants."

"Believe me, lass — you don't want to go charging up the mountains with anything *less* than a horde of giants. And even with all that, our innards could still wind up dressing

135

the castle walls." Morris's eyes narrowed in their pouches. "Titus is a monster."

At Lysander's order, a thick pair of boots had replaced Nadine's customary sandals. Now her feet thudded clumsily as she marched towards the helm. "He will not take *my* insides. The mots have defended themselves against far more fearsome —" She tripped over her boots and nearly fell. Strange words flew from her mouth in a heated string as she kicked the nearest railing. "Why must I wear these?"

Lysander raised his brows. "They're for your protection."

"They are for your amusement," Nadine countered with a glare.

He gripped his chest. "My dear lady — you wound me. I think only of the journey ahead. Where we're going, your toes could very well freeze if they aren't properly covered."

"Aye, and then there'll be nothing left to do but pop them off one at a time," Morris added with a gap-toothed grin, "like barnacles."

"You are both liars! Toes do not — oof!"

She'd tried to stomp over to them but wound up tripping, instead. With another fiery string of words, she flopped to the ground. She tore at the laces and buckles for several moments before finally giving up.

"Better than any lock or key," Lysander muttered as he passed by the helm.

"Aye, Captain," Morris said with a wink.

The sun had slipped beyond noon when Jake finally called: "I see Eveningwing!"

Lysander had been glaring at the ever-widening gray line to the south. But at Jake's cry, he spun around. Eveningwing screeched as he fluttered into the crow's nest. A moment later, his head appeared over its top.

"They're two miles from the village!" he said excitedly.

"How many are there?" Lysander called.

"Thirty-seven!"

136

"They've cheated us," Morris growled. "Blast — I knew it! Never trust a giant. They always try to find some way out of their promises."

"Once again, thank you for keeping it to yourself," Lysander muttered. Then he spun to his men. "We're going to have company aboard this vessel, dogs. Lower the ramp and make ready!"

The pirates flew to their work with a barking chorus of *ayes*.

It turned out that Eveningwing's announcement hadn't exactly been necessary. The noise of the village shrank back as a rhythmic thumping sound filled the air. The louder the thumping became, the quieter the merchants fell. Soon they'd stopped their bickering altogether and parted — stumbling back from the road to let a horde of towering men tromp through.

The giants' thick chests were plated in armor and helmets capped their massive heads. The collective thumping of their steps drowned out all other sound.

"Eh, thirty-seven might just be enough," Morris said.

Lysander slapped a hand to his forehead. "Oh, good Gravy. They've got the whole village staring at them. I told Declan to be *subtle!*"

Morris laughed. "I'm sure they're doing their best, Captain. How subtle could you expect a stomp of giants in broad daylight to be?"

The giants' march slowed considerably when they reached the docks. Planks groaned and buckled beneath their weight, sagging in dangerous arcs. The giant at the front of the pack was quite a bit smaller than the rest — hardly any taller than a man. When the dock's groaning reached a dangerous pitch, he hollered back:

"Step lightly now, you clodders. *Lightly!*"

The giants spent the next several moments painstakingly shuffling their way down the docks. With the merchants standing hushed on the shoreline, the shrilling of the wood filled the air at such a pitch that even the gulls stopped to listen.

By the time they reached *Anchorgloam*, Lysander's hand covered his face completely. The pirates were trying desperately to muffle their laughter in their shirtsleeves. Morris chuckled through the gap in his teeth.

The smaller giant paused at the ramp. He lifted the visor of his helmet, but the cleft of his brow still shadowed his eyes. He wore a deadly, glinting scythe across his shoulder. His head turned from one end of the ship to the other before he said:

"Where's Kael?"

"Thank you for coming all this way, Declan," Lysander said carefully. "I'm sure Kael will be very happy to see —"

"Ahoy there, gents!" A lanky forest man slipped out from between the giants' hulking bodies. His mouth bent in a wild grin as he waved up at the ship. "Fancy meeting you here."

Lysander's brows arched high into his waves. "Ah ... I had no idea you were coming along, Jonathan. Though had I known, I might've reconsidered the whole thing," he muttered through his grin.

Jonathan shrugged. "I've just come to make sure the ole army made it here safely. His Princeness wants me to report back to him as soon as you're on your way."

"I see. Is Brend not coming with us?"

"This is a task for his General," Declan said firmly. After a moment, the line of his mouth became slightly less severe. "He'll stay in the plains and tend to his people — and care for his new wife and daughter."

Lysander grinned. "Darrah had a little girl, did she? How wonder —"

"Enough talking! Our friends are in danger. We should be sailing by now," Nadine cried, thrusting her spear at the horizon.

"What friends?" Declan said.

Lysander shot Nadine a rather potent look. "I was getting to that —"

"Where's Kael? He called us here. Jonathan read the letter," Declan said.

138

Lysander dragged a hand down his neck. "No, it wasn't Kael who wrote to you — it was me. But I wrote on his *behalf*," he added quickly, when the giants began to grumble.

The sunlight cut across the steel in Declan's eyes as he tilted his chin upwards. "I knew it. This was one of your pirate tricks. Kael would've never made such a clodded mistake. We haven't even had a chance to forge new suits of armor — we've had to make due with what we managed to scavenge from the bloodtraitors. And it's not exactly fit for battling," he added, pointing to the large, shining hole in the steel above his heart.

The giants grunted in agreement. Much of their armor was either patched or badly dented.

"Winter always strikes the mountains first, and it'll be striking before we know it," Declan went on. "We'll never have time to reach the top, fight a war and climb back down. The snow'll bury us to our clodded necks. Save your breath, pirate. We'll go to war when *Kael* calls us. That was the deal."

At his signal, the giants turned to march away.

"Kael left for the mountains on his own."

Thirty-seven pairs of steely gray eyes settled onto Jake. His gloved hands balled into fists at his side and he glared from over the top of his spectacles.

"Oh, he's telling tales," one of the giants said.

The cleft in Declan's brow deepened as he frowned. "No ... he's telling the truth. Why would Kael go off on his own when he knew he had the strength of the plains at his back?"

"Because ..." Jake cleared his throat. "Because he's a stubborn mountain rat who would rather die than have to ask anybody else to fight for him."

For a long moment, the giants did nothing but glare through the slits in their helmets. Then all at once, they burst out laughing.

"Yeh, that sounds about right," Declan said.

Morris leaned against the helm. "So what do you say, lads? Are you going to help us or not?"

Declan shook his head. "The deal was to fight for Kael when he asked us to. He hasn't asked, so I can't order my men to fight. I won't hold them to that."

Nadine waved her spear in an arc. "Fine. Then let us set sail without them!"

Jake's face crumpled. "How can you say that? Think of what he's done for you — Kael freed your people! Doesn't that mean anything?"

Declan shrugged. "Sorry, but those are the rules. My men can all turn around and go home."

"Very well, then. I suppose if there's no convincing you …" Lysander spun and clapped at the pirates. "Set sail, dogs! We leave at once."

"Aye, Captain!"

Morris glared down at the crowd of giants and snorted through his wiry beard. "Great dirty lot of cowards. Aye, and I hope you can live with yourselves. Now get off of those docks before you snap them."

"All right," Declan said.

He broke from the crowd and marched directly up the ramp onto *Anchorgloam*. One by one, the giants followed him. They filed onto the lower deck and stood, watching with interest as the pirates raised the sails.

Jake's chin nearly touched his chest. "But didn't you just say …?"

Declan shrugged. "What would you have me do, wee mage? I can't order them *not* to fight."

Lysander, for his part, didn't look the least bit surprised. "Welcome aboard, gentlemen. Follow Jake — he'll help you get settled."

"As long as they settle quickly. I have led armies of *women* who have spent less time chatting," Nadine said.

Declan waved a hand at her. "We'll be settled long before you've finished squawking about it, sandbeater."

"I do not beat the sand!"

As the squabbling on deck continued without any signs of ending, Captain Lysander took his place behind the helm. He raised his brows when he saw that Jonathan had materialized at his side.

"Ah, the fresh wind of adventure! Gets the ole heart pumping, doesn't it?"

"Aren't you supposed to report back to Brend?" Lysander said.

Jonathan nodded. "I am."

"Then why are you still aboard my ship?"

"I'm not. I'm *strictly* not."

When a long moment passed and Jonathan still hadn't moved, Lysander crossed his arms. "Clairy doesn't want you taking off on her, does she?"

"There was some talk about cracking me over the head with my own fiddle," he said with a nod. "I know it'd be nice to have someone like me in your party — a fellow with his footprints in all the familiar places, and possessive of a certain roguish charm," he added with a wink. "But I'm sorry, mate. I can't go with you. As much as I'd love to lend my skills, I'm afraid the duty to my woman comes absolutely first."

Lysander sighed. "Well, that's regrettable. We'll certainly miss you. Raise the ramp and shove off, dogs!" he hollered behind him.

They were drifting out to sea, sails filled with the gusts from the storm brewing in the south and eyes set north when Lysander said: "There's no avoiding it this time, fiddler. Clairy's going to have your head."

Jonathan's lanky shoulders rose and fell. "Oh, I think she'll come around — especially once she hears the whole story."

Lysander nodded out at the waves. Seconds later, his smile had melted into a rather concerned look. "Wait a moment ... what story? What are you going to tell her?"

Jonathan grinned. "That I was kidnapped by pirates, of course!"

# CHAPTER 14
## WILDMEN

Days dragged across Kael's eyes like the swipe of a hand against a frosty window. The hours were smeared and blurred. He only remembered pieces of them — the grayish outline of things beyond the frost. The higher up the mountains they climbed, the more his memory blurred.

He was afraid to see too clearly, afraid to look too closely. They walked the path of the mountains' scar through one blackened village after the next, and he knew what was coming. Somewhere along this road there would be ruins he recognized, trails he remembered. There would be bones he knew the names of.

With each passing day, they crept closer to the middle of the mountains. It would be only a matter of time before they came to Tinnark.

"Do you hear that?" Baird stopped suddenly, jerking Kael by the straps. He cupped a knobby hand against his ear and smiled widely when a chirping sound came from the woods. "A little redbird! Let us follow for a bit."

Before Kael could stop him, Baird had wandered into the thicket — whistling and waving his hands about. He stumbled between the trees, bouncing off their unforgiving flesh like a drunkard through a crowd. He even apologized to a few.

"Oh, for mercy's sake," Kael muttered as he watched the beggar-bard nearly tumble over a rock. He didn't have the energy to go chasing after Baird. He'd hoped Kyleigh would do it — it was her turn, after all. But when went to say as much, he saw that she'd disappeared.

She'd melted into the woods with the same silent disregard as air through the trees. There wasn't so much as a print or a snapped twig to signal which way she'd gone. Kael sighed heavily.

She'd been doing that an awful lot, lately.

"Come back, little bird!"

Kael turned just in time to see Baird yelp and tumble out of sight. Judging by the number of crashing bounces he heard, the beggar-bard rolled quite a long ways down.

"Don't worry about me, young man. I'm all right!" Baird called from the bottom of the slope.

With a heavy sigh, Kael went after him. He knew this slope: it was a hill covered in shoal that would lead to a small spring. Roland had showed it to him once while they were out trapping.

Kael slid down carefully and found Baird crumpled at its bottom. He laid spraddled against the trunk of a tree, his bandaged face turned skyward. "I don't hear him anymore. Drat and blast it — I think he got away."

"It's probably for the best," Kael said as he helped him up. "I don't know what you planned to ..."

Hairs stood tall down his neck, as if a cold breath had blown across him. His limbs froze and his fingers tightened around Baird's arm as he felt the weight of eyes upon him. They were two black pits sunk into a furry brow. Watching hungrily.

Even though he tried to force himself to be calm, Kael could practically feel the fear wafting off his skin. He heard the wet snorting sound of an animal breathing in and turned around slowly.

There was a brown lump in the corner of his left eye. It stood beside the spring. He tried not to breathe as he turned, and tried not to gasp when his eyes focused and he found himself staring into the face of a monstrous bear.

Water dampened its muzzle and dripped out between its thick, grasping lips. On all fours, it was nearly a man's height. The wet nose twitched and it took rumbling, gasping breaths — as if the bear *tasted* his fear as well as smelled it.

"What was that sound?" Baird said loudly. "A woodsman's saw, perhaps? Are we finally near a village?"

143

The bear's mouth draped open as it turned its monstrous head in the direction of Baird's prattling — a head nearly the size of Kael's chest.

"We could use some fresh supplies. There's nothing quite like a ..." Baird's head tilted to the side and he breathed in. "Hmm, wet fur. But it hasn't rained in days. What could — ?"

"Bear," Kael said between his teeth. He stared at those tiny black eyes, small portals sunk into an enormous head. Bears were stupid brutes: slow to start, but fierce once they picked up speed. There was still a chance it might turn away and lumber back into the woods.

But it was a small chance.

"Yes? I'm right here."

"No, *bear*," Kael hissed. "It's a bear." An awakening heat surged over his skin as the bear rose on its hind legs. The animal in him knew what was coming. He knew there was no point in being afraid. The bear was going to attack.

Kael ripped an arrow from his quiver, locked it onto the pink, gaping hole of the bear's mouth, and fired. The arrow struck true — and at the exact same moment, its great furry chest exploded.

There was a muffled crunching sound as something erupted from the bear's ribs. It groaned around the arrow, its beady eyes rolled back. Kael felt the tremble in the ground as its body collapsed. A gory object tumbled from the gaping hole in the bear's chest and rolled to a stop at Kael's feet.

It was a large, jagged rock. How in Kingdom's name had a *rock* burst through the bear? He was in the middle of wondering how it was even possible when an inhuman cry cut over his thoughts.

"You've spoiled it!"

A woman stomped from the brush. She wore a rough tunic made of animal skins that covered her almost to the knees, and kept her fiery red hair cropped above her shoulders. Thick boots wrapped around her shins, the buckles carved from bone.

Black paint covered the woman's face in a vicious pattern. It made her eyes stand out and her teeth seem sharp. The paint swirled down her bare arms, but Kael could still see the lines of muscle carved into them.

In one of her clenched fists she carried a very serious-looking axe. It was a strange weapon with a bone shaft. Kael had to look twice to be sure, but he was fairly certain the axe's blade was made of solid gold.

Then he saw the red ripples coursing down its surface, and he blanched. "Is that —?"

"I had him!" the woman cried. The heels of her boots clomped loudly against the rocks as she marched to the bear's corpse. She ripped the arrow from its mouth and glared. "One of the wooden birds ..." She thrust its bloody point at Kael's chest. "Do you fight for the Man of Wolves?"

Kael had no idea what she was talking about. "I —"

"Answer me!"

"I'm trying!" he snapped.

"So much yelling!" Baird moaned. His knobby hands slapped against his ears. "First the bear, now Fate's sent a harpy from the treetops to torture us!"

The woman turned the arrow's point on Baird. "What's wrong with him?"

"It would take too long to list it all," Kael said. He studied the woman for a moment. Her furs, her hair, the swirls of paint on her face — it was like something out of a story.

Wait a moment. She *was* from a story.

"You're one of the summit people, aren't you? One of the wildmen."

Amos had told him stories of the wildmen. They were a clan of whisperers who lived at the top of the Unforgivable Mountains. One of the Kings had sent them into the Valley long ago to rid the land of monsters. The wildmen had chased the monsters up the mountains to the very top, where legend had it they'd been locked in a final battle ever since.

"They're dangerous men," Amos had warned. "You remember that if you ever meet one."

145

He'd always wanted to meet a wildman, but he'd never had the chance: they hardly ever left the summit. "What are you doing this far down?"

"That's none of your concern." The wildwoman's lips were stained a bluish black. They bent into a smirk as her eyes scraped the length of him. "Look at you — with your thin clothes and soft skin."

"It *is* rather soft," Baird agreed. "Like the crest of new-fallen snow."

Kael didn't think it was *that* soft. He was about to say as much when the woman interrupted him.

"You aren't from the Man of Wolves, that much is clear." She waved the arrow at his head. "You're some mutt from downmountain — a strange mutt with strange weapons. Why are you climbing *up* when everybody else is running down?"

"We have business in the mountains," he said vaguely.

The wildwoman narrowed her eyes. "What business?"

"We've come to flay the hide off a spoiled Thane-child in desperate need of a beating." Kyleigh materialized from the woods and stood cross-armed between them. "Hello, Gwen."

The wildwoman's mouth fell open. "Impossible."

Baird gasped so loudly that it made Kael jump. "Thane? Did I hear mention of a Thane?" He slung his filthy pack off his shoulders and began digging through it with gusto. "Oh Fate, what fortune! I have a letter here for a *Thane Evan*."

Kael had to wonder who in their right mind would ever trust Baird with a letter. "What sort of —?"

"Argh!"

He spun at the cry and saw that Gwen was charging for Kyleigh. She had the golden axe — the axe he was fairly certain was made of dragonsbane — raised over her head. Kael didn't have a chance to think: he sent an arrow hurtling for Gwen's face.

She turned as the arrow flew. Her eyes narrowed onto its head. Kael saw the shaft tremble in mid-flight, saw it

146

streaking for the gap between her eyes. She moved ever so slightly, jerking back so that the fletching nearly brushed her forehead as it whipped by and thudded into the tree behind her.

"A good shot," she said while he gaped. "Mind if I try?"

"Move, Kael!"

He heard Kyleigh shout, saw her eyes widen and at the same time, saw Gwen's arm sling backwards. But he didn't understand why. What could the wildwoman do with a single arrow?

He got his answer quickly.

Gwen hurled the arrow like a spear, and it flew every bit as forcefully as if it'd been loosed from a string. Had he not been so shocked, he might've been able to dodge — but as it was, he turned just in time to catch the arrow on the fleshy top of his thigh.

Pain shocked him. He fell back on his rump. His fingers snapped open as he tried to catch himself. He was vaguely aware of the sound of his bow clattering onto the ground.

The arrow stuck through the tender skin on the top of his leg, having missed the thick vein in the middle by inches. His flesh puckered around the shaft and blood leaked out in a steady trickle. Black spots burst across his vision, threatening to pull him under.

When he managed to blink them back, he saw that Kyleigh and Gwen were tangled upon the ground. Blood trickled from a split on Gwen's lip. She had Kyleigh pinned on her back, one arm above her head. The golden axe dug against the pale skin of her throat.

"Kyleigh!" He rolled back, gasping as a fresh wave of pain pushed down upon his skull. His bow was nearly in arm's reach. He dragged himself forward by his elbow. He reached for it; his fingers brushed its weathered surface ...

A thick boot came down on top of his hand. It held him pinned, but didn't crush down. When Kael squinted up, he met the curious eyes of a boy.

The boy was no older than ten, painted and dressed in furs. A patch of red hair cut down the middle of his head like a badger's stripe — the rest was shaved clean.

The golden sword he had wedged in his belt was badly chipped. It was clearly a man's sword: it likely would've scraped the ground, had the tip not been broken off. One of the boy's arms was wrapped tightly against his chest in a makeshift sling.

He hardly glanced at Kael's bleeding leg before he nodded to Kyleigh and Gwen. "Trust me — you don't want to get in the middle of that. They've flattened the hills with their battling."

Before Kael could even begin to grasp it, Baird emerged from the depths of his pack. "Ah! *Aha*! I've got it!" He waved a yellowed scroll in a triumphant arc over his head. "Nearly twenty years late, but here at last. I'm sorry I didn't tell you sooner, young man." His bandaged face swung to the trees at Kael's left. "But I wasn't sure I could trust you — and a courier must protect his mission at all costs! Now, if someone will lead me to Thane Evan, I'll happily deliver his letter."

Nobody paid him any attention. Gwen was bent low over Kyleigh — growling some highly unpleasant things into her ear. The boy kept Kael's hand pinned under his boot as he watched them struggle. He grinned when Kyleigh wrenched Gwen's head aside by her fiery hair.

Even if he hadn't had an arrow hanging out of his leg, Kael likely wouldn't have cared enough to listen. He believed that Baird had a letter for the wildmen about as much as he believed in fire-breathing frogs.

But that didn't put a stopper in the beggar-bard's prattling. "Yes, the words might've faded a bit, but the message should still ring true. Now if you'll just take me to Thane Evan, I'll —"

"Thane Evan is dead," Gwen snapped.

The clearing fell silent immediately. Baird's arm froze above his head. There was a light crunching sound as the boy lifted his boot. Kael realized just how loudly he'd been gasping for breath.

Kyleigh stopped with one fist still tangled in Gwen's hair. "I'm sorry to hear that."

The wildwoman shrugged — which must've been a difficult feat, judging by the way Kyleigh had her neck twisted. "He died fighting. It's what he always wanted."

"Who ...?"

"Berwyn."

That word had no meaning to Kael, but both women broke into wide grins. Kyleigh let go of Gwen's hair and the wildwoman took her axe away. For a moment, they seemed almost on the edge of laughter.

What in Kingdom's name was going on? First they were trying to rip each other's throats out, and now they were suddenly all grins. If Kael had been confused before, he was absolutely baffled now.

Kyleigh nodded to the stripe-haired boy. "You've certainly grown into your boots, Griffith. Are you doing all right?"

"Well enough," he said with a nod. Then he grinned. "Better, now."

"My brother's learning the way of the warrior. In time, I expect he'll outstrip me," Gwen said with a smirk. Then she stood and pulled Kyleigh up by the front of her jerkin. "You're coming back with me, pest. We've got a lot to talk about."

"What about the letter?" Baird chirped. "I've carried it all this way. It seems a shame not to have it opened."

"Griffith will read it. I've got my hands full," Gwen said, with a long look at Kyleigh.

At her nod, the boy stepped up and took the scroll. He fumbled one-handed with the wax seal for several moments, rustling so loudly that Kael found it difficult to concentrate on not passing out. "Oh, for mercy's sake — give it here."

"Really? You don't mind?"

"Well, until the world stops spinning, I doubt I'll be good for much else," Kael grumbled as he took the letter.

He broke the seal and rolled it open. It was difficult to read with the black spots dancing across his vision. He could only pick out one or two words at a time: *"Before you ... stands ..."*

And that was as far as he got. No matter how hard he stared at the next word, no matter how fast the world spun or how badly he wanted it to change, the word was still there. It was stamped straight onto the parchment — pressed down by a firm hand.

As his silence dragged ·on, Gwen scoffed. "Can't you read, lowlander?" She jerked her chin at Griffith. "Finish it."

Kael laid back and tried not to be sick as Griffith read the letter's one, simple sentence: *"Before you stands Kael the Wright — see to it that he's awakened.* It's signed by someone named *Setheran."*

Baird gasped loudly. "Well, now — isn't this a surprise?" But instead of putting the two very obvious things together, the beggar-bard thrust a finger at the trees to Kael's right and exclaimed: "There're *two* Kaels wandering the Kingdom. Ha! Before I met you, I hadn't met a single one. Now I know two!"

Griffith gave him a strange look before he turned back to Gwen. "What does that mean, sister?"

"It means the pest has been at her mischief again," she said with a glare.

Kyleigh did a rather convincing job of looking surprised. "I swear I had nothing to do with that."

Kael didn't believe her.

And it was obvious that Gwen didn't believe her, either. She twisted her fingers in Kyleigh's hair and tugged back, forcing her to look at the trees. "That pretty little face doesn't work on me, *pest*. Let's head back to the village, Griff — and bring the blind one along for questioning."

Griffith hesitated. He held the crumpled letter tightly in his good hand and stared unrelentingly at Kael. "But shouldn't we bring him with us? If he's really a Wright —"

"If he was really a Wright, he'd be on his feet with a hand around my throat by now. Instead, he's laying on the ground, sniveling like an infant."

"I'm not sniveling!"

"Get up, Kael."

Kyleigh was glaring at him. A curious red burned across her face — not quite scarlet enough to be pure anger. There was something else mixed with it ... a muted pink that took the edge from the red and made it bleed further across her cheeks. He'd seen this look before: sometimes on Roland's face, but mostly on Amos's. It was the sort of red that took the fire from his veins and made his courage slink back.

Kyleigh was disappointed in him.

"Get up," she said again. "You've survived a great deal worse. Pull the arrow out, seal it shut, and let's get moving."

She had no idea what she was asking. "It hurts —"

"It *hurts*?" Gwen jerked her chin at Griffith. "My brother nearly had his arm chewed off by a monster so wicked, it would likely make *you* soil your breeches. He's been running down the mountains for days with one arm hanging on by its sinew, and you're whining about a scrape. Either you've lived too softly," her eyes narrowed, "or you're even weaker than I thought."

That seemed to settle it. Kyleigh made no attempt to defend him. If anything, the shame spread further down her neck. After a moment, Griffith stuffed the letter inside the filthy rucksack and slung it over his shoulder. Then he pulled Baird forward with his good arm.

"Kael isn't coming?"

"No."

"But what about the other Kael?" Baird gasped when Griffith didn't answer. "Is *neither* of them coming?"

Gwen kicked him in the rump with the flat of her boot. "Move, or I'll snap your legs. Let's go, pest." She grabbed Kyleigh around the shoulders and pulled her against her chest, so that the axe's blade rested under her chin. "Take one last look at your little sniveling fr — omft!"

151

There was a sickening *crack* as Kyleigh slung her head into the middle of Gwen's face — and a *thud* as the butt of the golden axe slammed down onto the top of Kyleigh's skull.

The black spots fled Kael's vision as he watched her body crumple to the ground. Numbness surged through his limbs. He didn't remember getting up, he didn't remember charging. The next thing he knew, he was swinging for Gwen's face.

He more heard than felt the blow that landed across his jaw, as if he was merely watching from a distance. He tried to swing again, but his arm wouldn't move. Needles stung him as Gwen bent his hand backwards. His wrist creaked like a bow drawn too far. It stretched until he could fight it no longer, and he fell to his knees.

Gwen held his wrist taut, a fraction from breaking. Blood fell in torrents from her broken nose, staining the paint on her chin. Her eyes stayed glued to his face as the numbness faded and the pain gripped him once more.

Kael wanted to scream — he wanted to open his mouth and let the agony out. But that was precisely what Gwen wanted, too. So instead, he ground his teeth and choked it back.

"I hope Fate's fingers move swiftly across your last thread. But in case they don't ..." Her boot heel came down hard on his wounded leg. "May the mountains take you."

Blackness crashed over him like a wave. Kael felt as if he was lying on his back in the sand with the surf rushing in. A pain so thick he could actually see it washed over his mouth and eyes — choking him, trying to pull him out to sea. But he dug his nails into the sand. He held his breath. And after a moment, the blackness receded.

When he opened his eyes, he saw Gwen striding away — Kyleigh's unconscious form slung across her shoulders. She carried her as if she weighed nothing; her boots clomped loudly as she disappeared into the woods.

Kael forced himself up with a grunt. His hands shook as he broke the feathered tail away and pulled the arrow's shaft from his leg. His next breath rattled against his lungs. A few breaths more, and he was ready to go to work. He put his hands on either side of the wound and focused.

If Gwen had wanted to leave him for dead, then she shouldn't have taken Kyleigh.

# CHAPTER 15
## THE MAN OF WOLVES

Kyleigh knew better than to open her eyes. She reached to the top of her head and felt gently for the source of the throbbing. A lump the size of a robin's egg had risen along her scalp, but at least the skin wasn't broken.

She'd certainly had worse.

Rough wooden slats dug into her back. The air around her was musty and close. It reeked of pine and something else — something familiar ... and obnoxious. When she finally cracked an eye, her vision was gray. Wherever Gwen had her locked up was pitch dark. She scanned the room and stopped at a lumpy figure crouched nearby.

The odor of ash and soot wafted off its shadowy skin, but beneath all that was a scent that made her bare her teeth. "Silas, you stupid c —"

"Shhh!"

Her head swam horribly as she jerked out of his grasp. "If I'd wanted you to come along, I would've brought you."

"I will be *brought* nowhere, dragoness," Silas purred. "I go where I wish. It's lucky for you that I chose to trouble myself with following your trail. Had I not been so generous with my time, your humans would be dead."

Kyleigh said nothing. She remembered what Kael had told her — about how Silas had led them away from the fires of their camp just before Blackbeak and the hounds could discover it. She'd hoped that he'd been mistaken, that he only *thought* he'd seen Silas. But now there was no mistaking it, and Kyleigh knew she was in very serious trouble: she owed him.

Silas crouched over her. "Now that I've helped you ... you're going to help me."

"What makes you think I ... I ...?" The reek of ash tickled her nose. She sneezed — and very nearly lost consciousness.

"Gently, dragoness," he crooned as he pushed down upon her shoulders. "It's regrettable, but if I'm going to have any chance to save my mountains, I'm afraid I need you alive."

"What do you think we've hiked up here to do, you stupid cat?" she muttered, cinching her eyes closed to keep the room from spinning.

When she opened them, Silas's face was hardly an inch from hers. "You *will* save the mountains — of that, I'm certain. That's not what I'm asking." The tip of his finger bumped down the little ridges in her throat, and the haughty glow of his eyes grew sharp. "As I've been so kind to *your* humans ... you will be kind to mine."

Kyleigh's head throbbed so horribly that she wasn't certain she'd heard him. "Come again? You mean to tell me that *Silas* — the great King of all beasts and hater of men — has ... humans?"

He clamped a hand over her grin and the glow of his eyes grew fierce as he growled: "Yes, though I do not want them. Fate has played a cruel trick on me. I owe their Thane a life debt."

She grabbed his hand — more out of shock than anything. "*Gwen?*"

His mouth twisted as if he fought against a dagger. "A few seasons ago, I was hunting near the summit when I was set upon by a pack of wolves. Those stupid, slobbering brutes stole my kill out from under my claws — but that wasn't enough for them. They attacked me," he growled, the light in his eyes dulling. "Though I could've easily crushed three or four on my own, this pack was far too many. They circled me in as the wolves always do, biting and tearing at my flesh. I could not escape them. I thought I was meant to die. Then the Thane charged in.

"I'd never seen such power," he whispered. His eyes trailed to the wall and as he went on, it was as if he spoke to

155

someone else. "She broke those mongrels with her fists and crushed their heads beneath her heels. She snatched their alpha around his neck and held him out before her. Oh, the fury in her eyes as she crushed his throat ... I can still hear the bones crackling ..."

Silas wore what was easily the most unsettling grin Kyleigh had ever seen. "Gwen could've killed you like she'd killed the wolves, but I'm guessing she spared you, didn't she?"

He nodded. "She carried me to her great stone den, bound my wounds and brought me food. She even made a bed for me out of the wolves' skins," he added, with a flash of that vicious grin. "But in exchange for my life, I've been forced to follow her around like a ..."

"Pet?" Kyleigh finished. "Well, I'm sorry, cat — but you might as well get used to it. There's no way you're getting out of a life debt with Gwen."

He smirked. "I *will* get out of it. This Earl Titus has given me my chance. These people are like us, dragoness," his finger traced a line down her jaw, "wild, dangerous. Strong, yes — but a little ..."

"Stupid?"

He pinched her chin. "They need your mischief, dragoness. I left the mountains to find you because I'd heard how you tormented the rulers of men. You will repay my kindness by helping the Thane reclaim her den."

Kyleigh made a point of glaring at him before she let out a heavy sigh: "Fine. I'll help you."

The fact of the matter was that she'd already meant to help the wildmen — for her own reasons. But as long as Silas thought she was going out of her way to help him, it would free her from a very uncomfortable debt.

"I still don't understand how your saving the mountains is going to settle things with Gwen," she said after a moment.

"The Thane's heart is split into halves — one belongs to her wilds, and the other to her people. Titus has stripped them both away. She will die if she faces him, and die if she flees. So by saving the mountains ... I save her life. Methinks there's too much room inside your scaly head, dragoness."

"That's a bit of a stretch, cat." She held her breath as he leaned over her again. "Why do you smell as if you've been rolling around inside a hearth?"

"I came in through the den's fire shaft."

"The chimney?"

"Yes."

"Why wouldn't you just go through the door ...?" Then it struck her. "Gwen found you as a lion, didn't she? She has no idea what you really are."

He glared, but didn't deny it.

"That's a very bad thing you've done, kitten."

His fingers tightened about her throat. "When she found me, I lacked the strength to change into my human skin."

"And after?"

His hand loosened.

"I know it's hard to admit, but seeing as the two of you are going to be together until one of you gives up and dies, you've got to tell her."

"No, I don't. And if you breathe a word to her, I'll — I'll eat the blind one!"

"You wouldn't dare."

"Don't test me, dragoness," he growled.

He stared her down, and she stared back. It was a battle of wills: a silent fight that neither was going to lose. Their eyes pushed against each other. They didn't blink. They never looked away. Voices drifted in from outside, growing closer. They passed by the door without ever knowing of the battle raging within.

Finally, a distinctive pair of steps reached their ears — clomping, purposeful steps. Silas's eyes shifted ever so slightly. They twitched less than a hair's breadth towards a crack of light in one of the charred walls.

"I wonder what Gwen will think when she finds you behind a shut door?" Kyleigh said without blinking. "Will she be pleased that her little pet has learned to work the latches?"

His lip curled above his teeth in a silent snarl before he bolted for the hearth. No sooner had his feet disappeared up the chimney than the door burst open.

Sunlight crashed in behind it. The light went through Kyleigh's eyes and struck the back of her head, starting a wave of pain that began at her scalp and sank down to her teeth. She clenched her eyes shut as a pair of hands grabbed her around the waist.

There weren't many people in the Kingdom who could make her feel like a helpless child, but Gwen was one of them. She could do nothing more than hang limply as the wildwoman toted her to the wall.

The door closed with a noise that stabbed Kyleigh's ears. There was a *whoosh* from the hearth and the smell of burning wood filled the room. Soon a much softer light pressed against her eyes. Kyleigh gave herself a few moments to adjust before she opened them.

Griffith sat cross-legged before the hearth. He snapped branches in half with his good hand, breaking them against the floor. There was a fire growing steadily in hearth's middle. If Silas had managed to escape without getting his tail singed, it would be a very near thing.

Fingernails dug into the scruff of Kyleigh's neck. She knew the pressure of that hand all too well — and the pressure of the blade even better. She sat very still as Gwen pushed the axe against the vein in her neck.

"One chance. You get one chance to convince me not to kill you, pest."

"You know you could never kill me, Gwen," Kyleigh said evenly. "You'd miss me."

"I *did* miss you. That's the only reason you still draw breath. My aim will be better this time ..."

Gwen's words trailed into a grimace and the axe fell away. A red flower blossomed across her shoulder. Its petals stretched tentatively from the ragged hole in her tunic, crossing the hardened brown stains around the edges and seeping into new territory beyond.

Kyleigh leaned back as the tang of blood filled the house. It was a strange smell — sweet and bitter all at once, thickened by pain. "It's a shame you left Kael in the woods to die. It looks as if you need a healer."

"He won't die. He'll come charging back in here with an iron up his arse before evening." Gwen's voice was thick around her swollen nose, but confident nonetheless.

Kyleigh wasn't so sure.

It was hard to believe that the man who'd just been fretting over an arrow wound was the same one who'd led a ship through the tempest, who'd slain the Witch of Wendelgrimm and sacked the Duke.

That was one of the most frustrating things about Kael: he would've thrown himself on a sword for any one of his friends. He would've caused himself no end of pain just to spare them from a little. But for some reason, he wouldn't fight for himself.

Though they'd traveled for weeks through the forest and the mountains, he hadn't even tried to come up with a plan to take on Titus. In fact, she'd begun to fear that he never meant to. She'd begun to worry that his greatest sacrifice was yet to come, that he would trade the ones he'd loved for those he'd *come* to love — that in order to spare his friends, he would give up on his home.

Yes, she was certain that was what he'd had planned. And had he been left to his own devices, it likely would have worked. There was just one problem: Kyleigh had a different plan.

Gwen eased herself onto the ground, pressing the side of her fur gauntlet against her wound. "My father is dead, my people are broken and sick. A few days ago, we were sitting untouched inside our castle," she said with a hard smile. "Now look at us — forced to deal with the *pest*. Tell me what you know of the Man of Wolves."

Kyleigh wasn't going to let her off that easily. "Whatever happened to questioning the blind man?"

"He's talking to the trees. When we try to ask him something, he tells us not to interrupt."

"Then perhaps you should mind your manners."

Red burned beneath Gwen's paint. Even though she clearly would've liked to smack Kyleigh across the face, she didn't. Instead, she placed the golden axe on the ground between them.

It was an old weapon. A grayish rust crusted over it, nearly covering the dragon carved between its blades. The dragon's horns curved upwards and its mouth was open. Flame spilled past its tongue, falling in a bolt that ended where the boned shaft began. It was exactly how Kyleigh had remembered it, save for one thing:

The axe was supposed to have two heads — two blades forged to look like wings that burst unfurled from the dragon's back. Now there was only one. The second blade had been broken off, leaving a ragged nub behind.

Though she'd felt the bite of that blade on more than one occasion, Kyleigh couldn't help but feel sorry to see it broken. She studied the jagged edge and thought she could almost hear the rending blow still trembling inside the metal. "What have you gotten yourself into, Thane-child?"

"It's Thane now, actually. At least for a time." Gwen's eyes trailed to the hearth. Her voice fell to a whisper. "Griffith is only a child, and this is far too heavy a matter. I wouldn't burden him with it."

*But she would burden herself.* Those were the words behind her stare, the thought that dulled the edge of her scowl. Kyleigh leaned against the wall. "Tell me what happened."

By the time Gwen's eyes returned, it was as if they'd traveled a great distance: her stare was hollow and vacant. The unrelenting edge was gone, worn down by the wind. Had those eyes not been set into such a familiar face, Kyleigh might've thought she was looking at a stranger.

"We were beaten." There was a flash of that edge for a moment, a glint in the pit of her eyes as Gwen snarled. But it faded quickly. "At the start of last winter, just after Thane

Evan had perished in battle, my warriors and I went on a hunt. We came across some strange men in the meadows. They summoned fire in their hands, split the mountains' skin with their words. I'd never seen such power. I remember wanting to get close to them ..." Gwen swallowed hard. "We killed them, I suppose. They were in so many little pieces that I don't think I could've counted them all. There was a stench about them — more infuriating than anything I've ever felt."

"Mages," Kyleigh said. "What you smelled on them was their magic."

Gwen nodded slowly. "*Mages*. Yes, I've heard stories about them. I suppose I just expected them to be more ... difficult to kill. So few people ever make it into our lands that I was certain the mages were a sign from Fate," she went on. "I thought it meant the winter would be harsh, or the wynns planned an attack. But it was worse than I feared: it meant the Man of Wolves was coming.

"He marched in a few days behind the mages. When we told him to leave our lands, he refused. So my warriors and I stormed from our castle to drive him away. His army carried strange weapons — swords the color of storm clouds, wooden birds with beaks that pierced our skin like ice. They wore shells of stone over their heads and chests." She thrust a hand at the broken axe. "Our weapons shattered against them. His army was everywhere. They kept moving to our sides instead of meeting us at the front. Soon, everywhere we turned there were enemies at our backs.

"It was by our strength alone that we managed to escape. I gathered what was left of my warriors and closed the gates behind us. We were beaten, and the Man of Wolves knew it. He smiled at us as his army stripped our dead of their sacred weapons." Gwen's fists pounded into her knees. "He stole them!"

Kyleigh groaned inwardly. Titus had done worse than steal the weapons: he'd melted them down and turned them into collars. But she didn't have the heart to tell Gwen.

"Long weeks of silence passed. The Man of Wolves waited near the bottom of the summit. His army camped among the trees. Day after day, Fate's die landed in their favor. My pet fled the castle," Gwen added sullenly. "Animals can always sense a coming storm, and so I knew this was yet another sign of our misfortune."

"He's back now — perhaps that means our fortunes will change," Griffith called hopefully.

Gwen smiled at him. "I hope so, Griff." But by the time she turned back to Kyleigh, she was glaring once more. "When the snow's fury had passed, the Man of Wolves attacked us again. I knew better than to charge him a second time — we would use our castle. His soldiers beat against our gates, but my warriors shored them with their strength. We were prepared to hold them off till summer, if we had to ... then we heard the screams."

Gwen's eyes went dark and her voice dropped to a whisper. "Monsters had appeared inside our castle. They were horrible things — beasts and men twisted into one. Somehow, they'd gotten behind us. They tore the defenseless apart with their teeth and claws. Our craftsmen, our children ... I've never seen such cruelty, not even among the wynns. I begged for their lives, offered my surrender, but the Man of Wolves ignored me. He watched from afar, smiling as his creatures devoured my people.

"I had no choice but to abandon the gates. We ran to save the helpless, and the Man of Wolves smashed through. His army crushed our backs, his monsters waited with open jaws. My warriors managed to hold their ground long enough for us to escape through a hidden path. We fled down the mountains with those twisted creatures howling after our trail. A few days ago, we finally lost them. Last night, we arrived at the ruins of this village. And just when I hoped we'd reached the end of our misfortunes," her brows dropped to a glare, "*you* turn up."

Kyleigh didn't reply. Gwen's story raked a raw line across her heart. She hadn't always gotten along with the wildmen, but they were honorable humans. They cared for their people. They certainly hadn't deserved what Titus had done to them.

"I've told you what happened to us." Gwen took her under the chin. "Now you're going to tell me what you know of the Man of Wolves."

"His name is Titus," Kyleigh said. "He's one of the King's rulers."

Gwen pushed her away. "You're lying, pest. The King was the one who charged our ancestors with the task of cleansing the mountains. Why would he attack us?"

There was no way to explain it. How could she possibly tell Gwen that the Kingdom had forgotten about the wildmen? That their task had fallen into legend? That everything she'd built her life around was only a story to the rest of the realm?

She couldn't. It would've been far too cruel.

"The King didn't order this. Titus is trying to take the mountains for himself."

"Traitor," Griffith hissed.

He crept from the now-roaring hearth and sat cross-legged beside Gwen, careful not to bump his broken arm. A blue marble rolled between the fingers of his good hand. It was a trinket he always carried with him. If it was out, Kyleigh knew he was concentrating.

"We're going to stomp him, aren't we?" When Gwen didn't reply, he nudged her gently. "Sister?"

She took her gaze off the wall long enough to ruffle his stripe of hair. "Sure we are, Griff. And the pest is going to help us. Tell me everything you know about Titus," she said, turning back to Kyleigh. "How do I fight his army of monsters? How do I break his ice swords? Tell me, and I might let you live."

The wildmen had made their homes at the summit for centuries on end. Their only enemies were impervious to every normal sort of weapon — and would've made short work of armor. The dragonsbane the wildmen carried was passed down from parent to child. Any knowledge of how to forge from the earth had likely slipped through the cracks between generations long ago.

Kyleigh's walk among the humans had been a mere blink of time compared to the long years she'd spent living as a shapechanger. Trying to teach the wildmen what she knew was going to be no small task.

"Titus's swords aren't made of ice — they're made of *steel*."

"*Steel*." Gwen's lips formed the word tentatively, as if she learned a foreign tongue.

The marble danced faster between Griffith's fingers. "Where do we find steel?"

"I can teach your craftsmen to make it," Kyleigh offered.

Gwen narrowed her eyes. "In exchange for your life? No. If I'm going to spare you, then I'll be requiring more. You'll teach us how to make the stone shells as well."

"Armor," Kyleigh corrected her. Blazes, this was going to be more difficult than she'd thought. "I'll teach you everything I know about steel and armor."

Gwen nodded. "Good. Now that we've got all that settled ... there's the matter of this so-called *Wright*. I don't know where you heard of Setheran, but his name's no good among the wildmen. My father's told me stories of that troublemaker," she added with a glare. "*He's* the reason the wynns still haunt the mountain's top. If it weren't for his meddling, we would've cast them into the seas years ago."

This was the first Kyleigh had heard of it — of any of it. Setheran had never mentioned anything about the wildmen, let alone the wynns. She didn't know what he could've possibly done to anger them. But she knew one thing for certain:

"I had absolutely nothing to do with that letter."

# CHAPTER 16
## COMING HOME

It was with no small amount of dread that Kael took his first steps into Tinnark.

The charred houses watched him through hollow eyes. He caught himself waiting to hear the noises of the villagers. He listened for the familiar song of their work. But the path was quiet.

Painted, fur-clad wildmen gathered in clumps among the ruins. Some had limbs bound in slings, others nursed festering wounds or had bandages wrapped clumsily about their heads. A few watched him from the depths of small wooden litters. All looked as if they'd been half-chewed and spat back out.

The weight of the wildmen's stares slowed Kael's pace considerably. His anger faded back as he met their darkened eyes and saw the exhaustion on their painted faces. These weren't the fearsome warriors Amos had told him about: they were gaunt and sickly-thin. He couldn't believe they'd once battled monsters.

"Where's Kyleigh?"

One of the wildmen turned and pointed to a house that was a little less ruined than the others. It was slightly charred, but still intact. The warped door swung open before he could take more than a few steps towards it.

Griffith came out first. His golden sword was drawn and gripped in his good hand. "Stay back," he warned.

Kael froze. It wasn't the sword that stopped him: it was the look on Griffith's face. The skin behind his paint was deathly pale. Beads of sweat popped up across his brow.

Kael's healing instincts took over. "You're feverish. That arm has probably gotten infected. You ought to let me look at it."

Griffith said nothing. If anything, his hand twisted tighter about his sword. Then his eyes traveled down to the ragged tear in Kael's trousers — to the hole Gwen's arrow had left behind — and his mouth fell wide open.

"It's true," he gasped.

"What's true?" Gwen appeared in the doorway behind him, dragging Kyleigh against her chest. The skin beneath her paint went scarlet when she followed the line of Griffith's finger to Kael's leg. "Take one step closer, and I'll kill her," she snarled, planting the golden axe against Kyleigh's middle.

Kael wasn't fooled. "No, you won't. Kyleigh's planned this whole thing out."

"I'll slice her in two," Gwen warned.

Kael ignored her. "I can't believe you," he said to Kyleigh. "I really can't. This is exactly what you did with the pirates. After all we've been through, you still think you have to trick me into going along —"

"I swear I'll kill her —"

"Do it, then!" Kael snapped. "Quit threatening and take a swing."

He thought that would be the end of it. He thought Gwen would give up her act and start being reasonable. But instead, her bluish-black lips twisted into a smile. "All right —"

"Stop!" Kyleigh squirmed away from the axe. Her fingernails went white where they dug into Gwen's arm. "Please, this isn't a trick — she *will* kill me."

He didn't understand. He had no idea what was going on between these two. Sure, Gwen had clubbed Kyleigh over the head with her axe — but then again, Kyleigh had broken Gwen's nose. The fact that neither had killed the other could've only meant one thing:

"I thought you were friends."

Gwen snarled in Kyleigh's ear. "How many times have I got to tell you, pest? We aren't friends — friends don't try to bite each other's arms off."

"Oh, please. That was barely a nibble."

"It ruined my winter! I had to sit inside all season while the other warriors — you know something? I'm tired of explaining it to you."

She raised the axe, and Kael ripped an arrow from his quiver. "Stop it! Look, I haven't got a clue what this is. But if you hurt her, if you split one hair on her head —"

"You'll kill me?"

"I'll destroy you," he growled, when Gwen brought the axe close to Kyleigh's throat. "You'll be nothing more than a bloody smear on my boot heel. There'll be so little left that not even the maggots will bother with you."

"Is that so?" The axe's blade touched Kyleigh's neck.

Kael locked his arrow onto Gwen's eye. "I'm warning you. There won't be enough mercy to save you if you hurt her — not in this life or the next."

Her skin burned scarlet as she snarled: "I'll take my —"

"Stop!" Griffith threw his sword upon the ground and held up a hand. "They're only playing. Please — don't shoot my sister."

"Then tell your sister to get her axe away from my friend," Kael growled.

At his nod, Gwen shoved Kyleigh forward. She raised a brow as he lowered his arrow. "Would you have really shot at me?"

"I've shot at you once already. It wouldn't take much to convince me to do it again."

For some reason, this made Gwen smile rather widely.

"Are you hurt?" Kael said as he pulled Kyleigh towards him. "Is your skull —?"

"It's fine," she muttered, knocking his hand away. Then she waved to Gwen. "Come on, let's get started."

167

"Wait a moment — get started on what, exactly?" He grabbed her arm before she could turn away. "I'm not letting you anywhere near that madwoman —"

"*Wild*woman," Gwen cut in.

Kael honestly didn't see a difference.

"The pest has committed crimes against our people," Griffith said, waving at the wildmen.

Kael groaned. "What did you do to them?"

"Nothing they didn't deserve."

"You led the wynns against us!" Gwen said.

Kyleigh shrugged. "It seemed like the thing to do at the time."

Griffith quickly stepped between them. "Once the pest repays her debts, all will be forgiven. But until then, she'll stay here with us as our prisoner."

"Like Death, she will," Kael growled. "Come on, Kyleigh. Let's find Baird and —"

"And what?" She raised her brows. "Where are we off to, exactly? What's the plan?"

He didn't know. He couldn't go down the mountains, and he couldn't go up. Once again, he found himself trapped in their middle. And Kyleigh seemed to know it.

"From where I'm standing, it looks as if you've got two choices," she said, crossing her arms. "You can either float around the mountains for the rest of your life, moaning through the trees like a lost spirit, or you could do something useful. I'm choosing the latter."

"No, you aren't choosing anything. You've gotten yourself into trouble, and now I'm stuck here while you pay off your debts. How long is that going to take, by the way?"

"It'll take as long as it takes."

She grinned over her shoulder at him as she walked down the hill. Gwen followed her with a smirk, leaving Kael alone with the wildmen.

They clung to their wounds and stared through the weary film on their eyes, waiting. Kael sighed heavily — sighed, because then he wouldn't have to feel the strange ache in his heart.

He took Griffith by his good arm and led him up the hill. "Come on. Let's get those wounds patched up."

*******

The hospital sat by itself at the top of the slope. Its elongated walls looked like witches' teeth: blackened and chipped, sticking up at odd angles. The roof was completely gone. Kael didn't want to go any closer, but his legs seemed to have a mind of their own. They dragged him until he stood inside the ruins.

Mangled remains of cots littered the floor. Many had been overturned or broken. The only things left inside the tonic cabinet were a few broken bottles of ointment. Heat from the fire must've devoured the rest.

Planks creaked under Kael's weight as he made his way to Amos's office. A knot rose in his throat when he saw the warped desk and the ashen frame of Kyleigh's cot. But what hurt him the worst was something he'd never thought he would miss.

Amos's healing tomes lay scattered across the floor — empty covers with their titles burned away. Charred nubs of pages still clung stubbornly to their spines. How many times had he wandered in late at night to find Amos bent over one of those books ...?

"Well?"

Griffith was standing behind him, waiting patiently — along with a whole company of wildmen. Kael had been so wrapped up in his thoughts that he'd actually forgotten about them.

"Right. I'll tend to the most serious wounds first," he said, thinking back to the days when the hospital had been full. "Head wounds, broken bones, mangled limbs and the like. Then I'll take care of anybody with a scratch or scrape. Oh," he fixed the wildmen with what he hoped was a severe look, "and if you think you've got something lodged where it shouldn't be, let me know first thing. There's nothing worse than sealing somebody up only to find out that you've got to split them open again. Understood?"

When he received an acceptable number of nods, Kael got them all lined up — and tried not to think about how much he'd just sounded like Amos.

His first patient was an old man with a gash that looked as if a sword had come down on the top of his head. Kael had to spend several minutes draining the curdled blood and infection from the wound before he could start the sealing.

"Another day like this and you would've been dead," Kael muttered as he rubbed his thumb along the white scar on the old man's scalp, smoothing it away. "You should've taken care of it sooner. I'm shocked that it didn't kill you."

"What choice did I have?" the old man grumbled back. He checked Kael's work gingerly with the tips of his fingers, mouth parted slightly.

"Well, you could've gone to one of the other healers."

"Other healers? How many healers do you think we have?" The old man leaned to glare at Griffith. "If I'd known he was rattled, I wouldn't have let him split me open!"

Griffith shook his head, smiling. "He isn't rattled. He's just daft."

Kael wasn't sure that *daft* was much of an improvement over *rattled*, but it seemed to put the old man at ease. The moment he'd wandered away, Griffith explained:

"There hasn't been a healer born among the wildmen for years. It doesn't happen often, and they don't stay for long."

"Because they're weaker than the others?" Kael guessed.

Griffith raised his brows. "Weaker? No, there's no weakness among whisperers — only balance. We need each other. The healers don't stay because it's too rough on them, I think. They get all weepy around wounds." He shrugged. "At least that's what my father used to say."

Kael wasn't sure if his father had gotten it right. As far as he could remember, wounds had never made Amos weepy.

If anything, he'd only gotten grumpier around them. But he saw no point in trying to explain this to Griffith.

The line of wildmen seemed endless. Kael covered himself in such a fog of concentration that after a while, he didn't see their faces anymore. He would slip out for a moment as they approached, like a sea creature breaking above the waves. Once he'd found where they were wounded, he would duck back under and lose himself to the depths.

Not long ago, the healing would've exhausted him. There would've been no chance of him patching up an entire village without getting some sort of whisperer's headache. But after his time in the plains, this sort of work seemed ... simple. He was certain nothing could've ever exhausted his mind quite as much as the endless days he'd spent dragging lines across the Fields. Sealing skin together was an easy thing, by comparison. And though the wildmen kept coming, he found he always had a little more to give.

Though he grew paler by the minute, Griffith refused to be healed until all of the other wildmen had been taken care of. "To be Thane is to put the needs of my people first. I may not be Thane yet, but one day I will be. This is good practice," he said with a smile.

Kael thought it was ridiculous for Griffith to have to suffer any longer than necessary. But at the same time, a small part of him understood. "All right. Just tell me if you start to feel faint," he grumbled.

The last clump of wildmen was mostly just flesh wounds. Several of them had punctures on their arms and chests — the marks of Titus's hounds. They went deep, sometimes scraping the surface of bone. It was remarkable that so many of the wildmen had survived their wounds.

At last, the final patient left the hospital, and it was Griffith's turn. He stood stiffly, his wounded arm turned out of Kael's reach. "If you're a healer, why do you have so many scars? I've seen you wiping them away all day," he added.

Kael thought about it for a moment. "I suppose I don't erase them because they remind me of things I don't want to forget."

171

"What kinds of things?"

"Stories."

He pointed to the scar that split Kael's eyebrow. "What's the story behind that one?"

Griffith was dragging his feet. Kael had seen that same wide-eyed look on the faces of Amos's patients before. And he wasn't going to waste time answering pointless questions. At his order, Griffith reluctantly untied the sling around his neck.

Rags covered his arm from elbow to wrist. They seemed to be made out of the same rough material as the wildmen's garb. "Didn't you have any proper bandages?" He frowned when Griffith shook his head. "Well, these skins are too thick to use for binding. They won't let your wound breathe. Next time use a little moss if you don't have anything better."

The first layer of skins was stiff with dried gore. He knew from the smell alone that Griffith's wound was badly infected. But it wasn't until he pulled the last few strips away that he realized just how serious things were.

Misshapen lumps warped the line of Griffith's arm. Purple bruises blossomed down the length of it, swelling against the sharp hills pressed up against his flesh. His hand sagged over his wrist, hanging uselessly at the end of his mangled arm.

Puncture wounds dotted the lumpy flesh in twin arcs: one line on the top of the limb, and one underneath. They were swollen and puffed, weeping a mixture of white and red. Any other healer would've cut it off at the elbow and been done with it. But Kael thought he could fix it.

The trouble was that he would need Griffith to stay awake. His arm was so badly mangled that at some point, he would need him to move his fingers just to make sure he'd gotten it all put back together properly.

It was going to be a long, painful process — more than any child should have to bear. But Kael had a plan. "I'll make you a deal: you tell me about your wound, and I'll tell you about mine." He gestured to the mangled arm. "How did *that* happen?"

Griffith shrugged. "It was the red devil — the King beast of Titus's army. He was taller than my father, his body was covered in blood-red fur. His claws were nearly the size of my chest. Gwen clubbed him over the head — otherwise, I think he would've finished me. The devil got a taste for my blood, though." His voice dropped to a whisper. "I could hear him chasing me the whole time we ran down the mountains. But I'm not worried. Gwen's going to hunt him down and make me a necklace of his claws."

"What makes Gwen think she can kill him?" Kael said.

"She kills everything. And if she says she's going to do something, she will. So I've told you about mine." Griffith jerked his chin up at Kael's scar. "Now tell me about yours."

"Fair enough. Well, one day, I was sailing off to fight the Witch of Wendelgrimm when this nasty storm blew in ..."

Kael drifted in and out of his story while he worked. He pressed the infection from the punctures and sealed them closed. Then came the tricky part: Griffith's arm was so severely broken that he had to split his skin open and patch the bone together from the inside.

Though it must've been incredibly painful, the boy never flinched. He asked Kael every detail about the tempest and his battle with the Witch. Then once that story had been told, Kael showed him the scars on his leg — the rounded marks left by the wolf monster that'd mauled him in Bartholomew's Pass.

He grimaced when Kael told him about the wolves — though it probably had more to do with the bits of bone floating around in his arm than the story. "You got bitten too, then. Did it hurt?"

Kael slipped out of his concentration for a moment to mumble: "Of course it did." He was trying desperately to figure out which pieces fit where. It was like working on a very slippery, bloody puzzle —

"Did it hurt a *lot*?"

"Yes, it hurt a lot."

"Did you cry?"

"No."

Griffith snorted. "Be honest. Did you —?"

"No, I didn't cry," Kael snapped. He jerked himself out of his trance completely, with every intention of telling Griffith to kindly shut it. But the look on the boy's face stopped him short.

His chin was pointed stubbornly upwards; the freckles across his nose stood out like stars against his pale skin. "I cried when the red devil did this to me. I didn't mean to, but it hurt so badly and we'd run so far ..." His good hand trembled as it balled into a fist. "I hate it here. I want to go home."

It was difficult not to hurt for Griffith. Kael had spent his whole life dreaming about running away from Tinnark, going off on an adventure through the lowlands — perhaps he would even accomplish something so great that he would be made a knight of the realm. But at the end of every dream, Kael had always imagined what it would be like to come home.

He'd imagined the looks the Tinnarkians would give him when he walked through the streets. Marc and Laemoth would burn at the sight of him; Brock would have to eat his words. Roland would be overjoyed. He would wrap Kael against his boney chest and say he'd known all along that he was bound to do great things.

And Amos ... well, Amos would be so proud that he would have to actually admit it — out loud and for all to hear.

Tinnark was where Kael's adventures always began. It was the reason he left — but it was also the reason he returned. In many ways, growing up in such a miserable blot of village had given him a reason to dream in the first place. It had taken him a long while to realize it, but Kael finally understood just how important Tinnark had been.

So many of his dreams hadn't been about the adventure, at all ...

They'd been about coming home.

Once Griffith went quiet, Kael was able to finish quickly. He pieced the bone fragments together and sealed them into place. Griffith was able to wiggle his fingers and move his wrist around, so he figured he'd set it properly. Now all he had left to do was seal the split he'd made down Griffith's arm.

He was just about to begin when he felt a pressure on his hand. Griffith traced the jagged scar that Eveningwing had left behind, the one that cut between his fingers. "What about this?"

"That was given to me by a man who thought he wanted to kill me, but we wound up being good friends," Kael said simply.

He sealed the gash shut and had gone to smooth the scar when Griffith jerked his arm away. "No, I want to keep it. Maybe someday I'll give *you* a scar," he added with a grin, "then you'll always remember me."

The brightness in his eyes darkened Kael's heart; the daring edge of his smile cut him like a sword. Griffith's face was a painful reminder of one he would never see again. He could do nothing more than nod stiffly back.

He was relieved when the boy finally left.

Then Gwen walked in.

"Don't get too comfortable, mutt. You've got one more patient," she said as she strode towards him. She stood with her hands on her hips, eyeing him through the purplish bruises that spread out from her busted nose.

Kael set it quickly, cracking the bone back into place. He reached to seal the split on her mouth, but she knocked his hand away. "I'll tell you when you can touch my lips, mutt."

He had no interest in touching her lips. "Fine. Was there something else?"

She pointed to a mass of dried blood near the top of her shoulder. When she pulled her shirt taut, he saw a hole about as big around as a man's finger torn through the furs.

175

Kael scowled — a flimsy defense against the sudden burn in his face. "I can't work through that small a hole. You're going to have to unbutton your shirt."

"Sure I have to." Gwen's hands went to her tunic. She looked him in the eyes as she undid the first bone clasp. "You men are all the same, always trying to catch a glimpse —"

She looked rather shocked when Kael reached across and ripped the hole open, tearing it to fist-sized. "I'm not trying to glimpse anything. Now hold still."

"Whatever you say, mutt."

He tried to ignore the way her words slid across his ears.

There was a hole in Gwen's shoulder. Her skin was puckered around it and the edges were swollen red. He could see a nasty infection growing in its center. But the most unsettling thing was the ring of deep cuts that surrounded it.

They reminded him of the scars he'd seen on Baird's eyes. The cuts fanned from her wound like bursts from a star — jagged in some places, raised and scabbed along their ridges. Some of the lines had slipped and been cut too deeply. One of them wept red drops down her skin.

"There's a piece of something lodged in there," she said.

Kael placed his hands. His toes curled as he felt the depth of the cuts. "How many times did you try to dig it out?"

"Several," she growled.

Gwen sat still while he worked. Kael had to split her skin open to get the object out. It took him several tries to latch onto its slippery surface. But when he finally did, the object came out cleanly: it was the full head of an arrow.

"Are you finished?"

"Just about." Kael sealed the last bit of her skin closed and smoothed the scar away. "There."

Gwen rolled her shoulder a bit, testing it. "Good work." Her skin was quite a bit paler than it'd been before, and it made the black design on her face stand out sharply. "You're free to go."

176

Kael followed her to the door. "I'm not going anywhere without Kyleigh."

"Suit yourself. But if you stay, you'll be expected to work. I won't have any layabouts squatting in my village."

"Fine." Kael followed her down the hill, past the charred houses and into the heart of Tinnark. "Where's everybody gone?"

Gwen looked at him as if he was stupid. "It's dinner time."

"All right, but where are they ...?"

The words stuck in his throat. A shadow of a building lurked at the top of his eyes, and he realized they were headed towards the Hall.

Memories rushed out of the darkness: the Hall's roof was ablaze, its walls were warped against the heat. Brock, the head elder of Tinnark, lay dead beside it. After what had become of the hospital, he didn't know if he had the courage to look at the Hall. It was only after several deep breaths that he forced his gaze up.

Nothing could have prepared him for what he saw.

The Hall was restored. New shingles lined its sloping roof and the air was heavy with the scent of fresh pine. The oaken doors had been re-carved and set into place. Twisting images of dragons and warriors adorned their surface, locked in an epic struggle.

"How ...?"

"How what?" She followed his gaze to the Hall and snorted. "Please, that's nothing. Give them a couple of weeks, and my craftsmen will have this village looking decent again."

"You have craftsmen?"

"Of course I have craftsmen. Who do you think does the cooking?" she said with a smirk.

Kael's pace slowed as his eyes wandered over the Hall. The two large beams that stood on either side of the doors had been carved into the shapes of bearded men. They were dressed for battle, each with a rounded shield across his chest and his axe raised high.

He recognized the axe immediately: it was the same weapon Gwen carried ... wait moment. The bearded men's axes had two heads — Gwen's only had one. He glanced down at her belt and saw there was ragged nub where the second blade should've been.

Before he could ask what had happened to it, Gwen spoke: "That's Cadwalader, our first Thane. And my father, Thane Evan," she said, pointing to the carved warriors. "They were the greatest dragonslayers in our history."

Kael snorted. "There aren't any dragons in the mountains."

"Have you been to the summit?"

"Well, no —"

"Then you ought to keep your mouth shut. Otherwise, people might figure out how stupid you are," Gwen retorted. "There *are* dragons in the mountains — well, I suppose they're more like the frost-breathing castoffs of dragons. But they're the closest things you'll find on this side of the northern seas." She arched her chin at the images carved into the doors. "*Wynns* is what we call them. They've lived in the mountains for so long that they've lost their wings. Their breath bites like winter and they've got these great heavy claws they use to burrow through ice."

Roland had always said there were monsters living at the summit. Still, Kael had a difficult time believing they were wingless, burrowing dragons. "Are you cert — would you stop that?"

He tried to move away, but Gwen stepped on his heel. "Fate's fingers, you walk too slowly. Move, mutt!"

She clomped on his heel again, and Kael was tired of playing. He outran her easily, reaching the Hall doors several paces ahead. He stopped to open the doors — but Gwen didn't. Instead, she lowered her shoulder and smacked into him from behind.

There was a loud *crack*, a roar of cheers, and the next time Kael blinked, he was lying on the floor inside the Hall. His limbs were splayed in every direction; a large chunk of the door was trapped beneath him. Splinters the size of his fist ringed his body in an arc. The wildmen seated around the many tables grinned down at him though their beards.

Kael heard steps clomping up behind him and flipped over quickly. "What," he howled, "in *Kingdom's* name is wrong with you?"

Gwen leaned against the man-sized hole in the door, her bluish-black lips pulled back from her teeth in a grin. "How was your trip, mutt?"

"You could've killed me!"

"Are you dead?"

"No —"

"Got any scratches? Bruises? I bet you're not even sore."

Never, in all of his life, had Kael wished to be wounded. But Gwen was right: he'd just been launched through several inches of pine, and he had absolutely nothing to show for it. "Well, still … you've ruined that door."

Gwen shrugged. "The craftsmen will have it rebuilt before you've finished sobbing about it." She ducked through the hole, and the Hall fell silent. "Do you know why you're not hurt, mutt? Because you didn't have a chance to doubt it, this time. You didn't have time to see it flying towards you, didn't have time to fret about how badly it would hurt. Fate shoved you through a door —"

"*You* shoved me through a door."

"— and your warrior strength protected you. I don't know what those lowlanders taught you, but it wasn't whispering." She stepped over him — nearly crushing his fingers as she went — and marched to the back of the room.

Most of the wildmen returned to their cups immediately, but a few stared him down. And rather than simmer under their gazes, Kael got to his feet.

Heavy tables ringed the Hall, their legs carved into the coiling shapes of beasts. The fire pit that used to sit in the middle of the room had been pushed against the back wall. Dishes piled high with mountain fare sat in rows stretching to either end of each table. Empty plates circled the dishes, waiting to be filled.

The wildmen seemed to quickly forget that Kael had just erupted through their door. The air came alive with chatter as they handed the plates around, piling them with food.

Kael went for Kyleigh at a stomp. "I know what you're up to."

She was the picture of innocence. "Me?"

He frowned at her. "You knew the wildmen were around. Don't tell me you couldn't smell them," he added when she started to protest. "You knew very well we were headed straight for their camp."

"You're right. I did."

He hadn't expected her to admit it so easily. "Well, just ... why, then?"

"Why? Because it was the right thing to do. You see, I'd been so very bad to them for so many years. And my poor heart could barely hold the guilt —"

"Come off it, Kyleigh," he growled at her.

And just as he'd suspected, she grinned. "All right, maybe I missed them."

"*Missed* them? They're completely insane!"

"Don't be ridiculous. Would I keep friends who were in any way unstable?"

"Those seem to be the only sort you keep."

"Then what does that say about you?" She smiled when he glared. "Oh come now, they're not all that bad. Once you get used to the frivolity —"

"Is that what you call it? I just got launched through a door!"

"I know," she bit her lip, but couldn't stop the corners of her mouth from turning upwards, "I saw."

Kael didn't think it was funny. Not in the least bit.

# CHAPTER 17
## A New Beginning

It turned out that Gwen was serious about putting him to work.

Kael had spent the night on the Hall floor, curled on top of his bedroll and surrounded by wildmen. He hadn't slept very well: the wildmen seemed to get up at all hours of the night. The front doors creaked open and gasps of cold air whipped in, chilling him nearly every time he was about to drift off.

Then at dawn, Gwen woke him with a sharp kick.

Kael groaned and clutched his side. "What was that for?"

"You looked peaceful," she said with a shrug. "It was making my breakfast come up a bit. Now get out and get moving — we've got a village to rebuild."

Kael didn't know the first thing about building houses. Tinnark's carpenters had always taken care of that sort of thing. He was sure he wouldn't do the wildmen any good.

Gwen dogged him the whole way out of Tinnark and into the woods, stepping on his heels each time he slowed. It wasn't until they'd arrived at the base of an enormous tree that she finally relented.

Kael had climbed this tree once as a child, and he remembered it well. He'd been focusing so hard on the limb just ahead of him that he'd lost track of time — and of where he was. He wound up climbing much higher than he'd ever meant to.

When he'd thought to look down, the earth spun beneath him and the houses of Tinnark looked like toys. Fear froze him to the branch he perched on. He'd wrapped his arms and legs around it and shut his eyes tightly, trying to forget where he was, regretting that he'd ever climbed so high.

It was evening before Amos finally came looking for him. When he saw Kael's plight, he'd been less than sympathetic. "You got yourself up there, so you can get yourself down," he'd said.

Though he refused to help, Amos hadn't abandoned him: he'd sat beneath the tree, tending to a small fire he'd built as darkness closed in. The moon was full that night. Kael had been able to see the next branch a mere arm's reach beneath him.

He knew that once Amos put his foot down, that was the end of it. If he ever wanted to touch solid earth again, he'd have to get there on his own. "You got yourself up here, so you can get yourself down," he'd whispered as he stretched for the nearest branch.

He'd taken the tree one limb at a time, inching his way down. He forgot about the height and the spinning earth beneath him. He'd put all of his concentration into the climb, into reaching the next branch. When his boots finally touched the solid earth, he'd collapsed in relief.

"See? I knew you could do it. Though it would've been a blasted lot easier if you'd done it in the daylight," Amos had grumped from across the fire.

The tree had only grown taller with the passing years. Now when Kael craned his neck to search the highest branches, the view made him dizzy. He brought his eyes back to earth and saw handful of wildmen crouched beneath its evergreen arms.

Gwen swept a hand at them. "These are our craftsmen. They've been hard at work repairing this miserable little village —"

"Tinnark," Kael said.

She raised a brow. "*Tinnark?* That's a stupid name."

"No, it's history. This village was settled years ago by a man named Tinn," Kael explained. "His house had a large, pointed roof that was simple to build and could bear the weight of snow. As more settlers arrived, they called the sloping roof *Tinn's arch.* So the village became known as *Tinnarch.* But after a few generations, people began confusing the *arch* with *ark.* They said it wrong for so many years that it just wound up being known as *Tinnark.*"

Kael had thought it was an interesting bit of history — but Gwen must've thought otherwise. She rammed the butt of her axe into his middle with such surprising force that he lost his breath.

"Don't bore me again, mutt," she warned. "I don't care if you're a Wright. You'll still be expected to do chores. Nobody sits idly in my village."

"It's not your village — you didn't even know its name!" he gasped.

She smirked. "Well, I've given it a new one: *Misery.* Rather fitting, don't you think?"

Kael was about to tell her exactly what he thought when Gwen shoved him roughly to the side. She strode towards the craftsmen, and Griffith followed along in her shadow. He shot Kael a quick grin when his sister wasn't looking.

"Stand tall, craftsman. The Wright's going to get you a fresh tree."

The craftsmen scattered at Gwen's command, tittering excitedly to each other.

Kael was wondering just which tree he was going to be expected to fell. "All right. But I'll need an axe."

Griffith frowned. "What for? All you have to do is knock it down."

Kael couldn't believe it. "Knock it down? With *what*?"

"With these." Gwen spread her fingers wide. "They're the only tools a whisperer needs."

They were joking. They *had* to be joking — either that, or the wildmen were even more cracked than he'd thought. He looked all around the craftsmen, but there wasn't a hint of a smile on any of their faces. They were being completely serious.

"It isn't possible. I can't —"

183

Gwen clamped a hand around his throat, tightening until he could hardly squeeze out a single breath. "Don't tell me you *can't* — not when you haven't tried. Take that tone with me again, and I'll stuff your tongue so far down your gullet that you'll be talking out your gut."

Kael believed her.

When she released him, he went reluctantly to the tree. Though he was certain it was going to be a complete waste of time, he threw his body into its calloused side. He slammed up against it a few times, bruising his shoulder and rattling his skull. But the tree didn't budge. "There. You see? I told you it couldn't be done."

Gwen shook her head as she stalked past him. "Worthless."

For some reason, the craftsmen were staring at him as if he really *had* knocked the tree over. Their mouths hung out the bottom of their painted faces and they exchanged wide-eyed looks.

The skin on either side of Griffith's stripe of hair burned red at their mutterings. "You have to try harder," he whispered to Kael.

"How do I do that?"

"I don't know. You just ..."

Griffith reached inside one of his furry pockets and drew out a blue stone. It was perfectly round and rather small — perhaps only a quarter the size of his palm. Kael watched in amazement as the stone rolled between his fingers, weaving over and under in complicated patterns.

"You have to be stronger than the tree."

"Believe me — I'd *like* to be stronger than the tree. But I'm not," Kael said.

"You are," Griffith insisted. "I know you are —"

"Why don't you show the Wright how it's done, brother?" Gwen called. Sometime while they'd been talking, she'd started to climb. Now she was perched high in the branches of the tree, feet balanced one behind the other and arms stretched across the limbs on either side. She looked as

184

comfortable as if she reclined in one of Lysander's cushy chairs.

Griffith's face brightened immediately. "I can? Really?"

He whooped when she nodded.

As Griffith marched up to the tree, Kael crossed his arms. He was determined not to fall for it. Sure, he'd seen Gwen kill a bear with a rock, and she *had* sent him flying through the Hall doors. But the idea of a child knocking down a monstrous tree was completely different. He was certain it was altogether impossible.

Griffith looked tiny beside the tree — hardly any larger than the scales of its bark. He took a deep breath and stretched his arms out in front of him. For a moment, he held them poised before the tree's trunk like a knight guarded against his opponent. Slowly, the craftsmen stopped their tittering and fell silent. Then with a cry, he lunged.

His palms slammed into the tree and he bounced back hard. Kael expected the wildmen to give up their joke. But instead, Griffith lunged again. Three times he struck the tree, and three times he was knocked away. Then on the fourth blow, something strange happened.

There was a rustling sound as needles began to tremble across its limbs. His next blow shook the smallest twigs. Soon the air was filled with groaning as the branches rocked back and forth. The tree's top waved as the thunder of his blows traveled up the trunk.

Griffith kept pounding. He slammed himself into the tree until his skin was red with the effort. The craftsmen watched silently, their eyes burning as if they willed him on. Gwen held tightly to the branches as the tree shook harder, the white edges of her grin cut out sharply against the swirling lines of her paint.

Griffith timed each blow carefully. He forced the tree to tremble harder, catching it at just the right bend. When the weight of its top put too much strain on its bottom, the tree could hold itself no longer. At last, it fell.

A sound like the sky splitting into two cracked across Kael's ears. He watched, breathless, as the tree bent too far

185

backwards and the trunk snapped in half. He threw an arm over his face as jagged bits of wood spewed from its flesh. The tree groaned the whole way down; its branches seemed to grasp helplessly at neighboring trees — trying one last time to catch itself. But nothing could stop its fall.

Gwen let out a wild cry and wedged herself into her perch, holding on as the force of the earth tried to rip her free. With a rumble Kael felt in his chest, the tree crashed to the ground. Black clouds of birds erupted from the woods. A storm of dust, rocks, and shattered limbs exploded upwards before raining back down, leaving nothing but silence in its wake.

Dust hung thick in the air; the murky tendrils curled away like curtains as they settled. The quiet was so thick that Kael could hear little bits of soil tinkling as it rolled down between the scales of bark. When the dust finally cleared, he saw the great tree lying on its side — felled, with spines broken all down its back.

And he could find no words.

Gwen stepped out from behind the curtain of dust. She walked along the massive trunk with the steady legs of a pirate at sea, eyes bright behind her paint. She swung from the branches and landed among the wildmen without a sound.

Kael could hardly think to speak. "How ...?"

"Because nobody ever told him he couldn't," Gwen said simply. "Children are dreamers, but men have doubts. If you shut your mouth and try, you might grow to be one-fourth the warrior my brother is."

Kael bit his lip. He remembered the days when he'd been able to do extraordinary things simply by imagining them. Now it no longer seemed possible. The power he'd once had was gone — not quite lost, but misplaced somehow ... as if he knew where he ought to go, but could no longer recall which path to take to get there.

Perhaps Gwen was right: perhaps he had too many doubts. When he tried to untangle his thoughts, dark

186

memories flashed behind his eyes — Bloodfang's dying gasps, Thelred's screams ... the wings of the black beast ...

Kael wasn't sure when his doubt had begun, but as he stood staring at the toppled tree, he could feel it sitting heavily in his limbs. "How did Titus beat you?"

Gwen's smirk fell into a hard line. "He didn't beat us — he merely pushed us back. When the time comes, we'll stomp him."

"You could *stomp* him, now. You could shove down his walls, smash in his gates —"

"Let me worry about the Man of Wolves, mutt. For now, your only concern is rebuilding my village." She shoved past him to clap Griffith on the shoulder. "That was well done. Get some of the warriors together to help with the lifting — I'm going on a hunt."

"Yes, sister." Griffith waited until Gwen had clomped out of earshot before he snatched Kael by the shirt and whispered: "See? If I can do it, you can do it."

Kael didn't think he could. In fact, he didn't even know where to begin. But before he could say as much, Griffith darted back towards the village — leaving Kael alone with the craftsmen.

They'd fallen on the tree the moment it struck the ground. Now they hacked busily at the branches and peeled the tree's skin away in curling strips. He watched them for a long moment before he realized that they weren't using any tools: the wood split, cracked, and chipped beneath their bare hands.

Kael was so entranced by the rhythm of their work that several moments passed before he realized that none of the craftsmen spoke. Not a word, not even so much as a grunt or sigh left their lips. Instead, the noise of their work filled the woods like a song.

For some reason, the craftsmen's song drew him in. His hands itched madly as he watched them work — as if they knew which notes came next, and wanted very badly to join in. He'd taken several steps forward before he managed to catch himself. "How are you doing that?"

"Whispering," one of them grunted. Then he leaned to hiss at his companion: "Can you believe that? What Wright doesn't know about whispering?"

Kael tried to ignore their snickers.

He was beginning to realize that he didn't know as much as he'd thought. The only other whisperer he'd met was Morris — and he'd certainly never mentioned anything about toppling trees. He might never be able to do what Griffith had done. But maybe if he shut his mouth and tried, he could learn how to knock the walls off Titus's castle ...

*No*, he told himself, shoving the thought aside. *Don't even think it.*

Kael watched the craftsmen work for a moment and slowly began to figure it out. He remembered the day when Morris had asked him to tie a sword into a knot — how he'd imagined his hands to be hot like a forge and how the iron had bent beneath his fingers. He saw the craftsmen chopping at the wood with the sides of their hands and realized that must've been what they were doing.

Kael gave it a try. At first, he imagined his hands were sharp as an axe's blade. He swung a few times and hardly managed to chip the bark. Cutting through the tree with an axe was going to take a lot longer than he cared to wait. He needed to think of something sharper ...

That was when he thought of Harbinger.

He'd only had a chance to wield it once, but he remembered the blade well. It'd sliced through the bones and rusted armor of the Witch's army with ease. He thought of the sword's curved edge — so sharp it was practically invisible. He remembered the lightness of its weight, how it'd felt in his hand, how it moved so viciously through everything in its path.

As he concentrated, his hands began to change. The sides of his palms turned white and sharpened. He dragged them down the tree and the bark peeled off in thick, curling strips. Branches fell away with a single swipe of his hand. He worked as far as he could reach, shaving the roughness away until all that was left was the smooth white flesh beneath it.

When he was finished, he let the memory fade and dragged himself back to reality.

"How did you do that?"

Kael had attracted an audience. The craftsmen gathered around him in a half-moon, their eyes wide with interest. "I just ... I thought of the sharpest thing I could remember." Kael glanced down the tree and noticed that the craftsmen's sections were barely scraped. "What were you thinking of?"

"We learn to whisper with tools made from the shells of wynn eggs," one of them, a young woman, said.

"Of course you do," Kael muttered. "And what does a wynn egg look like, exactly?"

A boy pulled a flat bit of stone out of his pocket and held it up to Kael's face. "This is a shard of a wynn's egg. I found it in the ice caves."

It looked suspiciously like a piece of flint to Kael. "How do you know it's a wynn's egg?"

"Because if we strike it against a certain kind of stone, it sparks!" an old man crowed.

That was the moment Kael realized that Baird wasn't the only lunatic whisperer wandering around the Kingdom: he'd managed to find a whole nest of them.

He was just about to walk away when the young woman grabbed his hand. "What did you see? Teach us how to work faster."

He jerked out of her grasp. "I don't know how to teach you."

"*Show* us! That's how Setheran taught the warriors," the old man crowed again. "He showed them things — made them stronger. Oh, I would've loved to see what he saw ... but he couldn't teach us anything. He was a lousy craftsman. All brute force and not an ounce of finesse."

Kael couldn't believe what he was hearing. These people spoke about Setheran as if he was nothing extraordinary — as if they had no idea what he'd done for the Kingdom. He couldn't help but be a little curious.

"Did you really know Setheran?" When the old man nodded, he still couldn't quite grasp it. "Why would he go to the summit?"

"To be *awakened*," the young woman said impatiently. "I've heard stories of how Setheran climbed the mountains to learn from us. Thane Evan made him sleep naked in the ice caves outside our castle for a full week before he taught him anything. And he didn't get his clothes back until the day he left. You have it much easier than Setheran did," she added, frowning at his tunic. "Yet you've already complained so much more."

It seemed strange to Kael. He'd always just accepted that Setheran was great — he'd never wondered about where his strength might've come from. And he certainly never imagined him living naked in ice caves.

But *awakened* ... he'd heard that word before. It had been in the letter Baird had given the wildmen. For some reason, his insides began to twist uncomfortably.

"What do you mean Setheran wanted to be *awakened*?"

"He came to us because the ways of the whisperer had been lost in Midlan. He told us they learned from books and lessons — like common manfolk," the old craftsman said, wrinkling his nose. "By the time Setheran joined them, the whisperers of Midlan were so full of book-learning that they'd lost their imagination. They'd been hobbled by doubt! He climbed the mountains to find a way to set them free."

Kael swallowed hard. That sounded an awful lot like the way Morris had taught him to whisper — with readings and sparring practice and limits. He hadn't even wanted Kael to do any whispering without his permission. Perhaps the wildmen knew of a better way.

After what he'd seen Griffith do to that tree, he was certainly willing to try. "All right, I'm listening." He wasn't sure what to do next, so he spread his arms wide. "Awaken me."

The old craftsman grabbed his hand and mashed it against the young woman's. "Now someone take his other hand, and someone take *her* hand ..."

He went around, mashing them together until all of the craftsmen were linked, holding hands in a large circle. Kael wasn't used to being so closed in. By the time the last craftsman joined the circle, his palms were beginning to sweat. "I'm not sure this is helping anything."

"This is what Setheran always did!" the old craftsman insisted. "I remember — I was there. Now show us what you saw."

"How do I ...?"

Kael's words trailed away as a strange feeling washed over him. Slowly, he lost track of the hands twined in his. The film of sweat no longer separated them, he couldn't tell his fingers apart from anybody else's. It was if he was alone ... yet surrounded. As if he read a book while a dozen eyes watched over his shoulder.

He could see the dark silhouettes of the craftsmen gathered around him — shadows set to a background of gray. All feeling left his body and pulled apart from his skin, fleeing into the middle of the circle.

He could hear the craftsmen's thoughts like whispers in the backs of his ears. Their questions flicked across his eyes in faded pictures. He knew they were waiting for something — waiting for *him*. Waiting to listen, waiting to be shown ...

Shown. *Show them.*

Kael suddenly knew what to do. He thought carefully, drawing up an image of Harbinger. The vision appeared in the middle of the circle — *his* vision, his memory. His thoughts were no longer flat pictures that crossed behind his eyes, but living things brought alive in the center of the circle.

He could feel the craftsmen's recognition as images of Harbinger flashed by. Chills ran down their backs when he showed them how the blade felt and how fine its edges were. Their excitement thickened as they watched the sword slice through armor and bone. They followed the trail of his thoughts as if ripped by the force of the tide — creatures content to be carried along the ocean's path.

When he tried to bring Harbinger to the tree, the image wavered and the circle suddenly broke. It was like running full-tilt just to be jerked back by the belt. Kael snapped out of his vision with his teeth already bared.

"What's wrong?" he growled.

"We can't use a sword to shape trees," one of the craftsmen scoffed. "Swords are for fighting. *Tools* are for building."

"I've never carried a sword once in my whole life! War isn't our business," the young woman said.

Others murmured their agreement.

Kael couldn't believe it. They were so put off by the shape of something that they couldn't see its potential. "Whether it's a sword or an axe doesn't make any difference. Focus on the blade."

"How can —?"

"Just pay attention," Kael said shortly. "I'm going to show you."

He grabbed the hands on either side of him and the craftsmen followed suit, linking reluctantly until the circle was whole once more.

Kael focused on the blade, showing them how he imagined his flesh changing from skin to the strange material of Harbinger. He dragged them through every small step. Fighting against the rifts of their doubt was like weaving down a hallway that was all corners: his shoulder struck the edges and bounced him back, but somehow he managed to grind himself forward.

Finally, understanding settled about them like a cloak. Kael felt it slide into place and seal one perfect idea away. Something told him his task was finished. He let his hands fall to his sides, and the world rushed in.

The craftsmen blinked as if they'd just stepped into the light. They smiled and flexed their hands, the last of Kael's memories flickering behind their eyes. The old craftsman broke from the circle and stepped up to the tree alone. He held a hand poised over a branch as big around as a man's waist. Then with a cry, he brought it down.

The craftsmen let out a collective howl when the branch struck the ground, hewed in a single perfect stroke. They fell on the tree and began to strip it of bark and limbs, eyes bright by the fury of their work — hands sharpened with the things they'd learned.

Kael watched without really seeing them. His mind was consumed by the memories of what he'd just experienced in the circle: being a part of the craftsmen and yet somehow at their middle.

As completely impossible as it sounded, he'd felt more alive in that moment than ever before. In fact, it made him feel as if he'd lived his whole life ridiculously — as if he'd been trying to put both feet through one leg of his trousers all this time and had only just figured out how to wear them right.

Now as he watched the craftsmen work, he realized something had changed. He wasn't quite sure what that something was. He didn't know if he'd ever be able to find a word to describe it.

But for some reason, it felt like a new beginning.

# CHAPTER 18
## GROGNAUT THE BANDIT LORD

"Are you entirely certain we're headed the right way?" Lysander said.

Jonathan whirled around — so suddenly that the torch he wielded spewed a tail of sparks into the night. "Of course I'm certain! Bartholomew's Pass is the quickest way into the Valley. Any bloke with half a brain could tell you that."

Lysander's chin trailed down the jagged line that split the mountain into two — but his feet stayed planted. "Shouldn't we at least wait until dawn?"

"Nah, there's no point. It's blacker than the gap between Morris's front teeth in there. Day or night'll make you no difference."

The army of pirates and giants stopped behind Lysander. They traced the narrow opening with their eyes; their faces mirrored the captain's worry. Only Nadine seemed indifferent.

She shoved her way out of their ranks and snatched the torch from Lysander's hand. "Go back to your ship if you are afraid. I would hate for you to soil yourselves," she said as she passed.

Declan was next to shove through.

"You aren't really going in there, are you?" Lysander called.

"I'm sure as summer's breath not going to let that tiny terror go anywhere I'm not." Then he raised his voice. "What if she needs someone to shove her off a cliff and I'm not around to do it?"

"I would crack your head in two were it not made of stone," Nadine shot back.

"Yeh, and if you could reach it." Declan trudged off after her and the giants followed close behind.

Lysander hardly flinched as Morris waddled in beside him. "What are your orders, Captain?"

When he didn't respond, Morris nudged him with the flat of his arm. "I'm sorry, what was that?"

"We're all waiting for your orders, Captain."

"Ah, right." Lysander straightened the collar of his shirt and wrapped one hand tightly around the Lass's whittled hilt. "Well, dogs — we've come this far. So I suppose we should just ... press on, then."

"You heard the Captain. Move your nubs, you louts!" Morris called back.

They replied with a shaky chorus of *ayes*.

Lysander had barely managed a few halting steps when Eveningwing shot past him. "I'll watch the skies!" he said. He burst into his feathers and took off — leaving his clothes behind.

"Why don't you enchant that lad some breeches or something?" Morris grunted as he stooped to gather Eveningwing's things.

"I've tried. He won't wear them," Jake said distractedly. He had his palms pressed together and was steadily pulling them apart. A very bright something glowed between his hands.

"Why in high tide not? Does he *like* flitting around in his skin?"

"I haven't perfected the spell. His trousers shrink a little each time he changes, and he doesn't like to ..."

Jake's sentence trailed off as he pulled his hands apart. Something like a large soap bubble popped free of his palms and floated into the air above them — putting off such a glare of yellow light that the pirates staggered backwards.

Morris threw a stubby arm over his face. "Put that thing out! It's burning the backs of my eyes."

"No, leave it." Lysander's pace quickened as the light touched the earth around them, illuminating the jagged walls. "It'll guide us through the Pass."

195

"It could guide a blind man's soul through the under-realm," Morris retorted.

Jake took a few steps, smiling to himself as the light followed overhead. "Well, this worked better than I expected ... though you probably shouldn't look at it directly," he added after a moment. "Oh, and nobody touch it — just in case."

Morris's eyes widened in their pouches. "Just in case of what?"

But Jake didn't answer.

They walked for an hour or so between the high reaches of the Pass before they came across a small mass of graves. The graves were little more than hills of rock arranged in a row on the side of the path. One grave was stacked a little higher than the rest. Trinkets covered the stones piled at its top: jewels, coin, and little glass baubles shimmered in the torchlight.

"Take a look there, would you?" Morris croaked when he spotted them.

The pirates clustered at his back. "Who'd leave all that loot behind?" one of them said.

"It isn't loot — it's a merchant's burial. Caravans pass through here all the time. They must've stopped to pay their respects." Jonathan's customary grin had vanished. He stood half-turned from the graves, eyes fixed on the sheer wall in front of him.

"Why do they cover their graves with jewels?" Nadine said.

Declan shrugged. "Seems mightily strange to me. Jewels don't grow, you can't eat them —"

"Not everything is about eating!" Nadine said.

Lysander knelt at the grave. His hand moved slowly, hovering just above the tops of the trinkets. "Who's buried here?"

"It's my fault!"

The whole party spun in the direction of the cry and saw Eveningwing crouched above them. He was slumped over a boulder — his face buried in his arms and his bare chest pressed against the boulder's skin. When he lifted his head, his eyes went straight to Jonathan.

Tears streamed from them unchecked.

"It isn't your fault. It isn't anybody's fault but the King's," Jonathan said.

Eveningwing shook his head. "No — it's mine. I found you. I followed you. I ... I told the King where you were. I led them here!"

"You led who where?" Lysander said. His eyes went from a sobbing Eveningwing to a scowling Jonathan. "What is he talking about?"

"*You* set those monsters on us?" Jonathan said.

"I had no choice! The King's spell was too strong. I didn't want to," Eveningwing pleaded. "I had followed you for days before. Your music made me smile. I remembered your faces —"

"Yeah, and once we were trapped inside the Pass, you set the wolves on us," Jonathan spat. He made as if to turn away, then turned back. "They ripped his heart out!"

"I know. I saw —"

"You *watched*!" Jonathan hurled his torch at the rocks above Eveningwing's head. It struck the wall and exploded in a shower of sparks. "You watched, and you did absolutely nothing about it."

"I wanted to help. But the spell was too —"

"You're an animal! A bloody barbarian, that's all you are — because no decent human being would've ever sat by and watched an innocent man be slaughtered."

"That's enough," Lysander said sharply. He tried to get between them, but Jonathan spun out of his grasp.

"That grave belongs to Garron the Shrewd — your wife's father, in case you didn't know. And he was a hundred times the man that *creature* will ever be." Jonathan spat the word. His dark eyes burned with a fire that likely would've set the whole Pass ablaze, had it escaped.

The halfhawk shrank miserably beneath it. His head fell below his shoulders like the curling of parchment caught in the flames. He pressed the heels of his hands against his streaming eyes and whispered: "I'm sorry."

Then without another word, he sunk into his feathers.

"Come back, lad! Just give him a breath to cool off," Morris called, but Eveningwing didn't stop. He shot out of the light and disappeared into the thick black ceiling above them.

Lysander grabbed Jonathan by the front of the shirt. "When he returns, you *will* apologize."

Jonathan swatted his hand aside. "Sorry, mate. I'm not apologizing to that thing."

He made to stomp off when Jake stepped into his path. "He's telling the truth. There's no way he could've fought the King's spell. He couldn't help it —"

Jonathan shoved him. "What do you know about it?"

"I've lived it."

The fiddler's pace slowed under the lash of Jake's reply, but he recovered quickly. The whole party watched in silence as he marched away.

"Go. Follow him," Lysander said with a wave of his hand.

Nadine and the giants went first, followed closely by the pirates. Jake wandered along at the rear, his yellow orb lighting up their backs.

"Aren't you coming, Captain?" Morris said.

Lysander sighed heavily. "I'll be along in a moment. Go on without me. That's an order," he added, when Morris hesitated.

"All right, all right. No need to go snapping at me," Morris grumbled as he wandered off. "There's something odd about this place, I tell you. It's turning us against each other, sucking all the sunshine from under our boots. Gives me the shivers, it does ..."

As Morris's muttering grew faint, Lysander knelt at Garron's grave. The light from Jake's orb still shone brightly enough to illuminate the treasures decorating its top.

Lysander's hand clenched at his side. "Ah, I don't suppose you'd remember me. I was only a little thing when we met, and you were neck-deep in glory. I'm afraid I don't have much to offer you, either. It seems strange for a pirate to leave a friend something as silly as gold. But I can offer you this."

He drew the Lass from its sheath and dragged the edge across his palm. Dark red lines bloomed from between his fingers. They slid from his fist and spattered on the rocks, glittering alongside the trinkets.

"I'll love her till the day I die, and I'll defend her with my life — even if she gives me nothing but daughters. I'm sorry," he said with a smile. "You probably didn't find that too terribly funny, but I'm scared out of my wits about becoming a father. I'm nervous as a man tied to the bow of a sinking ship —"

"Are you coming, Captain?" Jake called. He peered at the graves from over the top of his spectacles. "Who are you talking to?"

Lysander sprang to his feet and thrust his sword back into his belt. "Nobody. I was just, ah, paying my respects."

*******

At last, the long dark of Bartholomew's Pass gave way to the cheery green of the Valley. The pirates and the giants stepped out from the shattered gouge in the mountains with a sigh of relief.

Warmth and the bright yellow sun greeted them; thick carpets of grass swayed on either side of the road. The pirates smiled and stretched their arms high overhead, drinking in the calm beauty before them.

But the giants struggled magnificently.

The rolling lands of the Valley were quite a bit different from the flatness of the plains, and it wasn't long before the giants' steps grew heavy. They panted as they trudged up each new hill — and complained heartily the whole way down.

"It makes the journey twice as long, having to climb up and over. Somebody ought to flatten this mess out!"

"Take a look there, would you? They've done their planting all along the bumps. Their crops are growing sideways!"

"Plains mother, I'd hate to be the poor clodder who had to plow my way up that."

"I'd rather be him than the clodder who had to plow his way *down*. You'd have to run mightily fast to keep the blade off your heels."

They grumbled for three days straight before Nadine finally put her spear down. "Enough! You would chase the crows away with all of your squawking. These are not tall — this is nothing. How will you ever climb the mountains if you cannot even climb a hill without losing your breath?"

"I haven't lost it," Declan panted from behind her. "It's just a little short, is all. And you ought not to stick your head where it doesn't belong, mote —"

"*Mot!*"

"Yeh, well when we need to learn about sand-raking, we'll ask you." He held up one thick finger. "But farming is a giant's business."

Nadine raised her chin. "My people carved their farms from a mountain's flesh. If you saw how steeply they sat, your large hearts would burst with shock. It does not matter how flat the land is. It only matters how *good* it is." And with that, she strode away.

"I think she may have had a point there, General," one of the giants panted.

Declan watched after her, eyes hidden beneath the shadow of his brow. "Yeh, and the point is we'd better get moving. I'm not letting some cricket-legged sandbeater walk out in front of me."

Though the giants certainly did their fair share of stomping, they made good time. Jonathan led the way at his usual loping pace, whistling a horrible, off-key ballad in time with his stride — while the pirates spent most of their time swiping fresh rations from obliging fields. When night fell, they camped off the road and slept beneath the stars.

Or rather, they *tried* to sleep. But Jake's light made things difficult.

"My spells for lamplight never quite worked," he explained. "They always just wound up becoming fire bursts — which of course burn very brightly, but can be rather ... destructive, in closed spaces. This is a spell of my own invention: a blinding spell for light, a shielding spell for containment, and a some very minor levitation."

"That's all well and good, lad. But couldn't you at least snuff it out while we're sleeping?" Morris grumbled. He lay on his back with a stocky arm thrown over his eyes, frowning through his beard.

Jake fiddled with his gloves. "Ah, I'm afraid that's the problem. I haven't exactly figured out how to take it down."

"You mean it's stuck up there?" one of the giants said.

They laughed when he nodded.

"That's nothing to chuckle about," Lysander said severely. His eyes flicked to the shadows around them. "We'll be spotted for miles. You might as well write our names in the sky while you're at it. I'd hate to catch our enemies by surprise."

"This is the Valley, mate. The only trouble you're likely to run into around here is a few tinheads from Midlan or a ragged bunch of bandits," Jonathan said. "Either way, it's nothing a stomp of giants couldn't handle."

They grunted in agreement.

"So just relax and try to work that bunch out of your fancy white knickers, will you?"

Lysander frowned at him. "Keep that up, fiddler, and I'll replace you with a map."

Jonathan grinned.

"Why do you not simply knock it down?" Nadine muttered from under her blanket.

Jake straightened his spectacles. "Well, that's complicated — or rather, it could cause some very serious complications. At the very least, you could expect some discomfort."

Lysander raised his brows. "Such as ...?"

"Permanent blindness to anybody within a quarter mile who's got his eyes open. But if we're lucky, maybe only temporary blindness."

"Nobody touch that thing," Declan commanded. "Just cover your wee heads and sleep tight. If anything wanders into camp, leave it to the giants."

After a few days of an empty sky, Eveningwing finally reappeared. They caught glimpses of his great wings as he soared behind the rolling clouds. Sometimes he flew so low that his shadow crossed their boots. At night, he roosted in the trees at the edge of camp. But nothing anybody said could convince him to come down.

"You need to apologize," Lysander insisted.

Jonathan's whistling had stopped the moment Eveningwing returned. Now he spent nearly as much time glaring up at the sky as he did watching the road. "I've got nothing to say."

"He couldn't help it."

"He knew what he was doing."

"I'm not so sure he did."

"Well, he sure remembered it clearly enough. Look," Jonathan stopped, and the merry glint of his eyes turned dark, "I know you think good of him. And I know you'd like to believe he's human, but he's not. Garron warned us a long time ago to never trust a barbarian. He was the one who convinced Countess D'Mere to keep them pinned in the swamps, after all. He wouldn't have done that if he didn't think it was for the best. And now I see why."

"There's good and evil among the shapechangers just like there is among men. The curse might've forced him to do some dreadful things, but Eveningwing is a good hawk. Give him a chance to prove himself," Lysander said quietly.

But Jonathan didn't relent. If anything, his eyes only grew darker. "There's honor among humans, but animals think only of themselves. When the time comes, you'll see it. You might think he's your friend now, Captain — but he's going to do whatever he can to save his own skin. Even if that means trampling you flat." Jonathan watched Eveningwing's

202

looping path for a moment before he muttered: "He's probably got some sort of trap in mind for us. If he wasn't flying out of bow range, I would've already shot him down."

Lysander said no more after that, and Jonathan seemed content to shove it aside. Slowly, the merry glint came back to his eyes and he spent less time glaring at the clouds.

But if Eveningwing's shadow ever crossed overhead, his face would darken quickly.

*******

The pirates and the giants traveled for days without incident, rarely meeting another soul on the road. Then one afternoon, Eveningwing startled them with a screech.

"What is it?" Nadine called up to him.

Morris grunted. "Eh, he's probably just after a rabbit."

Lysander's chin jutted out as he traced the hawk's frantic pattern of loops. "No, we worked that signal out before we left. It means there's trouble up ahead. Form ranks, dogs!" he barked, and the pirates fell in behind him.

Declan rapped his scythe across his breastplate. "Giants to the front! Keep those wee pirates out of harm's way."

"That won't be necessary. We're quite all right on our own," Lysander said.

He led his men through the gaps between giants, forming an uneven mass of bodies that sloped off either edge of the road. Lysander and Declan marched side by side, each trying to out-order the other.

"Easy does it, dogs. We don't want to give ourselves away —"

"Easy does nothing. Pound your feet, clodders! Let them hear what's coming!"

"Let them have a chance to arm themselves, you mean? Whatever happened to the element of s —?"

The rest of what Lysander had to say was swallowed up by the ear-rattling thud of the giants' march. While the men tried to out-yell each other, Nadine broke away and sprinted up the hill. Her mouth fell open when she reached the top.

"What is it, lass?" Morris called.

Nadine waved them forward. "Come quickly!"

Lysander and Declan sprinted to her side, their armies close behind. They spread out along the top of the hill and stared down at the land below.

The giants fell silent. The pirates swore.

A line of people filled the road beneath them, winding back as far as the eye could see. Dirt rose in clouds behind their shuffling feet. Many of them staggered under the weight of hefty rucksacks. They led livestock by their reins — some pulled carts filled with what looked to be all of their possessions.

It was an endless, miserable exodus: men and women in tattered clothes, gasping between coughs, staring through glassy eyes. Several limped along in the ditches, their feet wrapped in bloody cloths. But no matter how they struggled, the whole broken line moved stubbornly towards the Pass.

Behind them, the green of the Valley gave way to ashen gray, and black smoke overtook the horizon.

"Plains mother," Declan hissed. "Who's done this to them? Was it Titus?"

Morris shook his head. "He doesn't burn the land like that. Oh, he'll level their homes and murder their children, but I've never heard of him wrecking good soil. He's always thinking about what he can gain, see." He waved a stocky arm at the gray horizon. "There's nothing to gain from this."

When the people at the head of the line spotted the army standing above them, they slowed. Their eyes widened and they muttered to one another. A few reluctantly drew their swords.

"Get away from the road. You are frightening them," Nadine said. She shooed the pirates into the ditches and made the giants stand a good distance further.

Slowly, the line began to move again. A man dressed in leather armor walked at the head of the tattered crowd. He used his sword for a cane, digging the point into the earth as he plodded up the hill. His other arm was wrapped in a bloody sling.

"Hang tight a minute, gents. I'll see what I can find out." Jonathan slipped up to the armored man, wearing his most charming smile. "Ahoy there, mate. Mind if I walk with you a bit?"

While he talked to the armored man, the rest of the party watched in disbelief as the line of people trudged by.

"It's mostly Valley folk, but there are some mountain folk here, too," Morris said as his watery eyes flicked across some heads of flaming red hair.

"There are children with them," Nadine moaned.

She watched as a clump of redheaded children stumbled along behind their mother, clinging to her skirts. Exhaustion ringed their eyes and made their mouths sag. They seemed able to stand only by the will of their tiny legs.

"We must do something. We cannot let them suffer." Nadine took a step towards them, but Jake held her back.

"We *will* do something," he said quietly. "These people have a clear path to the seas — they'll soon have food and a safe place to sleep. We're going to guard their backs." His thin fingers tightened about her shoulder. "We're going to make sure they make it to safety."

"Aye. And the less they have to do with us, the better," Morris agreed. "What we're planning is treason, in case you've forgotten. They're going to want to pass us fast and forget us quickly."

While the others murmured to each other, Declan said nothing. He stood with his thick arms crossed over his chest. A shadow cloaked his eyes.

Suddenly, a crazed laugh drew their eyes back to the armored man. He cackled hysterically and slapped Jonathan on the arm before he went back to plodding his way up the hill.

"Well? What did he say?" Lysander said as Jonathan came back to them.

"I knew that fellow. He was one of the guards at Crow's Cross — I used to swindle him pretty good at cards. But I think he might've ... cracked." Jonathan frowned as he glanced over his shoulder.

Lysander raised his brows. "Cracked how?"

"You know ... he was crazed. Running on rusted wheels. A few rungs short —"

"Yes, yes I know what *cracked* means," Lysander said impatiently. "But *why* was he cracked? What happened to him?"

"Was it Titus?" Declan called.

Jonathan shook his head. "All he kept saying was that some fellow named *Grognaut* did this. Grognaut the Bandit Lord."

# CHAPTER 19
## THE CADDOCS

Kael spent the next several days learning everything he could about carpentry. He cut planks from logs, shaped chairs from branches, and carved stories into wood. When the craftsmen thought he was ready, they taught him how to build a house.

It was an exacting task. Every notch and peg had to fit together perfectly. Every layer of the wall had to sit firmly on the one beneath it, and every crack had to be sealed to keep out the winter frost. Though the building was certainly complicated, it was actually the *sealing* that gave them the most trouble.

The craftsmen used a thick paste to set the logs of each house together — a sticky resin that dried quickly and set like stone. And unfortunately, it was one of the few tasks Baird could do.

He terrorized them constantly. The craftsmen's song broke whenever he wandered in; the steady rhythm of their work cantered off-pace and dissolved into chaos. Baird wielded his mop and bucket every bit as effectively as a dragon's flame, stirring up panic wherever he went.

Planks were set crookedly, doors got stuck to walls. More than once, a craftsman had his feet glued to the floor. Kael looked away for five minutes and Baird had managed to slather a generous portion of resin to the wrong end of an unset plank. When Griffith tried to lift it, the plank stuck to his fingers. They had to spend several minutes chiseling through a thick layer of paste just to get his hands free.

Kael begged Gwen to put the beggar-bard somewhere — *anywhere* — else, but she refused. "He's a craftsman, so he'll do a craftsman's work."

"But he's blind," Kael said evenly. "He can't *see* to do a craftsman's work."

She shoved him aside. "I don't have time to solve all of your petty little problems, mutt. Figure it out for yourself."

It had become clear very early on that he could expect no help from the wildmen: the craftsmen didn't seem to know much of anything beyond their carpentry, and the warriors were downright mean. So Kael knew that if he wanted to do something about Baird, he'd have to figure it out for himself.

He was working on digging a knot out of one of the logs when he suddenly had an idea. He remembered what Griffith had said about how healers always cried around wounds, yet Kael had never cried. Perhaps he hadn't been healing like a healer at all ...

Perhaps he'd been healing like a craftsman.

It was a wild idea, a single loose thread that'd popped free of a tangled mass, and Kael tugged on it carefully. When he sealed a wound, he thought about the flesh and bone like clay — a material he knew well and could manipulate easily. Was it really that difficult to believe that instead of *healing*, he'd simply been putting the skin *back together*? No, it wasn't difficult. In fact, it made perfect sense. And if he could turn *flesh* into clay ...

Kael stopped. He stood and went to the nearest section of wall, nearly tripping over his boots in the rush. Once he had his hands placed firmly on the seam between logs, he concentrated.

*You are clay.*

Slowly, the unrelenting flesh of the wood began to soften. He held onto his memories of clay and kneaded them into the logs, forcing it through the first several inches of pine. When they were soft, he pulled them together. He dragged their skin over one another until they fused into one solid plank.

By the time he came out of his trance, he was sweating — but it was a good sweat, the sort of damp that used to

208

cover his brow after dragging the first line in a field. He still had plenty left to give.

"Come here, Baird." Kael grabbed the beggar-bard before he could cause any more trouble and plucked the mop and bucket from his hands. Then he placed them against the sealed logs.

His brows arced high over his bandages. "Something odd has happened here. What magic is this? What strange trickery?"

"It isn't magic, you lunatic. It's whispercraft."

"Whispercraft ...?" Baird gasped. "It was Kael the Wright, wasn't it? He was here! Lead me to him straight away!"

Kael sighed. "All right, come with me."

The wildmen gathered around him eagerly when he called. It had been several days since he'd shown them Harbinger, and the memories of their circle plagued him like an itch. He wanted badly to go there again, to feel the awakening he'd felt before.

Excitement coursed through the craftsmen's hands as they joined. It raced all around the circle and came back to Kael in jolts. He was vaguely aware of the warriors who gathered behind him, watching in interest. But their presence slipped far into the distance as Kael drifted away.

He knew what to expect, this time — the sensation of his body being one place while his mind was in another no longer felt strange. His thoughts flared to life in the circle's middle ... but they didn't glow for long.

The craftsmen were confused. They didn't understand how one material could become another. Their doubt put knots between them. Kael felt his grip slipping as the circle bunched, dragging his mind kicking and screaming back inside his body.

When he could hold it no longer, their connection broke. "You have to trust me," he growled when the world came back.

"It isn't possible," one of them said. "Wood can be burned, carved or chipped. Its shape can be changed, but it can't become clay."

The others mumbled in agreement, and Kael knew what he had to do. "Get together again. Move!" he snapped when they hesitated.

He'd learned from watching Gwen that about the only way to get the wildmen's attention was to shout at them — as if the loudness of his voice was a measure of how serious he was. And he must've sounded very serious, indeed: the craftsmen joined hands immediately.

This time when he went to the middle of the circle, Kael showed them proof. He drew up his memories of the day he'd spent healing them in the hospital. They watched the insides of his head as he cleaned and sealed every gash, how he snapped bones together and smoothed away their scars. They could see how his hands worked while his mind held memories of clay. Many of them saw their own wounds healed.

And they could doubt no longer.

When he showed them what he'd done to the wood, they accepted it. A new corner of their minds opened up — revealing a power they never knew they'd had. The possibilities rose like floodwaters and spilled over the banks. They were ready to work, eager to put their skills to the test. So Kael released them.

The craftsmen went immediately to the walls. Their hands ran up and down, dragging the edges of the logs together, smoothing them until they became one solid mass of wood. Their lips moved all the while they worked, alive with excited words that Kael couldn't hear.

When they had one full section of wall done, the craftsmen stepped away. Griffith slapped a hand against it. "Fate's fingers — we aren't going to have to worry about the frost anymore," he said with a grin.

They didn't even have to cut notches into the next log: the warriors lifted it into place, and the craftsmen sealed it together. Then the wildmen howled and beat their chests, dancing around like they'd won a great victory.

Kael knew they could go on like that for hours if he didn't stop them quickly. "All right, all *right* — back to work! We've got a lot to do."

And with no small amount of grumbling, they drifted away.

Kael was so busy glaring at them that it took him a moment to realize that Baird hadn't left the circle. He held his knobby hands out in front of him, his mouth a black hole beneath his rags.

Kael touched his shoulder lightly. "Do you think that'll work better than paste?"

A little gasp escaped Baird's throat before he burst: "I — I could see again! For a moment, I could see them! Wonderful colors, alive in the caress of shadow and light ... I'd forgotten what a gift the eyes can be. But Kael the Wright has reminded me." His voice dropped to a whisper. "Who is this man who can bring color to the dark? Who bids flesh to mend and molds the trees to his will?"

"I'm not sure. But he probably isn't nearly as great as you think he is," Kael said roughly. "Now come on — we've got crafting to do."

He tried to go back to his work, but found himself watching Baird out of the corner of his eye, instead. The beggar-bard traced his way around the walls — there wasn't a crack his knobby fingers couldn't find.

And all the while he worked, his mouth stayed fixed in an open grin.

*******

"Follow me, young man. I know the way!"

Baird had latched onto Kael's tunic when they'd finished their work. He'd prattled along behind him the whole way to dinner. But the moment they stepped inside the Hall, the beggar-bard took the lead.

He marched boldly into the mass of wildmen, swinging one arm about him and dragging Kael along with the other. They bounced and bumped their way though the crowd until they finally arrived at a table dressed with a wild boar.

"I smelled him the moment we entered. The muck and spiny bristles have given way to the sweet flesh beneath. He was well-fed and fleet — the perfect blend of lean and grease. Hmm," Baird slapped his hands together excitedly as they sat, "yes, he'll do nicely!"

For once, Kael agreed.

He wanted nothing more than to tear into his dinner, but the wildmen had a strange ritual: none of them would start eating until after Gwen had entered. So Kael was forced to wait.

"You're in for it now, whisperer," Kyleigh said as she sat beside him.

She gave him a look that made his stomach stop mid-grumble and flip onto its side. "Why am I in for it?"

Before she could answer, the door slammed open and Gwen marched in. Half a bear pelt hung off her back like a cape, the massive front claws wound in a clasp at her neck.

It seemed just about every evening Gwen had a new animal to add to her collection. She'd stalked around in wolf, bear, badger, fox, and nearly every other sort of beast. But strangely enough, the one creature she'd never reduced to boots was a lion — which must've been good news for Silas.

Kael was rather surprised when the halfcat had first appeared to him — so surprised that he'd jumped and nearly broken a finger in the trap he'd been trying to set. But Silas had been far from remorseful.

"I'll tell you the same thing I told the dragoness — the wildmen believe I'm nothing more than a common beast, and I want it to stay that way," he'd growled. "If you cross me, Marked One, I will devour you from the outside in ... beginning with your fingers."

Kael had no intention of crossing him. After Silas had kept them from being cornered by the hounds, he supposed

212

shutting his mouth was the least he could do. Though he didn't have a clue as to *why* the halfcat was so intent on keeping his human shape a secret.

He supposed it must've had something to do with Gwen: Silas followed her around like a shadow. At dinner, he curled beside her boots. Tonight, his powerful legs had to move quickly to keep up with Gwen's storming pace.

"What have you done to my craftsmen?" she barked when she reached Kael's table.

Oh, *that* was what she was upset about. Well, that wasn't his fault. "I told them to pace themselves, but they wouldn't listen," Kael said.

A trick he'd thought would make the building go by faster had actually ground it to a halt. The craftsmen had insisted on trying their newfound powers out on absolutely everything: they'd flattened branches into shingles, twisted solid pieces of wood into furniture, and bent the doorways into arches — simply because they'd *always wondered what it would be like to have a door with no corners on top.*

The warriors didn't help matters, either. They goaded their fellow wildmen into doing all sorts of ridiculous things. Kael had to yell at three separate craftsmen who were braiding rocks together instead of working. Then while he was trying to concentrate on fixing the roof, one of them had snuck up behind him and sealed his boot to the shingles.

Kael's next step had jerked him backwards, and he lost his footing. He wound up being trapped upside down, half-hanging from the roof, until Griffith finally wrenched him free.

The wildmen might've been colossal pains most of the day, but Kael had gotten the last laugh. As he looked around the Hall, he realized several of the craftsmen were absent from dinner. The few that remained were either passed out in the middle of their plates or very near to it. They stared through puffy eyes and clamped hands to their ears, wincing at every small sound.

"I warned them. I *told* them they'd get headaches if they kept on like that," Kael insisted.

But Gwen's neck only burned redder. She grabbed Kael by the roots of his hair. "My village had better not sit in ruins all summer while you fool about. Keep them on task, or you'll answer to me." She twisted his curls roughly before shoving his head away.

Silas drifted along behind her as she marched for the back of the Hall — stopping to hiss at Kyleigh as he passed.

Kael felt as if he'd just been beaten over nothing. "So while she's off running through the woods all day, *I* get to be the one in charge of keeping her people on task. Shouldn't that be the Thane's job?"

"It should be," Kyleigh said, leaning around him to make a face at Silas.

Kael didn't exactly feel like she was paying attention.

"You did good today," Griffith said as he slid in across from them. "Honestly — two houses a day is a good pace for the craftsmen."

"Well, we could've had the whole village done by now if they'd stop digging rounded windows into everything," Kael muttered, rubbing the sore spot Gwen had left on his scalp.

The tables in the Hall formed something like a rectangle with a large, empty space in the middle. Gwen's table sat at the back near the fire pit. The wall behind it was covered in the snarling heads of beasts. Her chair was adorned with designs that made it look as if it housed a dragon — with its high back carved into an image of the dragon's head and the arms chiseled to look like a set of massive claws.

Though it was certainly a menacing beast, at second glance Kael wasn't certain it *was* a dragon. The beast's horns curled backwards instead of up, and it didn't seem to have any wings. The designs on its torso made it look as if it had a chest full of hair. Perhaps it was supposed to be one of the *wynns* the wildmen kept talking about.

He was still trying to figure it out when Gwen stepped in front of the chair, blocking his view. The wildmen rose with their Thane and held their cups high. Kael scrambled to mirror them.

"Fate's die has fallen in our favor once more, my wildmen," Gwen declared, her voice ringing through the Hall. "We've lived to see another day. May we live to see many more."

It wasn't a celebration, and it certainly wasn't one of Uncle Martin's toasts. Kael hadn't figured out what it was — he just knew it meant they would get to eat.

After they'd taken a drink from their cups, dinner began. The wildmen passed their plates around in a circle, each scooping a portion of whatever dish sat in front of him until every plate was full.

"What a glorious feast!" Baird cried. Then he began shoveling roast pig into his mouth with both hands.

"Have you figured out the caddocs?" Griffith said around a large chunk of boiled goose egg.

Kael thought he had.

The wildmen were thrilled to have a healer among them once again — not for the fact that it would make their lives any easier, but because it had given them the chance to revive the ancient tradition of *caddocs*.

From what he could gather, there were often ice storms at the summit. The storms raged so fiercely and for so many days that Thane Cadwalader had come up with a way to both entertain his people and keep his warriors sharp: fearsome skirmishes designed to push the battlers to their limits.

Kael had gotten an up-close look at the caddocs during his first dinner with the wildmen. He'd been deep into his food when the warrior sitting beside him had flung the icy contents of his cup directly into the face of the warrior across from him.

They'd then proceeded to stand in the middle of the Hall and beat each other with their fists — striking one blow each on the top of the head, back and forth until one of them finally lost consciousness. Kael had spent the rest of his dinner trying to flatten out the knots on their heads. But instead of learning from their bruises and easing back, the caddocs had only gotten worse.

The night before, a whole table of warriors had erupted into a fight. They smashed their benches into clubs and chased each other around, turning the Hall into their personal battlefield. The other warriors had cheered for their mates while the craftsmen beat their hands upon the tabletop in a charging rhythm.

Even Kyleigh had seemed to enjoy herself. She'd stood on their bench and hurled dishes into the fray — cheering each time she managed to smash a plate across a warrior's head.

Kael, on the other hand, thought he could've done with a little less chaos at dinner. He and Baird had taken refuge beneath their table for most of the evening — and after the battle was finished, Kael had spent several hours more trying to paste the warriors back together.

Now he choked down his food as quickly as he could, watching out of the corner of his eye for trouble.

Griffith held up a finger. "What does the water represent?"

"Washing away ill will," Kael said thickly. "It's all in good fun."

"Right. And why is it important to pay attention to the rules?"

"They're different for every caddoc."

Griffith smiled widely. "Very good. I think you're ready."

Kael nearly choked. "Ready for w —?"

An icy lash slapped across his skin. It washed over his face and slid in chilly lines down his neck. Kael blinked the water from his eyes and saw Griffith standing before him, an empty cup in his hand.

"What in Kingdom's name was that for?" Kael gasped.

"You know very well what it was for. Now get out there," Kyleigh said. She shoved him off the bench with her boot heel and Griffith dragged him into the middle of the room by his leg.

216

"It seems we have a caddoc," Gwen said, eyeing them from her table.

Kael didn't think it seemed like that at all. "He's only a child!"

"Scared, mutt?" someone hollered.

Kael's face burned as laughter filled the Hall.

"Why have you called this man to caddoc?" Gwen said.

"Because he's a filthy mutt and I plan to slap his face off," Griffith replied — with what Kael thought was an alarming amount of enthusiasm.

Gwen's finger trailed a line down her jaw and across her bluish-black lips before resting, curled, beneath her chin. "That seems reasonable."

The wildmen's excited howls drowned out Kael's protests.

Griffith spread his fingers wide. "Open-handed, and you have to keep your boots planted. If you move your feet, I get to punch you." He smiled. "Last man standing wins."

Kael couldn't believe it. This was mad — even for the wildmen. "I'm not going to fight him. I'm not going to hit a child —"

A stinging pain cut his words short. The world hadn't even come back into focus before Griffith slapped him again, jerking his head to the side.

"Keep those feet planted," he warned. "I'd hate to have to punch you."

Kael felt as if two enormous bees had stung his face. He hadn't even realized Griffith could reach him. "I don't want to — oomft!"

Griffith slapped him across the mouth. "Then you can stand there till you pass out. Makes me no difference."

A blow across his ear made Kael realize that he had to do something. He caught Griffith by the wrist and tried to put him to sleep, but the boy twisted out of his grasp.

"No healer's tricks!" he crowed, slapping him hard in the side of the head.

The skin across his jaw was beginning to swell horribly. Kael didn't want to hurt Griffith, but it was also

217

clear that the boy was never going to relent. Perhaps he could just tire him out.

He turned his skin to stone and waited. Griffith seemed to realize that he was up to something. His hands hovered out in front of him, bobbing like the heads of snakes. Kael didn't even see him move: he just heard the hollow thud as Griffith's palm struck his hardened skin.

The boy swore and wringed his hand out in front of him. Kael heard howls he recognized and knew the craftsmen were cheering for him. Out of the corner of his eye, he saw Kyleigh leaning over Baird — no doubt telling him every detail of the fight.

Griffith flexed his hand, grimacing as he studied Kael's face. "What was that?"

Gwen had her boots propped on the table and her arms resting upon the claws of her chair. "Do you withdraw your caddoc?"

Griffith shook his head.

"Then keep fighting. You're beginning to bore me."

Kael stood still as Griffith slapped him again. Once, twice, three times his hands struck Kael's stoned flesh and bounced away. But the fourth blow was different.

The thudding sound was louder. It rattled his insides a bit — like the tremor of a giant's steps. He felt a hairline crack begin to snake its way down his chin on the fifth blow, widening on the sixth and seventh.

Kael concentrated hard on fixing the cracks in the stone, but Griffith's blows came faster than he could seal. They fell in a steady barrage, jarring his thoughts before he had a chance to collect them. The fissures widened as his concentration slipped. The slaps began to sting through the cracks in his armor.

Griffith's eyes grew brighter; his blows grew stronger. A strange, twisting grin bent his mouth as he struck Kael again and again. It wasn't exactly a cruel look ...

But it wasn't a merciful one, either.

At last, Kael could hold on no longer. His concentration slipped and the chipped edges of his stoned flesh cracked, falling away just as Griffith's hand collided with his face.

One moment Kael was standing there, gritting his teeth against what he knew would be an ear-ringing slap to the jaw — and the next, he was sailing through the air.

A strange feeling coursed through his body as he landed, more shock than pain. The wildmen pounded their fists viciously against the tabletops. They whistled and howled.

Even Gwen seemed excited. She leaned forward in her chair, fists clenched on the table in front of her. Red bloomed behind the swirling lines of her paint as she cried: "The mutt has lost his footing. Finish him!"

Her face disappeared, then — blotted out by the flesh-colored lumps of steel that collided with Kael's face.

He threw up his arms, but Griffith knocked them aside. His fists pounded in a merciless beat. They slammed into Kael's nose, cut his lip against his teeth, tested the hinges of his jaw — they rattled him so badly that his ears struggled to keep pace. The crazed thunder of the wildmen's pounding faded back until all he could hear was the steady *thud* of Griffith's fists.

The pain was too much. His mind couldn't tell him how badly he ached because there were simply no words to describe it. Kael stopped fighting. He lay back and his hands fell limply to his sides.

One final blow sent him into the darkness.

# CHAPTER 20
## THE GREATEST POWER

Kael woke to the warmth of a fire and the cool grace of the morning sky. The beams of the hospital's roof were black lines against the gray dawn. The craftsmen had been working on rebuilding it since they first arrived. Though they'd set and sealed the walls, they hadn't quite gotten around to finishing the roof. Perhaps he would do that today ...

Provided he ever managed to get his face arranged back to the way it'd been before Griffith scrambled it.

"Good dawn to you, young man!"

Kael groaned as Baird stumbled over to him. He carried an earthen bowl filled with water. It sloshed out the sides as he walked, splattering onto the floor. By the time he made it over to Kael's bed, the bowl was nearly empty.

"Did you hear the news? Kael the Wright claimed a mighty victory last night. Oh yes, just when he was doomed to perish, he called forth the fires and the wind — escaping the jaws of Death! Who is this man who tames the earth's fury? To whom even flame must ans —? Oh, dear."

He'd tried to set the bowl on the edge of Kael's bed but missed fantastically. It struck the floor and cracked like an egg, spilling what was left of the water.

"What are you doing here?" Kael said as he eased himself onto his elbows.

Right now his bed was more like a table than anything: four legs with a flat space in the middle. He'd begun stitching a mattress from the skins of the animals he trapped, but hadn't quite gotten around to finishing it. At least the bed's frame kept him off the icy ground.

220

Baird smiled widely. "I've been hunting for a place to keep my treasures, and that room in the back has plenty of shelves."

Kael groaned again.

He waited until Baird had shuffled away before he tried to sit up. His face sloshed forward as he dragged himself from bed. Swollen lumps covered nearly every inch of him. They sat so heavily that when he leaned over, he swore they nearly fell through his skin.

Bile rose in his throat as his fingers traced the damage. His nose was off-center, his lip was split, and he thought his jaw might've come a little unhinged. But at least he still had all of his teeth. Kael remembered the sharp lines of his face. He knew exactly how it fit back together — he just hoped he could stay conscious through the healing.

There were a few moments when he had to stop and take a breath, but he eventually managed to get his features rearranged. The bruises faded beneath his fingers, his nose slid back into place, and his jaw was tightly hinged. Soon there was no trace of what Griffith had done to him.

Still, he didn't think he would ever forget that beating.

No sooner was he finished than the door creaked open and Griffith ducked in. "I brought you some moss ... Fate's fingers." He dropped the hairy bundle he'd been carrying and leaned to look at Kael's face. "You can't even tell." He perched at the end of the bed, hands twisting in his lap. "I just wanted to stop by and say ... uh ..."

Kael watched as he wound the blue marble through his fingers. "Why do you do that?"

He waved a hand. "It helps me keep my thoughts in order. I just wanted to say that I'm sorry — not because I beat you, but because I beat you so *badly*."

Kael thought that was about the worst apology he'd ever heard. But he nodded anyways. "It's all right. No harm done."

"Good. It's just that when I know I'm winning, I get a little excited. Though I don't have to tell *you*," he said with a wink. "You know how it is — your blood bubbles in your ears, your chest swells up and you feel like you can topple the whole blasted mountain!"

Kael had never felt like that. Not once. The few times he'd managed to do anything remotely strong, it had been because he had to — because he'd had no other choice. He didn't enjoy fighting and he certainly never remembered feeling as if he could topple a mountain.

In fact, he couldn't remember a time when he'd known for certain he was going to win.

"Your muscles must be made of stone," Griffith went on. "By the time I knocked you back, I felt like I really *had* toppled a mountain!" He slammed a fist into one of the bedposts — and the floor trembled in protest. "Oops. Gwen's always yelling at me for wrecking things. She says the control will come in time, but I'm still a little raw. Sorry, again." He slapped Kael on the knee and got to his feet.

"I'm just glad it's all done with," Kael said.

Griffith paused at the door. "Done with? Oh no, it isn't done. Look — I know you were going easy on me because I'm not as strong as you, but Gwen wants to see what you're made of. You've got to really beat me tonight. I'm not going to stop until you do," he added cheerily. Then he whipped the door open and disappeared.

Oh, for mercy's sake — Griffith thought he'd *let* him win. He had no idea that he'd truly beaten Kael to a nub. He didn't care what Gwen thought of him: there was no way he was going through that torture again.

As if that thought had summoned her, Gwen came bursting through the door. The latch slammed against the wall and shook it dangerously. "On your feet, mutt. We've got work to do."

"What sort of work?"

It was the wrong thing to say. Gwen jerked him up by the fleshy part of his arm and hurled him towards the door — throwing in a sharp kick to the rump for good measure. "We're going on a hunt."

"Well, then I'll need my bow."

222

Her fiery hair seemed to stand on end as she snarled: "I'll tell you what you need, mutt. You need to shut your mouth — or I'll clobber you so hard it'll seal your lips together. Understood?"

She shoved him out the door before he could answer.

"Farewell, young man. Breathe the air and feast upon the flowers' bloom!" Baird called from the office.

Kael had no intention of doing that. In the mountains, any flower that wasn't poisonous was thick with thorns.

He'd made to follow Gwen up the hill when he glanced back and saw something rather alarming: a trail of smoke rose from the middle of the village. When he looked closer, he saw that the Hall's roof was gone. The shingles lay scattered and the beams curled upwards like the ribs of a carcass, charred on their tips.

Kael's heart stuttered inside his chest. He tried to sprint towards it, but a thrust of Gwen's boot sent him to the ground. "It's nothing. The craftsmen'll have it fixed before supper."

"What hap —?"

"It's *nothing*." Each word was a warning of its own — a promise carved into the flint of her eyes. "Now shut your mouth and follow me."

They traveled deep into the woods, jogging until the noise of Tinnark had faded and they were surrounded by the voices of the wilds. Then quite suddenly, Gwen stopped.

She sat cross-legged upon the rocky ground and Kael sat before her, wary. He'd learned the hard way never to relax around Gwen: the moment he thought he was safe, he'd usually get a slap across the ears.

"Griffith's been hanging off my jerkin for days now, begging me to teach you to fight like a wildman. He's convinced that you're something special. But we know the truth, don't we?" she said with a smirk. "You're too far gone."

Kael sank back. He'd been thinking a lot about what the craftsmen had told him — about how the whisperers of Midlan had filled themselves with knowledge until their doubt had crippled them. The wildmen didn't seem to know much about anything. Just the other day, one of the craftsmen had asked him how he'd managed to tame the *little wooden birds* he carried across his back. And yet ... they were capable of extraordinary feats.

The wildmen worked tirelessly, fought fearlessly, rode monstrous trees to the ground — it was like they'd never learned to doubt. Being a wildman meant leaping without looking ... and in the time he'd been among them, Kael had begun to realize that he'd spent his whole life looking without leaping.

He wasn't sure if he would ever find that sort of reckless strength. But he was determined to try. "I'm not too far gone. I can learn. I *want* to learn."

Gwen didn't reply. Instead, she drew a wooden triangle from her pocket and set it upon the ground. There were no designs carved into its surface, no words or explanation. The triangle stood on its base between them, pointing at the treetops.

"Do you know why the triangle is in the symbol of the Wright? Because it represents balance — the need to think with three different minds. But no matter how balanced you are, one side is always greater." Gwen waved a hand at the carving. "Which is it?"

Kael's first thought was that all the sides were equal. They were all the same length, after all. But if that was the case, why hadn't Gwen laid it flat? Why did she have it sitting up?

"This one," he said finally, pointing to the base.

"And why's that?"

"Because it's the side that holds the others up."

She snorted. "A typical craftsman's answer — always trying to find some deep meaning behind every little thing. That's your problem, mutt: you can't just ball your fists and crack a boulder in half. You have to have a *reason* to. Weakness," she grunted. "A healer would've told you all the sides were equal, and a warrior would've said that this here," she touched the tip that pointed skyward, "was the only place worth reaching."

224

Kael hadn't even thought of the point. "I'm not much of a warrior."

"There's war in your blood, mutt. You may have a craftsman's mind, but you've also got a warrior's eye and a healer's heart."

Though he hated to admit it, what Gwen said made sense. There were times when Kael thought he might've felt a bit like a healer — especially when he mind-walked. A couple of times, he'd dived past the memories and stumbled into something deeper. He'd burned with Declan's rage and cried Kyleigh's tears.

Yes, the healer he could believe.

But he was less certain about the warrior.

"A bird may be born with wings, but that doesn't mean it hatches knowing how to fly. What you need is a swift kick from the nest," Gwen said with a grin that made his toes curl. "There's no thinking involved in war. It's all about what you see. Haven't you ever done anything without thinking?"

He certainly had — more times than he cared to remember. He'd held the sails down during the rage of the tempest, fallen through fire to gouge the heart of the Witch. A numbness had covered him after he'd murdered Bloodfang. He'd felt as if he watched through a cloud as Duke Reginald's guards fell under his knives and arrows.

But that had been long ago, long before the reign of the black beast. His battle with Holthan was the last time he remembered doing anything without thinking. He had no idea how he'd managed to kick the sword so high, or how it'd wound up falling just right ... but he could still hear the wet crunch of the blade cutting through Holthan's chest.

Now that he thought back, he wasn't certain that it'd been strength at all. It had probably only been luck.

"I can't fight like I used to," he admitted. "Somewhere along the way, I'm not sure when, everything became more difficult. The world's not as simple as it used to be. I'm not sure I could ever fight without thinking."

Gwen snorted. "Then you might as well get used to cooking and chopping up trees, because that's all you'll be good for. A Wright who doesn't know how to war is about as useful as a bird without wings."

She got to her feet and had started to clomp away when a swell of something pushed Kael forward. "Wait — I want to try."

"I'm not sure you're worth it. But if you insist ..." She thrust a finger over his shoulder. "Go snap that in half."

A tree hung over the path behind him — the skeleton of a giant that'd been toppled by a storm long ago. It was wedged against the limbs of a neighboring tree, forming a bar that hung at about shoulder height.

Kael pressed his palms against it, testing it, but the tree didn't budge. He rammed his hands into it like Griffith had done. Once, twice, three times he struck. He'd expected something amazing to happen on the fourth blow, but it didn't. Even by the seventh, the tree still hadn't budged an inch.

He was beginning to get frustrated. "Why don't I just turn my arms into blades and hack through? What's the point of —?"

He had to duck suddenly to avoid getting his head knocked off. A rock thudded into the toppled tree, burying itself an inch into the bark. Gwen casually reached for another.

"A craftsman's power ends at his fingertips. If he can't touch it, he can't change it. War is different from craft." She turned the stone over, studying its jagged edge. "War is the ability to walk the earth with force — to send tremors that topple your enemies." Her arm cocked back. "Now try it again, or I swear by Fate's tattered robes that I'll put a fresh hole between your eyes."

There was no point in huffing and stomping his feet. Arguing with Gwen wouldn't get him anywhere. He knew he had strength inside him. He'd used it before. The problem was that the only times he'd *meant* to use it, it had been for simple things.

It wasn't that far of a stretch to believe he could hold his own in a pirate's gauntlet, or pull a giant's plow. That sort of strength came easily. But what about the impossible things he'd done? *That* was the strength he needed to find. If he could figure out someway to summon that power at will, then there might be a chance, however small ...

No. No, he wouldn't think about that right now. It was like Roland had always said: *There's no point in planning a journey if you can't even open the door.*

So he tried again.

He slammed his palms into the tree so many times that his arms went numb. The insides of his head rattled against his skull. Sweat poured from his scalp and stung his eyes. The tree's weathered skin rubbed raw patches into the undersides of his fingers. They swelled into blisters and burst, weeping down his wrists.

He pounded furiously, stepping back and charging into the tree with open palms. *Find your strength*, he said to himself. *Come on, you idiot — find it!*

Gwen's eyes burned the back of his neck as he lined himself up with the tree and prepared for another charge. Then, just before he could take off, she muttered something under her breath:

*"The greatest power I have is that which I give myself."*

The words came alive as they struck his ears. They mingled with another chant he knew, twisting together until he heard them both at once: *The greatest power I have is that which I give myself ... and in the quiet of the darkness, I see only what must be done.*

Another thread popped loose. There they were — every line of his story, every impossible thing he'd ever done lay in a tangled mass before him. Each one was bound to the next by its ends, held down the line by a single knotted something ... an idea he cleaved to so forcefully that it'd been enough to hold his strength together. But what was it?

*I see only what must be done ...*

That was it. Every remarkable thing he'd ever done hadn't been about trying to reach the highest point. He had no desire to topple the mountains or become the greatest. The moments when he'd found his power had been when he was doing what needed to be done ... mercy's sake — the tangle was coming loose.

*But* why *had those things needed to be done?*

That was the question he had to answer now, the reason his mind needed to finally let go. Kael held onto that single, fragile thread of thought as if it was the one thing keeping him from drowning in the depths of the sea. He studied it, watched as it trembled under the force of his gaze — trying desperately to understand what it was that the thread had him anchored to.

Then all at once, a storm broke over his thoughts.

The tangle of his memories, his weaknesses, his fears — all rose up before him. His doubt was a leviathan of the deep. The reflection of his every foolish mistake glistened inside its gullet. All of the frozen bodies of the pirates and the giants made up its scales. Noah's wound gaped at him from a hole in the leviathan's chest. When it breathed, it spewed Thelred's blood across his face.

*Your fault*, it hissed at him, speaking in Bloodfang's strangled, dying voice. *Fool ... weakling ... murderer*! *Your fault.*

His doubt stormed from between the leviathan's teeth. It ripped across the fragile thread, trying to wrench it from his grasp — trying to send him hurtling into the waiting, gaping jaws of the black beast.

But Kael held on. His mind trembled with the effort. There had to be someway to silence the leviathan, to drown the black beast. It would take something extraordinary. He had to find the power Gwen had spoken of — the power he'd given himself, the strength to do what needed to be done ...

And then all at once, it struck him.

Beautiful shores glowed against the horizon. He saw their warmth through the rain, heard their promise whispered in the gales. In that moment, Kael forgot the dangers. A knot formed in the fragile thread above him — the same knot that'd held all the impossible things together. Kael braced his grip against it and pulled himself back onto the ship.

He stared at the familiar faces that watched him from the deck and felt heat begin to surge inside his limbs. There were blots in his story, blood on his hands, holes in his heart. The seas before him were shadowed in uncertainty. But here, he found his purpose ... wrought clearly in the eyes of those who remained, of those watched him ...

Of those who needed him to sail on.

Here was a reason to face the leviathan, to sail across the jaws of the black beast. Here were the howling winds that would carry him over the darkened waves and to the shores beyond. After all, the things he'd done hadn't ever really been about *him* ...

He'd done it all for ... *them.*

He'd been pushing them away all this time, trying to focus on the task before him — only daring to think of them in the darkest of moments ... all the while failing to realize that when the moment was darkest was precisely when he discovered his strength. *They* were the reason he forced himself to do what had to be done.

They were the rising sun.

They were the source of his power.

Kael charged with a cry. The leviathan shrank back beneath the waves and the tree rose in its place. This time when his hands slammed into its weathered surface, he thought of Amos.

He thought of all the many years his grandfather had spent defending him against the Tinnarkians, all the many lessons he'd driven through Kael's thick skull. Then he thought of Amos shivering inside Titus's castle ... thought of shackles hanging off his thin wrists.

And it gave Kael all the reason he needed.

His love and his fury collided — two fires that burned equally bright. They raged behind his teeth; they chewed through the leviathan's scales. When he slammed into the tree again, something remarkable happened.

It was like a shutter had been opened over his eyes. He could see everything — every strip of bark, every ringed layer of skin. He could see the thousands of hairline cracks that cold, wind, and age had left behind.

Weakness filled the tree like a web. Here were the gaps of white flesh and the chinks in the armor — the places he had to aim. Kael forced his will into the cracks with hundreds of tiny arrows. He held his focus as long as he could, stretching the web to its limit.

The tree groaned, but didn't quite give way.

Kael slammed into it again. This time he already knew its weaknesses. He knew exactly where to aim. The cracks shrieked under the surge of his power. He watched through his mind's eye as they bent like the arch of a bow — stretched and creaking in panic. At last, they could hold no longer.

The tree snapped beneath his hands. Kael fell forward and saw the ground rising up. His eyes took in the pattern of the rocky earth and he rolled quickly onto his shoulder, popping to his feet.

A broken half of the tree lay beside him. Its weakness showed clearly through its shattered end, and he couldn't resist. With a cry, he smashed it beneath his heel.

Gwen tackled him. Her fist thudded into his jaw and he quickly struck back, flinging her to the ground by her shoulders. They grappled with one another, their punches charged by excitement and their bodies numb to pain. Their howls scared the birds from the trees.

Then Kael shoved Gwen hard in the chest.

She slammed against a tree and its trunk cracked loudly. The howls dried in his throat as the top half of the tree split and thudded to the ground. He blinked the warrior edge from his eyes and searched her for wounds.

"Are you all right?"

"Of course I'm all right," she snapped. She looked strangely flustered as she got to her feet — though Kael supposed he would've been flustered too, had his body just been used to knock down a tree.

He'd taken a step towards her when a strange feeling froze him. His limbs felt ... odd. When he rocked back on his heel, he swore he could feel every strand of muscle in his calf. They pulled tightly along the bone and tensed as he took a step back.

They curved at his next step. They wanted to twist his heel to a precise angle — and instead of fighting, he let them. He didn't understand why they'd curved that way until his foot came down on top of a rock ... and his heel fit against it perfectly.

This was what Gwen had meant when she said his warrior strength had been protecting him: it'd been there all along, silently watching over him, swelling when he needed it most. Now he could feel it — and if he could feel it, he knew he could control it.

"I don't think I'll be tripping over things nearly as often," he said. He walked around, grinning as he felt his muscles curve and tense. His strength had been hidden in an unexpected place. He didn't think he would've ever found it, had it not been for the thing Gwen had said to him. "Those words ... they were some sort of whispercraft, weren't they?"

"I was getting tired of watching you fail, mutt," Gwen said as she brushed the splinters from her tunic. "I thought a craftsman's chant might help move things along."

"But you're not a craftsman."

"No, I'm not. Those were Setheran's words. He was the last Wright to live among the wildmen, and my father taught him our ways. He told me once that Setheran hated craft — but every once in a while, the craft would come out of him. Sometimes the things he said would take on a life of their own. They'd ring on every tongue that spoke them, and ring on even now. The wildmen already knew the warriors' strength," she smirked, "but Setheran's words forced us to look deeper. He helped us find true power."

Kael tried to fight his exasperation back. But when he saw the many blisters that wept down his hands, he lost quickly. "Then why didn't you just tell me how to find it in the first place? Why did you make me fall on my rump so many blasted times?"

She shrugged. "Words do no good unless you're ready to hear them."

# CHAPTER 21
## THE TAIL

Kael returned to Tinnark late that afternoon — toting the first mountain deer he'd ever slain across his shoulders.

It hadn't happened quite the way he'd imagined it would. He never thought it would involve Gwen hurtling into a clump of deer and snapping one of their necks. He never thought the largest one would come charging towards him in a panic, or that his only weapon would be a rock.

But when he'd slung his arm back and felt his muscles coil, holding his strength at the perfect tension, he hadn't doubted. He knew before the rock struck that he'd won.

"I still can't believe you got the biggest one," Gwen said, glaring at him from around the hooves of her doe.

He *was* a rather large buck. Kael thought a man could've sat quite comfortably between his antlers. "If you would've waited a moment instead of charging right in, we might've been able to figure out how to get more of them at once," he muttered.

She rolled her eyes. "I would rather eat less than have to wait for anything."

That was one of the most ridiculous things he'd ever heard. But when he considered the source, it seemed about right.

They left the deer at the Hall: the craftsmen would keep the meat for dinner, but Gwen said he could have the pelt and antlers if he wanted them. "You ought to use it to dress up the hospital. It looks pretty grim on the inside," she said, turning to frown up the hill. "In fact, I want you to work on finishing it today."

Kael was fine with that. After all the time he'd spent yelling at the craftsmen, he could use a day to himself.

When he arrived at the hospital, he saw that Baird had made a fantastic mess of things. Somehow, the beggar-bard had discovered where Kael had stashed his rucksack and had dumped all of his belongings out in a pile. Now he sat cross-legged upon the bed, gripping the dragonscale gauntlets.

Kael had decided to take them off. There were too many dragonsbane weapons around, and the warriors were always attacking him at odd times of the day. So he thought it best just to store them rather than risk having them ruined.

"These are special," Baird murmured. His bandaged face was turned towards the wall, his mouth open in concentration. He ran his fingers tentatively across the gauntlets' ridged tops, as if he was stroking a pair of living things. "Special, indeed. *Very* spec —"

"All right, that's enough." Kael snatched the gauntlets from his hands and set them aside. "Why is it that I'm not allowed to go through your things, but you're allowed to go through mine?"

"Because *you* allow it!" Baird cackled.

Kael hadn't allowed it — not in the least bit. He was about to say as much when he saw that Baird had a new object clutched in his knobby fingers: the *Atlas of the Adventurer*.

He plucked it smartly from his grasp. "That isn't yours."

Baird's lips bent in a piteous downwards arc. "But ... but ... I *like* it. The words speak to me with the voice of an old friend."

"You can't even see the words."

"I can feel them! Let me show you." He waved about him frantically, trying to find the *Atlas*.

Kael was curious. He put the book in Baird's hand but held tightly to his wrist. "This is very dear to me, understand? It's my greatest treasure."

The beggar-bard was surprisingly gentle as he opened the *Atlas* to a random page. His fingers pressed against the arcs of each letter. They were written starkly, in a firm and simple hand. Even though they'd faded a bit, Kael could see the shallow indents the quill had left behind. He supposed that was what Baird was feeling for.

His lips moved silently as he traced the letters. "Oh dear me, I've landed directly in the middle of *Scarn*, haven't I?"

That was exactly where he'd wound up. "You can really feel them?"

But Baird didn't reply. "Let's find the beginning," he muttered as he flipped the pages back. "It's only from there that we can do your story any justice. Yes, yes — we must start at the start ..."

Kael had every intention of finishing the hospital's roof. But instead, he found himself wrapped up in Baird's readings. One story after another wove its way through his ears, given new life by the beggar-bard's voice.

Not all of the heroes had great strength. Perhaps it was because he was worried about his fight with Griffith that he paid special attention to those who'd had to outwit their enemies rather than cross swords.

It wasn't that he thought he couldn't beat him — it was that he didn't want to. Throwing a rock through a deer's chest was one thing, but the idea of having to hit Griffith put a sour taste in his mouth. There must be someway he could win without having to hurt him ...

"I'm going to keep this with my treasures," Baird said, hugging the *Atlas* close to his chest. "It should be in the company of other great things. Don't worry, young man — I'll keep it safe." He shuffled off, then, feeling along the walls until he disappeared into the office.

Kael sighed heavily when he looked up through the unfinished roof and saw it was nearly sunset. He stuffed his things away, dragging his feet a bit. He picked the dragonscale gauntlets up and turned them over in his hands.

They had a complicated texture: light, yet impossibly hard — spiny and smooth at the same time. The scales fit comfortably, breathed well. And yet, they could shatter swords. He bet even Griffith would have a difficult time ...

Mercy's sake — that was it.

235

"Baird, come on!" Kael hollered back at the office. "Let's get to dinner before I start thinking sensibly again."

"It takes very little effort to think sensibly, young man. The real challenge is in thinking *well*," Baird chirped in reply.

Somehow, Kael managed to get the beggar-bard wrangled and on his way to dinner. His mind was so filled with thoughts that he didn't even remember pushing through the heavy front doors.

The Hall was fuller than it'd been the night before. Kael noticed that the craftsmen had added several new tables to the inside edge of the rectangle. The people who filled them weren't dressed in the furs and paint of the wildmen, but wore the same rough-spun clothes the Tinnarkians had worn.

"Folk from downmountain."

Kael jumped. He hadn't even realized Gwen had come up behind him.

She wore a cap made of a fox's hide. Its feet dangled at her ears and its tail draped down her neck. The bright red pelt matched her wild locks perfectly. "They fled the mountains to escape Earl Titus. Now trouble in the Valley has chased them back up. They're mostly children — little more than empty bellies to feed, in my opinion."

After a moment, her frown softened. "I've put them to work gathering firewood. They aren't exactly safe making camp with us, but it's better than most fates. What can we do?" She nodded to a table that was packed full of redheaded children, and sighed. "The mountains would swallow them up if we left them on their own. Your heart would have to be colder than a wynn's underbelly to turn them away."

Kael agreed.

The children stared openly at the wildmen. One of the craftsmen grinned at them through her paint and sat down at their table. Cautious smiles spread across the children's windburn faces as she told them a story. Soon they'd clamped hands over their mouths, trying desperately to hide their giggles.

Kael couldn't help but smile as he watched. Laughter was as rare as warmth in the mountains.

Gwen marched for her table, and Kael let Baird tote him to a dish he liked the smell of — venison drowned in rich brown gravy. "Ah, the skies are closed once more," Baird said, inhaling deeply as they sat. "How quickly the craftsmen work."

Kael glanced up and saw that the Hall's roof had indeed been restored. The pine beams were hung back in place and new shingles hid them from the stars. "You don't happen to know *how* the roof got blown off, do you?"

"I told you — Kael the Wright summoned the earth to aid him in battle." Baird's fingers clamped down tightly upon his arm. "I heard the roar of thunder and a great storm wind threw me against the wall. Then heat — oh, such terrible heat! It was all around me, scraping, swirling. I hid my face from its rage and did not stir until the fires had passed."

At first, Kael had ignored the beggar-bard's tale. But now he was beginning to wonder. The roof had obviously been blown off by *something*. He sifted through Baird's rant, trying to piece it all together: *thunder, storm winds, fire …*

Quite suddenly, Kael figured it out.

He was doing a fairly good job of keeping his grin at bay when Kyleigh burst through the doors — and he quickly lost the fight.

Her armor was gone. She wore a rough-looking fur tunic and absolutely no boots to speak of. Her bare arms swung out beside her and the pads of her feet slapped against the floor as she marched across the Hall.

"Evening, gentlemen," she said as she sat beside them. There was a purplish ring around one of her eyes — and it made the green blaze all the more furiously.

Baird dipped his head in greeting. "Good evening, young lady."

Kael glared at her black eye. "All right — who do I need to throttle?"

"Nobody. Honestly, I'm fine."

She wasn't fine. And he was fairly certain he knew exactly who'd punched her. He'd had every intention of strangling Gwen with the bushy tail of her cap when Kyleigh grabbed him by the front of the tunic.

"I deserved it, all right?" she said, pulling him back into his seat.

"How could you have possibly —?"

"I lost my temper. I behaved badly, and if Gwen hadn't punched me ... well, things could've gotten out of hand." She touched her bruise gingerly with the tips of her fingers. "It's my own fault, really. Now Gwen's taken my armor away and forced me to wear *this*." She pulled down roughly on the hem of her skirt — a skirt, Kael couldn't help but notice, that showed far more of her legs than usual.

Baird's knobby hands slapped against his face. "Hmm, there's a strange warmth beneath your skin. Almost ... feverish. You haven't come down with a fever, have you?"

"I'm fine. I haven't got a fever," Kael snapped. He spent the next several moments staring pointedly at the far wall, taking long drinks of icy water.

Fortunately, Kyleigh was too busy swearing at her skirt to notice.

"What did you do to get into trouble, exactly?" Kael said.

Her mouth snapped shut and a strange pink blossomed across her cheeks. "Leave it."

"No. I don't want to leave it." He was almost positive that Kyleigh was being punished for blowing the roof off the Hall. He wanted to hear her admit it — but most importantly, he wanted to know *why*. "What did you —?"

A lash of icy water cut him short. It blurred his vision and splashed up his nose. Griffith grinned from beside him. "Are you ready for me to slap the skin off you again?"

He was.

Kael walked out into the middle of the Hall. While Gwen made her speech about the caddoc, he focused. He imagined that dragonscales popped up along his skin. Black, interlocking discs covered his knuckles, his palms, and wrapped around his fingers. He flexed his hands and waited, watching as Griffith took his place.

"Same rules as last time: open-handed, and keep your feet planted. Last man standing wins." He smiled. "Are you ready?"

Kael said nothing — which seemed to put Griffith on edge.

His eyes swept the length of Kael's tattered clothes. He was searching for weaknesses, looking for cracks in his armor. There was just one problem: he couldn't see Kael's armor.

While they stared at each other, the wildmen's mutterings grew to a hum. The craftsmen's fists began to pound against the tables. Gwen leaned forward in her chair, legs splayed and elbows balanced across her knees — staring sharply through the lines of her paint.

The wildmen seemed to realize that something was about to happen. Kael could hear their excitement thrumming through the air. For some reason, the craftsmen's song thudded more fiercely than it had the night before. He swore he could feel his heart slow to match its beat …

No. The warrior in him tried to force its way to the front, but he held it back. He wouldn't let the craftsmen's song get to him. He watched, waiting for the thrill of the fight to take Griffith over — for the moment when the wildmen's thumping drove him to attack.

And when he finally lunged, Kael was ready.

He thrust his hand up just as Griffith swung hard for his face. The boy yelped when he slapped the hardened back of Kael's wrist. He slung his hand out to the side, just like he'd done the night before — and Kael saw his chance.

He thrust his hands forward and shoved Griffith hard in the chest. The boy's feet came unglued. He stumbled backwards, swinging his arms for balance. Kael stuck a foot behind his heel and shoved again.

Griffith tripped and fell hard onto his rump.

"Finish him!" one of the wildmen cried, but Kael shook his head.

"The fight's over. I hit him with an open hand, and I'm the last one standing." The Hall went silent as he turned to Gwen. "That means I win."

Her hand moved from her lips to rest beneath her chin. "I suppose it does ... though that was easily the worst caddoc I've ever seen."

"It was clever!" Griffith said as he got to his feet. "It was exactly the sort of thing the Man of Wolves would've done."

"It was a trick, nothing more. We aren't going to stomp the Man of Wolves with *tricks* — we're going to stomp him with our swords."

The wildmen cheered loudly at this.

Gwen waved them back to their table with a flick of her hand, and Griffith scowled as he marched away.

Dinner went on as if nothing unusual had happened. The wildmen passed their plates in a circle around the table, each one scooping a portion of whatever dish sat in front of him before handing it off down the line.

The mood in the Hall was undeniably light. The wildmen buried themselves in their meals, eating in the same silence they worked, chewing through their grins. Baird downed his venison and then dunked his scraggly face directly into the middle of his plate, slurping down the gravy.

Kael was halfway through his dinner before he realized that Kyleigh's arm was pressed against his. He had no idea which of them had moved closer — and frankly, he didn't care.

For now, Kyleigh was here, sitting next to him when she could've been sitting anywhere else — pressed against him arm to elbow when she could've moved away. And even though he knew she'd probably been responsible for the roof, he didn't press it.

For now, he would sit calmly and enjoy the moment.

When dinner was finished, the wildmen left their benches and sat in a ring upon the floor. Silas curled up next to Gwen. He rested his great furry head in her lap and she

240

stroked him absently, her fingers running down between his ears.

Kael's face burned as he watched them. "He's got to tell her sometime. He can't keep lying to her."

Kyleigh had her fist pressed against her lips. She stared for a moment, her face inscrutable. "He will, I think. Though you never can tell." Her gaze narrowed to daggers' points as she added: "Nothing's too low or despicable for a cat."

Silas must've heard. His glowing gaze slid over to them and a deep, rumbling purr trembled inside his chest. It was clearly a taunt ... and Kyleigh gave him a gesture to think about.

"Tell us one of your stories, bard," Gwen commanded.

Baird immediately got to his feet. Griffith led him into the center of the ring where he sat, cross-legged. His head sagged forward and he took a deep breath. His exhale hissed loudly through the silent Hall.

"In a dark age long since passed, the realm was ruled by dragons. They were fierce and fiery lords. The dragons breathed their judgment upon the holds of men in singeing bolts, driving them to seek refuge deep beneath the earth. Only one brave soul dared to stand against them — Sir Gorigan, a knight of the realm and champion among men."

Kael had heard this story so many times he could've recited it by heart. It was a yarn so well-loved that it should've been worn thin. But Baird's voice gave the words new life. Kael closed his eyes and let the dragons rise inside his head.

"Sir Gorigan forsook the safety of the earth and charged out into the light, sword drawn and heart bared for battle. He brought his blade down with a mighty cry. But," Baird gasped, "it broke against the dragons' scales. The fiery monsters mocked his plight. Their wriggling tongues coiled inside their molten throats as they closed in around him — already singing of his death.

"It was in that desperate moment that Sir Gorigan turned to Fate." Baird raised his arms and shouted to the rafters: *"My lady, my light — keeper of the threads of men. If I've found favor in your sight, help me quell the dragons' din!* Fate heard his cry and answered. Her gift fell to his feet: a sword forged from a ray of the burning sun. As Sir Gorigan drew her aloft, he called her *Daybreak* — for by her edge would he lead the world of men to a new dawn.

"The dragons fled Daybreak's power. They took to their wings and soared into the Unforgivable Mountains — where they hoped their great father could protect them. For three days and three nights, Sir Gorigan battled the King of dragons. He was a fearsome beast with teeth the size of men and black wings that cloaked the sky. But even *he* was no match for Daybreak. Fate sent a howling wind across her blade, stoking her fires to a roar. All the power of the sun descended upon the dragon King in a fearsome gale. It melted his bones and turned his flesh to ash."

Baird reached down and touched the floor in front of him. The soft tap of his fingers was the only sound in the Hall. "Do you ever wonder, friends, why this mountain sits a little higher than the rest? It's because the dragon King is buried here. Oh, yes — the ridges are his bones and the rocks are his ash. Only one thing remains of him, the only proof he was ever here ... his tail." He raised a finger, holding it still as his audience looked on, breathless. Then he smiled.

The wildmen's laughter broke Kael from his vision. "It isn't a joke," he mumbled to Griffith.

"Sure it is. The only dragons buried in these mountains are the ones we've put there," he said.

"The Tail is real — I've seen it," Kael insisted.

Griffith's mouth fell open. "Really? Will you take me to it?"

Kael didn't see why not.

*******

They left early the next morning. Kael watched the world through his warrior eyes: leaping over rifts and streams, coasting down rain-slickened slopes and picking his

242

way across fields of jagged rock. It was like a dance — except instead of music, it was the pattern of the land that told him where to put his feet. His eyes watched and his body listened.

At long last, he led Griffith around a narrow, toe-curling ledge and straight to the base of the Tail. It stood alone at the edge of a cliff — a narrow, wind-worn tower that hung over the edge of oblivion. There were clouds above and mist below. All they could see of it was a smooth section the height of a castle.

"Fate's fingers," Griffith murmured when he saw it.

"Now do you believe me?"

Griffith nodded. He crept up to the Tail and slapped his hands against its base. Then he leapt. His fingers curled and the toes of his boots scraped against the rock, but there wasn't a crack to hold onto.

He slid back to the ground, frowning. "I wonder what's up there?"

Kael shrugged. "There are some sights no man is meant to see."

It was something Roland had told him years ago, back when he'd first taken him to see the Tail:

"There's no way of knowing," Roland had said. "There's no way to tell how high it goes, or what it would take to get there. And even if a man *did* manage to make the climb … would he have enough left in him to climb back down? When you think about it, I suppose it's really a *question* that keeps us grounded — not the height." He'd smiled as he ran a swollen hand down the rock. "Maybe there are some points men aren't suppose to reach, some sights we aren't meant to see. It's good to know the earth still has her secrets."

A howl jolted Kael from his thoughts. Griffith's cry echoed around them for several moments before it faded. "You'd have to be more than rattled to climb this thing," he declared.

Kael crossed his arms. "Weren't you just trying to charge up it on all fours?"

Griffith shrugged, grinning. "Well, you can't blame me for trying. Gwen says that I'm supposed to try things — that I'm never to let anything hold me back."

He stretched his thin arms high above his head, yawning up at the clouds. Then suddenly, he bent and picked a rock up off the ground. It bounced between his fingers as he tested its weight. Then he hurled it straight into the air.

The rock whipped through the clouds and disappeared. They waited for so many long moments that Kael had actually begun to forget about it. He was rather surprised when they heard the faintest of *clicks* from high above them — the end of an echo.

"So there *is* a top," Griffith said.

Of course there was a top. There'd never been a chance of there *not* being a top. When he said as much, Griffith rolled his eyes.

"You don't get it, do you? Warriors don't care about answering questions — we do things because we can." He stared up at the Tail for a moment more, and the blue marble rolled between his fingers. "If I show you something ... will you promise to keep it between us? You can't tell Gwen I've told you about it — otherwise, she'll skin me."

The worry in his voice put Kael on edge. "All right, I promise."

"Gwen doesn't want the others to worry. She says if we keep quiet, it'll eventually go away. But I'm not sure." Griffith took a deep breath. "The Man of Wolves is building something near the village."

# CHAPTER 22
## IMPOSSIBLE

A few miles up the slope from Tinnark, Earl Titus's soldiers were hard at work.

They'd chosen a steep portion of land and had begun building what looked to be the start of a rather large wall. It was made of stone, held together by thick lines of mortar, and was already more than a man's height.

Behind the wall, a rounded tower was almost finished. Large piles of wood were scattered around its edge. They were being nailed together — each one forming a stout base topped by a long, deadly arm. Kael recognized the weapons immediately as catapults.

He and Griffith lay on their stomachs beneath a thick tangle of shrubs, watching through the leaves from a distance. "How long has Gwen known about this?" Kael said, staring in disbelief at the tiny dots of soldiers that worked along the tower's sloping roof.

"A while, I suppose. They came down the mountains behind us."

"And you didn't do anything about them?" Kael said incredulously. "You just let them hover over you and build?"

"*We* didn't want that land. And what does it matter if they're building?" he said defensively. "It's not as if having a castle is going to help them much."

"You don't think so?"

"Well, it didn't help us."

Kael dragged a hand down the side of his face. He knew it would do him no good to try to explain that having a castle built on the slope above them would give Titus every advantage. If the wildmen ever tried to attack, they'd quite literally be fighting an uphill battle.

"I just thought since you showed me something, I'd —"

"I showed you a harmless old rock." Kael thrust a hand at the tower. "*This* is serious!"

Griffith's scalp burned red on either side of his stripe of hair. "Gwen says there's no point in worrying about it. Those soldiers aren't going to attack us — and if they ever try, we'll stomp them." He slid back on his elbows and disappeared into the woods without a sound.

Kael lay still long after he'd gone, watching the soldiers at work. There was no doubt in his mind that if the Earl's men ever came into Tinnark, they *would* be stomped. Surely Titus must've known this.

Perhaps he'd only built the fort in the hopes of goading the wildmen into an attack. Perhaps Gwen had done the wiser thing by not falling into his trap. Kael hoped that was all it was.

But his stomach still twisted in worry.

*******

When he returned to Tinnark late that afternoon, Kael found a surprise waiting for him at the hospital: sometime while he'd been gone, the craftsmen had finished the roof.

"Yeah, Gwen got tired of listening to that beggar moan about how his treasures were going to get ruined at the first sign of rain," one of the warriors called when she saw him looking. She had the bodies of two boars tucked under her arms, their legs swung limply as she marched down the hill. "A storm's coming tonight. Can you smell it?"

Kael didn't have to smell it. He could already see the army of charcoal clouds bearing down on them from the mountain's top. It must've been near the end of summer — the rest of the season would be one long string of storms. They'd soak the ground through just in time for winter, when the cold would turn it to ice.

A clanging sound filled Tinnark like a song. When Kael glanced down the slope, he saw a clump of craftsmen gathered outside the forge, beating iron plates into suits of armor.

They'd come to him a few days earlier, asking if he knew anything about forging. He'd told them all he knew: he'd led them through the pages of *Blades and Bellows* and showed them his memories. He'd even taught them how to trap a forge's heat and use it to bend iron with their hands. After they'd been taught, the craftsmen drifted away — going one by one to join Kyleigh at her forge.

As part of her punishment, Gwen had ordered her to craft steel weapons and suits of armor for her warriors. "Once my men are fully equipped, we'll be ready to stomp the Man of Wolves," she'd sworn.

Kael was rather looking forward to that day. The warrior in him stirred to life at the thought of marching on Titus, stoking fires that'd sat dormant for so long — summoning flames he'd been certain would never rise again. The craftsmen's new skills had quickened their task, and he knew the day would be upon them before long. Soon, Titus would pay for what he'd done to the mountains.

With the rain creeping towards them, Kael knew he'd have to spend the day in-doors — which meant his thoughts might drive him mad if he didn't find someway to distract himself. So he slipped inside the hospital and went immediately in search of Baird.

He stopped in the office doorway. There a strange man sitting at Amos's desk — a man with short-clipped hair and a neatly trimmed beard. There was no dirt under his nails, no grime on his skin. Kael likely wouldn't have recognized him at all, had it not been for the bandages over his eyes.

"For such a young man, his steps are heavy," Baird murmured. "These should be his brightest years — filled with hope and dreams and love."

"Yes, well, I've got a lot to think about," Kael muttered.

Baird had the *Atlas* opened in front of him. He ran his fingers down its weathered pages, his lips moving silently. "Hmm, it isn't the thinking that wears you down — it's the worry. Fretting too much about one thing or another can age you quickly, young man. It'll twist your spine and crush your knees. You'll hobble through the tail end of your life wondering why you've given so much of your time to worry. That's no way to live."

Kael supposed he was probably right. And had he known how to live any other way, he would've gladly done it. "Are these your treasures?" he said, waving to the many books that now adorned the shelves.

Baird smiled widely. "Marvelous, aren't they? I've spent my whole life collecting them. To be a bard is to be a beggar. Rarely did I ever have two coins to rub together, but I've always been rich in friends. Each of these books was a gift. There's a story behind every story."

Kael stepped closer to the shelves, a faint hope tapping inside his heart. "Have you got anything about dragons?"

"There should be a copy of *Tales of Scales* in there ... between *Types of Trolls* and *Griffins: Fact or Fiction?*. I always try to keep all my beastly books together."

There was a noticeable gap between the two books Baird had mentioned. Kael wasn't at all surprised. "Kyleigh was here."

"She helped me with the trimming," Baird said cheerily, slapping a hand to his face.

"Of course she did," Kael muttered.

"There are whispers swirling around the village, young man."

"Aren't there always?"

"But these are *troublesome*," Baird insisted. "The craftsmen say that Kael the Wright has abandoned them — that he refuses to step inside the forge. Has something powerful driven him away?"

"He hasn't abandoned them. He just doesn't want to get too close to Kyleigh."

Baird snorted. "The Swordmaiden? Why should he fear her?"

"He doesn't *fear* her. He just …" Kael sighed heavily. "He loves her. He's desperately in love with her, but she won't have him — he understands why, though. He knows it's because they're too … different. That she would never even think of him. But still, he can't help himself. He isn't quite strong enough …" Kael gripped a fistful of his hair, trying desperately to keep his anger at bay. "The thing is, he *knows* it's going to hurt — he blasted well knows it! And if he had any sense at all, he would forget the whole thing. But he's too big an idiot to let it go. That's precisely Kael the Wright's problem: he's a stubborn, irredeemable idiot."

For some reason, speaking about himself as somebody else to a beggar-bard who likely wouldn't remember his own name in a moment — much less anything Kael told him — made admitting the troubles of his heart much easier.

Baird raised his head from the *Atlas*. His mouth parted beneath his bandages in what was very likely shock. "Oh dear, oh me, that *is* a problem. Yes, a broken heart is a powerful enemy. Every time I hear of one, it reminds me of Calhamos the Healer. Have you ever heard that story?"

Kael hadn't. But he realized he could certainly use a distraction. "Tell it."

"Very well. Calhamos was a man from this very mountain. He served the Kings for two lifetimes of men, tending to their wounded —"

"Wait a moment — *two* lifetimes? How could a healer live that long?"

Baird's head tilted to the side. "Healers are masters of the flesh, young man. There is nothing a craftsman imagines that he can't create, nothing a warrior can't topple, and if a healer whispers for his heart to beat on, there's almost nothing that can stop it. Almost." Baird raised a finger. "Like so many healers before him, Calhamos grew weary of the Kingdom's pain. He fled to the mountains in search of peace — but instead, he found love.

"When his wife died in the throes of birth, Calhamos lost hold of his heart. Only one thing kept him from falling into Death's embrace: the cries of his newborn child. Part of his heart had died and broken away, but he lived on for his child's sake ... lived on with half a heart." Baird smiled. "Love can kill a man, but it can also save him. What a strange thing love is."

Kael nodded absently. Maybe if he'd been more of a healer, he could figure out someway to keep his gut from squirming every time he thought of Kyleigh. He was sorry he'd ever brought her up. "Do you have any books about Ben Deathtreader?" he said, hoping to change the subject.

"Now that's interesting," Baird whispered.

The deathly hush of his voice made the hairs on the back of Kael's neck stand on end. "What's interesting?"

"*Deathtreader* was the name he gave himself. A strange name, a secret name. Most people in the Kingdom didn't know it. But you do. Hmm," he murmured into the pages of the *Atlas*, "I wonder what that means?"

Kael had no idea what it meant. And he doubted if Baird knew, either. "Well, what name did you know him by?"

"He tricked them." Baird sat up suddenly. His knobby fingers twisted into his tunic. "He ripped their secrets out! He pulled them away strand by strand until he knew them all. They didn't know any better. How could they? It had never been done."

"Who didn't know any better?" Kael said carefully. Baird was on the brink: one wrong word would tip him over into madness.

His rant dissolved into groans. He buried his head beneath his arms and rocked back and forth. Kael was just about to give up when he suddenly spoke:

"He claimed to have fallen through the eyes of a dead man — chasing after the last light of his life. But he wasn't dead, and so his soul couldn't pass on. He walked the wastes between worlds for a thousand years until Fate finally took pity on him. But instead of sending him to the green lands beyond the rift ... she sent him back. That's why he called himself *Deathtreader*.

"And they *believed* him!" Baird cackled and slapped his hands upon the desk. "The man claimed to have walked through death for a thousand years — a *thousand* years — and they believed him!"

Kael certainly believed it. Deathtreader was a powerful healer — the adventures he'd written about in his book defied all possibility. No time passed in the realm of the mind, after all. So it was possible that Deathtreader could've walked for ages without a single moment passing in the Kingdom. But there was no way he was going to try to explain that to Baird.

"At least we know Kael the Wright isn't false," he chirped from the desk.

Kael thought that was a strange thing to say. "Why would he be false?"

"He *isn't* false. Otherwise, Setheran wouldn't have given me that letter ... gah!" He slapped his hands to the sides of his bandaged face. "I wasn't supposed to tell you that. A courier must never reveal his source!"

Kael rolled his eyes. "Come off it, Baird. I know Kyleigh gave you that letter. She just wanted to trick the wildmen into teaching me."

Baird smiled widely. *"Men expect the great, the bold, and the strong. But Fate never uses the obvious things,"* he whispered. "He knew that I'd be able to wander the realm without question, to stand in the very ranks of his enemies and never be noticed. I suppose that's why he chose me ..." He grinned. "At least, I like to think it is."

Those words tingled inside Kael's ears — faint, but strangely familiar. "Who said that to you?"

"Setheran." Baird's smile widened to a grin. "Four others stood beside me — each a great warrior in his own right, each far more worthy than I. We were all to take different paths to the mountains. I only got as far as Oakloft. No one I asked was willing to take me any further. So for nearly twenty years I sat —"

"And I just happened to be the first one to come along?" Kael said. He was angry, but he wasn't sure why. Something strange rumbled inside his chest as he growled:

"Stop lying to me, Baird. There's no way any of that's possible. There's no way Setheran could have known —"

"He stole her future!" Baird cried.

"Who's future?"

"He *stole* it!"

All of Kael's anger burned at his front. He felt it spread across the top of his chest and arms, as if he was using it to guard against the thing that squirmed behind it — the thing that said it *could* be possible.

There was only one way he could ever know for sure: "Show me the letter."

"I don't have it."

"I saw Griffith put it in your bag."

"Gah! *Fine.*" Baird reached inside his tunic and slapped the crumpled parchment upon the table. "But you mustn't tell a soul."

Kael tore the letter open. His eyes scanned across the words. He read the simple message over and over again: *Before you stands Kael the Wright — see to it that he's awakened.*

There was something familiar about the lines of the letters. The way they'd been printed on the page was careful and sure, more simple than beautiful ... and they were eerily familiar.

Kael's hand shook as he reached across the table for the *Atlas.* He turned it around and read them side-by-side. His eyes went back and forth between the letter and the *Atlas,* studying the lay of the words and the angles at which they'd been drawn. It only took him a moment to realize why the words had looked so familiar:

They'd been written by the same hand.

Kael felt as if he'd just taken one of Griffith's fists to his chin. He rocked back on his heels, swaying under the force of his shock. He didn't know if anything Baird had told him was true — but there was one thing he knew for certain.

And it made everything else seem small.

"Where are you going, young man?"

He heard Baird calling after him, but Kael didn't stop. He shoved through the hospital doors and out into a thick curtain of rain. Icy drops thudded onto the top of his head as he ran, washing down his back and shoulders. It mixed with the chill in his skin and made his joints seize up, but Kael ran doggedly for the forge.

A bright yellow light glowed beneath its door. When he shoved it open, a wave of heat knocked him backwards.

"Kael!"

He heard the lid slam shut over the trough of fire and the heat mercifully abated. Kyleigh's hands grasped his shoulders, but he knocked them away. "Why did you lie to me?"

As the glare from the yellow light faded, he saw her face. Her gaze was steady, her arms hung at her side. Their eyes locked and he watched the passing of the flames behind the green, not daring to look away.

"I didn't lie to you," she said finally.

"You told me that Setheran's child was dead."

"No, I said that Fate took him away. I never said he was dead."

He wanted to fall through the floor. He wanted to yell. He wanted to punch the wall as hard as he could. But Kyleigh's gaze kept him steady. "Why didn't you just ... tell me?"

She frowned. "It was too dangerous, at first. You were wide-eyed and fresh off the mountains. I didn't want to burden — fine. I was being selfish," she said when she saw the angry words forming on his lips. "It wasn't that I didn't trust you, or didn't think you were ready. I just ... I wanted to protect you."

"Because that was your task?"

"Because it's my purpose."

He didn't understand the sudden change in her eyes, how the flames could calm and yet lose none of their light. It was a look that made heat pool inside his middle. When he could bear the fires no longer, he looked away — seeking the cool relief of the floor.

She gripped his shoulder. "And I suppose that, if I'm being completely honest, I didn't want Seth to change you. I wanted you to find your own way."

"Well I haven't, have I? Not really." He could feel the anger coming back, dulling the pressure of her hand. "It was Setheran's chant that got me through the tempest. Those *were* his words, weren't they?" He bit his lip when she nodded. "Setheran was in my head when I fought Gilderick. Baird swears that he wrote that blasted letter — and I *know* he wrote the *Atlas*."

"He's been helping me all along. If it hadn't been for him, I would've died a thousand times over. And you ..." He paused, thinking. "You're only here because he sent you."

She grabbed him under the chin. "I resent that. He might've been the greatest warrior of our age, but that doesn't mean I let him order me about."

"Oh? Then why were you searching for me?"

A shadow crossed her eyes. "I don't remember — well, I don't," she snapped when he snorted. "The last thing I remember is attacking Crevan. The rest is all bits and pieces ..."

She released him and turned her glare on the wall. "The harder I try, the further my memories get. I don't remember who sent me, but I knew that I'd been sent. Sometimes I got off on other errands," she admitted, smirking. "The wildmen chased me down the mountains, and the Sovereign Five chased me back up. But every once in a while, I remembered that I was searching for someone — someone very important.

"When you said your name," she snapped her fingers, "I knew who you were. All of my memories of you came rushing back, clear as glass —"

"Your memories of me? You mean we'd met before?" His mouth went dry when she nodded. "That's not possible. I would've remembered."

She smiled. "You were only a few days old."

He took a step back. "You knew me when I was an infant?"

"Of course I did. Who do you think carried Setheran into the Valley so that he could meet you? I wouldn't have done that for just anybody, by the way. We dragons don't take well to being saddled and flown about. We're very proud creatures."

She laughed as he sank to the ground, but he didn't think it was funny. Not in the least bit. He leaned against the wall and stared out the open door, watching as the rain pounded the earth. He hardly felt it when Kyleigh slid down beside him.

For a long moment, they sat in silence. Kael just stared — stared, and tried to wrap his head around it.

"You were adorable, by the way."

He groaned. "Kyleigh, please."

"What? You were. But you wouldn't sleep. I suppose you must've been excited about coming into the world."

"Probably. Let's just leave it at that."

"So I stole you away —"

"I really don't want to hear this."

"— and we played for hours, just you and I."

The sudden softness in her voice made him look. She was smiling, her head tilted back against the wall. Her eyes brightened as she watched a distant memory.

"We sat by the fire and I told you stories — mostly about how frustratingly stubborn your father was. Little did I know," she added with a raised brow. "You were far too young to speak, of course. But your eyes were open. Most infants have this sort of glassy shine over their eyes. Bloodfang used to call it the *reckless flame of new life*. But the light in your eyes was different.

"Your stare went deep. You were so focused ... I remember thinking how serious you looked. When I sang to you, it was like you already knew the words. You understood the story before I'd even finished singing." Her eyes snapped back suddenly and she cleared her throat. "I suppose it was just the Wright in you."

She got to her feet, then — leaving Kael feeling something he'd never felt before.

Heat spread from his chest to his fingertips, but didn't quite burn. That space in his middle held the warmth like hearthstones. It pushed all of his worries aside and pinned them back. They'd keep swirling in a corner of his mind, building as they wove themselves into questions. But for now, he would enjoy the sudden lightness of his heart ...

The sudden, unexpected, completely impossible lightness.

"I'll see you at dinner."

"Are you certain there's nothing else you'd like to ask me?"

He thought she might've sounded a bit surprised. "No, I think I've got the answer I wanted." And with that, he stepped out the door.

The rain that struck him as he walked back to the hospital wasn't nearly as icy it'd been as before. It warmed as it rolled down his skin, fed by the heat that spread from the center of his chest. He imagined that each drop would burn hotly by the time it struck the ground.

And as the rain soaked into the earth, it'd carry enough fire in its crystal innards to melt the layer of frost beneath the mountains' skin.

# CHAPTER 23
## POISONED DARTS

Days passed while the pirates and the giants traveled on. They walked along the rough ground beside the road, marching against the exodus of the Valley.

Most of the ragged line hardly seemed to notice the army passing by: they kept their chins anchored to the ground, only lifting them to see how much further they had to go. Their eyes squinched at their bottoms as they took in the Pass. Some looked worried, others afraid. But most were empty.

Jonathan tried to gather information from the people they passed. But no matter how he asked it, the Valley folk all said the same thing: Grognaut the Bandit Lord was to blame.

"He attacked us in the dead of night. The bandits set fire to our homes while we slept. When we managed to escape the flames ... they were waiting for us."

"One of them got my finger — chewed it right off. And look how the nub's festering, will you? I've kept herbs on it for three days and it's still turning black as dusk."

"Terror is all it is. It's all the bandits ever want. Thieving is just an excuse to spill blood. And now that they've got the Earl's protection, they can spill as much as they please —"

"What was that, mate? You say the Earl's been protecting them?" Jonathan interrupted.

The man he'd been talking to was a shopkeeper from Crow's Cross. His eyes dulled at Jonathan's question. "Yeah, I suppose that's what you'd call it. He gave them weapons and armor, let them have the run of the land. Grognaut's even settled into the Earl's old castle — word is that Titus has got himself perched at the top of the mountains. Fate only knows why."

He kept walking, and Jonathan bounded to catch up. "But what about the King? Hasn't he sent his army crashing through here, yet?"

"The King? Huh. No one's heard from the King since last autumn," he said with a snort. "The Cleft fills with snow during the winter. But usually his blasted patrols are back to taxing us by spring. Now here it is, summer, and I've not seen so much as a glint of gold on the horizon. Either His Majesty doesn't care about what's happening here, or he's got a hand in it. Us free folk can do nothing but walk on and hope things are better on the other side."

It was nearly nightfall before Jonathan caught up with the rest of his party. They'd passed the tail end of the line of Valley folk and were only half a mile from the ashen land beyond.

They spent the evening setting up camp and gathering wood for the rest of the journey. For, as Morris put it: "Most things have only got one burn in them."

Once their camp was made, Jonathan told his companions everything he'd learned. "So it's true, then. Bandits really *have* taken over the Valley," Lysander murmured.

"And Titus had a hand in it," Declan added with a furious grunt. His eyes began to go dark. "I knew it. I knew he'd have something to do with all this! There's not a tear shed in the Kingdom that wasn't Titus's doing. I'll put such a dent in his head —"

"Take a deep breath now, General," one of the giants said as Declan's eyes turned darker. "You'll have your chance to dent him. There's no need to go getting upset —"

"No need? No *need*?" Declan roared. "There's every need! I'll waste no more time — I'll have him throttled before dawn!"

The pirates scattered in all directions as the giants fell upon Declan. He roared and twisted beneath them, trying to throw them off. But they held on tightly.

"Somebody give him a shock! Wake him up!" one of the giants cried.

"Stand clear!" A small jolt of lightning sparked from Jake's fingers and struck Declan in the chest.

The wad of giants convulsed as the jolt jumped between them, arcing along the path of their connected limbs. Their bodies stiffened as they rolled helplessly off of Declan — finally collapsing in separate, twitching balls.

"Not an *actual* shock, you clodded mage! That'll only make him angrier."

"Oh. You meant something more along the lines of a surprise?"

Declan got to his feet, eyes black as ever — and Jake moved quickly.

He flexed his hand and a blast of icy air struck Declan in the face. Frost crusted over his hair and brows. He staggered backwards, and the darkness quickly faded. His stony eyes roved from the pirates — who stood in ranks with their swords half-lifted from their sheaths — to where the clump of giants lay sprawled and twitching upon the ground.

"We're all right, General. Just a wee bit of a shock," they assured him.

His thick shoulders sagged. "I'm going to have a walk around camp," he mumbled. Then he slumped away.

"Keep that spell handy, lad," Morris said as he ducked out from behind a nearby tree.

Jake nodded.

Lysander thrust the Lass back into its sheath. He began to pace, a finger propped on his scruffy chin. "This Grognaut fellow has taken over the castle in the Cleft, you say?"

Jonathan nodded. "That's what I've heard. Which might put a bit of a kink in our rope, if it turns out to be true."

Morris snorted. "A *kink*? Try a knot the size of a dragon's belly. And there'll be no sating it, Captain," he warned. "Bandits don't bargain."

After a moment, Lysander sighed. "I suppose you're probably right. There's nothing for it, then —"

"We've come too far to turn back." Jake's eyes were sharp behind his spectacles. "Don't even say it."

Lysander raised his brows. "I wasn't going to."

"Oh. Well, then what —?"

"Save your breath, lad. He's already got something brewing," Morris said as he watched Lysander pace. "What're your orders, Captain?"

"We're not going to go around Grognaut, and we're certainly not going to treat with him. There's only one way to deal with a barnacle," he said, holding up a finger. "We're going to dig him out."

Jake's spectacles slid down his nose as his brows shot up. "Dig him out? How do you plan to dig out a castle?"

"That's just a figure of speech, lad. He means we're going to pop him off his throne and stick a knife through his belly so he don't grow back."

"Sounds like a plan to me," Jonathan said with a grin.

While the rest of the party talked bandits and war, Declan took a slow walk around the edge of camp. The orb glowed in a ring to the outskirts, and Declan traced it carefully — half in the light, and half in the darkness.

A young tree sat by itself a few paces from the shadows. Its canopy was just large enough to shelter a single man. Eveningwing roosted in the branches near its top. A slight breeze moved the limbs gently, bobbing him up and down.

Nadine sat beneath the tree. She had her knees drawn up to her chest and her head buried in her arms. Her shoulders shook gently.

"Are you all right there, wee mot?"

She wiped impatiently at her eyes as Declan stepped in beside her. "I am fine."

"Those don't look like happy tears."

"They are nothing."

"Well that's a mightily odd thing. You don't strike me as the sort of woman who'd cry over nothing. And I'm never wrong about my strikings," he added when she looked up.

"Why must you always plague me with your words? You will walk for days and never say anything to the pirate captain, or to the strange man you still call *fiddler* even though he plays so horribly. Why is it always me you bother? Is it because I am small?"

He shook his head. "I would never plague anybody over being small."

"Then what is it?"

"I suppose it's because of your voice."

"My voice?"

"Yeh, you sound so odd — like you're stumbling over every word. And then if I can get you mad enough, your face turns red and you start muttering all these silly little things nobody knows the meaning of," he said, lips twitching in the tiniest of smiles. "I like the way it sounds."

"You would not like them so much if you knew what they meant," she said vehemently.

He thumped down beside her, and she jerked the blanket over her feet. "What have you got under there?"

"It is nothing," she said again.

"Then why's your face gone all sandy-pale?" His arm shot out and ripped the blanket back.

Blisters covered Nadine's toes and the sides of her feet. Some were red and swollen. Others had burst. They wept openly between the ragged flaps of her skin.

"Plains mother," Declan hissed.

"I was going to let them breathe before I cleaned them. Eveningwing has been helping me," she said, pointing to the canopy above them. "It took us a while to figure out how to untangle and tangle them back. But I believe we —"

"Why didn't you say something, you great stubborn sandbeater? Every man in this camp knows how to work laces!"

"I did not think — what are you doing?"

He dumped her rucksack on the ground and pawed through its contents, digging until he came up with a bottle of ointment. "Stubborn, clodded ..." His thick fingers fumbled at the cork until she grabbed his hands.

261

"You are going to break it!"

"I'm going to break *you*! No wonder you were crying. You've been marching for days with your wee little toes all red and weeping. Why didn't you speak up?"

"What good would that have done? Lysander is right — I must learn to walk in them before we reach the icy paths of the mountains. Someday my feet will harden and I will not have this trouble. Now hand me the bottle."

He let go. His lip curled as he watched her dab thick white ointment onto her blisters. "Doesn't that sting?"

"You are asking if it hurts?"

"Yeh."

She shrugged. "It is uncomfortable."

He snorted. "Be honest, mite. It's a bit more than that."

She gave him a hard look. "My flesh will heal. These wounds will close and pass away. But there are marks on my heart that will never heal. Those are the only wounds worth my tears, giant. They are the reason I weep."

Declan opened his mouth, but a flapping sound interrupted him. Eveningwing bobbed on his branches. His head jerked to the side.

"What —?"

Declan clamped a hand over Nadine's mouth. His shadowed gaze turned to the edge of camp; his brows creased as he squinted. Slowly, he got to his feet. Eveningwing hopped into the upper branches, head bobbing along the light's edge.

Nadine took her spear and went to stand next to Declan. "What is —?"

His arm shot out and knocked her to the side just as a barrage of objects flew from the darkness. They looked like tiny arrows: bone shaved into needles with dyed feathers as their fletching. They peppered Declan's arms and neck, sticking firmly into his skin.

He jolted the camp with a roar.

"Bandits!" Jonathan cried. "Don't let those darts hit you! They've got numbing pois — ah!"

He took a dart in the neck and stumbled backwards. Morris got one in the leg and Lysander got hit twice in the chest before he managed to draw his sword. When the wave of darts ended, the bandits leapt in.

Yellowed bone adorned nearly every inch of them. They wore it around their necks and wrists, wove in tangles throughout their beards. Sharp bone ornaments pierced their ears, noses and lips. Breastplates with wolf heads were strapped over their filthy leather tunics. Steel blades hissed as they flew from their sheaths.

"Make them bleed, boys!" one of the bandits cried. Then he charged straight for Lysander.

Morris hurtled into the bandit's side, knocking his slight body to the ground. The hapless bandit took several rolls, his bone ornaments clattering with every turn. Finally, he came to a stop near the base of a tree — where another pirate ran him through.

"Form ranks, dogs!" Lysander yelled over the din. He managed to slice one of the bandits in the side before he collapsed, breathing heavily. "I can't feel my ... it's all ..."

"That's the poison," Jonathan grunted, stumbling over to him. He swung his sword in drunken arcs, trying to hold the bandits back.

Colored darts peppered the giants' thick skin. They swung their scythes furiously; the rage of the battle seemed to be holding the poison back. After a few unsuccessful attempts to break their line, the bandits retreated into the shadows.

They slipped to the edge of camp and hung out of the giants' reach. Without the fight to fuel them, the giants slowed quickly. Even Declan's rage was no match for the poisoned darts. Slowly, he sank to the ground, collapsing amid the mangled bodies of his foes.

Jake's magic weakened as the poison took its toll. The spells barely sputtered off his gloves. Soon his fireballs were reduced to little more than wisps of flame. He moaned as he sank to his knees. "What are they doing?"

"Waiting," Jonathan grunted. "Once we're all numb, they'll hack us to bits."

When the last of the giants had collapsed on all fours, the bandits crept in. "I wonder if the mage's bones have got any magic in them?" a bandit close to Jake whispered.

"Lots of giants, here," another said with a grin. "Just think of what we'll be able to make with *their* bones."

The bandits' circle tightened around the camp. The pirates and the giants watched through glassy eyes, their bodies swaying under the poison's bite. Not a one of them had the strength to draw his blade.

They all likely would've perished that night, had it not been for Nadine.

She lay curled upon the ground where Declan had thrown her, still as a rock. Her tiny form had been of no interest to the bandits: they'd walked straight past her, their eyes set on bigger game.

When the last of her enemies had gone by, Nadine stood with her spear poised over her shoulder and cried: "Cover yourselves!"

The bandits spun, but the spear had already left her hand. It cut through the air and shot for the orb of light that hovered above Jake. The pirates and the giants shut their eyes. Someone threw a blanket over Declan's head. They bared their teeth as the spear's point struck and burst the orb.

Piercing light erupted over the camp. It chased the shadows from under every leaf and blade of grass. The ashen lands before them were stricken white. For a breath, everything around them was perfectly and clearly illuminated — including the insides of the bandits' eyes.

Smoke trailed from their sockets. They screamed and threw their arms over their faces, but it was too late. When the burst of light receded, all of the color had been stricken from their eyes. The bandits stared unseeing through orbs of murky white.

Eveningwing darted out of the shadows. He raked the bandits' skin with his claws and his screeches drove them into a frenzy. They trampled over one another, trying to get away from him. Nadine picked up a fallen sword and swung it at their backs. She managed to bring two of them down while Eveningwing led a third straight into the low-hanging branches of a tree.

The bandit's neck snapped with a crunch.

The rest fled blindly into the darkness, where the shadows swallowed their screams. Nadine and Eveningwing stood sentry over their numbed companions throughout the night: she put ointment on their wounds while the halfhawk circled overhead. It was dawn before the poison finally loosened its grip.

"What a fight that was, Captain," Morris said as he rolled onto his side. He wedged a stocky arm beneath Lysander and, with Jonathan pulling on the front of his shirt, managed to prop the captain up.

Lysander flexed his hand tentatively. "Oh, thank Gravy — I can move my fingers. Are you all right, dogs?"

"Aye, Captain," they mumbled.

"Giants?"

They answered in a rumble of grunts.

"I'll be better once somebody takes this clodded blanket off my head," Declan said.

Jake reached over and pulled it free.

Lysander stared worriedly down at his legs. "Are you certain this isn't permanent?"

"Nah. It just takes a while, is all," Jonathan said cheerily. "I got grazed in the rump one time. I couldn't feel my left side for a couple of hours. Made sitting a bit of a challenge — but I managed. Don't be surprised if you find yourself on the ground an awful lot today." He slapped Lysander on the shoulder. "Two in the chest'll do that to you."

"Excellent," he muttered. His stormy eyes swept through camp. "Where's that desert woman?"

They called, and Nadine appeared beside them.

Lysander held out his hand. "I owe you my thanks."

"Why?"

"Ah, well … had it not been for you, we wouldn't have seen the dawn. And I daresay a few of our bones would be missing, as well," he added with a grimace. "You saved our lives. I don't think I could possibly thank you enough."

She shrugged. "We have work to do, Captain — work we cannot do if we are dead. You may thank me by getting to your feet."

He grinned. "Fair enough. Give me a hand, will you?"

*******

The ashen wastes of the Valley stretched on for miles.

Black grass curled beneath their boots as they traveled. Every breath of air was thickened by ash. A few of the trees still crackled. Sometimes a strong wind would rip across them, stoking their bark into bright red scales. Smoke was an ever-present enemy: their eyes streamed against its acrid breath. They covered their mouths and noses, but the fumes still made them cough.

After a day or so, the smoke abated. The pirates and the giants trudged out of the still-burning lands and into a stretch that was already dead.

Here, the ash had settled and the trees were blackened shells. A few miles more, and they began to see a bit of green: small patches between the ruins of houses and farms. Soon the only signs of destruction were in the things men had built — the land itself had been spared.

When they reached a large orange grove, Jonathan ordered them to a halt. "I'll bet my left foot the bandits are holed up in Crow's Cross."

"What makes you so sure?" Lysander said.

Jonathan shrugged. "The land hasn't been so crispy, of late. Not even the bandits would set fire to their own front door. They've always wanted to get into Crow's Cross, anyhow. It seems like the guards were always fighting them off. So if they ever got the army to do it," he shrugged off his pack, "then I'll bet that's the first place they went.

266

"There'll be no slipping by them, either — they'll be able to spot us for miles if they've taken the city. So we'd better prepare for a skirmish." He unbuckled his scabbard and dropped it next to his rucksack. Then he fixed a cloak about his shoulders and wedged his fiddle into his belt. "Well, gents. I'll see you in a bit."

Lysander grabbed him by the cloak. "Just where do you think you're going?"

"To check things out, of course. The bandits who attacked us weren't from the mountains — they were from the forest," Jonathan explained when Lysander glared. "Mountain bandits and forest bandits hate each other. So either one of them has finally killed the other off, or they're working together. That's what I'm going to find out. I know you're probably going to be worried sick about me —"

"That's not the first thing I thought of."

"— but I know what I'm doing. Charming my way into things, spying on the enemy. I've done this for Garron loads of times."

"Oh? You've snuck into a village packed with individuals who'd like nothing more than to wear your bones around their necks and emerged unscathed?"

Jonathan paused. "No. But I lived in Gilderick's castle for a full season and left with all my innards. That's got to count for something."

"He's got a point there, Captain," Morris said.

Lysander frowned. "I still don't like it."

"There's not a thing to worry about, mate. It's nearly sunset." Jonathan rolled his eyes at Lysander's blank look. "This is the hour of day when the corks start popping! It's prime sneaking time," he added with a wink. "The whole village is going to be too boggled to even notice I'm there. An hour or so in the tavern, and I'll have all the information we need. You want to know what we're up against, don't you?"

"Well, yes."

"Then leave me to my work." And with a rather dramatic swoop of his cloak, Jonathan marched away.

Lysander paced as the fiddler disappeared over the hill. He walked between the trees, hands clasped behind his back. He paced long after the rest of camp had settled down for dinner, an edge of his eye turned always towards the road.

"He'll be all right, Captain," Morris said. "That fellow could charm his way out of a hangman's noose."

"One dart — that's all it takes. One careless word. They're probably boiling the flesh off of him as we speak."

"Oh, why would they bother with all that? There's not enough on him to make it worth the effort. He'll be fine, Captain," Morris said when Lysander glared. "You brought him along because he knows the land."

"No, I brought him because he wouldn't leave my ship." At last, his pacing relented. "Though I suppose you're right. He *did* survive a stint in Gilderick's castle."

"He sure did, Captain."

"And how many bards could say that?"

"Not many, I'd wager."

Lysander sighed. "Perhaps I'm only —"

A screech from Eveningwing cut across his words. The hawk darted down into camp, brushing the top of Lysander's head with the flat of his wing before he shot back into the sky. His form stood out like a hole in the stars as he circled over the direction Jonathan had headed.

"What's he squawking about?" Morris grunted.

Lysander's mouth pressed into a grim line as he answered: "Trouble."

# CHAPTER 24
## THE RAT'S WHISKERS INN

"We have to go after him. Give the order to move —"

"Are you mad, Captain?" Morris cut in. "We haven't got one foggy clue about how many of them there are or what it is they're doing. If they see the horde of us crossing over that hill," he snorted, "well, it'll be all darts and darkness."

"We could go in quietly," Jake suggested.

"*They* do nothing quietly," Nadine said, jerking a thumb over her shoulder at the giants.

Several of them grunted in agreement.

Lysander snapped his fingers. "A small party might be able slip in and pull him out. We'll have to leave our armor and most of our weapons behind — anything that says *I'm part of a larger force waiting over the hill to sack your village.*"

Morris watched him unbuckle the Lass, mouth hanging open beneath his wiry beard. "This is madness, Captain! How do we know he isn't already dead?"

"That wasn't the signal for death," Lysander said, as if it should be obvious.

"Well, then what was it?"

"Ah, it was either extreme peril or imprisonment. I'm not sure. Now," he propped his fists on his hips, "who's coming with me?"

Nadine volunteered immediately, but Declan shook his head.

"If you're aiming not to be noticed, you shouldn't bring a woman."

"I'm afraid he's right," Lysander said when she started to protest. "A lady *does* tend to draw the eye. I'll admit I've certainly noticed one or two in my time. We can't have anything odd or memorable about us. Which I'm afraid puts you out of it, Morris."

He held up his nubs. "Aye, Captain."

"Jake's going, of course. That's a given." Lysander studied him carefully. "He's slight and unassuming."

"And I'm a mage, which some people might say is useful," he muttered.

Morris's watery eyes swept between them. "You can't go in with only two. What about Declan? He's man-sized."

Nadine rolled her eyes. "Not many men have arms bigger around than their heads."

"I'm built even," he growled, jabbing a finger at her.

Lysander shrugged. "We'll throw a cloak over him. If we're lucky, nobody will be able to tell what's wool and what's bulk."

*******

Crow's Cross was a beacon in a sea of darkness. Yellow light streamed from every window and beneath every door. Shouts and drunken laughter billowed over its walls and out into the silent night like fog off the sea.

The front gates hung open. The thick oaken planks had been smashed in at their middle, snapping the massive beam that'd held them closed. Now the gates sagged on their hinges — leaving the way open for all manner of villains.

Bandits weren't the only plague in Crow's Cross. A pile of charred corpses near the front gate marked the end of any order, and warned travelers of the sort of evil they might find inside.

The reek of death was everywhere — a tang so potent that most who braved the city's streets wore thick scarves around their noses and mouths. Bodies hung half out of broken windows and filth clogged the alleyways. Nearly every puddle was murky with either blood or sick.

Men in ragged cloaks stumbled down the cobblestone streets, knives drawn and eyes searching. They came across a bandit passed out over his drink and swarmed around him.

270

Their knives went in and out; they cackled when he tried to fight them off. Two stripped his corpse of armor and weapons while three more stood sentry.

A couple of thieves watched in interest. As soon as the cloaked men had moved on, they slipped in and took whatever trinkets had been left behind.

At the center of all the chaos was the *Rat's Whiskers Inn*. Bandits, thieves and murderers alike flowed through its doors in a constant stream. Wild shouting emanated from the shattered holes in its windows — along with the noise of a familiar, shrilling instrument.

Lysander and his cloaked companions followed the many off-kilter notes to the inn's crooked front door. "Heads down, gentlemen," Lysander said as they approached. "Speak as little as possible and try not to meet any eyes. We don't want to be remembered."

The doors swung open and three bandits tumbled out. They only managed to make it a few steps before they collapsed upon the ground in a mass of gurgling swears.

"These clodders won't be remembering what their mothers named them in the morning, much less anything about us," Declan grumbled as he shouldered his way inside.

Lysander followed after him, but Jake hung back. His eyes wandered over the front door in a slow, meticulous line.

"Come on, pick up your feet," Lysander hissed. When Jake still didn't move, he spun impatiently. "What is it?"

"There are latches on the outside of the door. Why would there be latches on the *out*side?"

Lysander furrowed his brows. "I haven't got a clue, and I'm afraid there's no time to wonder." He grabbed Jake by the front of his robes and pulled him inside.

They followed the fiddle's screams through a stinking sea of bodies to the hearth at the back of the room. Jonathan stood beside the fire, a lively tune shrilling off the end of his bow. Sweat drenched his hair and left dark rings beneath his arms. He kept a forced grin plastered on his face as he played.

Declan tried to wave but Lysander grabbed his wrist. "We don't know him."

"Of course we do — that's the wee fiddler."

"No, we have to *pretend* we don't know him. We're just three ruffians stopping by for a drink. Now follow my lead."

Lysander wove his way to the head of the line and led them in a wide circle towards the hearth. They were nearly there when a redheaded serving girl stepped into their path.

"Have a drink, sir?"

"Thank you, my dear." Lysander swiped three tankards from the tray she carried and slapped some coin into her other hand.

She narrowed her eyes at him before she walked away.

"What was that look for?" Jake hissed as Lysander passed them each a tankard.

"Maybe it had something to do with Captain Dashing and his fancy manners," Declan grumbled.

"*Dashing*? I didn't even smile."

"Well, you can't go sweeping and bowing to everybody. You've got to be a bit gruffer in a place like this. Watch." Declan threw his arm out and shoved a hapless thief hard in the back. "Out of my way, you!"

He tumbled over a bench and landed flat on the floor. When he tried to get up, a passerby kicked him smartly in the ribs. Someone else dumped a full tankard of ale on his head — much to the amusement of the nearby tables.

"See?" Declan said.

Lysander pursed his lips. "Let's get our man and get out quickly. I'm not sure this place is fit for a pirate."

At long last, they made it to the hearth. Declan and Jake pretended to be warming themselves by the flames while Lysander slipped up to Jonathan — cloaking himself in a black patch missed by the fire's light.

He brought the tankard casually to his lips while his stormy eyes roved about the room. "All right there, fiddler?"

"Never better," he replied through his teeth. "I would've come back sooner, but these chaps asked for a song. Of course, I couldn't refuse."

272

He raised his leg slightly, revealing the shackle clamped around his ankle. A thick rusty chain ran from the shackle to the wall, where it wrapped several times around a torch sconce that had been bent forcibly against the mortar — forming an inescapable loop.

"Is it a standard irons lock?"

"Standard as they come. The picking should be easy enough." He leaned to the side and the flap of his coat opened a bit, revealing the many rows of lock picks sewn into it. "I've got a few things stashed for a rainy day."

"Or a tempest," Lysander muttered.

"The iron's only half of it," Jonathan hissed through his grin. "They'll know the moment I've stopped playing. I tried to take a breath about an hour ago and wound up taking the backside of a bowl straight to the ole jewels, instead. They said they'll throw knives next time," he added with a grimace.

Lysander raised his brows. "Gravy. Well, we certainly can't have that. I'm sure we'll be able to think up something clever. But for now, let's see if I can't get you out of this shackle." He waved behind him. "Declan? Put those uncannily large shoulders to use and block for me, will you? No, don't stand there cross-armed like a guard at His Majesty's castle!" he hissed. "Sit down somewhere. *Blend.* Just make sure nobody can get a good look at what I'm doing."

Declan thumped over to the table directly in front of them and shouldered his way onto a bench filled with mountain bandits. Instead of bones, red scars adorned their skin — branded into the shapes of letters and symbols.

The bench groaned as Declan sat. The bandits seated on either side tilted slightly inwards — while those across the table were lifted until just their toes scraped the ground.

They stared, open-mouthed, as Declan drained his tankard in two gulps. He thumped it down when he was finished — so roughly that it left a shallow dent in the tabletop.

"How'd you do that?" one of the bandits said.

Declan shrugged. "It's ale, isn't it? There's no point in savoring it — just up you tilt and down it goes."

The bandit exchanged a quick look with his companions before he slid a full tankard across the table. "Do that again."

"A copper says he can't!" one of them cried.

They slapped their coin onto the table.

While Declan kept the bandits occupied, Lysander chose one of the picks and stuck it into the shackle's mouth. It rattled uselessly against the tumblers.

"What's taking so long, mate? My poor fingers can't keep this up much longer," Jonathan said, raising his voice to be heard over the wavering notes of a jig.

"It's rusted," Lysander grunted back. "They haven't taken very good care of it."

"Well, what'd you expect? They're villains! Before one of them came up with this chain, they were going to just nail my foot to the floor."

Lysander let out an exasperated sigh. "Maybe Jake has a spell —"

"Hang on a second, there." Jonathan's eyes went wide and he jerked his leg away. "I think we ought to consider chopping my foot off, first. No telling what one of those spells would do. He could blow me off at the knee!"

"It doesn't matter," Lysander said after a moment of craning his head around. "It looks as if he's wandered off. You and I are on our own."

While his companions had been focused on the lock, something across the room had caught Jake's attention. He left the hearth and wove his way through the crowd. His slight body was tossed this way and that by the masses, bouncing him from one hardened shoulder to the next. He rode the waves of passersby until he finally stumbled into a clearing.

One of the serving girls was headed in his direction — a forest woman with loose, dark hair and eyes to match. Her lips sat calmly, but she wore a scowl that could've melted flesh. She'd tried to sweep past him when he reached out and grabbed her arm.

It was a mistake.

274

Jake's head thudded into the top of a nearby table and he groaned as she twisted his arm behind his back. "Hello, Elena."

She released him immediately. "Jake? What are you doing here?"

"Well, I — I ought to be asking you the same thing!" he sputtered, rubbing his arm. "What in Kingdom's name are you doing in such a dark, horrible —?"

"He's with me," Elena interrupted, waving to a redheaded serving girl who'd crept up behind Jake.

She walked away with a nod ... slipping whatever sharp, glinting object she'd been holding back into her belt.

Elena waited until she'd gone before she turned her scowl on Jake. "I'm here because I happen to own this place."

His mouth fell open. "*You* own it? How ...?"

"It was given to me," she said shortly. She gathered up her tray and stepped past him, heading for an empty table.

He followed at a trot. "Who gave it to you?"

"The man who owned it before, of course."

"And he just handed over the keys, did he?"

"Well, I suppose it's more accurate to say that I inherited it — it's sort of a tradition." She plucked the empty tankards off the table with both hands, flipping them and setting them in a balanced ring upon her tray. "The man I got it from inherited the inn from the first owner, who was executed by Midlan for harboring criminals, or something."

"I see." Jake crossed him arms. "And what happened to the fellow before you?"

She waved a hand. "Oh, he ... died. It was all very sudden. And tragic."

"*Elena!*"

He glowered at her from over the top of his spectacles, and she frowned back. "Let me show you something, mage. You see those girls over there?" She pointed to the bar, where three redheaded serving girls were busy loading their trays with tankards and pies. "They're sisters. They fled from the Unforgivable Mountains after Titus burned their village and had no choice but to try to find work in the Valley. The man who owned this inn before me … he was horrible to them. He hurt them.

"I came to the Valley because it was the most peaceful place I could think of. I only meant to stay in Crow's Cross for the night. But when I saw how that man treated those girls …" Her eyes glinted like daggers' points. "I took matters into my own hands."

Jake shook his head in disbelief. "But how have you managed to survive all this time? What about the bandits?"

Her hand dipped beneath her collar and returned with a small, flat bottle of murky liquid. "The locals call this *dragon spit*. I haven't got a clue what it's made of, but it works about a dozen times faster than ale. Every time they sober up, the bandits storm in here swearing they're going to burn us to the ground. So I offer them a drink. And before you know it," she waved a hand about the room, "we've got ourselves a peace treaty."

Jake frowned. "You know you can't keep that up forever."

"Sure I can. The cellar's full of this stuff." She slipped the bottle beneath her collar and swept the full tray effortlessly onto her palm. She'd gone to walk towards the bar when Jake stepped into her path.

"Your cellar is going to run dry eventually, and then what will you do? What if Titus sends his men through here — or Crevan sends his army? They won't be so easily fooled."

"I know what I'm doing."

"You can't possibly be happy here. Look at this place!" He stretched a hand towards her, but recoiled at her scowl. "Come with us to the mountains."

Her lips parted slightly before she shook her head. "No. No, my fighting days are over. I left to find peace, and I've found it."

"*Here*? This couldn't be the furthest thing from … is that fellow dead?" Jake pointed to a dark corner of the room, where the body of a bandit was sprawled facedown upon the floor.

Elena shrugged. "He's probably just asleep."

"There's blood coming out of his throat!"

"I'll sweep it up in the morning," she said impatiently. "The point is that I run an honest establishment and make an honest living. It's all I've ever wanted."

"You mean you want to stay here and be a — a common tavern wench? That's right, I said it," he snapped when she glared. "A *wench*."

She held his eyes for one deadly second. When she spoke again, she growled each word: "I'm happy here. In fact, I couldn't be happier. Good day to you, sir."

He stood, slack-jawed as she brushed past him and marched away. His feet carried him to the hearth. By the time he made it back to his companions, Jake's thin shoulders had slumped considerably.

Lysander, on the other hand, had made some real progress. "Almost ... ah, there!" He grinned as the shackle snapped open. "I just had to be a little rough with her."

"That's all well and good, mate," Jonathan took a deep, gasping breath, "but how're we going to get out of here? I haven't been able to feel my fingers for two songs and my poor fiddle's just about to catch flame. I think there might actually be some smoke whisping off it!"

Lysander's stormy eyes swept around the room. "We need a distraction — something loud enough that they won't notice the music."

Jake had been staring at the floor while they talked. But quite suddenly, his chin shot up. "I'm going to start a brawl."

"A brawl would certainly do it," Lysander agreed. "But wouldn't a nice spell be just as —?"

"I want to punch somebody."

Lysander's brows arched high. "All right. Have at it, then."

Jake strode purposefully to the middle of the room, rolling up the sleeves of his robes as he went. A lone bandit sat at a nearby table, surrounded by a passed-out ring of his companions. Though he was still on his feet, he'd begun to slump over his tankard.

277

With a deep breath, Jake tapped him on the shoulder. "Excuse me, sir. But your manners offend me." When the bandit turned, Jake slung a fist into his forehead.

The result left Jake yelping in pain, while the bandit erupted in gurgling laughter.

"Why'd you hit him there for?" Declan hollered from his table. There was an alarming number of overturned tankards scattered before him — but remarkably, he was still conscious.

Jake grimaced as he wrung his hand. "I don't know. I've never hit anybody before!"

"You've got to smack him in the nose, right here on the side," Declan said, pointing.

Jake slung his fist again. The bandit's nose crunched and a little trickle of blood ran out. But he stayed sitting up — still cackling.

"Eh, that's no good. You're going to have to hit him with something else." Declan swooped an arm out to the side, nearly flattening his branded benchmates. "Grab one of those chairs and smack him over the head with it. Go on — give him a proper walloping!"

Jake frowned at him. "Have you been drinking?"

"So what if I have? Even a drunk giant still knows his brawling."

With a heavy sigh, Jake pulled a chair out from under one of the bandit's unconscious companions and drew it over his head. "Sorry about this," he muttered. Then with a cry, he brought it down.

It struck the top of the bandit's head with a hollow *thud*. For a moment, it looked as if Jake would have to hit him again. Then quite suddenly, the bandit began to tilt. His cackling stopped mid-stream as his eyes rolled back. He tumbled from his chair, flopping hard onto the ground.

Declan guffawed heartily and pounded his meaty fists onto the table. The bandits, on the other hand, seemed far from impressed. They hardly glanced at Jake before going back to their tankards.

Just when it looked as if they weren't going to get their brawl, Declan's bench groaned and finally gave out. It snapped under his massive weight, sending him straight to his rump. His benchmates tumbled on top of him, swearing the whole way down. With one side suddenly so light, the table flipped — dumping a whole bench of mountain bandits directly onto the heads of bandits from the forest.

That did it.

Swears became insults, insults became punches, and soon they'd started to brawl. The two tables grappled with each other; their cries drew bandits from all corners of the room. They rushed to the center in a swell of shouts — pulling hapless bystanders in along with them. Soon every bench was emptied and the tavern's belly was a writhing, tangled mass of flying fists.

Elena and her serving girls stood behind the bar as the chaos unfolded. At her signal, they separated: the three sisters went upstairs while Elena ducked into a room behind the bar. Moments later, three cloaked figures drifted down the stairs and out the back door — full rucksacks across their shoulders and heavy purses at their belts.

The moment they'd disappeared, Elena emerged.

Her tavern clothes were gone. She wore her black and scarlet armor once more, with the slitted mask tied firmly around the lower half of her face. She grabbed several bottles of dragon spit from behind the bar and uncorked them. Then she headed for the hearth ... leaving a trail of murky liquor on the planks behind her.

"You should leave," she said when she reached Lysander.

He and Jonathan had been throwing themselves desperately at the edge of the wall of brawling bodies, trying to force their way inside. His eyes widened at the sight of Elena. "You? What in high tide ...?"

"You need to go."

He shook his head. "Never — not without my battlemage!"

Elena rolled her eyes as he went back to shoving. "You there — giant!"

Declan stopped laughing and paused, a wriggling bandit hanging in his grasp.

She snapped her fingers. "Put that down and get your friends out of here. I'll find the mage."

Declan slung the bandit into the sea of fists and gathered Lysander and Jonathan under his arms. "Hold tight, wee things!" he slurred. Then he charged sideways into the fray, scattering all in his path.

Elena followed in his wake for several feet. Dragon spit trickled out of the bottles in her hand and onto the floor behind her as she walked. It wasn't long before she spotted Jake.

He'd taken refuge beneath a table. His thin arms snapped over his chest at the sight of her. "I don't care what you say — I know you aren't happy. And I'm not leaving here until you admit it!"

She ripped the table onto its side — along with the handful of bandits who'd been warring on its top. "Get moving, mage."

He scrambled to his feet.

Elena shoved Jake out in front of her, smashing bottles of dragon spit behind them. When they neared the front door, she grabbed a lantern from among the ruins of a toppled bench.

"Come with us," Jake pleaded.

Her brows cut low over her eyes. "Are those my gloves?"

"Ah," he flexed his hands, "yes. I thought you meant for me to keep them."

"I'd hoped you would keep them. I didn't realize you'd want to ... *wear* them."

His face turned slightly pink. "It's not that I wanted ... nobody was more surprised ... and how do you think I feel about it?" he sputtered when she raised a brow. "Do you have any idea how embarrassing it is to walk around with a leather impetus? *Leather.* Other mages will think I'm some sort of gutless, slimy warlock —"

"Gripping," Elena interrupted. "Would you light this for me?"

Jake snapped his fingers over the lantern's wick and a small flame blossomed on its end.

The dark of Elena's eyes reflected the light like a mirror. "Thank you," she said. Then she hurled it to the ground.

Flames sprang from the shattered lantern in a roar, following the path of the dragon spit. Elena shoved Jake out the door and slammed it shut behind them. She clamped the bolts down and snapped locks onto the latches.

"I put these on weeks ago," she said as she worked. "It's strange, but not one person ever asked me why there were latches on the outside of the door."

Jake's mouth hung open. "You've been planning this all along, haven't you?"

She shrugged. "I suppose the peaceful life *was* beginning to get a bit dull. Now come on," she grabbed him by the arm, "we've got to save my Braver."

*******

Declan thundered through the crowd and out the gates — Lysander under one arm and Jonathan under the other. Most scattered from his path, though an unlucky few struck his massive shoulders and were knocked aside.

Only when they were a safe distance from Crow's Cross did he stop.

"Put us down!" Lysander cried. He beat his fists against Declan's massive arms but the giant only laughed. "Jake's still in there! We have to —"

Jonathan reached across Declan's middle and smacked him in the face. "I think it's too late for that, Captain."

Lysander looked to where he pointed and gasped when he saw smoke rising from the city. A ball of fire erupted from its middle. It bloomed violently, scattering bits of the

281

inn in every direction, spreading as its flames caught to the roofs of nearby houses.

"Jake ..." Lysander's mouth parted in disbelief. "No, it can't be."

A thick stream of tears ran unchecked down Declan's face. "Poor wee mage!" he bawled.

Fire leapt from one house to the next, lighting their roofs like torches. A crowd of bandits swelled between the gates. Screams filled the air as they tried desperately to escape the flames. They beat each other, crushed heads beneath their heels and climbed over bodies in a panic.

Lysander watched dully for a moment more before his head sagged low. "Jake ..." He hung there for a moment, limp beneath Declan's arm. Then a second blast made his head snap up.

Something like a mighty gust of wind struck the crowd. It ripped the frayed gates off their hinges and sent the bandits flying — spewing them into the night in a flailing, terrified stream.

A dapple-gray horse charged through the empty space left behind. On his back were two riders: one dressed in night-black armor, and the other ...

"Jake? Jake!"

Lysander and Jonathan waved their arms and the dapple-gray horse galloped towards them. More cries split the air. A force of pirates and giants charged over the hill and struck the bandits who'd managed to squeeze through the gates. The pirates darted in with their swords drawn while the giants moved their scythes in steady, sweeping lines — felling their enemies in rows.

With an army standing in their way, the bandits had nowhere else to turn: they stumbled drunkenly towards the mountains, leaving the Valley behind.

The flames rising from Crow's Cross grew so furious that the pirates and giants had to move further down the road to avoid being overtaken by the smoke. They charged to the top of a nearby hill and watched as fire dragged the city to ruin.

The moment she caught her breath, Nadine marched straight for Lysander. "What happened? You were supposed to go in *quietly*!"

"Yes, well, things got a bit out of h — oh by Gravy, put me *down*!"

Declan opened his arms, dumping Lysander and Jonathan onto the grass.

Morris chuckled as he watched the city burn. "That's more than a *bit*, Captain. I suppose we'll have to add this to the list of places you aren't allowed back."

"That's probably for the best," Lysander agreed, grimacing as he massaged his ribs.

Jonathan's hand uncurled slowly from around his fiddle. "Oh, my poor fingers. They're burning worse than a desert bloke's backside!"

Nadine jabbed her spear into the ground. "You were supposed to go in quietly and get him out. Instead, you set fire to everything!"

"Oh, calm yourself, wee mite," Declan said.

Nadine gaped at his uncharacteristically silly grin for a moment before she narrowed her eyes. "You are drunk."

He shrugged. "A little bit, yeh. That mountain ale is heady stuff. But it's a wonder, I tell you. There was battling all around me and I didn't go mad!"

"I cannot believe y — let me go!"

Declan spun her around by the shoulders, laughing when she tried to kick him. He'd gone to lift her higher when the pommel of a knife struck his head with a *thwap*.

"Set her down," Elena growled as she pulled another knife from her bandolier, "or I'll hit you with the pointy end."

Nadine let out a cry at the sight of her. Elena slid off her dapple-gray horse just as Nadine hurtled into her chest. "I knew you would come back to us." She pulled away and took both of Elena's hands in hers. "Did you find your peace?"

"Briefly," she said with a sigh. "Then Jake set fire to my inn."

"I did no such thing," he said indignantly. He'd been trying to dismount, but wound up with one foot on the ground and the other tangled in the stirrup. Braver stood patiently as Jake tried to tug himself free. "You were the one who started the fire —"

"Odd. I seem to remember *you* were the one who lit the lantern."

"Well, I had no idea you were going to use it to burn down a city. Otherwise I never would've given — could somebody *please* get me free of this confounded beast?"

Nadine pulled his boot out of the stirrup and he stumbled backwards.

Elena crossed her arms. "Consider this, mage: because of your spell, we've purged the land of a bunch of murderers and thieves. Is that such a bad thing?"

Jake turned back towards the city. For a moment, his spectacles reflected the dancing flames. "I'm not your tool, Elena. I won't be used. There's too much blood on my hands already."

Elena glared as he stalked away, shaking her head. Then she turned to the waiting crowd. "So, I hear you lot are on some sort of hopeless quest to free the mountains ... mind if I come along?"

# CHAPTER 25
## WHERE THE DARKNESS BEGAN

Life in the mountains followed a harsh rhythm.

The gray hours of the morning stretched longer here than anywhere else in the Kingdom, simply because the sun had so much further to climb. Daylight passed above them briefly — though by the time it'd fought its way through the clouds, there was very little warmth left to it. When the sun fell back behind the peaks, the long, cold night began.

Kyleigh often woke to the sound of the mountain's voice. It was fainter this far from the summit, but no less menacing. Winds howled through the darkest hours of the night. They rattled under her door and made bumps crawl across her skin. She wasn't supposed to be there. The mountains wanted her out.

It was like living each day with a knife pressed against her throat.

Her task was only half-finished — for now, there would be no escaping the voice. So she spent her time at the forge, letting the noise of her work drown out the mountain's ghostly taunts.

The things Kael had taught the craftsmen took their skills to extraordinary heights. They had no need for the anvil or flame: they shaped swords with their hands and pounded out armor with their fists. It wouldn't be long before the wildmen were suited and ready for battle.

There was just one problem.

"I've acted rashly," Gwen said as she clomped around the forge. "I see that, now. Were it only my own life at stake, I would gladly risk it — I would fight until I had nothing left to give, as I once did. But things aren't how they used to be, are they?" The words were almost spiteful. She took a deep breath. "My father would've thought first of his people. The wildmen are happy here. And more importantly, they're safe."

"You're camped right in the middle of his great bloody road, Gwen," Kyleigh said through her teeth. "Rest assured that Titus knows exactly where you are. If he hasn't attacked you yet, it's only because he's got something worse in mind."

"Why would he come down? He has the summit. He won't bother us again."

"He's not a bear — he's a man. Territory isn't the only thing he cares about. One of these days he *will* attack you, and then his game will begin."

She thrust a red-hot blade into the water trough. It hissed and spat as it cooled. Gwen watched the steam rise, smirking. "I'm not afraid of him. The day he strikes us here will be a very sore day, indeed."

"Sore for you, perhaps," Kyleigh muttered under her breath.

Gwen turned. "What would you have me do, pest? My craftsmen are useless, my army is a ragged strip of what it was, and each day more of these soft-skinned downmountain folk come to my village, begging for shelter. Sometimes being Thane means you've got to do what's best for your people — even if it costs you your home."

The swirls of paint on her face twisted as she pursed her lips. Kyleigh couldn't help but feel a bit sorry for her. "Kael will think of something."

"Really? Is he going to carve a thousand warriors from the trees?" Gwen shook her head. "He's taught my craftsmen some entertaining tricks. But he isn't like our last Wright — he can't fight worth anything."

"I think you're scared."

Kyleigh didn't move when Gwen stalked over. She leaned in until their faces were hardly a hand's breadth apart. "What was that, pest?"

"You heard me. Stop dragging your arse, Gwen — you know what he's capable of."

286

"I know only what you've told me. I haven't seen it for myself. And until I'm convinced, my people will stay put."

Kyleigh struggled to keep her voice even as she growled: "How do I convince you, then? Tell me what I have to do, and I'll do it."

"Well ..." Her eyes brightened as they scraped down Kyleigh's throat. "Perhaps if the mutt could manage to do something I never could, something I'd always wanted to do ... I might find *that* impressive."

She knew what Gwen meant — she read it in a dark, glinting corner of her stare. And she bristled against the thought. "I'm not doing that."

"Why ever not?"

"You'd win either way."

"Don't act as if you didn't see it coming, pest. You knew I wasn't going to let you off so easily. I want to see you truly, *thoroughly* punished. I want you to suffer the same humiliation I've suffered. I want you to know my pain." Gwen pressed a thumb against Kyleigh's chin. She turned her head this way and that, smirking. "I'm looking forward to adding you to my collection. I've already got a spot picked out."

"Provided I don't snap you in half before then. Or maybe I'll swallow you whole — that way you'll have plenty of time to think about what an absolute pain you've been while you're melted down."

Gwen slapped her. It was more playful than anything: just hard enough to give her something to think about. She grinned over her shoulder as she strode from the room.

It was nearing midday when an obnoxious scratching sound drew Kyleigh back to the door. "Why can't you go for a walk in the woods like a normal creature?" she muttered as she let Silas in.

He stretched quickly into his human skin, gasping as if he'd been holding his breath. "I would have to walk for hours to escape their eyes. These Marked Ones are always sneaking about, lurking behind boulders and high up in trees. Is there nothing they can't climb?"

"I doubt it. Just have a look around before you do any changing."

"Their human scent mixes with the animals they wear. I can never get a clear smell ..." His words dissolved into grumbles as he paced about the room. Every few steps he would shake a leg out behind him — as if he had something sticky on the bottoms of his feet. "These pants only have a few changes left in them. Soon they'll be so tight —"

"Just take them off, then. You were always moaning about how you'd rather run around in your skin. So find yourself a quiet patch of forest and have at it," Kyleigh said distractedly.

She was trying to measure a hilt for fitting, but her mind was so lost on other things that she could barely concentrate. It was several moments before she realized that Silas hadn't replied.

His pacing steps were suddenly much lighter. He walked as if he feared he might tumble through the floor — which Kyleigh thought was rather interesting. "Why are you still here?"

"Why do I do anything? It's because I choose to. Save your stupid questions, dragoness." He was quiet for a moment. Then he blurted out: "Your Marked One angers me."

She hadn't been expecting to hear that. "Why? What has he done?"

"I don't know," Silas growled. His fists clenched and his pacing grew even more dangerously light. "He's *done* nothing. Yet, he angers me. I want to kill him — but in the same breath, I feel that crushing his body will never rid me of his spirit. My anger will not burn out. It will haunt me always. I feel it ... in here," Silas said, gripping at his chest in surprise. "I didn't know my chest could be empty. What is this feeling?"

Kyleigh knew what he felt. She knew it all too well. "Jealousy — it's a human emotion."

Silas raised his brows. "I see. And what is *jealousy*?"

*Selfishness*, the dragon in her said. *Refusing to do what's best for those you love.* But for all the dragon's wisdom, it was the human that spoke aloud:

"It's when you want something so badly, but it's always just out of reach. Then somebody else comes along, someone who knows nothing of your struggles. They don't understand the heartache you've had to endure. They simply walk up, and they take it — they take the thing you wanted so badly straight out of your grasp. And you can't even be angry because deep in your heart, you know they're better suited for it. That's what it feels like to be jealous."

Silas's glowing eyes had gone wide while she spoke. "Hmm ... perhaps I was only hungry."

Kyleigh said nothing. He could deny it all he wanted, but she'd felt the same thing. She'd felt it every time Gwen and Kael returned from a hunt, every time the Thane goaded him into a fight ... every time she did something that made the red burn his face.

Jealousy was a strange feeling — fiery and cold all at once. Her dragon wisdom was a flimsy defense against it, a thin pane of glass stretched over a growling storm. But for now, it was enough.

It would *have* to be enough.

*******

Kyleigh didn't go to dinner that night. She spent the long hours of the evening thrashing at her forge — letting the dragon stuff her bothersome human worries aside.

Night passed. Morning came and went. Her hammer fell in careful strokes. The tones that struck her ears were sharp at first, but rang sweetly at the ends. She found herself humming along with it — sometimes matching the pitch, sometimes just above or below. Her voice danced with the beating of the hammer in an unbroken song.

Then the music ended with a sharp hiss and a cloud of steam.

"Is that why Harbinger sings?"

Kyleigh's heart leapt into her throat. She'd been trying so desperately to drown everything out that she hadn't been listening for the door. Now Kael stood directly behind her.

Something strange had happened to him. It had all started with his gait: he used to walk with his shoulders slightly forward, like he meant to ward off every eye. But now they'd crept back so far that anybody who didn't know him well might accidentally mistake him for someone who was all right with being looked at.

It wasn't long after his shoulders straightened that bits of his rough-spun clothes had begun to disappear — only to be replaced by the furs of the creatures he hunted. Now even most of *those* were gone.

He stood before her now in nothing but boots and patchwork trousers. There was dirt on his limbs, scruff on his face, and little bramble scratches across his chest. He looked positively wild.

And it suited him.

Kyleigh tore her eyes away quickly. "How long have you been standing there?" She'd gone to pull the lid shut over her forge when she noticed Kael wasn't sweating. He wasn't squinting or coiling back. The heat didn't seem to bother him at all.

"I've been trying something out," he said when he saw her gaping. "You didn't answer me. Does Harbinger sing because you do?"

"I ... I suppose so. I forged him from my scales, inside my flame ... perhaps he was already so much a part of me that my songs gave him a voice of his own. I've never really given it much thought."

He studied the yellow fury of the flames, his eyes bright with interest. "Your forges are different from the others I've seen. In *Blades and Bellows* it says that a forge should be opened so that the flames can feed on the air."

"Well, that book is about forging with regular flame. Dragonflame is different."

"How so?"

Kyleigh knew she had to be careful. His question seemed innocent enough, but it might dip into deeper things — things better left unsaid. "Air feeds regular flame, but it'll suffocate dragonflame."

"Why?"

"I suppose it's because our fires sit inside our bellies most of the time. A dragon's breath is certainly hot, but it burns out quickly in the open air. That's why I have to keep my forge covered."

He stepped closer to the flame, his brows furrowed in concentration. She was certain there wasn't a single bead of sweat on his face. "How long does it last?"

"Forever, if the air doesn't get to it. I have to close it up every now and then to let the flames grow back — Kael!"

She grabbed him just before he could reach the fire. She tried to pull him back, but his arm slid only so far before it stopped. A new strength twined through his limbs like cords — pulled taut beneath his skin. She knew that to move him an inch would be like trying to pull a rope tied to the mountains.

"It'll melt your flesh off the bone," she said, glaring to mask her surprise.

He pulled her hand away. "No, it won't. Trust me."

She had to cross her arms very tightly as Kael reached for the flames. She realized she could no longer stop him. The days when she'd been able to pull him from danger were over. Now there would be no contending with his stubborn will.

*He's strong enough on his own*, the dragon reminded her. *You should be happy for him.*

She *was* happy for him ... though she was also a little sad. Watching how he'd grown was like weathering the change of seasons: half of her was excited for summer, but the other half would miss the spring.

Her toes curled as Kael's hand went into the flames. She reached for him instinctively, expecting him to yelp in pain. But his smile stopped her short.

It was one of his rarest smiles: an involuntary mix of confidence and joy — a moment when his spiny shell peeled back to reveal his secrets. His fingers ran through the flames, making them dance across his palm. The thrill that wafted from him thickened the air like a pirate's grog. It made her feel numb and powerful all at once.

A few seconds later, Kael took his hand away. He reached up and shut the trough of flame, plunging the forge into darkness. As Kyleigh's eyes adjusted to the dim light, she saw his hands flex at his sides. It was a subtle movement — she wondered if he even realized that he'd done it. But she knew immediately what it meant:

"You were whispering. How in blazes did you figure out how to stick your hand into dragonflame?"

His eyes darted away as he shrugged. "It wasn't that difficult."

She didn't press it. She'd learned never to come at Kael from the front: he would raise his guard and fend her off with an eye-rolling amount of stubbornness. She would have to circle him carefully and wait for the opportunity to present itself.

"Are you ready to talk?"

He raised his brows. "About what?"

"Aren't there questions you'd like to ask me?"

"None that I can think of."

His mouth stayed serious, but there was a strange lilt to his words — one that seemed familiar ... yet out of place. He turned his shoulder to her; his face was suspiciously innocent as he trailed his gaze about the room. It was so unusual that it took her a moment to realize what was happening:

Kael was playing with her.

"I once knew a boy who would've died rather than walk around without his shirt," Kyleigh said as she watched him pace.

"Well, he's got far more important things to worry about, now."

"Really? You aren't worried someone's going to tattle on you for being a whisperer?"

"No. Who would they possibly tell?" Kael paced to the end of the room and turned. His hands stayed noticeably inside his pockets as he paced back — leaving his chest exposed.

The last time she'd seen him like this, there'd been bones sticking out of him. But now those bones were covered over in a layer of flesh. New lines had appeared along his skin, lines that carved shadows into the pale — lines, she was quite certain, that weren't bones at all.

It was rather ... unexpected.

With no small amount of effort, Kyleigh forced her eyes back to his face. "So there isn't a single question bouncing around inside that red head of yours?"

"I supposed there isn't."

"Why do I find that difficult to believe?"

"Maybe you aren't trying hard enough," he said.

She had to try very hard indeed to keep from shoving him as he turned.

"Do you spend all your time here?"

He was back to being serious once more. She was slightly relieved. "Yes. Well, except for dinner."

"You weren't at dinner yesterday."

"I was ... busy. I'll be there tonight," she said when he looked at her.

His brows furrowed and his lips clamped together tightly as he glared about the forge. "Where do you sleep?"

"In that corner over there. I promise it's more comfortable than it looks."

A dangerous patch of red sprouted across his face as he glared at the floor planks. "That couldn't possibly be comfortable."

"It isn't bad. I've certainly had worse."

"You have?"

She smirked. "I know you're going to find it completely shocking, but this isn't my first time in prison."

"I'll bet it isn't," he grumbled. Then he straightened. "Well, I'll see you at dinner."

"Kael, wait."

He stopped in the doorway, brows raised.

She took a deep breath. "Are you certain you're all right? There's nothing you want to ask about ... your past? I'd be happy to answer anything."

"I know you would. It's just ..." His fist pounded into the doorframe — calm, but firm. "I'm not ready yet."

That was all he was going to say about it. The way Kael handled his emotions always reminded her a bit of how caterpillars handled the spring: he would bury them away, letting them wriggle and grow until they finally burst free.

The problem was that by the time Kael wanted to talk about anything, it'd become a six-legged creature with bulging eyes and a frightful set of wings.

*******

Kael came late to the Hall that night. Dinner was already halfway over by the time he finally turned up, and Kyleigh intended to ask him where he'd been. But no sooner had he shoved through the doors than the wildmen sprang their trap: half a dozen warriors armed with swords bounded over their tables and surrounded him.

After seeing how handily he'd dealt with Griffith, most humans would've left him alone. But the wildmen weren't like most humans. They would never let a monster sleep in the brush — they'd much rather poke it awake.

"You don't belong here, mutt. Leave now, or we'll kill you," one of the warriors said. It might've been a convincing threat, had he not been grinning.

Kael sighed heavily. "Can I have a moment to think about it?"

It was a strange answer, given the fact that he was unarmed, shirtless, and facing the prospect of having to fight his way through a half-dozen swords. Not surprisingly, it seemed to confuse the warriors.

In the second it took them to adjust, Kael did something strange. His hands passed over his limbs, down his chest, across his neck and over his head. His fingers dragged as if he was trying to scrape something off his skin.

"What is it? Why is there such an odd, unsettling silence?" Baird hissed.

"Kael's about to clobber them," Griffith said. The battle hadn't even started yet, and the blue marble was already rolling between his fingers.

Finally, Kael made a motion that looked as if he was washing his hands. Then he shook his head. "Sorry, I'm not leaving. I suppose you're going to have to kill me."

The warriors attacked in a swarm.

Kael darted to the edge of their circle, swinging his limbs out beside him as he went. Two of the warriors were knocked onto their backs. Their mouths parted in surprised Os as they struck the ground.

"That one wrestled a boar by his tusks yesterday," Griffith said, pointing to a downed man. "Pinned him and put him to sleep with his fist. Now look at him — knocked on his rump like a piglet! Ha!"

Kael sprinted for one of the tables. He vaulted over the heads of some craftsmen — who quickly scattered out of the warriors' charging path. Kael stood on the table's top and waited calmly as the warriors formed their ranks. Then he attacked.

The first warrior took a plate to the top of his head and stumbled back in surprise. The rest threw up their arms, trying to shield themselves against his blows. Kael defended his ground with dishes and cups, platters and plates. They shattered across the warriors' skin, sending blinding pieces into the air. One warrior climbed the far end of the table and tried to attack him from behind.

Instead, he took a hambone to the face.

"What a walloping that was!" Griffith's painted fists slammed into the tabletop and he howled. His arms trembled as if it took everything he had to keep from charging into the fray.

Other wildmen joined his cries, their voices rising in a peculiar song. The warriors fed on the thrill of battle. The craftsmen fed on the excitement in their cries, and the pounding rhythm of their fists traveled back to their warriors — carrying their frenzy to new heights.

Setheran had always said that to be a whisperer was to be understood. The differences in their talents gave each other everything they needed. They were like a flame that didn't bow to the wind, a fire that fed itself. Kyleigh had never seen anything like it — not among beast or men. Together, the whisperers made the perfect creature. And in the very center of it all was Kael.

The warriors quickly grew frenzied by the craftsmen's song. They lost themselves in a wild attack. One grabbed the table and heaved it onto its side — launching Kael over their heads. He landed on one foot and swung the other out behind him, catching a warrior under the chin. Kael had already added a new victim to his count before the last had finished crumpling to the ground.

He stepped in a careful pattern: turning to escape the warriors' traps, darting out of the path of swords and dodging their grasps. It was a mesmerizing dance — one that made Kyleigh's heart thrum in time with his steps. She watched, breathless, as Kael battered every hole in the warriors' defense.

If an arm was raised too high, his fist collided with their ribs. If a foot was off balance, he knocked it out from under them. He swiped his arm against the flat of a warrior's blade, popped it free, and caught it by the hilt. Then he flung it from his hand.

It wound up stuck in the wall above Gwen's head — buried firmly between the ears of her prized bear.

"Kill him!" she screamed.

Only one warrior remained. His sword swooped down and Kael's hand shot up to meet it. Kyleigh held her breath as they hurtled towards one another. They were going to collide — and no matter how clever he was, Kael's flesh was no match for steel. She didn't even have a chance to gasp as the blade struck him ... struck, and promptly shattered into pieces.

What in blazes ...?

She watched through a fog as Kael knocked the final warrior unconscious with a quick punch. He said something to Gwen that made the wildmen cheer; she replied with something far less savory. But it all felt like foam in Kyleigh's ears.

She'd figured out what he'd done — how he'd shattered the sword and how he'd been able to stick his hand inside her flames. She'd figured it out ... but she still couldn't believe it.

As the wildmen filed out of the Hall, Kael stayed to wake the warriors and make certain their wounds were healed. They chattered excitedly as he woke them. They hounded him with questions. He gave answers that made them frown and walk away, disappointed.

Finally, his steps halted beside her.

"What have you done?"

His eyes went wide at her question. "I haven't told anybody — I swear I haven't. It's your secret to tell."

It was far more than a secret. "You've done the impossible," she said quietly. "You've managed to find someway to conjure dragonscale armor out of nothing."

His glare burned her. "You don't trust me."

"Don't be ridiculous. If I didn't trust you, I wouldn't have given you those gauntlets in the first place."

"Then what are you worried about?"

She was worried about the future. She was worried that something she'd done would change the course of history — that the scribes would be able to trace a red line across a bloody final chapter to her name and say: *Here's where the darkness began.*

"Nothing," she said after a moment. "I suppose I'm just asking you to be careful."

They left the Hall in an uneasy silence. He didn't speak, and she couldn't think of anything to say. So she listened to his breathing and the steady beat of his heart.

"Goodnight," he said as they reached the forge.

He walked up the slope, never breaking pace. Kyleigh watched after him for a moment before she opened the door … and she took a startled step back.

There were strange smells inside the forge: the scent of pine mixed with the musk of animal. Kyleigh's eyes adjusted quickly to the darkness, and the strange, shadowy mass in the corner of the room took shape.

It was a bed.

The bed's frame was carved from pine and dressed in animal skins. A soaring dragon had been carved into the headboard; the legs had curled claws at their ends, each wrapped around an orb. An assortment of furs stuffed with what smelled like the down of geese padded its center. Folded on top of the fur covers was a pair of deerskin trousers.

Kyleigh stood there, staring at the bed and the trousers for nearly a full minute. Kael had never given her a gift before. She tried to remind herself that human gifts had many hundreds of meanings.

But as she studied the careful lines of his work, saw how each stitch sat so tightly, how it all seemed to come together in one stunning picture, almost alive in its beauty — she began to realize that some gifts had meanings that rang true across all sorts of hearts.

Sometimes, the message was clear.

# CHAPTER 26
## LIGHTNING BEHIND THE CLOUDS

The summer trading season dragged on to such exhaustive lengths that Thelred had begun to wonder if it would ever end.

Muggy air hung thickly over the chancellor's island castle. It was one of those windless days — the sort of day that left the sails empty and the deck baking hot. The weather would've been death to any man trapped at sea. His ship would drift sideways along the current, helpless and at the mercy of the waves while the sun drained him of his strength. Yes, to burn alive in the middle of the sea would've been a slow, humiliating way to die.

But it still wasn't the worst fate Thelred could think up.

Blue flags draped from the castle, slack and still. Heat rose in waves all around them. He could see it shimmering off the cobblestone and along the arched tops of the merchants' carts. Bodies moved in a line through the scant maze of earth left uncovered by the stalls.

Feet rolled beneath trousers and skirts, carrying with them a mass of frilled, colorful sludge that never seemed to end. Mouths moved constantly: opening and closing, blasting more hot air into a space that was already miserable enough. What could they possibly have to say? How could anybody stand to wander around with his mouth hanging trap-open in this miserable, awful —?

"Where's the battle?" Aerilyn called from behind him.

Thelred wished there *had* been a battle. He'd rather have a sword hanging from his middle than have to endure this blasted heat. "There isn't one," he muttered.

"Exactly. So would you please quit stalking about like we're expecting an invasion from the north? You're scaring off all of our customers."

That was easy for her to say. Aerilyn had traveled with merchants her whole life. She was used to the crowds and the stink — and the stifling heat, apparently. There wasn't so much as a dark patch on her pale pink dress.

No, she lounged in a chair behind their stall, feet propped on an empty crate and one arm draped absently across the now-noticeable bump on her belly. She waved a blue fan with the other hand, keeping the heat off her face and neck.

She might've felt at home in this baking under-realm of a castle, but Thelred was used to a certain kind of life — one in which he'd bargained with his sword. "I'm not stalking. And I haven't scared anybody off."

Aerilyn pointed over his shoulder with her fan. "Really? Then what are *they* rushing off for?"

Thelred turned in time to see three young ladies cutting out of his way. They squealed when they saw him staring and darted off — cramming themselves and their frilly trappings down a passageway lined with baubles.

Aerilyn's brows rose in mocking arcs. "They must've seen a mouse."

Thelred tugged roughly on his trousers, even though he knew the peg would still show. "Well, what did you expect? Nobody's going to get anywhere near us with this leg sticking out."

"Nobody's going to get anywhere near us with that *frown* sticking out," Aerilyn retorted. "The leg is fine — charming, even."

"It isn't charming. It's monstrous." Thelred pulled on his trousers again, baring his teeth as he felt his raw skin scraping against the leather ties. "Who wants to buy anything from a one-legged man?"

Aerilyn pursed her lips. "If you'd stop being so beastly, I think you'd find that people are *more* willing to buy from a one-legged man. It's all in how you limp." She glanced down the stall, where a middle-aged merchant was inspecting a barrel of apples. *Observe,* she mouthed.

The merchant picked up an apple, turning it this way and that. "How much for a sack of these?"

"Twenty," Aerilyn said.

He snorted. "No sack of apples is worth twenty. I could buy full-cooked tarts for less than twenty. I'll offer you six."

"Six?" Aerilyn said quietly. Her hand moved from the arm of her chair to the bump on her belly. "Could you do ten?"

He stared at her hand. Slowly, his brows went up and he let out a heavy sigh. "Very well. Ten it is — but not a copper more."

"Oh, wonderful!" Aerilyn waved, and a grinning pirate stepped up to take the merchant's coin. "Make sure he gets the best we have to offer."

"I'll pick them out myself," the pirate said.

The moment the merchant and his apples had wandered out of earshot, Aerilyn gave Thelred a rather smug look. "See? Having a condition can improve your bargaining — if you use it properly, that is. No one's going to feel sorry for you if you insist on scowling the skin off of them."

"Good. I don't want them feeling sorry for me. And I don't have a *condition* — I'm a bloody cripple," Thelred snapped. Sweat dripped off the end of his nose. He pulled roughly on the neck of his tunic. "I don't see why we've got to be here again. We were just at this blasted castle!"

"A month ago," Aerilyn reminded him.

"Right. And we made plenty of gold. So why do we have to drag our ship out here again if we've already got enough to feed the Bay?"

Aerilyn jabbed her fan at the blue shield on the chest of his tunic. "The chancellor's council is in session — and like it or not, being the only merchant allowed in the Endless Plains makes you a part of that council," she added when he started to argue.

He didn't need to be reminded. Having that thing stitched to his tunic was reminder enough. It reminded him that he belonged to Chaucer — that he had to answer his every beck and call.

He had no idea what they were voting on. He never knew. All the other councilmen seemed to have at least some idea of what to expect, but Thelred didn't care enough about the politicking and rumor-chasing to find out. To him, a session meant having to sit in a stuffy room for however long it took to draft a law and pass a vote — which, he'd quickly discovered, could take ages.

At their last meeting, Chaucer had kept them locked up for nearly an entire day. The servants weren't allowed inside if the doors were closed. And in order to open the doors, the chancellor's cabinet needed to be in agreement — which they weren't. So the whole council had gone without food or drink for hours while Chaucer droned on about taxes.

Aerilyn had said it was some sort of trick: Chaucer had been trying to starve the votes he needed out of the opposing councilmen, and it'd worked. But by the end of it all, Thelred was furious — and having to sit in one place for so long had given him the chance he needed to plan his revenge.

So when it came time to open the voting chalice, he'd had some of the pirates drop Chaucer a little ... gift, from the balcony.

"No mischief this time," Aerilyn warned, as if she'd been reading his thoughts. "We've been lucky so far, but Chaucer already suspects that one of us was responsible for the bee incident — it isn't funny!"

She batted at the pirates who'd been snickering behind her, swatting them away with her fan.

"Dropping an angry hive into the voting chalice isn't appropriate councilman behavior! It wasn't even that clever ... all right, it was *slightly* clever." Aerilyn's brows dropped quickly over her smile. "But no more tricks. One toe out of line, and Chaucer will lock you all straight in the dungeons."

"Let him try," Thelred grumbled. He could feel the heat settling in the nub of his leg. It was pounding. Sweat rubbed him raw, scratched him against the leather. If he stood still, he would do nothing but think about it. So he started to walk.

"Where are you going?" Aerilyn called after him.

"To stretch my blasted leg out," he snapped.

Thelred lurched through the crowded streets. The sludge peeled out of his way. Eyes scraped across him. Everyone was watching — no, they were staring. Their eyes were drawn to the clatter of his leg and they gaped at him openly, as if he deserved to be gaped at ... and perhaps he did.

Thelred gasped against the stabbing of his knee for as long as he could before his breath grew too short. He stopped and balanced himself against a nearby cart, closing his eyes as the throbbing relented. The ache was still there. It would always be there, just as people would always be staring at him. But with his eyes closed, at least he couldn't see the people.

There was nothing he could do about the ache.

The footsteps around him followed a pattern: the strollers, the rushers — the stomping of spoiled children. It was such a familiar racket that Thelred didn't even realize he was listening to it until he heard something that sounded out of place.

Authoritative steps — the march of a guard about his duties. This was a sound Thelred had always had to be especially wary of, and he focused on it immediately.

A young forest man stepped out of the crowd and headed purposefully towards the gates. He wore a deep green tunic with the grand oak of Countess D'Mere stamped upon his chest — stamped right there in the middle, shining like a beacon. That dark-haired codpiece hadn't even tried to hide it.

When the guards at the gates spotted him, Thelred expected him to get thrown out on his arse. But instead, they parted to let him through.

Thelred took a few halting steps forward. The guards had seen him. They knew full well what he was — and they'd still let him through. They waved him on like he had every right to be there, as if the Countess had any business at all in the seas. What were they think ...?

Chaucer.

Bloody Chaucer, that idiot.

Pain stabbed him with every step, but Thelred willed himself towards the gates. The guards saw the badge on his chest as he approached and had moved well out of his way by the time he reached them.

"Councilman," one of them grunted.

Thelred didn't reply. He kept his eyes on the dark back of the forest man's head. Everything else was a blur: the people, the carts and wagons, the guards who paced about their watches — they were nothing more than shadows in the corners of his eyes. He could follow at a distance in the courtyard. But when the forest man ducked inside the castle, Thelred had to hurry to catch up.

Blasted leg. He cursed as he swung it up the steps and to the large front door. The grand room in the heart of the castle was teeming with servants. They swarmed here and there, laying out the tables and chairs in preparation for the session.

Thelred knew it would be a dull evening. He was beginning to understand why Lysander had dumped the whole business on him in the first place: sitting through rump-numbing meetings was about the only thing he was good for.

The forest man's head bobbed through the crowd, and Thelred followed closely. He glanced away when a familiar clanging sound caught his attention. A small army of servants was busily working a new piano out of a crate. He was certain the pale wood the instrument had been carved from couldn't be found anywhere in the High Seas.

*Chaucer, you idiot.*

Thelred followed the forest man out of the ballroom. Deeper down the passageway, the noise of the servants faded — which made the clumping of his peg echo all the louder. Soon he had no choice but to slow and step carefully.

304

He cursed under his breath at the next corner — and swore aloud when he saw the hallway was empty. The forest man was gone.

Countless passageways twisted around the castle. If Thelred didn't hurry up, he could lose him for good. He'd managed to go a few paces down the hall when he heard familiar steps coming from behind him. He turned in time to see the forest man cross the end of the hallway.

How had he gotten behind ...?

Thelred didn't have time to think about it. He moved as quickly as his leg would allow, lumbering to the hallway's end. When he glanced around the corner, he saw the forest man standing outside a door. At his knock, a muffled voice bid him inside.

Thelred waited until the door had closed behind him before he ventured out.

He knew this hallway. This was where Chaucer kept his office. After what had happened to the Duke, the chancellor seemed unwilling to take risks: he kept his office in a windowless room on the bottom floor.

There was a brass keyhole set into the door. Thelred bit his lip against the stabbing in his leg as he bent to look through it. All he could see was a tapestry of a ship and the hem of a woman's dress. She was sitting, one leg crossed over the other. He could see the slight heels of her pale blue slippers from beneath her skirt.

"I thank you for the gifts," a voice said — a voice so solemn and undisturbed that he knew it belonged to Chaucer. "The instrument is very fine, of course. But I'm rather looking forward to discovering what's inside those bottles."

"My gift to the council — for welcoming me on such short notice," a woman replied. "It's an oak-aged liquor. I was hoping you might use it to open the session."

"I see no reason why not. Having a bit of drink in us can only make the vote go smoother." A moment of silence. Then, quite suddenly: "But I don't understand why he sent you. I've already spoken with His Majesty's envoy. He knows I'm open to an alliance."

305

Thelred's breath caught in his throat.

"The forest and the seas were allies, once. I hope we'll soon be allies again. Consider my presence an act of faith," the woman said. "The King wishes you to understand that there are lands that must be reclaimed — empty thrones that wait to be filled. The Sovereign Five squabbled over the mountains for years. You have a rare chance to extend your reach, Chaucer. The King would like for you to consider it."

She spoke with all the deadly hush of lightning behind the clouds. A long moment passed before Chaucer replied: "I have absolutely no interest in a throne. A man who sits upon a throne is exposed to his people, but a man who sits behind a desk is protected. As chancellor, there are dozens of votes between me and any misfortune — and dozens of goats to shoulder the blame. A ruler has no such luxury. This business of new lands, however ..." There was the tapping of papers being arranged; the clearing of a throat. "Are the rumors true, then? Has Titus really managed to carve a road through the mountains?"

"Yes," the woman said. "The Earl believed he would be out of the King's reach at the summit. But in trying to make his army's path easier, he's slit his own throat. Titus's road runs directly to the gates of his castle. A well-stocked army will have no difficulty reaching it.

"The reign of the Sovereign Five has ended, chancellor," the woman went on. "A new order has begun — one in which all who defy Midlan will be destroyed. You have a rare opportunity to earn the seas a little power over the other regions." Her hands spread wide. "Don't waste it."

There was a creak as Chaucer shifted his weight. "It isn't that simple. None of this will pass without a vote — and there are still plenty of councilmen against it. I'm afraid I'm little more than a mediator."

"Reginald's death left you in a dangerous position, chancellor," the woman murmured. "You know this, and your people know it as well. You wouldn't have offered Crevan your allegiance if you believed you had any other choice. There will be some resistance, I'm sure. But the King's terms are not unreasonable, and there's much to be gained. All you have to do is make sure the council sees it."

There was a sound of fingernails raking across stubble. "And if it fails ... what then?" Chaucer said after a moment. "The King won't wait forever. What if I do everything in my power —?"

"You won't have to do anything. The vote will pass." Thelred could almost hear the smile in the woman's voice as she added: "I'll see to it."

Chaucer's harsh laugh grated against Thelred's ears. Then came the rustling of parchment. "I'm going to keep these conditions close, if you don't mind. It's not that I don't trust His Majesty's word —"

"I'm a daughter of the seas, in case you've forgotten," the woman murmured. "You don't have to explain your reasoning to me."

Chaucer laughed again, and the woman stood. Thelred was leaning to look through the top of the keyhole when a pair of strong hands grabbed him around the shoulders.

They swung him back — then hurled him through the door.

# CHAPTER 27
## ON GOOD TERMS

Splinters showered down Thelred's neck as the latch gave way. His ears went numb against the sound of his head slamming into the door's hardened flesh. He fell flat on his chest and gasped at the sudden emptiness in his lungs.

No sooner had he struck the ground than the hands came back. They flipped him over roughly, forcing him to stare at the ceiling. The tip of a sword bit the middle of his chest. Thelred followed the steady line of the blade up to its wielder ...

Impossible.

The forest man stared back at him — the very same man he'd seen enter Chaucer's office. He heard the noise of a second blade sliding from its sheath and saw the forest man's reflection standing at the other end of the room.

"There're two of you," he said without thinking.

"Twins," a woman replied.

She stood before of one of Chaucer's gaudy chairs, hands clasped at her middle. Golden brown hair flowed past her shoulders. The soft lines of her face drew him to her crystal eyes ... but her stare made him shiver.

He knew without a doubt that this must be Countess D'Mere.

"What's the meaning of this, chancellor?" the Countess said, without ever taking her eyes off of Thelred.

Chaucer hardly glanced up from the parchment he'd been reading. "That's nothing more than a common sea thief, Countess. We've tried our best to civilize them, but it's difficult to train rats."

The Countess's icy gaze never faltered. "I see. Shall I handle it?"

Chaucer sighed heavily as he stood. "No, you'd better let me."

Thelred knew the moment he met Chaucer's eyes that he was in very serious trouble — mostly because the left one was still a bit swollen.

It had been nearly a month since the bee incident. When Chaucer had opened the voting chalice and that hive had come crashing in, he'd thought it been worth it — worth the trouble, worth having to endure Aerilyn's squawking for three days after, worth the few stings he'd gotten himself to watch the councilmen hike up their girth and run for their lives.

It'd certainly been worth the wait to see just how horribly Chaucer's head would swell: he wound up having to wrap his face in bandages and call the session short.

But now, as that still-swollen eye glared down at him, Thelred realized that it was Chaucer's turn to do the stinging. He was about to find out if it'd all truly been worth it.

Chaucer's boots dragged as he stepped around to the front of his desk. He spent a long moment folding up the piece of parchment he'd been reading. His fingers slid along each crease with deliberate slowness, pinching them tightly at their ends. When he'd finally shoved the parchment inside his coat pocket, he *tsk*ed and shook his head.

"Tell me, thief ... why were your little rat ears planted against my door?"

*Why were* you *allying with our enemies?* The words leapt to the tip of Thelred's tongue just as the sword at his chest dug in. He grit his teeth. "I wasn't listening. I was just —"

"Thelred!"

Aerilyn swept in, her eyes already wet with tears. She threw herself upon Chaucer and gasped: "Please don't hurt him, chancellor. He isn't well —"

"Aerilyn?"

She spun as if she'd just taken an arrow to the back. "Countess D'Mere! What a surprise. I didn't expect to — oops." She went to drop into a quick curtsy and tripped

309

— barely managing to catch herself on Chaucer's h my, I'm so terribly sorry!"

"It's fine, it's fine. Stand up, girl," Chaucer grouched as he propped her onto her feet.

Thelred realized that the only thing that might save them now was the fact that Aerilyn and the Countess seemed to know each other. He hoped they were on good terms … though judging by the look on the Countess's face, they weren't.

Her hands curled into claws at her sides. She stared at the bump beneath Aerilyn's dress with her lips sealed shut. The skin around her eyes had paled … yet the arches of her cheeks burned a furious red.

"What happened to you?"

Four words. Four simple words, and the room filled with ice.

Chaucer — that complete and total idiot — chose that very moment to let out a laugh. "This is what becomes of a pirate's whore," he said, waving a hand at Aerilyn's belly.

The Countess's eyes snapped up to him. "Indeed."

Two syllables — two thrusts of a knife. Thelred could hear each flick of her tongue twisting in and out. But Chaucer went on laughing, deaf to the danger.

Aerilyn placed her hands over her stomach protectively. "My husband and I are expecting our first child, Countess."

"Husband?" she hissed.

"Yes, Countess. I've got a few months left to go. I expect I'll get quite a bit more swollen before then — but we're ever so excited. Please, Countess," tears sprang into her eyes as she looked down at Thelred, "please don't hurt him."

There weren't enough swears in the Kingdom. Had he known every mage-word and half the desert tongues, Thelred didn't think he would've ever been able to express his profound … *displeasure* with Aerilyn.

The whole icy edge of the Countess's gaze swept across him. "Your husband is a pirate?"

310

Her stare made the backs of Thelred's eyes ache, but he tried to meet it. He knew full well that Aerilyn was bargaining for their lives — whether she realized it or not was another matter.

"Yes, Countess — well, at least he used to be a pirate. Now he runs a merchanting business out of the Endless Plains."

Chaucer snorted. "He *stole* the whole business, more like. The giants refuse to deal with anybody else."

Slowly, the Countess's lips slid out of their harsh line and bent into a purse. "He runs the whole plains, does he?" When Aerilyn nodded, her fists unclenched. "Your father would be pleased to hear that."

"I'd like to think so, Countess," she said quietly.

A long moment passed and Thelred could hardly stand to look. He glared at the ceiling and tried not to breathe too deeply. After a moment, the Countess waved to her guard and the sword lifted from his chest.

"You may leave."

Thelred couldn't believe it.

Apparently Chaucer couldn't believe it either, because he sputtered and said: "Wait a moment — there's still the question as to why that thief was listening at my door."

All eyes turned to Thelred. And as he had nowhere else to look, Thelred turned to Aerilyn.

*Limp*, she mouthed.

"I ... was headed to my chamber when my leg began to ache. I stopped for a moment to catch my breath, and your guard must've thought I was up to something."

Aerilyn raised her brows, silently urging him on.

So as much as he hated it, Thelred forced himself to groan. "It's sore every other day, but that blasted damp heat makes everything worse. I'm sorry if I've caused you any trouble."

He made a great show of wincing as he pulled himself to his feet. Aerilyn stepped up and draped one of his arms across her shoulders. "I'm sure he'll feel better in time for the session," she said as she helped him towards the door.

311

"I do hope you're right." When Thelred turned, he saw the Countess watching him through a smooth mask. "You ought to go upstairs. Lie down for a while and give that leg a rest."

The words burned his tongue like venom, but he forced himself to spit them out: "Yes, Countess."

With Aerilyn helping him, they limped down the hall and into the ballroom. A few chairs were gathered in a corner of the chamber. Aerilyn sat him down and propped his leg up before she settled in beside him. One of the servants must've seen the sweat drenching Thelred's tunic: he brought them both a goblet of water before returning to his duties.

"Listen to me carefully," Aerilyn said the moment he was gone, "I need you to tell me everything you heard exactly as you heard it."

Thelred didn't see what good talking about it was going to do. But he'd dealt with Aerilyn long enough to know that she'd just squawk at him until she got her way. So he told her everything he could remember.

When he was finished, she looked slightly disappointed. "That's it? That's all they said?"

"What? Were you expecting it to be *worse*?" Thelred hissed. "Chaucer's signed on with the King!"

Aerilyn waved a hand. "That was bound to happen eventually. We can't exactly bargain our way out of trouble, now that the Duke's dead. So Chaucer knows it's either war or surrender."

"I'd choose war!"

"Then it's a very good thing you aren't chancellor," Aerilyn retorted.

Thelred couldn't look at her. He was far too furious. He took a steady drink of water, wishing it were something a little stronger. When he turned back, he saw Aerilyn had a leaf of parchment clutched in her hands.

It was the very same leaf he'd seen Chaucer stuff into his coat. "You snatched that when you tried to curtsy, didn't you?" Thelred guessed.

She smirked. "I'm a little uneven at the moment. That doesn't mean I've suddenly gotten clumsy."

"Where did you learn —?"

"Lysander teaches me all sorts of things," she said impatiently. "Now be quiet while I read."

Thelred looked her over. "But where did you hide it?"

She made an indignant sound. "You aren't allowed to ask a lady about her hiding places! Honestly, Thelred — I don't think your manners could be any more ghastly."

While she read, Thelred hunched forward and tried to block her from view. They'd been sitting for no more than a few minutes when one of the forest twins appeared across the room.

He stood, bold as a southern wind, and watched them without blinking.

"One of the Countess's dogs is following us," Thelred growled.

"I'm not surprised. She's got an awful lot riding on this vote." Aerilyn sighed and leaned back. "They've already drafted a treaty. This," she waved the parchment, "is a detailed list of all the things the King expects to get from the seas — not the least of which is an invasion of the mountains."

So *that* was what they'd been talking about, the claiming of new lands and the stretching of reach. Crevan had lost his grip on Titus ... and he was planning to use the people of the seas to get it back.

"That isn't a treaty — it's a trap," Thelred growled. "If they haven't starved to death, they'll be beaten to scabs at the summit. Any man not lucky enough to die in battle will freeze to the mountainside trying to climb back down. It's madness."

"Especially since there's already an army *in* the mountains," Aerilyn muttered, her eyes on the twin.

Thelred had forgotten about that. He had to stuff a fist against his mouth to keep from swearing aloud. "We have to do something ... what if I have the men steal the voting chalice?"

"Then they'll just put their votes in a bowl, or something. The chalice makes no difference."

"Well, then we'll tamper with the votes."

"How? Unless I'm very much mistaken, you and I have gone to all the same meetings," Aerilyn snipped. "There's no secret room anymore — after Colderoy got elected, the council decided it wouldn't risk another tampering. The chalice sits straight at the front of the ballroom and Chaucer never lets it out of his sight. And, since that nasty incident with the bees, he makes certain to keep it well *beneath* the balcony," she added with a glare. "Fiddling with the votes isn't going to be an option."

Thelred glared back. "Fine. Then why don't you think of something?"

She watched the servants bustle about for a moment, her lips twisted in a frown. Then she gasped so suddenly that it made Thelred jump. "Yes, there it is! See here." Aerilyn pointed to a line on the conditions list. "*All forces shall be supplied with weaponry and armor in the fashion of Midlan.*"

Thelred thought about it. "Crevan's going to send them marching up the mountains dressed like a lot of scabs from Midlan ... why would he do that?"

"I haven't got a clue. But that isn't really what's important, is it? We can't stop the vote, but I think ..." she smiled as she glanced over the list, "I think I might've figured out a way to buy us a little time. The last thing we need is for our friends in the mountains to get caught between Titus and Crevan."

For once, Thelred agreed. "What do you need me to do?"

"Just sit somewhere and stay out of trouble."

Thelred didn't like the idea of slumping around and leaving everything in Aerilyn's hands. But if she was going to be running around the castle all day, he knew he couldn't keep up. "I'll just go upstairs, then —"

"No!" She grabbed his shoulder tightly. "Um, I mean, it would probably be best if you stayed around people at all times. Never be alone, not even for a moment."

"Why?"

"Because I've got every reason to believe the Countess will kill you the second she gets a chance."

Thelred's throat went dry.

"My father was one of her top merchants," Aerilyn explained. "She used to visit us often. Once, when I was a little girl, I told her that a boy from the village had kissed me on the cheek. He disappeared a week later and was never heard from again. I can't prove it, but I think my father might've ... paid her to protect me."

A chill rose up Thelred's spine. "It was probably just a coincidence."

"It wasn't," she insisted. "I knew the Countess was a bad woman. I'd heard all sorts of nasty rumors. When I asked my father why he kept working for her, he said: *I owe her a great deal. In fact, I owe her everything.* That was the only answer he would give me. I don't like to think about it," she said, cutting over the top of Thelred's question. "Just please ... don't go anywhere alone for a while. At least until I return."

She stood — then promptly sat back down. "Oh, and you should probably find some excuse to stay in the ballroom. I expect Chaucer will come looking for you shortly. He's going to offer you a spectacular deal: your life for the Endless Plains. Don't take it."

She tried to stand, but he snatched her down. "What in high tide are you talking about?"

She made a frustrated sound. "D'Mere thinks you're my husband, but Chaucer knows you're not. So why didn't he out you immediately?"

Thelred groaned. "Because he's going to use it for leverage. Things would be much simpler if you merchants just killed each other off like civilized people."

She smiled wryly. "Simpler, yes. But not nearly as fun. Now, if there are no more questions, I really must —"

"Wait." Thelred grabbed her wrist. "You think the Countess killed a boy for kissing you on the cheek?"

"I can't prove it, but yes."

315

"Perfect. And now she thinks I did *that* to you," he thrust a hand at the bump beneath her dress, "so I suppose it's only a matter of time before I'm slowly tortured to death."

She smiled sweetly. "Don't be ridiculous — it could be quick. Farewell, my dear, dear love." She grabbed him by the hair and planted her lips against his forehead.

He wiped it away with his sleeve.

She was wrong. He could tell by the way that blasted forest guard was staring at him that his death would be a long and torturous affair. The Countess's knife probably wouldn't start at his important bits ...

But he bet she'd get to them eventually.

# CHAPTER 28
## THE LURCH

Countess D'Mere couldn't sit still. She paced back and forth through her chambers, listening to the surf as it crashed against the rocks beneath her window. The rhythm reminded her to breathe deeply. She tried to time her breaths to match the waves.

And she waited.

The high-pitched moan of her door stopped her pacing. One of the twins had come to fetch her. She glanced to see which hip he wore his sword on. "Is it done, Left?"

He turned sideways, and she knew he meant for her to follow.

D'Mere's heart beat faster with each step through the winding halls. She didn't know who that cripple was, but he wasn't Aerilyn's husband. The pirate captain she'd written about in her letters was a handsome man — she remembered his face had been drawn on the back of one of the pages.

The man Aerilyn was with now was a scowling lurch — probably one of her servants. Had he been the Captain Lysander she loved so dearly, D'Mere might've considered sparing him.

But the lurch knew too much.

Left broke from the side passages and led her down the main hall. She grew more frustrated the closer they got to the ballroom. "You had very specific orders to keep things quiet ..."

Music drifted over the top of her words. It wasn't part of a ballad, or even a ballroom dance. No, this song coursed through the halls like a single, powerful thought — the inner musings of the man who played it.

Left walked straight into the ballroom, turning to glance at D'Mere over his shoulder. He caught her eye and led her with his chin. Then he marched to join his brother.

It was the lurch who played the piano. He was hunched over the keys; sweat hung thickly in the creases of his tunic. That horrible stump of a leg creaked each time he shifted his weight. The rough red on the back of his neck stained him against the finery of the room.

And yet ... that music.

It covered over everything else — it hushed the councilmen and slowed the servants' work. Ladies wandered in from all corners of the castle, peeking at him from behind their fans. Slowly, the ballroom began to fill.

They pulled chairs from the tables and turned them around so that they faced the piano. Councilmen in their gold-embroidered garments sat next to merchants' wives. Maids gathered at the back of the room, their chores half-folded in their arms. All were united in their gazes, their silence. Every ear equally captivated by the music's spell.

While the lurch sat under the watch of so many eyes, there would be no dealing with him. So D'Mere resolved to wait.

The front of the room had suddenly become the back. She took her place at a table near the head and turned her chair around. Before long, Chaucer appeared. The music seemed to have no effect on him: he strode straight through the crowd, arms clasped behind his back, and halted beside the piano.

"What a charming ballad," he said loudly.

The music stopped.

"Is there something I can do for you, chancellor?" The lurch's voice was like two stones grinding against each other — every bit as unrefined as that whittled lump that hung from his knee.

Chaucer smirked. "Yes. I was wondering if I might ask you to join me in my office. There are some things I'd like to —"

"Oh, there'll be plenty of time for business later," one of the councilmen said. "I was actually beginning to enjoy myself. Let the lad finish his song!"

Others murmured their agreement. One of the ladies started an applause that drowned out Chaucer's protests. The stern line of his lips snapped upwards for a moment as he surrendered. He raised his hands and walked away ... the skin beneath his beard turning redder with every step.

Now *this* was a song that made D'Mere smile. A clever trick — one designed to keep the lurch out of her grasp and away from Chaucer's office. As she listened with her mind tuned to this realization, she began to enjoy it.

Music poured from the lurch in a rush, softening his edges. It was a burst of white water against the rocks, a contrast that drew her attention. And perhaps it was because the music and the lurch were such an unlikely match that D'Mere felt her lips bending into a smile.

She rather liked surprises.

The lurch's hands danced across the piano's keys for an hour more. People drifted in and out — disappearing upstairs before returning clad in their session garb. Councilmen donned blue coats over their tunics, while councilwomen wore broaches adorned with delicate blue shields.

As the chairs began to fill, D'Mere traded idle chatter with her tablemates — a small delegation of soldiers from Midlan.

Their leader had a beard that curled down to his chest. He introduced himself as some captain in the King's army, and then proceeded to go on endlessly about how he'd been chosen to head up the envoy:

"The King doesn't let just anybody handle these sorts of things. There're too many dolts lumbering around the barracks. Most have got skulls thicker than their arms, if you want my opinion."

D'Mere didn't.

319

"When do we get to eat, anyhow?" The captain lifted the plate in front of him, as if he expected to find some morsel tucked beneath it.

"After the session opens, I believe," D'Mere said.

His eyes traveled down the curve of her back, glinting. "I can think of something else we can do after the session opens."

It was so easy, almost as natural as breathing in. D'Mere turned and arched her chin high. She slid her gaze from the dragon on his chest and along the matted strands of his beard — settling at last upon the greedy light that flooded his eyes. "So can I, Captain. In fact, I mean to give you a night you'll never forget."

His eyes moved more boldly. "I can't wait to see if the legends are true."

They were. They were truer than that oaf and his ratty beard would ever know. D'Mere forced herself to keep smiling, to deflect the captain's many offers while keeping the hunger burning in his eyes.

It was a light that reduced all men to stumbling fools: their greed made it easy to disarm them. She could shatter them with a smile, a touch. For all their great strength, they melted far too quickly beneath her powers.

Perhaps that was why she'd always found men to be such ... *disappointing* creatures.

D'Mere kept her ears tuned to the music as she weathered the captain's prattling. When the song ended, she glanced back and saw that Aerilyn was helping the lurch into his coat. She draped it over his shoulders and smoothed the wrinkles out of his back. They talked for a moment, their heads close.

Aerilyn had painted her lips. How many times had D'Mere told her not to? Paint might've hidden flaws in other women, but against Aerilyn's skin the bright red was a blemish, a nuisance — a smear on an otherwise perfect picture.

"Councilmen, I thank you all for joining this session," Chaucer bellowed. He stood behind the head table, one hand

320

resting on the enormous silver chalice next to his plate. "In a few moments, dinner will be served and the doors will be sealed. Once we've eaten, we'll get straight to the v —"

"Ah, just a moment, chancellor. I'm afraid I have a question."

A man two tables behind D'Mere got to his feet. He was a small man with far too large a nose and a shining spot at the top of his head.

"Councilman Alders, a representative of Harborville," he said, with a slight bow to the tables around him. "As many of you know, my ships do a great amount of trade with the people of the Valley. We've spent years dealing in weapons and armor forged of mountain steel — first for the Duke, and now as loyal members of the free people's council of the High Seas."

D'Mere couldn't stop herself from smiling. Chaucer's face was about to get a great deal redder.

"I'm afraid I've heard a rather unsettling rumor," Alders went on. "I was hoping you might be able to lay it to rest."

"I'll see what I can do, councilman. But you know how quickly rumors become monsters, in the High Seas," Chaucer said lightly.

Alders chuckled along with the others for a moment, an unconcerned smile on his face. Then: "Is it true that you've been privy to a list of treaty conditions drafted by the King, and one of those conditions is that we wear Midlan's armor during our acquisition of the mountains?"

The laughter went out like a candle's flame.

"What's this about conditions?" the woman on D'Mere's left said. "I've received no such list."

"Nor have I," a man piped in.

"We haven't even agreed to *join* Midlan, yet. Why are there already conditions?"

The woman bolted to her feet. "Surely you haven't agreed to a treaty without the council's consent. That would be a serious breach of office, sir!"

Chaucer held up his hands before the murmuring in the ballroom could grow too fierce. "Ladies and gentlemen, please. If you'll all take your seats, I'm certain we can sort this —"

"I have the conditions list right here," Alders declared. He whipped a folded square of parchment from his pocket — sparking a round of gasps from the others. "It came to me from a very reliable source and I must say, it certainly looks official. Shall I read it aloud, chancellor?"

To his credit, Chaucer did a remarkable job of keeping his face calm. "Please do, councilman. I'm very eager to hear it for myself."

While Alders rattled off the list, Chaucer's hand went to his coat pocket. He clenched the fabric so tightly that his fingers looked almost skeletal in the white.

D'Mere had seen him put the list inside that pocket. How it had wound up in the hands of Alders was a complete mystery. She turned ever so slightly and had to prop a hand over her lips to hide her smile.

Aerilyn.

Her face was innocent, but her chin jutted out defiantly. It reminded D'Mere of a little girl she used to know: a girl who would swear up and down to Garron that she was only going for a walk — and return hours later with her hems covered in mud. She'd stand wide-eyed under his interrogation, melting him with the innocence in her gaze ... but the point of her chin always told clearly of her mischief.

The ballroom grew steadily noisier as the list went on. The councilmen were concerned that their various trades would be overlooked in favor of those from Midlan.

"These conditions will cost us gold that we could be putting back in our own coffers."

"Yes, keep our coin in the seas!"

"I vote to put this matter on hold," Alders declared. "Before we vote on an alliance, the council shall draft a new list of conditions — one that benefits us all. The seas are happy to join His Majesty's cause," he raised the parchment high, "but as his allies, and as a free people. Our voices *will* be heard!"

The thunderous applause that followed his words drowned out anything Chaucer might've said. He kept his hands raised until the room fell silent. "I agree with councilman Alders. Under the circumstances, I move that we put the signing of a treaty on hold until we've added our own conditions to the list," he said with a forced smile. Then he waved to the envoy of Midlan. "Our concerns must seem strange to those outside our region. I'm sure the King meant no offense."

The captain, who'd been staring with his mouth open for quite some time, sprang to his feet. "Uh, none, chancellor."

"There you have it. Now to open this session, Countess D'Mere of the Grandforest has offered us a case of spirits from her region."

She stood at Chaucer's gesture and turned to smile at the rows of tables behind her. "A liquor from my personal cellar — it should pair well with sea fare and spirited debate." She bowed slightly at their chuckles. "My thanks to you for allowing me to join this session."

They applauded as she sat.

Chaucer gave the order and dinner was brought in — along with the bottles of D'Mere's liquor. She watched as the servants poured the amber spirits into the waiting mouths of goblets. Everything was going well. There was just one final matter that needed settling.

She excused herself from the table and made her way to the back of the room. Aerilyn and the lurch were still standing by the piano. They tucked their smiles away as she approached.

"I suppose you think you're clever, don't you?" D'Mere said.

Aerilyn pulled out of her curtsy. "What ever do you — ?"

"Spare me, girl. You know I'm not easily fooled." She waved a hand. "And I know that *thing* isn't your husband."

Her face flushed pink.

323

The lurch glared at her. "If you're going to kill us, then go on and be done with it. Otherwise, get out of our way."

"Thelred!" Aerilyn hissed.

"No, I'm tired of all this chattering and sneaking about. I'm not afraid of her." He reached out and snatched a goblet off a servant's tray without looking. "To your health, Countess."

The goblet was an inch from Thelred's lips when D'Mere slapped it out of his hand. "You might've won this battle, *pirate*, but you can't save the seas." Then she turned her glare on Aerilyn. "Out of respect for your father, I won't kill you tonight. But if I see your face again — either of your faces — I will carve them from your skulls." Though the revelry around them was loud enough to drown out a battle horn, she dropped her voice to a whisper. "Now you will return to your ship and you will sail home immediately."

Aerilyn tilted her chin. "I'm afraid we can't do that, Countess. We still have the vote."

D'Mere had to fight hard not to smile. She looked so much like Garron when she was angry. "No, my dear — there'll be no vote for you tonight. My guard will see to that."

Left appeared out of the shadows and placed a hand on Thelred's shoulder.

"He'll be standing at the docks all night, so don't even think about turning around." She grabbed Aerilyn by the arm — not hard enough to bruise, but hard enough to prove that she *could* bruise her if she wanted to. "You're a sweet girl, Aerilyn ... and I know you'll do what's best for your men."

Her chin trembled as it slid down. "Yes, Countess," she said through her teeth.

Slowly, Thelred turned and limped towards the passageway — Left following close behind. Aerilyn tried to spin away, but D'Mere held onto her arm.

"Please, Countess. I —"

"Are you happy?"

Her bright blue eyes widened at the question. "Of course I'm happy, Countess. I still miss Papa. But everything else is —"

"Good." D'Mere pressed the sleeve of her dress against Aerilyn's lips, wiping the red away. "What have I told you about face paint, girl?"

"*It's a mask for lesser women,*" she said sullenly.

"Precisely. And don't forget it." When she was done, D'Mere waved her away. "Now go. Leave before I change my mind."

Aerilyn curtsied slightly, one hand placed on the lump beneath her dress. Then she swept down the hall.

D'Mere watched long after she'd gone, staring at the shadows cast against the torch-lined walls. Somehow, they seemed darker than they had before. It was only when Chaucer gave the order to seal the ballroom and begin the session that D'Mere returned to her table.

She stared at the amber liquid in her goblet while the councilmen raised theirs in a toast. They agreed the liquor was very fine, indeed. Several of them took second and third gulps. D'Mere nodded absently at their applause, forcing herself to smile.

Dinner began, and soon the noise in the ballroom faded. There was the occasional *thump* as a councilman's head struck the table, the occasional clattering of knives upon the floor. When all was finally silent, D'Mere looked up.

The problem with the men of the seas was that they relied far too heavily on their politics. They were so afraid of having their fingers nicked that they'd grown reluctant to fight. They preferred to argue rather than use their swords. But D'Mere had always done things a little ... differently.

She stood slowly and turned, gazing around the hall. The council laid lifelessly all around her: hanging against their tables, sprawled upon the floor, or slumped in their chairs. Oh, they weren't dead — she'd seen no reason to kill them, not when their fear of Crevan would make the council such willing allies.

No, they were merely paralyzed.

It was one of the first poisons she'd ever learned: a simple compound of numbing herbs made more potent by the headiness of spirits. The council was alive and awake.

Many of them followed her with their eyes as she stepped out from behind the table. They could see her, they could hear her ... but they could do nothing to stop her.

D'Mere turned at the march of footsteps and saw Right walking down the stairs. He'd hidden in the second level before the start of the meeting. Chaucer should've never held a secret council in such an open room. That was his second mistake — his first had been in trusting D'Mere.

"Bag the heads," she murmured as she strode down the line of tables.

Right drew his sword and advanced on the envoy from Midlan. The soldiers' eyes rolled in panic when his blade bit their necks. Their mouths hung slack, filling the petrified air with silent screams.

D'Mere watched for a moment as Right lifted the captain by his matted beard and stuffed him into the sack. She'd given him exactly what she'd promised: a night he would never forget.

Tears streamed unchecked down many of the councilmen's faces. She could practically hear them begging through their eyes as she swept towards the head table.

"I'm not going to harm you, councilmen," she assured them. "The King meant to lead your armies into a trap, to buy a victory against Titus with the blood of our people. Yes, councilmen — *our* people. I've not forgotten the loyalty I owe the region of my birth. So I came here tonight to prevent this council from making a very serious mistake." She smiled at them. "But politics work far too slowly ... I hope you won't mind it if I speed things along."

When she reached the head table, she drew a leaf of parchment from the folds of her skirt. "Why would you kneel to a madman when you could easily stand on your own? The Grandforest will not bow to Crevan's commands."

D'Mere took one of the candles from the table and tilted it, dribbling a good amount of wax in the corner of the parchment. Then she slipped the chancellor's crested ring off Chaucer's finger and pressed it firmly into the wax, forming a seal.

When she was finished, she held the parchment up. carry with me a declaration of war — a declaration signed by your chancellor. You will repay my kindness by joining in our fight, when the time comes. I assure you Crevan will be much less willing to treat with you once his envoy is delivered back to Midlan." She placed the ring onto the table and cast a smile around the room. "I'll leave you to your council, ladies and gentlemen. You have much to discuss."

Footsteps on the balcony told her that Left had returned.

"Have they gone?"

He nodded.

"Good." Her gaze returned to Chaucer. "Bring the chancellor along. There's one last thing I'd like to do."

They left the council frozen upon their seats and climbed two stories to the ramparts — Left with the limp form of Chaucer slung over his shoulders, and Right with his bag of heads. All of the guards were gone from this section of the wall ... her twins had made certain they wouldn't be disturbed.

Left bound the chancellor's hands together. He grabbed one of the wall's teeth and pulled, ripping it free of the mortar. D'Mere watched as he tied the stone to Chaucer's feet. He hefted his limp body to the edge of the wall and held it out over the crashing waves —

"Wait."

Left set him down and stepped away quickly.

D'Mere wound her fingers through Chaucer's hair. She lifted his head from where it slumped against his chest and knelt so that their eyes were even.

They were desperate with panic. His eyes were the eyes of a man who would've offered her anything. She could have any portion of his wealth, every inch of his castle. She could've chopped off any part of his body — just so long as she let him live.

But D'Mere hadn't come to the seas to bargain.

His eyes widened and his lips peeled back in a silent scream as he felt the bite of her dagger. She twisted it,

)lade against his ribs. Then she pulled it out ...
'r planned to kill you. In fact, you could've been
But I'm afraid you made one too many

The dagger bit his flesh again. She watched the veins bulge out along Chaucer's neck as he fought the pain. She pulled the dagger free and balanced the blade against the ridges of his throat, feeling for the perfect angle. She wanted him to be alive when he struck the waves.

She wanted him to suffer.

"You didn't *have* to die tonight, Chaucer." She brought her lips to his ear and whispered: "But you also didn't have to call my daughter a whore."

# CHAPTER 29
## STRATEGY

Kael wasn't sure how it'd happened. One moment he'd been wandering through the Kingdom, quite certain that some things were impossible — and the next, nothing seemed to be.

Knocking over trees and killing bears with rocks no longer seemed strange. Things that used to be necessary — like wearing a coat or a tunic — suddenly just got in the way. He'd hardly blinked the last time he saw a child carrying a boulder down the road. Having to fight his way through dinner had become so much a part of his routine that he felt uncomfortable when he *wasn't* attacked.

And had he stopped running through the wilds long enough to look, he probably would've been shocked by his reflection.

He was certain the mountains hadn't changed. The deer were just as swift, the slopes as unforgiving. The rocks weren't any softer. The nights certainly weren't any warmer. And yet, here he was — bounding across the most perilous corner of the Kingdom as if he had every right to it.

Perhaps the mountains hadn't changed ...

But Kael had.

What would Amos say if he could see him now? Would he smile when he saw the hospital had been rebuilt? If he could show Roland how well he hunted, it would erase his disappointment forever. His mouth would never sag, and his shoulders would never slump again.

Now that Kyleigh and the craftsmen had finished their work, that dream was finally, at long last, within his grasp. The wildmen had everything they needed to face Titus and win. There was just one final obstacle in his way, one impenetrable wall of flaming red stubbornness:

Gwen.

"I've already told you, mutt — when the time comes, we'll stomp him."

"And when will that be, exactly?" Kael said through his teeth.

He'd been trying to get her to rally the wildmen for weeks, now. He'd done everything she'd asked of him: the warriors had furs to keep in the warmth, oilskins to keep out the damp, and enough dried provisions to survive the wastes at the mountain's top. But no matter what he did, it never seemed to be enough.

Every time he'd asked her when she planned to march on the summit, she would say something about stomping the *Man of Wolves*. She'd get the wildmen so stirred to roaring that anything Kael tried to say was completely drowned out.

So today, he'd followed her into the woods.

It hadn't been difficult to find her. Gwen's heavy, clomping steps made the tracking easy, and she couldn't outrun him. Now that he finally had her cornered, he was determined to get an answer.

"If you'll just tell me what you have planned, I might be able to help."

"We plan to crush him," she said with a shrug. "And after I'm finished, there'll be little for you to help with."

He leapt into her path. "All right, but *how* are you going to crush him?"

"With my fist."

The blow she slung into his chest likely would've shattered an average man's ribcage. But Kael had gotten so used to her punches that he hardly flinched. Instead, he grabbed her arm and twisted. "You know what I mean, Gwen. How are you going to fight him? What strategy will you use?"

Red blossomed behind her paint as she fought his grip. Her strength swelled against him, gaining her an inch. "Strategy?"

"Yes. Strategy is how you move an army." His muscles were shaking. He lost a little more ground as he thought of how to explain it. "Fighting a war is like battling with two enormous beasts: you've got to tell your beast where to go, tell it where to bite — ouch!"

She'd slowly taken over while he'd been talking. Now *he* was the one with his arm twisted back. "I'll tell my army when to crush him — and that'll be the end of it."

"If he beat you once, he can do it again."

"My army is better equipped, this time. I'll bring the Man of Wolves to his knees," she growled — forcing Kael to his.

"Then why don't you get on with it? What are you waiting for?" he grunted.

"I've already told you — the time hasn't come."

Kael relaxed. He slumped against her hold and for half a breath, let her think she'd won. Then he pulled himself free with a burst of strength.

He slammed the heel of his hand into her middle. She swung for his head and stumbled forward when he ducked. He took the opportunity to rip her over his shoulder. There was a *thud* as her back struck the ground. He sprang up and tried to put some distance between them — but somehow, she'd already gotten to her feet.

She tackled him from behind. Her hand wound in his curls and ripped back, forcing his eyes to the trees. He knew he couldn't wrench his way out of her grasp from that angle. So he tipped backwards and let his body fall to the ground.

Her gasp was strangled at his ear. He knew he'd knocked the wind out of her. By the time he flipped over, her boots were under his chest. She would've launched him clear across the woods, had he not thought to turn his skin to stone.

Sweat trickled down the furious lines of her paint. Her breathing was sharp as she struggled to hold him up. Kael knew he'd won — but he wasn't finished with her, yet.

"Tell me how Titus beat you."

She managed to raise him a hair's breadth before he concentrated on making the stone denser, even thicker. Her legs shook as he sagged towards her.

"If you tell me how he beat you the first time, I can make certain it won't happen again. Just tell me what you know."

"I can't!"

"Quit being difficult. Tell me how Titus beat you, or I swear I'll crush —"

"I don't know! I don't know how he beat us!"

Kael's surprise lifted him an inch. "What do you mean?"

Her face burned scarlet. Sweat rolled down her neck in molten lines as she roared: "I ... don't ... *know!*"

His ears rang with her cry, but it wasn't the words that shook him: it was her eyes. The angry red veins bled pink into the white. A dangerous film covered them — one that was every bit as clear and fragile as glass. He could sense what was about to happen, but he was no less surprised when it finally came.

He watched in horror as a tear slipped from the edge of her eye.

Gwen clamped down upon it furiously, turning her head away. But the damage had already been done. That single tear coursed down her cheek and onto her jaw, where she wiped it away. "Get off me."

Kael rolled aside. "I'm sorry ... I didn't kn —"

"Well, now you do. Now you know that I'm a failure *and* an idiot."

"You're not —"

"I'm the only Thane in our history to lose the mountain's top," she snapped over him. "And I've got no idea how it was even taken from me. All I know is that I'd rather be a blot on my fathers' throne than risk destroying my people. I hope one day our children's children will laugh about what a shame I was," she added with a hard look. "Because at least that'll mean we lived."

Kael watched as she clomped away, his chest heavy with her words. He wished he could've been there when Titus attacked — he wished he could've seen what the wildmen saw. He was certain that if he'd only known how they'd been beaten, he could unravel Titus's plan ...

Wait a moment — perhaps there *was* a way he could see it. Perhaps there was a way he could watch the battle through their eyes. It was a mad idea, and he would need help.

So he went in search of Griffith.

*******

"You want us to do *what?*"

Kael thought he would go mad if he had to say it again. "I need you to stand in a circle and —"

"I'm not doing it. We're *warriors*, not fairies," one of the wildmen said, rapping his knuckles on the shining top of his breastplate.

Most of the warriors were gathered outside the forge. They'd just been fitted in their new armor and had fresh edges ground into the steel swords at their belts. There was probably no worse time to ask them to link hands — but then again, there would probably never be a better one.

"All I need is two moments."

Another wildman snorted loudly. "When was the last time you saw a bunch of warriors standing around holding hands?"

"I only want to help you."

"You'd do well to listen to him," Kyleigh said as she strode from the forge. "I can always tell when he's got something exciting planned."

She smiled at him from over her shoulder — and Kael had to wonder if she could also tell when his heart was about to burst from his skin. He hoped she couldn't.

"Do you really have something planned?" Griffith said.

He didn't. Not yet. But if he could get the warriors to work with him, he was certain he would have one before evening. "I just ... need your help," he said evasively.

A determined red sprang up behind Griffith's freckles as he held out his hand. "And the rest of you will do it, too — or I'll tell Gwen about the animals," he added with a glare.

Now that the village had been rebuilt and all the weapons and armor had been made, the wildmen had run out of things to do — which meant they often got into mischief. A few nights ago, some of the warriors had snuck into the Hall and, with the craftsmen's help, had wreaked havoc on the many stuffed animals that adorned the back wall.

Gwen had marched into dinner that evening to find that her prized creatures had all been rearranged: the boars had foxtails hanging off their chins, the wolves wore antlers, and most of the deer had sharp, pointed teeth. A few badgers had even been settled into some rather compromising positions.

When Gwen saw her favorite bear shooting her a rude gesture from where it sprawled in her throne, she'd lost her temper — and the wildmen had all fled the Hall rather than risk getting a pair of antlers shoved anywhere they couldn't reach.

Though the craftsmen had returned the animals to their places, Gwen was still completely livid about it. So the warriors joined hands rather than risk having Griffith out them.

Kael hadn't circled with the warriors before. He'd hoped the fact that they didn't question every little thing might make it a bit easier. But he was wrong.

The warriors' excitement bubbled up when Kael showed them how his thoughts came alive in the circle. He showed them a memory of one of his caddocs and then stepped back, asking to see *their* memories of battle.

Things quickly got out of hand.

"Stop it," Kael growled, breaking the circle. "I don't care about who's survived the highest fall, or which of you killed the biggest bear —"

"Especially when mine was clearly biggest," Griffith said.

One of the warriors snorted. "Oh yeah? Why don't I show you the wynn I stomped while you were still in nappies —"

"No!" The word burst from Kael's lungs so loudly that the warriors actually flinched. "We're not going to waste time bickering back and forth. I need you to focus. Show me what you remember of your battle with Titus."

The warriors fell silent immediately. They scratched at the tops of their heads, dragged their fingers down the lines of their paint. Not a one of them reached to clasp hands. All wore the same dangerous scowl.

"We were beaten," one of them finally said. "It's done. There's no point in living through it again."

The others murmured in agreement. They'd turned to leave when Griffith spoke up: "I'll go first."

He held out his hands, waiting — and one by one, the warriors crept back in. Griffith's hand shook furiously as Kael grasped it. But when the circle closed, he kept his word.

Screams raked across their ears. They heard the shriek of splitting wood and saw the Earl's men burst through the shattered gates. Through Griffith's eyes, the army was a stone monster: a beast with an impenetrable shell and hundreds of shining, pointed teeth. His gasps filled their lungs as he tried to keep up with the other warriors. He was nearly there when something knocked him off his feet.

They heard the *thud* as his back struck the wall; saw the great, red shadow that loomed before him — a devil with an iron head and hollow pits for eyes, a beast twisted by Griffith's nightmares. The world spun as the monster slung him about. They heard him cry, heard the crunching of his bone.

A howl, a sharp *thwap*, and the monster fell aside. Gwen was there — the tail of an arrow hung from her chest and her tunic was drenched in blood. Even so, she scooped Griffith onto her shoulder.

"Hold tight, Griff! We're going to make it out. We're going to make it ..."

Her voice trailed away and the middle of the circle went dark. Griffith's hand trembled so violently now that Kael could feel it through his trance. He was about to break their connection when another image rose in the middle.

The warriors went around the circle, each one offering up his memories of the battle. They showed him everything: the shattering of their dragonsbane weapons, the deaths of their comrades ... the bleeding, mangled bodies of the ones they loved. Orange-blue fire burst all around them, adding to their panic.

He felt their fear, their anguish — felt how those unfamiliar edges dragged across their hearts. And slowly, he understood.

For all their strength and chasing monsters about, the wildmen had never warred with a human enemy. They had never known what it meant to fight in a real battle. Through their eyes, Titus was the Man of Wolves — a wicked, grinning nightmare shrouded by a cruel, impenetrable cloak.

The wildmen were like children: terrified of something they didn't understand, haunted by an enemy they had no idea how to defeat. To them, the battle was hopeless. Each of their visions ended with a crushing blackness — a hood that shuttered their flame. But Kael was determined to bring their fires back.

They needed to see what he saw — they needed a new vision.

So he gave them one.

Their fists would shatter Titus's walls. Their strength would fill its cracks like ice and stretch until they crumbled. They would peel back the iron shell of his army and batter the soft flesh beneath. They would break the steely points off its teeth. Their hands would wrench the monsters apart by their jaws. And at last, they would crush Titus, himself.

No, they would *stomp* him — they would drive his body so deeply into the rock that not even the wynns would be able to dig him up. They would own the mountain's top once more, and it would never again be taken from them.

He knew the moment the warriors started to believe because they added themselves to his vision. They charged through the walls and set upon Titus's army, fighting through Kael's imagination. When he was convinced that he had them blazing once more, he let them go.

They leapt around each other; they howled and beat their chests.

"We're going to stomp him!" Griffith bellowed over the others' cries. "We're going to crush the Man of Wolves!"

Their fires were there, but the flames glowed weakly. The warriors needed more than kindling to stay bright. They needed a fierce wind that would stoke them to a roar, as the storm gales had done to Daybreak. They needed to taste the blood of the Man of Wolves — they needed to know that he could be beaten.

"Come with me," Kael said.

And the warriors followed.

*******

Earl Titus's fort leered at them from the slopes above Tinnark. It was nearly complete. Another week or two, and it likely would've been finished. But Kael wasn't going to let that happen.

His army was spotted the moment they left the trees. The Earl's men shouted in warning and began to scurry along the ramparts; the arms of their catapults disappeared as they bent dangerously beneath the wall. A moment later, something small shot into the air.

It was a stocky clay jar — one of the same vessels Kael had seen in the Earl's camp. There was a rag hanging from its mouth and its tail was ablaze. Kael hurled a rock at it before it could travel too far, exploding it in the air.

"That's where the Man of Wolves' fire comes from," Kael called as the orange-blue flames rained down upon the field between them. "It's weak while it's in the air. Knock it down!"

When the next catapult swung, the warriors answered with their own barrage. They ran as they threw — exploding the Earl's fire and gaining on his fort. Their hands and eyes moved so quickly that they began to strike before the jars could clear the wall. Screams pierced the air as the soldiers' own fire devoured them.

The wildmen charged up the hill in a single unbroken line. They stepped easily around spear points, ducked beneath a hail of arrows. A cry ripped from Kael's throat as the first of the wildmen reached the gates. He heard the wood crack beneath the thrusts of their hands — saw it tremble, shudder.

Then finally, it gave way.

"Stomp them!" Griffith roared as he charged inside. "Peel their armor back — crush their flesh!"

The warriors did exactly that: they did everything Kael had showed them. They destroyed the Earl's men, smashed his catapults, flattened his walls — and then they turned their eyes upon the tower.

Their hands slammed into its sides together. Half of them pushed from the ground, and the other from the ramparts. One, two, three times, they struck. And on the fourth, it toppled.

Howls and whistles filled the air as the warriors roared over their victory. They leapt around each other and beat their chests. It was only when his throat began to burn that Kael realized he'd joined their cries. It was only when he felt the bruises on his chest that he realized he was pounding right along with them.

A tiny voice in the back of his head warned him that he probably looked ridiculous. It shrilled that he was behaving like a wildman, that he ought to calm himself. But Kael didn't listen.

He howled all the louder. He pounded his chest even harder. And the warriors' song drowned out that little voice.

338

# CHAPTER 30
## HAPPY NEWS

"You, Sir Wright, are in very big trouble," Kyleigh said when he stepped inside the forge.

Kael was well aware of this. Gwen had made it abundantly clear when she'd ripped the hospital door off its hinges and flung it at him. She likely would've beaten him to death with one of his bedposts, had Griffith not stepped in.

"Don't you see what this means, sister?"

"It means you've disobeyed me," she'd snarled. "I told you to leave that fort alone. Had we not attacked, the Man of Wolves —"

"He would've come after us anyways!" Griffith cried.

"Well, he certainly will now. There's no doubt he'll call his monsters down upon us again — on our craftsmen, on those children from downmountain. How do you plan to protect them, Griffith?"

The edge in her voice had drained all the red from her brother's face, but his chin stuck out stubbornly. "Kael will know how to protect them. He knows how to fight the Man of Wolves. You've seen what he —"

"*Kael.*" She'd hardly glanced at him as she spat his name — as if he wasn't even worth the trouble to scold. "All Kael's proved today is that he's a fool as well as a weakling."

"He's stronger than you think — he's strong enough to lead us!" Griffith cried. He'd glared at her back as she marched away, and the blue marble rolled madly between his fingers. "Don't worry, Kael. I'll think of something. I'll prove you're ready."

And before Kael had a chance to get a word in edgewise, Griffith had stalked from the hospital.

By that point, Baird had begun to complain loudly about all of the noise — and warned that if he didn't have some peace, he'd be forced to do something *drastic*. So rather than have to find out what that might be, Kael had hung the broken door back into place and jogged straight for the forge.

He didn't know what Gwen planned to do with him ... but he knew there was safety in numbers. "She thinks I forced them into it," Kael muttered as he paced. "She said I *entranced them with my Wright visions*."

Kyleigh raised her brows. "Well, did you?"

"Of course not. I only wanted to see how Titus beat them. Then the things they showed me were so ... horrible. They were so badly broken. I could *feel* they'd given up, and they had no reason to!" He pinched the arch of his nose, trying to hold his frustration back. "I just — I wanted them to see what I could see. I wanted them to know what they're capable of."

"Frustrating, isn't it?" Kyleigh muttered.

He didn't think that was entirely fair. "I never would've known what I was had it not been for the wildmen. It was like trying to look at a map through a pinhole! And I don't think — oh, give that here."

He grabbed the axe and shaft she'd been trying to fit and pushed them together. The metal swirled into the wood as he twisted it, sealing them tighter than any blacksmith could've possibly done. When he was finished, he held the axe aloft. It looked exactly like Gwen's axe, except it had two heads — and it was made of steel.

"The end of an era," Kyleigh said with a sigh. "The wildmen will have to learn to be something other than dragonslayers."

Kael had doubted before. But after seeing the warriors' confusion for himself, he was starting to believe. "It's really true then, isn't it? They've done nothing but chase monsters through the mountains for centuries on end."

She nodded. "One of the old Kings sent their ancestors into the Valley long ago. He swore that if they could drive the monsters out, they could keep the land for themselves. That's why they call their leaders *Thanes*."

Kael supposed it made sense. "But they never finished their task, did they?"

Kyleigh shook her head. "The dragonslayers chased the monsters straight up the Unforgivable Mountains and to the very top, where they planned to shove them off into the northern seas. But the monsters put up a desperate fight — and as the battle raged on, the eternal winter slowly warped them both. The monsters became the wynns, and the dragonslayers became wildmen.

"Gwen's people have wasted ages fighting an ancient battle," Kyleigh said with a sigh. "The wynns lure them out of their castle, and the wildmen chase the wynns to the cliffs above the northern seas. Back and forth they've gone for generations, neither side ever gaining much ground over the other. The wynns won't leave and the wildmen won't give in. Their children grow up knowing that they'll likely die at each others' hands."

Kael groaned as he sank to the ground. "How am I ever going to convince her to go to war? How *do* you convince somebody with mules for forefathers?" An idea came to him suddenly. "Am I allowed to caddoc Gwen?"

"Oh, Kael — you don't want to do that. Not if she's really sworn to salt your heart and eat it."

He was certain she'd only been joking about that ... well, he was *half*-certain. Still, he didn't see another way around it. "If I beat her in front of all the wildmen, she'll *have* to listen to me. She's probably going to attack me anyways, so I might as well get her first."

Kyleigh gave him a serious look. "Speaking as somebody who's had many fond battles with Gwen over the years, let me offer you a warning: there *is* an end to her goodwill. She's spitting mad right now, and if you push her any closer to the brink, she'll kill you."

Kael didn't understand. "I thought the two of you were just friends who sort of hated each other. Has she really tried to kill you?"

Kyleigh was silent for a long moment. "Do you remember the day you found me in the woods and my head was all bashed in?"

His gut twisted into a knot. "Don't tell me ..."

"I never saw it coming," she said with a sigh. "One moment I was soaring over the battlefield, leading the wynns into her flank. And the next," she slapped her hands together, "Gwen had knocked me out of the sky. She jumped from one of the castle towers and clubbed me over the head with that blasted great axe of hers. Then she rode me into the ground.

"I managed to escape, of course. I still don't think she realizes just how badly I was wounded. I don't think she ever *meant* to kill me. Part of me likes to think that she regrets it ..." Kyleigh smiled hard. "But the other part isn't entirely sure."

Mercy's sake. He'd always wondered how Kyleigh had gotten wounded. He'd imagined a dozen different ways it might've happened — but none had involved a wildwoman leaping from a castle.

"The Gwen you know might be sagging a bit at the breeches. But if you prod her, you'll regret it. Look ..." Kyleigh tugged hard on the end of her pony's tail, and the blaze of her eyes went dark. "I know what to do with Gwen."

"Really? What?"

She shook her head. Her smile didn't quite reach her eyes as she said: "Don't worry about it, whisperer. Just leave it to me."

\*\*\*\*\*\*

Nothing he said could convince Kyleigh to tell him what she had planned. So when evening fell, he followed her rather grumpily to dinner.

"Hmm, quail stew. Ah!" Baird spat the broth back into his bowl and waved a hand over his tongue. "Oh, it's hot!"

"Well, what'd you expect? It's been bubbling in a cauldron for hours," Kael said impatiently. Then he turned back to Kyleigh. "Are you going to fight her?"

"No, I'm not going to fight her."

"You are though, aren't you? You're just going to say it was *mischief*, or something."

An amused half smile bent her lips, but she didn't reply.

Kael knew he wasn't going to get it out of her, no matter how he tried. So he busied himself by glancing around the room for trouble. "Where's Griffith?"

"He said he had chills," Baird mumbled from around a mouthful of stew. Sweat beaded furiously over his bandages as he forced it down his knobby throat. "Gah! Oh, that's hot! Young Griffith said he had the shivers, so I put him in one of the cots."

Kael sighed. Gwen was probably going to blame him for that, as well.

Kyleigh tapped him on the shoulder, interrupting his thoughts. "I just realized that I never thanked you for the gifts."

"And you'll never have to," he said firmly.

"But I want to. Thank you for the bed, and the trousers."

He glanced down absently. "They seem to fit well."

"They do. Remarkably so. Which makes what I'm about to do all the more difficult."

Kael didn't have a chance to reply — he didn't even have a moment to fully grasp her words. All at once, a familiar icy-wet slap to the face blurred his vision. He wiped the moisture from his eyes and saw the empty cup in Kyleigh's hand. He saw it, but his mind struggled to grasp it.

The empty cup was in Kyleigh's hand.

*Kyleigh's.*

The wildmen shoved him off the bench and into the middle of the room. Had it not been for their urging, he didn't think he could have made it there himself. Black clouds filled his chest. Their fumes made his head light while the rest of his limbs sagged as if they belonged to a giant.

He didn't hear what Kyleigh said to Gwen. He didn't know what joke she made that had the wildmen laughing while Gwen's face burned red. When Kyleigh turned around, the sound of her bare feet scraping the floor was the only sound he heard; hers were the only eyes he saw. And he could think of only one word to say:

"No."

She raised her fists. "Hand-to-hand combat, and no shortcuts — you can't put me to sleep." She smiled hard. "We fight until one of us is knocked out."

"Kyleigh, no. I'm not —"

Her fist collided with his jaw. Every thread of her impossible strength, every cord of iron-bending muscle charged hot behind her blow. His head snapped back, but he stayed on his feet.

He felt the familiar looseness in his limbs as the warrior edge of his mind tried to take over. His eyes wanted to search her stance for weakness, but he forced them to stay still. "I'm not going to hurt you."

More blows came, but he hardly felt them. He tried to understand the confusion of being struck so hard by someone he loved. He tried to separate the sudden fury in Kyleigh's eyes from the warmth he was certain was still there.

And while his mind struggled to make sense of what was happening, his warrior edge protected him. It grew stronger and more insistent with every blow. He fought to hold onto his reason, but it was becoming more difficult to push the numbness back.

"I'm not going to hit you." The words felt strange on his lips. Perhaps it had something to do with the wet warmth that trickled down his chin. "I'll stand here all night if I have to."

The fire in her eyes swelled as she circled him. "Then I'll beat you again tomorrow night," she whispered. "And the night after that. And while you stand there with your arms crossed, Titus will rule the mountains. This is what Gwen wants — it's the only way to convince her that you're strong. You've got to defeat the one beast in the mountains she never

344

could." Her fist slammed into his nose. "You've got to beat *me.*"

Hot blood rushed down his face like a cleansing fire, driving out his confusion. The blaze in Kyleigh's eyes assured him: she was strong, she was ready. She could shoulder his blows. If this was what had to be done, then he would do it. He would break his heart once more if it meant some greater good might rise from the pieces.

With that thought, the warrior in him took over completely — its roar rattled the insides of his ears. The black clouds gave way to its fury and a cool wind filled his lungs. The earth dissolved beneath his feet until the only thing left was Kyleigh.

Then Kael struck back.

He clipped her chin, but she darted away. He ducked beneath her next swing and tried to kick her feet out from under her, but she leapt. He had to roll to miss the fall of her heel — a blow that splintered the wood where his head had been only moments before.

Her movements were all there — they were branded into his memory from the hours he'd spent fighting her aboard *Anchorgloam*. Each tilt of her chin and dart of her eyes had meaning. He read them and reacted quickly. The patterns of her steps were the words of a familiar song: he knew which line came next. He followed the verses patiently and tried to leap ahead.

But she was ready for him.

Her elbow came down into his palm. He twisted, but she was gone — popped out of his grasp and already circling at his back. A blow aimed for his head was only a feint. He realized this when he heard the thud of her fist striking his middle. It wouldn't happen again. He stored that verse alongside a hundred others and waited for the next.

Slowly, he became aware of the drumbeats that'd joined their song. The pounding of the wildmen's fists upon the table boomed beneath the noise of their fight. It thrummed in the silence between blows; it drowned out the grunts and desperate shuffling of their feet.

*Boom. Boom. Boom. Boom. Boom.*
Fists crashed against flesh. Elbows pounded into ribs.
*Boom. Boom. Boom. Boom.*
She whirled to the right, but he was already there. He swung an arm for her face, but she knocked it aside. The kick she aimed for his ribs stuck against his palm. Her heel lashed out as he flipped her, clipping his jaw.
*Boom. Boom. Boom.*
Sweat lathered her face and neck. Her chest rose with heavy breaths. He circled, hungry and waiting — his head fogged with the thrill of the fight. She lunged.
*Boom. Boom.*
Her feet moved in a familiar pattern. He was two steps ahead. When he cut her off, she swung for his face.

He read the tilt of her chin, followed the line cast by the corners of her eyes and knew instantly what was coming next. The blow aimed for his head was a feint — her other fist would come crashing into his middle at any second. She would expect him to block it, to step back or dodge. But instead, he would bring his fist overhead.

He saw himself standing high above her, the power of the earth quickening his blow. His fist cut downward — the tail of a star trailing a white-hot line across the sky. The fire in her eyes dimmed as her fist struck his middle ... the flames sputtered back into the green when she saw that star screaming towards her face ...
*Boom.*
Either complete silence or a noise beyond reckoning had enveloped the Hall — Kael wasn't sure. He saw the wildmen's mouths open; saw the fire in their eyes and the trembling of the tables as their fists came down. But for some reason, he couldn't hear them.

The numbness left his limbs as he struggled out of his trance. The fog drained from his ears and the pure, deafening noise rushed in. Wildmen leapt from their benches, chanting his name. They formed a wall of bodies, howling and leaping over one another. Even some of the downmountain folk joined in.

Slowly, the noise faded and the wall of bodies drifted apart. Gwen stepped out from between them, fists clenched at her sides. By the time she came to Kael, the Hall had fallen deathly silent.

She wasn't angry. There was only the slightest pink tinge behind her paint. There was an edge in her eyes that he thought might've been trouble, but he realized it was more excitement than anything. When she spoke, her voice was calm — and loud enough for all the wildmen to hear:

"You've managed to do something I never could, not in a lifetime of trying — and you've done it without a weapon. She's too proud a creature to have let you win." She looked down at the ground between them, and her smirk was tempered slightly by her surprise. "I honestly never thought she'd face you. But now that she has, I suppose I'll have to keep my word. The wildmen will follow you to the summit, Kael the Wright."

The Hall erupted again, but Kael wasn't listening.

All at once, he remembered what he'd done. He looked down and saw Kyleigh's unconscious form crumpled beneath him. Her brows and lips were smooth. He might've thought she was only sleeping ... had it not been for the angry red lump that swelled over her jaw.

"Kyleigh!"

The wildmen swarmed in before he could reach her. Their laughter stung his ears. Their celebration made him sick. They wrapped their hands around him and tried to pull him away. They tried to separate him from Kyleigh.

It was a mistake.

"*Move!*" Kael roared. The word rang sharply at its end and the wildmen stumbled away, shoved back by the force of his command.

The Hall fell silent as he picked Kyleigh up from the ground. The heat of his anger made her light. He held her with her head resting against his chest.

"Open the doors."

It wasn't whispercraft, but the wildmen still leapt to obey.

347

Mutters filled the Hall as he left, but Kael didn't care. The village passed in a blur. He kicked the forge doors in and slammed them shut behind him. He laid Kyleigh out on the bed and gently touched her jaw.

Her hand shot up.

"No, stop that. I'm going to heal you."

Her eyes burned defiantly.

"Do you want me to put you to sleep?"

The blaze died down.

"I didn't think so." He moved her hand aside and placed his fingers at her jaw. "Hold still."

He didn't want to hurt her any more than he already had, so he tried to make her numb. He concentrated on the muddled feeling just before sleep and watched her eyes fall hooded. When her glare had softened a bit, he went to work.

Her jaw was badly bruised. He massaged the swollen skin carefully, easing the traumatized flesh beneath it. The red retreated and the lump shrank down under his fingertips. When he was done with her jaw, he found other bruises: there were lumps on her forearms, ribs and shins. He bit his lip hard when he found a red mark on the side of her face — a mark he could match perfectly with the flat of his hand.

"I'm sorry," he whispered when he was finished. "I'm so sorry."

"Don't be. You were lovely."

He thought that was an odd thing to say. When he looked up, he could tell by the silliness of her grin that she was still numb — lost on the shores of sleep. He realized that she probably wouldn't remember anything when she woke ... and he saw his chance.

"Why did you blow the roof off the Hall the first time I fought Griffith?"

Her hand came up, clumsily brushing his lips. "I'm fond of you, Kael. I don't want to see you hurt."

Lightness flooded him in such a rush that he feared his heart might actually float from his chest. He twined his fingers in hers and whispered: "Sleep. It's time to sleep."

He watched her eyes close and held her hand long after she'd drifted off. Then he pulled the fur covers up to her chin and slipped outside — pausing to fix the shattered door on his way.

His broken nose throbbed horribly. Blood dried to his teeth and chin. But he didn't care. The moon could've tumbled straight from the sky and he probably wouldn't have noticed. His head was miles high and away, lost somewhere above the clouds.

After what she'd said to him in the forge that day, after the way her voice had softened as she spoke of the first time they'd met — he'd suspected. But now he knew for sure.

He pushed through the hospital door, past the lumpy cot that was probably Griffith, and sprinted back to the office. By the time he stopped in the doorway, he was grinning so widely that his busted lip had split anew.

Baird's head lifted from the *Atlas*. "Ah, I hear the eager steps of a man with happy news. Come on, then — out with it."

The words burst from between Kael's grin before he could stop them: "She's fond of me."

Baird slapped a hand upon the desk. "Good for you! Who's the lucky girl?"

Kael was too warm to be frustrated, too light to care. "Goodnight, Baird," he said as he turned away.

"Sleep well, young man."

And for the first time in a long while, he did.

# CHAPTER 31
## THE MYTH OF DRAEGOTH

"Your Majesty? Are you all right?"

The darkness peeled back and the worried face of a guard came into focus. Rough fingers pressed against Crevan's neck. He knocked them away. "What are you doing in here?"

"The Seer called us. He said you were in danger." The guard held his spear protectively over his chest as Crevan got to his feet.

He had good reason to be afraid.

Their screams were distant now, but Crevan still remembered the faces of the men he'd slaughtered in his chambers. They'd come crashing in, blathering something about trouble in the seas ...

No, not only trouble ... *disaster.* Treason! He remembered it, now: the chancellor's promise of an alliance had been a trap — a ploy to murder his final ruler. Countess D'Mere's panicked message still rang clearly through the fog of his memories. She'd barely escaped with her life.

The High Seas had joined with Titus. Crevan's vision had gone red at the sight of the gold medallion tied around a stinking, gore-soaked bag — redder still when he'd torn the medallion away and the severed heads of his envoy rolled out.

He'd hardly been able to read the sealed note the guards handed him, hardly been able to grasp the fact that all his plans for Titus had just crumbled out from under him. The red cloud enveloped sight, and he knew no more.

Now as he glared around the room, he saw an empty goblet laid a few stones from his boots. The chair near the hearth was toppled over onto its side. He must've drunk his liquor too quickly — *that* was what had caused the sudden darkness ... that was when his latest bout of madness had begun.

The Firecrowned King had come to him again. Flames had spouted from between its teeth and its skeletal face waved in the heat. Crevan had swallowed the contents of his goblet as quickly as he could and shut his eyes tight. But he'd found no peace.

No sooner had the Firecrowned King vanished than the Dragongirl's face rose from the darkness. Her hands reached inside Crevan's gut, twisting his innards about her fingers while her eyes burned green. The last thing he'd seen were the fangs that had sprouted from between her lips — sharp and glistening as they stretched for his throat.

A handful of guards crowded around him, now. Worry marred their features. The deep lines worn into their brows were arched in pity. Crevan's eyes swept away from them and directly onto Argon the Seer.

He stood calmly before the guards, dressed in blue robes. Blood matted the bits of his long gray beard that sat beneath his nose. His deep eyes were swollen and red-rimmed. But Crevan didn't care. Seeing Argon made his anger boil all over again.

"You've disturbed my peace, Seer."

"My apologies, Your Majesty," he said with a slight bow. "I thought I Saw you in the presence of an enemy. But it appears I was mistaken."

The presence of an enemy? Crevan's mind turned back. The vision of the Firecrowned King had been so potent ... he could still smell its charred bones and see the hollow caverns of its eyes. He felt the heat of its breath.

It wasn't impossible, then. If the Seer had sensed the specter's presence ...

No, *no* — it was madness! A vision brought on by the red mist and nothing more. Crevan wouldn't be tricked. He wouldn't let the mist take him ...

But what if ... what if it *hadn't* been madness at all? What if the Firecrowned King had truly sat before his hearth?

351

What if it'd given Crevan everything he needed to defeat his enemies, to reclaim his throne?

With his last hopes lying in ruin, he was finally mad enough to look.

The guards stood warily as Crevan turned. "Come with me, Seer — and the rest of you follow."

He marched out of the throne room with Argon at his side and the guards close behind. It was a number large enough to protect him, but small enough to be … dealt with, afterwards. They wound quickly through the brightened halls of Midlan. Servants ducked out of their path, guards stood at attention. Crevan felt their curious eyes flick across his back.

He led them down a narrow hallway and stopped at its end. A golden shield hung on the wall before them. It bore the black dragon of Midlan on its front, but the crest was backwards. The dragon's head faced the wrong direction. It was a small detail, one that likely went overlooked by most. But Crevan had noticed it immediately.

"What is this?" Argon had been about to reach for the shield when his fingers recoiled sharply. "It bears a warning, Your Majesty. An old magic guards this place."

"How old?"

"Centuries."

Crevan rolled his eyes. "Impossible. A spell dies with the mage who cast it. No magic could last for centuries."

"There are ways, Your Majesty," Argon muttered, gazing at the shield.

But Crevan ignored him. "Stand aside."

He muscled his way past Argon and gripped the shield at its bottom and top. Then with a grunt, he moved it. The shield turned like a ship's wheel. His arms strained against the centuries-old rust that coated its hinges. When the dragon had turned so that it was upside down, a loud *click* echoed down the hall.

"Swords drawn and ready, men," Crevan said as the wall slid open. "If any of you try to run, I'll have the Seer blast you into the under-realm."

The soldiers drew their swords quickly, muttering to one another as the wall slid away. Their whispering only grew louder when they saw the mass of trees that stood in the opening the wall had left behind.

The trees grew thickly, their leaves unfurled and full. The vines that draped down from their tops hung between them in a thick, tangled web. Some bore the scars of Crevan's first visit. He could still see the years-old marks of his sword in the thickest branches.

He'd charged in so foolishly, so unaware of the horror that lay just beyond. This time, he wasn't going first. "Clear us a path," he ordered, and the soldiers obeyed.

They slashed their way through the vines, grunting while they worked. He knew when they made it to the other side because their voices suddenly fell hushed.

"Kingdom's name," one of them gasped.

Crevan snapped his fingers. "Come, Seer."

Argon hesitated, wincing when the shackle around his wrist glowed hot at the command. Finally, he could stand the pain no longer. He clutched his robes tightly and followed Crevan through the trees.

This chamber was one of Midlan's greatest secrets: a space of land the size of a small village hidden in the very center of the inner keep. The ground was covered in a thick layer of grass; trees squatted here and there, their trunks bulging over their roots. But in between the wilderness were ruins left by men.

Shells of houses, bits of road, the crumbling limbs of enormous statues — all were the ghostly remains of an ancient city. They jutted up from the earth like shattered bones through flesh. The ruins must've laid undisturbed for quite some time: a large tree had sprouted up boldly through the center of one house, knocking its roof aside.

"What is it? Some sort of ... courtyard?" one of the guards muttered.

A man at the front of the line ventured a few steps ahead before coming to a stop. He stood, frozen, a hand wrapped tightly around his sword. "Kingdom's name — it's a graveyard!"

There were dozens of them, dozens upon dozens. Pale stone chunks cleft from the ruins, shaped into rounded markers and arranged in perfect lines across the grass. They filled the deep shadows beneath the trees, spreading ever outwards, like ripples in a pond.

The pale stone markers shone white in the moonlight. Argon planted his hands on one of them, tracing over its smooth surface with his fingers. "It has no name, no writing of any kind. There must be hundreds ..."

"This castle was built on the ruins of another," Crevan said. "Monsters once ruled these lands. When the first King defeated them, he razed their city and built his keep atop its ruins."

"Draegoth," a wide-eyed guard whispered to his fellows. "It *does* exist."

Crevan had doubted the legend as much as anybody. Except for a very vague passage in the Kingdom's history, there was no other mention of the monsters called *draega*. So Crevan had grown up believing all of Draegoth was a myth.

Then one day, as he'd been exploring Midlan's tunnels, he'd come across these ruins. There'd been no doubting what they were. He supposed the draega's powers had been so great that the first King had wished to strike them even from the pages of history.

The moment Crevan saw the countless lines of graves, he'd known the land was cursed. He felt the spirits of the ancient dead. He felt the land trembling with their cries for vengeance. And so he'd fled through the door and shut it tightly behind him — swearing never to return.

Now he stood on the edge of Draegoth once more. A full moon hovered overhead. The pale light cast from its skin did little to illuminate the tangled land around them. There were plenty of shadows ahead.

"Go." Crevan shoved the nearest guard, forcing him into the backs of his companions. "Move quietly."

They did as they were told.

354

The soldiers crept across the graveyard with Argon and Crevan following at their backs. Tangled branches grasped at them; the earth was damp from a heavy rain. A slight breeze toyed with their senses: it made the vines swing and the ruins whisper strangely.

"Your Majesty." Argon's sleeve slid back from his arm as he pointed upwards. "There are symbols written across the sky."

All Crevan could see were stars. "What do they say?"

"It's an ancient tongue. I can't understand all of it, but it looks to be a ward. They are powerful symbols, Your Majesty." Argon tugged on his beard. "Make no mistake — whatever lies in these ruins was meant to be bound for eternity."

A cold chill raced down Crevan's spine, but he forced himself to press on.

The soldiers' heads swiveled on their necks; the rattling of their armor was hushed. They'd been walking for several breathless minutes when the whole line came to a halt.

"What's that?" One of the men spun to Crevan. "Your Majesty — do you hear that? It sounds like ... a song."

Crevan didn't know what sort of hunter lurked among the ruins. But the Firecrowned King had said that even the Dragongirl would fear it. He wasn't going to take any chances. "Ready your spells, Seer."

Argon drew his Seeing stone from the folds of his robe. The stone rose into the air and its marbled black surface glowed a pale blue. It hovered before them as Argon and Crevan stepped to the head of the line.

At the next breath of wind, Crevan heard it: the hum of a man's voice filtered softly through the air. It rode the wind, rising and falling to match the whisper of the trees.

Crevan signaled for the guards to move forward — *silently*. The blue glow of Argon's stone dulled as it floated ahead of them. The man's song grew louder with their every step. His voice stroked their ears with cold, chilling fingers.

"Spirits," one of the guards said. "Spirits of the de —"

Crevan's sword swung back and stopped a hair's breadth from his throat.

The guard clamped his mouth shut.

They moved quietly towards the song, picking their way around the undergrowth until they came to a thick grove of squatting trees. The singing drifted out from behind the wall of their limbs.

One of the guards crept close to the vines. After a moment, he signaled that he couldn't see anything. Crevan gave them a silent command, and the soldiers nodded. They braced themselves for a count, knuckles white about their weapons. Then with a cry, they charged.

Crevan burst through the grove behind them. Argon's stone shot above the trees and belched rays of blue light from its middle, illuminating a creature that hunched alone near a white stone marker. The creature moved like a shot from a bowstring — a man-sized flash of furry brown that darted for the trees, easily outstripping the guards.

"Stop it!" Crevan bellowed as his men sprinted ahead. "Don't let it out of your sight!"

Argon's Seeing stone fell from the sky and crashed down among the trees. Rays of bright green light burst through the foliage, knocking the guards backwards.

"The creature's been hit!"

Tangles of vines and men passed in a blur as Crevan shoved his way to where the stone had fallen. When he saw the creature's body crumpled upon the grass, the stone lying beside it, he let out a roar.

"You killed it! You worthless Seer —"

"It's not dead, Your Majesty. The creature's only been petrified," Argon said calmly as he joined them.

"I don't think it's a creature at all, Your Highness." One of the guards had edged close to the crumpled body. He reached down and snatched quickly at the fur over its head.

"Impossible," Crevan breathed.

What he'd thought to be a monster was actually a young man. He was dressed head to toe in a strange garment — one that looked to be made up of the furry skins of rats.

There were dozens of them: stitched together side-to-side and head to rump. The brown, black, and gray bodies formed a full set of clothing, complete with a thick fur cloak.

The young man's fingers were curled slightly; his legs raised one over the other, as if he'd been struck mid-run. His face, though frozen in shock by Argon's spell, was remarkably handsome. The crop of his hair was dark like a forest man's, but his skin was strangely pale. Crevan took a step closer and balked at the color of his eyes.

They were a cold, furious blue. Flecks of white drifted in a burst from his pupils — like caps of ice across the northern seas. There was the same strange mix of danger and allure in his stare as there had been in his song.

"What is he, Your Majesty?" Argon said.

Crevan wasn't sure. Was this what the Firecrowned King had sent him into the ruins to find? Was *this* the hunter he'd spoken of? This — this, *child* of a man?

Red mist clouded his eyes when he realized he'd been tricked. He grabbed the young man by the front of the shirt, enough rage coursing through his limbs to rip him in half. But just before the madness could take hold, something caught his eye.

A half-moon of wood peeked out from behind the young man's cloak. Crevan dropped his body on the ground and cast the cloak aside, revealing the wooden medallion that hung around his neck.

There was a symbol carved into the medallion's surface: a pair of trees sprouting from the same root. Their trunks wound together like a braid until they met at the top, their foliage bursting in a single, indistinguishable bloom.

Crevan's hand shook as he flipped the medallion over. When he saw the image carved into its back, he laughed. It was a wild, booming laugh — one that echoed across the graveyard and made his men take a hasty step back.

"What is it, Your Majesty?" Argon said. Even *he* sounded worried.

Crevan ripped the medallion from the young man's neck and stuffed inside his pocket. "Have the beastkeeper

357

send word to Countess D'Mere — I plan to meet her in the swamps."

The Seeing stone rose from the ground and shot off towards the castle. "Done, Your Majesty," Argon said. His eyes went back to the young man. "What about —?"

"Take that whelp to Ulric," Crevan said, motioning to the guards. "He'll keep an eye on him while I prepare for the journey north."

Argon watched as the guards hoisted the young man between them, a strange look on his face. "Ulric...? But Your Majesty, there's no need to trouble your archmage with so small a task. Why don't you allow me to look after him?"

Crevan thought about it. "I suppose that makes more sense. A worthless task for a worthless Seer. Take him to the tower, then."

The guards marched away, but Crevan held Argon back. "Once they've delivered the whelp, send them to Ulric. He knows what to do."

Argon's gray brows rose high. "But —"

"The longer a man lives, the more secrets he tells. I've discovered that the only way to keep their mouths shut," Crevan said quietly, "is to blast them to pieces. As for you ... you'll never speak of this place to anyone. People can't know that the ruins of Draegoth exist."

Argon's shackle glowed red-hot with the command. He had no choice but to nod. "As you wish, Your Majesty."

Crevan smirked as he marched away. The mist of his madness had lifted. His mind was sharp. He strode from the ruins, arms swinging beside him — moving with all the ill-intentioned haste of a rogue fresh out of prison.

He wouldn't have to wait much longer. The hour was nearly here.

Soon, the Dragongirl would trouble him no more.

# CHAPTER 32
## IN THE COUNSEL OF THE MOUNTAINS

When Kael woke the next morning, his mouth was stuck in a smile. He'd felt no pain as he'd fallen into bed. Now as he woke, he could feel the twinge of his busted lip against his smile. But his wounds didn't bother him. They *couldn't* bother him. Even when he rolled over and saw Gwen scowling at him from the hearth, it did nothing to shake his mood.

"My brother's lost his marble."

"Well, that was bound to happen eventually. He only had one to begin with."

The world turned sideways and Kael found himself dumped upon the floor — buried beneath a small mountain of pelts and a heavy mattress of goose-stuffed skins.

A hollow *thud* shook the planks as Gwen dropped the bed onto the ground. She dragged him out from under his covers by the heel. "He's hidden it somewhere, and he says *you're* the only one who knows where to find it."

Kael wrenched his leg out of her grasp and rolled onto his feet. "Well, I don't have time to find it. Why don't you ask ...?" He ripped the covers off the cot and realized that the lumps he'd thought were Griffith weren't actually *Griffith* at all: they were a rucksack and a set of Baird's ragged clothes.

"He tricked me. He said he wasn't feeling well and then he slipped out the moment I left him alone with that blind old fool," Gwen said, scowling back at the office. "The pest found him in the woods this morning."

Kael didn't understand why she looked so concerned. "It's only a marble. I'll make him a new one."

"It isn't *only* a marble. It's a perfectly rounded piece of stone-ice."

"Stone-ice?"

"Yes, mutt. Parts of the mountain's top have stayed frozen for so long that the ice has turned to stone. All of Thanehold is built atop a hill of stone-ice. It's the one thing too dense for the wynns to tunnel beneath — the marble has healing powers!" she snapped, cutting over the top of his next question. "That's all you need to know. Now hurry and help me find it."

She was being ridiculous. He doubted very seriously that a marble had any sort of power and even if it did, there was no way they were going to be able find it out in the woods. If he ever wanted to see his marble again, Griffith would have to give up his game and tell them where he'd put it. "I'll go talk to him."

"You can't." Gwen's voice was suddenly hard; the edges of her eyes were sharp. "You can't talk to him. He's too far gone."

*******

Kael found Griffith inside the forge. He was sprawled upon Kyleigh's bed, his head resting on Silas's tawny back. The halfcat's tail flicked sharply when Kael burst in. His eyes glowed in warning.

So he inched carefully up to the bed. "Griffith?"

There was dirt under his nails and the stripe of his hair was slightly damp. But aside from a few bramble scratches, the boy seemed unhurt. He stroked Silas roughly between the ears, mumbling through his grin.

"Griffith?"

"Walk to round it wants, Silas."

Kael froze. "You know about Silas?"

A rumbling growl drew his eyes back to the halfcat. Silas's tail flicked angrily. He wanted Kael to notice something, to pay closer attention. It was when he leaned to look at Griffith's face that he saw his eyes were strangely empty.

His pupils were stretched wide, as if he sat in darkness even though the morning light streamed in. He breathed heavily through his mouth — a mouth that seemed to dip constantly between a frown and a manic grin. If that wasn't enough proof that something was amiss, Silas didn't growl when Griffith flattened his ears.

"Walk to round it wants, Silas?"

His words didn't make any sense. "What are you saying?"

"He keeps calling my cat *Silas*," Gwen said as she entered. She glanced around outside before she shut the door. "Sometimes he'll laugh and say the cat's naked. I don't know why."

"Well, neither do I," Kael said quickly — perhaps a little too quickly.

Gwen narrowed her eyes. "Why would you? This isn't your brother and that's not your cat. The pest is out trying to make some sense of Griffith's trail," she went on while Kael breathed a sigh of relief. "But I doubt she'll find anything. It looks as if he stumbled through the woods for half the night."

"Walk to round it wants, Silas."

Gwen pursed her bluish-black lips. "His words are scrambled. Gah ... it just keeps getting worse, doesn't it?" Her fingers left red lines down the side of her face. "The moment I think we've finally made it into the sun, Fate sends another storm."

Kael thought that was probably his fault. Rotten luck seemed to follow him wherever he went. "What's wrong with him?"

"There's nothing *wrong* with him," Gwen said vehemently. She stepped over and parted the stripe of Griffith's hair — revealing the raised, purplish scar beneath the red. It was nearly as long as a man's finger. "When he was five years old, Griffith lost his footing and cracked his skull on one of the rocks outside the castle. He shouldn't have lived. But my brother's stronger than he looks.

"When he finally woke, his eyes were out of focus. His words were always mixed. Thane Evan locked him away and told our people he was ill. He never paid Griffith much attention after that. If my brother tried to speak, Evan would just ruffle his hair and say: *Poor, scrambled Griff.* But I didn't give up." Gwen's hand pressed down firmly as she ran it across his hair. "I asked Fate for an answer, and she led me into one of the caves beneath our castle — where I found that stone-ice marble. Its powers keep him focused. As long as he has it with him, he'll be all right."

Griffith had once mentioned the blue marble helped him gather his thoughts. Now, as Kael met that strangely blank stare, he found himself believing. "Why did he think I would know where the marble was?"

Her shoulders rose and fell. "I'm not sure. Knowing Griffith, it was probably another one of his blasted tests. He kept trying to convince me about you, kept putting you through the caddocs, trying to prove that you were ready ..." Her hand dragged down her face again and she let out a frustrated growl. "I should've listened sooner. He knew it — he could see it all along. Why didn't I listen? Why did I have to be ...?"

She went on, but Kael didn't hear her.

He'd thought that the wildmen had been caddocking him for their own amusement. He hadn't realized there'd been any purpose behind it. But as he thought about it, he realized it made sense.

Griffith had been pushing him all along: he'd believed Kael could topple a tree, led him into his first caddoc — he'd even begged Gwen to teach him how to use his warrior's edge. Kael realized that all the while he'd been focused on climbing the mountains, Griffith had been right behind him, pushing.

Now he lay stark-eyed and empty upon the bed, and Kael knew there must've been a purpose behind it. Griffith must've had a reason for hiding his marble. Kael was certain he'd been intending to give him one final push ... but how?

He combed frantically through his memories, trying to think of anything that might lead him to where Griffith had stashed the marble. He remembered the last thing Griffith had said to him — about how he was determined to get Gwe to listen.

He'd hidden the marble somewhere in the woods. He said that Kael was the only one who would know where to look ...

And all at once, he knew where the marble was.

*******

Gwen took one look at the Tail and snorted. "It can't be climbed."

"Don't tell me you can't when you haven't tried," Kael retorted.

She glared at him. "I *have* tried. I know every inch of forest around my village. Do you honestly think I would've let such an interesting rock go unconquered? Of course I've tried." She walked beside it, tracing her hand around its perfectly smooth surface. "How high does it go?"

Kael squinted through the clouds. "I'm not sure. You can't exactly see — no, don't hit it! If you knock it over, that marble's going to go sailing into Kingdom knows where and we'll never find it again. Honestly, don't you think?"

She paused mid-swing. "No, I don't. That's the problem. Griffith's much better at thinking — obviously," she added, glaring up at the Tail. "But if the others know he's scrambled, they'll never let him be Thane. Then *I'll* have to do it."

Kael could hardly believe what he was hearing. "You don't want to be Thane?"

"That's the last thing I want, mutt. I'm my mother's daughter, and I want to live as she did — freely, with the wilds at my feet."

As far as he could remember, Gwen had never mentioned anything about having a mother. He'd begun to imagine that she'd simply hatched from the ice. "What happened to her?"

"She was mortally wounded during a battle with the wynns. And so she grabbed their Queen by her horns and off the mountain's top, sending them both into s of the northern seas." Gwen smiled fiercely. "If ell, I'll be pleased."

.... ...idn't doubt it. But though she was mad in at least a dozen other ways, there was one thing they could both agree on: the wildmen would be better off with Griffith.

So as he walked the Tail again, his eyes searched for weakness. His hands memorized the smooth texture of its hardened skin. The climb itself wouldn't be all that difficult. What made the Tail such a challenge was the fact that there was absolutely nothing to grasp onto. If there'd only been some holds ...

"I have an idea," Kael said. He waved Gwen back and stepped up to the Tail alone. "Wait here —"

"Not in a thousand rolls of the die, mutt. I want to see what's up there."

"Well, one of us needs to survive. If I don't make the climb, you'll be the only one left who knows where the marble is. Think of Griffith," he said quickly, when he saw the argument forming on her lips.

Her scowl hardened and froze. "Fine. I hope your bones rot in the under-realm, mutt."

"I hope I'll see you there," he said back.

He could practically feel her grinning behind him as he placed his hands on the Tail. He tried not to think about the infinite drop beneath him. Instead, he focused on the cloud of mist that covered the Tail's top. He remembered the day when Griffith had thrown a rock up there, how so many long moments had passed before they finally heard the faint echo of it striking the top.

There was no doubt in his mind that was precisely what he'd done with the marble.

Kael was staring up at the impossible task before him when Roland's words struck his ears: *There's no way to know how high it goes, or what it would take to get there ... when you think about it, I suppose it's really a* question *that keeps us grounded — not the height.*

364

If he wanted to reach the top, Kael knew he had to focus. He couldn't climb if he was worried about the journey down. So he wouldn't worry. He wouldn't leave anything to chance — he wouldn't trust the rock to give him the holds he needed.

Kael would carve his own path.

He dug his hand into the smooth side of the Tail, molding its flesh like clay. It curved into a hold beneath his grip. He latched onto it and his muscles tensed. They tightened around his bones and held him firmly as he reached to form the next hold. Then the next. He wedged his feet into the holds that his hands had left behind and focused on the patch of rock above him.

The warrior and the craftsman worked together: one part of his mind carried him up the path while the other carved it out. It was an easy rhythm, like putting one leg in before the other.

He felt the cool breath of mist on his neck and across his bare chest. White fogged his vision, but he didn't panic. The rock was above him: he could feel it. He mapped his next move one-handed, letting his fingers see what his eyes could not — trusting his strength to hold him.

On and on he climbed. He pulled himself up the Tail, making a way where there'd been none. He'd gotten so used to the motion, so entranced by the rhythm of the climb, that he nearly lost his balance when his hand swung up and touched nothing.

He felt tentatively through the empty air until he came to a lip of rock. He crawled over the final ledge, dragging his knees across the earth. When he pulled himself out of his trance, he saw that there was nothing left to climb. He'd reached the top.

Kael stood on a shelf of rock — a platform no wider than a table. Wind hissed across his ears. It whipped through his hair and tugged on his trousers, making them flap like a pirate's sails. But that was the only sound for miles.

Rolling gray clouds crowned the sky. They hung all around him, marching on a thousand silent, wispy feet towards the land below. Peaks of the neighboring mountains stood in a watchful ring. Their jagged white tops pierced the clouds like a set of monstrous teeth.

He stood in the mouth of the earth. Here was another world entirely, a sight no other man had seen. Kael was alone in the counsel of the mountains.

There was simply no grasping it. When he tried to understand, the feeling was too strong for his grip. It was a sight too powerful for his eyes. So he didn't try to contain it. He didn't try to take it in. Instead, he spread his arms wide.

He breathed deeply as the wind whipped across his face. It swept by, following an invisible path across the bowl of clouds — dancing towards the silent peaks ... taking the cry of his heart along with it. After a moment, Kael brought his eyes back to the platform beneath him. It was time to finish his task.

He found the blue marble wedged between two rocks. He stuffed it deep inside his pocket before he headed back to the ledge —

"I told you to stay put!"

Gwen rolled her eyes as she pulled herself over the lip. "Like I'd do anything you tell me to, mutt."

She slipped past him, walking until the toes of her boots hung off the very edge of oblivion. Red blossomed down her neck and spread across her bare arms. Her fists trembled as she raised them over her head. Then she howled.

Her cry echoed all around them. Kael had expected it to shatter the silence — to grate against the raw, quiet beauty. But if anything, her voice added to it. The way her howl was both sharp and deep, the way it traveled along the wind's whipping path ... that, more than anything, convinced him that Gwen belonged among the mountains.

They were as raw and wild as she was.

"This place reminds me of The Drop," she said, propping her hands on her hips. "It's what we call the back wall of our fortress. Our keep hangs over the edge of the mountain's top, and below it is a straight fall to the northern seas. I watched the pest leap off of it, once." Her head turned slightly, and he saw she was grinning. "I had her cornered at The Drop. She was mine for the taking. Then she spread her arms and fell backwards over the edge, growing her wings mid-fall ... Fate's fingers, what it must be like to see the world through her eyes."

At last, Gwen strode from the edge and took the marble from his hands. She turned it absently, its blue skin reflected in her stare. "I wasn't very kind with Griffith," she said after a moment. "I didn't know if he truly *would* make a better Thane. My own desires drove me to seek Fate ... but she wouldn't have led me to this marble if she didn't have some great plan for Griffith. And so she turned my selfishness into a mighty gift." Gwen jabbed him hard in the chest with her finger. "I'll bet even *you* couldn't do that, mutt."

She spun around and Kael's toes curled as she dropped over the ledge. He leaned out and saw she'd caught herself a few holds down the path.

"Move, mutt!" she yelled when she caught him staring.

The angle of the drop made his stomach flip. He had to take a step backwards and breathe deeply. Fear had nearly gripped him when he remembered the words Amos had spoken to him the last time he'd been stuck up high.

It chased his fear away; it steeled his limbs. And so a small lesson he'd learned long ago gave him the courage he needed to take that first step:

Kael had gotten himself up there. And he would get himself down.

*******

"I knew you'd find it," Griffith said, practically beaming.

After just a few minutes of twining the marble between his fingers, Griffith's mind had come back. Kael never would've believed it, had he not seen it for himself.

"Is Gwen going to fight the Man of Wolves?"

"She is," Kael said carefully.

He had to brace himself against Griffith's excited shout: "We're going to stomp him! We're going to topple him just like we toppled his castle, aren't we?"

Silas was pretending to be asleep, curled up near the head of Kyleigh's bed. He cracked a glowing eye as Kael sat heavily beside Griffith. "You're a brave boy, Griff."

"But you're not going to take me with you," he finished sullenly.

Kael couldn't — not again. He wouldn't risk Griffith's life or the lives of the folk from downmountain. He had a plan to keep them safe. Their battle with Titus might drag a little longer because of it, the journey up might be a little more difficult, but he could think of no better way to protect the wildmen.

"You're going to stay here and look after Tinnark. Gwen's going to leave you with most of the warriors. Make sure they listen —"

"Wait — if I have the warriors, who will you fight with?" Griffith said, with no small amount of concern.

That was the tricky bit. He'd spent most of the journey back convincing Gwen to listen. He'd quite literally had to pound it into her skull before she would believe him. And he doubted very seriously if Kyleigh would be pleased. But mad as it sounded, he knew it would work:

"I'm going to use the craftsmen."

"The *carpenters*? But ..." Griffith's incredulous look suddenly melted as he shook his head. "You're mad, Kael the Wright. And I'm probably mad for believing you, but I do." He smiled hard as he popped onto his feet. "Just keep my sister out of trouble, will you?"

Kael promised he would try.

Fortunately for Silas, Griffith didn't seem to remember knowing his name — or anything else he might've discovered while he was scrambled. So perhaps it was out of relief that the tawny mountain lion obeyed when Griffith snapped his fingers and said:

"Come, cat."

Kael watched as boy and lion sauntered out the door. The moment they were gone, he slumped onto the bed. He wasn't sure how long he waited, though it was probably the weight of his dread that made the minutes scrape by. When Kyleigh finally opened the door, a cool afternoon breeze came in behind her.

"Have you heard the good news, then? Griffith's ..." Her smile vanished when she saw him, and for a heart-stopping moment, he feared she might've been able to read the plan on his face. "Oh, look what I've done to you!"

Kael had honestly forgotten about his caddoc wounds. He flinched when her fingertips stirred the ache from a bruise on his cheek. "They don't hurt."

The fires in her eyes swelled as she traced a narrow cut on his chin. "I was horrible to you."

"We were horrible to each other — I just patched you up."

"Well, I wish you'd patch yourself up," she growled.

"I will ... but first, I need to talk to you. And it isn't going to be pleasant, and you're going to be furious —"

"You want to teach the craftsmen how to whisper themselves into dragonscale armor."

She wasn't glaring, but she wasn't exactly smiling, either. Kael swallowed hard. "And weapons. Though I ... I may have already, sort of, showed them Harbinger. A bit."

She gave him an amused look. "How's that, exactly?"

"They only think of him as a tool for chopping up trees."

"Well, don't let *him* hear that. He'll be highly offended."

Kael stiffened when she sat down beside him. He was certain the storm was going to break; the rage was going to come. He just wasn't sure *when* she would finally decide to throttle him.

But to his great surprise, she spoke gently: "You're a strange creature, Kael. Few men would've wrung the magic from a piece of dragonsbane, and even fewer would've tossed the gold aside. No man would've done the things you've done

369

and asked for nothing in return — believe me. I've seen every type of man there is.

"You've got the rarest of hearts. And I hope you'll take this the best way possible, but sometimes I don't believe you're human," she added with a wry smile. "Perhaps I didn't exactly know what I was doing when I made you those gauntlets. But there's one thing I know for certain: I trust you."

Her words burned him. He wasn't like that at all — in fact, he felt impossibly small standing next to the Kael she'd built. For some reason, her praise broke him even more thoroughly than a scolding. "I don't have a rare heart."

"I beg to differ."

"Well, what if I don't want you to trust me like that?"

"You haven't got a choice, have you? It's my trust, and I'll put it where I please," she retorted. "But before you go off and get the craftsmen suited up ... I want you to know why I asked you to keep it a secret for so long."

Kyleigh took a deep breath, and Kael forgot about being angry with her. He knew by how her face was twisted that she was about to tell him something important.

"During the Whispering War, the rebels were led by a very powerful whisperer," she began quietly. "He knew the minds of the warriors, the craftsmen and healers. He knew how to guide their powers. He was even able to awaken them — but he wasn't a true Wright."

"The Falsewright," Kael breathed, remembering what Baird had told him before ... what *Baird* had told him. Mercy's sake. "That beggar-bard isn't nearly as mad as he lets on, is he?"

"Oh, he's mad," Kyleigh assured him. Then she pursed her lips. "He just has a long memory."

The question practically burst from Kael's mouth: "So was what he said about you true, then? Did you really kill the Falsewright?" His heart thudded furiously when she nodded.

"The rebels knew all of the King's tactics, they knew every detail of his army — even down to the material of their weapons and armor. With the rebels' knowledge combined, the Falsewright knew everything. His army could defend against any of our attacks, break any of our shields —"

"But he didn't know about dragonscales," Kael guessed.

She smirked. "Setheran told me to keep my powers a secret from everyone, even from the King. Oh, word got out eventually," she admitted. "But not in time to save the Falsewright. Setheran said that if I would be patient, if I would wait until the last possible moment, he would give me the chance I needed to end the war.

"We spent months trying to lure the Falsewright out. And when he finally showed his head, I sent it rolling. Not even the whisperers were prepared to do battle with a dragon," she said, smiling at the memory. Then her face went serious. "Keeping my scales out of their reach prevented the rebels from stopping me. If a whisperer doesn't know how something feels ..."

"He can't break it. Just like what Titus and his steel did to the wildmen." Kael thought for a moment. "I don't think we have to worry about the wildmen ever trying to take the throne."

"Neither do I," she said dryly. "I supposed this is just the end of another era ... I'll have to give up one of my greatest secrets."

She patted him on the knee before she stood, but he hardly felt it. He was too busy combing through everything he knew about the Whispering War. Then he measured it against everything Kyleigh had just told him.

For some reason, an eerie feeling twisted in his gut when he thought of the Falsewright. There was a loose thread at its end — something a dusty corner of his mind had already put together, but that he was still trying to draw into the light.

All at once, Baird's voice rose inside his head:

*I knew too much. They planned to turn me over to the Falsewright — and he would've got it out of me. Oh yes, he had his ways. I had no choice ... he tricked them ... he ripped their secrets out! He pulled them away strand by strand until he knew them all … a strange name, a secret name. Most people in the Kingdom didn't know it …*

*But you do.*

Kael couldn't feel his legs. The earth had fallen out from under him and the sky had peeled away — leaving him floating, helpless, snared inside a horrible, gut-twisting realization. His tongue was too swollen to move. He shouldn't have been able to form the words, but he somehow forced them out:

"Kyleigh … did the Falsewright have another name?"

"Only the name the rebels gave him."

"What was it?"

She shrugged, as if it was merely a line scrawled in history and nothing more: "Deathtreader."

# CHAPTER 33
## NO OTHER CHOICE

They left Tinnark in the early hours of the morning.

Kael was more surprised than anybody at how difficult it was to leave the wildmen. They'd spent their last evening feasting in the Hall. The wildmen had eaten and caddocked as if nothing exciting was going on — as if they preferred to spend their final night together as normally as possible.

The warriors Gwen had chosen to stay behind and watch the village were none-too-pleased about their duties. They'd been even less pleased when they realized that a horde of craftsmen was marching up the mountains in their place.

But fortunately, Griffith had known just what to say to silence their arguments. "The lives of our people are the most important things — more important than our castle or our lands. Fate had to club me over the head a few times, but I can finally see it." He'd waved a hand around at the tiny, pointed houses and said: "We don't need a castle to be a people. As long as we stay together, the wildmen will have a home wherever we settle. I'm honored to take on such an important task."

Kael had watched in amazement as the warriors calmed. They'd nodded stiffly and gone on about their business, their backs a little straighter than they'd been before. "That was well done, Griff."

He'd shrugged. "It was the truth. They knew it — they just needed me to smack them with it. Here."

Kael held out his hand, and Griffith had pressed a fistful of curled roots into his palm. "What are these for?"

"We call them *night-fingers*. They're sweet like berries, but you can eat them raw. They only grow at the summit — I had some in my pocket when Titus sacked us. I've been rationing them, but I'm running low. Will you bring some back for me? I'd ask Gwen, but they probably wouldn't make it down the mountain in her pack."

"All right."

"I knew I could count on you," Griffith had said, clapping him on the shoulder. "Keep these with you so you'll know what they look like. Oh, and you should pack them somewhere they won't get squished." He'd grinned widely — revealing the purple splotches that covered his teeth and the arches of his gums. "They stain."

Kael wasn't certain that he'd have any better luck getting the night-fingers down the mountains, but he promised he would try.

Though he was impatient to reach the summit, the morning still seemed to come all too quickly. He'd risen long before the sun and had gone back to the office, hoping to spend a few moments talking with Baird.

The beggar-bard was already waiting for him. He sat at the desk, all of Kael's belongings spread out between his hands. "Whispers swirl around the village. Kael the Wright is leaving us today. I hear you mean to join him," he said as Kael entered. "You're one of a small company that follows the Wright up the mountain, their spirits bent on reclaiming its top."

"I can't hide anything from you, Baird," Kael said as he stepped up to the desk. "What are you doing with my things?"

Baird clasped his knobby fingers around the rough-spun garments and boots. "A woodsman's garb, a traveler's soles — loved for so long, and now they lie unused. You've wandered from where you began," he said as he passed them over.

Kael couldn't help but smile.

Baird's hands wandered until they came across the bow. His fingers traced the strange, swirling lines that had been carved into the grayed wood. "Whispercraft," he said.

"The whisperer who carved this bow meant it to be as smooth and supple as the breeze. A shot fired from this string will never be knocked aside by the wind — as long as the archer's hands are steady and his sight is firm, the arrow will always fly true."

Kael was speechless. He'd known that the bow was special: it had bent so easily the first time he'd wielded it. The arrows followed the line of his eyes without question. The few times he'd missed, it hadn't been because of the bow — it'd just been bad luck.

"Such whispercraft requires nothing short of absolute concentration," Baird murmured, as if he could sense the question forming on Kael's lips. "He must allow his mind to be consumed in the thought he desires and push it out through his craft, weaving it along the path of his hands in a single, focused thread. If his mind wanders for even a moment," Baird slapped his palms together, "the thread will be broken. Such a skill requires years to master.

"But even the greatest bow is useless without its arrows," he went on as he reached for Kael's quiver. "You remember that, young man."

He promised he would.

Baird had gone through each of his things one by one, spouting of their virtues and warning of their weaknesses. At last, there were only two items left on the table: Kael's hunting dagger, and the *Atlas*.

Baird took one in either hand. "A blade and a book ... hmm, more like a lock and a key."

"What do you —? Wait!" Kael grabbed Baird's wrist before the dagger's point could reach the *Atlas*. "You're going to ruin it."

"No, *you're* going to ruin it. He needs to learn to keep his mouth shut and listen," Baird mumbled at the ceiling. "Surely he knows by now that I would never harm a book."

Kael supposed he had a point. He let go of Baird's wrist and kept his fists clenched tightly as the dagger advanced on the *Atlas*.

375

"An old trick," Baird said. "There's always a little space in the spine — just enough for a note ..."

Baird's mouth parted slightly as he worked. His knobby fingers traced the *Atlas*'s worn leather spine. They felt inside the narrow U between the pages and the binding. His brows scrunched over his bandages as he stuck the tip of the blade inside.

He pried the dagger upwards, and something that looked like a tiny brass fingernail appeared over the top of the spine. It must've been some sort of latch: at Baird's slight urging, the whole spine slid out of the U like a panel — revealing a folded bit of parchment that'd been tucked inside.

Baird tilted the *Atlas*, and the note fell out. "Well, what does it say?"

Though the ink was faded brown, he could still read the careful words scrawled across its front: "*For Kael.*"

Baird's head tilted to the side. "Which Kael?"

"Kael the Wright," he said without thinking, even though there had been no mention of a Wright. The note was clearly and simply addressed to *Kael*.

"Well, then you ought to make sure he gets it," Baird said. His knobby fingers found the note and pushed it across the desk. "Safe travels to you, young man."

Kael thanked him absently. He stared at the note for several long moments before he finally tucked it inside his pocket.

As he left Tinnark for a second time, he kept his eyes on the backs of the wildmen in front of him and tried to keep his mind turned to other things. But the note still sat heavily inside his pocket.

*******

Gwen made a frustrated sound. "Why do they travel so *slowly*?" she growled from up ahead.

"They're craftsmen — not warriors," Kael said back. "If you'd stuck to the road, things would've been a lot easier."

376

They'd gone no more than a few miles and the wildmen had already managed to make a mess of things. Though a good deal of their force was made up of craftsmen, the warriors spoke loudly.

"The road curves around here," Gwen had said, gazing down the path. She wore a fitted breastplate over her fur tunic, and her gauntlets were capped in iron. The steel axe that hung from her belt looked even more menacing than dragonsbane: the sunlight glinted dangerously off its twin edges.

There was a rounded, wooden shield strapped across her back. The iron cap in its middle had been molded into a thick spike, and she'd insisted that the ring around the shield's edge be ground sharp.

"I'm not sure that's such a good idea," Kael had said, glancing back at the craftsmen.

While the warriors were all dressed like Gwen, the craftsmen didn't have the strength to carry heavy armor. The first time Kyleigh had tried to fit one of them with a breastplate, his skinny legs had collapsed beneath the weight. So they'd had to settle for boiled leather and furs.

Kael knew how perilous the raw mountain could be, and he'd doubted very seriously if the craftsmen could survive a jaunt through the thicket. But Gwen wouldn't budge.

"You wanted to bring them along, mutt. See to it that they keep my pace," she'd barked as she clomped into the brush. "This cut will save us at least two hours."

But instead of trimming two hours off their journey, it'd wound up tacking at least two on.

Kael learned quickly why Gwen had thought the craftsmen were useless: away from their work, they were frail, stumbling things. They panted heavily and complained often. If they took their eyes off the ground for even a moment, they'd trip over their own feet.

One of them slipped and broke his arm at the first boulder. Kael had to spend several minutes setting it back.

"How could you have possibly outrun Titus's army with this lot?" he said to Gwen.

She looked at him as if he was stupid. "We were going *down*hill, mutt. Save your breath for climbing."

By midday, it became obvious that they weren't going to make up any time. In fact, they seemed to be losing it at an alarming rate. Kael's companions weren't any help: Kyleigh and Silas had disappeared into the woods almost the moment they set out, and the warriors did nothing but laugh at the craftsmen.

Gwen's only solution seemed to involve a good amount of yelling. She yelled for the wildmen to move faster, yelled at the rocks and trees in their path, yelled at Kael for bringing the craftsmen along in the first place. If she stopped hollering for more than a minute, he'd begin to hope that perhaps she'd fallen off a cliff — only to have his hopes dashed when her squawking started up again.

Kael groaned aloud when the narrow trail they'd been following suddenly ended at a steep, jutting wall of the mountain. It was twice the height of the Hall and covered in jagged stones. The warriors scampered up its side without a problem. But the craftsmen struggled magnificently.

Kael lifted the first man onto the rocks and held him up for as long as he could reach. But as soon as he was forced to rely on his own strength, the craftsman toppled straight off the edge. Kael knew there was no chance they could make it up on their own. Something had to be done.

He called the craftsmen, and they gathered at his side. "Look — if you can't find a good place to hold on, then do exactly what you did with the houses." Kael pressed the wall's skin in and down, forming a step. "Make them close enough, and it'll be no more difficult than walking upstairs."

The craftsmen gave it a try, and things seemed to be going well enough that Kael thought he had a few moments to heal a man who'd gotten a nasty cut on his knee.

He was wrong. By the time Kael turned back, the craftsmen had already gotten themselves into very serious peril.

The man in the lead had obviously never done any climbing. He'd molded the steps up in a straight line, leading them directly to a dead end. He was stuck, frozen beneath a jutting edge of the cliff.

To make matters worse, the craftsmen below hadn't waited for him to reach the top. Now there were hands and feet packed into every hold, forming a straight line of craftsmen from the bottom to the top. And they were all completely stuck.

"Oh, for mercy's sake," Kael growled when he saw them.

"Help!" the craftsman at the top cried. "My — my arms are shaking!"

"At least you can *feel* them shaking. Mine have already gone numb!"

"My hands are all sweaty!"

"What's going on up there? Why have we stopped?"

While the craftsmen clung to the wall for their lives, the warriors howled with laughter. They grinned down at the desperate line beneath them — and inexplicably, the craftsmen grinned back.

Gwen wedged her feet against a rock and swung her upper half over the lip, hanging cross-armed like a bat. "How long do you think you'll be able to hold?" she said to the craftsman at the top of the line.

"Go away!"

"But we're taking bets."

"I don't care," the craftsman gasped. "Stop making those faces! You're going to ..." He pressed his face against the wall and started laughing.

Kael didn't think it was funny. "What in Kingdom's name are you doing? Help them up before they fall, you idiot!"

Gwen arched her neck to glare at him from above. "I'm no idiot, *mutt*. And who cares if they fall? You'll just patch them up anyhow. The day's completely lost. We might as well have a bit of fun —"

"*Fun?* Do you think this is about having *fun?*" Kael roared. He didn't want to have to yell, but he knew it would be the only way to get her attention. "We've been hiking all day and we haven't gotten anywhere. At this rate, we've got weeks of hiking left to go! *If* we ever manage to reach the top, there'll be an army of bloodtraitors and monsters waiting for us — an army that *thrashed* your hides the last time you met them.

"And on top of all that, winter's rushing down to meet us. *Winter*, Gwen. We're going to be trapped at the top of the mountains with no shelter and no way home." He jabbed a finger up at her and said, as loudly as he could muster: "The next time I hear the word *fun* escape your lips, it had better be because Titus is lying dead in a bloody pool at the bottom of the mountains. Otherwise, I'll crack your skull across my knee. Got it?"

Any ruler across the six regions would've had his head for that. Had he spoken to Captain Lysander in such a manner, he probably would've spent the night in the brig.

But instead of ordering him to his death, Gwen only smiled. "All right."

"Well ... good," Kael muttered. "Now help them up."

She dragged herself to her feet. "If you insist."

"I do." She raised both fists, and Kael suddenly realized what was about to happen. "Wait —!"

But it was too late. Gwen's fists came down and shattered the cliff's jutting edge. Bits of crumbled rock rained down among the craftsman. Miraculously, only one man got hit: a rock bounced smartly off his head and sent him plummeting to the ground. He cracked a rib, but Kael still considered it lucky.

The craftsmen climbed to the top of the ladder and the warriors pulled them up the gap left by Gwen's fists. They moved in a steady line, one behind the other. Once they got moving, it was amazing how quickly they worked. If he could only get them to focus, there was no telling what they might accomplish.

Kael was the last one to make the climb. When he reached the top, Gwen pulled him up by the hand. Even after he was on solid ground, she didn't let go. "Sorry, mutt."

Calluses roughened her fingers and her grip was often too tight. For some reason, the pressure of her hand was gentler that day — present, but not painful. He knew it was probably killing her not to crush him ... and yet, he saw no struggle in her eyes.

He tried to mask his surprise with a frown. "We need to get moving."

She nodded once before she released him. She strode to the wildmen and crouched on one knee. They sat cross-legged before her, their painted faces open and waiting.

Kael stood back and watched as Gwen pressed a thumb between her eyes. She grimaced, rolling her head this way and that. All the while, not a word passed among the wildmen.

Finally, she looked up. Her eyes wandered all about them, meeting each of their gazes in turn. "Now, for the rest of the day, I don't want to hear anymore foolishness. I want you all to shut it," she jerked her chin at Kael, "and do as he says. Understood?"

"Yes, Thane," they replied.

Then all eyes turned to Kael.

"I ... the warriors will travel at the front," he said, thinking quickly. "Figure out the best way through the woods and lead us on — and when I say *best*, I don't mean the most exciting, or the most dangerous," he added with a glare. "I mean the easiest."

With no small amount of grumbling, the warriors set out.

Then Kael turned to the craftsmen. "Your bodies are weak."

"Don't you think we know that?" one of them moaned. "I'll be sore in places I didn't even know I had tomor —"

"Listen," Gwen growled, snapping her fingers.

He shut his mouth.

381

"Your bodies are weak," Kael went on. "So you're going to have to use your minds. If there's a log in your path, don't try to jump over it, don't waste time going around it — just cut through it. Use the tricks I've taught you to make climbing easier. If anybody gets hurt, let me know. Now get moving," he waved them ahead, "follow the warriors."

The day went surprisingly well after that. The warriors chose simple paths and the craftsmen made them even simpler: they carved ladders into the rock, turned boulders into steps, and slashed through the undergrowth with ease.

When they came to the banks of a rushing river, the warriors knocked a tree down across it and helped a few of the craftsmen to the opposite side. They worked quickly from either end, stretching and molding the wood under their fingers. By the time Kael arrived, the fallen tree had become a full, arching bridge.

"Well done," he said when he saw it. "Keep moving, now. We ought to make it back to the road before nightfall."

Though he tried to stay severe, it was difficult not to grin when as he watched the wildmen go about their work. If only Roland could see him now — traveling with a band of men who could shape the mountains at will. They were coming along even better than he'd hoped.

They were near the end of their sunlight when they finally made it back to the road. Gwen ordered them to make camp immediately. "Never again," she snapped at the warriors. "No more shortcuts."

"Yes, Thane," they mumbled when she glared.

The craftsmen shaped a number of small lean-tos for them to sleep under, using nothing but logs and bits of rotted wood. They got the fires roaring and the coals were piping hot when the warriors returned, their shoulders laden with game.

Kael drew the craftsmen aside. "Before you start cooking, there's something I want to show you."

"More tricks? A way to turn water into fire?" one of the craftsmen said — drawing a round of excited tittering from the others.

Kael shook his head. "Not quite."

He gathered them into the circle and began to show them how he'd used the dragonscale armor to win his caddocs. He'd hardly gotten through the first bit of his explanation when the circle broke.

The craftsmen were totally, completely against it.

"We aren't warriors!"

"What use could we possibly have for armor?"

"Even if we *could* use it, we wouldn't know how."

Kael had expected this. In fact, he'd planned on it. "If the Man of Wolves attacks us, that leather isn't going to do you any good," he said, gesturing to their shirts. "His swords and arrows will go straight through it."

"The warriors will protect us!"

Kael shook his head. "There are too few of them. They can't hold off Titus *and* protect you. If you want to survive, you're going to have to learn to defend yourselves. This armor will protect you against fire, iron, and steel. Even the claws of his beasts will be no good against it."

They bickered amongst each other for a long moment. Their resolve had lost some of its edge, but it was still there. Finally, they seemed to reach an agreement: "Half of us will return to the village — then the warriors will be able to protect those who remain."

Kael smiled. He gestured at the dark, winding path that stretched behind them and said: "Have at it."

Not one of them so much as shifted in his boots.

"Could some of the warriors —?"

"No, I'm afraid I can't spare them," Kael said as he strode away. "If you want to go back, then you'll go on your own."

After how they'd balked at the thought of swinging Harbinger, he knew getting the craftsmen to even consider thinking like warriors was going to be no small task. They could do it, though — he had a plan. But first, he needed them to believe. He needed to give them a *reason* to try war. And so he'd given them the best reason he could think of:

He'd given them no other choice.

# CHAPTER 34
## The Fiddler and the Hawk

With Crow's Cross smoldering in ruin, word spread quickly: there was an army marching through the Valley — and it meant to topple Grognaut the Bandit Lord.

"Our reputation precedes us," Lysander said as they passed another abandoned camp.

Its occupants must've left in a hurry: bone ornaments were scattered, tents lay half-packed on their sides, and a large pot sat directly in the middle of a still-smoldering campfire, its contents burnt to its bottom.

Morris crouched to look at the trample marks left in the dirt. "Aye, even their footprints look panicked."

"They are right to panic." Nadine jabbed her spear among the prints, glaring. "They will answer for what they have done to these people."

The pirates and the giants traveled for days, following a disheveled path of abandoned camps. The Unforgivable Mountains grew ever closer in the distance: the jagged spires of its peaks loomed before them like the wall of a monstrous castle. The closer they got, the grayer the sky became — as if the gloom of the mountains had seeped into the Valley.

Elena spent most of her days riding out well ahead of the main camp, occasionally returning with some news of what lay before them. On one particular day, she brought them a gift: the severed head of a forest bandit, mounted onto a spear.

"Look what I've found!"

She flung the spear towards them and Jake leapt back when it landed at his feet. "Why have you always got to kill everything so ... dramatically?"

"I didn't kill him. He was like that when I found him," she said. Braver trotted off to drink from a nearby stream while Elena stepped in beside Jake. "There was a whole line of them pinned up around a camp to the east of here — all weepy and rotting in the sun. I rather liked the effect. Maybe that's how I'll decorate my next inn."

"I don't doubt that, not for a breath," Declan murmured when Elena left to join Braver. "She's got eyes like Death, that one."

"I'm sure she was only joking," Lysander said. He pulled the collar of his white tunic over his nose as he leaned in to inspect the bandit. "Gah, good Gravy!"

"Got a reek on him, don't he?" Morris had the lower half of his face buried in the crook of one stocky arm. His eyes seemed to be watering more than usual. "What do you suppose it means, Captain?"

"It's good news for us," Jonathan said. The cheeriness of his voice was a bit strained from having his nose pinched shut. "Only the mountain bandits do their heads like that. Oi, dead-eyes! Were all the headless blokes from the forest?"

"From what I could see through the goop —"

"There's no need to be so *descriptive*," Jake cut in from around the sleeve of his robes.

Elena stared at the green tingeing his face, and her brows became slightly less severe. "Yes. As far as I could tell, they were all forest bandits."

Jonathan let out a whoop. "They're fighting amongst each other — I'd bet it on the back of my fiddle! And while they're frayed at the edges ..."

"We'll step in." Lysander's sudden grin made the shirt slip off his nose. He gagged immediately. "Excellent. Now let's — *gah* — let's press on, shall we?"

By mid afternoon, they were able to smell the camp Elena had spoken of — and they took a wide path around it. Soon the green began to fade from the earth and the rocks grew more numerous. The dirt path was swallowed into the terrain, leaving them no choice but to map their way by the mountains.

In less than a day's time, Eveningwing began to circle above them, screeching at the tops of his lungs.

"What's he going on about, Captain?" Morris said.

Lysander glared up at the sky. "Trouble."

"I am beginning to think that is the only signal you taught him," Nadine grumbled from behind them.

Declan laughed.

As they crossed the next hill, they saw immediately what Eveningwing had been so frantic about: at long last, they'd arrived at the Earl's old castle.

It sat in the shadow of the Unforgivable Mountains — half in the Valley and half in the mouth of the Cleft. Thick stone towers squatted at each corner of its walls, their tops cut into squares like teeth. Behind the castle was the beginning of a road that carved its way up the mountains.

"That's where we're headed," Lysander said, pointing it out. "Now all we have to do is leave through the back door."

It was a task more easily said than done. For while the pirates and the giants stood watching upon the hill, a war was being waged for the castle. An army of forest bandits laid siege to the walls. They'd stripped a thick pine of its branches and sharpened its top into a dull point. It took dozens of them to lift it. They carried the tree across their shoulders and hefted it into the castle gates in a steady rhythm.

Meanwhile, bandits from the mountains had gathered along the ramparts. They hurled stones the size of skulls over the high walls and down upon the forest bandits — leaping up for a quick barrage before ducking to avoid an onslaught of darts and arrows.

One of the mountain bandits stood a head above the rest. His thick beard curled about his chin and he had a monstrous wolf's head branded into the middle of his chest. A rock the size of a small child flew from his hands and onto the head of a forest bandit beneath him — reducing it to a red spatter.

"Get them, boys!" he howled, beating his chest. "Send those leaf-weavers back to where they came from. Crush them! Beat them down! Knock them —!"

An ear-piercing whistle cut over the top of his commands. Both armies stopped their fight and slapped their hands against their ears. The bandits carrying the pine tree let it slip — accidentally crushing several of their companions' legs beneath it.

When they'd all turned towards the hill, Jake took his fingers from his mouth. "We don't really have to kill them, do we?" he said as Lysander stepped forward.

"I'm afraid it's going to come to that."

"But what if they agree to go peacefully?"

Lysander snorted. "They'll never go peacefully."

"But can't we at least ...?"

They hissed back and forth for a moment before the large bandit on the ramparts reared back and bellowed: "What are you doing on my lands, scum? Leave before I mount your skulls on my spear!"

The bandits all thundered in agreement.

Lysander waved a hand at them. "See?"

Jake twisted his gloves. "I still think —"

"Move." Elena shoved between them and walked until she stood alone at the crown of the hill. "Are you Grognaut the Bandit Lord?" she hollered at the ramparts.

The large bandit pounded his chest. "*I* am Grognaut, Lord of the Bandits!"

"I see. Well, my friends and I are rather peeved about what you've done to the Valley. So if you could leave these lands and never return, that'd be wonderful."

"Why do I feel as if you're mocking me?" Jake hissed when she turned around.

Elena's dark brows arched high. "I haven't got a clue."

He frowned at her. "You're still doing it, aren't you?"

Anything she might've said in reply was drowned out by the sudden boom of Grognaut's command: "Crush them!"

The forest bandits forgot their siege and sprinted for the hill, swords drawn. Behind them, the castle gates burst open and a horde of mountain bandits joined their charge. The pirates' swords were hardly out of their sheaths before the giants were already thundering down the hill — led by a battle-maddened Declan.

Nadine raced after them with a frustrated growl. "They will crack their large heads open upon a rock before they even reach their foes!"

The pirates followed after her, led by Lysander, with Jonathan whooping and waving his sword somewhere in their midst.

Elena turned back to Jake, arms crossed over her chest. "I don't think that worked, dove."

"I knew it! I knew you were mocking me."

"I would never mock you — I'm genuinely, utterly crushed that they didn't accept our offer."

He glared at her from over his spectacles. "Why can I never tell —?"

"We'll have plenty of time to figure out who's mocking who later. Right now we could use one of those spells!" Morris said.

When Jake hesitated, Elena's dark brows tightened over her eyes. "Someone's going to die today, mage. You can't stop that from happening, but you *can* make sure that fewer of your friends wind up among the dead."

"Aye, send one of those fiery balls out there, lad! Chase them off," Morris croaked.

Below them, Declan had reached the first line of bandits. His eyes were black with fury; scarlet ribbons followed the sweeping trail of his scythe. It wasn't long before his hulking body disappeared within the crush of bandits.

Grognaut stalked along the ramparts, howling for blood. As Jake watched the Bandit Lord, his eyes suddenly dulled. "I'm not a sword," he said firmly as he raised a hand towards the ramparts. "I'm a free man ... and I'll make my own decisions."

Something like a red spear shot from his palm and hurtled for the ramparts. It crackled like a thunder's boom as it struck Grognaut in the chest. The bandits spun in time to see Grognaut's flesh crumble away, fluttering into the wind like ash. His skeleton stood by itself for a moment, swallowed in the bulk of his armor. Then it toppled forward.

The battlefield quieted as Grognaut's bones tipped over the ramparts. The *clang* of his armor striking the ground seemed to ring through the Valley — and the battle ended just as suddenly as it'd begun.

The bandits screamed and tore for the Cleft, trampling each other in their haste to get away from Jake. The giants followed at their heels. Their long steps swallowed the gap between them and their scythes worked quickly. Only a small portion of bandits managed to escape — the rest were hewed and split like wheat.

"Well, I suppose that settles *that*," Lysander said. He tucked the Lass into its sheath with a flourish and led his men inside the castle gates.

There were chips of stone missing from the floor of the courtyard and char marks nearly everywhere else. Large strips had been carved from the mortar in places. They were deep and easily the width of a dagger's blade.

Morris ran the toe of his boot along them and whistled. He shot a look at Lysander, who grinned.

"Blimey, this isn't the work of bandits," Jonathan said. He crouched and ran his fingers down a set of marks. "They look like … claws. What sort of creature leaves a mess this size?"

"Maybe it was a dragon," Morris said, wagging his brows.

"There's no such thing as a dragon left. Those wee beasties took off a long while ago," Declan called from the gates. His feet dragged as he stepped into the courtyard. His gray eyes were heavy from the exhaustion of battle.

And he was covered head to toe in blood.

The pirates nearly tripped over their boots in the rush to get out of his path. Even the giants hung back behind him. They made a great show of checking their scythes for chips, glancing everywhere except at their General.

Declan stood square-shouldered as the courtyard went quiet. Gore trickled off the end of his scythe and fell in steady drips to the ground. After a moment, the deep cleft in his brow swallowed his eyes. He mumbled something about going to clean up and had made to turn when Nadine leaned out from behind one of the tower doors.

"There are barrels of water in here. You should wash if you mean to go inside," she added, frowning at Declan.

"I'll do as I please, woman," he growled at her.

"Then it must please you to sleep beneath the stars, because you will not be setting foot inside until you are washed."

Though he made a great show of stomping for the tower, Declan's glare wasn't nearly as severe as it'd been before.

Jake and Elena were the last to arrive in the courtyard. They walked slowly, tangled in some sort of heated discussion. Jake glared and straightened his spectacles an awful lot while Elena's eyes stayed deadly calm above her mask.

Lysander waved as they approached. "Well done with that spell!"

They split away immediately, like two drops of oil accosted by water. Jake tugged uncomfortably on his robes. "I … I wanted the battle to end quickly. I don't think it was *well* done, so much as simply … done."

"It was one of the most fantastic things I've ever seen," Elena called over her shoulder. She strode through the ranks of pirates and straight into the castle.

Jonathan nodded at her back. "You ought to go take a closer look at that, mate," he said with a wink. "Go sidle up and see what she meant."

"She meant to exasperate me. And it's working." Jake cleared his throat under the others' stares and waved a hand about him. "What happened here? Why's everything so … ruined?"

Jonathan's gaze took on a dark edge. "Eh, it was probably just another one of the King's monsters."

Eveningwing, who'd been watching from his perch upon the ramparts, ruffled his feathers miserably.

391

Morris frowned. "You need to let that go, lad. He's already apologized for it, *and* he saved your skin at Crow's Cross. If you keep digging at an old wound you'll get nothing but sick."

Jonathan shrugged, but didn't relinquish his glare.

They camped inside the castle's throne room that night: a large, circular chamber with a shallow stone platform set at its rear. The throne lay on its side at the top of the platform. Its high, worn back was shattered beyond repair.

It looked as if tapestries had once adorned the walls, but they'd been torn from their nails — leaving large holes in the wooden paneling that covered the stone.

Jake got a fire going in the hearth while the rest of the party set up their bedrolls. The giants hefted barrels of water in from outside while the pirates refilled the canteens. Declan returned after a while, cleaner than he'd been before the battle. A smile bent his lips as he approached the throne room — though it disappeared the instant he crossed the shadow of the door.

Dinner was well underway and the chamber was filled with happy chatter when Nadine finally arrived — leading Eveningwing the boy in by his arm. His strange yellow eyes flicked over every face in the room and he walked stiffly at Nadine's urging.

When Lysander caught sight of him, he raised his canteen. "There's my favorite halfhawk! Come warm your feathers by the fire — that's an order, by the way. Don't force me to lock you in the dungeon," he added with a grin.

Two pirates scooped Eveningwing under the arms and sat him in the middle of their ranks. They shoved food into his hands and filled his cup to the brim. Under their cheerful care, the hard corners of his mouth bent quickly into a tentative smile.

While the rest of his companions seemed thrilled by Eveningwing's return, Jonathan's eyes grew darker. His food went uneaten. Jake watched the fiddler from over the top of his spectacles for a moment. The leather of his gloves

392

squeaked as he clenched his fists. Then he marched to Jonathan's side.

"May I sit?" When Jonathan didn't reply, Jake sat anyways. He tugged his robes tight over his knees and cleaned the lenses of his spectacles. When he finally spoke, his voice was quiet: "You know, I spent a great deal of my life under the King's spell, bound in service to the Duke. Mostly it was just a matter of sailing here or there, protecting his ships from, well," he waved a hand at the pirates, "that lot. But there were a few times when I got sent on other errands.

"I remember this one errand in particular ..." Jake's thin fingers wrapped absently around his wrist. "The Duke was very angry with one of his managers. He'd lost a large number of shipments, you see — and I was ordered to punish him. Though I fought against the Duke's command, I ... I wasn't quite strong enough.

"I lost the fight that day," he said quietly, his eyes distant. "I went to that manager's house, blasted in the door ... and I burned his wife alive. I burned her right in front of him, slowly, one layer of flesh at a time ... I was ordered to do it slowly."

For a long moment, Jake was silent. His mouth fell in a grim line; the hand around his wrist tightened. "You don't get to sleep after something like that — not really. Because every time you close your eyes, you see the flames. The screams burst your ears and you can still hear them ringing in the quiet. You come to fear the silence and the darkness. Sleep offers you no reprieve ... it's merely the stage upon which your nightmares dance."

Slowly, his fingers relented their hold. He placed a tentative hand upon Jonathan's shoulder. "Try not to judge Eveningwing too harshly. Believe him when he says he couldn't help it. Kingdom knows I've fought and lost ... we all have."

"Well, maybe you didn't fight hard enough."

Jonathan got to his feet, and Jake stood right behind him. "Is that really what you think? Do you think I burned that woman alive because I *didn't fight hard enough*?"

"I don't know, mate," Jonathan said, marching on. "Maybe you're right — maybe Eveningwing really *was* under some sort of spell. All I know is that I wouldn't have given up so easily."

"You think you could've done better?"

"Better than letting a pack of wolves slaughter an innocent man? Yeah, I think so."

"Then let's put you to the test."

They spoke so loudly now that the rest of the room had gone silent. All eyes were split between Jonathan and Jake. The fiddler burned under their looks for a moment before he turned, slowly, and said:

"All right, mate. I'll let you magic me. And if I can't beat the spell, I'll apologize. But if I can," he jabbed a finger at Eveningwing, "he goes."

"Fair enough." There was a strange light in Jake's eyes as he stretched a gloved hand forward. "Walk."

One of Jonathan's legs jerked out in front of him. His eyes widened. He stumbled two more steps before he started to fight back. His brows furrowed and his next step was much shallower. It wasn't long before he'd ground to a halt.

Jonathan raised a fist in triumph, grinning through the beads of sweat that'd popped up across his face. "See? That's not so bad. It'd take more than that to —"

"Silence."

His mouth snapped shut immediately — though judging by the bulge of his eyes, he hadn't meant it to.

"This spell is commonly known as *borrowed legs*. It was originally used to transport livestock over short distances. Levitation is better suited for the inanimate," Jake explained. "Living things tend to squirm too much when lifted off the ground.

"The problem, as you can see, is that *borrowed legs* is a rather weak spell — having to control so many muscles and joints means that one's powers are stretched rather thinly, and the effects often lose their potency quickly. Unless," he raised his other hand, "you add pain."

He flexed his fingers and Jonathan's mouth opened in a silent yelp. He stumbled forward, eyes white around the dark.

"Or rather, I suppose you add the *illusion* of pain — a madness that tricks the mind into believing the body is on fire," Jake mused as he forced Jonathan another step. "It's a spell the old Kings used to torture information from their enemies. It weakens the mind's hold over the body and makes resistance ... difficult."

Jonathan was walking smoothly now. His legs swung out in front of him as if he moved of his own accord.

Jake's thin lips bent into a smile. "See? If you don't fight it, it doesn't hurt."

"All right, you've made your point. I think the wee fiddler's had enough," Declan called.

But Jake shook his head. "No, I haven't. Not quite yet ... but I'm about to."

All at once, Jonathan changed course and began marching towards Nadine.

Declan got to his feet, but Nadine never budged. She sat cross-legged with her spear in her lap and watched Jonathan approach with interest.

"Can you truly not speak?" she asked him.

He shook his head.

Jake kept both hands stretched towards Jonathan. His spectacles began sliding down his long nose as sweat beaded upon his face. "Someone, I'm not sure who, figured out a way to contain these spells inside an object and bind that object to a specific voice — so that even those without magic could command them. I was bound to the Duke's voice. Eveningwing was bound to the King's. And you, fiddler, are bound to mine."

Sometime while he'd been talking, Elena emerged from the shadows and drifted to Nadine's side. Jake gave her a weighty look before he turned his eyes back to Jonathan and whispered a command.

He fought. Veins bulged from Jonathan's neck and across his forehead. His hand trembled as it moved, but move it did. His arm ground in its socket as he reached down.

"What are you making him do?" Lysander said cautiously. By now, half the room had gotten to its feet. "Jake?"

But Jake didn't answer.

Tears streamed from Jonathan's eyes. The skin on his face turned ashen. His hand trembled for a moment more, as if he was fighting with every ounce of his being. Then suddenly, he lost the fight.

He ripped his cutlass from its sheath, raised it over his head, and brought it screaming towards Nadine. The blow likely would've split her head into two, had it not been for Elena.

Before Nadine could even flinch, she'd caught Jonathan's sword on the hilt of one of her black daggers and wrenched it from his grasp.

"What in high tide was that about?" Lysander barked.

"Aye, there was no cause to do all that!" Morris piped in.

Declan was far less calm. He snatched his scythe from the ground and roared: "I'll kill him! I'll cleft his head from his scrawny neck —"

"Don't!"

The room fell silent at Jonathan's cry. He'd collapsed when Jake released him and now lay in a panting mass upon the floor. When Nadine helped him to his feet, he stumbled immediately to Eveningwing.

The halfhawk stood his ground as Jonathan approached. His strange eyes never blinked.

"I was wrong," Jonathan said when he reached him. "I was wrong, mate. I didn't know ... I had no idea what you'd been through, what it must've cost you. I'm sorry." He held out his hand. "You're a good hawk, and I'm lucky to count you as my friend."

Eveningwing raised his brows. "You're going to be my friend again?"

"I'd like to, if that's all right."

He cocked his head to the side. "You aren't angry at me anymore?"

"Not in the least bit. Why don't we just shake hands and —? Oof!"

Jonathan stumbled backwards as Eveningwing sprang onto him. He wedged his toes into the fiddler's side and wrapped his scruffy face tightly between his arms, smiling to either ear.

Lysander frowned at him. "What have I told you about perching upon others in your human form?"

"It's all right, Captain," Jonathan said from between his arms. "I probably deserve a bit of this."

Jake watched quietly as his companions returned to their dinners. The slight smile that'd formed upon his lips quickly turned serious when Elena appeared at his side. "Do you think I was too hard on him?"

She shook her head. "He's been huffing around and swearing at the skies for days on end. If I'd come across him on the road, I would've slit his throat and buried him in a ditch." She pulled her mask down — revealing the hard line of her mouth. "That was a dangerous game you played."

His spectacles slid down his long nose as he raised his brows. "What do you mean?"

"You know very well what I mean," she said sharply. She turned her shoulder from their companions, grimacing before she turned back. "How did you know I'd stop that sword?"

Jake shrugged. "There are very few things you care for, Elena. But that little woman from the desert is one of them."

Her brows dropped into a dangerous glare. "You aren't nearly as smart as you think you are, mage."

"And you aren't half as heartless," he murmured as she stalked away.

397

# CHAPTER 35
## AMELIA

For two days straight, Kael weathered the craftsmen's endless storm of grumbles. They muttered at his back about how pointless it was to learn to whisper themselves into armor. It wasn't as if *they* would ever be any good in a fight. He was ridiculous to ask it of them, it would be ridiculous to even try.

"Then go — march straight back to Tinnark," he'd snapped when their moaning wore his patience thin.

They *would* have gone back, and gladly. But they couldn't be expected to make the journey on their own. There were all sorts of wild beasts roaming the woods, and the weather often made the roadways treacherous. It was a task more suited to the warriors. Perhaps if he would consider —

"No," Kael said firmly, cutting over the top of their pleas. "The warriors aren't going to hold your hands down the mountain. You can either go back on your own, or you can stay. But if you choose to keep marching then you'd better listen to me — you won't last two minutes in a battle without armor."

He put his foot down and kept it firmly upon the ground. No matter how they pleaded with him, he refused to lift it an inch. The craftsmen quickly realized that he was never going to budge, and they didn't hold their ground for long.

By the time they'd stopped to make camp on the third evening, the craftsmen had finally given up. Kael fixed them with a glare as they gathered sheepishly at his side. "Are you all going to shut it and listen to me?"

"Yes," they muttered.

So he circled them and showed them how to form the dragonscale armor. They watched tentatively as he explained their texture, as he brought the memories to the tips of his fingers and let them travel along the links of their hands. They gasped when they saw how the soldiers' sword had shattered against Kyleigh's middle. Slowly, their excitement began to creep in.

It was a reluctant emotion — a spark born from the warring of flint against steel. They still doubted in their ability to fight, but they accepted this small piece. They took the knowledge of how to form the armor and turned it over in their heads. He could practically hear the scraping, see the sparks flying. Once he was certain they'd grasped it, he set them loose.

Most of the craftsmen had never donned so much as a gauntlet, and it showed. They teetered around for an hour or so, their brows squinched tightly in concentration. They took heavy, spraddled steps. A few lost their balance and simply tipped over. From a distance, Kael thought they looked like an army ... an army astride some rather uncomfortable invisible horses.

"What's the point of all this, then?" a young craftswoman said. She had to wave her arms madly to keep from tripping. "What good'll this do us if we can't —?"

Kael swung a sword against her middle, and the noise of its shattering cut across her words. Her shocked gaze went from her unscathed middle to the empty hilt in Kael's hand. And her face turned red.

"*That's* the point," he growled. "The longer you work on this, the easier it'll come. Soon you'll be able to hold the vision with hardly any effort. You'll be able to run *and* defend yourself. Then I'm going to teach you to carry swords."

"*Swords?*" she squeaked.

"I'm going to make warriors out of all of you, whether you like it or not." He tossed the hilt at her feet. "Fix that back to the way it was. Tomorrow, I'm going to crack you all with a sword. So you'd better practice."

They grumbled magnificently at his back. But when Kael had slipped out of the fire's light, he glanced over his shoulder.

Now that they thought he was gone, several of the craftsmen wore wide grins. They turned their arms over and thumped their fists into their chests, testing their scales. Their smiles only widened as they bent to inspect the shattered sword.

Perhaps it was only the light from camp, but Kael thought he might've seen a bit of fire in their eyes.

Night was falling quickly. He watched the shadows spread like inkblots, expanding until they finally overtook the earth and sky. Though his vision dulled, his body hadn't: his feet still knew where to step, his flesh could sense if he wandered too close to a tree.

They'd been traveling the Earl's road for days, and in all that time he'd only gotten a few glimpses of Kyleigh. She and Silas had all but disappeared. At least Silas returned in the evenings to Gwen's tent. But though Kael had waited long into the night, Kyleigh never showed.

He was determined to find out where she'd been hiding.

He'd only gone about a quarter of a mile when a dark shape sprang into his path, nearly startling him to death. "Silas! You can't just go leaping out at people. What if I'd shot you?"

He looked less than concerned. He sat on his haunches in the middle of the road, cleaning one of his massive paws lazily with his long pink tongue. Kael couldn't help but notice that his muzzle was covered in blood.

"Is that where you went? Were you on a hunt?"

He shut his glowing eyes and rumbled contentedly to himself as he went on with his cleaning.

Kael wasn't amused. "Where's Kyleigh? I know you can hear me, Silas. Just point, or something. Tell me if I'm headed in the right —"

"Why are you talking to my cat?"

400

Kael spun and his heart charged up his throat when Gwen sauntered from the trees behind him. "I ... well, I'd already asked everybody else. So I figured I might as well ask the cat."

"Did you expect to get an answer?"

"Um ... no."

Fortunately, Gwen didn't press it. She crossed her arms and took a few clomping steps towards Silas. "You've done better than I expected, mutt. My wildmen aren't an easy lot to manage. Thane Evan always had a time of it."

She stood and watched the night march across the sky for such a long moment that Kael wondered if she was waiting for him to respond. "I know what you mean. My grandfather used to say —"

"Don't bore me with your stories, mutt," she murmured at the stars. "And the next time you speak of my cat, you'll use his name: *Silas*. It's a handsome name, don't you think? Griffith chose it well."

The gasping breath Kael had just sucked in became a sigh of relief — which he quickly turned into a cough when Gwen narrowed her eyes at him.

"Fate's fingers, you're an odd one," she muttered. She clomped away, then, shaking her head.

Kael waited until she was gone before he went after Silas. He saw the curled end of his tail slipping in amongst the brush and chased after it. The earth was so dark beneath the trees that he quickly lost sight of him.

That was when a strong hand grabbed him around the neck. "What were you thinking, you stupid human?"

Kael didn't know what to think. Silas stood in the middle of a large bush. Its leafy branches covered him above the waist and his bare feet stuck out its bottom. "You aren't ... naked, are you?"

"Of course I'm naked. My pants shrunk too far."

Kael had no idea what that meant, and he wasn't sure he wanted to. "All right —"

"No, it's not all right. The Thane can't know what I am. And you, you stupid human," his hand tightened about Kael's throat, "you almost gave me away."

"I'll be more careful, next time," Kael promised, and Silas released him. "But you're going to have to tell her eventually."

His glowing eyes burned like twin coals as he spat: "*Never.*"

"You can't lie to her forever —"

"I will lie as long as it takes."

"As long as what takes?"

His fingers clamped onto the bush, snapping several of its branches between his fists. His lips twisted around angry, half-formed words. Then quite suddenly, he dropped on his haunches — disappearing into the bush.

Kael wasn't going to let him off that easily. He grabbed a stick and thrust it sharply amongst the leaves. "What's going on?"

"None of your human bus — ow!"

Silas hissed and swatted furiously, but Kael jerked the stick out of his reach. "Fine. If you're not going to tell me about Gwen, then at least tell me where Kyleigh is."

He didn't reply.

For some reason, the silence that hung in the air between them made Kael feel uncomfortable — like he was hearing something he shouldn't have been listening in on. "She thinks your name is handsome," he offered.

"I heard," he muttered. The leaves rustled with a heavy sigh. "The dragoness is sleeping in her scales, tonight. She's perched on a hill behind me. If you keep walking straight, even *your* weak human eyes will be able to spot it. Now go away."

Kael left — more baffled than ever about Silas.

It didn't take him long to find Kyleigh. She was curled upon a rocky slope in full dragon form. Her head rested on her massive foreclaws and her wings were tucked against her sides. Her white scales drew her sharply against the night, practically glowing when the starlight touched them.

402

She cracked an eye as he approached, and the ferocity of the green nearly stumbled him backwards. He had to watch the dancing of the flames for a moment before he realized that she wasn't angry — in fact, she was rather pleased. The fires roared with her excitement more than anything.

She was happy that he'd *finally* found her.

He forced himself to look severe. "I thought you said it was too dangerous to be wandering around as a dragon."

An edge of her scaly mouth bent upwards, and he read the answer clearly in her eyes: she wasn't *wandering* anywhere, thank you very much. As long as she stayed put, there wouldn't be a problem.

"Clever," Kael mumbled as he stepped up beside her.

They stared at each other for a moment. He wasn't sure how to talk to her when she was like this, and it was obvious that she wasn't going to come back into her human form. He was about to give up and bid her goodnight when she tilted her wing back slightly — a gesture he knew meant that she was beckoning him to her side.

Heat spread quickly across his face. "No. That wouldn't be decent."

Her rumbling laugh made his skin burn all the hotter.

He wanted to sit close to her. He wanted to curl up beside her and feel the warmth in her scales. But he was also terrified — not of Kyleigh ... well, not of the fact she that was a dragon. It wasn't the things he felt for her that had him frightened, nor the things he was fairly certain she felt for *him*.

It was the idea that one wrong word might undo everything ... that he might break the fragile, trembling thread between them simply by stepping on it. When he forced himself to think about it, he supposed it wasn't the prospect of having to sit close to Kyleigh that terrified him — it was having to sit so close to the *edge*.

And perhaps it was because he had all of these little worries bouncing inside his head that he blurted out: "I'm ready to ask you a question."

Her eyes brightened with interest.

Kael put his hands inside his pockets and felt the worn back of Setheran's letter scrape against his fingers. A wall rose inside his heart, shoving that question aside. "Did you ever meet my mother?"

She had.

Kael's stomach flipped and flopped. Cold caked its leathery bottom — but somehow, warmth bubbled beneath the ice. "Could you ...? Do you think ...?"

The words wouldn't quite come out, but Kyleigh took his meaning. She dipped her head down to his reach. Kael's hand trembled as he touched her scaly brow.

An image rose before his eyes. Snow swirled around him, the world bounced with Kyleigh's jog. A thin man kept pace beside her. His breath came out in frozen puffs and his cloak trailed at his back, whipping in the wind.

"Are you all right, Seth?" Kyleigh said over the thudding of their feet. Her voice rang calmly inside Kael's head. But for some reason, Setheran howled in reply.

He tossed his head back and a gust of wind blew the hood from his face. A wide grin split his features. His booming voice cut through the air: "I feel no pain, Swordmaiden — not even the winter can bite me!"

Kyleigh laughed. When she turned back, the gates of a small castle filled her vision. A line of warm light appeared between the gates, widening until they hung open. Guards thundered down the rampart steps behind them. The two men at the keep's front door flung it open and leapt quickly out of their way.

Kael only saw glimpses of their faces as Kyleigh and Setheran charged by, only heard the echoes of their cheers. Setheran's pace slowed to a trot. He took one sharp turn and thrust a second set of doors open.

A young woman waited just inside the room. Kyleigh's vision narrowed onto her face: she had dark hair and dark eyes — a forest woman. Worry lined her every feature. Her lips sagged beneath its weight and her brows twisted in tortured arcs. For the few paces it took Setheran to reach her, Kael was absolutely miserable.

The forest woman was nearly two heads shorter than Setheran. He had to stoop to embrace her. His long arms wrapped around her waist and her hands went immediately to the back of his neck. They stood there for a moment, neither speaking a word.

Slowly, the woman's brows relinquished their hold and slipped upwards. A smile bent her lips; her eyes brightened and she gasped in relief. "You're well."

"Of course I'm well, Amelia. I promised I would be." Setheran pressed his lips against hers, moving gently. Kael was relieved when Kyleigh looked away.

They stood at the edge of a large, circular room. Instead of tapestries, the walls were lined with oaken shelves. Books covered their every surface, packed in as tightly as they would fit.

Kyleigh followed the light winking off their gilded titles to a small hearth at the side of the room. Her eyes rested briefly on the timid flames, on the padded chair and the small, whittled crib settled in front of it before she looked away.

A strange, twisted lump lodged itself in Kael's throat when he saw the roughly-carved desk settled against the room's back arch. The desk sat atop a slight platform — one that had likely been meant for a throne. He realized with a jolt that this room was a reflection of his Inner Sanctum. *This* was the place he'd held for so long inside his heart.

Kyleigh glanced briefly at the still-twined Setheran and Amelia before her eyes shot back to the floor. Kael wasn't at all surprised to see the symbol of the Wright carved boldly into its surface, stretching nearly to the edges of the shelves until it looked as if the whole room watched through a bottomless, triangular pupil.

"How is he?" Setheran said, drawing Kyleigh's eyes once more.

Amelia was still a little breathless from his kisses. "He's strong, Seth. He's calm, and sweet, and ... perfect." Her hands twined across her chest — as if bracing them might somehow keep the light inside her eyes from bursting out.

Setheran squeezed her tightly before he inched his way over to the crib. His large hands dipped inside and drew a bundle wrapped in white cloths from its depths. "Oh dear, he's going to have my skin, isn't he?" Setheran said through his grin. "I'm sorry about that, little one. I was so hoping you'd have your mother's looks."

"He could've come out green and you wouldn't have cared one bit," Kyleigh said.

Setheran laughed.

Amelia looked as if she'd just noticed Kyleigh was there. Her gaze traveled up and down. The softness in her features hardened into something a little more cautious. "Is this the warrior I've been hearing about?"

"It is, my love," Setheran said distractedly. He cradled the bundle tightly in the crook of his arm and pestered it with a finger. A tiny, pink hand reached out and curled about the tip.

When Kyleigh looked back, Amelia had stepped closer. "You're ... surprised?" she murmured.

Amelia's brows slipped upwards. "Setheran didn't tell me you were a woman."

"Did he tell you I was a man?" Kyleigh made a frustrated sound and her gaze shot back to Setheran. "You know I've been working on my manners."

"Yes, and soon you'll be able to eat dinner in His Majesty's hall without everybody wrinkling their nose at you," he sing-songed in reply, his eyes never once leaving the bundle.

"Well, since I've at least been trying, you might stop calling me a *man*."

"Never!"

Kyleigh said something under her breath that made Amelia laugh. Her gaze turned back at the sound and Kael saw that every last troubled line had vanished from her features. "Sorry. We haven't been anywhere civilized for quite some time. I really *have* been working on my manners."

She waved a hand. "Please, I've heard far —"

"When was he born?" Setheran cut in.

Amelia smiled softly. "He came with the snow."

Setheran's fiery brows rose high. He *tsk*ed as he shook the bundle's tiny hand. "One of Fate's Forsaken," he whispered mockingly. "Had you been born in the mountains, people would've thrown rocks at you. Most folk think it's a cursed thing to be born on Death's Day — but I say it's lucky." His eyes glinted as he lowered his voice: "You can do all sorts of naughty things and never have to worry about that wrinkly old bag giving you a slap on the hand —"

"*Seth!*" Amelia hissed. "We aren't going to let him grow up thinking he can do whatever he pleases. He'll spoil before he learns to speak."

"And you certainly shouldn't mention Fate's wrinkles," Kyleigh added, her voice tinged with amusement. "That's a good way to get your hand slapped, whisperer."

He scoffed at them before turning back to the bundle. "Have you looked?" he said after a moment.

"No, I've been far too nervous. You haven't even named him, yet," Amelia scolded when he took a step towards the hearth. "Give the poor boy a name before you go looking for his gifts."

Setheran held the bundle high, smiling to either ear. "Kael," he whispered. "That's a good name — a woodsman *and* a warrior's. You'll hear both of us, that way. You'll have a foot in both your homes."

He strode towards the hearth, and Kyleigh's gaze went back to Amelia.

After a moment, a slight pink tinged the forest woman's cheeks. "Why are you looking at me like that?"

"It's strange," Kyleigh murmured. "Seth talks about you so often ... it's strange to finally get to see you for myself. It's like a story come to life." Her finger appeared in Kael's vision, pointing to the pink in Amelia's cheeks. "You're blushing, aren't you? Setheran said you would."

As if simply the mention had spurred it on, Amelia's face turned all the redder.

"He says you blush a lot," Kyleigh continued. "Especially when —"

"How about I run to the kitchens and fetch us a late dinner?" Amelia turned quickly. "Are you hungry, Seth?"

He didn't reply. He stood before the hearth, holding the bundle in his arms. His body was so unnaturally still that Kael thought he might've turned to stone.

"Seth?" Amelia took a half-step towards him. "Seth? What is it? What's wrong with the baby?" She rushed to his side, leaning to look when he tilted his arms. A moment later, she'd stumbled backwards. Amelia clamped a hand over her mouth and her eyes widened above her fingers. "What ...? What does that ...?"

"It means we're going to fail," Setheran said harshly. He was glaring at the bundle now — glaring with something that was a mix between anger and pain. "Why else would my son have been born a Wright?"

He placed the bundle into Amelia's arms and stalked back to the desk. His fists came down with such force upon its top that Kyleigh actually flinched. Amelia gasped. The bundle began to wail in fright.

"It's all been for nothing!" Setheran shouted over its cries. "Everything I've worked for, fought for, *bled* for — it doesn't mean anything now, does it?"

"Seth," Amelia said, her voice trembling. "Please, you're frightening the baby!"

"He *should* be frightened!" Setheran raged on, pounding his fists. "He has every right to cry! Let him have his fear, for mercy's sake — because he'll be stripped of everything else! I took up my sword ..."

His elbows bent sharply and he slumped forward, as if a mighty weight had just fallen across his back. When he turned, Setheran's eyes burned red. But it wasn't anger Kael saw in his face — it was sorrow.

"I broke my oath ... I did it all for *him*, I did it all for Kael," he whispered, his voice barely climbing over the bundle's wails. "It was the one shred of good I thought would come of all this death. But he's going to be just as broken, just as miserable ... it's all been for naught."

Setheran bared his teeth, as if he was fighting a desperate battle against the words that swelled behind them. Finally, he could hold them back no longer: "Every drop of blood I've shed and spilt was wasted."

"Seth — please!" Amelia called, but Setheran marched away.

Even from down the hall and over the bundle's wails, Kael heard the keep doors open and slam shut behind him. Amelia's worried pleas were for the bundle — her worried eyes for Setheran.

"Let me hold him a moment," Kyleigh said. "I'm very good with pups — ah, children."

Amelia seemed too grateful to notice. She passed the bundle gently into Kyleigh's arms. "He's not angry at anybody —"

"He's angry at everything. I know: I've had to put a few fires out, myself. Go and see if you can't beat the knot out of his knickers. I've got the child."

"Thank you." Amelia squeezed her arm tightly before she hurried out the door.

The moment she was gone, Kyleigh's gaze went down to the bundle of cloths. She *shhh*ed quietly and peeled them back, revealing the little red-tinged face and the tiny, wailing mouth beneath.

"Hush, little one," she whispered. "You father's just got a bit of fire in his breeches, at the moment. Maybe he ought to sit in the snow for a while."

The wails began to quiet at the sound of her laughter. The tiny mouth closed and a pair of tightly-shut eyes came into focus. Kyleigh's finger brushed gently across the little wet lines that stained the pink skin, drying them.

Slowly, a set of fingers came up and grasped blindly for hers. They were so small that they were hardly able to wrap the full way around — and yet, Kyleigh froze at their grasp.

He could feel them. Kael could feel the warm, soft fingers wrapped about his. He could feel the shallow breaths against his chest. He felt the child's slight, insignificant weight in every single fiber of his arm. And when those eyes opened, when the lids cracked and those two brown orbs locked sleepily onto his, he fell through —

Kael gasped as Kyleigh pulled away and the stark light of reality rushed in. For a moment, the chirping of the nighttime creatures sounded impossibly loud; the scents of the forest were too thick for his lungs. He blinked. He took deep, steady breaths. And slowly, the power of the vision eased back.

"She was a healer," he said quietly, remembering how Amelia had grasped Setheran, how her worry had only lifted after she'd held him for a moment — how she seemed to know by merely touching him that all was well.

Kyleigh inclined her horned head. He'd guessed correctly.

There was another question in her eyes, but he pretended not to see it. Kael turned away as a memory of Setheran's face rose unbidden. His hand twisted in his curls, pulling painfully on his scalp — but the memory of that look raged above the pain.

He'd been unlucky from the beginning. The symbol Setheran had seen in his eyes had turned his face from merry to dark. Had Kael been born any other way, Setheran and Amelia might've lived happily. He might've been able to grow up inside that castle with two people he knew as nothing more than *mother* and *father* ...

But that wasn't at all what had happened — he'd been born a Wright. He'd messed it all up from the very beginning ... and that was precisely why he hadn't wanted to look.

Dark things swirled inside him — their bubbling muses an angry, painful mystery. Kael would've spent all night with them churning beneath his skin, had it not been for Kyleigh.

"No, I don't want to," he growled when he felt her pointed teeth clamp around his shirt.

410

The garment was simply made — nothing more than a thick leather jerkin with iron studs clamped down its front. But Kyleigh had made it for him, and he rather liked it. So he told himself it was for the jerkin's sake that he allowed her to drag him back against her, that he only fought a little when one of her wings pinned him to her side, and didn't grumble at all about the heat that radiated from her scales.

He could feel the rhythm in her chest: calm, steady, and remarkable deep. Most of the time he forgot she was supposed to be ancient. But when he listened to her heart, he believed it. There were centuries of depth in there — a calm beyond human.

With the song of her heart and the warmth of her scales, it wasn't long before Kael's eyes began to get heavy. He pushed the darkness cast by his shadow aside and instead, he focused on what lay before him ... beside him ...

And slowly, he fell asleep.

# CHAPTER 36
## HUNDRED BONES

For mornings on end, Kael rose with the gray dawn and followed at the back of the wildmen's march.

The treacherous climb seemed to carry them quickly through the seasons. One day they crossed summer's edge and passed into a land that looked like autumn, where the trees had burst in fiery shades of orange and red. They'd trekked through a snow of fallen leaves for miles after — a snow that hissed as it fell, a snow with flakes that danced in each gust of wind and often got themselves lodged in Kael's hair.

The higher up the mountains they climbed, the sharper the weather became. Oaks shrank back under the chill; they grew bare and bleached as bone. The evergreen arms of the pines sagged on their limbs, as if the cold had drained them of their marrow.

Though the trees creaked miserably at every gust, the wildmen only grew stronger. Their laughter came more frequently. Their chatter filled the air in a near-constant, white-puffing stream. The warriors seemed to gain breath as the air grew thinner; the craftsmen stopped their moaning. Every time Gwen turned to bark an order, her teeth were bared in a grin.

The wildmen's eyes brightened beneath their caps and helmets — as if the frigid air had somehow warmed their spirits. Occasionally, the brightness grew so fierce that they seemed unable to contain it: the warriors would break into a dead sprint with Gwen at their lead. They would howl and run with their weapons raised high while the craftsmen followed, beating their chests with their fists.

"Mountain folk," Kyleigh muttered as she watched them gallop off. "The more miserable things get, the happier they are. I'll never understand it."

Not so long ago, Kael would've rolled his eyes and agreed. He would've said the wildmen were behaving like children, and that they ought to save their strength for walking.

But now as he watched the whole thundering, fur-clad lot disappear around the next bend, it felt strange *not* to run after them. The craftsman in him studied the wilderness: he saw the beauty in the sharp terrain, read the secrets that the mountains' wild, untouchable spirit had cleft into the rock. The warrior in him was tuned to every deadly shift in the mountains' temper. He felt the danger in every step.

He wanted to sprint along the rocks and streams, to battle against the slapping force of the wind, to dance the wild dance of the mountains ...

"Oh, go on, then."

Kyleigh was watching him — her exasperated look slightly muddled by amusement. "Go on where?"

She waved up the road. "I know you want to chase them."

He did. Very much. His leg took one lurching step before he shook his head. "I should save my strength."

She rolled her eyes. "Yes, because that's far more exciting than spending it. Ah, well ... it's probably for the best."

"Why's that?"

"Because you'd only lose."

She took off like a shot, and Kael was determined not to let her win.

He chased after her. He charged in behind her as they tore around the next bend. He stayed directly at her back, so close that he could've reached out and touched her.

Ahead of them, the wildmen had come to a stop. Some of the warriors spotted the dust flying up from their charge and they formed a wall — holding their arms out, goading them into a faster sprint. Kael stayed behind Kyleigh until the last possible second. He matched her pace-for-pace, keeping his head ducked even with her shoulders. He waited until she risked turning back to see where he'd gone, and then he shot past her.

He whipped by her blind shoulder and thudded into the warriors' arms. She thudded in beside him — just a half-pace behind.

The wildmen howled and shoved him roughly. Gwen hurled him away by the roots of his hair, laughing. "He stomps dragons, he beats them in a footrace. Is there anything he can't do?"

Kael's face burned under their looks. "Well, I can't stop the snows from coming. So we'd better press on," he said gruffly.

The wildmen glanced around each other before they shrugged in agreement. Gwen got them all moving with a snap of her fingers. They filed in behind her, heading straight for a section of the road that sat so precariously over a rift that it looked as if it'd been carved from the edge of the earth.

Kael waited until they'd gone before he turned back to Kyleigh. "You let me win, didn't you?"

Her hands went to her hips; her elbows bent into dangerous points. "Kael of the Unforgivable Mountains," she growled, "you know very well that I would never *let* you win at anything."

"So you're admitting I beat you?"

The fires in her eyes blazed hot. They glowed with that strange light he'd seen once before — with the fury he was certain wasn't rage, with the heat that didn't quite burn. There was a fierce and terrible danger there …

One that made his heart quicken its stride.

"If you force me to say it aloud, you'll be sorry."

His chest was pounding so violently that he was sure anything he might've said would've come out as a stutter. So instead, he offered her his arm.

And to his great surprise, she took it.

*******

More days passed, and Kyleigh walked beside him more frequently. When he asked her why she'd suddenly decided to stop running through the woods, she looked away.

White mist trailed from between her parted lips and the frozen air seemed to make the green in her eyes stand out all the more sharply as she gazed around the woods. "I thought Titus might have something planned for us after the ... incident," she said, giving him a smirk. "I thought for certain he would've answered by now, but he's been quiet."

"He's frightened of us," Gwen called as she passed. She pushed through the line of wildmen, the limp carcass of a badger hanging from her pack. "After my warriors were finished with him, the Man of Wolves had to use rocks to pound the stains from his breeches!"

"It seems like only yesterday she was hurling a door at my head," Kael muttered under the wildmen's cheers. "And now it was suddenly all brilliant."

Kyleigh didn't reply. When he glanced at her, she was tugging at the end of her pony's tail.

"You still think Titus has something planned," he guessed.

She nodded. "To him, war is a game. Titus doesn't charge out with his teeth bared: he circles, he waits, every move he makes is a step towards victory — no matter how sideways it seems. He doesn't attack unless he knows he's going to win. When he finally strikes, it's with a blade measured to fit his enemy's neck. The only blow he deals is the ending one," she said quietly. "Mages are bothersome, but Titus is the real reason I've always given Midlan a wide berth."

"How do you know so much about him?" Kael asked, trying to smother the chill that'd suddenly crept up his spine.

"I used to fight with him."

"You fought *against* him, you mean." When she didn't reply, Kael felt as if he'd just had an iron fist clamp around his stomach. "You mean you've fought with Titus before? *On his side*?"

"I once fought alongside all the Sovereign Five, and Crevan. They were our allies during the Whispering War. I told you I was a knight of Midlan," she said testily, scowling at his look. "What did you think that meant?"

"You were only a knight for a day! What about all the days before? What in Kingdom's name were you thinking, fighting with the Sovereign Five?"

"They were all the Kingdom had left," she said sharply. "Most of the whisperers had abandoned Midlan to join the Falsewright, and King Banagher had tossed the rest out on their ears because he feared they might be spies. By the time Setheran and I joined the fight, war had been raging for two years across the realm. And who do you think held the rebels back all that time?"

"The Sovereign Five," Kael said quietly, piecing it together.

The only story he'd ever read about the Whispering War had been the one at the end of the *Atlas*, and it hadn't exactly been detailed. Now it was beginning to sound as if some bits had been intentionally left out.

"Why would Setheran have waited so long to fight?"

Kyleigh shrugged. "He'd given up his title in Midlan long before I met him, and he'd sworn never to shed blood again. When I asked him why, he said it was because he'd been broken. He would never tell me anymore than that," she said with a hard smile. "The memory I showed you was the most he ever spoke of it."

There must've been lead inside Kael's boots. *That* was the reason he could hardly lift them. "But Setheran ... I can't believe he would ever side with villains, not even to save the Kingdom."

Kyleigh sighed heavily. "They weren't *villains* in those days. Crevan and the Five wanted power, but no more or less than any other humans. It's what they did with their power that turned them villainous."

Kael couldn't believe it. He couldn't grasp it. The whole idea was far too hot to wrap his head around. If he tried, it would burn him up. So he didn't. He forced his legs to move, hoping the mountain air would cool him.

"Don't stomp off," Kyleigh called from behind him. "I don't want you to think badly of me —"

"I don't. In fact, I don't know what to think. Even if you thought the rest of the Sovereign Five weren't villains, you can't tell me you didn't see it in Titus. You can't tell me you didn't know he was wicked from the start."

"You're right. I can't."

He whipped around to face her, matching her glare with one of his own. "Then just answer me one thing," he said through his teeth. "If you knew Titus was a monster, why didn't Setheran kill him? Why didn't he save the Kingdom seventeen years of pain and suffering? Why did he let Titus live?"

Kyleigh studied him for a moment. "Titus was a hero during the Whispering War. His tactics were unbelievably cruel, I'll give you that. But he kept the rebels from taking Midlan. Setheran always said that Titus was a necessary evil."

With that utterance, a thing Kael had held onto all his life crumbled between his fingers. A hero he'd fought beside in his dreams, a warrior he'd aspired to be — a man who'd been such an unwittingly large part of his childhood perished before his eyes.

"I could never do that," Kael said quietly. His eyes were on Kyleigh, but behind them he watched the last of the earth cover Setheran's face. "I could never stand by and let a man with so much blood on his hands go on living."

Kyleigh grabbed his arm before he could turn away. "I know how all the stories painted him, but the truth is that Setheran preferred to *spare* lives rather than end them. He wanted Fate to have her say. Setheran was very much a reluctant hero ... a bit like someone else I know."

*I'm nothing like him.*

Those were the words he wanted to say — the ones that waited on the edge of his tongue. Kael wanted to twist out from under Kyleigh's hand and sling his fist into the nearest tree. But then he would've been no better than Setheran.

So he swallowed the words back and instead of swinging, he placed a hand on top of hers. "I'm not angry," he insisted, when he saw her searching. "I suppose I'm just a little ... disappointed. I've spent my whole life thinking that Setheran the Wright was the greatest warrior who'd ever lived. Now I'm beginning to realize he was just an ordinary Wright who was very lucky in friends."

She smiled at this — which made it much easier to forget his anger.

*******

One day, the wildmen marched out from between a forest of sagging pines and into the opened mouth of a field.

Here, the land was completely flat — as if the peak they stood upon had been cleft of its top. The nub it left behind was a gap between fall and winter: perched above the autumn slopes and cradled in the shadow of the mountains' frosted peaks.

Three of the peaks stood higher than the rest, with the tallest, most formidable in the very center. "That's the summit," Gwen said, pointing. Then her finger trailed to the left, where the second-highest peak rose beside it. "Thanehold — our lands. And over there," her finger went to the smaller peak on the right, "is Wynndom."

Kael was more than a little surprised: he thought the wildmen would've put their castle at the very top of the mountains. The fact that they hadn't made him wonder if perhaps the wynns truly *did* exist. Something powerful was obviously keeping them from the mountain's top.

As he studied the harsh, frozen edges of the summit, he began to think that the *real* mystery was why anybody would want to claim it in the first place.

A scant layer of grass covered the field's rocky skin. It was surprisingly green, though it wasn't the crisp, healthy green of the Valley: it was a deep, defiant green — a green

418

nearly blackened by its depth. Sickly-thin blades whipped violently in the wind, their roots clinging to their rocky perches. It was if the grass was green here because it *wanted* to be, as if it'd flexed the tiny fibers of every blade and willed itself to turn.

Tuffs of snow-white reeds dotted the rocky earth. They grew several hands apart, surrounded by patches of greenish-black. Kael had seen fields like this before. Roland called them *stubble fields*, because the way the white reeds clumped together made them look like the sprouts of an old man's beard.

This patch of land was like a valley dug out of the mountains, the sort that seemed to droop down and suck everything else in along with it. Even the clouds got caught in its snare: the gray marching beasts sat so closely above them that Kael swore he could feel them scraping the top of his head. They covered the points of the trees and draped over the land in front of them like a blanket. He could see the peaks of the mountains in the distance, but the land before them was hidden in cloud.

He knew where they were. This low point near the mountain's top, with its ghostly field and the low-hanging clouds was a place he'd read about in the *Atlas*. The air seemed colder here — as if it was made of ice. Though it wasn't the cold that chilled him so much as the spirits: the ghosts of one hundred of the King's noblest men, all drowned at once.

They were near the banks of Hundred Bones.

"It's the only way across, mutt," Gwen said when he voiced his very serious concern. "The river's been frozen over for centuries. It's not likely to crack under us."

Kael knew very well that Hundred Bones was always frozen over — but only because it fed upon the souls of the King's men. The river would need new souls, eventually. He just hoped it would hold for one more crossing.

"*Move*, mutt!" Gwen barked from up ahead, startling him.

she falls in, do we have to pull her out?" he
.nder his breath to Kyleigh.

didn't answer. While he'd been arguing with
Gwen, Kyleigh had fallen behind. Now she wandered several
paces away, staring wide-eyed at the shaded bellies of the
clouds. She didn't look frightened, exactly. But she certainly
didn't look comfortable.

"Do you feel the ghosts?" he wondered.

When her smile came, it was disturbingly frail. "You
could say that, I suppose."

Her eyes finally dragged to watch the wildmen from
over his shoulder. The clink of their armor faded as they left
the banks and stepped carefully onto the river's icy back. But
Kyleigh didn't move.

Her teeth dragged across her bottom lip as she stared
emptily at Hundred Bones. "The mountain's voice is so much
stronger here. I can hear it screaming at me. Do you ever feel
like it's ... after you? Am I mad to think that?"

No, she wasn't mad.

Kael had often felt the mountains' spirit. It was always
after him, always throwing tricks in his path and trying to
claim his life. As a boy, it'd frightened him. But then Roland
had showed him his woodsman's tricks — how to read the
weather's moods and glean bounty from the wilds. Amos had
taught him how to find healing roots beneath the mountain's
unforgiving flesh, how to press ointment from the prickly
leaves. And as he'd grown, Kael had begun to realize
something:

"The mountains really aren't as unforgivable as we
think. If they truly meant to keep us out, they could. But
instead, there's a path around every trap, a salve for every
sting — a way across every river. Sure, the mountains will try
to kill you ... but they'll also make you stronger." An
involuntary smile bent his lips. His heart lurched as his hand
reached out to her, as if it hadn't quite realized what he'd
been about to do. "Come on."

He tried not to burst into flame when her hand met
his, when their fingers twined and their palms pressed

420

together. The fires roared for a moment. They tried to scare him off. But he held on tightly.

They trekked through the stringy grass, with the clouds hovering like the roof of a cave and the cold wind lashing their scalps. Kael battled the flames all the while they walked. He grit his teeth against the voice that whispered he wasn't strong enough, that he had no right to hold her. After a fierce, silent battle, the fires abated.

The flames that'd bitten his skin now sank beneath it. There wasn't any pain here — only warmth. He slowed until he walked beside her instead of at her front, and their arms twined as closely as their hands.

All too soon, they arrived at the frozen banks of Hundred Bones.

The river lay still and silent among the reeds, frozen like a monstrous corpse from long ago. It was several ship-lengths wide: Kael could barely make out the edges of the opposite shore in the distance. The land beyond sloped upwards, where the clouds quickly swallowed it.

By the time Kyleigh and Kael arrived, the wildmen had already begun to cross. The warriors slid surely along the ice, testing the safest paths. The craftsmen followed in their wake. Their thin legs shook and they grumped to one another as they took careful steps.

One man lost his footing. His feet slipped out from under him and he took a fantastic spill, landing directly onto his rump.

A warrior slid over and offered a hand. "Careful — that patch is slippery."

"Yeah, thanks for telling me *after* I'd already cracked my backend," the craftsman said. "It's like walking on hog's fat out here."

"Why don't you just give yourself some pointed toes, then?"

"What — and tease this ice? Are you mad? We can't go digging out our steps."

"One crack won't hurt anything," the warrior insisted, grinning.

"One crack is all it takes," the craftsman said with a glare. "Now help me over this next bit, here. Don't —!"

The warrior shoved him hard in the back and the craftsman slid, waving his arms like a gull fighting its way from the sea a few feet before he hit a rougher path of ice and went spilling over onto his chin.

"Be careful with my craftsmen," Gwen called, glaring at the warrior.

He stopped laughing immediately.

While the rest of the wildmen fanned out in clumps, Gwen walked alone behind them. She strode easily along the rough patches of ice and slid across the slippery bits. Her head turned each time there was a slip or a stumble, watching to make sure the craftsman who'd fallen wound up all right. Her axe was drawn and swung loosely at her side — which Kael didn't think was a particularly good idea, considering how treacherous the ice was.

Silas, as always, padded along in her wake. Even from a distance, Kael could hear the scratching of his claws as he dug into the ice. His limbs trembled with every step. He struggled over a slippery bit with his foreclaws. He dug his nails in and the rough fur on the back of his neck bristled as he regained his footing.

He'd arched his chin and gone to plod on as if he'd won a great victory when his back feet slipped out from under him. They splayed in opposite directions. The muscles in his shoulders coiled as he quickly righted himself. His glowing eyes flicked over his shoulder, as if to make sure no one had seen. When he saw Kyleigh and Kael grinning at him from the shore, he hissed.

Gwen turned at the sound of his spitting. Her eyes went to Kyleigh and Kael's clasped hands — and narrowed. "Move, pest!" she barked.

Kael couldn't be sure, but he thought the back of her neck might've been a good deal redder than usual. He supposed the wind must've burned her. Without any trees for shelter, it lashed them mercilessly. It howled across their ears until they had to shout to be heard.

Kyleigh and Kael had gone several yards from the shore when the ice suddenly groaned beneath them. He glanced down — and froze when he saw the many hairline cracks that fanned around her boots.

"Dragon bones," she explained with a grimace. "We ought to spread out."

She let go of his hand, and the air immediately felt chiller. "Why don't you just fly across? We'll meet you on the other side."

"It's a bit late for that, isn't it? If I change now, I'll fall straight through. It'll be fine," she insisted. She took another step, and the ice made only the faintest protest. "See? As long as we don't add your weight to it, the river ought to hold nicely."

He thought *nicely* was a bit of a stretch. But he knew there was no point in arguing with her. Instead, he kept several paces to her left — and glared anytime the ice so much as muttered.

Blue-green waters stretched before him in a field of their own, frozen in the traps of time. Kael couldn't help but stare down at them as he passed. The river's halted swirls were every bit as entrancing as the shapes of the clouds above the seas.

A magnificent scene played out beneath his feet: he saw knights warring with dragons, woodsmen climbing the tops of the mountains. Deer bounded over hills and birds spread their monstrous wings. He watched the frozen shapes beneath him for so many long moments that the next time he looked up, they'd made it to the middle.

Hundred Bones stretched out in every direction, barren as the wastes. Had it not been so cold, he might've thought they were standing in a desert. Kyleigh walked a few reaches beside him. She moved slowly, and the ice didn't complain beneath her feet. The wildmen were stretched ahead of him in a line, barking insults at each other. Their harsh laughter warmed the air.

Ahead of them, the land sloped upwards. The cloud that sat atop their heads hid all but the faintest line of the shore. Its gray underbelly worried him. Right now the clouds were hoarding all their snow, but they could let loose at any moment.

He was watching the feathered edges of the clouds when he saw movement along the shoreline. He heard the stomping of feet and the rattling of armor — followed by a sight that chilled him swifter than the river's breath:

A horde of Earl Titus's soldiers.

# CHAPTER 37
## THE EARL'S GAME

The soldiers made no move to cross Hundred Bones. They stood in a line on the opposite bank and raised their swords high in warning. The thundering call they let out seemed practiced to Kael, and he was immediately wary.

But the warriors must not have noticed. They let out howls of their own and took off after the Earl's soldiers, their boots moving surely against the ice. They cut the distance between them quickly. The soldiers waited until the warriors were a ship-length from the banks before they turned and fled up the shores, heading north.

The hair on the back of Kael's neck was standing tall. His eyes went from the warriors' charge back to the middle of the ice, where the craftsmen were still trying helplessly to wobble their way across.

And he suddenly realized what Titus had planned. "Stop! Gwen — stop them!"

Ice sprayed from her heels as she ground to a halt. The light of battle left her eyes and the skin beneath her paint went white as she gaped at something over his shoulder. "Look out!"

Kael's worst nightmare came hurtling from the shore behind him.

Twisted creatures with armor melded into their skin thundered across the ice. Dogs, badgers, weasels, cats with no tails and tall, pointed ears — all locked their crazed black eyes onto the craftsmen. Gwen's cry only made them quicken their pace. They howled and screeched for blood. Wet trailed from their jagged teeth.

Harbinger screamed as Kyleigh ripped him from his sheath. Kael drew an arrow from his quiver. "Remember your

425

armor, craftsmen!" He said as he locked onto the eyes of the first beast. "Put on your armor!"

A small horde broke from the pack, drawn to Harbinger's song. Kyleigh swung her blade in dizzying arcs, cleaving the first monster's head from its furry neck. They circled her carefully after that — darting in and leaping back. They screamed each time the white blade bit them.

Gwen crashed into the front of the line. She leapt and brought her axe down with a cry, splitting a badger's head like a log. Her shield dented a weasel's iron skull. A thrust of her heel shattered a dog's ribs. She slung the skewered body of a cat into the monsters in front of her, rolling them in every direction.

Creatures fell beneath Kael's arrows. He kept the first line from reaching the craftsmen, but by the time the second wave broke through, his quiver was empty. There was nothing for it.

Black scales popped up along his skin as he ran. The first monster swiped at the line of craftsmen with its massive claws, knocking a clump of them across the ice. Their armor held well: though the monsters bit and slashed, they couldn't break the craftsmen's skin.

One of the weasels tried unsuccessfully to crack a craftsman open with its teeth. When that didn't work, it scooped the poor man up and began slamming his body into the ground. The craftsman's armor didn't yield ...

But the ice did.

Kael was several yards away when he saw the angry, white-blue web forming beneath the weasel's feet. He knew that if the river cracked, it would drag them both to an icy grave. The craftsmen could no longer hide beneath their shells. It was time to fight.

Kael's warrior edge held him in a sprint while the craftsman worked on his swords. The armor and the swords were made of the same material: it wasn't difficult to imagine that the scales sharpened to points at the tips of his hands, or that edges grew along his arms.

"Remember your blades, craftsmen!" Kael hollered as he ran. "Remember how they felt — sharp enough to cleave the pines, light enough to wield."

His eyes clamped down upon the weasel. He was nearly there. The words grew louder as they left his lips, charged by the fury of his sprint: "Use them now, craftsmen! Swing your blades against the Man of Wolves — split his army as you split the trees! Fight, craftsmen! *Fight!*"

Kael roared and thrust his arm into the weasel's middle. He felt warmth, wet, then cold once more as his hand burst out the other side. The craftsmen caught in the weasel's grasp charged his hand through its throat, and its wriggling body collapsed. Then with a howl the warriors might've been proud of, the craftsmen fought back.

Beasts fell beneath their hands — hewed and split, curled away. The craftsmen's eyes burned with the fires of their work. Their lips moved with silent words. The beasts couldn't stop them; they couldn't break them. The craftsmen ripped through Titus's army as if it was no more fierce a thing than nettles.

Kael slung his arms in arcs around him. Hot droplets spewed onto his face and the front of his jerkin, where the wind struck them cool. A dog lunged for him, its jaws gaping, and Kael held out his hand.

His arm went down its throat and out the back of its neck.

He'd turned to destroy a circle of badgers when a massive claw struck him in the small of his back. Clouds whipped overhead as he slid across the ice. His elbow ground against the river's flesh until he struck a rough patch, and the sudden jolt flipped him onto his stomach. He was about to jump to his feet when he caught sight of the creature that'd flung him.

It towered over every other beast: a monster with blood-red fur sprouting through the gaps between its tortured human flesh. An iron helmet capped its head — a head that was far too small for the hulking shoulders that crowded it on either side.

Between its fur, its size and the large dent in the front of its helmet, there was no mistaking who this monster was: the red devil.

The devil looked as wicked as it had in Griffith's nightmares. A pair of tiny black eyes lurked behind the slit in its helmet. A wolf-like mouth almost overtook the monster's face — though the massive, hooked claws curled at its side looked as if they belonged to a bear. Its red tail was short, but thick and bristled.

Roland used to tell him stories of animals that looked like this. They had a wolf's speed, a bear's appetite, and a badger's temper. They preferred to live alone, and Kael had hoped to never cross paths with one.

But he supposed that hope now lay dashed alongside countless others.

He got to his feet and prepared himself to charge. Even when it draped back on its hind legs and stood to its full, towering height, Kael wasn't afraid. This beast would fall like all the others.

The monster's lips pulled back across its teeth. Its pink tongue lolled clumsily between them, forming two gurgling words: "Hello, Twiglet."

Kael froze. The devil's twisted mouth curled into a snarling grin. A patch of blood red fur sprouted from its lower lip. The beady black eyes that stared him down were even properly dim. Still, he could hardly believe it.

"Marc?"

Before the monster could reply, Gwen slammed into its middle. She chased its rolling body with her axe raised beside her, shouting: "The red devil is *mine!*"

It roared and swung a massive claw, forcing her back. She howled and beat her axe against her chest. The monster bristled for the charge. Then all at once, the collar around its neck glowed hot.

The red devil, *Marc*, whipped away from Gwen and galloped out of her reach. He charged for the shrouded banks, as if he'd been summoned by whistle. Titus's monsters followed. They shoved past the craftsmen and lumbered

428

away. No sooner had they slunk into the cover of the clouds than the warriors returned.

They sprinted from the northern reaches of the shore, their fur-clad bodies stained with the marks of their victory. Behind them, the bodies of the Earl's soldiers lay crumpled and scattered.

The warriors stood along the banks and howled.

The craftsmen howled back.

Gwen raised her axe high: "We've beaten him again! We've clobbered the Man of Wolves!"

The wildmen pounded their chests in triumph, but Kael wasn't so sure.

Kyleigh slid in beside him. The ice creaked under the burden of their weights, but she didn't seem to notice: her eyes were on the clouded shores. "This isn't over," she murmured.

No sooner were the words out of her mouth than Kael heard something strange — a creaking sound, followed by a *whoosh* of wind. It was faint, like the noises he used to hear when *Anchorgloam* passed other ships. Kael looked at the clouded roof instinctively.

A dark spot had appeared among the gray. He thought it might've been a bird at first, but then it grew larger. Was it a shadow? A storm? Then the dark spot broke from the clouds and the blunt teeth of a monstrous boulder came streaking towards him.

Kyleigh slammed into his side, and the unexpected force launched him several yards away. He landed hard on his shoulder and rolled onto his feet, but not before he heard the ground-shattering noise of breaking ice — and a splash.

"Kyleigh!"

Breath hissed from Kael's lungs when he saw that she'd managed to escape the boulder's fall. A large hole had been knocked out of the ice behind her. She'd been drenched by the splash, but was otherwise unharmed.

"That was close," she said, grimacing as she leapt away from the hole. "Are you all —?"

A black bolt fell from the sky and knocked her to the ground. Glossy wings beat against her head and a pair of large black eyes gaped at her through a falcon's twisted face. She drove her elbow into the top of its feathery head, and the pointed end of her gauntlet silenced its screeching forever.

Kael had made to run towards her when she thrust a finger behind him. "Don't worry about me — the craftsmen!" she cried.

Boulders fell from the sky in steady arcs. They crashed into Hundred Bones, shattering its icy shell and sending waves of water splashing high into the air. The craftsmen tried desperately to escape. A chasm of churning water cut them off from the shores behind them. They had no choice but to move forward.

Gwen ran among them, slinging the craftsmen one at a time across the ice and towards the warriors — who had charged out immediately at the sound of their panicked cries.

"No! Half of you go back!" Kael shouted at the warriors as he ran. "Find the catapults and destroy them! The other half form a line — slide the craftsmen down. *Move!*"

The warriors scrambled to do as they were told. Half peeled away and sprinted into the clouds while the other half formed a chain to the shore. They slid the craftsmen from warrior to warrior, passing them quickly across the ice.

Boulders thudded mercilessly all around them. The river awakened with a roar — it began to gnaw hungrily on the cracks in its frozen shell, chewing them off in chunks. The warriors slung the craftsmen out of the boulders' paths. They carried their thin bodies across their shoulders and tossed them over swirling, blue-green rifts.

The wildmen were going to make it. They were nearly there. Kael went to tell Kyleigh to run for the shores, and saw with a jolt that she hadn't followed him.

She was under attack.

Falcons fell from the clouds like bolts, tearing with their claws and beaks. They struck with such blinding fury and in such a constant stream that Kyleigh hadn't gotten a chance to draw her sword. No sooner had she reached for

430

Harbinger than she was knocked away. One falcon shot dow and rammed hard into her back. Its neck snapped under the force, but its body still managed to knock her to the ground.

The falcons swarmed.

The world went red.

A howl ripped from Kael's throat as he sprinted towards her. A falcon shot down and tried to deal the ending blow. It fell for Kyleigh, talons outstretched — and met the spurred heel of her boot. The falcon's head was crushed immediately. It seized up and toppled over as if it'd struck a castle wall.

But the damage had already been done.

The combination of Kyleigh's weight and the sudden jolt of the falcon seemed to be too much for the ice. Time slowed as Kael watched the spider web of blue-green cracks blossom beneath Kyleigh's middle. Talons came down, thudding into her upraised arms — widening the cracks.

He yelled for her to roll aside, but she couldn't hear him over the screeching of the falcons. She swung her fists, unaware of the fact that she was about to be sucked into an icy oblivion. The seconds seemed to last an age. Kael's legs thundered at a speed he never knew he had. His arms swung furiously beside him; his fingers clawed at the air.

But he was still too late.

The ice gave way with a *crack* and Kyleigh fell through. Kael heard the *thud* echo inside his head as his body struck the ice. His eyes were on her hands; her fingers dug into the last solid edge, her knuckles stark white with the effort.

He saw the fierce, blue-green monster erupt around her body. Its spray looked like thousands of tiny hands — grasping, pushing, trying desperately to thrust her under and out of his reach. But Kael was far too quick. He dove and grabbed, finally snatching her by the wrists.

The world rushed back. A ghostly cold had already settled into Kyleigh's armor. His skin ached against it. Her hands stayed curled as he pulled, as if they were so stiff with

: couldn't get them to bend. Her full lips were
d. White showed around the green in her eyes.

 now, Kael managed to drag his feet beneath him.
...e felt hairline cracks forming around him as he pulled,
heard the thudding of boulders as they crashed through the
ice beside him, fought against the river's grasp and against
the numbing cold in his hands and slowly, he managed to pull
Kyleigh halfway free.

The ice groaned dangerously, and he froze. With even
the slightest shift of his boots, it groaned again. It couldn't
support both their weights — one of them was going to fall
through.

And as long as he drew breath, it wasn't going to be
Kyleigh.

She must've seen the plan forming in his eyes. The
battle raged around them. The howls of the wildmen, the
screech of the falcons and the river's roar all seemed distant.
His hands tightened around her wrists, preparing to throw
her to safety.

She tried to shake him off.

"Don't," he begged her. "Please, don't fight me. I'm not
going to let you die —"

The insides of his head slapped against his skull as a
falcon crashed into him. Half a breath, a blink, a single thud of
his heart — his concentration broke for a shred of time too
small to measure. But that was all the opportunity the river
needed.

It ripped Kyleigh's frozen, soaked arms out from
between his aching fingers and swallowed her whole. Her
hands disappeared beneath the rapids. The white foam swept
over her head.

And then she was gone.

*******

The cold was Kyleigh's greatest enemy. It froze her
muscles to her bones, curled her limbs. An ache enveloped
her: it seized her joints and made her head pound. She could

432

feel the river's glee as it dragged her further — as it tightened its icy embrace.

Her lungs convulsed, throbbing against their cage. The pressure of their begging strained the edges of her throat — her last breath of air threatened to burst up and through the feeble seal on her lips at any moment.

Thunder rumbled across the ice above her. It boomed loudly every few seconds — a knock upon the door. A voice called to her, muffled through the ice:

"Kyleigh ... *Kyleigh!*"

Her lungs screamed. Her limbs were frozen solid. She couldn't open her eyes. She had enough strength left for one reply, and then the river would take her. The icy crust that'd formed across her skin broke as her arm swung upwards. She heard a *thump*, but didn't feel anything as her fist struck the frozen ceiling.

Her last breath gave way to the urging of her lungs. Air left her lips in a stream of bubbles and icy water filled her mouth. It numbed her teeth and tongue. Her chest tightened, preparing to expand — and when it did, water would fill her to the brim. The river's spirit would freeze her from the inside out.

Light struck the backs of her eyes. Something anchored her arm, halting her body's plunge down the river. The mountain's voice roared inside her ears. Ice shattered over her head and spilled down her back. When she gasped, it wasn't water she breathed in:

It was air.

"Come on, Kyleigh!"

The world spun as Kael lifted her onto his shoulders. He moved like wind across the river. She watched in horror as Hundred Bones' icy flesh cracked beneath his heels. Little holes opened up behind him. The waves slurped and snapped, trying to pull him under. But Kael was far too quick.

"Hold on!" he cried as he ran. "Hold on, Kyleigh! Please — we're almost there. Just a little further!"

She tried to hold on. She would've done anything for him. But the spirit of the mountains raged too fiercely. Its voice shrilled in delight as the wind whipped across her — as the frozen air finished what the river had started. Her vision blurred and dark shapes danced across it. Numbness had so claimed her that she could no longer feel to fight.

Her eyes closed ...

"Stay awake, Kyleigh. You have to stay awake!"

Kael's face swam blurrily above her. Warmth spread across her flesh where he touched, but it was faint — a candle's warmth. The ice beneath her skin quickly snuffed it out ...

And the cold dragged her off to sleep.

*******

"Kyleigh!"

He kept his hands on her face, trying to will her eyes to open, trying to force her back into the light. When they closed, he felt the black beast rushing in. He felt its monstrous jaws about to crush him. He started to panic —

"What do we do?" Gwen gasped. She fell in beside him; the drenched body of a craftsman lay shivering in her arms. "Heal them, mutt! Heal them!"

For some reason, the panic in her eyes destroyed his own. He realized that he couldn't afford to break — he was the only one left who knew what to do. If he let his panic take him, then the wildmen ... Kyleigh ...

"Craftsmen to me!" Kael roared, and they stumbled to his side. He put some of their hands on Kyleigh's armor. "Use your forge fires to keep her warm, heat her exactly how you would heat steel."

Another group of craftsmen gathered around Gwen and began trying to warm their frozen companion. Their fires would have to burn more gently to keep from singeing his flesh. Kael hoped the heat would be enough.

He heard screams of terror and the noise of splintering wood. Up the slope, the warriors had destroyed the catapults. They ripped the wooden arms apart and hurled boulders at the fleeing backs of the Earl's men, crushing them. Just when he thought they might have earned a breath, a roar from Silas drew his eyes away.

Titus's beasts had returned.

They tore from the cover of the mist and charged in a straight line, their blackened eyes locked onto Kyleigh. "Form a ring around the wounded!" Kael said, and the craftsmen moved obediently. "Use your armor, use your blades — don't let the monsters through!"

They held the beasts off for only a few seconds before one of them sprang clear over their heads. The craftsmen turned to cut it down, and their circle shrank back. Kael ran around its inside edge, cutting down the beasts that managed to leap over their wall, but he couldn't stop them. The circle shrank further as more beasts made the jump.

Warriors poured down the slope and threw themselves into the fray. The monsters moved too quickly. They found every opening, every gap. If a craftsman stumbled for half a breath, he was overtaken. They were punished for every flinch.

It wasn't possible. Not even the warriors with all their speed could've reacted so quickly. Several of the beasts leapt into holes without even turning to look. They moved as if they could see behind them, from all sides. Their collars would flash red and they would jump — gaining advantage. It was almost as if ...

Kael tore his eyes away from the battle and saw a handful of falcons circling overhead. They made no move to attack: instead, they kept a looping pattern — their large, glassy eyes locked unblinkingly on the battle beneath them.

All at once, Kael figured it out. He wrenched a melded chunk of armor off the body of a dog and hurled it at one of the falcons. Blood rained down upon them as the iron struck true. The falcon's body crashed amongst the warriors — who took one look at its wound and began scooping rocks up off the ground.

Stones flew from their hands in such a furious barrage that only one falcon managed to escape. It tore off, squawking at the tops of its lungs, and Titus's beasts followed. Their collars burned red and they bolted for the slopes, moving as quickly as their twisted legs could carry them.

"No — stay together!" Kael bellowed when the warriors started to give chase.

They'd managed to beat the monsters back for now, but he wasn't going to let the wildmen split up again. That was all the opportunity Titus needed.

He pushed through the large clump of wildmen that'd formed around Kyleigh and Gwen. The Thane's eyes burned red. She clung tightly to the now-frozen body of the craftsman, her teeth bared in a snarl.

"Dead," she managed to whisper.

Kael tore his eyes from the wildmen's crumpled faces and fell on his knees beside Kyleigh. Her skin was blue and she shivered miserably, but the heat from the craftsmen's hands had kept her from freezing to death.

She was alive ... but fading quickly.

# CHAPTER 38
## DOUBLE-EDGED

A deer lay on the ground before Kael. There was a fist-sized hole over its heart: the jagged mark his stone had left behind. The deer's dark eyes were vacant; its tongue lolled out of its muzzle. Though the bare trees creaked with the wind and the shadows of the clouds roamed across the slopes, the deer was eerily still.

It had once been a part of this world. There had been a place for it in the mountains' song, somewhere among the notes that bounded high and fast. Now the hooves would clatter no more. The body wouldn't dart and the eyes wouldn't close against rare glimpses of the sun. It was still, empty — lines on a page that would never again be sung ... dead, for lack of its voice.

The deer's tawny head flopped suddenly as Gwen lifted it onto her shoulders. "A good shot," she said.

She waited for something. Gwen stared, her brows arched high and expecting. Was she waiting for Kael to reply? To offer something in exchange for what she'd said? Wait a moment ... what *had* she said? The longer he thought about it, the less he remembered.

Gwen shifted the deer across her shoulders, making its head flop again. "A shot like that's got to make you feel better about things. Don't you feel better?"

Better? He wouldn't have known what *better* was even if it'd splattered across his boots.

Kael was stung and sore, but living. He was prepared for the pain, but longed for the impossible. His hope was double-edged: it cut him deeply, but the agony kept him alive. Perhaps there would come a day when he would hurt no longer, when he either healed or died.

Perhaps he would feel *better*, then.

The mountains dragged out of corners of his eyes. His boots drifted down the path that had become so familiar the last ... well, he didn't know exactly how long it'd been. He wasn't sure if he should measure it in terms of days or weeks. The clouds still hung above them, threatening and gray. No snow had fallen, yet. But it didn't matter. It had been half an eternity, by his reckoning ... and Kyleigh still wouldn't wake.

No matter how many pelts they draped across her, or how warm they kept her shelter, she lay shivering through all hours of the day and night. Her limbs trembled pitifully. The red was gone from her lips, replaced by a purplish blue. When he'd touched the side of her face, he found all the warmth was gone. There was only cold.

Kael had spent his every waking moment flipping through the pages of his memory. He poured over the words he'd read in Lysander's library, drew up every lesson Amos had taught him about the cold. None of the remedies had worked. None of the broths, herbs, or warmth had done anything to calm her shaking or bring the color back to her face.

Sometimes, sleep shut his eyes and he spent a few hours in darkness — but even then he saw the pages in his dreams.

His legs stopped moving suddenly. He realized it was because Gwen had grabbed him by the shoulder. "This has to stop."

Stop? What had to stop?

Gwen's brows dropped low, but there was something in her eyes that Kael hadn't remembered seeing before. A softness ... a sad sort of softness. "Her bones are frozen, mutt. There's nothing you can do to thaw them."

Pity. *That* was the softness in Gwen's eyes.

Her hand tightened on his shoulder. "I lost one of my craftsmen to the river. He shook himself to death, died right there in my arms ... you saw him pass. Now listen to me closely, mutt: it's been ages and she hasn't so much as cracked an eye. The wildmen are depending on you, and you haven't spoken a word to anybody in days."

Gwen stopped. She was waiting for something again. Her brows rose hopefully for a moment under Kael's gaze. Then they snapped down low.

"It's time. She's never going to wake — she's just going to get colder and more miserable. She was a decent creature. But it's time to put her out of her —"

Kael's palms slammed into Gwen's chest and she went flying backwards, crashing into the trunk of a tree. The force slung the deer's body aside; the branches trembled dryly. They were silent for a moment. Gwen stared in shock while Kael tried to glare a hole through the middle of her head.

"She isn't a *creature*. She's my friend."

Gwen held up her hands. "All right, all right — she isn't a creature."

"And I'm not putting her anywhere." The wind picked up as Kael spoke, as if the mountains were agreeing with him. "I'll stay beside her until she wakes or Death claims her. If you don't like it, then you're welcome to ..."

They caught it at the same moment: a familiar, moldy scent on the wind. It brushed across Kael's face and made the insides of his nose itch horribly.

"Magic!" Gwen cried. She was on her feet in an instant, tearing through the woods. And Kael followed close behind.

He knew Titus was keeping an eye on them — watching and waiting. He'd known it was only a matter of time before the Earl sent another group of soldiers after them. This time it smelled as if he'd also sent one of his mages ... and that was a mistake.

Thorns scraped his face and arms as Kael charged through the brambles. He burst from the thorny wall several paces ahead of Gwen and spotted the mage immediately. He was a thin man wearing a robe of furs. There was a pair of rounded spectacles perched at the end of his long nose ...

Dirt sprayed from beneath Kael's heels as he ground to a halt. He saw his own open-mouthed shock reflected in the mage's thin, familiar face.

439

"Kael?"

"Jake? What are you —?"

"Arrrr!"

Gwen burst into the clearing and tore for Jake, her fists clenched and ready to strike. Kael yelled for her to stop. Jake stumbled backwards. Gwen kept coming. She was an arm's reach away when a black blur slammed into her shoulder, knocking her aside.

It was Elena — the strange forest woman who'd traveled with Kyleigh into the plains. Rage must've blinded Gwen. She tried lunging for Jake even though Elena had a knee in the middle of her back. She was pinned with an arm twisted behind her in half a blink

"Wait — stop!"

Elena's black dagger halted just as it was about to glide across Gwen's throat. She glared at Kael from over the top of her mask. "A friend of yours?"

"A friend of mine, actually," Silas purred.

Sometime in the middle of all the chaos, the halfcat had appeared behind Jake. He strode barefoot across the rocky ground, wearing nothing more than a plain set of trousers. His glowing eyes narrowed as he took in the scene before him.

"Take your hands away from my Thane, you stupid Elena."

"Tell your Thane to keep her hands away from our mage, cat," she growled, "or I'll slit her throat."

"Cat?" The purest, most fearsome red Kael had ever seen bloomed behind Gwen's paint. Her eyes traveled up his bare chest and at last came to a stop at his haughty eyes. "Silas?"

"We have much to discuss, my Thane," he said with a smirk.

Elena released her, and Gwen's arms shook as she pulled herself to her feet. Red spread across the bridge of her nose and down her neck — a scarlet storm that raged in a hundred different shades of fury.

Kael wouldn't have been surprised if she'd throttled Silas. He wouldn't have been surprised if she'd screamed at him or burst into tears. What *did* surprise him was the fact that she chose to do none of those things.

She simply turned and clomped away.

Silas's shoulders fell heavily with his sigh. "There are too many eyes that have seen my shapes, too many mouths who might reveal my secret. I knew there would be no more hiding it."

"What do you mean?" Kael said. He was still trying desperately to grasp it — still blinking, afraid that Jake and Elena might disappear, terrified that it'd all been a dream.

"I've returned from my hunt, Marked One," Silas said, giving him a rather haughty look. "And I've found some game that I think belongs to you. The holes your battle left behind made the journey more difficult, but I managed to lead it up the river and across a frozen path." His voice dropped to a growl. "Now you will deal with it while I look after my Thane."

He slunk away, kicking dirt at Elena as he passed — and before Kael had a chance to grasp what was happening, he heard footsteps crunching up the frosted trail.

Several heads appeared over the top of the slope. Their faces were wind-burned, their breaths wheezed out in puffs of white, fur caps tipped over several of their brows. But he still thought he might've recognized ... no, it couldn't be. It couldn't possibly ...

"Kael!"

Lysander reached him first. Never, in all his life, had Kael expected to feel relieved at the prospect of being crushed against a pirate's chest, but that was precisely what he felt. Jonathan's lanky arms wrapped around his head; Nadine's wrapped about his middle. Declan scooped them all up together and squeezed until they nearly broke.

"Keep that up and there'll be nothing left for the rest of us!" Morris croaked. When Declan set them down, the helmsman slapped a stocky arm across Kael's back and said: "You'll have to run faster than that to lose *us*, lad!"

A hawk's cry rang above them as Eveningwing sounded his agreement.

More people stepped up to greet him. The pirates smiled as they clasped his shoulders. One of the giants plucked him off the ground and passed him through their hulking ranks. They ruffled his hair with their meaty hands and guffawed loudly in his ears. Kael didn't think his feet touched the ground for a full minute.

When the shock wore off and the giants finally set him down, Kael realized all of his companions were dressed like wildmen: fitted in heavy furs and armor, caps pulled tightly over their heads.

"Ah, yes. We came across your village on the way up," Lysander explained, pulling on his chainmail. "I thought it was a rather charming place —"

"Yeah, once those painted blokes stopped trying to kill us, it wasn't half bad," Jonathan said with a wink.

Kael groaned. "They tried to kill you?"

"I really think they would have, to be honest. But once some of us put our daggers away," Jake said with a pointed look at Elena, "they turned out to be rather civil."

She rolled her eyes. "If by *civil* you mean they graciously stopped trying to tear you limb from limb, then yes."

Jake produced a vial from the depths of his pocket and held it aloft. It was half-filled with a rather sickly looking yellow liquid. "The odor my skin puts off seems to be the one unbearable thing about me. I thought if I could somehow manage to cloak my natural scent, I might not be such a bother. So I've been carrying this around with me for ages, waiting to test it on an unfamiliar whisperer," he said with a slight smile. "I'd hoped it would be useful in an emergency."

"It's skunk oil," Elena said, when she saw the confused look on Kael's face. "It certainly kept the whisperers away —"

"And everybody else, I might add," Lysander said with a grimace.

Jake frowned. "It wasn't all that bad."

"It's still burning the back half of my throat!" Jonathan insisted.

"Aye, and there was no saving his robes, either. We burned them up a few miles past the village." Morris chuckled. "The smoke was worse than the smell! Knocked a bird straight from the trees, it did."

"That was just an ... unfortunate coincidence, I'm sure. There's no possible way a smell could knock something dead." Jake's eyes roved away and he pushed his spectacles absently up the bride of his long nose. "Or is there? I wonder ..."

Elena shook her head at him before turning back to Kael. "Even with Jake *cloaking* his way out of trouble, they probably still would've killed us."

Lysander nodded. "But a little charisma goes a long way. Luckily, I thought to introduce us —"

"*Luckily* they knew our clodded names!" Declan said with a glare.

"One of the children remembered us from your stories," Nadine explained. "When he heard our names, he called out to the others and said: *I know these people — they are friends of Kael the Wright.*"

Kael dragged a hand across his curls; a smile pulled at his lips as he tried to keep the rest contained. "Griffith," he said.

"Aye, that's the one. Things got especially friendly after that." Morris thumped his chest. "Warm clothes, new armor —"

"A nice stall for Braver. They've promised to keep him fed and brushed while I'm away. I hope for their sakes that they do," Elena growled.

"They even tended to our weapons. The giants' scythes have never been so sharp." Declan hoisted the weapon once before he slumped forward, planting his hands against his knees. "Plains mother, all the climbing and stomping about ... it may be twice as tall here, but I swear the air's only half as thick!"

443

The giants let out a grunt in reply — though it wasn't nearly as enthusiastic a cry as Kael remembered it being.

"Well, now that we've got our Wright, all that's left is to find our favorite mischief-maker," Lysander declared. "Where's the Dragongirl?"

Every fleeting shred of happiness he'd felt was gone in an instant, drowned in the depths of their stares.

Kael fell heavily on his knees and his eyes sank to their boots. Their voices swam in his ears. They asked him things — he couldn't answer. He barely heard it when Morris thumped down beside him. He barely felt the stocky arm that draped across his back.

"What's gone wrong, lad? Whatever it is, we'll sort it out," he croaked. "You've got the whole clump of us here, now. We'll do whatever we can."

Slowly, Morris coaxed the story from him. Kael told them of the wildmen's battle at Hundred Bones, how the Earl had trapped them, how Kyleigh had fallen into the river. He told them everything he'd done to try to save her.

"Her bones are frozen. She won't wake ..." Kael clenched his teeth and Morris's arm tightened its grip, steadying him. "Nothing I've tried has worked. I don't know what to do. There's nothing I *can* do. She's just ... Kyleigh's ..."

A tiny pair of hands clasped either side of his face. They turned his chin upwards, lifting him until he found himself staring at Nadine. "Take me to her," she said softly.

The firmness of her stare made Kael's heart lift a little — made the hope come back.

"I promise you I will not leave her side until she wakes."

*******

They'd made their camp a few short miles from Hundred Bones. Beyond the river's crossing lay the final season: now the wildmen stood in the winter reaches of the mountains.

444

Only a few scraggy trees still clung to the slope. The sparse grass was shrunken back against the rocks in surrender. And everything, from the trees to the grass was sealed in a shell of ice.

It looked as if the land had been encased in glass. Branches hung perfectly preserved, their buds frozen in time. In some places, faded blooms sat in drooping clumps — evidence that life once blossomed in the wastes. It was as if the winter had struck them so fiercely that the land hadn't had a chance to wilt. Now it was frozen forever, trapped in a cage of ice.

Kael had the pirates and the giants set up camp at the top of a hill, while the wildmen spread out beneath them. His friends' bodies weren't as accustomed to the cold. He had the craftsmen mold them shelters from stone. They used the armor they'd scavenged from the Earl's men to make little firepots, and turned their swords into spits. Even with the icy earth spread all around them, the camp was warm and well-fed.

Their biggest worry was Titus.

In the days following their battle at Hundred Bones, Kael had begun to realize that he'd made a very serious mistake. He remembered what Kyleigh had told him about how the Earl stalked his enemies. She'd said that he would only strike once, and the only blow he'd deal was the ending one.

Now as Kael thought back, he realized the fort outside of Tinnark had only been a test. Once Titus knew what the wildmen were capable of, he'd done exactly what Kael had done to Griffith: he used the warriors' battle lust against them. He'd goaded them into a fight, knowing they would follow — he'd tricked them into leaving the craftsmen vulnerable.

But Kael had struck back. He'd countered in a way the Earl hadn't been expecting ... he hadn't been expecting it because he'd known the craftsmen were weak. Mercy's sake, *how* had he known about the craftsmen? Had he been spying on them?

445

And even though Titus had clearly hoped to destroy the craftsmen at the river's middle, he'd been prepared for the worst. He'd brought his catapults along, knowing full well that he might have to use them — prepared to break the river and strand his army at the mountain's top, just so long as he sank the wildmen first.

The more Kael dwelt on it, the tighter his stomach twisted. Perhaps Titus had meant to end them at Hundred Bones ... but perhaps that'd merely been another test. Perhaps the *real* battle was yet to come.

For all he worried, there was one thing the Earl knew for certain: Kyleigh marched with the wildmen. He'd sent his falcons on her the moment his army began to lose its grip. Kael realized why the birds had been attacking so frantically now. Those had been Titus's blows — he'd been trying to force her into the river, to eliminate his greatest enemy.

And unless he was completely blind, he now knew that Kael would do anything to save her.

"The thing about Titus is you've got to get him quick, lad," Morris said. "You've got to get him before he gets you."

Kael was beginning to understand this. He'd come to realize that every moment he sat idle would allow Titus to add another detail to his plan. But he couldn't march on — not without Kyleigh.

Nadine had made good on her word. She'd spent the last several days with Kyleigh, tucked right in beside her. Sometimes Elena lay on Kyleigh's other side, sometimes it was Gwen. But Nadine insisted it be someone she knew.

"A woman as strong as Kyleigh will not lose the will to fight, not even in her sleep. Familiar voices, the beating of familiar hearts — these things will heal the wounds within. If the cold is truly in her bones," Nadine had said with a determined smile, "it will not last for long. I will speak to her until it melts."

Kael wasn't sure he believed that being surrounded by familiar bodies would heal her. But as he'd tried everything else, he was willing to do whatever Nadine said — even if that meant he was only allowed to visit twice a day.

The first morning he'd gone to see Kyleigh, he swore there'd been a little color in her face. That evening, he'd held her hand for as long as Nadine would let him. He wasn't allowed to tell her how badly he wanted her to wake, or mention how furious he was with her for having tried to fight his hold at the river. Instead, he told her stories. He said things he thought would've made her laugh.

And slowly, it began to work.

That morning when he'd gone to hold her hand, there'd been a tiny bit of warmth beneath the frost. He'd pressed her palm against his chest and kept it there for an hour, trying to will more warmth into her blood. It was only after Nadine had stomped her tiny feet at him that he'd reluctantly gone outside.

Now it was nightfall, and Kael had circled the whole camp once already because he was far too thrilled to sleep. On his second turn, Morris had waddled out to join him.

"Titus is like a bit of arrow," the old helmsman croaked on. "Pull him out right away, and you've only lost a little blood. But let him sit, let him fester, and he'll kill you. That's something the rebels never figured out."

Kael nodded absently.

The clouds had retreated and frost-covered blades of grass shimmered in the moon's unfettered glow. The fires from their camp were little more than dots in the distance. He'd wandered too far out, listening to Morris. He knew he ought to turn back ... just a little further, and he would.

"I underestimated him," Kael said bitterly. "I thought the wildmen lost because they didn't know how to battle a real enemy. I had no idea Titus was so ..."

"Smart? Aye, that he is, and he *knows* he is — and it's a cruel sort of smart, too. That's the worst kind, if you ask me," Morris muttered. "But you've held him off well, lad. If anybody's got a half-chance against him, it's you."

Kael wasn't so sure.

They walked in silence for a moment — which seemed to be about the only amount of silence Morris could handle. It wasn't long before his chattering billowed up once more.

447

"I saw an old friend of mine back in that little village. Never thought I'd see him again." Morris's mouth cracked into a wide grin as he looked up at the stars. "I'd always wondered what'd become of Baird."

Kael's stomach twisted into a knot. "You knew him?"

"Aye, he was a bard, back in the old days. When the Whispering War broke out, he signed on as a courier. He was a blasted good one, too," Morris muttered with a shake of his head. "He carried the King's secrets across the realm. He'd stride straight to the front lines with an order to pull back, if he had to. There wasn't a thing he wouldn't have done to save Midlan, and he proved it ... did he show them to you?"

Morris touched a nub to the corner of his eye, and Kael's throat tightened. "He said he cut them out himself."

To his horror, Morris inclined his head. "Gouged them with a rock, he did. Baird could've talked his way out of anything — the rebels only caught him because they stuffed rags in their ears. They were going to turn him over to the Falsewright —"

"Deathtreader, you mean."

The harsh edge of his voice wasn't lost on Morris. The old helmsman sighed. "Figured that out, did you? Well, you're a smart lad. You were bound to find out eventually."

"I wish you would've just told me," Kael said, quickening his pace. Instead of turning back, he marched higher up the slope.

"You wish that, eh?" Morris grunted as he tried to keep up. His breath came out in wheezes. "Well, then ... how come ... you never asked?"

"How could I have thought to ask whether Deathtreader was the one who led the rebel whisperers?" Kael said hotly. "How could I have possibly guessed?"

"I wasn't talking about ... Deathtreader." Morris's crunching steps came to a halt. "I meant ... about *these*."

When Kael turned, Morris was staring at him. He held his gauntlet-capped nubs before his face — a face that Kael likely wouldn't have recognized, had it not been attached to Morris's stocky body. His eyes had sunk so deeply into their

448

pouches that he could barely see them. The mouth beneath his wiry beard hung slack.

"I know Baird's told you," he whispered, his croaky voice broken. "He started singing it the moment Lysander said my name."

Kael felt as if he stared at Morris from the lip of cavern, as if the man he'd known was tumbling out of reach — as if he would soon be lost forever. And more than anything, Kael didn't want that to happen.

He would rather hear a lie.

"It doesn't matter what Baird said to me. If you tell me it isn't true, I'll believe you — or don't say anything at all." Kael took a step towards him, as if that might somehow keep the cavern from devouring his friend. "I'll never ask. I don't have to know."

"It don't work that way, lad."

"No." Kael took a step back. The cavern opened its jaws. "You didn't."

"I did," Morris said quietly. "I did, lad ... I wrote those letters."

# CHAPTER 39
## CHOICES

Kael could think of only one thing to say: "How could you?"

Morris's stocky arms sank lower as his shoulders fell. "I was a fool, simple as that. Crevan asked it of me —"

"And you wagged your tail and went along," Kael said scornfully. "Baird was right to call you the Dog."

"He was. They all were. When Crevan asked me to write those letters, I did just that. But I'm no traitor," Morris said sharply, thrusting a nub at the middle of Kael's chest. "That's something you got to understand, lad."

"Well, I'm having a difficult time believing it."

"The Kingdom was in a bad state," Morris insisted. "The whisperers all scattered after the Falsewright's death. The ones still loyal to Midlan had lost their faith in the crown, and the rebels thought they'd be rounded up and executed —"

"And they were."

"— but Crevan said he wanted the whisperers to come back. He said it was for the Kingdom's sake. He said the regions couldn't survive without their aid, and that the only hope he'd ever have of convincing them is if I did a bit of whispering." His shoulders rose and fell. "I thought they had a chance, lad. What would you have done if you thought your people had a chance of saving themselves? And what if you thought they might miss that chance out of fear?"

Kael said nothing. He didn't know what he would've done, but he was certain he wouldn't have lifted a finger to help Crevan.

"He was different in those days," Morris said quietly, as if he could read the thoughts flickering behind Kael's eyes.

"Banagher did a bad thing, driving the whisperers off. Crevan stood for Midlan when most others fled. He and this sorry clump of outcasts got the nobles rallied and brought the Kingdom back together. They were heroes, lad."

"Kyleigh could see it in him," Kael said vehemently. "She knew Crevan was a liar — she attacked him for it."

"Aye, up in the towers where it was only just the two of them. Nobody in the King's court knew what Kyleigh was. They didn't like her, they didn't trust her. So when Crevan stumbled down the stairs with his face sliced open, who do you think they believed?"

"*You* knew what she was. You told me you knew."

Morris looked away. "Aye ... and so I had more reason than most not to trust her. Look, lad — being a ... a ... well, being what she is didn't exactly help things. We only went along with her because of Setheran. But when we saw what she done to our new King, we thought she was the enemy. It was only after Crevan started to turn that we realized we'd made a mistake.

"He called me into the throne room the evening after Kyleigh fled, I'll never forget it," Morris said somberly. "Crevan begged me to write those letters. He said he wanted to bring the Kingdom back together. And after everything he'd done, I ... well, I believed him.

"Once I'd sealed the last letter, Crevan turned on me. He made sure I couldn't undo it," Morris said, holding up his nubs. "He made sure I couldn't stop him. Then he locked me in one of the tower rooms. He was going to make me watch, see — he was going to stand me up in front of all the whisperers, just before the sword came down, and he was going to make sure they knew it was *me* who'd sold them.

"By the time Setheran found me, it was too late. The letters had already been sent. I told him what I'd done, and he could've killed me then. But instead, he snuck me out. He handed me off to Matteo and told me to keep with the pirates. Then he gave me that wallet," Morris thrust a nub at the throwing knives strapped around Kael's arm, "and he said to

451

me: *you make sure he gets these.* 'Course, I didn't know who *he* was —"

"Wait a moment." Kael had already marched several paces away when a thought struck him. "Setheran died fighting in the Whispering War. There was no way he could've found you *after* ..."

He spun to Morris, who raised his bushy brows. "Died in the war? No. Where'd you hear a thing like that?"

He'd read it in the *Atlas.*

Something that was a mix between anger and shock burned across his face as the realization sank in. "How, then? How did he die?"

"You really want to know, lad?"

He wasn't sure. After what he'd learned about Morris, perhaps it would've been best not to find out. But his curiosity won out over his worry.

Morris sighed when he nodded. "Setheran died in Midlan. He died right there alongside all the other whisperers —"

"But he knew about the trap!" The words burst from Kael's lungs, furious and shocked. "Why in Kingdom's name would he go if he knew? How could he have been so foolish?"

Morris was quiet for a long moment. "I wondered that, too. I couldn't believe it when I heard. Haunted me for years, it did. And then one day, this little redheaded lad from the mountains showed up aboard our ship ... and it all came together."

Kael's mouth went dry. He knew what Morris was going to say before he even spoke. The horrible, icy weight crushed across his back. It made his knees bend in shock ... sagged his heart with anguish.

"His son was dead — leastways, that's what Setheran told us. Said he'd died just days after birth. His whole village mourned him for weeks. I thought maybe he'd been so hurt by it that he'd gone to Midlan as a way of ... ending things," Morris croaked, his voice broken by his whisper. "But the moment I saw you, I knew what they'd done."

"*They?*" Kael's stomach was gone. It'd finally slipped out the bottom of his chest — leaving a ragged, gaping hole behind.

"Setheran and Amelia were well-known in the court," Morris said quietly. "Crevan expected them to come to Midlan. If they hadn't turned up, he would've known something was wrong. Had they run, he would've chased them. The only way they could give you a chance, the only hope they had of keeping you a secret ... they had to make sure Crevan would never go looking for you. They had to let him think he'd won. Don't you see, lad?"

Kael did. He saw it through such a fearsome, angry burst of light that he could hardly think to stand.

There was nothing left inside him ... for he realized that not one thing he'd done was truly his. Every victory belonged to Setheran — payment for the blood he'd wasted. And if he'd ever done anything worth an ounce of good, deserving of the light, then it belonged to Amelia. It all belonged to her.

Kael was a ghost standing upon borrowed ground — one foot supported by the mounds of each grave. And he realized with an anguish that sank him to his knees that he would never be able to repay them. Nothing he ever said or did could possibly measure up to the gift they'd given him.

He would be forever in their debt.

Morris must not have been able to hear the shocked gasps of Kael's heart, because he croaked on without pause: "I know what you're thinking, lad. It's easy to turn your nose up at a story once you've closed the book. You can shake your fists and call us fools — but when you're stuck between the pages, you can't see what's coming. I'd give anything to go back there," Morris whispered, his eyes imploring. "I'd give anything to change what I'd done. But time don't turn back. It only goes forward. Now you know the truth ... so do what you got to do. It'll be what's fair."

He spread his arms to either side, leaving his chest exposed. But Kael shook his head. "I'm not going to kill you."

His mouth fell open beneath his wiry beard. "But, I ... it's my fault, lad. If I hadn't wrote those letters, they never would've had to —"

"It isn't your fault," Kael said sharply — sharp, because he knew the fault was his.

As he stared at the ground between them, he began to understand the weight of blood. It couldn't settle every score. It couldn't right every wrong. Blood, when spilled for a purpose, could be worth its weight in gold. But he'd never much cared for gold.

No, there were far greater treasures to be had ... gifts that only life could give.

"You told me once that I shouldn't regret things, and now I see why. Mistakes are just part of our stories, aren't they? We can't always choose which monsters will rise in our path, but we can choose to face them. Our choices carry us to our ends." Kael looked up and met the old helmsman in his watery eyes. "Time will run out on both of us eventually, Morris. And when it does ... well, I'd rather have you by my side than buried somewhere in the mountains."

Relief washed out over his eyes. He slammed Kael into the middle of his chest, crushing him in a stocky-armed embrace. "And that's right where I'll be, lad. Aye — that's right where I'll be!"

The way Morris had him crushed forced Kael's chin up at the stars. He was staring at the pale flesh of the moon, wondering how he was going to untangle himself, when a shadow crossed through the light.

He recognized the twisted silhouette of one of the Earl's falcons. Its short wings beat furiously and its body bobbed up and down — dragged by the weight of the dark object hanging from its talons.

Kael quickly pulled away from Morris and pointed upwards. The old helmsman's eyes widened. He waved a stocky arm, gesturing for Kael to follow. "Come on, lad. If we're lucky, that little devil'll lead us straight to where Titus is hiding."

"Shouldn't we go back and get the others?"

454

Morris shook his head. "No time. You said you've been wondering why the Earl's gone quiet — this might be our only chance to find out. Pick up your feet," he called as he lumbered up the slope. "You can't let a fellow with no hands and too much belly get out ahead of you!"

*******

The falcon didn't travel far. Kael had expected to jog half the night. But instead, it flapped hardly a mile up the slope before it came back down to earth.

There was a small stone cottage hidden against a rocky face of the mountain. It was only large enough for a handful of men. Kael figured it must've been home to one of the Earl's scouting troops, or perhaps it was worse — perhaps the cottage was merely the head of a larger force. It was close enough to their camp that Titus's men could've traveled there with ease.

The falcon landed clumsily. It hopped up and rammed its head against the cottage's small wooden door. "Rest!" it screeched. "Tired — rest!"

Light streamed sleepily onto the frozen ground as the door's latched window cracked open. Then the whole thing swung on its hinges and one of the Earl's soldiers leaned out. "Have you got it?"

"Yes!"

"Good. There'll be another bird coming by to pick it up in the morning." The soldier bent to work on the object attached to the falcon's claws. There was a muffled *click* and the clink of chains as the object came free.

"Sore!" the falcon screeched as it hopped inside. "Hungry!"

"Yeah, there's vittles on the fire. Make sure you're ready to take off at dawn," the soldier grumbled as he straightened. "Someone's got to keep an eye on those savages over the hill. They've been lurking around here for weeks, now. Makes me nervous. Don't know why his Earlship doesn't just sack them and be done with it ..."

455

His grumbling went on as he ducked through the door, and Kael saw there was a small wooden box hanging from a length of chain in his right hand. He only caught a glimpse of it before the soldier disappeared into the cottage — shutting the door tight behind him.

"What do you suppose that is, lad?" Morris whispered.

Kael wasn't sure. He was thinking about what the soldier had just said — about how he wished Titus would attack them and be done with it. If he'd known where they were camped, why *hadn't* he attacked?

"He's planning another trap," Kael said as he studied the cottage. "And I'll bet it has something to do with whatever's inside that box."

The soldier had said that another bird was coming to retrieve the box in the morning, and dawn was quickly approaching. They didn't have time to return to camp. If he wanted to find out what Titus had planned, he knew he'd have to act quickly.

Morris kept an eye on the door while Kael circled around. The cottage backed up so close to the rock wall behind it that Kael had to turn sideways just to edge through. There were no windows and no other doors. There was only one way in or out of the cottage — and Kael sealed it up.

He molded the door to the frame, molded the frame to the stone. He pressed on the hinges until they were little more than flattened strips of metal. He sealed the door's window to its latching — just enough let it shift, but not enough to open. Then he crept back to Morris.

"I have a plan, but I'm going to need your help."

He was met with a wide, gap-toothed grin. "You know I'll do my bit, lad. Just point me to it."

Once Morris was ready, Kael crept to the back of the cottage. The stone and mortar bent like clay beneath his hands. He dug until there was hardly a fingernail's breadth of wall between himself and the inside of the cottage. Then he waited.

It wasn't long before he heard the hollow *thud* of someone pounding on the door.

456

"All right, all *right!*" one of the guards shouted over the din. There was the stomping of steps and then some frantic rattling. "One of you maggots get up and help me — the blasted latch is stuck again!"

Another set of steps marched towards the first. They struggled for a moment before two more joined them. The latch rattled furiously under their efforts, and the thudding never stopped.

"Clamp it, will you? We're working as fast as we can!"

"Bloody latch ..."

"Well, you can't just rip on it!"

"What does it matter? The blasted thing's probably frozen to the do — ah!"

Kael's arrow struck the nearest man in the back of the neck. He fired through the hole he'd made in the wall, bringing the other three down in a quick series of shots. A fifth man charged wildly into the middle of the room, sword drawn. He wiped at his eyes as if he'd just been sleeping.

An arrow pinned his hand to his face.

"Attack! Fight!"

Kael lurched back and narrowly missed having his face split open by the falcon's twisted beak. It snapped at him, trying to cram its way through. But the hole was too small. It'd leaned back to charge its head against the wall when Kael's arrow struck its middle.

He waited, breathless, in the moments that followed. But he couldn't hear anything over Morris's pounding. When another moment passed and not a shadow moved inside the cottage, he widened the hole and slid through.

The falcon was still alive. Terror ringed its large black pupils and its wings flopped helplessly beside it. Kael didn't want to look — he didn't want to have to watch the light leave its eyes ...

Wait a moment — that wasn't *light*, at all. Kael crept closer, leaning in until he stared straight into the falcon's eyes.

A man's face stared back. His head was suspended in the black depths of the falcon's gaze, floating there without a body. The image wavered like flame battered by the wind. Kael could barely make out the tangled mane of hair, the ragged beard — the cruel mouth that twisted into a grin.

The man's face dissolved into the blackness as the falcon's last breath hissed out of its lungs. Kael was staring so intently at the fading image that he didn't notice the shadow creeping up at his back. He heard the floor planks groan and spun, slinging an arm out behind him.

A sharp, pinching sting bit the flesh below his left shoulder. Kael ripped the hunting dagger from his belt and plunged it blindly through the mass in front of him. There was a moan, a gasp, and then an armor-clad body fell across his chest.

There'd been one more soldier in the room. He stared over the man's shoulder and saw he'd been hiding in a corner behind the jutting edge of the hearth. Kael had just managed to fight his way out from under the soldier's body when the pain struck him.

It was sharp, burning with such a rage that it nearly blinded him. No, it wasn't the pain that made his vision dim: a strange numbness filled his head. It traveled down his limbs, made his hands droop at his sides. His body felt as if he'd just woken from a heavy sleep — as if he had no real control over it, as if his head merely sat atop a tangle of limbs.

Cold whipped through the crack behind him. He could feel the wind's every pointed tooth as it raked down his skin. His teeth chattered uncontrollably. His body shook even though he told it to stop.

There was a dagger stuck below his left shoulder, its blade half-buried in his flesh. Blood wept from the ragged hole at its base — he knew from how steadily the drops came that there was more blood waiting behind it. If he tried to pull the dagger free, he might very well bleed out. Perhaps if he sealed an edge of the wound closed ...

Kael gasped and slumped back. His fingers had done nothing more than pinch fire from his skin. No matter how fiercely he concentrated, he couldn't turn his wound to clay.

He couldn't remember how it felt to mold flesh back together. He couldn't remember how he'd done it.

"Is that all of them, lad?" Morris hissed from around the hole in the wall.

Kael's teeth chattered too badly to answer. What in Kingdom's name was wrong with him? Why had everything gone so cold?

"Are you all right in there? Have you got the —? Kael!"

Morris ducked through the hole and stumbled to his side. His nubs circled helplessly over the half-buried dagger. His eyes went from Kael's chattering teeth to where the soldier had been hiding. He stared inside the small wooden box that lay opened in a shadowed corner of the hearth, and he swore.

"What ...? What's ...?"

"Easy now, lad. Try not to fuss." Morris scooped up armfuls of the soldiers' bedding and began stuffing it inside the hole, silencing the howl of the wind. "You've been poisoned lad — it won't kill you," he said quickly, when he saw the panic on Kael's face. "It's a poison called *mindrot*. Puts us whisperers in a bad way, it does. Mindrot muddles your head. It'll make you human for a bit. You won't be able to use your powers until it wears off."

Once Morris had the hole blocked, he pinched the box between his arms and toted it over to Kael. There was a large vial inside of it, filled nearly to its top with a dangerous-looking purple liquid. The wax seal had been broken over its cork. Kael realized that must've been where the soldier had gotten the mindrot for his dagger.

"One drop is enough to muddle a whisperer ..." Morris swore loudly, gaping down at the box. "There's quite a few drops in here. I don't know what Titus traded for it, but it must've been something grand, indeed. D'Mere's the only one who knows the formula for mindrot," he explained. "And she doesn't hand her vials out lightly."

Kael sank to his knees. So *that* was how the Sovereign Five had managed to keep the rebel whisperers at bay all those years. If mindrot had been able to defeat the whisperers once before, it could do it again.

Titus knew this. He was planning to use it on the wildmen. He hadn't attacked them because he'd been waiting for this vial of mindrot. Now that he had it, he planned to crush the wildmen exactly as he'd crushed the rebels ...

"That isn't blood, is it?"

Kael looked to where Morris pointed and mumbled a curse when he saw the purplish stain spreading over his trousers. "Night-fingers. I promised Griff that I'd ..."

He stopped.

A mad thought came to him suddenly. He fought against the searing pain in his arm and reached inside his trousers. One of the curled roots had burst. It leaked a large amount of purplish juice down his fingers and stained the beds of his nails. But the rest of the roots were intact, still bulging with their liquid innards.

Between his poison and his beasts, Titus had the wildmen trapped. If Kael moved one way, Titus would leap to block him. There would be endless layers to his plan: he would adapt to every shift in their strategy, mold his army to fit against their charge. If the wildmen met Titus in the field, they could end up fighting a battle every bit as eternal as their war with the wynns.

Kael knew he couldn't possibly hope to outwit the man who'd brought the Kingdom to its knees, and so he wouldn't try. He wouldn't fight back.

Instead, he would take a leaf from Setheran's book: he would do exactly what Titus expected him to.

Kael would walk straight into his trap.

# CHAPTER 40
## HERE AT THE END

"Ho, that was a wicked thing you done, lad!" Morris panted, half-laughing as they stumbled down the frozen slopes. "Are you sure he'll find it?"

Kael was positive. He was certain the Earl had been watching him through the falcon's eyes. He'd seen what Kael had done to his soldiers, and he'd likely sent a force to retrieve the vial of mindrot the moment the falcon had perished. When his soldiers arrived, they'd find the vial exactly the way it'd been delivered: corked and with its wax seal melted back into place by the hearth fires. Titus would have no reason to believe anything was amiss.

"How're you holding up, lad?" Morris gasped as they picked their way down a particularly nasty slope.

With darkness shrouding it, he hadn't realized just how treacherous the path to the cottage had been. Now a gray dawn had begun to creep over the horizon. The edge of the path that he'd thought dropped a mere few feet actually dropped several hundred — and there was a field of sharp, ice-covered rocks waiting at its base.

Kael's head spun when he glanced down. "I think I need ... a rest," he managed to say. He felt as if the insides of his throat had frozen over. His breaths slipped clumsily out, and his lungs never seemed to get enough air.

He sat on his knees, careful not to jostle the dagger. They'd managed to bind his left arm against his chest. Morris had held a strip of the soldiers' bedding in place while Kael had woven a very clumsy, one-handed knot around it. The binding wasn't as tight as he would've liked, but at least having his arm pinned would keep the wound from tearing.

"Aye, take a breath," Morris said, propping his nubs on his knees. "But let's make it a quick one — I'll feel better about things once we're back amongst those rock-hurling lads."

Kael agreed. "It shouldn't be far, now. Just a few more ..."

A howl rose over the top of his voice. It trailed faintly in the gray dawn, falling until it disappeared. He hoped he'd only been imagining it, but then it came again — and this time, two others joined it.

Morris's eyes went wide. "What in Kingdom's name — ?"

"Hounds," Kael cried, scrambling to his feet. "It's the Earl's hounds! Run!"

The yelping grew frenzied, rising as the hounds picked up the scent of his blood. Soon the separate wails molded together. They became a never-ending chorus of screams — a tide rising to take them.

Kael urged his legs into a run. He hobbled across the slickened rock, trying desperately to will them on. Every breath stabbed his lungs. The dagger in his arm dug painfully against the ragged ends of his flesh. He felt as if a second dagger had been thrust between his ribs.

Soon his legs shook as he brought them down. The motion of his jog beat his body too roughly. He felt an unnerving warmth trickle down his chest as his wound spat out a fresh helping of gore. Beside him, Morris wasn't faring much better: the old helmsman's gasps had grown so labored that his face was white with the effort.

They might've made it another half mile or so, had Kael not lost his footing.

Rocks beat his back. He curled up as he rolled across the frozen ground, trying to protect his wound. But somehow, he managed to catch the edge of a stone at just the right angle — and he was hurled on top of the dagger.

The blade bit deeper into his flesh; the ragged wound wept freely. Kael cried out as the pain clamped down upon him, trying to fight against the blackness.

462

"Come on, lad!" Morris wheezed. "Come on — throw your arm across me ... there's a good lad. We'll get there ... don't you worry ... we'll ..."

They didn't get far.

Screams burst up the slope. The hounds were so close that Kael could hear the panting between their frenzied cries. At any moment, they would be overtaken. "Morris, you have to go."

"No, lad. I'm not —"

"Go!" Fury raged above Kael's pain, turning his words white-hot. "The hounds can smell my blood. That's the only reason they're after me. They won't stop until they've killed me!"

His shoulder was far too mangled to draw his bow. So he chose a knife from his wallet and tried to ignore the fact that his hand didn't seem to remember how to throw it. Without the warrior in him, he wasn't sure he *could* throw it. But he had to try. "I'll hold them off as long as I can. Once they've got me, they'll go back to Titus. But you've got to run, Morris. You've got to tell the others what we've done."

He took a deep breath. He braced the knife against his knee, holding the point upwards. If he couldn't throw it, then at least he might be able to skewer one of the hounds. If he held it against his chest when they attacked ...

Morris's stocky arm thudded across his shoulder, chasing the darkness back. "All right, lad. I just want you to know ... I want you to know that I was happy to be at your side, here at the end."

Kael took in every edge of his features, every line on his face and every wire of his beard. The light in his watery eyes steeled him, gave him courage — it reminded him of what needed to be done. And he was proud to do it.

Screams split the air between them; the hounds were at the crest of the hill. He could hear their clawed feet scraping against the ground, but he wasn't afraid. "Tell Kyleigh that I love her, all right? Make sure she knows."

Morris gazed up the slope, where three twisted, screaming bodies were tearing down to meet them. And he smiled. "No, I'm not going to do that, lad. You tell her yourself." Then he slammed the blunt of his arm onto the top of Kael's knife.

The blade went through Morris's leather gauntlet and deep inside his wrist. He stood and ripped the knife out with his teeth. A red torrent spewed from the ruptured veins as he lumbered for the cliff. The hounds screamed. Their dark-pitted eyes burned beneath the folds of skin on their faces. Their claws screeched against the rocks as they turned from Kael and headed straight for Morris.

The old helmsman stopped at the edge. He turned his back on the hundreds-foot drop and the jagged rock field beneath him so that he could fix Kael with one final, gap-toothed grin.

"You finish it, lad!" he called, raising his blood-soaked arm. "You finish what we started!"

The hounds crashed into him. They swallowed his stocky body and tumbled over the edge, ripping the whole way down. The faint *thud* at the bottom of the cliff broke Kael from his shock.

He screamed.

*******

"No! *No!*" Titus's fists pounded into the arms of his throne as the last of his hounds perished and their windows went dark.

He'd had him. He'd *had* him! Stupid, blood-mongering beasts. He'd led them straight to the Wright, he'd held so tightly to their chains — he'd *willed* their legs to pound! Then they'd ripped from his grasp at the last moment, charging after that worthless, crippled pirate ...

Titus pulled roughly on his tangled beard, trying to force himself to calm. This chance might've been taken from him, but there would be others. His greatest weapon had yet to be unleashed. One of the falcons had arrived at the cottage ahead of the hounds. He'd found the vial intact.

464

*The moment will come,* he reminded himself as he paced. *The victory is all but assured. Be patient.*

"Your Earlship?" A soldier leaned cautiously around the door. "It's one of the beasts, Earlship. He wants to speak with you."

"Send him in." Titus leaned back on his heels as his most powerful creation stalked into the room.

He'd been right about the man named *Marc.* The weakness of his spirit meant his body had been easily twisted. Sorrow and hate had devoured him at the Tree — spitting out a creature that was a reflection of everything Titus could've ever asked for in a warrior. Had he been able to split his soldiers open and pull out their souls, he imagined they'd all look like Marc.

"What is it, beast?" Titus said.

Marc sat on his haunches before the throne. His monstrous claws rested, curled upon the ground beside him. He spoke clumsily around his fangs: "I have information for you, Earlship."

Odd. Titus hadn't remembered seeing anything through Marc's eyes that he thought might be useful. Then again, he rarely looked. For all his hulking size, Marc's vision was disappointingly dim. He feared the pain that might come from his collar if he ever disobeyed a command, so Titus never had to hold his chain too tightly.

"What do you have to offer me?"

"Memories," Marc grunted. "I know the boy who leads the savages — I remember him."

Titus leaned forward, trying to keep his face as smooth as possible. "I see. And how are your memories supposed to help me?"

"You want him stopped. I know how to stop him."

Titus snorted. "I've already got him beaten. His army will be helpless against the bite of my poison. Once I've weakened them, I'll have my pick of skulls to crush."

"He's too sly, Earlship," Marc said. "You've got to dig your fangs into his throat and keep them there. Give him a breath, and he'll crush you with it."

These were echoes of the worries that plagued Titus's sleep — the whispered ends of all the little things that might go wrong. The Wright had already proven himself to be rather slippery. If there were any way to ensure he would fall, Titus would gladly take it.

"Tell me, beast — how do I hold him by the throat? How do I make sure he never breathes again?"

"You've got something of his, Earlship ... you've got Amos. March that old coot outside, and he'll walk straight into your hands."

"The healer?" Titus breathed. "What would the Wright want with a common healer?"

"That's not just any healer, Earlship." Marc's fanged lips twisted into a wicked grin. "It's his grandfather."

*******

Kael wasn't sure how long he walked. It seemed as if he collapsed at every few steps — and each time he fell, he swore it took the last of his strength to pull himself up. But somehow, he found more. There was always more. No matter how much he'd given, he found he always had a little left to give.

Kael's knees struck the ground again. He clutched at the dagger in his shoulder, holding it in place as he prepared to drag himself to his feet. *Finish what you started*, he thought to himself. *Finish it — do it for Morris.*

The force of that thought pulled him up, held him steady. He shoved the little black spots aside and willed his legs to carry him on. They were numb — either from the cold, the loss of blood, or the crushing weight inside his heart ... he wasn't sure.

His legs fumbled a paltry few steps before he found himself sinking again. The ground was rushing up; the black was creeping in. His knees were inches from the rock when a pair of strong hands caught him under the arms.

"Well, look what I've found — a ragged little mountain mutt."

"Gwen," Kael moaned.

She grabbed him under the knees and scooped him into her arms, carrying him like a child. Her neck arched back and she let out a sharp whistle.

A hawk screeched in reply.

"Evening ... wing ..."

"He went out looking for you this morning — followed your trail, saw what a state you were in, and came screeching to the first person he could find. Lucky for you, I was hunting nearby," she said with a smirk. "I'm disappointed, mutt. I thought you'd grown out of moaning over flesh wounds."

Kael's anger cut through the pain. "It's not just a wound ... it's poison."

Gwen pursed her bluish-black lips. "Like wynn venom? Then why aren't you dead?"

"It's not that kind of poison," Kael said evenly. "It's like venom for whisperers ... a poison that keeps me from using my powers."

Her pace slowed considerably. "I think you'd better explain yourself, mutt."

He did — or he tried to, anyways. It wasn't easy to get Gwen to understand what he'd seen at the cottage, and how what he'd seen meant that Titus had a plan for them. When he got to the part of what he'd done to the poison, she let out a frustrated growl.

"Why didn't you just throw it in the fire and be done with it?"

"Things will be better this way. You'll see," Kael insisted when she rolled her eyes.

At least she understood what had happened to Morris. Her grip on him had tightened to the point it was almost painful by the time he'd finished speaking, but he didn't mind it. Focusing on how hard her fingers dug in kept the darkness from swallowing his heart.

"We're going to stomp him," Gwen snarled.

For once, Kael didn't argue: "We're going to do more than that — the mountains will run red with Titus's blood."

They walked in a smoldering silence for a while before a rumbling growl made him flinch. Kael raised his head enough to see Silas the lion striding out in front of them.

"Have you forgiven him, then?"

Gwen sighed heavily. "When my brother got ... lost, it was the cat who found him in the woods. That's how Griffith knew his name — Silas must've stayed with him all night. So as much as I wanted to crush his furry little skull for deceiving me," her hands tightened again, "I couldn't. Not after I realized that he'd protected Griffith. Instead, I've decided to punish him by binding him in service to the wildmen. He'll do exactly as I say until his debt is paid. Or I *will* crush him."

Silas's eyes glowed haughtily as he glanced over his thick shoulders, and his tail swished in an unconcerned loop.

# CHAPTER 41
## MISGUIDED COURAGE

High in one of Midlan's winding towers, Argon the Seer was more frustrated than ever.

The book that'd once been so troubling now lay open before him. The words were no longer sealed, but written plainly. He'd read *The Myth of Draegoth* once already, expecting some great secret to come pouring out from between its pages. But instead, he'd found the tale to be disappointingly vague.

There was very little information at all about the monsters called *draega* — the beasts that'd inhabited Draegoth before the rise of the first King. A precious few lines mentioned the draegas' *savage ways* and their *dark, terrifying magic*. Even the pictures showed them as nothing more than the shadows dancing around yellow flame.

No, Argon realized early into his reading that he would gain very little knowledge of the draega from this book. He wished there'd been more lines dedicated to the history of the tale ... and far fewer on the illustrious nature of the first King.

The book droned on about him, talking of how he'd come to the Kingdom from the barren Westlands — seeking a new life for his people. The historians bemoaned the fact that no matter how the King tried to befriend them, the draega refused to turn from their savagery. And so he'd been forced to lay siege to their royal city of Draegoth:

*By his magic had the King conquered the whole Wildlands, but not even his mages could stand against the draega. Their champion would rise from the city's white walls, using the deep night as his cloak. He laid waste to the King's army with a single spell — devouring both flesh and steel. So great were the champion's powers that whole of the King's mighty army trembled at his coming.*

*As night passed into day, mankind was forced to see how the draega had ravaged them. The King knew he could not breach the city's walls until the champion was slain. So in his wisdom, he sought the advice of his archmage — who knew at once what must be done.*

*From the bonds of magic pure and earth's most gleaming vein, the archmage did forge the King's salvation: a protection called the Dragonsbane.*

This was the part of the story that had Argon most puzzled. He wondered what sort of magic the draega might posses that a mage would not. There was no doubting that the chamber Crevan had led him to was heavily spelled — crusted in symbols written to seal in a powerful enemy ... but which enemy?

Surely not the child they'd discovered hiding in the ruins. Argon was certain he had no gift for magic of any sort, least of all one that might strike fear into the hearts of mages. No, he was certain the boy was perfectly, completely harmle —

A loud *whoosh* startled him, followed by a flash of light from under his door. Argon cursed as he threw it open. He stumbled out into the tower's main room and clawed his way through a cloud of rather foul-smelling smoke — already dreading the damage.

A handful of young mages clumped tightly in a far corner of the room. They whirled around at the noise of Argon's shuffling steps. He knew things were going to be dismal when he saw the guilt staining each of their faces. But it wasn't until they parted to let him through that he saw their latest mess.

How many times had he warned them? *You can't drop lion's teeth into a cauldron with troll blood*, he clearly remembered saying. But of course, they'd had to try it for themselves.

He supposed he should've expected nothing less from a roomful of young mages — especially ones who'd spent their lives bound in service to the King. Their studies had been neglected straight though their most formative years. None of them had developed enough to forge his own impetus. Each one still carried a wooden staff: a coarse vessel whittled by an older mage and inscribed with only the most basic of spells.

As the last of the mages parted and Argon got a clear look at what they'd done, he couldn't help but be a little proud. One of mages had actually thought to cast a shielding spell around the cauldron. It was very crudely-drawn and leaking slightly out the bottom. But for the moment, the bulk of the disaster was contained within an orb of swirling, foul-looking smoke.

"Now do you understand why I warned you not to do this?" Argon said, fixing as many of them with a scolding look as possible. "You're fortunate that shield survived the blast. Otherwise, you might've put a hole in the tower's roof. That certainly would have attracted the King's attention. Do you want him locking you up again?"

They shook their heads, and several of them glanced nervously at the smoke orb. After a considerable amount of tugging on the curls of her hair, one mage-girl finally worked up the nerve to raise her hand.

"Not until I'm finished," Argon said firmly.

Her hand slid down.

"I need you all to pay very close attention. My neck is stretched out just as far as it will go. The King's only allowed you in here because he believes we're working to solve his problem. One more misstep and I'll have no choice but to — in a *moment* young lady!"

"Please, Master Argon, I think you should know ..."

When the mage-girl glanced anxiously at the orb, it finally struck him. "Who's in there?" Argon said, doing a quick head count. When he noticed which head *wasn't* among them, he let out a string of curses and sent an arrow spell into the side of the orb.

It popped like a soap bubble, bathing them all in a thick cloud of smoke. Argon pinched his nose closed against the odor of burnt troll and stumbled his way towards the cauldron. "Devin ... gah! Devin, can you hear me?"

"I'm right here."

Half a step more and Argon collided with what appeared to be a man-sized stuffed doll. The young mages had Devin wrapped in several layers of gauze. Ice spells and shielding charms had been scrawled clumsily across each layer. It took Argon nearly a full minute of unwrapping just to find Devin's face. When he finally managed to pull the last layer free, he was relieved to see that the boy looked mostly unharmed.

For all the mischief they caused, the young mages had proven themselves to be very useful in one matter: they'd gotten Devin to speak.

Argon had known nothing at all about the boy they'd found living inside the fortress's hidden courtyard. He'd tried several times to ask him questions, to no avail. For days on end the boy had simply gazed around the tower, his mouth opened in wonder at all of Argon's books and instruments.

But he seemed to enjoy magic, and he liked the young mages. It wasn't long before Argon heard him chatting with the others, asking all sorts of questions about the spells they cast. And he'd made it a point to listen in whenever he could.

That was how he'd discovered the boy's name was Devin. Other than that, he'd learned precious little — except that he'd lived with his mother inside the courtyard, and they had a garden where they grew fruits and vegetables.

Argon stripped the rest of the gauze away and bellowed for someone to open a window. When he'd sent the last of the foul smoke out into the weather, he fixed the young mages with an iron gaze.

"He is *not* a plaything."

"We're sorry, Master —"

"*Sorry* won't bring him back," Argon said over the top of them. He let them stew in their guilt for a moment before he dropped his voice to a more scathing level. "I'm disappointed in you — every one of you. You all know better than to use a human for an experiment. The next mage I catch tampering with Devin will have his impetus locked away for a week. Understood?"

They nodded stiffly. Several of them clutched their staffs tighter against their chests.

"Good. Now I would like you all to march down to the library and compose an essay on the dangers of mixing maleficent ingredients — by *hand*. No writing spells," he added, stirring up a fresh wave of groans as they filed out the door.

Once they were gone, Argon dropped the gauze into the cauldron and set its contents ablaze. It was a cleansing fire — a spell of flame linked to one for drawing poisons out of wounds. It ate the potion and the spells off the wrappings, all without producing one wisp of smoke.

He could feel the weight of Devin's strange blue eyes upon him while he worked. "It isn't their fault. I volunteered."

Argon snorted. "Yes, in the same way a fledgling volunteers to be first out of the nest — with a good deal of misguided courage."

"What does that mean?"

Argon gestured at the smoke-soiled walls. "When you volunteered, did you know that you might die in a fiery blast with enough malevolent heat to turn your very bones to ash?"

"Well, no."

"Then I would say you were misinformed. And your courage, then, misguided."

It wasn't only magic that Devin seemed oblivious to: it was as if ... well, as if he'd been locked up somewhere that stood still while the Kingdom grew up all around him. When he thought about it that way, Argon supposed he should've expected nothing less.

And he knew he should try to be a little more patient.

Devin was missing most of his left eyebrow — which gave him a rather quizzical look. He touched the raw skin around his brow and cheek. There were other patches down his arms.

Argon sighed. "You were fortunate, child. Very fortunate, indeed. Those young ones can hardly stitch two spells together without causing some sort of fiery burst."

Devin shrugged, as if a violent magical death was simply a part of life. He wandered over to the cauldron, scratching madly at his collar as he went.

One of the first things Argon had done was throw Devin's rat-hide attire into the hearth. He replaced them with a plain tunic and breeches — and though Devin seemed to like the breeches, he often went without his shirt.

The male mages didn't seem to notice. In fact, Argon doubted if *he* would have ever noticed, had a young female mage not wandered into his office one day and asked if he knew anything about mixing love potions. When Argon had looked up to frown at her, he'd noticed that a small crowd of tittering mage-girls had gathered around Devin.

They'd been pretending to have trouble opening their vials and had all but trapped Devin in a corner of the room, begging for his help. The giggling that ensued each time he pulled a cork free had been enough to make Argon grind his teeth — and poor Devin had looked absolutely terrified.

The whites had shown the whole way around his stark blue eyes as he uncorked the next vial. He'd offered it to a mage-girl at the head of the line and flinched under the others' giggles — as if he expected them to swarm at any moment.

Most young men in the Kingdom would've been thrilled with half of the attention, but Devin had seemed to be on the verge of tears. And Argon realized he would never get any studying done with so much laughter billowing up every few minutes.

So he'd told the curious mage-girl that he actually knew a great deal about love potions — and warned that if he ever caught her trying to mix one, he'd make sure she fell madly in love with the royal beastkeeper.

That threat alone would've likely been enough to keep the girls from toying with Devin's heart. But Argon had ordered him to wear his shirt at all times, just in case.

Now the strange young man from the courtyard seemed perfectly at home amongst the mages. He dug through the wrappings Argon had set ablaze — searching for char marks. When he found none, he shook his head. "Amazing."

A few of Argon's instruments had tipped over during the blast. He was settling them upright when he suddenly had an idea. "Have you not seen magic before, Devin?"

He shook his head.

"Really? None at all?" When he shook his head again, Argon decided it was time to simply ask — the worst the boy could do was ignore him. "That courtyard where you lived ... were those truly the ruins of ...?"

He couldn't say it. The shackle around his wrist burned hot the moment he thought of bringing the word *Draegoth* to his tongue. Crevan had ordered him never to speak of it to anybody, and his command burned hot. Still, he thought there might be a way around it. "Were those ruins truly your home?"

"That *is* my home," Devin muttered as he fiddled with the dials on a golden spyglass. "It isn't ruined."

"Are you one of the draega, then?"

Devin froze. His ghostly stare wrapped tightly about Argon, measuring him. "My mother warned me this would happen someday. She said the people who locked us away would come for us, and they would question us ... and she said that I wasn't to answer them."

From the way he'd spoken, Argon half-expected him to turn on his heel and march into another room. But he didn't. Instead, he stayed frozen in place. "Forgive me, child. You've spent enough time around the mages to know what curious creatures we are."

After a moment, Devin sighed. "I know."

"Would you permit me one final question?"

His gaze seemed to churn as he considered it. The little flecks of white set against the blue appeared to drift slowly in an arc around his pupil. "I trust you more than I trust Your Majesty. One more question."

Argon thought carefully. He'd spent hours trekking through the courtyard at the King's command, searching for others who might've been hiding amongst the ruins — wondering if perhaps he would come across the mother Devin had spoken of. But though he'd cast spells for light and life, there'd only been Devin.

"What happened to the ... others? What became of your family?"

He shrugged. "They died. My mother used to say all her children were like the wildflowers: beautiful while they bloomed, but lasting only a season. I've already lived half my life."

That couldn't be possible. Devin was only just a man — he hadn't even quite gotten his beard. "Forgive me, but you must be mistaken. If your lives were truly so short, your people would've perished centuries ago."

Devin smirked. "You didn't know my mother." All at once, the calm blue of his eyes coiled tightly. "That token Your Majesty took from me belonged to my father — it's the only thing I have of him. I promised my mother I would keep it close. I want it back."

It took Argon a moment to realize what he was talking about. "I can't help you, child."

"Why not? You can use magic."

Argon sighed. "There are chains on my wrists as well — you just can't see them."

No expression crossed his face. There was no anger, no frustration or fear. Devin simply walked away.

He went to the window and laid his hands upon the seal. He pressed his head against the glass and leaned heavily, as if he wished he could tumble out into the world beyond. The stark eyes beneath his brows roved to watch the courtyard.

Soldiers were gathered around a team of carts. They hauled supplies up by thick ropes and covered them in tarps. They were preparing for the King's journey into the northern swamps, making certain that all their food and shelter would be protected from the damp air.

"It's a short journey," Argon said as he watched over Devin's shoulder. "The King has made it many times."

That was as comforting as he dared to be. It would've been unkind to say that the journey would be easy, or that Devin would return. He wished he could scry the boy's future, but Fate's presence sat too heavily upon the Kingdom, now. The waters of his bowl remained pitch black and still.

"Will I ever see you again?"

It wasn't a question Argon had been expecting to hear, and he wasn't exactly prepared to answer. "I don't know, child. The future is a fickle thing ..." He cleared his throat. "But I hope you will."

"I hope that, too," Devin said quietly. "You've been kind to me."

After that, the days passed all too quickly. The young mages kept including Devin in their experiments, blissfully unaware that he would soon be taken from them. Argon listened to their chatter as often as he could. When the curtains caught flame, he didn't scold them quite so harshly.

Perhaps it was cruel to keep them from the truth. But he thought it would've been far crueler to force them to live with the knowledge that Devin was going away ... and that even if he returned, he would never be the same.

When the sun finally dawned upon that dreaded morning, the young mages were still asleep in their chambers. Argon woke to pounding upon the door and opened it reluctantly. A pair of soldiers pushed their way through and grabbed Devin by the arm.

"Not until I've said my goodbyes." Argon spoke calmly, but the look on his face made the soldiers think twice. They released Devin and waited grumpily by the door.

"Farewell, child."

He didn't reply. But then again, he didn't have to: the boy's deep blue stare pierced Argon straight through the heart. He felt reluctance in every fleck of white, sadness buried in the rifts that burst from his pupils. There was a reflection of all the chains that wrapped around them both — that forced them into tasks they'd never wanted.

After a silent moment, Devin walked to the soldiers without fear. One of them grabbed him roughly. But instead of trying to pull away, he latched onto the soldier's arm — like a child might've latched to his mother.

"Be kind to that boy," Argon said when the soldier looked up in surprise.

He wasn't sure if it was the warning in his voice or Devin's stare that did the trick, but the soldiers were much more careful than usual as they led him away.

Argon watched the King's caravan from the window. He frowned as Devin was hobbled and tossed inside one of the carts. When the caravan rolled from the courtyard, Argon's hands curled rather unexpectedly into fists. He'd watched the King haul countless men to meet the same fate — and though he'd hurt for them, he knew in his heart it would do no good to be angry. Everything happened on a roll of Fate's die, after all. In the end, she had a purpose for all living things.

But as the caravan's tail disappeared through the gates, he began to feel something he'd not felt in a long while. It was an emotion he preferred to cover over with peace — the knowing that all would be as Fate intended.

Now that peace had vanished, replaced by a doubt that burned dark and fierce. Argon was not content to simply allow the die to fall. For the first time in a long while, he hoped that Fate knew what she was doing.

# CHAPTER 42
## REMARKABLE FRIENDS

*Kyleigh ... Kyleigh!*

The ice broke. A spray of bubbles clouded her vision as something plunged beneath the flow. They hissed and dissipated into the blue, revealing the spread fingers of an outstretched hand.

Kyleigh flew towards the hand, ripped along by the river's fury. If she could grasp it, she'd be saved. She tried to will herself to move, will her arm to stretch and her hand to reach. But the cold was far too great. She couldn't feel her muscles well enough to urge them on.

And while she struggled, the hand whipped by.

It was the only dream she seemed able to have — this one flash of color in an eternal darkness, this one chance to pull her soul from sleep. Each time she missed, Kyleigh was plunged into the black once more. There was no sight or sound, nothing to grab onto. She hung listless in the depths for countless hours, waiting for the dream to come again.

An age passed before she heard the waters roaring against her ears. Pressure filled her nose and pulled hard against her lips. Her eyes flashed open to a world wrought in shades of greens and blues.

Twin shadows passed above her, the gallop of footsteps across the ice. She heard the muffled sound of her name as the shadows thundered overhead, and she ... she turned to follow them.

This was new. Instead of waiting for the river to twist her around, she'd twisted on her own. Now she watched as the shadows stopped ahead of her. She knew that hand would be plunging into the water at any moment — and this time, she would be ready.

Her fingers cracked open, bursting through the frosted shell that'd settled over her skin. Her mind felt sharper: she was no longer a listless thing passed between the worlds of light and darkness, but a prisoner mindful of her cage.

She would escape. She would pull her soul from the depths.

With the force of this thought came a little warmth. Heat pressed against her palms and circled, spreading out to her fingertips. She moved her hand. Her arm followed after. She heard the ice shatter and saw the spray of foam. Her lips parted and a stream of bubbles *whoosh*ed out as she swung herself forward.

In the split second before she reached the hand, the world went dark once more ... but she'd made it. She must have. Even in the dark, she could feel the hands in hers. They were numb at first: things she thought didn't belong to her. When the fingers brushed against her palm, she knew it for certain.

Feeling came back to her slowly. A song drifted across Kyleigh's ears — muddled by the distance, growing clearer as she listened. Strange words carried by a familiar voice. They sunk beneath the dream and teased her with their dancing notes. She followed the voice to the edge of darkness, chasing until a seal broke over her lungs.

They expanded, breathing in an air with taste and scent. Her first breath surprised her. The second carried with it a wakefulness that spread quickly to her limbs.

Kyleigh's body was trembling, shivering with cold. There were warm patches on either side of her. They'd begun to thaw her at the edges. Her lungs took in an air that smoldered with heat. It spread warmth through her blood and melted the frost that'd formed inside her chest.

Flames grew in her middle until they touched the warm patches on either side. Fingers pressed against her palms in slow, circling movements. The smallness of their touch matched the strange words in the song. Kyleigh thought she might've fallen into another dream. Just to be sure, she closed around the hands twined in hers, brought them closer ...

The song stopped with a gasp.

Kyleigh groaned as the warm patch in front of her pulled away suddenly. Cooler air rushed in, startling her eyes awake.

Dark strands of hair fell loose from her silver clasp, but couldn't quite shadow the sparks in her eyes. Nadine wrapped her arms about Kyleigh's neck and plunged her head forward until her ears were filled with the wild thudding of a tiny heart.

"She is awake!" Nadine cried.

"Thank Fate. I was about to die from the heat." The warm patch behind Kyleigh rolled away. A hand came up and patted her lightly on the shoulder. "I'm glad you didn't die."

"Me too, Elena," Kyleigh said. Her voice was hoarse — half from sleep, and half from being pressed so tightly against Nadine. Her scent was much stronger than it'd been before. She realized her ear was pressed against bare skin. "Nadine, are you ... naked?"

She pushed Kyleigh away and pulled a fur blanket up to her chin. "We had to keep you warm."

"Oh dear, I can see I've been a very bad influence on you," Kyleigh teased. "Now you've gone and broken all sorts of rules."

Nadine scowled at her grin. "This does not count. They said there was ice on your bones, and that the warmth of other bodies would keep your blood from freezing —"

"I'm honored." Kyleigh braved the cooler air outside the blankets to clasp Nadine on the shoulder. "Truly, I am. In all my years, I'm not sure I've done enough to deserve such remarkable friends." She lay back and closed her eyes against the orange light. "Now ... would you care to tell me how in blazes the two of you came to be in the Unforgivable Mountains?"

It sounded as if they'd had a rather wild adventure. Kyleigh's heart fell when she heard of the Valley peoples' plight, but rose again at the battle with the bandits. She laughed outright when Elena told her that Jake had unwittingly burned Crow's Cross to the ground.

"He was angry with me for ages about that," she muttered, staring up at the stone ceiling. Her arms were propped behind her head and the furs pulled over her chest. The dark edge of her eyes softened a bit as she spoke. "I think he realized after a while ... well, death is just a part of life, isn't it? The more evil we get out of the way, the happier life will be. *That's* what gives us peace."

They talked for a while more, trading stories while Kyleigh tried to remember how to use all of her limbs. Then a sudden knocking on the door threw her friends into a panic.

Elena tossed a heavy pelt over Kyleigh's head and held her close while Nadine shouted: "Come in — *quickly*! Do not leave the door open for long."

There was a creak and a blast of icy air. Kyleigh realized that her body hadn't quite recovered from the frost. Her joints remembered the ache of cold and seized up quickly, even with Elena covering her.

Fortunately, the door slammed shut as quickly as it'd opened. The familiar noise of boots clomping across the floor told her it was Gwen. "Supper's here. It got frostbitten on the way over. I'll set it in the coals for a while, but ..."

Elena pulled the pelt off Kyleigh's face and the pot Gwen had been holding slipped out of her hands. It hit the stone floor with a *clang* and broth splattered in every direction.

For a moment, the whites around her eyes showed starkly against the black swirls of her paint. Then she glared. "I groan to think of how many spools of thread Fate wasted on your tapestry, pest."

"I've missed you too, love," Kyleigh said with a grin.

Surprisingly, Gwen smirked back. "Yes, and speaking of ... tapestries," she said, holding the word with an edge that made Kyleigh bristle, "the mutt will want to know that you're awake. I'll go get him."

"No, I'll go."

Elena ripped the blankets aside and — judging by how quickly Nadine covered her eyes — she wasn't wearing much.

Gwen made a frustrated sound. "How many times must I swear on the graves of my fathers that your companions are safe?"

There was the rattle of armor, then a *click* as Elena strapped her daggers into place. "I don't trust you around my mage — *the* mage. That mage, I mean ..." Her words trailed into a string of curses and she stormed away.

"That's still going on, is it?" Kyleigh whispered.

Nadine grinned from behind her hands.

Gwen scooped the pot off the floor and set it in the coals. "Fine. Then I'll at least tell my wildmen that you're awake," she muttered.

Grit rained down from the ceiling as Elena pounded on the door. This time when it opened, Kyleigh kept her head above the covers.

From a distance, the door seemed to be made from a solid slab of wood. As she watched, the wood peeled back like a curtain and Gwen and Elena slipped through the narrow opening left behind. She saw the painted hands of a craftsman molding the door back into place, sealing out the cold.

"This used to be a cave with a mouth opened to the weather. But Kael and his people — these wildmen — shaped it until that hole was all that remained."

Nadine pointed up at the ceiling, where a gap the size of a man's torso stood out against the rock. A pit of burning coals sat in the middle of the cave's floor. Smoke trailed from its fiery bed and drifted out the hole in steady tendrils.

"They have sealed the door to the stone so that not even a cold breath may enter. It is remarkable, this magic. Now, you will cover your eyes while I dress — I would hate to have to gouge them out," she said with mock severity.

Kyleigh sighed, but did as she was told.

Once Nadine had pulled on her clothes, it was time for the challenging bit. The cold had done more than freeze

Kyleigh: her muscles were weak and her joints groaned in protest at even the slightest movement. She felt as if she'd been lying around on the floor for years. But she was determined to stand.

No sooner had she risen to her feet than Nadine clothed her with furs, pulling on such a variety of dead animals that Kyleigh couldn't quite pick out all of their scents. Her knees bent with the added weight and she sat down heavily, struggling to catch her breath.

Though Nadine was vehemently against it, Kyleigh got back to her feet. She leaned against the wall for balance while Nadine swathed her in yet another layer of furs. She'd just wrapped a pelt about her shoulders when a wild chorus of howls sounded from beyond the door.

"Gwen has told her people. It will not be long before Kael is here." Nadine's hands gripped Kyleigh's arms and when she spoke, her voice was in earnest: "I know you must be grateful to him, but do not do anything ... rash."

It took Kyleigh a moment to understand the worry behind her eyes. "Wait — so you're saying I *shouldn't* chop off my hair and ask him to marry me?"

"Your insolence knows no bounds!" Nadine said. She smiled the whole way to the door. "I am glad to see you again."

"I'm glad to see you too, Nadine."

The door opened and her little friend from the desert vanished with a blast of cold. The moment she was gone, there was nothing left to distract her. Kyleigh nearly collapsed against the wall.

Twin rivers raged inside her chest, warring against each other. One was deep and calm: the dragon in her knew what Kael had done, and accepted it with love. But the human side of things was a different matter.

Kyleigh wasn't used to being saved. She hated feeling weak — hated the idea that, had it not been for someone else's pity, she might've drawn her last breath. This river raged more furiously than its brother. Its white-capped waters plunged over jagged rocks and slapped against the shores. It would not bend, would not be swayed. Its flow would break for no one.

*Shallow, though*, the dragon in her said. *For all its fury, those waters are shallow — more foam than depth.*

Half of her heard the wisdom, but the other half still worried. She wanted to be able to keep Kael's stride. She didn't want to slow him down. Would he think less of her now?

Was *that* what the river had been roaring about?

A sudden creak of wood peeling from the cave's mouth startled her. She watched as Kael stepped inside — watched the careful movements of his hands as he sealed the door behind him. She stared at the high arches of his brows as he spun because she was too afraid of what she might see in his eyes. She plugged her ears against the proud roar of the river and took a deep breath.

"Kael, I want to thank —"

Her words caught in her throat. His arms were wrapped about her middle. Their hearts collided as he pressed his chest into hers. His grip was stronger than it'd been before, but no tighter. She let her face rest against his neck and steeled herself against the things that might be rushing through his veins.

Relief was all she felt: the song of rain striking the barren earth, a burst of the sun's light as it broke from behind the clouds. His joy rose beneath her and filled her to the top, straining until she could no longer hold it in.

"Why are you crying? *I'm* the one who should be crying!" Kael said with a gasping laugh.

"You should be, but you're too stubborn," Kyleigh said back. "Someone's got to cry. So now I'm crying for both of us!"

He pressed his sleeve against her cheek, drying her tears. Tiny white flakes clung to his jerkin.

"It's snowing?"

He nodded. "It started falling about an hour ago. The wildmen had this mourning ceremony all arranged, with drums and songs — it was supposed to be a very solemn thing, mind you. They were going to weep all afternoon about

485

how Fate has forsaken the earth and let winter in." Kael shook his head. His lips tightened around his smile, and she knew he was fighting back a laugh. "Then Jonathan got involved. Now they're singing about pirate grog and toothless women — and bosoms, of course."

"Naturally," Kyleigh said with a grin. "It wouldn't be a proper mourning ceremony without at least one mention of bosoms."

Kael groaned and shook his head, but his smile never faded. He eased her onto the ground — which was rather alarming, given the fact she hadn't realized he'd been holding her up. "You ought to rest."

That was the last thing she wanted. "I've been lying around for days. Why don't ..." She cleared her throat, pushing the dragon's wisdom aside long enough to force out a few reckless words: "I don't suppose you'd stay with me for a while, would you?"

He glanced at the door. "I don't know ... I might get my head cracked open."

The lights in his eyes flared brightly — a playful smirk. He was teasing her again. Blazes, she hated when he did that. It made her want to grab him by the curls and draw his smile out, to bend his lips with hers.

But she couldn't. And she found that to be rather ... frustrating. "Let me worry about Nadine." She slapped a hand against the floor beside her. "Sit, whisperer."

He did. They talked for a few moments, their conversation trailing as lightly as the smoke. But it wasn't long before their words grew solemn.

Kyleigh clenched her fists tightly in her lap when Kael told her of what he'd found inside the scouts' cottage a few miles from their camp. He spoke of how he'd been wounded, how he'd stumbled down the mountain, and her fists clenched tighter.

"If it hadn't been for that blasted slip, I could've kept going. It wasn't as bad as it sounds — honestly," he added when he saw her glare.

She knew it'd been far worse than it sounded. Whisperers crumbled so easily under the mindrot poison. Had his body not been so strong, Kael might've been unable to move. The winter might've frozen him to the rocks.

Her heart pounded weakly as his story went on. When the hounds barreled towards them, his eyes grew dull. The light faded back and she could sense how the tale would end. Her heart dropped when he told her of what had become of Morris.

"Did you ... know?" Kael whispered, his eyes on the coals.

She'd known some of the story, but hadn't known all of it. For some reason, her memories had stopped the moment she attacked Crevan. She'd heard bits of what had happened to the whisperers and the nobles over the years. The fractured edges of what she'd known and what she'd heard made the truth seem muddled.

But there was one thing she knew for certain:

"Morris always regretted his role in the whisperers' trap. He was a good man. I wouldn't have brought you to him if I didn't trust him. But he'd lived with his regret for years. In a lot of ways, I think his teaching you gave him a chance to ... make amends."

"I hope so." Kael gripped the top of his legs tightly as he added: "I would speak for him."

"I know you would. And you'd be right to."

Kael nodded slowly, his gaze still distant. His hand went inside his pocket and returned with a small, black jewel — the two-headed crystal Kyleigh had found among the ruins of Baron Sahar's castle. "It was in your armor pocket. I kept it with me while you slept. And as you're always nicking things from me, I didn't figure you'd mind," he added as he handed it back. "Is it special?"

"It's called starlight onyx," she said quietly. There were a few stars peeking through the hole in the roof. Kyleigh held the jewel up to them and its blackened flesh began sparkling with their light. "I thought it was a clever thing."

"It is," he agreed. His mouth parted slightly and as he leaned to look through the jewel, his shoulder brushed against hers. "Setheran wrote me a letter."

It was such a sudden thing, and she'd been so focused on *not* edging closer to him that it took her a moment to grasp what he'd said. "Well ... what did he write about?"

"I don't know. I haven't opened it." Kael pulled a small, folded letter from his other pocket. She smelled the heavy musk of its age and saw how the color had faded from its seal. "He'd hidden it inside the *Atlas*."

Kael held the letter strangely. It sat in the middle of his palm instead of between his fingers. "You don't mean to read it."

His mouth fell in a stern line. "No."

"Why not?" When a moment passed and he'd done nothing but glare at the letter, Kyleigh touched his arm. "Whatever you might think of him, he was still your father."

Kael shook his head. "Setheran might've carried me up the mountains, but then he left. That isn't what a father is. A father is someone who stays, who spends years teaching you everything he knows. And by that reckoning, I didn't grow up without a father: I had two fathers. Their names are Amos and Roland — and more than anything, I want to see them again.

"I'm grateful for what Setheran did for me. I'm grateful he gave me a chance, and he'll always be my favorite hero. But I can't read this." His hand closed tightly around the letter. "He's been there at every fork in the road, urging me along. I'm not sure if I've even taken a step on my own —"

"You know that isn't true, Kael," she said fiercely. "He might've helped you a bit, but you chose your own paths."

The determined edge in his eyes only sharpened. "What if it's whispercraft? What if he tells me to turn my back on everything and march down? I don't trust him. If he was willing to die for me, he'd be willing to do anything — maybe even sacrifice the mountains. Morris told me the truth," he said when she froze beside him.

He glared into the flames, fixing them with all the harsh light trapped behind his eyes. And Kyleigh realized that perhaps she should've been more insistent. Perhaps it hadn't been a decent thing, letting him avoid his questions for so long.

"I would've told you," she whispered, touching his arm. "I *wanted* to tell you. After I showed you Amelia, I expected you to ask why she hadn't ... why you never ..."

"Knew her?" Kael sighed heavily. His brows tightened at their ends, creasing miserably above his nose. "I wish I hadn't looked."

"Kael ..."

"I mean it — I wish I'd never seen her. My gut kept telling me that no good would come of it, and I should've listened. Now there's all this ... no, it doesn't matter." Kael sat straighter; he dragged a hand through his curls and his eyes flickered with thought. "All that matters now is that I finish what I started. No matter what he's done for me, I can't risk falling to another one of Setheran's tricks. I can't read this letter."

His hand opened and for a moment, Kael held the letter as if he meant to read it. The rough edge of his thumb dragged across the faded words on its front. Then he leaned forward and tossed it among the coals.

Flames spouted from its skin. They curled and blackened its edges. Bubbles writhed inside the wax, popping with muffled shrieks. A few moments later, and Setheran's words had turned to ash.

Kyleigh leaned back against the wall. So many things twisted inside her head ... she wanted very much to sort them out, but the weariness in her bones made it difficult.

The touch of Kael's shoulder kept her anchored in wakefulness. He was stuck beside her, pressed in as tightly as he would fit. His neck arched away from the wall. His gaze was focused. Lights danced in the dark of his eyes, whipping beneath gales of thought.

Kyleigh couldn't help but smile. "I feel sorry for Titus."

"You should," Kael growled. "I have a plan."

489

She wove an arm through his and held on tightly. She was determined to stay awake just a moment longer. "I hope you'll have a happy birthday, Kael," she whispered.

His hand closed over hers: warm, but not stifling — not demanding, but firm. He held her, and he let her be. His touch hadn't changed because he'd had to save her. He felt no debt between them. They were tied together, as they'd always been.

And in that moment, Kyleigh realized that she'd worried over nothing.

# CHAPTER 43
## THE BRAIDED TREE

At the northeastern reaches of the Grandforest, the land began to change. The great trees languished into drooping weeds and the ground became a treacherous bog.

Water pooled between the narrow stretches of grass. Deep pits of mud waited hungrily on all sides — their tops covered so thickly in moss that they might easily be mistaken for solid ground. One of Crevan's scouts discovered this quickly when he took a wrong step and was dragged into the bowels of the earth.

At least his screams warned the rest of the caravan away.

Black ponds festered in the gaps between trees. The water was still, reflecting the sickly landscape like a mirror. Occasionally, the reflections would break into ripples as the scaly beasts that lurked within them ducked from the noise of the King's march.

Crevan hated the swamps. It was a useless plot of land that seemed to exist only to breed insects — great, bloodsucking pests that drove him mad with their needles. They left itching welts down Crevan's neck and across his back, sipping during the day and swarming to feast at night.

To make matters worse, the whole air stank like a dead man's breath. The odor hung so thickly that Crevan began to think there *wasn't* any air. Perhaps their lungs simply filled with the stench of rotting travelers.

No road crossed through the swamps. The land was in a constant state of decay: its skin rotted and festered with such vigor that any paths they might've built would've been swallowed up immediately. Instead, Crevan's men were forced to travel along a few narrow pathways of solid earth.

Muck and slime oozed from the stringy grass at their every step. The mire grasped wetly at their boots, sank its jaws across the carts' wheels — always trying to drag them to a slow and murky death. It was with no small relief that Crevan and his soldiers finally made it to the mouth of the northern seas.

The great river that cut through the Kingdom split at the seas' mouth, forming two smaller currents. They flowed on either side of an island caught between them and disappeared into the icy blue beyond.

Countess D'Mere waited for him at a camp along the northern riverbank. She wore a deep green tunic and tight-fitting black breeches. Her boots came up to her knees. Crevan was alarmed to see that they were covered in mud.

"You should've brought a horse, Countess," he said as he dismounted. He patted the creature's warm, muscled neck and smiled. "If the swamp muck begins to drag you down, their sacrifice will give you a moment to escape."

"A clever ploy, Your Majesty. I hadn't thought of that."

The Countess kept her smile sharp. Her lips could charm like a serpent's eyes — Crevan had seen it done. And he'd promised that if she ever tried her tricks on him, he'd lop off her head. "Where's the shaman?"

"Here, Your Majesty," Blackbeak crowed. There were gashes on the side of his warped face and a number of his feathers were missing. "Unfortunate! I had an unfortunate accident, Your Majesty," he explained.

Crevan was certain that he'd had gotten whatever he deserved. He might've looked like a monster, but the crow shaman was clever: there was little his beady eyes didn't see. It would've been dangerous to let him wander around the fortress of Midlan. So Crevan had left him in the charge of Countess D'Mere.

Blackbeak approached from the river, hemmed on either side by young men dressed like the Countess. Both of the guards carried swords at their hips and had the golden, twisting oak of the Grandforest stamped upon their chests.

Crevan glanced at their faces — and then he had to glance again.

From their dark eyes to their frowning lips, the boys were identical. Both had their hair cut close to their scalps. They even had the same knot on their nose, as if both had been broken and healed at the same crooked angle.

"I hope you're well, Your Majesty," D'Mere said, her eyes searching.

Crevan shook his head. "I'm more concerned for *you*, Countess. I should've realized that Titus would use a treaty with the chancellor to lure you in — he knew I would send you to the seas on my behalf. I don't know what I would've done, had you shared the same fate as my envoy."

She returned his smile with a hardened one of her own. "I was pleased to serve, Your Majesty — and I look forward to paying Titus back."

"As do I, Countess." Crevan smirked again as he signaled behind him. "Bring the boy, Ulric."

So many of the mages were unwilling to use their magic for anything other than simple tasks — and the few who had gifts for battle were often cowards. But Ulric had seized the opportunity for greatness.

No sooner had the crown been settled upon Crevan's head than he'd offered Midlan a mighty gift of allegiance: a spell that would bind any creature with magic in its blood to Crevan's will. Ulric had bound himself in homage, and all he'd asked for in return was to serve Midlan in the ancient ways — as the mages had served the Kings of old.

So Crevan had gladly granted him the title of archmage.

"Good to see you again, Countess," Ulric called as he strode forward. The archmage was a desert man. His head was completely bald and he wore gold robes with the dragon of Midlan embroidered across his chest. His voice was charming.

But his face was not.

Ulric's eyes sunk deep inside his head — dark, and glittering. He always smiled with an open mouth, letting the

493

sharp edges of his teeth crop out from over his lips. His ears were twice the normal size: the skin was stretched to near transparence. Little blue veins webbed out from their middles, snaking all along the dips and rivets.

Crevan supposed his ears had grown from the strain of listening to the many voices of his mages and beasts.

For years on end, Ulric had done little more than sit cross-legged inside his chambers, sifting through the wails of the Kingdom's slaves. He could hear their every gasp and plea, each desperate thought that bounced inside their heads. He plucked all the useful bits away and handed them over to Crevan. More than once, Ulric's ears had saved his throne.

But though his magic was among the most powerful Crevan had ever seen, his archmage had one weakness that kept him tethered to the crown: a love for cruelty.

He was always trying to create new ways for his victims to suffer, always weaving a more painful, devastating spell. Being able to hear their thoughts gave Ulric a clear window into the fears of the beasts … and so Crevan had given him the authority to break each one.

D'Mere stiffened under Ulric's gaze. "Archmage," she said with a nod. "Shall we begin? I don't want to keep His Majesty waiting."

Ulric turned and stretched an arm out behind him. It was adorned with a silver impetus: a chain that wrapped around his wrist several times and was made up of dozens of tiny links — each one tied to a particular mage or beast. The impetus glowed as Ulric beckoned with a finger, and the strange-looking forest boy stumbled out of the cart.

His name was Devin — a fact he'd reminded them of every time the soldiers had called him *whelp* or *maggot*, or anything that wasn't his name. He'd squawked about it until Ulric finally sealed his mouth shut.

With a wave of his hand, Ulric released him. The bonds fell from Devin's wrists and he stumbled forward as he regained use of his legs. He massaged the muscles of his jaw, wrapping them all up in his stark blue gaze.

"He's too stupid to run," Ulric said in answer to the question on D'Mere's face.

Her icy gaze swept over him. "What ... *is* he?"

Devin's eyes widened when he saw her, but he didn't speak. He craned his neck over her shoulder to stare at her guards. His stark eyes traveled between them, and his face fell. "You're brothers, aren't you?"

They didn't answer. In fact, they didn't even blink.

"You look too alike not to be brothers," Devin went on, speaking as if the twins were the only people in the swamps. "I wish I'd gotten a chance to know my brothers. I would've liked to know them, I think." His eyes widened at Blackbeak. But instead of stepping back, he stepped forward. "Are you a man or a bird?"

"Yes," he crowed. Then his neck bobbed to Ulric. "Surprising! I'm surprised he still has his tongue."

"His Majesty wished him to arrive ... unspoiled," Ulric muttered.

D'Mere's brows arched high. She craned her neck over his shoulder to look at the cart. "You've only brought one, Your Majesty?"

"Yes. I searched for others ... but there was only *one* left. Enough chattering," Crevan growled before she could ask another question. "Get to work, shaman."

The collar around his feathery neck glowed red with the command, and Blackbeak hopped to obey.

Two shriveled hands curled at the tops of the shaman's wings. Devin stiffened when one of them latched onto his wrist. There was a small flint dagger clutched in the other. His stark eyes followed dagger's path unblinkingly as Blackbeak passed it over his hand. Strange muffled words rolled off the shaman's gray tongue and out his beak. The wooden talisman that hung against his chest glowed faintly as he spoke.

Devin yelped when Blackbeak swiped the blade across his palm.

"Why are you hurting me?" he gasped. "What did I ...?"

Slowly, the blue of his gaze lost its sharpness. He stared at Blackbeak's talisman for a moment, watching as the light flickered and finally went out. Devin's mouth parted and his eyes went to the island in the distance — as if he searched for something.

"Get out of his way," Crevan hissed.

Blackbeak leapt to the side.

Without any words or so much as a glance behind him, Devin began to walk. He reached with his wounded hand as he made his way slowly towards the island between rivers.

And Crevan held his breath.

*******

It was a voice that drew him to the river. A woman's voice — strong and deep ... and kind. The words she whispered reminded Devin of his mother.

She hummed the same songs his mother used to sing, speaking with the river's roar and along the whistle of the wind. The earth trembled when she spoke, as if he was standing upon the chords of her throat.

*Closer, child. You must come closer.*

Her voice lured him to the rocky bank. Swift waters lapped the shores, but he was certain the woman wouldn't lead him to harm. The waters must not have been as angry as they looked. With a deep breath, he dipped his foot among the rapids.

The whole river seemed to be made from the same foam that covered its top: there was no strength behind the flow. It didn't try to pull him under. The water whipped harmlessly around him as Devin waded further out.

It was at the river's middle that he began to be afraid. The foamy swells came up to his neck, now. If it went much deeper, he wouldn't be able to breathe.

*Look up, child. My light will guide you.*

Devin's eyes left the swirling waters and locked onto the woman standing upon the opposite bank. She waited for him. He couldn't see her face, but her hand was outstretched. He wanted desperately to reach her.

With a deep breath, he forced his way across the river and pulled himself up the rocky slope of the bank. He didn't realize how the journey had weakened him until he collapsed on hand and knee.

*Closer, child. Closer.*

He was nearly there — her hand was almost within his reach. The fresh cut on his palm stung as he dragged himself across the pebbly shore. His skin burned against the many little rocks that ground into his flesh. With his last ounce of strength, he stretched out and grasped for her hand.

When he looked up, he realized it wasn't a woman that'd been calling to him: it was a tree. Its trunk was made of two smaller trees, twisted tightly around each other and spiraling towards the sky. They mingled at their branches — forming one great canopy of leaves.

Fear twisted inside Devin's throat. It shoved until it burst from his mouth in a panicked cry. The Braided Tree! His mother had sung of this place before. She'd shown him the picture carved into his father's talisman.

No. No, he couldn't be here. He wasn't supposed to be here — the draega weren't allowed! He tried to pull himself from the Tree, but his hand wouldn't budge. It was as if his fingers had melted into the roots.

*Peace, child. Peace.*

A great light began to pulse from within the Braided Tree. It went from blinding to dim in slow, steady breaths. Devin filled his lungs along with its rhythm and felt something like cool rain wash over his head. But his peace didn't last for long.

His arm went numb and his hand burned as the Tree sucked a great amount of blood out through his cut. The light in the center grew brighter — so bright that Devin had to shut his eyes.

"Let me go!" he cried.

The woman's voice was gone. A new sound came from the Tree — a sound like the thud of footsteps across a wooden bridge. It grew faster and louder as Devin tried to pull away.

"Let me go!" he said again. "I'm not supposed to be here — I didn't want to be here!"

*Thump thump thump thump thump.*

"Please, let me go!"

He shouted, he cried. He beat a fist against the roots. He tore at his palm with his other hand, trying to pull himself free. A few desperate minutes passed before he realized it was hopeless. He was trapped.

*Thump thump ... thump thump ... thump thump ...*

The pounding quieted as Devin gave in, slowing to a rhythm that didn't frighten him so badly. As he lay there listening, he realized the thudding within the Tree matched the noise inside his chest.

*He hears you, child. He accepts your challenge.*

"No! Please, I didn't mean to! I didn't want ..." But Devin couldn't finish his words. He collapsed, every bit of him finally spent.

Hot tears welled in his eyes as he realized what he'd done. It was the one thing he swore he'd never do — he'd broken the oath that every draega pledged to protect. He'd promised his mother, *promised* her that he would stay away from this place. He promised that no matter what, he would keep the draega's oath.

It was the only thing she'd ever asked of him. It was the promise he'd whispered to her when she finally took her Great Sleep ... when she'd gone to join his father and all of his brothers and sisters in the green lands across the river.

And now ... he'd failed her.

"Please ... I just ... I want to go home."

*The ritual is almost complete*, the Tree whispered to him. *Now you must face him in the Arena of Souls ... and face him bravely, child. For the victor is two lives, and for the vanquished — none.*

\*\*\*\*\*\*

498

When Devin looked up, the Tree was gone. The sky was gone. The island and the rivers were gone. He knelt in a strange place.

It reminded him of home: an open space of land ringed by broken things. But there weren't any trees. He couldn't feel the wind or smell the flowers' bloom. Everything was a mix of gray and shadow. The whole world shimmered like the air above flame.

A song drew his eyes to the other side of the land. It was the rumble of storm clouds — powerful and deep. It was the music of the wind, the whisper of the trees. The song was exactly the one his mother used to sing. Devin knew the sort of creature that waited for him before he even had a chance to look.

Curved horns and a long spiked tail, great wings unfurled proudly at its side — blurry like the rest of the world, but still shaped enough. A black dragon watched him from across the Arena.

Slowly, Devin got to his feet. In the world outside, the dragon would've towered above him. But in this world they stood at the same height. "I'm sorry," he said. The words didn't come from his mouth. He couldn't feel his mouth. When he reached up, he realized that he didn't have a mouth. His face was blank like the dragon's.

A low groan came from the depths of the dragon's scaly chest. It rose slightly towards the end, but never quite climbed from the depths. The song would never rise any higher. It wasn't meant to. The dragon's voice stayed low, like the sad tales his mother used to sing — the ones that ended in her tears.

Devin didn't understand the dragon's words, but he understood their meaning: only one of them could leave this place alive. They were going to have to fight.

Boy and dragon charged each other, colliding in the middle. The dragon raked its claws across Devin's chest. Tendrils of black leaked from his wound and into the dragon. To his horror, the beast grew larger. The earth came closer as Devin shrank.

499

He gasped as the dragon's jaw clamped down upon his arm. More black leaked away, pouring out in rivers. He tried to run, but by now he was too small: the dragon arched its long neck and bit him without even taking a step. The more it consumed, the larger it grew. Soon it was nearly the size of a hill — while Devin had shrunk to a child's height. One more bite, and he'd be finished.

For the victor is two lives, and for the vanquished — none.

Devin knew what was happening. His mother used to sing songs of the old days — the age when draega and dragon lived as one, but that time had passed. It was too dangerous a power, too cruel a practice. They'd sworn an oath long ago that man and dragon would never again be joined.

Now that oath was broken. Whether Devin won or the dragon consumed him, the oath would still be broken. To give up his life wouldn't change a thing. And so he wouldn't give up.

He would fight.

The dragon's head shot down, and Devin rolled to the side. He grabbed one of the beast's curved horns with both hands and slung himself onto its shadowy neck.

It roared and tried to shake him off, but Devin held on tightly. He wrapped his arms around the dragon's throat and squeezed hard. Black flowed into Devin as the dragon lost its breath. Soon they stood at equal heights once more.

The dragon twisted out of his grasp and sunk its teeth into his neck. Devin plunged his shadowy arm through the dragon's chest. They struck the ground together — so forcefully that it began to shake. Pillars toppled, the air wavered dangerously. They rolled, tearing at each other while the earth crumbled under their blows.

At last, the world could hold their battle no longer. The ground shattered beneath them — and both Devin and the dragon tumbled into the darkness beyond.

*******

Crevan paced a stone's throw from the rocky shore. He'd watched as the boy's body crumpled beneath the Braided Tree, but he hadn't worried. They'd all done that: fallen unconscious as they reached the Tree, only to wake a few moments later.

But now the sun had climbed on for almost an hour, and Devin still hadn't moved.

"What's taking so long?" Crevan growled.

"Perhaps the little whelp is dead." Ulric's eyes shifted to the sky above the island. "See? The carrion birds have already begun to circle."

D'Mere's lips were tight and she kept her arms crossed over her chest. She hardly glanced where Ulric pointed. "That's a hawk."

Blackbeak — who'd been inspecting the bald patches between his feathers for quite some time — suddenly leapt to his taloned feet. "Hawk? *Hawk*! Kill her! Blast her from the sky!"

Ulric raised his hand eagerly, but Crevan stopped him with a word. "No! You might strike the boy."

Blackbeak leapt up and down, stirring clods of dirt with desperate flaps of his wings. "But Your Majesty — not what she seems! She's one of the great shamans! Kill her, kill her n —!"

A thundering roar cut over the top of his words and a great black bear lumbered out of the woods. It stood on its hindquarters and curled its lips over its massive teeth. Crevan's men lowered their spears, forming a protective arch around him. D'Mere's guards drew their swords. Ulric stretched out his hand and a dangerous red light bloomed along the links of his chained impetus.

A cry from the island stopped them all short.

Devin had awakened. He writhed upon the ground, his chest bowed against the force moving inside his body. His back arched and his hands snapped into fists. His limbs trembled dangerously, and Crevan knew what would happen next.

He grabbed Ulric around the robes and shoved through the soldiers — running for the river. They'd only just reached the shore when Devin's body transformed.

His skin split open and black spots burst from the wounds — joining together until they covered him. His cries grew strangled around a set of enormous fangs. His voice deepened, rattling Crevan's innards. He watched as horns burst from his dark crop of hair and the blades of his shoulders stretched into wings. At last, the change was finished.

Devin crumpled to the ground — his body now that of a great black dragon.

"Chain him, Ulric! Do it now!" Crevan roared.

The archmage's face had gone ashen at the power of Devin's voice, but Crevan's command burned too hotly. The spell had nearly formed in Ulric's hand when Devin tried to lift himself from the ground. The great wind that came from his mighty wings knocked them all backwards.

Ulric tumbled over and Crevan struck the ground hard. He ripped at the stringy grass, trying to pull himself to his feet. He'd only just managed to roll over when a voice broke through the air:

"The time has come, Blackbeak — the shamans will purge the earth of your Abomination!"

A gangly man with sunken features had appeared from the swamps. He stood between a man with far-set eyes, and a woman whose eyes glowed a dangerous yellow. The bear lumbered to join them, becoming a hairy man in mid-gallop. When all four were aligned, they raised the talismans from their chests.

"It's time you answered, Blackbeak," the gangly barbarian said again. "It's time to cleanse your Abominable soul."

Blackbeak took to the skies with a squawk and a shower of feathers, but the light from their talismans brought him crashing back down. He squirmed under their chants, the light from his own talisman pulsing desperately against the shamans' attack. He screamed for help, but Crevan didn't answer.

His eyes were on Devin.

The great black dragon had collapsed upon the island. He was a beast far greater than the Dragongirl: each scale across his enormous chest was a large as a man's palm, his wings stretched to the island's ends. Even from a distance, Crevan could feel the terrible heat in his ragged breaths — it seared the skin across his brow and nose.

While he watched, the hawk fell from the sky and took a woman's shape. She grabbed Devin by his horns and shook him fiercely. "Fly! You must fly, sky-hunter!"

His stark blue eyes snapped open, lighting on her. The shaman raised her arms, Devin raised his wings — and Crevan let out a roar. He leapt to his feet and ripped Ulric from the ground. "Bind him now, you worthless mage! Stop him!"

With a blast of his mighty wings, Devin shot into the sky. His limbs curled beneath him as he turned for the northern seas. A few beats more, and he likely would've been free. But Ulric's spell got there first.

A red-hot strip of light burst from his hand as the archmage fell back from the blast of Devin's wings. It roared through the open sky and struck him in his scaly throat. His great voice made the earth tremble. His wings shivered as he tried to force himself on.

"I am your master, beast," Crevan thundered. "Kneel at my feet!"

The collar grew red-hot under the force of Crevan's command. Devin fought against the burning spell. He roared and slung his head about. For half a breath, he spun towards them. His blue eyes snapped shut and the scales around his lids squinched together tightly. When they opened, Crevan took a startled step backwards.

The cool blue was gone — replaced by a horrible, fiery yellow. A black, slitted pupil cut down each eye, guarded on both sides by a raging wall of flame. These eyes met Crevan's without fear. It was the defiance in each slit that gave the

503

fires their light. This time when Devin roared, his voice shook the trees and flattened the river's waves.

Finally, he seemed to break through Ulric's hold. His wings stopped their trembling and beat all the more furiously for the seas.

"Stop him! Bring him down!"

Ulric looked as if he held onto Devin by no more than a thread. His arm shook violently, his face turned purple. Words flew from his lips in a maddened scream as Devin winged further out to sea. The chained impetus writhed across his arm, squirming as it struggled to control its newest link.

Crevan couldn't even hear the furious words that tore from his throat. His life, his Kingdom — everything he'd worked for was tied to the clawed feet of that dragon. If Devin escaped, it would all be for naught. He roared for Ulric to stop his flight, to drag him in by his horns.

Their fates depended on it.

All at once, the collar around Devin's neck burst into flame. He roared and twisted against the pain, but Ulric had him. The archmage grinned as he pulled his hand towards the shore. Devin followed the line of his arm helplessly, as if there was a rope tied to his back.

The spell dragged him into the swamps and brought him crashing down. His body slid until his great, horned head came to rest a stone's throw from Crevan's boots.

"Your Majesty — the shaman!" D'Mere gasped.

Crevan looked up in time to see that the barbarians had given up their fight. They burst into their animal forms and scattered among the drooping trees, fleeing out of the reach of D'Mere's twin guards.

Blackbeak — or rather, what was left of him — lay in a deflated mass of skin and feathers upon the ground.

Crevan laughed. "What about the shaman? He served his purpose. I've no longer got a use for him — this is the last beast I'll ever need."

D'Mere's careful steps froze at his side. Her breath seemed trapped behind her lips; the ice in her gaze melted as she took in the sight of Devin's enormous, panting body upon the ground.

Crevan smirked. Very rarely was D'Mere ever stricken speechless. "What do you think of my newest slave?"

"Fate help us," she whispered.

He brought his lips to her ear and growled: "She already has, Countess ... she already has."

# CHAPTER 44
## UNDER THE STARS

At long last, the sun dawned upon the day Kael had been waiting for: the day his army would march for the summit.

Gwen had said they were only three days' journey from Thanehold. "Though it'll feel more like a week, with all this snow in the way," she'd added with a glare.

Winter had finally opened its gullet and the mountains belched snow upon them in a near-constant stream. When they left the frozen lands, the drifts were up to their knees. A day later, they'd risen to just below their waists. Kael knew if they wanted any chance of reaching the summit, he'd have to think of a way to make the journey easier.

He told the craftsmen to use the heat of the forge to melt the snows. He showed them how to imagine the fires consumed their skin, how to hold the image of white-hot flesh inside their heads. Then he'd stepped into the middle of one of the thickest drifts and it'd melted with a hiss.

The problem was that the snow turned to water, and water froze quickly. Kael looked behind him shortly after they'd started walking and groaned to see the giants sliding helplessly at the end of the line. Once they lost their footing, they didn't stop: a few managed to dig their scythes in, but most slid quite a ways before they finally crashed into a large drift at one of the bends.

The wildmen laughed uproariously.

"Instead of chuckling, why don't you clodded well help us?" Declan bellowed. He'd managed to dig the tip of his scythe in between two frozen rocks, stopping himself from sliding to the bottom. But the weapon's shaft creaked dangerously under his weight.

Gwen strode to the edge of the icy slope, rolling a large clump of snow in her hands. "How long do you think you can hold on, giant?"

"Long enough to clobber you, if you throw that," he said with a glare.

She rolled the snow down, where it got wedged against his arm. "How long, now?"

"Stop that, you paint-faced —"

Another ball rolled it into his mouth. He tried to spit it away and very nearly lost his grip. Soon Gwen had Declan so piled with snow clumps that they could hardly see his face. Though the shaft groaned in protest, he still didn't budge. When she made the mistake of trying to pack the snow in with her boot, he snatched her around the ankle and slung her behind him.

Gwen howled the whole way down. She slid on her rump and steered with her heels. She popped onto her feet at the bend and flipped, headfirst, over the scattered giants and into a large drift of snow.

A moment later she erupted from the bank, arms raised high. She let out a triumphant howl that the warriors rushed to answer — and it all very quickly dissolved into chaos.

The warriors crowded onto the icy slope. They slid on their backs and chests, trying to see who could go the fastest. They scraped the giants out of their holds, knocked them off their feet, and wound up in such a fantastic tangle of bodies at the bottom that Kael expected there to be at least a dozen broken bones. But there weren't any — at least not until Jonathan tried skating down on the back of one of the wildmen's rounded shields.

Then there were four.

"Do you see what comes of your nonsense?" Kael grumbled as he patched up Jonathan's ribs.

Gwen shrugged. "I didn't force him to do anything."

"I'd do it again!" Jonathan said groggily, swinging his fist.

Kael put him to sleep. Then he scooped the fiddler up and held his lanky body out to Gwen. "Here. You carry him."

She made a face. "Why?"

"Because I'm angry with you. And perhaps it'll teach you that not everyone in our army can take a beating like a wildman. Some of them are fragile — *no!*" he barked, when he saw a clump of warriors gathering at the top of the slope. "Nobody's having another go. If you slide down here again I swear I'll hurl you over the edge."

They slumped away, grumbling magnificently as they went.

The moment they were gone, he turned back to Gwen. "Carry him until he wakes — and think carefully about how you ought to behave, *Thane.*"

Her grin was sharp as she took Jonathan. "All right ... *mutt.*"

He didn't like the way her words slid across his ears. And he liked her smile even less. But there wasn't any time to worry about Gwen. He had more important problems to solve.

In order to keep the slopes from freezing behind them, he split the craftsmen into three groups. They walked in Vs: one at the head of the line, another in the middle, and the last towards the end. The heat coming off their skin kept the snows melted and the ice from forming back.

When they finally stopped to make camp that evening, Kael put the final few bits of his plan together. He gathered the craftsmen in a circle and had them show him everything they could remember about their fortress.

Between all of their memories, he got a pretty good image of Thanehold and the stone village surrounding it. Then he tried to see it all through Titus's eyes, tried to guess how the Earl would use it to his advantage. He played the battle over inside his head, combing through every possible scenario — knowing full well that the Earl would adapt quickly to anything the wildmen threw at him.

All the while he thought, Morris's words rang inside his head: *The thing about Titus is you've got to get him quick, lad ... you've got to get him before he gets you.*

Kael realized that there would be no days-long battle with Titus. In fact, he might only get one chance to strike. So he would have to plan his steps carefully; he could afford to hold nothing back. He would craft a blade and fit it perfectly against Titus's neck ... and the first blow he dealt would end him.

Once his plan lay unraveled, Kael went after his companions.

He'd expected some resistance from the pirates, but Lysander only nodded somberly at his part in the plan. "We'll do whatever you ask of us, Sir Wright."

The good captain's eyes had become considerably clouded in the days following Morris's death. He spent a large amount of time walking with his hand gripped around the Lass's whittled hilt, his customary grin lost far behind him.

Kael's heart stung miserably at the sight. "You don't have to drag the pirates into battle. I won't —"

"No. I've made a bargain, and I'll keep my word." His wavy hair stood on end as he passed a hand through it. "I miss Aerilyn. That's all it is."

"Are you certain?"

He sighed heavily. "I suppose ... if I'm honest, I *do* miss Morris. Uncle Martin told me to keep an eye on him, to keep him hidden from the Kingdom but always in my sight. He never trusted him. Yet, when Morris had the chance to ruin me, he didn't. He stayed loyal to me even while I was cursed." A faint smile bent Lysander's mouth as his eyes looked back. "He proved himself to me during those years. I'd actually forgotten that I was supposed to keep an eye on him. In fact, I think Morris wound up keeping an eye on *me*. I'll miss him as dearly as I miss any other pirate ... but we must march on, mustn't we?"

Kael forced himself to smile as he said: "Aye, Captain."

That brought the grin back to Lysander's face.

Though the pirates were willing to do their part, Declan was much less enthusiastic about the giants' role. "I brought my army here to battle — not stomp about and make a great lot of noise!"

Kael tried to be patient. "If everything goes well, there won't be much fighting. All you have to do is make sure Titus keeps his eyes on *you* and away from the craftsmen. And you can't go ... mad, all right? Things are likely to get pretty thick on that side. You'll be killed if you charge right in."

Declan nodded slowly. "Yeh, I think I've figured out a way to keep from losing my head. But it'll involve a good amount of pirate grog."

"Of course it will," Kael muttered.

He'd gone to turn away when Declan's thick hand thudded onto his shoulder. "I want the wee sandbeater on my side of things."

Kael followed the shadowed cleft of Declan's eyes across camp, to where Nadine and Elena stood. They'd exchanged weapons and were locked in a rather precarious battle beside the fire. Nadine swung the black daggers in clumsy arcs while Elena tried to knock them out of her hands with the butt of the silver spear.

Jake, who'd recently doused his fur robes in a fresh helping of skunk oil, seemed to be trying to chronicle their attacks in his journal. "Given the superior weight of the hilt, what's the likelihood that a dagger disarmed would land point down?" he called.

Elena responded by kicking one of the daggers from Nadine's hand. She swatted it with the butt of the spear and it shot towards Jake — thudding point-first into the skin of the mangy shrub beside him.

He gaped at it for a moment before he scribbled into his journal: "*Rather ... likely ...*"

It had come as no great surprise to Kael when he discovered Elena was a whisperer. She certainly had a warrior's strength, and she seemed capable of disappearing whenever she pleased. The wildmen had been so entranced

510

by her ability to meld into the shadows that she'd begun to teach them some of her tricks.

Consequently, Kael now had to assume that every darkened patch around camp was actually a wildman waiting to caddoc the skin off him.

No, he could understand Elena being a whisperer. What he couldn't understand for the absolute life of him was the way Declan smiled at Nadine.

He didn't even seem to realize he was doing it. The giant's mouth was bent at such an unusual angle that Kael felt as if his stern friend had vanished — only to be replaced by a man who hadn't frowned once his whole life.

Declan quickly stuffed his smile away when he saw Kael staring. "She's a wee terror, is all. There's no reasoning with her. She'll be a harm to herself if she's not looked after."

"Is that the problem?"

Declan grabbed him roughly by the front of his jerkin. "As far as you know, yeh — it is."

Kael managed to hold his smile back until after Declan had stomped away.

With the pirates and the giants ready to do battle, it was time to talk to Jake. Kael was still several yards away when the tang of skunk oil hit him. The stench was at least as much taste as smell: the oil's reek seemed to bypass his nose and drop straight down his throat.

"I've gone numb to it," Jake said when he saw Kael gagging. "A remarkable orifice, the nose — it's capable of adapting to nearly any amount of reek in a surprisingly short time."

Kael thought he would've preferred his nose to have simply fallen off and been done with it. "I need to talk to you about our attack on Titus."

Jake sighed heavily. "Yes, I've been giving it a considerable amount of thought, and I've realized there's only one thing I can possibly do: keep my magic to myself."

"No spells," Kael agreed. "None whatsoever. It'll be difficult enough getting the wildmen to do what I've asked

511

them. The last thing we need is the smell of magic driving them mad. I think it'd be best if you stayed with Declan."

Elena glared when Kael turned to her. "I'm staying with the mage. And that's final."

He leaned away as she leveled the spear's head at his chin. "I was going to say that, anyways."

"You were?"

"Yes. So there's no need to go pointing things at me," he said, shoving the spear aside. With the way things were going so far, he thought he was at greater risk of being killed in his own camp than by Titus's army.

When he told Nadine her lot, she stamped her tiny feet. "This is all *your* doing, giant!" she hollered at Declan. "I will not be made to sit idly while my friends do battle."

"You'll do what I tell you, mite."

"*Mot!*"

Kael could feel himself nearing his wit's end, and the worst was still to come: he needed to talk to Gwen.

They were camped beneath a cliff face that night. The craftsmen had spent the evening molding several large shelters into the rock: they bent the unforgiving stone back into caves and draped large, pelt tarps over their mouths to keep the snow out.

Kael was rather proud of how well the pelts had been melded together, and how they'd thought to seal the fur to the edges of the caves' mouths. For days now, the craftsmen had built shelters without his help — steadily improving their quality and speed. There was no doubt in his mind that the wildmen would thrive long after Titus lay dead, even if they insisted on living at the mountain's top.

A number of campfires ringed the space outside the shelters. Kyleigh and Silas sat near the largest one, busily devouring the carcass of a deer.

"Curse the mountain's breath — it bites at everything!" Silas hissed. He gnawed unsuccessfully at a chunk of red flesh on the deer's leg. Judging by how his teeth scraped against it, the meat had frozen solid.

Kyleigh held her portion above the flames for a moment, her brows bent in concentration. "It'll be much easier to get a decent bite if you warm it."

"I don't have to *warm* my meals, dragoness. My jaws are powerful enough."

"Suit yourself." Kyleigh took her meat from the blaze and tore off a large chunk with her teeth, grinning smugly at him while she chewed.

Silas finally relented. He thrust his deer among the flames and pulled it back with a huff. "It isn't working," he grumbled, jabbing it with a finger. "Why isn't it working?"

"You have to leave it in there for a moment, you silly cat. No, look ..."

She grabbed his wrist and bent him, forcing the leg to hang just right. His neck craned all around and he shifted worriedly on his haunches the longer Kyleigh kept it in. "Now, dragoness?"

"No, not yet."

"But —"

"Patience," she growled.

At last, she let go. Silas crammed the leg against his lips. "Ow! It's hot!" He stuffed a fistful of snow into his mouth and tried the bite again.

Kyleigh rolled her eyes at him. When she saw Kael approaching, she leaned back. "Where are you off to?"

He sighed heavily. "To battle all the forces of the under-realm and the winter."

She grinned. "Send her my love."

He tugged on her pony's tail as he passed.

Gwen had a small shelter to herself in the middle of the wildmen's camp. Its mouth was covered in a thick blanket of bear and wolf. The bear's head crowned the shelter's arch and seemed to snarl at him as he approached, bearing all of its jagged teeth in greeting.

The light from one of the craftsmen's makeshift lanterns glowed beneath the pelt door's bottom. "Gwen? Can I talk to you for a moment?"

"Fine," she growled.

513

"It's about tomorrow. I just wanted to make sure you remember what you're supposed to ..." His voice trailed off. He'd been so focused on battling his way past the pelt door that it took him a moment to realize what he was looking at.

Gwen stood before him, turned away — and she wore nothing but her leggings. Every muscle in her back was visible: they coiled as she bent to scoop her tunic off the floor. He could see where the swirling designs on her arms ended near the base of her neck, giving way to pale, slightly freckled skin.

A ring of scars bent around her right shoulder blade like a bow's arch. Each one was almost perfectly rounded — and about the size of a large tooth.

"Kyleigh really bit you," he said, though he could still hardly believe it.

"She could've sent me to the under-realm with a roar and a burst of flame. But instead, she slung me into a cliff side," Gwen muttered as she pulled the tunic over her head. The soft material fell down her back, covering the scars. "It took me an hour to dig out from under all the rock and snow — and my father kept me locked inside the castle for the rest of the winter while my wounds healed ... but things certainly could've been worse."

She smirked as she turned around. She rolled the tunic's sleeves up to her elbows, all the while keeping her eyes on his. "You must be the only man in the Kingdom who would walk up to a shirtless woman and ask after her *scars*."

Heat singed Kael's face. "Well, I ... you said I could come in."

"I did."

He didn't understand why she was still smirking at him, or why her eyes shone so fiercely. But it took every ounce of his courage to keep from sprinting outside. "I wanted to talk to you about —"

"I'm not pleased with your plan, mutt," she said, crossing her arms. "I don't see why we ought to spend so much time piddling around a battle we could easily win."

514

He'd lost count of how many times he'd had to explain it to her. "It's not just about winning — it's about keeping our people safe."

"*Our* people?"

"Yes. Your wildmen might be able to hurl themselves over the gates and come out unscathed, but my friends aren't as strong. I won't put them to harm when there's a better way to do things."

She raised a brow. "So destroying my castle is better?"

"Castles can be rebuilt," he said evenly.

"So can bodies."

"That's not ..." He tugged roughly on his hair, but his frustration still came out as a growl. "I'm doing what's best. For once, will you please just trust me?"

"I don't think so. I need to be convinced."

He was nearing the rather frayed ends of his patience, and anger bubbled in a pit beneath it. Still, he tried to hold on. "No, you don't need to be *convinced*. You need to shut it and do exactly as I say. And when all this is over, you can thank me."

She sauntered closer. "Why would I do that?"

"Because Titus will be dead, and you'll never have to see me again. You and I will shake hands and part ways — and your people can go straight back to chasing imaginary creatures through the mountains."

"Why don't I just thank you now?"

"I wish you woul ..."

Kael couldn't breathe. It took him a moment to realize *why* he couldn't breathe. He got his answer quickly when he tried to take a breath and Gwen's lips pressed harder against his. They were every bit as strong as she was, moved as roughly as her grip. Her fingers twisted his jerkin about his chest; her teeth scraped down his lip.

Then she shoved him away.

"What in Kingdom's ...? *Why*?" he gasped.

She shrugged. "I admire you."

"Well, that's no reason to just — just ... I don't love you, Gwen!"

515

She looked at him as if he was stupid. "I don't love you either. Love has nothing to do with it."

"Nothing to do with *what*, exactly?"

Her arms crossed over her chest. Her eyes were level with his. "Where will you go, when all this is done?"

He hadn't exactly thought about it. He supposed it would be best to stay in Tinnark, now that the Countess knew about him … but *could* he stay in Tinnark? After having seen the Kingdom in all its many shades, could he go back to shriveled brown and iron gray? What would he do with Amos and Roland? And Kyleigh hated the mountains — he couldn't ask her to stay with him in Tinnark.

"You have a home among the wildmen, if you want it." Gwen's eyes moved sharply across his face, picking his struggle apart with ease. "My people listen to you. My brother loves you. If you stay with us, you can teach him how to rule as Thane —"

"So you won't have to? So you can spend your days killing beasts and mounting their heads on your wall? No thanks," Kael said firmly. "I'm not going to give you an excuse to disappear."

"I won't disappear," she said with a smirk. "I'll come back … on occasion."

"What do you mean?"

A slight red blossomed down her neck as she shrugged. "You and I are a good match. Just because we don't love each other doesn't mean we can't … work together."

It took Kael a moment to figure out what she'd meant. But when he did, he couldn't believe it. "I'm not going to marry you, Gwen. I don't want to rule the wildmen or live in a frozen castle, and I certainly don't want to spend the rest of my life at the summit."

"Then what *do* you want?"

"Kyleigh." Her name burst from his lips like sparks from shifting coals. She was always there, always smoldering at the pointed base of his heart. He didn't regret admitting it — not even when Gwen laughed.

"The *pest?*" Her neck arched back as she laughed again, revealing the blue veins that snaked down her throat. "Oh, you poor fool."

Kael had to clench his fists to keep from punching her. "I'm not a fool. I happen to love her."

"You can't *love* her," Gwen gasped, still chortling. When she saw the look on his face, she stopped. Her voice immediately grew serious. "The pest is a beautiful creature, I'll admit that. But she isn't human. She can't give you what I'm prepared to: a wife to grow old with, children to carry your name —"

"I don't care about having children," Kael said vehemently. He thought back to the memory of Setheran and Amelia, about how heartbroken they'd been when they'd seen the symbol of the Wright in his eyes.

He certainly didn't want that life for his children. He wouldn't want them to have to carry the same weight that crushed across his shoulders even now, the guilt that made the ground go cold beneath his feet.

He'd rather they weren't born.

But Gwen wouldn't relent. "What will happen when your skin starts to wilt, and the pest stays as beautiful as ever? Will you let her hold you through your twilight years? Let her spoon broth past your toothless lips?"

"There are ways a whisperer can live for lifetimes," Kael said, thinking back to the story Baird had told him, the story of Calhamos the Healer. "I can tell my heart to keep beating."

"Not without a reason, *craftsman.* You're the mutt who couldn't topple a tree because you thought its roots went too deep." Gwen's lips bent into a smirk. "What reason could you possibly find to convince your heart to beat forever?"

He wasn't sure. But he knew one thing for certain: "I'll find one."

"Sure you will."

He could bear her smirk no longer. If he stood there another moment, he'd fight her.

"Have your fun with the pest," she called as he threw the blanket aside. "But someday you'll come to your senses — and when you do, my offer still stands."

Kael stormed out into the snow, trying to shove her taunts aside. He breathed deeply as the thick flakes melted against the rage boiling beneath his skin. His anger had so blinded him that he didn't see Silas coming until it was too late.

He slammed his shoulder hard into Kael's. "Out of my way, *human*," he hissed as he passed.

Kael was too furious to care. He sat on the ground beside Kyleigh and hardly noticed when the snow began soaking into his trousers. "If there's a more insufferable woman across the six regions, then I'll quit right now. I'll jump off the mountains rather than risk ever having to meet her."

Kyleigh said nothing.

So he ranted on: "How does she do it? How does she take a perfectly pleasant evening and twist it into the most frustrating, horrible — *she's* horrible. That's the problem. She's completely —"

"Right," Kyleigh said quietly. "She's right, you know. She's right about me, about ... everything."

He watched in disbelief as she tossed the deer's bones into the fire, as she stood and straightened the hem of her black jerkin as if nothing was at all out of place. "What are you saying? You think I ought to go be with Gwen?"

"I think you should consider it," she said curtly. She tossed the flap over her rucksack and set it to the side. Then she stooped to wrap her arms about his neck. "You and I will always be friends, Kael ... and more than anything under the stars, I want you to be happy."

# CHAPTER 45
## FATE'S SHAME

Kyleigh was gone.

She was gone before he could reply, before he could even fathom what she'd said. She was gone before he could tell her that she was wrong. Kyleigh slipped away into the frozen darkness, leaving Kael with all the things he wanted to say still burning upon his lips.

It took him a moment to realize why he hadn't spoken sooner: there were no words. All the many searing, twisting things that might've become words were still far too raw. They were glowing lumps he had no way to shape — a weight that sagged his chest. He didn't have the slightest clue what to do with them.

For a moment, he'd been certain ... he thought she might've, perhaps ... well, he thought she might've grown to love him back. He thought that if he was patient and didn't press her that she would finally admit it. At the very least, he'd expected to battle her over it for years to come.

But he'd never expected her to shrug and walk away.

The strange feeling in his blood might very well have consumed him. It might've crushed him with its emptiness. But at the moment when his head dropped its lowest, he saw Kyleigh's rucksack out of the corner of his eye.

Its flap lay clumsily over its opening — its contents weren't quite hidden. Kael didn't have to lean much closer to see the red spine of a familiar book sticking out of its top:

*Tales of Scales: The Complete Catalogue of Dragons.*

He realized it must've been the copy she'd stolen from Baird. She'd stolen all the dragon books from Lysander's library as well — he was fairly certain she'd nicked the first copy of *Scales* out from under his hammock. And it made him wonder …

What was Kyleigh hiding? If she truly felt nothing for him … why did she go to such great lengths to make certain he never read *those* particular books? Kael knew he might never get another chance to find out.

He glanced to make sure she hadn't crept up behind him before he grabbed the book. His hands trembled as he flipped it open, as he dug through the first few pages to the passage he'd drifted off trying to read a year ago:

*Long have the race of men warred with the dragon, long have they envied him. Though the King bears his image upon his heart, he knows not the dragon's strength. He is Fate's first child and the most ancient of all beasts. His life stretches into the thousands of years, sword nor arrow can pierce his skin. The fire that boils in his belly is more fearsome than the core of flame.*

*But even a dragon's breath is paled by the fury of his love. It burns in his heart, sets fire to every drop of blood. The dragon loves most fiercely: none but the one he chooses can withstand his inner blaze. He protects his chosen with all of his strength, with every mighty fiber of his soul. He will bear her pain as his own. He gladly suffers her wounds.*

*For though the dragon's eyes may gaze upon the passing of an age, his heart loves only once …*

*******

It was near dawn before Kyleigh worked up the courage to return to camp.

The last watch of the night greeted her sleepily from their posts. Hardly any noise came from the cavern shelters. Their fires had been doused by a heavy fall of snow. She'd sat so long beneath the stars that she'd had to brush several inches of white from her lap and the top of her hood. Now she faced the prospect of having to dig her rucksack from the drifts.

She thought she might've found it when Gwen emerged from her shelter. The wildwoman stretched her arms high above her and shot Kyleigh a wicked grin. "Have a good night, pest?" she called as strode towards the watch.

Kyleigh didn't smell any other bodies within the mouth of her shelter. "Where's Kael?"

"How should I know where that mutt's run off to? The last I saw, he was storming out and swearing vengeance."

Well, that was a relief. She'd been angry the night before — not at Kael or even at Gwen, but at herself. She shouldn't have listened in. She shouldn't have given the human in her any more reason to lose its grip. When she saw Kael marching away with black paint smeared upon his lips ... well, Gwen was fortunate that Kyleigh thought to be angry with *herself.*

It was in her anger that she'd shoved Kael towards Gwen. Now that the night had passed and the sun crept towards dawn, she realized that Gwen would never make him happy. It would be better if he waited for a human that could give him a life full of the love he deserved.

Kyleigh planned to find him and tell him all this. She planned to apologize for the way she'd behaved. But first, she needed to find her rucksack.

No sooner had she managed to drag it free of a pile of snow than Eveningwing greeted her from above. The chill morning wind whispered across his stormy-gray feathers as he circled overhead.

He had something to show her — and he wanted her to follow straight away.

She could read the excitement in the arches of his turns, and found it was impossible to refuse him. "All right."

He took off with a delighted screech.

Down the slope they went. Kyleigh picked her way across the mountain's slippery ridges and waded through knee-high drifts, a corner of her eye fixed upon the circling shadow up ahead.

Eveningwing led her to a monstrous rock. It stuck out of the ground like a fang, nearly swallowing the earth beside it. A narrow ledge protruded from the rock's base — just wide enough to edge around. Kyleigh caught the scent of open air and wide, boundless skies as she crept across the ledge.

"Have you come to show me the sunrise?" she called. "It's beautiful from up here, isn't it? With the peaks and the sky, and the whole realm beneath ..."

She stopped.

The sun *was* rising. Its blush spread through clouds between the peaks, staining their every bump and rift in shy swathes of crimson. A few paces ahead, the world simply ended. It plunged into the roiling clouds beneath the summit — the ironclad couriers of winter's rage. Had she not known where she was, she might've thought she stood upon an island between worlds.

But as beautiful as the sky was that morning, it was another sight entirely that stopped her short: the sight of Kael standing at the edge of the earth, smiling like she'd never seen him smile before.

Her next few steps were halting, startled. The smile she'd always known was there, the one he'd kept tucked so carefully behind his eyes was suddenly out for the world to see. It was a fierce thing, a sight carved into the mountains that made her feel as if she'd fallen through the clouds.

Then she saw the bright red book clamped between his hands, and her heart dropped to her middle. Every ounce of warmth fled her skin as she whispered: "Where did you get that?"

"I stole it out of your bag, you insufferable dragoness. Why didn't you tell me?" He held the book high, his voice suddenly accusing. "Why didn't you tell me you bloody well loved me?"

Her heart shuddered; her stomach twisted in a knot. "I'm not supposed to love you. It's Abomination."

He laughed.

"I'm serious, Kael." Had she not been so angry with him for laughing, she might've lost the struggle against her tears. This was the moment she'd been dreading from the

hour she first knew she loved him. This would be
all came to an end. "I can't love you. It's one of th
my people: *to bond with any but your own is Abomir
upon all Abomination, Fate will loose her brother — Death.*"

Kael didn't look at all troubled. In fact, he rolled his
eyes. "Well, I think Death will have a difficult time hunting me
down, given that Fate can't see me."

Kyleigh scowled at him. "Do you honestly believe that
Fate's forsaken you just because of the day you were born?"

"Do *you* honestly believe you can't love me just
because some great crone in the sky says it's Abomination?"
he countered with a smirk.

Her heart began to thud indignantly from where it'd
fallen. She couldn't believe he wasn't listening. *Why* wasn't he
listening? Why could he think everything twice over, and
twice again — but couldn't be bothered to take Death
seriously? "If I love you —"

"According to *this* you already do," he said, waving the
book. "That's why your blood doesn't burn me, why you can
heal me. You take my pain as your own because you love me
— that *is* how a dragon loves, isn't it? And that's why you've
been so desperate to hide these books. Well, it's all over,
Kyleigh," he said with a grin. "Now I know your secret."

In three strides and one furious swing, she'd knocked
the book from his hands.

His mouth fell open as he watched it flutter into
oblivion. "Baird's not going to be happy about that."

"I couldn't care less. I can't love you, and that's the end
of it. Because if I do ..." She glared to keep her eyes from
stinging. "If what I feel is truly Abomination, you'll die."

"*If*? How could it possibly ...?" The exasperated words
he'd been about to speak faded quickly. He looked at her if
he'd only just noticed the tears welling up in her eyes, the
anguish on her face. And he sighed heavily. "Sometimes it's a
*question* that keeps us grounded — not the height."

He spoke so quietly that she knew she probably
wasn't supposed to have heard him. But before she could
wonder what he'd meant, Kael went on:

523

"I know that you're worried about us not ... fitting. The fish know each other by their scales, the birds by their wings. Every creature in the Kingdom has got somebody it's meant to be with." He dragged a hand through his curls. The lights flickered madly behind his eyes. "By that measure, you and I aren't *meant* to be. There's nothing written in the stars that say we belong together, there's no predestination or prophecy. In a lot of ways, we simply don't fit.

"But in spite of all we've got against us," his smile returned as he took a step towards her, "to the shame of Fate and Death and every force in between, against all the laws of beast and man ... we love each other. And it isn't much, but I believe love can be a prophecy in its own right."

Sometime while he spoke, she'd lost track of her heart. It wasn't until his hands twined in hers that she was able to feel it beating again. "I won't let you die."

He shrugged. "What does it matter, Kyleigh? The wildmen are going to win. Titus is going to fall. Amos and Roland will be free men once more. Whether I live or die isn't going to make the Kingdom one bit of difference. We can spend the rest of our lives staring at each other, always a few paces apart ... or we can be brave."

There was a warmth beyond reckoning between them — an eternity wound through their fingers and made the lights in his eyes brighten for every year. He offered her all of that light, the whole of that eternity.

Kael was giving her a choice.

"If we die today, I want it to be because we fell. I won't let a question keep us from climbing. Be brave with me, Kyleigh," he whispered.

His lips formed so firmly around those words; his eyes held her with such certainty. They stood not only at the edge of this world, but at the edge of the next. And she realized with a fire she saw reflected inside his eyes that in whatever world they woke, she would love him all the same. She would never stop loving him.

And so she was brave.

Time halted. The mountains fell still. Kyleigh held him by the sides of his face, held his lips to hers. She felt Kael's arms wrap around her: he pressed her at her back, at her middle. He crushed her tightly against him, prepared for the fall ...

But it never came.

Slowly, time began to turn once more. Something roared through Kael's veins — she felt its fury rising as his lips moved against hers. Her body tumbled from the sky. Wind ripped through her flesh and the thrill of the plunge filled her heart with a scream.

All the fire in Kael's blood rushed to meet her. Its power consumed her — roaring, raging. The flames lifted her out of the plunge. They held her suspended over the world's edge; they stormed against her soul. She lost track of the earth, of the sky, of the heart thudding against her chest and the arms wrapped so tightly around her waist.

There were only those lips, that storm — the gales that sang the song her voice could not. Then all too soon, Kael pulled away.

She blinked against the harsh light of the rising sun and flinched at a murmur of the wind. For a moment, she feared he was gone. Then Kael's lips were at her ear. His voice was there, too. Her grip tightened about his curls as he growled:

"Who would've thought? I suppose Fate has better things to do than smite us."

He was teasing her again. Oh, he was going to pay for that.

"*What* is happening, here?" a voice called from behind her.

Sometime while they'd been tangled, Elena had sauntered out from behind the rock. Now she stood with her arms crossed and her mask pulled down to her chin, watching with a smile that made Kyleigh want to throttle her. She likely would have, had Jake not been standing at her side.

Kael pulled away. "I might ask you the same question," he said with a glare that didn't quite stifle the amusement in his voice.

Jake seemed to be in such a rush to shove his spectacles up his nose that he nearly jabbed himself in the eye. "Ah ... we, ah ... came to see the sunrise."

"Is that so?"

"If that's what the mage said we were doing," Elena cut in, "then that's exactly what we were doing."

A round of giggles drew their eyes to the rocks, where Eveningwing the boy perched among the crags. He clutched his knees to his chest and his grin was so impossibly wide that they couldn't help but smile back.

*******

"Are you ready, mutt?" Gwen said as she passed.

Kael *was* ready. The icy air slipped between his lungs and froze against the iron shell. It stirred the molten beast that lurked within him — the rage he'd had to keep pinned back for so long. Soon that beast would burst from its cage ...

Soon, Titus would meet the fury of the mountains.

They stood less than a mile from Thanehold — a squat castle perched upon a hill of angry blue stone, one lone mark of man in a sea of ice and snow. The castle looked as if it'd risen along with the mountains. Its walls had been chewed by the howling winds, its thick towers so lambasted by the ice until it took on the essence of the crags.

To its right stood the summit. The way the peaks curved at their points made them look like two colossal waves: Thanehold was perched atop the crest of one, barely clinging it to its edge while the summit towered overhead — prepared to slap all of its crushing weight down upon the fortress.

Here, the mountain's skin was too thick for trees, its flesh too cold for beasts. It was a marker, a warning — the very embodiment of the mountain's unforgiving spirit. White capped its every inch, but not even winter's jaws could do much to crack it. The summit seemed to rise with its crags crossed like arms over a chest. Though the winds scolded and shrilled, the mountains stood firm.

Kael knew Titus could see them. There was nothing for miles except the wildmen and their army. The giants, with their heavy armor and glinting scythes stood nearly as tall as the boulders. Lysander and his pirates swung their cutlasses about in practiced arcs, their eyes upon the fortress.

Jonathan had been so impressed by the craftsmen's pounding that he'd taught them how to make drums. Now a large handful of them stood in the force's middle, drums hanging from straps around their necks.

They were rough-looking things, crafted from scrap wood and the skins of beasts. But they thundered to life at the urging of the craftsmen's hands. The music was a monster all its own — one that swore death to Titus. Its intentions rumbled in the echo of every stroke.

Jonathan paced before the drummers. His fiddle shrilled a warning above their roar. His smile cut hard across his lips and had there been any words to his song, Kael imagined most of them would've been unrepeatable.

One of the warriors passed him a shallow clay bowl. It was filled to its top with the thick, black paint of the wildmen. All of his companions had their faces painted. Even Nadine marched among the giants, her brows bent over the thin designs Elena had scrawled across her cheeks.

Kael supposed there was no harm in joining them. "Here," he said, turning to Kyleigh. She stood patiently as he drew patterns around her eyes, stoking the green to brilliance. He was drawing a line down her chin with his thumb when she broke into a grin. "Quit flinching."

"I can't."

"Well, you're going to spoil it."

She grabbed him by the front of the jerkin and kissed him straight on the lips — directly in the middle of absolutely everything. When she finally released him, he could barely hear the pirates' cheers through the roar of flame.

"Scold me again, and I'll do something that'll *keep* you red," she warned.

He believed her. And so he stood perfectly still as her hands brushed down his face, painting lines and swirls. No sooner had she finished than Silas was pawing at her hem.

"Paint me next! I want to look menacing."

She obliged — though for some reason, Kyleigh seemed to be fighting back a grin the whole time she worked. When she was finished, Silas spun around excitedly: "Well, how is it? Does it look menacing?"

It looked suspiciously like a button nose and a set of long, curling whiskers to Kael. But he thought better of admitting it. "You look like a beast to be reckoned with, Silas."

He bared his teeth in a grin.

Soldiers gathered across the fortress's ramparts, the glint of their armor dulled by the fall of snow. The flakes fell sparsely enough that Kael could see them pacing worriedly from a distance. When the craftsmen's song ended, the mountains fell eerily still.

Kael's friends gathered around him. Lysander and Declan, Kyleigh and Gwen. They would be the four heads of his army, the snarling jaws of their attack — while Kael and the craftsmen knocked Titus's feet out from under him.

"Keep to your tasks," he said as they gathered. "He'll try to split you, but don't ..."

His words trailed away as a strange noise filled the air. It was the clacking of chain, the groan of wood. Kael turned and saw something he never expected to see — not in all the hours he'd planned: Titus was opening the fortress door.

It was Thanehold's only entrance. A monstrous gate creaked open over the thin strip of stone-ice that flowed up to the castle like a ramp. The gate widened just a crack, just large enough for a handful of men to march through. And standing at their head was none other than Earl Titus, himself.

There was an iron helmet clamped over his mane of hair, but Kael could still see the tangles of his beard. He dragged another man along at his side and held a dagger against the ridges of his familiar, frail back.

Kael's stomach fell from such a height that he thought it might've actually flopped out at his feet. He heard Kyleigh inhale sharply at his side, felt her hands clamp around his arm.

"You can't —"

"I have to," he said firmly. He knew he had to. One look at how Titus menaced the dagger, and Kael knew he had no choice. "At least it'll get me in a little quicker."

"He'll kill you," Kyleigh insisted, her eyes blazing.

Kael wasn't afraid. "He can try."

"At least let me come with you."

"No." He pulled her hands from his arm and brought them to his lips. He held her like that, trying to push everything he felt out into his stare so that she could see the things he saw — so that she could understand that Titus had just slit his own throat. "Keep to your task. Do exactly what we have planned and I swear I'll come back to you. Titus is desperate. This is all he has left ... and I'm going to turn it against him."

At last, she relented. He kissed her once, swiftly. Then before the fires could burn out, he marched alone towards the fortress.

"Where are you going, mutt?" Gwen hollered after him.

"To rescue my grandfather," he said with a sigh.

# CHAPTER 46
## THE WRIGHT'S ARMY

Earl Titus watched impatiently as the Wright climbed the ramp that would lead him to the castle gates. He took note of the halting steps, the way his toes seemed to drag against the ground. He reveled in the white rings around his eyes as he stared at his grandfather.

Amos, that old crow, was wise as ever. Titus had promised that if he didn't hold his tongue, he would gladly carve it out. He could see the warning stabbing from the darks of Amos's eyes. He glared, practically screaming for the Wright to turn back to his army.

Perhaps Titus would pluck his eyes out in punishment … after he'd gotten a good look at his grandson's mangled corpse, that is.

A narrow bridge of blue stone led from the frosted wastes and to the front doors of his castle. The Wright climbed it slowly, as if he expected an attack. He was right to be worried. Behind him, the many painted faces of his army watched without a sound. Giants, a few gangly seas men and those savages from the summit were all the Wright had with him. Titus could see the blankness in their stares from a distance. They would be powerless without their leader.

Even the Dragongirl would fall to his sword. He grinned at her scowl and thought: *I've got something planned for you. Oh, yes. Take to your wings, barbarian — I dare you to fly.*

At last, the heavy steps before him ground to a stop. Titus drew his eyes from the Dragongirl's blazing stare and into the depths of the Wright's.

He held his hands out to the side, his palms facing Titus. "There's no need to hurt him. Let your prisoners from the mountains go, and I'll order my army to retreat," he said loudly.

Titus laughed.

White blew from the Wright's nostrils in a frustrated breath. "I'm being more than reasonable."

Reasonable? Oh, it was far too late for that. Titus had to concentrate on the furrows between the Wright's brows to keep his dagger from twisting — because when he looked into his eyes, it was reminded of how he'd failed.

For years he'd languished in Banagher's army, tossed in among his last-born castoffs. He'd been one of Midlan's common foot soldiers — a human overshadowed by the whisperers' might. Nothing he said was heard; nothing he offered was ever quite enough. He was to salute and raise his sword, to charge at Midlan's head. He was to be willing to give his life for the sake of those who led him ... to fight for the *whisperers'* glory.

Crevan had worked for years to turn Banagher against the whisperers, and Titus had ridden the surge of unrest straight through the ranks. With the whisperers banished and the rebel forces gathering, the Kingdom was finally willing to listen. Midlan became a place where humans could toast their own victories rather than have to survive off the dregs of the more *talented* — a place where a common foot soldier might rise above his lot.

And so Titus had risen.

Crevan kept the title *warlord*, but it was only a name: Titus was the true commander of Midlan's army. Under his guidance, they beat the rebels back. The Falsewright himself had quaked rather than return to the fortress. It was by Titus's skill alone that Midlan was saved. But just when he was about to seal the Kingdom's fate, Setheran had returned.

In the final battle, Titus had the Falsewright trapped. The glory was *his* for the taking — the most powerful of all whisperers was going to die by his sword. Then Setheran and his *pet* had swooped in and stolen it out from under him. He'd snatched Titus's honor away and in a single act, undone all his years of fighting.

No one would ever remember what humans had sacrificed for the Kingdom. They would sing only of Setheran the Wright.

Now Setheran's flesh and blood stood before him. There was no mistaking it. Every defiant edge of his features lined up so perfectly with the memories of the face that tarnished his throne. Setheran was making one final move, a last thrust from the grave.

But he would fail.

The savages would wilt beneath Titus's poison and drench the summit with their gore — not a soul across the six regions would remember that the whisperers had ever existed. Then Setheran's son would be made to watch as his companions were lined up and destroyed; he would be forced to gaze upon the last flickering lights of their eyes, to hear their terrified screams ... to know that he'd brought them to their deaths.

Then at last, Titus would purge Setheran's blood from the earth. Flames would devour each crimson drop and he would scatter every flake of the Wright's ashes into the northern seas.

Yes ... the hour had come.

Titus smiled. He shoved Amos forward, into his soldiers' hands. "Very well, whisperer. Come take your grandfather — and then you and your army will leave my mountains and never return."

The soldiers marched towards him slowly. The Wright's eyes were so set on Amos that he didn't see the trap until it was already too late. An archer rose from the ramparts. He aimed carefully and at the slightest tilt of Titus's chin, he fired.

The Wright heard the bowstring. He tried to twist out of the arrow's path but its head ripped across the top of his arm. Titus watched hungrily as red seeped out into the leather of his tunic. The Wright's hand trembled as he clutched his wound. His eyes widened in shock as the mindrot took his strength.

"Grab him," Titus said, and two soldiers scooped his body up. He thrust a finger at Amos. "See to it that he lives, crow. I want the Wright to watch as I destroy his army." As Titus marched inside the fortress, he arched his neck to the ramparts and bellowed: "Seal the gates, ready the catapults. Bare your teeth, my wolves —drink your enemies' blood!"

*******

Kael focused on hanging as limply as possible as the soldiers dragged him away. They passed through the gates and into a tunnel — the belly of a short, thick tower that sat at the front of the walls.

The tower arched over the ramp and extended a good ways into the stone village beyond. A line of men rushed by, sap-filled clay jars clutched in either hand. Kael pretended to lurch back in pain and watched as they deposited the jars against an arch of the tower's wall — settling them alongside hundreds of others.

The Earl had packed the only entrance into Thanehold with enough firebombs to thaw the mountains' breath. With both the gates and the doors into the stone village sealed, the tower had become something like an enormous, sap-filled jar. One spark, and it would erupt with enough force to bury anybody caught beneath it ...

And he realized with a jolt that must've been precisely what Titus had planned.

He watched out of the corner of his eye as the Earl climbed the tower's steps and disappeared into the upper level — the one he remembered that would lead onto the ramparts. Titus would probably wait in the loaded tower for as long as possible, just to make certain he lured the wildmen in.

It was an extremely dangerous plan, but one that was bound to work. He expected no less from the man who'd brought the Kingdom to its knees.

The soldiers carried him quickly through the stone village. The squat houses had been converted into barracks for Titus's army. Shouts rang out from every direction as the Earl's men prepared themselves for battle. Kael hung limply when the soldiers dragged him into the keep, watching as the passageways twisted by, trying to keep track of where he was.

The soldiers hauled him up a narrow flight of stairs and into a room at the back of the fortress. "Lock them up tight," one of the soldiers hissed as they threw Kael inside. Amos muttered a curse as he was shoved in behind him. "Don't open the door a crack until his Earlship sends for you."

The door slammed, and Kael listened intently as the soldiers argued on the other side:

"... got a bad feeling about this. We ought to just gut him."

"His Earlship wants him alive, something about making him watch ..."

There was silence for a moment as the guards marched away. Kael flinched when Amos grabbed his wound. His weathered hands shook as he inspected the thin scrape on the top of Kael's arm. "Confound it, boy! What were you thinking? I'm not worth dying over. And I'm certainly not worth what Titus is going to do —"

"I'm all right, grandfather," Kael said.

He pulled gently out of Amos's grasp and leapt to his feet. The chamber door was made of solid wood. He got down on his belly and saw the shadows of two feet beneath its bottom crack. Then very quietly, he flattened the hinges, molding them so that the door wouldn't open.

When he turned, Amos was staring at him in shock. "You're not poisoned?"

"Why would I be? It's only a bit of night-finger juice."

Kael couldn't help but smile when he thought back to what he'd done: how he'd poured the mindrot into the cottage hearth and let the flames devour it, how Morris had held the vial wedged between his nubs as Kael crushed the night-finger's bright purple juice into it ... how one small gift from a child had become the weapon he needed to topple the Earl of the Unforgivable Mountains.

And in that moment, he knew he owed Griffith a great debt.

"Are you well?"

"I'm alive and in one piece, if that's what you're asking." Amos's sharp brown eyes flicked over Kael once more, and the lines around his mouth thinned as his lips drew tight. "I'd hoped you wouldn't come back here."

"Well, I did. I'm not going to leave you to rot."

"I'm old as they come, boy! The rotting is the only thing I've got left to look forward to. You ought to have gone and made a life for yourself. You ought to have left this whole mess behind."

"I will," Kael promised as he marched to the back wall. "Just as soon as I've taken care of Titus, you and I will go on our way."

He ignored Amos's muttering and focused on the wall. It bent under his hands, molding back until winter burst in. He squinted against the stabbing winds and the lashing of the snow as he widened the hole to something a man could squeeze through. He leaned out to get his bearings — only to nearly butt heads with a craftsman.

"Ha! I told you they'd stuff him in the larders," he called triumphantly behind him.

A chorus of howls answered and Kael saw a whole line of craftsmen waiting on the slope beneath him. The whole back end of the castle jutted out over The Drop, suspended over an infinite fall to the northern seas by little more than a ledge of stone-ice. It was a slick, jagged climb — nothing a human could've scaled. But under the craftsmen's hands, a strip of the angry blue ledge had been smoothed into a ramp.

The craftsmen clambered along their ramp and into the hole Kael had made for them. Their painted faces were frosted over, their breaths came out sharply — and their grins couldn't possibly have been any wider.

"You were right," one of them panted. "The Man of Wolves has his eyes set on the walls. He never thought to check his back."

535

He'd never thought to check because he'd been certain the wildmen wouldn't be able to think on their own. Titus was still treating them like children: he expected them to charge straight for his gates and never give any thought to strategy. So Kael was giving him exactly what he expected.

He was about to give the order to press on when Elena slipped in at the back of the craftsmen's line. "Jake said you might need someone who knows how to move quietly," she said, eyes darting over her mask to take in the room. "So, here I am."

He led her over to Amos — who was scowling at the craftsmen. "I can't believe you brought this lot with you. I can't believe you *got* them to come with you!"

Kael didn't have time to explain. If the craftsmen were already here, it meant they'd have to pick up their feet. "Do you know where Titus is keeping his other prisoners?"

Amos pointed. "Two rooms down." He watched in amazement as the craftsmen began digging a hole out of the next wall.

Kael latched Amos's weathered fingers around Elena's arm. "Take him back to Jake — don't let him out of your sight. I'll join you as soon as I can."

Amos looked as if he was about to argue when a low, groaning noise came from the back wall. It made the floors tremble and sent grit raining down from the ceiling. "What in Kingdom's name was that?" Amos sputtered.

Kael grinned; the molten beast swelled hungrily inside its chest. "It's the song of my craftsmen."

*******

Titus climbed the tower's weatherworn steps, bellowing orders as he marched. A set of narrow windows ringed its top. From here, he could see the entire battlefield spread out before him. He paced around the windows, taking note of the rampart doors on either side.

Those poor, fumbling savages hadn't learned a thing from their last beating. Their forces hurled themselves uselessly against his walls, wasting their breath in a wholly unimaginative attack.

The seas men lined archers up against his eastern edge, while the giants charged the western. The main force stood directly before his gates — led by the Dragongirl and a female savage who wielded a two-headed axe. He remembered her as the one who'd begged him to call off his attack.

She'd gotten no mercy the first time, and she would get no mercy the second.

Titus closed his eyes and touched his collar, letting the windows of his falcons overtake his vision. They circled the battlefield and watched the Wright's army through unblinking eyes.

The seas men's volley was merely a distraction. They stood well out of the reach of Titus's archers and their arrows clattered harmlessly against the castle walls, whipped away by the howling winds. His falcon sharpened its gaze at the wall's base, where a handful of savages were using the pirates' attack as an opportunity to try and scale the mortar.

"Eastern wall — a volley over the edge!" Titus commanded. He watched as his soldiers leaned over the walls and sent their arrows straight down.

The savages managed to dodge and went sprinting back to the seas men, their eyes wide with fear.

A few slings from the catapult kept the giants at bay. Those stupid oafs yelped and scattered when the first of the firebombs landed. They lumbered away until they stood safely at the edge of his range. One of them — their leader, judging by how much he bellowed — was several heads shorter than the rest. He also appeared to be drunk.

Titus watched the clumsy movements of the giant-leader's scythe and nearly rolled his eyes at how easy it was going to be. The giants might've been able to stand out of reach of his catapults, but their thick legs had no chance against his beasts. They would be overtaken and torn to shreds by evening.

Yes, the two edges of the Wright's army would be easy prey for Titus's wolves. The only real challenge of it all would be in dealing with the center.

Wedged in the middle of the three forces was the head led by the Dragongirl. Her savages had their eyes locked on the front gates. He watched in interest as some of them scooped up the blue stone at the base of the ridge. They molded it in their hands like clumps of snow before tossing it to others — who hurled them directly at Titus's gates.

He grinned as he watched large chunks of the wood splinter and fall away. The savages were going to make quick work of the gates. They'd be through in less than an hour's time. He thought it was a pity that whisperers couldn't be magicked into his service. There was no end to what he might accomplish, had he been able to control them as easily as he controlled his beasts.

The Dragongirl paced with her white sword drawn, bellowing orders to the craftsmen — while the woman with the two-headed axe stalked behind the warriors.

Her stare was fixed on Titus. It was strange to watch from above, to be able to see the fury in her glare and see himself through the window's grate — calm and close-eyed.

It'd been so easy to crumple her before. The moment she'd seen her people torn to shreds, she'd given up the fight. He'd expected her to be more cautious at this second meeting. The fact that her warriors stood so far from the gates told him that she was being careful.

But once the gates splintered and gave way, the temptation would be far too great. There'd be nothing left in her way, nothing to stop the fury behind those eyes from spilling out. She'd chase after her rage, follow it straight through the tower's maw.

Titus would let her pass ... but the savages behind her wouldn't be so lucky.

When she saw her army erupt in flame, she would be broken. She'd stare in shock as their blackened, mangled bodies were scattered across the ridge. She would lose her voice, and the remainder of the savages would lose their leader.

His beasts would rain terror down upon them. They would devour the giants and the seas men. The rest of the savages would fall to a slew of poisoned arrows. Whatever remained of the Wright's army would be driven into the frozen wastes, where winter would consume them. Titus would win this battle with a single blow — a single, calculated blast.

A screech sounded high above him, and Titus's eyes locked onto the window of one of his falcons. It circled the back wall of his keep. While his eyes had been on the giants' attack, a band of savages had darted out from behind their hulking shoulders.

They'd scurried between frosted boulders until they reached the back wall. Now they'd begun to scale the blue rock beneath the keep. Their hands worked with furious speed: flattening the jagged crests, digging a sloping path up towards the keep's base.

"Clever little savages," Titus murmured as he watched them reach the stone. Then he switched to a different window — one that overlooked a small army of beasts waiting in the courtyard. He found the set of eyes that towered above the rest and forced his command into them. "To the keep, Marc! Find those little rats and crush their skulls. Don't let them free the Wright!"

*******

Screams bounced off the walls. The shadows beneath the door's crack vanished as the soldier dove from his post. Seconds later, something heavy slammed into the door — testing its flattened hinges.

Kael stood just beyond the opening at the edge of the ramp. On his right, the villagers were scrambling down the slope to safety. On his left, a large group of craftsmen had all but disappeared into the rock. They dug like wolves, tearing huge chunks of stone-ice out from beneath the keep's base and flinging it behind them, straight into the bottomless mouth of The Drop.

They moved against the ledge like a gigantic axe: the craftsmen chipped away, widening the split between the keep's foundation and the ledge. It wasn't long before the weight of the keep began to put strain on the thin layer of stone-ice left at its base. The whole tower groaned dangerously; its broken top shifted against the shrieks of the wind.

Now the V that the craftsmen dug had grown so wide that large chunks of stone-ice began cracking from the ceiling. The keep moaned, swaying like a tree. Kael glanced up to see how much longer they might have to dig — and instead, he saw quickly that their time was up.

Screams split the air above them as Titus's monsters clambered over the keep's top. They galloped down the walls on all fours, digging in with their dagger-like claws. Their twisted muscles swelled against the pull of The Drop. Thick streams of white trailed from between their fangs as they howled for blood.

Kael watched the tower sway and groaned when he realized what would happen when the monsters reached the keep's base — when their collective, thundering weight put strain on the tower's weakness.

There was no time to waste.

"Move!" he roared, waving to the craftsmen.

They scrambled out from the V and charged down the ramp. Kael stayed to help pull the last of the villagers out of the keep. Their panicked faces passed him in a blur. He could hear the monsters' panting growing closer above him. And to make matters worse, whatever was crashing into the door was nearly through: the whole thing held on by its latch and middle hinge.

No sooner had Kael pulled the last of the villagers through the wall than the door broke — and Marc came bursting out.

Kael dove beneath his massive claws and back into the keep just as Titus's monsters reached its base. The floors rocked like a ship caught in a tempest. He heard the panicked wails of beasts and saw several of their twisted bodies fall into The Drop as the tower lurched. A mighty *crack* split the floors into two. He saw the bristled end of Marc's tail disappearing over the top of the hole, and Kael knew he had no choice but to run.

All the images he'd seen in the craftsmen's memories burst to the front of his mind, jolted to life by his panic. His legs thundered beneath him. His muscles bent and twisted, carrying him over man-wide splits in the floor — curving as the keep tilted.

The floors became the walls. The walls became the floors. Kael leapt over torch sconces. He ducked into an enclave to avoid a wave of soldiers. They screamed and fell down the hall, dragged by the weight of their armor. One man hurtled straight into the edge of the enclave. Kael heard a *clang* and a sickening crunch as The Drop swept the body away.

Kael was still several yards from the door when the keep tilted to its final angle — the only floor was suddenly a hundred feet beneath him. So he had no choice but to climb.

His holds were clumsy, dug out by the frantic grasping of his hands. The warrior in him calmed the craftsman. His eyes found the best places to hold, his feet moved surely. The keep door was directly above him — a gap of light at the top of a cellar's steps.

Kael hurled himself up the final few feet. His hands grasped. His arms pulled him over. The keep was still shifting, groaning towards The Drop. His legs jolted into a sprint. He ran across the keep's outer wall and dove for the ramparts. The guards stationed along its top cried out, scattering to avoid him.

The world shook violently as his boots touched the ground and the keep broke free, tumbling straight into The Drop. Kael's body flew forward — catching its weight on his shoulder and smoothing it with a roll. No sooner had he leapt to his feet than arrows hissed by his ears. He charged the

Earl's soldiers with a roar, donning his dragonscale armor as he went.

His arm exploded through the first man's chest and the rest of the soldiers tore off with a scream, shouting at the tops of their lungs:

"Fall back! The Wright's escaped! Fall back to the gates!"

# CHAPTER 47
## WOLFSTOMP

"Run! *Run*, you fools!" Titus bellowed the moment the keep began to shake. He had both hands clamped upon his collar. The gold bit into the pads of his fingers as he roared, as he tried to will his beasts to safety.

Half of the windows showed beasts that managed to cleave to the ramparts and the cliff side, to find their way to solid ground — a sheet of gray sky consumed the rest. Clouds whipped by. Dying shrieks raked against his ears as his beasts fell for an eternity. The last thing Titus saw was the maw of the northern seas. One by one the windows went to black as his beasts' bodies were crushed against the ice-capped waves.

Titus's eyes snapped open as he groped for the relief of his own sight. In a single blow, the Wright had destroyed half of his army of beasts. But he'd done far worse than that: nearly all of his army's supplies for the winter now lay in the depths of the northern seas, drowned along with the keep.

With the back of his fortress gone, the barracks were open and vulnerable to the howling winds. Titus felt its breath hiss through the windows and cross the nape of his neck, but steeled himself against it.

The Wright may have left him vulnerable to winter, but it'd cost him his life. He'd watched through Marc's eyes as the Wright scrambled back inside the keep and to his death. Titus would replace his army's supplies with the spoils of battle. They would take refuge within the stone village. All was not lost —

"Fall back! The Wright's escaped! Fall back to the gates!"

Impossible.

Titus lunged to the western window and saw a lone figure barreling across the ramparts. His arms swung furiously beside him, trailing arcs of red behind his every blow as he hacked his way through Titus's soldiers.

He watched a sword shatter against the Wright's chest and howled his curses. D'Mere had deceived him. Her poison hadn't worked! Now the Wright was as powerful as ever — and he was charging straight for the tower.

But he could still be stopped. "Catapults — aim for the ramparts! Bring him down!"

They scrambled to obey, working frantically to lower their aim while more soldiers raced up the steps to crowd the ramparts. With their keep destroyed, his wolves seemed to realize that the only way they would survive would be to kill the Wright.

And they would give their lives to stop him.

Titus was about to send his beasts into the fray when a familiar, earth-shattering roar broke him from his concentration. He lunged to the northern windows and saw the Dragongirl had taken to her wings. She rose over the walls and spat fire into the courtyard — heading straight for the catapults.

Titus bared his teeth in a grin. She'd just given him an unexpected opportunity to hobble the Wright. "Now, archers!"

He'd had a ring of soldiers hidden at the tower's top, crouched beneath the walls and waiting with a single purpose: to destroy the Dragongirl.

Their cries rang above him and he watched as a volley of arrows left the tower's top. They were arrows he'd made especially for her — tipped with dragonsbane heads.

Three of the arrows struck the Dragongirl's wing. Her flame stopped short of the catapults as she twisted in mid-air, writhing against the pain. Titus watched as her wings faltered — as she drifted clumsily over the wall and landed hard in the field beneath him. He growled in triumph when he heard the Wright scream:

"Kyleigh!"

He was broken now. Oh yes, his strength would wane just as it had at the river. He would be unfocused, vulnerable. And while his heart was broken, Titus would rip it from his chest.

Wood creaked above him as his archers drew the ending volley —

"Ah!"

The crunch of bone and the sharp clap of rock sounded overhead. Archers tumbled past his window, limp and trailing gore — bludgeoned to death by a volley of ice-blue stones. He heard the savages howl in triumph and at the same moment, heard his catapults loose their jars.

Screams rent the air as a sea of orange-blue flame consumed the ramparts — devouring his soldiers along with the Wright. He watched their writhing bodies for a moment, basking in the Dragongirl's agonized roar. Titus drank in his victory with a howl. Now that the Wright was finished, he could carry out his plan for the savages.

Titus was marching towards the rampart doors when one of his soldiers cried: "Your — Your Earlship!"

He sprinted back to the windows and watched in horror as his soldiers' burning corpses tumbled into the courtyard — thrust away by the Wright. His body was engulfed in flame, but he charged forward. He broke free of the corpses and burst into a sprint ...

"Move! Get out of my way!" Cold strangled Titus's limbs as he hurled himself out the door and onto the opposite ramparts. He ran as far and as fast as his legs would carry him, his teeth gritted against what he knew would happen next.

But no matter how he tried to brace himself, the blast still knocked him off his feet.

The earth shook and ice sprayed out in a wave as the tower exploded. Rocks the size of men burst out and tumbled down the ridge. The stone bit Titus's knees as the force of the explosion knocked him to the ground. The few soldiers that'd managed to escape the blast *clang*ed down hard behind him, dragged off their feet by the weight of their armor.

Titus twisted onto his back, dragged himself to his feet and saw, with a horror that froze his limbs, a burning streak erupt from the tower's remains and begin charging its way towards him. He heard the savages' wild cries. He watched from the corner of his eyes as they clambered over the blazing ruins and into the courtyard to battle what remained of his beasts. But the Wright's stare consumed the rest of his vision.

His eyes were made darker by the fires that danced across his skin — a blackened gaze untouched by flame. They stayed locked onto Titus the whole while he fought. Heads rolled from the sweep of his arms. Bodies crumpled at his feet. The orange-blue flame ate across his jerkin, but the Wright's stare never faltered.

At last, the final paltry line of his soldiers fell to the Wright's fury. Titus heard the wails of his beasts as they fought desperately against the savages, and he knew that victory was out of his grasp.

The last of the Wright's flames died to the breath of winter. The red mark that cut down his chest showed clearly through the charred holes in his tunic. His hands hung empty at his sides. His eyes glinted furiously from beneath the crop of his reddish hair.

Titus did the only thing he could do, the only defense he had left: he lowered his gaze ... and fell to his knees. "I could be a powerful ally to you, Wright. The Kingdom is ours for the taking. With my help, the crown could be yours —"

"I don't care a whit about the crown." His words were as biting as the winter, his voice no more forgiving than stone. "You've already taken the Kingdom, Titus. You've shed its blood and strangled its children. You've wrung the tears from its eyes. I've seen the scars of your *power* in every hold across the realm."

He took a step forward, and Titus brought his chin from the ground to meet his eyes. There had to be something there — some weakness he may have overlooked. He'd been able to find mercy in Setheran's eyes ... but there was no mercy in his son's.

Instead, the warrior's edge had been refined, sharpened until it glinted like steel. His fury lay unsheathed inside his glare, never to be covered. And Titus knew before he even spoke that he would not escape death that day ...

For Death looked him in the eyes.

"I'm going to kill you, Titus," the Wright growled. "Not for power, not for vengeance — but for the Kingdom's sake. For the simple reason that as long as you're dead, everything that's good in this realm has a chance."

In that moment, Titus knew he was beaten. He knew there would be no escape. The Wright raised his arm, brought it above his head ...

*No!* No, Titus refused to die this way. He wouldn't die kneeling before a whisperer — he would stand. He would fight to his last breath. He would fight once more for the glory of men!

His sword hissed as he drew it from its sheath. The blade struck the Wright's upraised arm and shattered. The hilt jarred from his hand. A resounding *crack* echoed in his chest as the Wright's fist shattered his ribs. Titus's back struck the ground hard.

Pain stabbed him with his every breath. He gaped at the swirling gray sky, blinked against the flakes of snow that drifted to melt against his skin. Blood coated his tongue with its peculiar, metallic tang. The agony in his chest railed so fiercely that his body began to numb rather than try to take it in.

The Wright's face appeared above him. His eyes watched mercilessly as Titus struggled to breathe. His boot came up, arching high over Titus's chest, and he knew what was coming.

When he tried to beg, a fresh spurt of blood clogged his throat. *Please,* he thought furiously. *Please — not like this. Allow me to stand. Let me take up my sword!*

But the Wright couldn't hear him. He never faltered in his stride. And so with a blow that shook the mountain's top, Titus went to meet Death.

*******

Kael watched as Titus's eyes darkened and his body stilled. The Earl's breastplate had collapsed beneath Kael's boot, crushing his ribs and innards. A scarlet puddle formed beneath the Earl's tunic. It spread eagerly across the mortar and stone, only stopping when it froze.

For a moment, Kael breathed deeply. The molten beast inside his chest cooled and sank beneath the rivers of his blood. He grinned when he heard the craftsmen howling from the field:

"Wolfstomp! Wolfstomp!"

He raised his fist, and they howled all the more.

Then he heard Nadine cry out in warning: "They are coming over the walls!"

With Titus dead, his beasts seemed to have found a new leader. Marc's great bristling body disappeared over the ramparts — followed quickly by the remaining horde of beasts. The wildmen gave chase but couldn't follow as the monsters vaulted over the walls.

Above them, the falcons screeched furiously. The first fell from the sky in a black bolt. Its pointed beak hung open, its talons stretched out. Both of its monstrous eyes were locked onto the villagers.

In the instant before it could strike its mark, Declan leapt into its path. The falcon split from around the upraised edge of his scythe in nearly two perfect halves. "Steady on, you clodders — protect the wee mountain rats!"

The giants wrapped tightly around the villagers, their scythes pointed outwards towards the hurtling bloodtraitors like the jagged maw of some gluttonous beast.

Kyleigh galloped towards them with a roar. Yellow flame spewed from her mouth and arced high, reducing the falcons to cinders. Their bodies tumbled out of the sky like fallen stars and crashed into the snow with hisses and puffs of steam.

The pirates were running to the giants' aid; the wildmen were leaping over the ruins of the shattered gate.

548

Kael sprinted as fast as his legs would carry him, prepared to leap from the ramparts and onto Marc's bristling back —

Snow and ice burst from the field before the giants in a monstrous wave. A beast with a dragon's head and a great, furry-white body lunged out and snapped at Marc. It was only by the panic of his long limbs that Marc was able to hurl himself to the side — and the beast's great jaws clamped around the body of a weasel instead.

Kael heard the crunch from the ramparts, watched the iron on the weasel's chest get torn and twisted between the monster's jaws before it spat its mangled body away and snapped down for seconds.

More snow burst up, more creatures lunged out. Their backs were covered in ice-blue scales. The spikes that ran down their stout tails crushed the bloodtraitors' twisted heads. Wherever their claws pounded down, they left crimson stains and mangled limbs behind. One drove its horned head into the snow like a battering ram, flattening three beasts beneath it.

In the midst of all the chaos, Marc had nearly escaped. Kael caught sight of his reddened body as he fled over the hill and charged after him. But Gwen got there first.

The two-headed axe flew from her hand, whistling towards Marc. There was a hollow *thud* as it struck him between the shoulders. His twisted body crumpled to the ground. He howled piteously, struggling under its edge as Gwen marched over to him. She wrenched the blade from his back and raised it high. Kael looked away as it fell.

Marc's screams were cut short. He heard the thud of the axe falling twice more. When he dared to look back, Gwen hefted Marc's severed claws above her head. "I've killed him! I've slain the red devil!"

The wildmen let out a triumphant howl.

Gwen's eyes darkened quickly as she began marching towards the dragon-like creatures. Their battle was done: the last of Titus's beasts lay slain in a twisted mass. Now the creatures stood noticeably before the giants — not threatening, but present. There was more warning in their ice-blue stares than bite.

Fortunately, Kyleigh reached them before Gwen could do anything rash. Kael's stomach twisted when he saw the arrows that stuck out from one of her great wings. He scrambled down the gate's ruins and through the ranks of pirates, listening to their confused murmurs as he went:

"Did you know that about her?"

"... always knew she was a strange one."

"Strange, aye — but *this*?"

It'd been so long that he'd forgotten how desperate Kyleigh had been to hide her second shape. Now as he saw the looks on the pirates' faces, he was reminded quickly. Their brows arched high and their mouths hung open. Some even clutched warily at their swords.

"Mind your manners, dogs!" Lysander barked as he fell in next to Kael. The captain's handsome face twisted in worry as he eyed the creatures standing before the giants. "Good Gravy. Please tell me we aren't going to have to fight those ... well, whatever they are." His concern quickly melted into confusion. "What *are* they?"

"I think they're called *wynns*," Kael said, though he could still hardly believe it.

Eveningwing the hawk perched upon Lysander's shoulder. He nipped playfully at Kael's curls as they walked. For some reason, seeing that the halfhawk wasn't concerned made him feel better about things.

"As long as Gwen behaves, there shouldn't be a problem," Kael said, more to assure himself than anybody.

The wildmen shoved him through their ranks, howling and pounding their chests. When he reached the head of the line, Gwen snatched him by the back of his shredded jerkin and threw him towards Kyleigh. "Make sure the pest doesn't trick us," she growled.

There was more concern on her painted face than he'd ever seen.

He jogged to Kyleigh's side, gaping at the arrows that hung from her wing. Their heads were made of dragonsbane and slightly hooked, which meant they'd stay latched into her flesh until the shafts were broken away.

Her fiery blood boiled in streams from each hole; the tip of her wing dragged against the ground. Seeing the pain in her eyes sent fire roaring to the ends of Kael's clenched fists.

It made him wish he could kill Titus a second time.

He reached immediately for Kyleigh's wounds, but she nudged him away. *Later*, her eyes said.

He glared at her. "Do you swear? I won't let you play the hero."

She promised she would behave. Then she lumbered towards the wynns, dragging her horned head in an arc that he knew meant she wanted him to follow.

The wynns were spread out behind their leader. Their pupils were slitted, cutting up like spear points across their frozen blue eyes. Deep breaths rumbled inside their furry chests — most of which were stained with fresh spatters of bloodtraitor.

Kael felt as if he stood before a second council, one every bit as ancient as the mountains. He wondered if any of them were as old as Kyleigh. Perhaps they were even older. His toes had begun to curl under their stares when he heard a sound that surprised him: a hum, low and deep.

The hum wailed like a storm and ended with the deep boom of a drum. The wynn leader's furry chest expanded, and he hummed again. Kael's heart leapt when Kyleigh answered. Her voice was lighter, but no less beautiful. Her hum trembled through the wynn's in a heart-stopping song.

Kyleigh looked down at him suddenly. Her blazing eyes drifted over his and her great, scaly arm shifted closer. Kael realized that she wanted him to touch, to listen.

His heart was pounding in his throat as he pressed his hands against her stark white scales. Her voice trembled across his ears and sank deep, until he heard the echo of its meaning from inside his soul:

*... pleasant day to you, Berwyn*, she said.

Kael's heart thudded as he looked at the wynn leader. *Berwyn? The one Gwen spoke of?*

*She is a worthy enemy, this new Thane-child.* Berwyn replied. His voice was growling and deep. It swelled across some words, faded back across others — his chest rumbled like thunder against the seas. *I should like to war with her for many passings of the sun.*

His bright blue eyes shifted over Kael's shoulder as he spoke. The slits carved through them narrowed as they lighted on Gwen. "Take one step towards me and I'll gladly lop off your head, you hairy lizard," she swore.

Kael grinned at Berwyn's rumbling reply. "He says he notices that you don't have your sacred weapons with you."

"But we do have magic!" Jake worked his way through the thick of the giants, squeezing his slight frame between their hulking bodies until he stood at the head of their army. His stare was sure as he pushed his spectacles up his nose — determination pierced his eyes.

Elena slipped in behind him. She stood with her arms crossed, glaring over her mask at the wynns.

Jake flexed his gloved hands in warning. "They're such fascinating-looking creatures. I'd hate to have to blast them out of their scales. But I'll do it. So, just ... stand aside, will you?"

An icy wind struck Kael in the face as Berwyn sighed. Frost crusted over his nose and brows, making them sting a little. *The wynns have no power against the fury of the mages. We will allow the humans to pass.*

At his utterance, the wynns parted and Jake marched through. Elena's dark eyes shone for a moment as they lighted on his back — but hardened quickly when she saw Kyleigh watching.

Declan's eyes were still red, and he reeked of pirate grog. His mouth hung open as he stopped before Kyleigh. "Plains mother, now I know why the manfolk called you *Dragongirl*. You really *are* a dragon-girl. Did you know about this, sandbeater?" he said, snatching Nadine as she passed.

"I would shock you with the things I know," was her curt reply. Then she prodded him with the butt of her spear. "Raise your heavy feet, giant!"

When Declan did nothing but stare, Kyleigh bent and nudged him on with the tip of her nose.

"She's warm!" Declan exclaimed as he stumbled forward. "Most scaly things've got cold blood — but she's warm! Did you know *that*, sandbeater?"

"Did you know I am not above jabbing you if you do not get your giant middle out of my path?"

"Oh, you aren't *above* anything, mite!" Declan said with a grin. He scooped her over his shoulder and charged away — bursting into laughter when she cursed in her strange tongue.

At Gwen's command, the pirates, the giants, and the warriors disappeared inside the fortress to set up camp for the evening. The craftsmen grumbled to themselves as they stripped Titus's beasts of their collars. They held the dragonsbane out before them and Kael could see the eagerness in their eyes. He was certain they'd have the collars shaped back into proper weapons before nightfall.

Once the craftsmen had finally slipped through the gates, Berwyn made a request. "He wonders if you'll speak with him, Gwen," Kael said.

He could feel the heat boiling off of her as she stood reluctantly at his side. "I don't care what he's done for the others — this changes nothing."

*Everything has changed, Thane-child*, Berwyn rumbled. *You know this. You sense the mountains' pain as clearly as I.*

Her stare hardened when Kael relayed his words, but she didn't argue.

Berwyn's deep blue eyes turned to where their companions had gone. He blasted them with another frosted sigh. *Humans have never climbed so high before. The mountain's top belongs to creatures who understand its beauty, who can brave its dangers.*

"The summit belongs to the wildmen," Gwen growled. "Sacred weapons or no, I won't let you shove us down."

Wind stirred the long mat of Berwyn's hair. Snow caught among its pale strands. *I love to fight you, Thane-child.*

553

*You are a most worthy foe. But for the sake of our mountains, I'm afraid our war must rest.*

He was quiet for a moment, and the other wynns began to shift behind him. They slumped to lie on their furry bellies, crossing their massive foreclaws. Kael could sense the surrender in the gesture.

Gwen must've sensed it, too. Her axe slipped from her hand and buried itself in the earth at her feet. Then to Kael's great surprise, she hissed: "I know."

*Our refuge is wounded*, Berwyn said, his voice heavy. *She aches with the mages' scar. Do not fear, Thane-child: she will heal. In time, the wilds will cover over her wounds and she will flourish once more. But while she is maimed, she will be weak.*

"Lesser humans will start coming in by the road," Gwen said, her eyes sharpening. "War-mongers and treasure-seekers — scourge like the Man of Wolves."

*Scourge far* worse, Berwyn murmured. He dipped his great head low until he rested on his belly. *We must be the rivers and the sky, the caverns and the peaks. Your people must guard her from below, and mine shall guard her from above.*

"I won't reduce my people to living downmountain," she spat, glaring.

Kael thought she was being pretty unreasonable. "Well, it's not as if the wynns can guard the bottom. If the King saw them, they'd be hunted down and chained."

"They want the summit for themselves," Gwen insisted, her face burning redder.

Kael saw Berwyn's chest expand and threw an arm over his face in time to spare himself from the wynn's frosty sigh. *To be anywhere in the Wildlands is a gift, Thane-child. Whether it is at the mountain's top or beneath it. We will guard our refuge with all of our strength.*

Gwen's chin jutted out. Her eyes burned fiercely. For a moment, Kael feared she might very well take up her axe and charge. But instead, she simply thrust a finger at Berwyn and snarled: "This isn't over, beast. One day when the mountains heal, my children's children will take up the wildmen's task once more. They'll march to the summit and reclaim what's rightfully theirs — and they'll cast your severed head into the northern seas."

Two lines of very sharp, pointed teeth appeared between Berwyn's scaly lips as he bared his grin. *I look forward to that, Thane-child. May Fate grant us many years of battling to come.*

# CHAPTER 48
## ATLAS OF THE ADVENTURER

"I still can't believe you bothered with all this," Amos grumbled as he shuffled around the hospital. "You knew there'd be no more Tinnark. Why waste time trying to fix something that'll be no use to anybody?"

For all the days they'd traveled down the mountain, Amos had done nothing but grump. He'd scowled at the snow, cursed the wind, and spat about the walk. He was a good deal crankier than Kael had ever remembered him being. And he didn't understand it.

"I thought you'd be pleased."

"Pleased? *Hmph.*" Amos muttered to himself the whole way back to the office. When he reached the door, he stopped. "Who in Kingdom's name are you?"

"Baird the Beggar-Bard!" came the chirping reply. "I speak with a voice like honey and make plain all of the forgotten whispers of the earth."

"Of course you do," Amos said. He shook his head as he made his way back into the main room. "Why have you got to keep so many blasted strange folk about you, boy? Can you not have one common man in among them?"

"They're my friends," Kael said — so sharply that he surprised himself. "If you'd take a moment to speak with them instead of snorting, you might find you like them."

Amos stared at the smoldering hearth for a moment before he slumped down onto the foot of Kael's bed.

He watched the furrowed lines between Amos's brows, watched how they suddenly became shallow — and all at once, he understood. Kael sat beside him. "I miss Roland, too."

He'd spent most of their last night in Thanehold mourning over Roland. His tears had felt as if they slid down familiar tracks ... as if somewhere deep in his heart, he'd been expecting it. They burned, but not as fiercely as he'd thought they would. Perhaps it was because Marc and Laemoth were dead that he hadn't hurt so badly for Roland.

Perhaps vengeance had softened the blow.

"Roland ..." The name came from Amos in a half-sigh. "You want to know why I won't meet your friends, boy? Because there's no blasted point in it. The moment you come to love someone, they're taken from you. Death is all we've got to look forward to."

Kael didn't like the far-off look in his eyes. "Grandfather?"

He shook his head. His hand came down roughly upon Kael's knee. "Don't let me make you miserable. You've got plenty to look forward to. Love can be as healing as it is cruel."

His words were eerily familiar. "Have you ever heard the story of Calhamos the Healer?"

Amos snorted, half-laughing. "The bards love to keep that one alive, don't they? They can't stop chirping about poor Calhamos the Half-Hearted. If they knew what it was really like having to plod on with a broken heart, they wouldn't be so quick to spew their rubbish." His wrinkled smile fell back into a frown when he saw the confused look on Kael's face. "Oh, don't tell me you're that thick, boy. Calh*amos* the Healer? Don't you remember me telling you about why I changed my name?"

"You never told me anything about that — you never told me anything about *anything!*" Kael sputtered. "Are you telling me that *you're* Calhamos the Healer?"

"Well I'm trying to, but you aren't listening!"

Kael couldn't believe it. "How old are you?"

"Too old," he grumped. His eyes narrowed at the question forming on Kael's lips. "No — no, it sounds like a decent thing, but trust me: you don't want to live forever. And besides that, you can't. You haven't got the gift for it."

"Odd. I seem to remember a certain grumpy old man telling me I had a *knack* for healing."

Amos let out a frustrated sigh. "What would you have had me do, boy? Tell the truth?"

Kael threw up his hands. "Yes, actually. I would rather have known it all from the beginning. I'm not a child — you don't have to protect me."

"All right, then. If you want the truth so badly, here it is." Amos reached inside his tunic and drew out a rumpled square of parchment.

Kael only caught a glimpse of the words scrawled across its front, but that was all he needed. He knew before Amos even started reading that the letter was from Setheran.

"*Raise him, protect him. One day, Kyleigh will come for him. When she does, you must let him go.* There," he muttered, tossing the letter aside. "There's your truth. Do you feel better about it all?"

No, he didn't. In fact, he felt as if he was going to be sick. "How did Setheran know? How did he know that Kyleigh would come for me? How did he know about ... everything?"

Amos snorted. "He said he stole her future. I warned him no good would come of it. There's a reason most folk can't tell —"

"Wait a moment," Kael cut in, his gut twisting. That sounded exactly like something Baird had told him. "*Whose* future did Setheran steal?"

"Kyleigh's," Amos grunted, scowling at the memory. "He said if he couldn't have yours, then hers was the next best thing. He said he knew she'd find you one day — and after that, you'd be *tied together*, or some blasted nonsense."

Had the bed not been between them, Kael was certain he would've sank through the floor. A thousand questions bounced inside his head — not the least of which being how it could even be possible to *steal* somebody's future. But one question raged above all the others.

"Why couldn't Setheran have my future?" he whispered, though his heart moaned as if it already knew the answer.

Amos's brows clamped down tightly over his sharp eyes. "You were born on Death's Day, boy. As far as Fate's concerned, you have no future. I had every mind to fold that letter up and forget about it," he grumped on, oblivious to the sullen ice that crusted over Kael's heart. "I wanted you to have a normal life. But you were too different. You were too much like ... *him*.

"When that girl turned up in the woods, I knew it had all ended," he muttered, shaking his head. "I made my peace with it and swore I'd see you off. That's it. I've fulfilled my every promise. My task is finished."

Dread sank past Kael's frozen heart and settled at the bottom of his gut. It pressed down harder as he watched Amos get to his feet. "What do you mean your task is finished?"

"You know what it means."

Anger boiled up Kael's throat. It rose, swallowing the other things that swelled inside of him: the dread, the ice — a new horror that fell as miserably as an autumn rain. "Is that all I was to you? A *task*?"

Amos's fingers curled about his shoulder. "One thing the bards won't tell you is *how* I managed to survive my sorrow. There's a price to be paid for shirking Death — calluses keep my heart together. Maybe it wasn't as soft a love as you deserved, but it was all I had left to give."

He shuffled for the door, and Kael got to his feet. "Where are you going?"

"To sleep."

"There's plenty of room here," he said, trying desperately to ignore the warning in his heart. "You can take my bed."

"I need the sleep that brings peace, boy." He pulled the door open and stood, staring at the frosted ground. "I need rest that lasts an age. *The woods have held your body all this time, so they ought to be good enough for your bones.* That's what Roland was always going on about. He didn't get to take his blasted woodsman's walk, so I suppose I'll have to do it for him. For both of us."

559

Kael could hardly breathe. "I fought for you, grandfather. You're the whole reason I marched back up the mountains!"

"Well, I wish you hadn't."

"Then I wish you would've gone ahead and given up," Kael said back. His face burned furiously, but his tongue knew no shame. "What was the point of *plodding on* this last year if you planned to give in the moment I saved you?"

"Hope." Amos turned to watch Kael from over his shoulder. "I'd hoped that you would come into your gifts, waited for the day when all the misery we went through in this blasted little village would finally mean something ... for the day when you'd prove the elders wrong. But more than all that, I lived on because I'd hoped to see you again.

"Your father gave me a remarkable gift the day he sat you in my arms. You colored a dull world, brought meaning to years I was certain would be altogether meaningless. When I watched my son march down the mountains to face his death, you were the one thing that kept my heart from breaking ... and you've made every beat worth the pain. I don't care a whit for the Kingdom," he smiled slightly, "but you've finally found your place, boy. And now your old grandfather can rest well knowing you're happy."

Kael sat down hard. He heard the door creak, felt winter's breath muffled as it closed.

And Amos was gone.

*******

He wasn't sure how long he stared at the hearth. Kael watched the flames chew thick branches down to coals, to cinders. One of the wildmen came by to take Baird to dinner, but Kael didn't follow.

There were no tears left for Amos. Even if there had been, he suspected they were buried so deeply that it might take him years to draw them out. For now, he was raw — like a patch of flesh exposed to the sun. But he would crust over eventually. Someday, he might be able to decide whether he was more furious or anguished by the loss.

Perhaps he'd been a fool to destroy Setheran's letter. Had he not thrown it into the flames, perhaps he might've spared himself some of the emptiness he now felt. But these were fleeting thoughts.

In his heart, Kael wanted nothing more than to press on. He couldn't erase the things he'd learned about his past, but he was determined not to let them haunt his future. After what Amos had told him, he realized that Kyleigh had probably known more than she let on. Perhaps she'd even allowed Setheran to take her future — hoping to weigh the die in his favor. But he didn't care.

Kyleigh could keep her secrets. He wouldn't spend another moment fretting about his past. The prints he'd left behind would eventually fade into the sand. He would concern himself with the greener lands beyond the wastes, focus only on the parts of his story that he might write for himself.

And there *would* be more to write. He was certain of it. In fact, he planned to live happily for many years to come. He was determined to live happily.

Kyleigh slipped in a few minutes after Baird had gone. Light flooded the hospital as she piled fresh wood onto the dying flames. Three shining marks stood out in a line across her back, from where the dragonsbane arrows had pierced her armor.

They'd left gaping holes in the scales — holes with edges that looked as if they'd been charred in flame. Kael had sealed them back the best he could, but the marks still showed.

Kyleigh sank down beside him. The hearth fires had roared to life under her care, crackling with hunger. He heard the sound of rumpling parchment as she pulled Amos's letter open, silence as she read. Then her hands were in his hair, against his neck. She coaxed his head into her lap and held him tightly, draping an arm across his chest.

After a moment, he found his voice: "Did you … see him?"

"He's taken his eternal rest," she murmured. Her lips brushed forehead, and warmth spread across his skin where she touched. "I've never seen a man more at peace."

That must've been precisely what he'd been waiting for; those were the words his heart needed to hear. When Kyleigh whispered for him to close his eyes and sleep, that was exactly what he did.

*******

It was with no small amount of grumbling that the wildmen began their march downmountain.

The snow fell lightly that morning. Thin flakes settled gently upon their packs. It covered the pointed roofs of the houses, streaked the proud beards of the Thanes guarding the Hall. As the wildmen slumped to the edge of Tinnark, the snow marked their every step.

Lines dragged behind the prints told of their reluctance. Tiny mounds formed where their toes dug in against their fates. But their heels came down firmly. They left craters in the drifts that would take the snow hours to fill. So it was by the force of their stubborn will that the wildmen took their final steps out of Tinnark.

Kael stood at the edge of the village as the last of his companions marched by. He allowed himself one final look at the tented homes, the hard-packed streets, and the solemn gray sky above it. The hospital sat by itself in the distance — he could just make out its long, sloping roof.

The sleepy murmurings of the wildmen faded down the road and for a breath, the gentle fall of snow silenced the earth. Kael felt as if he was headed out to sea and Tinnark watched him from the docks. He felt as if the tiny, pointed houses waved him on — as if the Hall raised its fist and the hospital wished him well.

But he knew in his heart he would never return from this voyage. He would sail on to new lands and leave the old

562

behind. This realization coated his tongue with something that tasted bittersweet.

He felt a familiar tug on his pack as Baird's knobby fingers tightened their grip. "Old trees must perish to give way to the new. Ah, but how sad to see a monster fall. I shall plant new roots among these howling men — their Thane has offered me warmth and a full belly for the rest of my days. I would be a fool to turn such a boon aside."

For once, he'd been so quiet that Kael had actually forgotten he was there. "I'm happy for you, Baird."

"Happy? Hmm, happiness takes on a strange smell about you, then. It reeks of something solemn." He dropped his voice to a whisper. "I hear Kael the Wright means not to settle. I hear he means to travel on and leave the howling men."

Kael was more than a little surprised. He hadn't told a soul what he had planned. "How did you —?"

"Ah, I shall miss him greatly!" Baird moaned over the top of him. "Do pass my sorrows on, when next you see him."

Kael sighed heavily. "Baird ... I *am* Kael the Wright."

He glanced over his shoulder and saw that the beggar-bard's grin had spread wide beneath his bandages. "I know that, young man — but I was beginning to wonder if *you* did!"

*******

By midday, what started as one of the gloomiest mornings Kael had ever seen had blossomed into full-fledged nonsense.

Jonathan struck up a particularly bawdy ballad and the pirates sang along, trying to coax smiles from the wildmen's faces. It was only after Lysander had them clapping out of tune for several moments that the craftsmen finally joined in.

They beat their drums in annoyance at first, trying to force the pirates back into rhythm. But soon the pounding was no longer forced: they played a wild tune that thrummed beneath Jonathan's fiddle, giving life to every bawdy line.

The song of craftsmen's drums swept the warriors in. They learned the pirates' jig with ease — though what started out as a harmless dance quickly became a caddoc.

They spun each other around with such terrible force that the whirling motion would cause one of them to lift his feet up off the ground. When that happened, his partner would take the opportunity to sling him into the nearest tree.

Lysander swore and dropped to the ground the first time a wildman went sailing overhead. "Good Gravy!" He swore again when a tree cracked and thudded into the ground. "Somebody's bound to get very seriously injured if you don't keep a tighter hold on your men!"

Gwen stopped laughing long enough to shout: "Make sure those trees fall *away* from the path! We're not trying to get anybody flattened."

"Yes, Thane!" Griffith cried. Then he hurled his partner into an oak.

The resulting *crack* had Lysander swearing all over again.

With the caddoc slowing the wildmen's pace, the giants marched well ahead. The force of the earth seemed to carry their hulking bodies quickly down the slopes. They still grumbled about the thinness of the air, but seemed to be happy about going downhill.

Nadine had taken it upon herself to look after the children from downmountain. They followed in a neat little clump behind her — many wielded staves with their ends sharpened to points.

Somehow, the whole lot of them had been surrounded by giants, and Nadine wasn't at all pleased about being trapped among their thick ranks. "I do not need your protection," she barked at Declan.

He glanced at her from over his shoulder. "Protection? What makes you think I'd bother protecting such a wee speck of woman?"

"*This*," she said impatiently, waving at the wall of giants that surrounded her and the children. "What is this if not protection?"

"It looks to me like you've drifted into the middle of our march."

"Your march has swallowed us! Everywhere we turn, we are followed. Your heads blot out the sky!"

"Well then, I suppose we ought to bring the sky to them."

There was a chorus of delighted squeals as the giants scooped the children onto their shoulders. Their little red heads bobbed above the crowd and their laughter filled the air.

"Be careful with them!" Nadine warned, though her glare faded quickly at the sight of their grins. She walked among the giants for the rest of the day, occasionally looking back to watch the children.

Though sometimes she glanced up at Declan.

*******

A few days of hard travel passed before Kael heard Lysander cry excitedly from down the slope: "Here it is! This ought to suit your people nicely."

The small castle that sat at the mouth of the Earl's road looked as if it'd seen better days. Gwen frowned as they neared the shattered gates. "It's a mess."

Silas, it seemed, had decided to take his punishment rather literally. He'd spent a large amount of time in his human skin as they traveled down the mountains, hardly ever more than a pace behind Gwen.

Now, when he saw how she glared at the castle, he leaned forward and murmured: "This den sits in the mountain's shadow and at the Valley's mouth. A Thane who rules from here will have one foot in the wilds, and the other in the realm of men."

"Keep your pretty words to yourself, cat," Gwen said sharply.

"Yes, my Thane." He smirked from behind her and his glowing eyes followed the path of her finger as it trailed from her jaw to her chin.

Her gaze shifted across the squat towers and thick, sturdy walls for a moment before she sighed. "I suppose it won't be too bad ... once my craftsmen clean it up a bit. March, wildmen!" she bellowed behind her.

They followed with a howl.

Kael recognized the heavy gates, the stone courtyard and the hallway beyond the keep's entrance immediately: this was the castle from Kyleigh's memories. He knew before he even stepped into the first room what he was bound to find.

Though that didn't stop his stomach from flipping when he saw it.

The shelves had been knocked from the walls so that only the oak paneling remained. In place of the whittled desk was an empty throne. The chamber was molded into a perfect circle, but there was no eye carved into the floor. Kael was beginning to think that perhaps he'd been mistaken when one of the stones shifted beneath his boot. He pulled it loose, revealing an older layer of stone — one that had a design carved across it.

With the craftsmen's help, they stripped the top layer off the floor and uncovered the Wright's eye buried beneath. When Griffith saw it, he gasped.

Gwen had made good on her word: no sooner did they return from Thanehold than one of the craftsmen had strung Marc's claws onto a leather cord, weaving beads of stone-ice in between them. Now Griffith wore the claws around his neck in a sharp, deadly-looking ring.

They clacked together as he crouched to run his finger across the symbol's large, triangular pupil. "We were meant to come here. Fate's turned our exile into a gift. She's given us a new place to call home."

"A great Wright once lived here," Kael said quietly.

"What happened to him?"

"He gave himself up to save the Kingdom."

Griffith sat back on his heels. His hand dragged down his stripe of hair, and his eyes were distant. "Gwen's going to leave us one day."

"Yes, she's told me," Kael said.

Griffith got to his feet with a sigh. He took the blue marble from his pocket but instead of sending it through his fingers, he merely stared. "She says she'll wait until I'm ready, but I wonder ... sometimes I'm afraid I won't ever be ready. How will I know which paths to take? How will I know what's best for my people?"

Kael watched Griffith stare at the marble for a moment, and a sudden thought twisted inside his head. Slowly, he drew the *Atlas of the Adventurer* from his pocket. He felt its worn leather cover and ran his fingers across the faded words that trailed down its spine. Then he held it out to Griffith.

"Here — this book will teach you everything you need to know."

He stuffed the marble away and took the *Atlas* carefully. "Really?"

"I've carried it with me since I was a boy," Kael said with a nod. "Its pages are filled with the stories of knights and heroes, all sorts of brave men who weren't afraid to forge their own paths. There are maps and histories, as well — everything you could hope for, really. It's a book fit for a Thane."

The *Atlas* sat heavily in Griffith's hands for a moment, as if he wasn't certain what to do with it. Then slowly, he opened the first page. His eyes trailed in a hesitant line across the poem about the six regions of the Kingdom before he turned to the next.

Kael spent the day with the craftsmen, helping to repair the castle. They hung doors into place and mended holes in the roof. Some of the hallways were so packed with rubble that they had to be cleared before the craftsmen could mend them. All the while they worked, Griffith sat in a corner of the throne room, the *Atlas* propped against his knees.

Soon his eyes had begun to move surely across the words. They burned with a light as he read. Once, Kael glanced up and saw that a smile had bent Griffith's lips. He was caught up inside the *Atlas*'s world — Kael could practically see the beautiful lands passing by as he trailed his finger across the words, swore it was the blaze of battle that made his eyes shine so fiercely.

He couldn't help but think that this was what Setheran would've wanted. He would've been pleased to have his book handed down to another whisperer. It would've made him proud to know that what he'd written could bring such a light to Griffith's eyes ... that his stories would ring on long after they'd ended.

******* 

"The Thane wishes to speak with you," Silas purred.

Kael had only just gotten settled for dinner. "Can't it wait?"

"Oh, it wouldn't do to keep the Thane waiting," Silas murmured. He *tsk*ed and drifted away, hands clasped smartly behind his back — and Kael had to fight the urge to roll his eyes.

From the way he strode with his chin arched so high above the rest of them, Kael began to think that perhaps Silas had confused the word *punishment* with *power*. Still, he knew Gwen would only come after him if he ignored her. So he abandoned his dinner and with a groan, marched up the stairs.

When he finally made it to the chamber Gwen had claimed for herself, he was surprised to see Kyleigh leaning against the window. She spoke to a woman he didn't recognize: a woman with short, fiery hair, full lips, and a band of freckles across her nose. She turned when Kael knocked on the open door, and he saw there were scars across her face.

They were red and slightly faded — little dots that clustered at her chin and spread out as they climbed up her cheeks to her forehead. Had he not known they were scars, he might've thought she'd just been spattered by something red.

"Hello, mutt."

"Gwen?" He could hardly believe it. Even after she spoke, he had to look into her eyes to be sure. "Where's your paint?"

"The wildmen only wear our paint in times of war. Now that the Man of Wolves is vanquished and our battle with the wynns must wait, I haven't got a reason to wear it." She touched the scars on her chin. "Come here and make it bearable, will you?"

"What happened?" he said as he placed his hands. "Were you burned?"

She smirked, and her eyes slid over to the window.

"You more than deserved it," Kyleigh growled.

"I still don't regret clobbering you, pest. I hope I'll have a chance to do it again. It happened when I cracked her over the head with my axe," Gwen explained. "Her blood sprayed across my face a bit. The winter cooled it quickly, but not before it left some nasty marks."

By this point, both women seemed to be fighting very hard not to grin.

Kael was more than a little confused. "Do you want me to heal the scars on your back, as well?"

"No ..." Gwen smirked at Kyleigh again. "No, those I rather like."

Kael shook his head as he went to work. He was certain he would never understand them — not if he had a thousand years to sit and wonder. So he gave up trying.

When he was finished, Gwen ran her fingers across her skin and nodded in approval. "Have you given any more thought to my offer, mutt? You don't have to marry me," she said, half-laughing when she saw the burn spread across his face. "But you're welcome to stay among the wildmen. Griffith would be happy to have you ... and I would be happy for Griffith."

Kael shook his head. Somehow, against every reasonable bone in his body, he'd come to like the wildmen. He knew he would miss them terribly. But he also knew that if he stayed, he'd spend the rest of his life yelling at the tops of his lungs, trying to keep them all in line. And he wasn't sure he had the stomach for it.

"I'm grateful for the offer, but I can't stay here," he said firmly.

Gwen frowned. "Where will you go, then?"

That was the problem. After what he'd done to Titus, Kael was no longer afraid. The worries that'd sent him away from his friends before now seemed like little more than nightmares — mere dreams compared to awakening that surged through his blood.

He realized he had the power to face any enemy, be it Countess D'Mere, Lord Gilderick, or even King Crevan, himself. And perhaps one day, he would.

But for now, he stood at the edge of a new season of life — a spring that blossomed behind the frost, a dawn filled with warmth, and light … and love. By the time his eyes made it to the window, he'd already lost the fight against his smile. "Well … I was hoping Lady Kyleigh might let me come to Copperdock, for a bit."

The blaze of her stare made the fires rise inside his middle. "I suppose there's room," she murmured.

But though she did her best to tease him for it, he could tell she was pleased.

# CHAPTER 49
## THE GIANT AND THE MOT

In a few weeks' time, Kael found himself sailing into the glittering mouth of Gravy Bay once again.

He hadn't wanted to return to the Bay — he'd wanted to go straight to Copperdock. But the moment Gwen's face was healed and she'd clomped out of the room, Kyleigh gave him some rather frustrating news: she was going to stay in the mountains for a few weeks longer, just to make entirely certain that things were settled between the wildmen and the wynns.

"They aren't going to go to war," he'd insisted.

But Kyleigh wouldn't listen. "Berwyn loves to taunt them, and Gwen always rises to the occasion. Both need to understand the fact that they aren't at the summit anymore. If they go waging war in the middle of the Valley, the Kingdom is bound to notice. And as I'm the only one who speaks both tongues, I'll have to do the explaining."

Kael didn't believe anybody could possibly be that foolish — not even the wildmen. But Kyleigh had seemed to think she was responsible for keeping them out of mischief, and she wouldn't be swayed. "Fine. I'll come with you, then."

She'd raised a brow. "And leave the rest of our friends to fend for themselves? Not a chance. You've got to make sure Lysander doesn't wreck his ship trying to get home. He's a man on the edge already."

Kael had known exactly what she meant. Lysander had done nothing but fret over Aerilyn for days on end. The moment they left Tinnark, he'd sent Eveningwing straight to the Bay. Then he'd struck such a pace down the mountain that he'd broken into an accidental run — and had only stopped when he crashed at the base of a rather large tree.

"I'll meet you in the Bay once I've finished here," Kyleigh had promised.

The way her lips moved against his had made it difficult to argue. "Then what?" he said when she released him.

Her hand had fallen in a burning line down his neck. The fires in her eyes swelled as she whispered: "Then you and I will go home."

*Home.* That was something Kael was very much looking forward to. And as long as Kyleigh was by his side, *home* was precisely where he'd be.

Now that they'd finally arrived in the Bay, he found himself faced with the near-impossible task of being patient one last time. He knew it would be weeks more before Kyleigh returned; he knew it would do him no good to worry. So he tried to keep his steps as light as possible as he dragged himself behind his companions — hoping to mercy that the time would pass quickly.

But he doubted it would.

No sooner had they reached the mansion's front doors than Uncle Martin burst out from between them. His hair stood on end, sweat drenched his brow, and one half of his mustache was bent fantastically out of place.

Lysander gaped at him. "What in high tide —?"

"She's here!" Uncle Martin cried, waving his cane at Jonathan in warning. "Run, by Gravy — save yourself!"

The fiddler whirled around on his spindly legs and tried to bolt, but he didn't get far.

Clairy stormed out the door, skirts whipping furiously about her. She caught up to Jonathan in just three of her long strides. "Where have you been? Out with it, fiddler — and don't you dare lie to me."

He yelped when she twisted his ear. "I could never lie to you, my sweet giantess! I love you far too mu — ow!"

"Is that why you ran out on me, then? Because you love me?"

Jonathan was bent at such an unnatural angle that Kael had begun to worry he might get stuck that way.

Fortunately, Lysander stepped in before the fiddler could suffer any permanent damage. "I'm afraid *I'm* the one responsible for all this. Ah — I mean, I asked Jonathan to come along," he added quickly when Clairy turned her scowl on him. "We needed a guide to lead us across the Valley, and I could think of no man better for the job."

"It was a right dangerous journey, too," Declan said. "Had it not been for the wee fiddler —"

"You were supposed to send him back!" Clairy fumed. "I sat all alone for months waiting for him to return! I had to listen to Brend go on about how he'd known it all along, about how he thought I was fool for believing *a clodded string-twiddler like that would ever stay for long.* I traveled across the seas to get here only to find that you'd gone off adventuring!"

"It wasn't an adven — ow!"

She twisted Jonathan's ear with one hand and swatted at Declan furiously with the other. Nothing Lysander said could convince her to call off her attack. Uncle Martin seemed more concerned with bending his mustache back in the right direction than anything else.

All Kael wanted was to go upstairs and sleep until supper — but the battle raging in the doorway made it impossible to get through.

At last, Jake stepped in. He brought his hands together and a sound like a thunder's clap rent the air. "Now see here, Jonathan did a very brave thing for us. He was even kidnapped by bandits."

Clairy cupped a hand around her ear. "What?"

"Something about having a nap," Declan said loudly. He slapped the side of his head. "What's that? What's all that ringing?"

"There's a bee in my ear!" Jonathan cried.

Uncle Martin swung his cane in an impatient arc. "Yes, yes — I *hear* you, Bimply! You can stop ringing that blasted lunch bell. *Stop*, I say!" He stormed into the mansion, shrilling at the tops of his lungs: "Cease your wails, you unrelenting harpy!"

"Why's everybody yelling?" Elena said.

Kael wasn't sure, but he'd been around Jake long enough to guess: "One of his spells must've gone wrong."

And right on cue, Jake threw up his hands. "Oh, blast it all. I knew that spell wasn't ready quite yet. I thought it might be a little less irritating than a whistle, but it appears I was wrong." He leaned until he was an inch from Clairy's ear. "I said Jonathan was *kidnapped*!"

Clairy gasped. "Kidnapped! Oh, you poor wee thing!"

The fiddler's scruffy face disappeared into the crest of her bosom as she crushed him against her. "Is it safe to come out?" he called, his voice slightly muffled. "Am I forgiven?"

Clairy didn't seem to hear him. She toted Jonathan through the door, yelling about how she planned to *put some meat on those skinny wee bones*, and the rest of their companions followed — slapping their ears and complaining loudly about all the ringing.

Jake sighed heavily. "I'm never going to be useful, am I? I suppose I ought to just stick with blowing things up."

"I'd be all right with that," Elena murmured.

"What?"

"I like to watch you destroy things. I like even better that you're reluctant to destroy them —"

"I can't hear you!"

"— because that means you've got a gentle heart." She crossed her arms and eyed him from over the top of her mask. "I like you, Jake. And I trust you. You're different from other men. One of these days I'm going to be able to tell you that, and I'm going to give you all the love you deserve."

He squinted at her. "I can't tell if you're talking to me or not! *Are* you talking to me?"

She pulled her mask down so he could read her lips. "Lunch!" she said, pointing to the door.

"Ah! Oh, good!"

He shuffled inside, and Kael tried to follow him quickly.

But Elena caught him by the belt.

"If you ever speak a word about that to anybody," she whispered, her dagger's edge against his throat, "I will murder you in your sleep."

Kael swore to keep his mouth shut.

*******

Though Lysander insisted they could stay as long as they wished, the giants were eager to return to the plains. And so the pirates readied a ship and took them off that very next morning.

Jonathan and Clairy sailed along with them. The fiddler kept his arms wrapped about her middle the whole way across the Bay — and his face planted very firmly against her chest.

To everybody's great surprise, Declan chose to stay at the mansion. "I've not spent much time in the seas," he said when they asked. "My men can find their way back without their General. Brend won't need me right away. There'll be no harm in staying here a while longer. I don't understand why everybody's going on about it."

"No one's going on about anything," Lysander said with a smile. "We're happy to have you."

Kael thought Declan's change of heart might've had less to do with spending time in the seas, and more to do with Nadine.

On the day they'd left the wildmen, her little flock of children had stood so miserably at the gates that Nadine hadn't seemed able to stand it. She'd hardly taken two steps down the road before she'd run back and gathered them up in her arms.

"I cannot leave them — not yet. I will return with Kyleigh," she'd promised.

Declan wasn't at all happy about this. In fact, he'd brooded the whole way across the Valley and the seas. His eyes had slipped so deeply into the cleft of his brow that Kael had begun to wonder if they'd ever see them again. But for all he moped, it turned out to be a very good thing that Declan chose to stay behind.

In the time they'd been gone, the bump on Aerilyn's stomach had swelled tremendously. She'd gone to throw her arms about Lysander's neck when they first arrived and had very nearly knocked him off his feet. But as dangerous as her belly was, her moods were even worse.

One moment, she would be perfectly happy. A blink later, she was sobbing and wasn't sure why. Then Uncle Martin would say something to try to cheer her up, and she'd laugh ... until she cried. Most of the time her tears were completely harmless. But if Lysander caught her at the wrong moment, they'd pour out burning hot.

"This is *your* fault!" Aerilyn cried as she stormed into the library.

For once, Lysander was innocent. He'd been doing nothing but reading over the shipping log for the last three hours — Kael knew, because he'd have to glance up from his book every few minutes to answer one of the captain's ridiculous questions.

"What's my —?"

"*This!*" she said, thrusting her favorite blue dress under his nose. "You did this to me, you horrible rogue! You're the reason nothing fits!"

"Ah, well I don't think that's entirely *my* fault," he said with a wink.

Aerilyn wasn't amused. In fact, she slung the dress at his head. "How would you like it, Lysander? How would you feel if I made you carry something for months and months, and it just got heavier and more uncomfortable — while I skipped around drinking grog like there was nothing at all the matter?"

Lysander was still struggling to fight his way out from under the frilly skirts, so the panic in his voice was slightly muffled as he cried: "But we're going to have a baby, my love! Think of how happy you'll be once you have him."

"Or *her!*" Aerilyn shrilled. "Quit talking about our baby as if it's a boy. What if we have a little girl? She'll come out thinking you don't love her. And that'll make me so ... oh, I'll just be so ... so *sad!*"

Before they could do anything to stop it, she melted into tears.

Kael saw his own horror reflected on Lysander's face: the good captain gaped and clutched the skirts to his chin. His mouth moved, but no words came out. They stood frozen under her sobs for several moments before Declan plodded in.

He took one look at Aerilyn before he snatched her around the arm and grunted: "Come on, let's walk."

She sniffed. "Where are we walking?"

"Around. You need to move those wee little legs and get to breathing some fresh air."

"Why?"

He thrust a thick finger at her belly. "That's coming out early. That's why you keep sobbing and flinging things about. My wee baby brother came early. The old women had my mother walking through the fields every evening. Helped keep her head on straight."

"You had a little brother?"

"Yeh. And if you promise to stop weeping for a clodded moment, I'll tell you about him."

Aerilyn dried her tears immediately and followed Declan out the door. Kael and Lysander watched in amazement from the window as the pair went nearly a full turn around the Bay without Aerilyn once dissolving into tears.

She hung off Declan's thick arm and he weathered her chatter — occasionally chiming in with a grunted *yeh.*

*******

A few weeks later, Kael hurried down the stairs for breakfast — only to nearly trip at its bottom. "Nadine!"

She stood in the middle of the grand circular room, smiling broadly — and surrounded by a horde of redheaded children. "There were too many of them. The wildmen could

577

not manage them all. So I have brought some of the youngest along with me," she explained when she saw his surprise.

"We're happy to have them!" Uncle Martin strode in from one of the halls, grinning through his mustache. He waved the children on with his cane. "Come along, now. No, no — don't be shy. We've got mounds of breakfast in there. More eggs than any man or beast could possibly devour. And while we eat, I can tell you about the time my dear brother stole the King's favorite pair of knickers!"

They giggled at his chatter the whole way down the hall, and Nadine beamed at their backs.

Kael didn't realize he'd been craning his neck over her shoulder until she grabbed his arm. "Kyleigh has gone to Whitebone. She promises she will not be long."

Kael's heart sank. "What could she possibly have to do in the blasted desert?"

"She says she must visit Asante. And she also says you are to keep your chin raised and not to scuff the floors with your moping."

That sounded exactly like something Kyleigh would've said. So Kael grit his teeth and tried to be patient.

Fortunately, his companions provided him with plenty of distractions. If he wasn't trying to stop Aerilyn from bludgeoning Lysander to death with one of her dresses, then he was fighting off Elena — who'd taken to hiding in various nooks and attacking him when he least expected it.

"Why?" he gasped as he tried to keep her arm from wrapping any tighter around his throat.

That particular afternoon, she'd ambushed him in the hallway on his way back from lunch. He should've noticed that one of the doors was slightly ajar. He should've realized that meant there was a masked forest woman waiting behind it to throttle him. But he didn't.

Now she clung to his back like paste. Her legs crushed his innards and her arm won ground against his throat. Little black spots burst across his vision as she cut off the flow of his blood.

"Why can't we just pass each other in the hall ... like normal ... people?"

"We're whisperers. Fighting keeps us sharp," she said, as if they were doing nothing more than discussing the weather. "Now hold still while I put you to sleep."

Kael had no intention of doing that. She'd strangled him unconscious once before because he hadn't remembered to check under his bed, and he'd woken with a nasty headache. Instead, he turned and slammed his back into the wall behind him, crushing her against it.

She didn't let go, and so he slammed her again. "You are ... the most ... *difficult* —"

The wall behind him gave way with a *crack* and Kael held his breath. He knew very well which room was on the other side, but Elena didn't.

Her arms snapped open and she coughed violently against the tang of magic as they fell flat into the spell room.

Kael leapt to his feet. "Sorry, Jake."

The mage hardly glanced at him from over the top of his spectacles before going back to his reading. "It's fine. Just mend it when you have a chance, will you?"

Kael bolted out of the hole in the wall before Elena could recover, promising he would.

After he'd so narrowly escaped getting strangled, he was hoping to have a few minutes to himself in the library. Unfortunately for him, it was already occupied.

Declan and Nadine had done nothing but argue since the day she'd returned. Any time he passed them, they were in the middle of some heated debate: they hissed as they walked, stood in corners with their arms crossed and growled. Even at meals, they scowled at each other from across the table.

They kept their voices so hushed that he wasn't sure what exactly it was that they argued over. But he knew he didn't want to get involved.

"Well then, maybe we need another ear on this," Declan growled. He reached over and snatched Kael before he could escape through the door. "Tell the sandbeater I know what I'm doing, rat. Tell her she knows full well they'd be better off somewhere open."

"It is about the children," Nadine explained when Kael sputtered. Then she turned back to Declan. "They are happy here! The Uncle has taken them out for fishing and a picnic."

"They're excited, is all," he said back. "Did you not see their mountains? They need somewhere to run and stretch their legs. The wee mice could never be happy packed onto some great floating tinderbox. Look at this one!" he said, rattling Kael by the shoulder. "Look at how wild he is! You can't force such hearty folk to sit trapped for long — it'll hobble them."

Nadine stamped her tiny foot. "You are wrong!"

"Am I? All right, then — tell us which you'd prefer, rat. Would you rather grow up on land or on a ship?"

Kael would've *preferred* not to be dragged into the middle of it. But as they were both scowling at him, waiting for an answer, he supposed he ought to be honest. "Land," he said firmly. "I don't mind spending a few weeks on a ship, but I'm much happier on land."

Declan thrust a thick arm at him. "See? There you have it."

Nadine's eyes shone fiercely. "What would you have me do? I am an exile. Kyleigh has given me a place in her village — I have no other home to offer them."

Declan's glare went shallow. There was something hidden in the depths of his steely gray eyes that Kael hadn't remembered seeing before, something that reminded him of the way the wynns had bowed to Gwen — a surrender that put him on his belly.

"They'd be welcome in my home, among my clan," he said quietly. "I'd teach them all I know about horses, about how to till the earth and raise their food from seed to sprout. They could chase the sun from one end to the next, if they wanted. I'd never see them hobbled."

Nadine's lips parted for a moment before hardening once more. "I will not leave them."

Declan leaned forward. "Well, then ... I suppose you'd better come with us."

They stared at each other for such a long moment that Kael began to sweat. He would've bolted straight for the door, had Declan's meaty hand not been clamped so tightly about his arm.

Finally, Nadine's head dipped in a nod.

"Yeh?"

"Yes."

Relieved smiles crept across both of their faces. Declan leaned closer. Nadine came up on her toes. Kael could see what was coming and tried madly to escape, but Declan's grip was far too tight. Just when he thought he would be forced to endure it, Uncle Martin came to his rescue:

"It's started! It's happening!"

He slung his picnic basket into one of the stuffed chairs and the little redheaded children swarmed in behind him. Their curls were still sopping from the waves. Several carried armfuls of shells. All were burnt an alarming shade of red.

"You have kept them out too long!" Nadine said when she saw them. She swore in her strange tongue and pressed her hands against their reddened cheeks.

"Eh, a little sun is good for them. It'll give them a nice crust," Declan said.

Uncle Martin waved his cane impatiently. "Quite right! Take them straight to the kitchen and have Bimply give them a salve — and tell that cake-snatching shrew to send my favorite decanter to the library. We'll soon have reason to celebrate!"

The children squealed in mock terror as Declan scooped up an armful of them and marched for the door. Nadine led the others out in a chain behind him. Kael had meant to follow, but now he was curious.

"What are we celebrating?"

Uncle Martin's eyes gleamed over the top of his mustache. "It's time, Sir Wright. Aerilyn's gone to her chambers — I'll be a great-uncle by evening!"

# CHAPTER 50
## A DANGEROUS PROPOSAL

"How much longer?" Lysander moaned.

It had been hours since Uncle Martin had burst into the library. Now evening had come and gone, the day had passed wholly into night — and there was still no news of Aerilyn.

No sooner had word slipped out the mansion's front doors than midwives had marched in from the village and taken over Aerilyn's care. They'd shut her chamber doors and absolutely refused to allow any man above the spiral staircase. Consequently, the men of Gravy Bay had gathered in the library to worry together.

"I never thought it would take so long," Uncle Martin said with a sigh. His decanter sat before him, unopened. The way the glass bent around its amber contents made the sag of his frown impossibly steep, and his eye impossibly large. "I never imagined that Aerilyn would have any trouble — she has the perfect birthing hips!"

"Yeh," Declan grunted from the hearth.

"Can we please not discuss my wife as if she's some sort of ... pasture animal?" Lysander mumbled.

He dragged his hands down his face — something he'd done so often in the last hour that his skin had actually begun to stay red. His wavy hair stood on end. The sleeves of his white tunic were rolled up to his elbows, the buttons at his collar undone. His trouser pockets were considerably rumpled from where he kept drying his palms.

His stormy eyes traveled to Thelred, who shook his head firmly. He stood before the door, arms crossed. "Don't do it, Captain."

"Just for a moment?" Lysander pleaded.

"No. The desert woman is in there with her, and the forest woman said she'd come get us if something happens. There's no point in you hiking up there, Captain. The midwives won't let you in, and you'll only get upset."

Lysander's fists clenched at his side. "I outrank you, cousin."

"That won't stop me from kicking you in the shin if you rush over here. Remember what happened last time? You limped around for a good half-hour."

"Yes, well, you've got a rather unfair advantage," Lysander said, glaring at his peg. "It's like being kicked by a tree."

"Don't worry. Your mate will be fine," Eveningwing called. He sat cross-legged atop the polished desk, grinning to either ear. "I sense it."

"Oh, well, as long as you *sense* it, I don't know what I've been worried about," Lysander muttered, throwing up his hands.

Jake sat rigidly in the desk's chair. He drew his nose from his book long enough to add: "Actually, there *is* something to be said for having extra senses."

"Yeh, like the way the birds go to roost before a storm," Declan agreed.

"You know, my wife had a cat that always seemed to know when I was coming home," Uncle Martin mused. "He was an orange tabby with a penchant for butter cookies —"

"I can't take it any longer!" Lysander burst. His eyes were wild as he charged for the door.

Kael tackled him around the legs, quickly earning himself a boot heel to the chin. Declan planted an elbow in the middle of Lysander's back. No sooner had they managed to calm him than Uncle Martin swooped in and began lashing them all with his cane, yelling:

"Run, Captain! Now's your chance!"

Eveningwing leapt into his feathers and tried to scare Uncle Martin back. After a few unsuccessful dives, Thelred finally stomped over to try and wrestle the cane from his father's grasp — thrusting his wooden leg in like a wedge

583

between them and swearing magnificently when the cane struck true.

Jake hardly glanced up from his book.

Sometime in the midst of all the chaos, the library door creaked open. Elena's dark eyes roved across the whole tangled, yelling mass of them, and she scowled. "What in Kingdom's name is going on, here?"

"Never mind about all this," Jake said, snapping his book shut. "Have you got some news?"

Declan shifted so that Lysander could stick his head out from under the pile. "Please tell me you've heard something. I can't bear it any longer!"

"It's finished," Elena said.

The room went so deathly quiet that Kael could actually hear Lysander's tongue as it scraped across his lips. "Is Aerilyn ...?"

"She's doing well."

"And ... and what about ...?"

She shrugged. "You have a son."

The library erupted in cheers.

They jerked Lysander to his feet and pounded him heartily upon the back. He seemed dazed as Eveningwing swooped to brush him across the shoulder. He stumbled forward when Declan ruffled his hair. The good captain likely would've sunk back to his knees, had Kael and Thelred not grabbed him under the arms.

"A son," he whispered, his mouth opened around his smile.

Uncle Martin rushed straight for his decanter. "Well done! Well done and congratulations!"

Lysander took the small glass of liquor they shoved into his hands and tossed it back in a single gulp. They cheered as he strode purposefully out the door.

When the midwives finally agreed to let the rest of them come up, Kael walked at the back of the line. He hadn't spent much time around infants, and wasn't entirely sure if Aerilyn would want them all crowding in. But the moment he saw her smile, he knew it would be all right.

Her golden brown hair was knotted loosely at the top of her head. Little strands escaped their clasp and matted against her neck. Pink crossed her face in a sunrise of color. But she was positively beaming.

"That was, and without a doubt, the most horrible, painful, *satisfying* thing I've ever done," she said when Kael reached her.

He wasn't sure what to say. He had no idea about anything she'd just done — other than what he'd read in books. And he doubted if any of that would've been at all comforting. So instead, he crouched at the side of her bed and held her hand while the others met the baby.

No man in the history of grinning had ever worn a more ridiculous grin than Captain Lysander's. He passed the little bundle in his arms to Thelred — whose stern expression actually gave way for a moment, melting into something that wasn't quite as harsh as usual.

When it was his turn, Uncle Martin bounced the little bundle in his arms and said, with his most mischievous grin: "A handsome lad, indeed! With a little help from your dear great-uncle, we'll have the ladies tripping on their skirts to swoon over you."

"You'll do nothing of the sort. I won't have you teaching him your tricks," Aerilyn said firmly. "He's going to be a perfect gentleman."

Uncle Martin's mustache bent as he pursed his lips. "Gentleman, eh? The problem with gentlemen, my dear, is that they keep the company of unicorns and griffins. *Gentleman*," he scoffed, grinning down at the bundle. "A mythical creature if ever there was one."

A few minutes more, and the baby had made nearly a full circle around the room. The only one who hadn't held him yet was Declan — and that was only because he flatly refused to. "No, I shouldn't be holding such tiny wee things. I don't want to hurt him."

"You will not hurt him," Nadine insisted, holding the bundle out.

Declan kept his thick arms firmly crossed. "He's too tiny! I don't want to clod it up."

"What have you named him?" Kael said, when their argument showed no signs of ending.

Aerilyn bit her lip, and her gaze went to Declan. "I want to thank you for walking me around all those days."

"It was a small thing," Declan insisted, leaning away as Nadine tried to hand him the bundle.

"No, it was an important thing. You were so very kind to me ... and I'll never forget the stories you told me about your little brother."

He went silent immediately.

"That's why ..." Aerilyn took a deep breath, "well, we've talked about it. And Lysander and I have decided that we'd like to call him *Dante*."

Declan's eyes disappeared beneath the cleft of his brow. His chin turned to the bundle. "Your little one? You want to name him ...?"

Lysander smiled. "Yes — if that's all right, of course. We wouldn't want to do it without your approval."

Slowly, Declan's arms slid from his chest. Nadine placed the little bundle in his meaty hands and he held it, unflinching, for several long moments. "I think that'd be a grand thing," he whispered finally, his voice unusually gruff. "A mightily grand thing."

*******

The celebrations went on long into the night. His companions were still toasting in the library when Kael finally plodded up to bed.

His room was bright and warm. The covers were folded back neatly and the window was opened a bit, letting the cool breeze in. Though it all looked very inviting, Kael knew better than to simply fall into bed.

He checked behind the bath and in the shadowed cleft of the hearth. He even stuck his head out the window and glanced down either ledge of the sloping roof. There was no doubt in his mind that Elena planned a swift revenge for how he'd thrown her through the spell room wall. Yes, he knew very well that she would be coming for him.

He just wasn't sure when.

The space beneath his bed was impenetrably dark. He was crouched on his hands and knees, trying to decide if one of the shadows looked a bit suspicious when he felt something creep up behind him.

It hadn't made a sound, but there was a fullness in the air at his back that hadn't been there before. He felt the weight of eyes on the nape of his neck — felt them drag down between his shoulders and all the way to the soles of his boots. And he knew he would have to act quickly.

Kael spun with a cry, fists raised and feet set beneath him — prepared to shoulder the first blow ... but it never came. He stared at the black-clad figure in the doorway and realized it wasn't Elena who'd crept up behind him.

It was Kyleigh.

Her pony's tail hung loose. Strands of raven hair had escaped their bonds and fallen across her eyes, but not even the shadows could dull their flame. They blazed as they locked onto his. Her chest rose and fell quickly, as if she'd just sprinted a great distance.

He realized that must've been exactly what she'd done. "I thought you said it was too dangerous to go winging about the Kingdom?"

Her mouth bent into an amused half-smile — a smile that somehow made him lose track of his feet. "I suppose I might've broken a few rules."

He forced himself to look severe. "Well, it wouldn't be the first time. What were you doing in the desert?"

"*That*," she growled, creeping forward, "is none of your business."

Before Kael even had a chance to be worried, she attacked.

His feet left the ground and his back thudded onto the bed. Kyleigh's lips moved against his. Flames burst inside his chest. The pressure of her body twisted the fires, forced them closer to the surface. They lapped against the under-edges of his skin and melted them together.

Two white-hot lines seared him on either side when her hands slipped beneath his tunic. They bumped along his ribs; the flames roared more furiously than ever before —

"Wait."

Kael grabbed her wrists, halting those burning lines. Her lips paused at his throat. He groaned when she pulled them away. He hated himself for drawing her hands out and holding them clasped at his chest — safely above his tunic. But it was what had to be done.

He loved Kyleigh with his every beat, his every breath. Her touch mended his all his rifts. She stretched to the very corners of his soul. He never wanted her to have to worry about anything — not even Fate's will. So Kael planned to bind himself to her.

They would be whole in flesh and law, in blood and spirit. They would be so bound that she would never doubt again. He didn't want her to be afraid. He wanted to prove that he was hers completely, that she had every right to love him.

So he took a deep breath and said: "Marry me."

She raised her brows. "You mean ... like humans do? With a ceremony and toasts and people gawking at us? Ugh," she said when he nodded. "I can't think of anything I'd like less."

When she bent to kiss him, he shoved her up and out of reach. "I'm serious, Kyleigh. I want to marry you."

"Are you worried about defending my honor?" she whispered with a grin that made the fires swell up. "Oh Kael, that's so ... *barbaric*."

He was absolutely determined to marry her, no matter what she said. Kyleigh sank down very heavily against his arms. She was trying to break his will — and he knew that if their chests touched again, it would be broken quickly.

With no small amount of effort, he flipped her over. He tried to ignore the swell of pink that blossomed down her pale throat, tried not to be devoured by the fires in her eyes.

He held her wrists tightly — and tried to ignore the way her blood thrummed against his fingertips.

"I'm not worried about defending your honor."

"Oh?"

"I'm worried about *my* honor."

Her lips bent into a smirk. "What if I promise to be gentle?"

That wasn't at all what he'd meant — a fact he had to remind himself of when he bent involuntarily for her lips. He was losing the battle with his heart. He knew he'd have to think quickly. "How else can I be sure you'll stay?" he said, hoping desperately to knock her off her guard.

She frowned. "You know I'll stay."

"Do I? How do I know you won't leave the second you've gotten what you want from me?"

Her lips pulled back from her teeth in a snarl. "I hope for your sake that you're only joking, whisperer."

"Am I?"

"You know I love you."

"Then you'll have no problem proving it." Kael leaned back, watching as the blaze in her eyes took on that dangerous edge — the one that thrilled and frightened him all at once. He knew then that he had her.

"Fine," she growled. "I'll marry you."

He wasn't going to let her off that easily. "I'm not sure I want to, now."

"Why not?"

"You've hurt my feelings."

He was certain her glare had never burned quite so fiercely. "I'm sorry," she said through her teeth. "How can I make it up to you?"

He shrugged. "Well, I suppose since you've wounded me so severely, the only way I might trust you again is if *you* do the asking. Go on, Kyleigh," he whispered, fighting desperately to hold back his grin, "ask me to marry you."

A look of such absolute horror crossed her face that he nearly laughed outright. She snarled as his grin broke free and tried to shove him away, but he held her down. "Marry me," she growled at last.

"I don't think that was very sincere."

"Fine. I'm going to *sincerely* pummel your arse if you don't say you'll marry me. How's that?"

He *tsk*ed, reveling in how dangerously the fires glowed. "I'm afraid I'm not convinced." It took every ounce of his will to get to his feet. When she tried to follow, he shoved her back onto the bed. "You can stay here for the night. I'll sleep across the hall —"

"No," she groaned.

He stopped in the doorway. "Yes. When you stop glowering and ask me gently, with *love*," he added when she bared her teeth, "then I'll consider marrying you. But until then, I'm afraid you'll just have to wait."

\*\*\*\*\*\*\*

He tormented Kyleigh for days on end.

Every time she asked to marry him, he would refuse. It grew steadily more difficult to shrug and say he wasn't convinced — especially when that burning edge in her eyes made him want to forget the whole thing and pull her into his arms. But no matter how she teased him, he was determined to wait.

Things weren't quite ready, yet.

Declan, Nadine, and their horde of redheaded children sailed back to the plains. Thelred took them on his way to pick up another shipment of goods — along with a list Kael had given him for the wedding.

He had enough coin from his time among the merchants for a few heads of cattle. Brend sent a whole herd, along with his congratulations and a roughly scrawled note insisting they were a *wee weding presant.*

"Where are we going to keep all these bloody beasts?" Thelred called down from his ship.

Kael wasn't sure. He'd only wanted a few — and he doubted if even Kyleigh could eat a whole herd. "You're always going on about how difficult it is to get red meat in the seas. Why don't you sell them at the chancellor's castle?"

Thelred nodded slowly. "Yeah, all right. It's probably safe to go back by now."

Kael had no idea what that meant, and he didn't have time to find out.

The giants had sent along everything he asked for: all of the ingredients Bimply needed for her cakes and cookies, as well as a few baskets of chickens. There were also plenty of things he *hadn't* asked for — like a mountain of fresh-baked pies and several barrels of malt beer.

"Well, you ought to stop helping people," Thelred grumped when he saw the surprise on Kael's face. "They'd be much less inclined to give you things."

With all of the items on his list delivered, Kael figured he could have everything ready by week's end. He'd only have to survive Kyleigh a few more days. Little did he know just how daunting a task that would be.

She asked him to marry her again at dinner. When he refused, Aerilyn shrilled that he was being completely unreasonable. She held little Dante in one arm and slapped Kael angrily with the other. Lysander and Uncle Martin threw gravy-soaked biscuits at him, and Thelred — though he knew full well what Kael had planned — exploded a mixed berry tart across the back of his breeches as he ran out the door.

Kyleigh found him in the library a few minutes later. She was armed with a soaked rag for the stains — and a new marriage proposal.

"No," he insisted.

She scrubbed absently at the gravy splotches across his chest. Her hand pressed down a little more firmly than necessary and moved in slow, agonizing circles. "Very well, if you're certain ..."

"I am," he croaked.

"Then I won't trouble you again tonight."

Her kiss was every bit as firm and agonizing as her scrubbing. He likely would've given in, had it lasted another moment. But she released him just before his resolve could melt.

He cursed himself silently as he watched her stride out the door.

Sleep didn't come to him that night. He stared at the pattern of the shadows across the ceiling and tried to forget the pressure of Kyleigh's lips. But even though his mind was consumed with all he had to do, his fingers kept returning to where they'd touched.

The memory roared back to life at the slightest pressure. It burned so insistently beneath the surface that he knew he'd never get to sleep. So he decided to go for a walk.

The mansion was silent that night. Even the many bustling maids had finally disappeared into their chambers. And it was perhaps because the silence was so intense that the faintest of sounds caught his ear.

Someone was humming a song. The notes were low and drawn out, like the mumbling of a summer breeze through the rafters. Then they rose, sailing to a height that somehow matched the depth. Each note was a line in a story, a piece that fit perfectly into the next.

Kael followed it down the hall and into the dining room. The great glass window that overtook the far wall was alive with stars and smeared in thin, wispy swathes of cloud. Kyleigh stood before the window ... her skin washed in moonlight, her hair loose and shining with the stars.

She'd obviously come from bed: she wore nothing but a tunic that covered her to the knees. The song she hummed drew Kael helplessly in. She turned from the window and he saw that she had little Dante wrapped in her arms.

His pink face rested gently against her chest, smooth with sleep. "They were having a difficult time getting him to calm. I thought a song might help," she whispered, smiling down.

Kael's throat had gone impossibly dry. Somehow he'd wandered in so closely beside her that his chest was pressed against her arm. Her hair smelled like flowers — the blooms that grew subtly and not too sweet. He could feel the

592

impossible warmth in her skin. The softness in her eyes as she gazed at Dante was altogether frightening. Her voice still carried remnants of her song.

And he realized that he was in very real danger of losing his resolve.

Kyleigh must've realized it, as well. No sooner had he managed to take a step backwards than she grabbed his wrist. "I've got you now, you stubborn whisperer. Will you *finally*, at long last, say you'll marry me?"

He couldn't quite get his tongue to move, so he nodded instead.

"Tonight?"

"No."

"Soon?"

Blast it all. He couldn't wait a week — not when she looked at him that way. "Give me another day to settle everything, and I'll marry you the next at sunrise."

# CHAPTER 51
## THE SUN RISES

Kael stood impatiently at one of his favorite spots in Gravy Bay: on the jutting ledge of a cliff that overlooked the sea. It wasn't the mountains by any stretch, but it was the closest he could come to the moment when they'd finally admitted to loving each other. And from this point, they would be the first to greet the sunrise.

"There's still time, you know," Uncle Martin whispered. He slipped a flask from his coat pocket and held it at the ready. "A quick nip for courage never hurt anybody."

Kael remembered his last experience with Gravy grog, and he had absolutely no intention of collapsing on his wedding day. "I think I'll be able to manage on my own, thanks."

"If he's got enough courage to take on Titus, then I think he'll have no trouble at all wedding a halfdragon. Besides, marriage leads to such wonderful things," Lysander said. He bounced Dante in his arms as he spoke, grinning to either ear.

"Does it?" Jake muttered. He glowered over his spectacles at Elena — who kept her mask pulled up and her dark eyes fixed pointedly on the sea.

Beside them, Eveningwing fidgeted with the high, stiff collar of his tunic. They'd had to cut the sleeves short so the feathers that sprouted from his elbows wouldn't get bent. Of all of them, he should've been the most comfortable. But he was still sweating.

"Why do humans dress up their skin for everything? And why are the dressings always so *itchy*?" he moaned.

Had Kael's insides been able to make a face, he imagined they'd be wearing one similar to Eveningwing's. His

594

palms were so sweaty that he felt as if he had his hands sitting in bowls of water. The air was muggy, but for some reason his legs kept shaking with cold. His heart was either beating too fast to count, or had seized up somewhere in the middle of his chest.

The villagers made a line down the slope of the cliff, all of their faces pointed eagerly towards its bottom. Behind them, the pink sky bloomed orange as the fiery crest of the sun appeared. Kael nearly leapt out of his skin when someone cried:

"I see them! They're coming!"

He'd told her she didn't have to wear it. He knew she hated it, and he'd wanted her to be comfortable — even if it meant wearing her armor. But when he first caught sight of Kyleigh striding up the hill, he saw she hadn't listened:

She was wearing his favorite emerald green dress.

Her raven hair was braided loosely over her shoulder. Little strands escaped their bonds and fell gently across her forehead, as they always did. White flowers had been woven along the path of the braid. She was smiling — laughing, even — as Aerilyn wept happy tears beside her.

The warmth of the sunrise did a remarkable thing to her eyes. When they lighted on him, he felt as if her gaze carried all the silent wonder of the dawn directly into the center of his chest.

"Is it too late for some of that grog?" he said weakly.

Lysander slapped Uncle Martin's hand from his coat pocket. "No, none of that," he said. Then he fixed Kael with a serious look. "Chin up, chest out. Smile and try to enjoy the moment — once it passes, you'll never have it back."

Kael knew he was right. He tried to remember everything — from the way Kyleigh smiled at him to her every graceful step. He couldn't believe that she was walking towards him. He couldn't believe that she'd chosen him.

Though he saw the unmistakable joy her smile, though his heart assured him with its every beat that her look was meant entirely and wholly for him, his mind still couldn't grasp it — it was a sight every bit as stunning as the mountains, a shock too vast to comprehend.

Him, of all people. She'd chosen *him*.

At last, she stopped at his side. Aerilyn drifted away, moving to stand near Lysander. And the only thing left on earth was Kyleigh.

"Um ... good morning," he whispered, because he couldn't think of a single blasted word to say.

Her smile brightened as she took his hands. "Good morning, Kael."

There was silence all around them. Why had everything gone quiet? Kael pulled himself from the depths of her eyes and realized the whole village was waiting. So he cleared his throat.

His heart hammered so violently that it made the words sound a bit unsteady as they left his lips: "Will you sail with me through the storms, hold my hand in the gales? Will you stand by my side in battle? Will you take me as your love?"

"I suppose."

Several of the villagers laughed.

Kael forgot his nerves. He couldn't believe she wasn't taking it seriously. "Say it right, or it won't count."

She raised a brow. "Is that so?"

"Yes."

His stomach twisted when she dipped a hand beneath her collar. When she drew it out, he saw there was a ring clasped in her fingers.

The band was made of a strange sort of gold — one so pale it was nearly white. As he studied the ring, he realized it'd been shaped to look like a twisting dragon. There were tiny, rounded scales carved into the band. Some of its braided lines were capped in deadly-looking spines. At its top was a dragon's snarling head.

A black jewel sat inside the dragon's mouth, shaped to look like a bolt of flame. Kael recognized it immediately. "Your onyx ... you've carved it up."

She nodded. "Asante did a marvelous job, didn't he?"

"Asante?" He gaped at her as she slid the ring onto his finger. "You had this planned all along, didn't you? You were going to marry me anyways."

She laughed at his scowl. "This is how the shapechangers bond — we trade tokens."

Kael's face burned as he stared down at the ring. "Well, I wish you would've told me. I haven't got anything for you."

"Check your pocket," she whispered.

He did. And he was rather surprised to find a second ring sitting at its bottom. This one was more delicately woven than the dragon. The white band was shaped to look like the symbol of the Wright, with the black jewel carved into a triangular pupil at its center.

"I promised Asante that I would keep the two heads of the jewel together, no matter what I made with them. So once you put that on," she said, holding out her hand, "I'm afraid you're stuck with me."

He couldn't have put it on any faster.

As soon as they wore their rings, she took his hands in hers. "I will be your sword, and you will be my shield. We'll face every battle side by side, and celebrate our every victory together." Her lips hardly brushed his before she shoved him back. "Oh, and there's one other thing I'll promise you."

He stood warily as she marched away. "What is it?"

"You'll always have me to make sure things don't go according to plan." She grinned at him from over her shoulder as she reached the cliff's edge. "I'll meet you at Copperdock."

And before he could stop her, she jumped.

He raced to the edge in time to get knocked backwards by a blast of her wings. She sloped down the cliff's face and up, darting above the waves.

Kael watched in horror as the ragged remains of the emerald green dress fluttered into the sea. "I can't believe you — I really liked that dress!" he yelled at her.

597

She replied with a roar that rattled his lungs. Then she swooped over their heads and took off, winging into the open seas and straight for Copperdock.

Aerilyn smacked him hard on the rump, jolting him from his shock. "What are you waiting for? Go after her!"

"I'll lead the way!" Eveningwing said. Then he tore off his shirt and flapped straight out of his trousers.

Uncle Martin wacked Kael with his cane; Lysander shoved him on. He stumbled down the line of villagers for a breath, carried only by the urging of their hands. Then he broke into a run.

Cheers filled the air on either side. Trees whipped out of the corners of his eyes and the slope shrank beneath the pounding of his legs. When Kael reached the docks, Thelred was glaring up at the sky.

"Where's she going?"

"Copperdock," Kael gasped.

"I can't row there."

"No, but we can sail there." Kael leapt into one of the Bay's fishing boats: a tiny, shallow-bottomed vessel that was more sail than deck. It was sturdy enough to get them to Copperdock, but small enough that two men could manage it easily. "Come on!"

Thelred stood frozen on the docks. "I can't sail that. Not with my leg —"

"I wouldn't have asked you if I didn't think you could do it," Kael said testily.

At last, Thelred seemed to make up his mind. He freed their boat from the dock. Kael helped him over the lip and onto the deck. "Take the helm — I'll manage the sails."

"Aye," Thelred grunted.

They took off with Eveningwing soaring happily at their head, sailing until the Bay and all of the villagers' cheers faded behind them.

*******

They were a ways out when Shamus spotted their boat — but Kael could still hear him bellowing *Witchslayer* from the docks. The moment they landed, a horde of shipbuilders rushed to tether them to the shores. They practically lifted Kael out of the ship and onto solid ground.

"She's waiting for you up at the castle. Go on, lad!" Shamus bellowed, grinning as he shoved him forward. "Best not to keep her waiting!"

It was nearly sunset, but the air was still hot from the afternoon. Sweat drenched Kael's tunic by the time he reached the castle's front gate. The door creaked open as he neared it. He leaned to thank the guardsman on the other side ... but there wasn't one.

He'd jogged a few paces away when a rather snide voice called from behind him: "Best of luck to you."

Kael turned. He swore there wasn't a soul near the gate, but it'd closed somehow. And its latch was done up tightly.

"Witchslayer," the guard at the keep's door said with a nod. "You go straight inside, now. Crumfeld will show you the way."

"Thanks," Kael panted.

He burst into the main hall, sighing in relief as the cool gloom cloaked his face. He glanced around for the man called *Crumfeld* but once again, there wasn't a soul in sight. He took off down the nearest hall, cutting between the rays of orange light that filtered in through the holes in the roof — and very nearly flattened a young woman coming down the stairs.

"You're all right, Master Kael. No harm done," she insisted as he helped her retrieve the damp cloths she'd been carrying. She had a round face and a warm smile. Her hand was surprisingly strong as she gripped his arm. "Right up these stairs, Master Kael. You can't miss it."

He thanked her breathlessly as he charged his way up.

A small landing awaited him at the top of the stairs. There was a chamber on his right, one that had its door hanging slightly ajar. To his left was a window cut out to face the falling sun. He hardly noticed its dying blaze, or the way its golden light set fire to the pointed tops of the trees. For there, standing before the window, was Kyleigh.

Her hair hung free of all bonds, waving and shining in the light. She wore a plain white dress with a hem cut just above her knees. Her eyes — mercy, the sun would never again bother to shine if it saw how they blazed.

And when she smiled, he was reminded with a jolt that each coiling flame trapped within them burned entirely for him.

"It's about time," she murmured.

Kael couldn't breathe. He was suddenly aware of how very drenched he was, of how the sea had crusted onto his skin and how his curls hung limply against his forehead. His wedding clothes were splattered with grit from the waves and mud from his sprint. Eveningwing had accidentally torn one of his sleeves when he'd dived down to wish him luck.

But none of that seemed to matter to Kyleigh.

Her thumb trailed across his jaw, her fingers gripped the back of his neck. She brought her lips to his in a kiss that sent his worries melting across his shoulders. He felt them wash down his back and pool somewhere in the mortar at his feet.

Kyleigh's hand traveled slowly while she kissed him. It slid from his neck, across his torn sleeve and down his arm, trailing an agonizing, white-hot line behind it. Finally, her hand came to rest. Her fingers twined tightly through his and she pulled away, drowning him in the fires of her eyes.

"Come on, you," she growled, smiling.

Then she led him through the chamber door ... and to the start of another grand adventure.

# ACKNOWLEDGEMENTS

First of all, nobody panic — there *will* be a fourth and final book in the Fate's Forsaken series. Y'all keep your fingers crossed for me, and maybe the writing will go by a little faster!

I just want to say again how much this opportunity has meant to me. When I published *Harbinger*, I thought it would be cool to be able to share a story with the world. Little did I know that the world would soon be sharing its stories with me.

You guys have touched my heart. You truly have. It's a remarkable thing to be able to communicate with people from all over the globe. And because of the passion with which you've shared, I feel I've learned not to take a single word for granted — for each one truly leaves a mark. Thank you to everybody who has so bravely written to me. It's an honor I won't take lightly.

Of course, I'd also like to thank my intrepid beta readers: Prudence, Markus, and Brad Coish — who trekked fearlessly through *Dragonsbane*, hunting for errors and helping me find all of those bothersome misspelled and downright *missing* words. The way y'all challenged the story helped make for a more polished final product. You guys are awesome!

Special thanks to Bene — whose concern for my characters helped bring the whole thing together. I was at a loss as to how to put it into words, until your questions forced me to look a little deeper.

Finally, since you all have shared so generously with me, I'd like to share something with you. It's something that was written in answer to a question from a reader — something that I feel is appropriate, given the tone of this third book (and if you don't like the mushy stuff, you should probably sign off here):

*Love is frustrating. That's the horrible, wonderful, messy truth of it. We read books like this because it's so unlike reality that it allows us some reprieve from the harsh light of truth.*

*In our world, hearts are broken often — sometimes beyond repair. People fall out of love just as suddenly as they fall into it. Sometimes the heartache is all our own fault, and sometimes it's beyond our control. Here, there is no such thing as "love at first sight." If there is any love in the real world at all, then it's because it was fought for, worked for. Love is a hard-won, and often bittersweet, reward.*

*But in spite of all of this, love remains a powerful salve for the weariness of our world. Someone once said that death doesn't stop love — it only interrupts it. And I think that about sums it up.*

# Map of the Lands in Dragonsbane

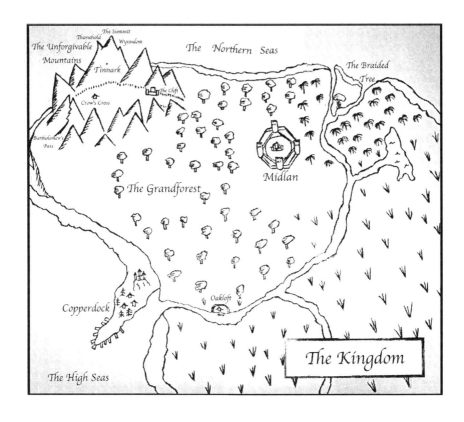

31685227R10336

Made in the USA
Middletown, DE
09 May 2016